SECRETS OF THE NINE
A FEAST UNKNOWN
LORD OF THE TREES | THE MAD GOBLIN

SECRETS OF THE NINE

A FEAST UNKNOWN
LORD OF THE TREES | THE MAD GOBLIN

PHILIP JOSÉ FARMER

Meteor House

SECRETS OF THE NINE

Meteor House
ISBN 978-1-945427-31-2
First Trade Paperback Edition

DEDICATION

Philip José Farmer dedicated *The Mad Goblin* to Jack Cordes. Meteor House was saddened to hear that Jack passed away on January 16, 2024 at the age of ninety-eight.

Jack was a World War II U.S. Army veteran, part of the force that went ashore at Normandy during the D-Day operation to liberate mainland Europe.

Jack's passion for cinema and science-fiction led to the creation of a magnificent collection of memorabilia, as well as a close friendship with Philip José Farmer. Jack and Phil enjoyed watching movies together and Jack would often accompany Phil at conventions.

Requiescat in pace, Jack Cordes.

PUBLISHER'S NOTE

A Feast Unknown has often been described as controversial (perhaps the politest description you are likely to find)—a thin euphemism for a story that prominently features murder, rape, bestiality, incest, animal cruelty, and a slew of sundry unsavory practices that even fifty years after its publication will still make your intestines squeak and your eyes narrow. This is not a book for the faint hearted, nor for those readers who are content to park to one side the more unpleasant traits that all men can have. And when these traits are amplified as a reaction to age extending drugs, we move from unpleasant to positively aberrant.

But, if you've ever asked yourself questions that you know you perhaps should not be asking, and if you are willing to accept that the piper must always be paid, then *A Feast Unknown* is the novel for you. As Theodore Sturgeon notes in his postscript, Farmer is always asking questions. Like "Why don't your superhumans, your heroic fighters, leaders, battlers for good and against evil, so seldom have a sex life—or, indeed, sex organs?" The answer, of course, is that they do, and Farmer wanted to bring this to our attention. Along the way you will get a fast-paced, action-packed, engaging (if violent) adventure that will leave you wanting more. And there is more. This volume is testament to that.

The first edition of *A Feast Unknown* had a tagline of "Adults Only." This book shocked readers when it was first published in 1969. And it still does today. But it also informs and entertains.

an Evolution
Strange
two tongues Touch
exchange
a Feast unknown
to stone
or tree or beast

—EVOLUTION, May Swenson

TABLE OF CONTENTS

EPIPHANIES IN PULP

The Philip José Farmer novel *A Feast Unknown* debuted in 1969, published by Essex House. I've told the story before of how I encountered it four years later, in 1973 at age fifteen. At that time I was living in the beach town of Ocean City, Maryland. Strictly speaking, my family was actually homeless, squatting in closed-down hotels in the winter, and shifting a little south to the wild island of Assateague to live in tents in more temperate months. I was no longer going to public school, and wanted, more than anything, to become a writer. I read incessantly . . . a mixture of classic literature and pulp fiction. I haunted any establishment in Ocean City that had books in it.

One of those places was a head shop called The Rainbow Tree. Head shops were holdovers from the '60s . . . places to buy smoking paraphernalia, incense, and best of all, badass literature. I was too young to actually be allowed in there, but at that age I could raise a thin mustache that made me look older, and so I slipped inside their beaded curtain to what felt thrillingly like a forbidden world.

Of course I went straight for their "book section," a motley collection of underground comics, revolutionary pamphlets, sex magazines, and outlaw lit. I had been an avid fan of the Bantam paperback Doc Savage books, but needless to say I was not looking to expand that collection *at* The Rainbow Tree. Nevertheless, I did a double take to see the cover of a used Essex House edition of *A Feast Unknown*, with its art clearly depicting a nude Doc Savage (who I would quickly learn had been renamed Doc Caliban) wrestling an equally unclothed Tarzan (named Lord Grandrith).

I was intrigued, in fact fascinated. But as I opened the book and scanned randomly through the pages, I was, quite frankly, shocked. Used to the sanitized world of the Doc paperbacks, I was unprepared for what was obviously a hammering narrative of nonstop sex and violence.

I almost put it back and walked away. Not because I didn't want to read it . . . but because I felt somehow naked myself. Pulp heroes were innocent . . . the adventures of their protagonists violent, yes, but never mixed with intense sexuality. To see those idealistic heroes in the context of brutal eroticism was jarring, unsettling. My own interest in sex (adolescent male, hormones raging) was intense, but I was shy around girls, and the social separation and isolation caused by homelessness only increased that shyness. Forbidden books and magazines were where I turned to explore, gingerly, that exciting, mysterious, superheated world. But it was a quest filled with stolen glances and secret thoughts. To be seen wanting *that* book, would surely be like wearing a scarlet letter on my forehead.

But I couldn't walk away. Used paperbacks were cheap at The Rainbow Tree—even though I counted every penny in those days, I could afford it. So I nerved myself up and brought it up to the counter, my heart pounding, fully expecting the checkout guy to look at the nude Doc and Tarzan on the cover, raise his eyes to look at fifteen-year-old me attempting to appear calm and cool and at least eighteen, and shake his head with an admonition to go home and read the Sunday funnies, kid.

However, he didn't bat an eye. I paid, fled back out through the beaded curtain, got on my bike, and rode to the nearby beach. With my back propped against a sand dune, I started reading.

I was conceived and born in 1888. Jack the Ripper was my father. . .

Reading on in earnest, my mind lost most of the notion that literature has as its purpose the basic ordering of the human soul. Could it be that its true, most noble purpose is to challenge and transform the reader, reaching into innermost depths and ripping out a thorny tangle of mores, beliefs, obsessions, and hopes? Those are forms of insight which might take a lifetime to unravel—or which might never be unraveled.

The French title for *A Feast Unknown* is *La Jungle Nue*, "The Naked Jungle" . . . In Italy it is *Festa di Morte*, "The Feast of Dead Men." But it seemed they missed the subtlety in Farmer's title. Not all editions have it, but most show this stanza from the poem *Evolution* before the story begins.

> an Evolution
> Strange
> two tongues Touch
> exchange
> a Feast unknown
> to stone
> or tree or beast

The poet, May Swenson, though not widely known today, was in fact a very influential creator in her day. The eminent critic Harold Bloom considered her one of the most important and original poets of the twentieth century. Born in 1913, she was a contemporary of Farmer—he might well have witnessed the whole of her literary career.

The poem, notably, contains further imagery on the theme that all things, even the inanimate, yearn for life. Its metaphors include a lion (and Grandrith would wrestle and kill a lion), and stones hungering to speak (bringing to mind excruciating images from the final Doc Savage novel, *Up from Earth's Center*). The question of what any creature might be willing to do in order to achieve life (or extended life, in the narrative of *A Feast Unknown*), also echoes strongly through both poem and book.

One French edition has a cover that depicts a lurid, arresting scene: a powerful hand stabbing downward with a knife, precipitating almost an explosion of blood. And yes, the violence is unrelenting in *A Feast Unknown*. Upping the stakes even further, the two main characters, Doc Caliban and Lord Grandrith, are in the grip of a condition which makes them impotent unless strongly contemplating or initiating violence themselves. They have become living engines of sex and violence, and the theme is literally "full-frontal" in the story, with every act explicitly depicted and described.

Certainly a compelling concept to explore in our time, where the linking of those two words in fiction and entertainment has been ubiquitous, but rarely with a goal that includes actually seeking to *understand* violent and erotic human drives. Farmer himself, a vigorous explorer of sexual themes throughout his career, framed the eros/thanatos equation in the context of it being a byproduct of an elixir the Nine and their followers (the antagonists of the story) take in order to extend their lives. They do so willingly, but at a great price to their humanity. The spiritual puzzle being one that Grandrith himself ponders: *I was forced to dwell a little on that which I had pushed away because it was too painful. Had I, by becoming a god, become less of a man?*

Interesting conjecture, when you apply it to the extremes human beings will go to in order to perpetuate personal power and life. By layering such deep seams of philosophical content under the action narrative, Farmer invests the story with a powerful, primal heartbeat.

Farmer, in interviews about the book, also stressed its black humor and elements of satire. Here is an excerpt from his interview about *Feast* presented in *Bakka* magazine. He recalls his thoughts when Brian Kirby of Essex House asked him to write some novels of science fiction erotica.

> *Farmer: "Well, I had never read a pornographic book up to that time. So I became kinda interested. I thought . . . well now, here's a chance to write a satire on my heroes Doc Savage and Tarzan, because Edgar Rice Burroughs and Lester Dent totally ignored the sexual content. I had done some thinking, extrapolating, if there was a real Tarzan, what would he actually be like? Well, all right, I wanted to write an erotic satire of these two gentlemen, also at the same time I was satirizing pornography. I had my tongue in my cheek, and I had a hell of a lot of fun doing it."*

Pornography is a strange thing . . . by definition, something that is created expressly for the purpose of stimulating sexual arousal (this is a bad thing?). By society's usage, the word is generally utilized to describe something erotic that the criticizer of that particular form of eros doesn't like. So in that context porn is cheap, exploitative, degrading. Why should that be so? It's rather like trashing a chef for succeeding in making something that stimulates an anticipatory, excited desire to eat, and to have that eating become a feast for all the senses.

One interesting point to consider is that very little of the sex in *Feast* is presented as pleasurable. Mostly it seems a form of agony. This, perhaps, reflects the deep and diverse fear and discomfort many people feel about sexuality.

And yet, Farmer brought counterpoint to that theme. It's not just the title and its provenance that echoes with poetry in the book. I've long considered that Farmer, either consciously or by unconscious inspiration, utilizes poetic language in a powerful way. Poetry often stirs emotion, and even a spiritual response, not directly, but with oblique imagery, which prompts a reader to a strong reaction though a sometimes unexpected, even mysterious beauty. Much adventure fiction is devoid of this kind of deeper layer within its narrative, but *A Feast Unknown* is filled with it.

Consider this passage from the beginning of the novel—the prelude to an exceedingly violent military attack on Grandrith. This passage utilizes a mixture of explicit description, stream of consciousness thought, and metaphor, creating a uniquely visceral reading experience.

> *The sun was no longer an old lion. It was the red eye of Death, the drunken always-dry sot who had thirsted for me for almost eighty years. Now the red eye was bisected by my penis, which reared with a piss hard-on. I was lying on my back, naked, and the scarlet ball climbed up the shaft and was on its way to being balanced atop it. From some distance, there was a click. The sky ripped as if it were rotten old cloth. The sun was on top of the head of my penis, seeming almost to spurt out. I knew what the ripping sound was the moment I heard it, and I knew what the click had been. As if it were red seed, the sun burst open from my penis. It disappeared in smoke. The walls*

flew apart as if they had become a flock of cranes disturbed by an eagle. The smoke poured into me and filled me to the backs of my eyeballs. The noise was squeezed out of me. I was turned inside out like a glove. I was a tuning fork trying to find the correct resonance.

A remarkable evocation of the male climax, using nature imagery, spiritual life/death allusions, wrapped in a slash-and-burn adventure narrative. Erotic writing (much less the more derogatory and dismissive term pornography) had never quite looked or felt like this before. As you will see when you read the book itself, the passage is typeset using short line breaks that also strongly evoke free verse poetic structure.

This type of style suffuses the novel, raising it to a dynamic artistic level. Later in the book, an erotic scene between Grandrith and Trish Wilde (a pastiche of Pat Savage) presents a much more ecstatic bonding:

I came several minutes after entry. Instead of withdrawing, I remained on top of her and left the semi-hard cock in her. She began to squeeze on it with her sphincter, which was powerful, and seemingly, tireless. It was like a weak but loving fist sending telegraphic messages. My peter swelled up again, and I began going back and forth with her legs over my shoulders and my hands around her hips and under her thighs so that the tips of my fingers caressed the edges of her labia. The second orgasm did not arrive until quite a few minutes later. I almost passed out from the intensity; I saw great red flowers shooting up from green stalks, exploding in scarlet, and collapsing.

Another poetic technique is being used here . . . instead of the stanza-like breaks of the previous passage, a continuous unbroken narrative is presented. This begins with prosaic (even clinical) language, which in the end suddenly pivots into fierce, even hallucinatory imagery. This is an adept use of the methodology of blank verse, which often grounds the reader firmly and then abruptly tips or propels them into vehement sensation.

The cover art of the French edition which I described above, in the light of these thoughts, becomes more than a slasher-scene. The knife Farmer wields to cut into intense, often shunned human themes does indeed cause splatters of hot blood to go everywhere, but the soul is being released in the sanguine fountain as well. Through the experiences of heroes like Caliban and Grandrith—who are so often equated with a nobility of action and spirit—we can viscerally feel our own blood pumping with primal power.

> *Nobody moved. They could not accept what they had seen. And when their senses thawed, they began to realize what they faced.*

That line from *A Feast Unknown* could well summarize the experience of reading the novel. It was, in essence, one hammer blow after another, leaving the reader stunned. This was not just because of the explicit content of the story. I believe it was because the novel achieved that rarest of literary accomplishments: it was *about something*.

What, exactly? I'm sure the question would raise lively debate even over a half-century later.

What was *A Feast Unknown*? Essex House wanted to add a prestigious name to their author list, and they wanted a speculative pornographic novel of the highest quality. Certainly they got it. Farmer, from his statement in the interview quoted earlier, wanted to explore the sexual component that had been essentially ignored in the canons of Doc Savage and Tarzan. He wanted to satirize pornography. Certainly he achieved that. But what happened ultimately was more. The story did not merely satirize and entertain, it *elevated* the much maligned and dismissed genre of erotically explicit creativity. It took icons of the twentieth century and unleashed in them—in greatly exaggerated form—some of the most primal behaviors in the human condition: sexual need and violent expressions of power. It linked the two, in a narrative of unrelenting intensity.

In an interesting parallel, 1969 (the year *Feast* was published) was also the year *Midnight Cowboy*, then an X-rated film, won the Academy Award for Best Picture. It has since been deemed "culturally, historically or aesthetically significant" by the Library of Congress and selected for preservation in the United States National Film Registry. It too elevated sexual themes out of the critical wasteland of the label "pornographic," giving the weight of intelligence, emotion, and countless nuances of troubled, messy humanity.

In 1981, the critic John Simon wrote (not in reference to *Feast*, but to all literature), "There is no point in saying less than your predecessors said." These are words I passionately believe. All literature is linked to a huge tree that we are just the most recent branch of. As creators, we have a unique opportunity (and responsibility) to go fearlessly as far out on a limb as we can. Farmer did that, using sheer literary muscle and audacity to dig deep, and in a bloody welter, rip secrets of the human soul out for us to see and feel.

What happened after that? Well, Farmer throttled back. The two books that followed, *The Mad Goblin* and *Lord of the Trees*, were a very different experience. In his essay on Farmer in the 2013 Sanctum Books reprinting of the Doc Savage novels *Murder Mirage* and *The Other World*, Will Murray states (referring to the Ace Double first printing of *Lord of the Trees/The Mad Goblin*) that ". . . editor Don Wollheim had censored all frank sexual content." And that was true. The two stories were engaging adventure fiction, rougher and more hard-edged than standard Doc Savage/Tarzan fare, but in film terms, the NC-17 content had been dropped to PG-13.

Had Farmer even wanted to go back to that fierce, exacting place through his writings? Possibly not. Even if Wollheim, managing the mainstream Ace Books, would not have allowed it, Farmer's own description of his plans for Caliban and Grandrith seem to indicate neither wish nor intent to return to laying bare raw essences of violence and nobility in the human soul . . . it would instead finish as a tough and clever adventure series, eventually even veering into Lovecraftian pseudo-science/supernatural themes (as outlined by Farmer in the program book of the 1983 World Fantasy Convention).

That does not dismiss the aftermath of *A Feast Unknown*. I love adventure fiction, am a devoted reader of the original Doc Savage canon, which I think is deserving of far more literary recognition than it receives. I take great pleasure in the works of those talented people who have explored the more playful of Farmer's concepts, like his literate mashups and cross-connections. But to quote another author/critic, Harlan Ellison (again, not talking specifically about *Feast*, but about the phenomenon of human creativity), "There was only one Machiavelli, only one Shaka Zulu, only one Alexander of Macedon. Name the highest and brightest and most accomplished until you get to Fellini or Billie Holiday or George Bernard Shaw and compare; and recognize how much higher thereafter is the high water mark. Suddenly, there is more sunlight in the world."

This, to me, is one of the great keys to a full appreciation of Farmer's contributions—across the wild arc of his long career—to literature. By 1970, the cultural zeitgeist had undergone monumental changes from the time of the pulps' heyday in the 1930s and '40s. Audiences were arguably more sophisticated, and it was a time of considerable experimentation in all forms of popular fiction. What would a more straightforward pulp look like in that era? Farmer, ever ahead of his time, offered an answer with the double book *Lord of the Trees/The Mad Goblin*.

Even without the erotic content, the narrative has more grit, more edge than traditional pulp storytelling. And its structure is fascinating in its crafting of two mirroring texts—one narrated by Grandrith, the other by Caliban (in the third person)—that intertwine with one another to tell the overall story. The first time I read the Ace Double, in 1974, I read the Caliban side of the book first, then flipped it over and read the Grandrith side. Insights from each bled skillfully into one another, so that by the time I finished, the original Caliban reading felt deeper, richer. The next time I read it, I reversed the order, and the experience felt deeper yet. In recent years (yes, I return to the book over and over) I've taken to flipping back and forth between the narratives while still in midstream . . . the result being a collage, which actually takes me as a reader to a unique place of heightened perception.

It was masterfully done. And when joined with *Feast*, it becomes a *gestalt* achievement . . . literally an experience greater than the sum of its parts.

Farmer chose an interesting characterization device in his presentation of the two stories: Grandrith's continues with the first-person narration of *Feast,* as another installment of his memoirs.

But for Caliban, the story opens with a remarkable little note from Farmer himself, explaining that Caliban has chosen to write his side of the story in third person, as he (Caliban) feels it allows him to be more objective. Farmer offers his own opinion that for Caliban to write in the first person would make him very uncomfortable . . . that Caliban does not like to get personal. This is cleverly consistent with the Doc Savage of the pulps, who was very restrained (at times to the point of awkwardness) about displaying emotion. And it also sheds light on an aspect of *Feast* that had previously puzzled me. In the grip of the madness elicited by the Nine's extended-life elixir, Grandrith actually changes very little from his personality/behavioral tendencies of everyday life . . . while Caliban goes off the deep end, prompting many characters in the book to perceive him as having "turned evil." Why the difference? It's a puzzle made clearer with the knowledge that Caliban, a very repressed man, would swing further into what might be considered psychosis during the elixir-enhanced experience.

One danger in dividing the authorial style between the two men to third person/first person is that the mirror-narratives will feel discordant, but instead it actually enhances the feeling of two perspectives enriching the story.

Farmer also gives some time to his supporting cast—on the Grandrith side, the Countess Clara Aakjaer (who also appeared in *Feast*) plays a dramatic part, as does a proto-human named Dick, who is one of Farmer's most inspired supporting players. On the Caliban side, the sons of Caliban's two aides provide a somewhat more mature version of the pulp-era Monk and Ham byplay. Also shining brightly in the scenes she appears in is Trish Wilde. Farmer, in his long (lovingly so) chapter on Pat Savage in *Doc Savage: His Apocalyptic Life*, clearly admits his literary affection for her, and that resonates in her scenes both in *Feast* and in *The Mad Goblin*.

The story dovetails to its conclusion at the same point in time for both books, and there is a feeling of both familiarity and immediacy at the end . . . as if the story will continue almost without pause.

But that was not to be. There was a long gap before the announcement of the next book. At least relatively long, though almost a blink of an eye in retrospect when compared to the *decades* that followed. As I mentioned, Farmer announced the fourth installment in the series in 1983, accompanied by an excerpt from the intended book to come. It was, to put it mildly, mind-bending. Once again boldly fusing genres, it had the Lovecraftian elements of ancient, malign entities (which tied in tantalizingly with the concept of the eon-spanning secret rulers of the world, the Nine) . . . a return to more darkly erotic imagery (though not quite to the extent of *Feast*), and a sequel to the final, somewhat legendary (as it had, at that time, never been reprinted) final pulp story in the Doc Savage series, *Up From Earth's Center*, where Doc—maybe—descended into Hell.

To my mind it also righted a fundamental imbalance in the original three books. *Feast* had been (brilliantly, insightfully) narrated by Grandrith. Then the balancing act of Grandrith/Caliban in each side of *Lord of the Trees* and *The Mad Goblin*. But a deep, focused dive into the psyche of Caliban had not yet been done. It was in fact consciously avoided in *The Mad Goblin*, through the third person distancing technique of Caliban's narrative. This, to me, would be the crowning achievement of the fourth book, as it was Caliban's story, providing an elegant sense of fullness to the saga.

1983 . . . going on forever. The fourth book in the series did not appear in Farmer's lifetime. And without him—the grand prime mover/trickster/high-wire walker of innovation—how could it be done? In my private thoughts, sadly, I was convinced it *couldn't* be done.

The Monster on Hold, a posthumous collaboration between Farmer and Win Scott Eckert, appeared after the unprecedented gap of almost forty years. Though not physically incorporated into this omnibus, it should absolutely be considered the essential final key to the doorways of perception opened by Farmer in *A Feast Unknown*, *The Mad Goblin*, and *Lord of the Trees*. Caliban, somewhat frustratingly an inscrutable figure in the earlier books, has his thoughts, emotions . . . his *humanity* . . . laid bare. Concurrently, a breakneck-speed adventure unfolds, and core story elements I would have considered impossible to merge, come together—successfully—at long last.

I was astonished—and grateful—that Win Eckert pulled it off.

Almost fifty years after I first had my life changed by plunking down fifty cents for *Feast* at The Rainbow Tree, I set *The Monster on Hold* beside it on my bookshelf—with *Goblin/Trees* in between—and experienced a feeling that popular literature had been transcended.

A Feast Unknown went to a pinnacle . . . it burns, and pounds, and stuns you even all these decades later. *The Mad Goblin/Lord of the Trees* made pulp reading into a uniquely interactive experience, encouraging readers to embrace many layers of perception. And *The Monster on Hold*—the ultimate high wire act—actually grounds all that had come before in a portrait of human complexity, bravery . . . and above all the dignity and strength that can come when we take the forbidden into our hearts. Through conscious, positive choice, we don't allow that feast to be one of degradation. We transform it, and are ourselves transformed.

R. Paul Sardanas
January, 2024

A Feast Unknown

Volume IX of
The Memoirs of Lord Grandrith

edited by Philip José Farmer

A Brief Introduction

In the summer of 1969 at the tender age of sixteen, I made my weekly trip to the Bookmaster's store in Times Square, Manhattan and I was shocked at what I saw in the Science Fiction section. There was a book from a publisher that I did not recognize with two naked men on the cover wrestling with each other. One of those men had bronze skin and blond hair with a pronounced widow's peak. The other man had lighter colored skin but wore his black hair long and feral-looking. The two looked suspiciously like Doc Savage and Tarzan, both of whom were favorite characters of mine. The blurb on the book described these characters as Doc Caliban and Lord Grandrith. I caught on that this must be a pastiche of my two favorite pulp heroes and was immediately hooked.

The name of the author was familiar to me. Philip José Farmer had written several strange science fiction novels and recently had won a Hugo award for the novella *Riders of the Purple Wage*. I was an avid science fiction fan, but up to that time the themes in Mr. Farmer's books were a little bit extreme for me. Now it looked like he had written something that I could not resist.

I read this book in a single day in one sitting. I was simultaneously intrigued, repulsed, disgusted, titillated, and entertained. I reread the book several times that week, at first trying to edit out some of the objectionable material. Ultimately I realized that the work was an integral whole that dealt with issues of life, death, sex, violence, mortality, immortality, religion, and moral responsibility. It was written for adults who had enjoyed the juvenile stories with the intention of introducing graphic material that would not have been permitted by the literary standards of earlier times. These were the pulps without censorship or moral limits. These were old heroes made into antiheroes and let loose into our world.

Reading this book was a turning point in my life. It not only got me thinking about what it really meant to be a superman among ordinary men. It also made me think about what it meant to be a hero in a world where there were no purely white or black hats. As in the real world, gray hats predominated. It also made me an instant Philip José Farmer fan and opened up an entirely new world of imaginative and weighty fiction.

I invite you to enter the wild and extreme vision of Philip José Farmer as he reimagined the world of pulp adventure for grownups in the late 1960s.

Arthur C. Sippo MD, MPH

Editor's Note

Lord Grandrith has written nine volumes of autobiography, totaling close to a million and a half words. Yet this volume, the latest, covering only a part of 1968, is the only one published. Lord Grandrith had planned to publish all the volumes someday, when it became possible to reveal his true identity and true story. However, Grandrith turned against the Nine who had given him the elixir of prolonged youth.

The first eight volumes are hidden in a place only Grandrith and his wife know. He made arrangements through the editor to publish Volume IX after he had failed to get it published in England, France, Sweden, South Africa, and at several houses in the United States. Grandrith states the Nine were behind the rejections and the various "accidents" to and "losings" of the mss. he sent out.

Fortunately, he had met the editor at the home of a common friend in Kansas City, Missouri. The editor did not then know the true name of James Claymore, as he was calling himself at the time. A letter sent from Lima, Peru, told the editor of Claymore's actual name and identity. It also outlined the danger that Grandrith, his wife, and several others were in. The next letter came from Dublin, Ireland. The third had no postmark and was left in the editor's mailbox between midnight and six A.M. The editor sent his reply to a man in Stockholm, Sweden, as requested. The ms. of Volume IX was mailed from Western Samoa.

The editor has Americanized various English terms, changing bonnet into hood, petrol into gas, lorry into truck, etc. The locations of various places in Kenya and Uganda were purposely made vague by Grandrith. This was not done to protect the Nine but to protect those foolhardy people who might try to seek out the Nine or the now-buried gold mines of the valley which Grandrith named Ophir.

In addition, the incident of the landing at Penrith is not quite accurate. Penrith has no airport. The events after the landing did happen as described, but the airport was created by Grandrith to obscure the actual event. He wants to protect a friend who set out lights on a meadow so the plane could land there. Grandrith refuses to change the incident to bring it closer to reality. We can only respect his reasons without understanding them.

In his last letter, Grandrith says that "almost nobody, will believe this. Not at this moment, anyway. But events conceived and brought forth by the Nine will soon convince the world. I hope then that it will not be too late for the world. Meanwhile, we are all alive and fighting, though doing more hiding than fighting. And I have added another book to the autobiography."

—*Philip José Farmer*

FOREWORD

Since the first eight volumes of his memoirs have not yet been published, Lord Grandrith has written a special foreword which encapsulates the early part of Volume I. Without this, the reader would be puzzled by some of the references in this volume.

I was conceived and born in 1888.

Jack the Ripper was my father.

I am certain of this, although I have no evidence that would stand up in court. I have only the diary of my legal father. He was, in fact, my uncle, although he was married to my mother.

My legal father kept a diary almost up to the moment of his death. Shortly after he had locked it inside a desk, he was killed. His last written words recorded his despair because his wife had just died and I, only a year old, was wailing for milk. And there were no human beings within hundreds of miles, as far as he knew.

I alone have read the entire diary. I have never permitted anyone else to read any of the diary preceding the moment when my uncle and my mother sailed from England for Africa.

My "biographer" would have been too horrified by the truth to have written it if I had been unkind enough to reveal it to him. He was a romanticist and, in many ways, a Victorian.

He would have made up a story of his own, ignoring the real story, as he did with so many of my adventures. He was interested mainly in adventure for its own sake, although he did describe my psychology, my *Weltanschauung*. However, he never really transmitted the half-infrahuman cast of my mind.

Perhaps he could not understand that part of me, although I tried to communicate it as well as I could. He tried to understand, but he was human, all-too-human, as my favorite poet says. He could never grasp, with the human hands of his psyche, the nonhuman shape of mine.

That part of the diary which I had forbidden others to read describes how my mother happened to be with her husband in Whitechapel on that fog-smothered night. She had insisted on going with him to look for his brother, who had escaped from the cell in the castle in the Cumberland County. Private detectives had quietly tracked John Cloamby to the Whitechapel district of London. His brother, James Cloamby, Viscount Grandrith, had joined the hunt. My mother, Alexandra Applethwaite, related to the noble family of Bedford, had insisted on accompanying him.

My uncle objected to bringing his wife along for several reasons. The strongest was that his brother had attempted to rape her when he had broken out of his cell after bending several iron bars and uprooting them from their stone sockets. Only her screams and the prompt appearance of two manservants armed with pistols had saved her. Alexandra, however, persisted in her insane belief that she alone could make him surrender voluntarily when he was found. Also, she said that she alone could locate him exactly. There was, she claimed, a psychic bond between them, "vibrations" which enabled her to point toward and track him as if she were a human lodestone.

I use the word "insane" in describing this belief because later developments (described by my "biographer" and by me in Vol. I) revealed her mental instability.

She also said that if she were not allowed to go with her husband in the search, she would inform the police and the newspapers of what had happened.

My uncle gave in to her. He had a horror of publicity of any kind and especially of this kind. Also, he might have been arrested for concealing evidence of murder. He was, in fact, an accessory after the fact of murder, if, indeed, there was a fact.

My uncle believed that his brother was responsible for the disappearance of two whores from villages only a few miles from the estates. A severed breast was found on the shore of a tarn; this was all. The locals presumed that somebody had done away with the two women and buried them somewhere. My uncle connected his brother to the murders because of his ravings while in the cell about killing all whores, including his mother. Especially his mother.

His mother, of course, was safe from him. She had killed herself when James, John, and Patrick, her three sons, were quite young. Her husband had killed himself because he suspected that a Swedish gentleman was the father of the boys and that she may have killed herself because her conscience made life unbearable. Their aunt raised the three boys and was much loved by them. But John Cloamby never forgave his mother, although he had never spoken of her until his madness took him.

Later, my uncle believed that John was Jack the Ripper. Before his breakdown, John had been a medical doctor. His real motive in becoming a physician was not in curing the sick. He wanted to know everything about the human body because he intended to find out the secret of immortality. To this end, he had meant to learn much more of chemistry and botany than any medical doctor had ever known.

This obsession was supposed to be the cause of his sickness. Instead, it was the symptom.

It was ironic that he did not find that secret but that I, his son, did. I supposed this, only to have to change my mind.

If my mother and uncle had not gone to Africa primarily to put my father behind them, I would not have become immortal (have a very long prolonged youth, to be exact). Or so I thought.

I am immortal in the sense that I will be thirty-two years of age in body for a very very long time. However, accident, murder, and suicide can reduce me to the rotting corpse which others usually become before their hundredth birthday.

I omitted disease from the fatal list. The same elixir that gives me a potentiality of 30,000 years or more also preserves me from disease. This does not, however, explain my seeming immunity from all the diseases so common in tropical Africa before I became thirty-two.

My uncle's diary recounts in an elegant style, reading like a prose Racine, a ride through the dark fog of the night on March 21. He glimpsed his brother after hours of driving through the mists, and he leaped out of his carriage and ran shouting after him. My mother sat shivering with cold and fear in the carriage while she tried to peer through the wet grayness. A gas lamp nearby shot a ghastly half-light through the swirls. She was alone. Her husband had not wanted a coachman because he might report the peculiar occurrences of the evening to the police.

For a while, there was silence. Then she heard the clicking of hard heels on the stones. A man appeared like a ship sailing through the fog. He stopped and turned, and by the dim light she saw her husband's mad brother.

When James Cloamby returned, he found his wife unconscious on the seat of the carriage. Her skirt and petticoats were up over her face, and her undergarments had been cut off, probably with the scalpel that later took apart the bodies of the Whitechapel whores in such grisly fashion.

My uncle was to reason that his brother had not killed her because she was not a whore. But John did hate his older brother, and he may have raped Alexandra for revenge, or possibly because she was not a whore and so was better than his mother, whom, in one part of him, he must still have loved. Also, since John loved Alexandra, or had said he loved her, it was possible that this was his act of love. Who knew what the madman was thinking?

My uncle lit a match when she did not reply to his cry of alarm. He saw the white legs, stripped of the black stockings, and the black, exceptionally hairy vagina out of which oozed my father's spermatic fluid and some of her blood.

The strange thing, to me, anyway, was that this was the first time my uncle had seen any of his wife's body below the shoulders.

Although they had been married for a month, the two had not had any sexual intercourse beyond some kissing and slipping his hand down her bodice and over her breasts. The day of the wedding, she had begun menstruating and would not stop. He, being a Victorian, could not bed her while she was "unclean." (Although there were plenty of Victorians who would have done so.)

The day before John broke loose from the cell, Alexandra had ceased to flow. My uncle (as recorded in his diary) was ecstatic. He could quit masturbating now and could stop eyeing his wife's maid.

Then my father-to-be got out of his cell in the north tower of the half-ruined Castle of Grandrith. He and his wife were too upset for some time to consider sexual intercourse. At least, she was.

Now, in the London fog, James Cloamby pulled his wife's skirts down and revived her. She became hysterical, and not until the next day did he discover that his brother had attacked his wife.

His wife seemed to recover. A few months afterward, they sailed for West Africa, where James was to conduct a secret investigation for the Colonial Office. (This was not the investigation which my "biographer" described, however. He knew the true reason, but he chose to give a spurious one.)

Alexandra now refused to have intercourse with James. She said that she was too "ashamed," felt "too unclean," and, besides, wanted to make certain that she was or was not pregnant. If she was to have a child, she wanted to be certain of its paternity.

Before they sailed, the first known murder by Jack the Ripper occurred on Easter Tuesday, April 3rd, 1888, on Osborn Street. My uncle heard about this (it was not reported in the *Times*) and wondered in his diary if it could be the work of his brother. Later, he was certain that it was. Yet, so great was his dread of the shame and disgrace if John should be caught, he did not inform the police.

He did continue the search on his own through private detectives. When he sailed for Africa, he sent an anonymous note to the police, describing his brother but not naming him. This note is not in the official records. Research has convinced me that it was suppressed by politically powerful influences.

My father disappeared when Jack the Ripper disappeared. It was not until 1968, the year of this narrative, that I found out what had happened to him.

Alexandra Grandrith was finally able to accept her husband in bed. But by then she was too big with child. My uncle continued to suffer and then backslid, as he put it, to masturbation and, once, a few days before sailing, to the maid. These necessary discharges caused much breast beating in private and many mea culpas.

The events that led to the Grandriths being stranded on the West African coast are familiar to the readers of my "biographer." The reality was somewhat different, but the result was much as depicted in the romances based on my life. James Cloamby built a strong house on the shore near the jungle, and they survived the first twenty months.

I was born November 21, 1888, at 11:45 P.M.

My mother's mind was never thereafter quite in Africa. She spent most of her time in a dream England, a country much better than the one she knew in reality, I'm sure. Despite this, she was very competent in taking care of me, if I am to believe my uncle's diary. James could not make love to her then because it would have been too much like taking advantage of an idiot. So my poor uncle suffered, and I think he may have been glad when death came at the hands of the chief of a tribe of The Folk. Any horror he felt would have been for his nephew, a twelve-month-old baby crying for food and for his mother's milk.

I was to get no more of that because she had died in her sleep a few hours before my uncle was killed. I did get a mother's milk, though it was not quite human milk.

CHAPTER ONE

The morning of March 21, 1968, was a fine morning. I was seventy-nine years old and felt, and looked, thirty. The sun woke me up that morning. Or so I thought. Sometimes the African sun sneaks over the horizon like an old lion on the prowl, the mists diffracting its rays into a mane. I awoke as if I had been tickled on the nose with a hair from that mane.

The silence was like a breath on my face. It was the silence that had quietly awakened me.

The whinnying of horses, the bellowing of cattle, the squawking of chickens, the chittering of the monkeys were compressed within lungs and sealed by mouths afraid to open.

The voices of the cooks, house servants, and yard men were there, but noiseless. They hung in the sky, turned to cold blue air. I could sense them fluttering the windpipe.

Fear?

Or stealth by some and fear of others?

Treachery.

Perhaps.

Jomo Kenyatta had said that I was the only white man he had ever respected. What he meant was: feared.

During the so-called Mau-Mau revolution, he told his men to stay away from me. My own tribe, the Blacks who had initiated me with blood-letting and buggering into their tribe and who had selected me as their chief, hated the Agikuyu. And they loved me. Not as a brother but as a demigod. They would have died to a man to defend me.

Besides, Kenyatta knew that though I was white, I was even more African than he. After all, I was adopted and raised by The Folk. My blood-brothers and warriors, the original tribesmen, had almost all died off. The survivors were creaking-boned whitehairs. I had been given the choice of becoming a citizen of this African state and declaring the source of my wealth or getting out. Old Kenyatta felt strong enough now to send me that ultimatum. Even though he was no longer the titular head of state, his voice was behind the order.

I had refused to do either. And so I had waited. But I had waited so long for action to be taken that I had become a little careless.

The sun was no longer an old lion. It was the red eye of Death, the drunken always-dry sot who had thirsted for me for almost eighty years.

Now the red eye was bisected by my penis, which reared with a piss hard-on. I was lying on my back, naked, and the scarlet ball climbed up the shaft and was on its way to being balanced atop it.

From some distance, there was a click.

The sky was ripped as if it were rotten old cloth.

The sun was on top of the head of my penis, seeming almost to spurt out.

I knew what the ripping sound was the moment I heard it, and I knew what the click had been.

As if it were red seed, the sun burst open from my penis. It disappeared in smoke. The walls flew apart as if they had become a flock of cranes disturbed by an eagle. The smoke poured into me and filled me to the backs of my eyeballs. The noise was squeezed out of me.

I was turned inside out like a glove. I was a tuning fork trying to find the correct resonance.

The first shell may have struck just outside the bedroom window. The second shell may have exploded at the end of my bed. By one of those freaks and coincidences that have caused many to mock my biographer, but have actually happened to me, the blast lifted my spring and mattress and me upward and backward and out the window behind me.

I must have landed in a pile of wood and plaster and bricks. I was still on my mattress, which was by what was left of the veranda. I crawled slowly out of the pile, like the naked body of a tortoise working through its shattered shell. I felt but could not hear other shells. None of these came close enough to damage me; they must have been striking other parts of the house. Through the smoke, I could see the stone foundations and these were sending off chips of stone and also pieces of wood were breaking off and flying into the air. Machine guns and rifles were trying to shred away all the stone and brick and mortar and wood and anything of flesh which the shells might have missed or failed to utterly destroy. Rock fragments struck me in many places.

I was half-stunned, but I had one thought. That was to get to the refuge prepared for such an emergency. More smoke poured over, obscuring my vision and making me cough. I had, however, seen that the thin stone shell which was actually a doorway, an exit, to the refuge, had split open. I reached inside the portion of foundation still standing, felt the steel handle, turned it, and slid inward.

Even as I closed the door it swung in hard, propelled by a bullet. I was in darkness and utter silence. I groped around until I found the oxygen bottles and cracked them to make sure they had a sufficient supply. I couldn't hear the hissing, so I felt out the nozzles. Cool air struck my palm.

I decided to use the lamp for a moment and examined the room. It was a box twelve feet by twelve by eight. It was double-walled steel with fiber glass insulation between the walls. It contained the oxygen bottles, five gallons of distilled water, medical supplies, some cans of food, pistols, two rifles, and ammunition. The main entrance was through a trapdoor in the bedroom above, but the two small exits could be used as entrances. The refuge had been built thirty years before and updated now and then, hence, the fiber glass stuffing. I had built it at my wife's insistence, who had pointed out that we would have been safe a number of times if we had had the refuge. So I had built it and it had not been used until now. In fact, I had almost neglected replacing the empty oxygen and water bottles and over-aged cans.

I hoped that no one outside there knew about the box. Since it had been built, I had taken great pains to get the stores into it unobserved and to never speak of it to anyone besides my wife. If the enemy got hold of an old Bandili who remembered it, and the old one talked, I would be as helpless as an elephant in a pit.

While I crouched in a corner, I discovered that I had spouted jism over my right leg. This probably occurred when the first shell exploded.

Hemingway and his imitator, Ruark, are usually full of shit when they speak of Africa. Or, as the Yankees say, they didn't know shit from shinola. But they were sometimes accurate in their observations of animals, particularly leopards, shooting sperm at the moment of violent death. Ejaculation is a form of protest of the body against death. The cells want to live forever, and they will try to impregnate the air in desperate copulation, to perpetuate themselves when faced with the end.

That is my explanation. I, personally, do not fear death, but my cells are not as rational as I.

What women do at the moment of suffering a violent death, I do not know. I never heard of a woman shooting out an ovum. Perhaps they do this, but the egg is so small it's unnoticed. Of course, there are so many days when no egg is available, and a man always has sperm. It's possible women substitute voice for sperm; their ejaculations are screams.

I waited in the corner. The box was dark now because I had turned out the lamp to conserve the battery. The silence continued for a long time. I had a sharp headache which I endured for some time and then took two aspirins to relieve. The relief did not come. From time to time, I felt the vibrations of explosions against my back. These, I imagine, were direct hits. The enemy certainly believed in overkill. To use a cannon against one man seemed superfluous, but it was also guaranteed to destroy me entirely. Like so many guarantees, it was worthless. So far. One or more of the direct hits must have blasted away part of the outer steel wall. Another direct hit removed the fiber glass and the inner wall. I felt as if I were buried under tons of dirt, and I lost consciousness.

Chapter Two

When I came to, I could hear somewhat. My sense of smell was as sharp as ever, that is, much more effective than a human's but not quite as good as a bloodhound's. (The reasons for this are explained in Volume I along with another explanation, in the appendix of Volume I, of my YY chromosomal mutation.)

There was, stronger than anything, the knife of gunpowder smoke. There was the needle of widely scattered food. There was the saw-edge of pulverized plaster and rent wood. Faint, the odor of human sweat and of a dog.

I opened my eyes. It was high noon. The sun blazed through a small hole in the mass of wood and bricks covering the ripped open upper corner of the box. I was covered with smoke, ashes, and dirt. The five gallon bottles of water had broken and spilled their contents over the room to make a fine mud. The cans were broken open. I think shrapnel had bounced off the walls and struck them. The weapons were buried under dirt that had fallen in.

On top of a pile of mud was a hunting knife. This was the knife I had found on my uncle's skeleton in the house he had built. I was ten then and had found out how to gain entrance. There were bones over the floor; The Folk invading the house had eaten my uncle and mother before leaving it and taken some legs and arms with them. I had used the knife much; hence, its thinness. It was now more of a stiletto than a hunting knife, but I cherished it and kept it in my bedroom, though I had not carried it for many years. A shell had lifted it up and cast it through the opening in the box before the opening was covered up again.

It seemed like a gift to me and cheered me up, despite my headache and earache.

I was also thirsty. I chewed some of the mud to get moisture, and I collected a thimbleful of food from the cans. Then I pushed the mud into the corner opposite the opening, smoothed out my tracks, and pushed the mud over me. Hours passed. My hearing sharpened. Drums beat. Voices shouted and laughed. I smelled liquor, faintly. I heard cattle mooing and bellowing and then smelled blood. After a while, smoke drifted to me and the odor of cooking flesh.

Once, I heard footsteps and the rattle of wood being pushed aside. Several men spoke in the tongue of the Agikuyu. I could imagine them looking down into the box. One said something about going down to see what it was and what was in it. Another said something about tossing a grenade into it just for fun. I did not move.

They talked among themselves in a much lower voice and agreed to come back tonight when no one would notice them and climb down. Perhaps the Englishman had hidden money down there, or the gold he was rumored to have in great quantities.

It became darker. The drums and shouts and stamping feet of dancing men became louder. The moon paled the night and made a skeleton of the wood laid over the opening. I arose, stretched and bent until my muscles were loose again, and then stepped on a ledge and opened a little door.

This was hidden by more debris, but I could see well enough through it. Capering figures in front of great bonfires were lifting bottles from my liquor stores or shooting at the empties when they tossed them into the air. Those who still wore their clothes were in the uniform of the army of Kenya. There was also a number of my own tribesmen, all young fellows.

At the nearest fire, 60 feet away, three men were holding down my pet bitch, a German shepherd named Esta. A young Bandili, Zabu, naked except for an ostrich feather headdress—which he had no right to wear according to tribal law—was holding the bitch by the flanks. His hips moved back and forth rapidly while the soldiers and Bandili laughed and clapped their hands in rhythm with Zabu's strokes. The dog was howling in agony and struggling frantically.

Zabu was a leader of the youth of the villages in this area. He hated all whites, and most of all he hated me. I don't bother to explain my position or views very often, but I had done so with the young racists of my tribe. I tried to explain that the color of my skin was not relevant. I was not as other men, Black or white. My rearing by The Folk had resulted in a lack of conditioned reflexes concerning skin color among men.

Nor had I exploited the Blacks, as other whites had. Actually, the Bandili had no cause to complain about any whites. I had kept whites from possessing, or even living in, this relatively broad territory. I had also kept the Agikuyu from attempting to run the Bandili out. And I had spent much money to establish local schools, bring in qualified teachers, and send young Bandili, male or female, to colleges as distant as England and America.

All of this made no difference to Zabu and his fellows. I was a white. I must go.

I don't like to be forced into doing anything. On the other hand, it would have been a great relief to get away from my duties and obligations as the owner of the Grandrith plantation and as chief of the Bandili. Especially, it would be a relief to get away from the over-crowdedness, noisiness, bickering, and hatefulness of the humans here.

Once, there were only a few small tribes here and much room to roam and great herds. Now . . .

I was stubborn, and I stayed.

I had recently sent my wife off to England to shop, visit friends in London, and inspect the ancestral estate in the Lake District. Thus, I did not have to worry about her. I had only myself to take care of, and that is the way I like it.

Zabu was not content with my death. He had to revenge himself on the poor dog because she was mine. There was nothing I could do for the moment to help her. I did, however, crawl out to hide behind a pile of bricks and stones. I did not want to be caught in the box if the three who planned on searching the box did return. I was covered with dirt and mud, so my white skin did not show. And I had the hunting knife in my hand.

After a while, an officer pushed the onlookers aside and violently yanked Zabu off the dog. Zabu arose and staggered back, turning, and I saw, by the light of the fire, that his belly and genitals were covered with blood. The slit of the animal had not been large enough for him, so he had used a knife.

The officer shouted at Zabu in his tribal speech and then in Swahili and drew his pistol. I thought he was going to shoot Zabu, but he turned and held the muzzle a foot from the bitch's head and fired. She jerked once.

Zabu had held up his hands in a pleading gesture, evidently thinking that the officer was going to kill him. The officer was a Mugikuyu and so hated the Bandili.

Seeing that he was spared, Zabu laughed and took a bottle from a man and swaggered off. The officer spat at Zabu's back. I didn't know whether he interfered with Zabu because of humane feelings or because he wanted to bug a Bandili.

I waited. I was hungry and thirsty, but I would be stupid to try to stroll out through that crowd in the light of the bonfires. If I could get past the fires, I might pass for one of them. I was taller than most, but a few were the equal of my six foot three, and at a distance, in the dark, I was muddied enough to look black-skinned. There was no chance just then, however.

I fixed my eyes on Zabu and hated him. After a while, as if he were hypnotized by me, he lurched very near. He was mumbling to himself, his head swinging low. I rose up behind him and chopped him on the side of the neck with the edge of my palm and dragged him back behind the pile. Nobody had noticed us. Everybody was looking at a group of young Bandili dancing a spear dance around the dead dog.

Chapter Three

Zabu awoke on his back with my hand over his mouth and my knife at his throat. His eyes widened like water boiling over. He shook. With a rip of gas, he shot out a long turd. His breath stank of my whiskey and of terror. The blood on his belly and genitals stank of the terror and agony of the bitch, and of the sperm he had loosed.

"Tell me how this happened, Zabu," I said. "Otherwise, I kill you right now."

He was willing to buy a few minutes of life, although his grandfather and father would have died rather than tell an enemy anything. His lips spewed Bandili. His eyes rotated as if he were looking for some device to appear from the air and give him a handhold whereby he could be whisked away from my knife.

Perhaps he thought I had been killed and my ghost had come back.

He had gone through school and college with my assistance. He had denied believing in ghosts. He was an educated man, he had said. *But he believed.* The hindbrain is almost always stronger than the forebrain, though in a subtle fashion.

Zabu said that the Kenyan army had moved in with the assistance of some of the young Bandili. At the last moment, the older Bandili in the nearby village had found out about the attack. They were told to keep quiet or die. Three of the old men had tried to warn me.

One was Paboli, the Spear-Launcher, Zabu's grandfather. All three did die.

A strange thing happened then. Zabu, speaking of his grand-father's death, wept.

The army units had moved in on three fronts, leaving the western open because I was returning from a hunting trip in that direction. After I got home, the units quietly closed the gap.

During the night, with utmost care, a cannon and six .50-caliber machine guns were hauled in by foot soldiers. The trucks were kept far out in the savanna to avoid noise. The young Bandili had told the army officers that the stories of my supersensitive hearing and sense of smell were not exaggerated.

Zabu talked on and on, as if enough words would build up a wall thick enough to bar my knife. He tried to justify his treachery, although he did not call it that. He called it patriotism and Africanism.

Humans are always labeling deeds. No doubt, he thought he was right. But he was moving his thoughts around in two boxes labeled BLACKS and WHITES, just as the whites he hated—with the exception of myself—moved their thoughts around in their two boxes.

What happened next surprised me. I did not intend to do it and had no thought of doing any such thing.

Looking back, I see that the treachery, so unexpected in those who had been my people for sixty years, combined with the shock of the explosions, had literally loosened something in me.

Rather, *loosed it.*

It had always been in me but shoved down as deep as deep was.

I stunned him with the knife hilt. While he lay half-unconscious, I cut his tongue off close to the root to keep him from screaming. The pain brought him to his senses. He tried to sit up, and his mouth gaped. The blood shot out.

I kissed him. One, to drink the blood, which I needed because I was thirsty. Two, to stop any sound he might have made. Three, I was compelled to do so.

The blood was salty and unpleasant, as if it contained the essence of a sea-bottom built up from the decomposing flesh and bones of a million poisonous fish. It contained a trickle of tobacco, which I hate. In other words, his blood was like most of the humans from whom I have drunk.

But the blood was strengthening, and I began to feel an excitement similar to that which I felt when in battle or making a kill. However, when it became more intense, it was obviously sexual.

Quickly, before I climaxed, I cut Zabu open with a stroke down his belly. It was not deep enough, however, to cut into the intestines. I know my anatomy well.

As the knife sank into the flesh, I spurted over his belly and the knife.

For a moment, I lost control. My arm straightened, and the knife went in to the hilt.

He writhed briefly as he died. I shook like a tree in a storm.

I sat back, gasping. I wiped off my knife on his hair. I wondered what had made me behave thus. I had intended to stick my penis into the wound and do to him what he had done to my dog.

CHAPTER FOUR

Finally, I quit trying to explain to myself my strange compulsion. I am a relentless hunter but only if there is a scent or track to follow.

I waited. The noise increased, and the celebrators staggered even more. When the moon had quartered the sky, the inevitable fights broke out between the Agikuyu and the Bandili. The few officers not thoroughly drunk separated the fighters and sent them on their way. Some soldiers, however, staggered into the village, a hundred and fifty yards away. They were after women, of course. The older men in the village were Bandili, as proud as ancient Romans and as courageous. They had been imprisoned by their youths, who had surprised them. Now, they were free, and they fought. And the Bandili youths could not stand aside while their sisters and mothers were raped and their elders killed by the Agikuyu. They attacked the soldiers. Presently, the two factions were killing each other and innocent bystanders, as in all wars, and the village huts were ablaze.

The battle gave me a chance to leave the ruins of my house unobserved. In a few minutes, I had worked my way through the shadows to the cannon. It was a British gun-howitzer of World War II, a 25-pounder or 88 mm, set on a two-wheel carriage and carrying a shield. The caisson held some shells and point-detonating fuses. These were inserted just before the shell was loaded into the gun and would explode on striking.

The crew of four were moving the cannon to a slight hill to fire upon the village. They were drunk and probably would have hit their own men as well as the target.

I took a semiautomatic rifle from a stack near them and killed each with one bullet. With the first shot, my penis began to rise. At the fourth shot, it was in the state where, usually, the orgasm was within ten seconds of arriving. Then it slowly subsided, and the pleasurable sensations diminished.

The cannon was too close to the soldiers. Before I could have fired two rounds, they would be at me from three sides. I picked up the end of the carriage and towed it off across a level of forty yards and then up a 25-degree incline for perhaps fifty yards. Past the top of the hill, I turned the cannon around on the wheels and inched it down the other, which was a 30-degree incline. I had to dig my heels into the dirt to keep it from getting away. The next hill was steeper and higher. Twice, the 900-pound cannon and carriage almost got away. A small flat space on top of the hill was large and broad enough for my purposes, and it commanded the side of the smaller hill and the village and the area around it.

I ran back and pulled the caisson, into which I had loaded the dead crew's rifles, ammunition, and some grenades, up to the hilltop. I then cached three of the rifles and ammunition behind trees at various places. I lined up the cannon, depressed the muzzle, inserted a fuse, loaded in a shell, and took one more look at the situation.

It was then that I saw dark figures coming out of the woods on the east side of the plantation, behind the soldiers. They advanced in an arc, and several times the moon struck something metallic. There were about forty men on foot, and two groups carried bulks which could be recoilless rifles on tripods.

Behind them, something big emerged from the woods. A long barrel of a cannon projected from a platform. It was a half-track, self-propelled cannon which I estimated to be a 90 millimeter.

The foot soldiers and the half-track reached a line of trees and stopped. They were out of my sight when they were behind the trees. Four dark figures ran out from the trees toward the cover of other trees near the village. They were scouts.

By then, the Kenyans had discovered that their cannon was missing. Four men followed the wheel tracks toward the smaller hill and soon were hidden by its bulk. The flames from the village were searing the skies. There were many bodies, men, women, children, sprawled between the burning huts. Machine guns were still shooting, but the rifle fire had died down.

CHAPTER FIVE

Suddenly, all firing ceased. The soldiers began to regroup on the east side of the village. I supposed that the officers had sobered up enough to bring the men under control. They were beginning to realize the consequences of their actions. It might be possible to get the government to consider this just an unfortunate incident, but justified, because the mission had been successful. It had obliterated me. But if the other Bandili villages revolted because of this massacre, the government might shoot them to satisfy the Bandili.

On the other hand, they might be re-forming for another attack on the Bandili survivors, entrenched in the woods on the west side of the village.

The newcomers were moving back. Their haste gave me the impression they intended to remove themselves at a great distance from the Kenyan army. It was evident that they were surprised to find the soldiers. I supposed they had come to attack me. For Revenge. For Wealth. For the Secret of Immortality. Perhaps for all three.

Their appearance here at the same time as the army attack was one more of the many coincidences which some readers of my biographer's novels have found incredible. These people do not know that some men are not only endowed with "animal magnetism," but some men also have what I call a "human magnetic moment." That is, some men, of whom I am one, are the focus of unusual events, of mathematically unlikely coincidences. They radiate something—a quality, a "field," which pulls events together. The field slightly distorts, or warps, the semifluid structure of occurrences, of space objects intertwined with the time flow. Whatever the reason for their being here, the newcomers were now leaving. I could, however, directly influence them now. I picked up the tailpiece of the carriage, turned the cannon, unconsciously estimating the distance and trajectory as if I were firing an arrow. I depressed the muzzle and then got down off the operator's seat and jerked the lanyard.

I had been vaguely aware that I was sexually excited. Now, as the cannon went off, so did I.

The orgasm, however, was not nearly as intense and ecstatic as when I had thrust my knife into Zabu's belly.

Thereafter, I was all action, intent on the "red business," as Whitman so appropriately and beautifully phrases it. If I had a hard-on or came during the next few minutes, I did not know it.

My first shell landed about ten feet ahead of the half-track. It stopped, backed up, and then turned to the left. My second shell landed on its right and drove it still more leftward so that it was heading toward the village again. The third shell exploded in the middle of a group of the newcomer foot-soldiers, which had hit the ground when my first shell struck. The three survivors got up and ran. About eight bodies were on the ground.

At this time, as I had expected, the four trackers came over the smaller hill. My rifle fire got two, because they were such fine silhouettes against the fires. The other two dived back behind the hill and began firing at me. I ignored the bullets, although some hit the cannon and some spurted dirt near me. My fifth shell blew up the top of the hill. The two men may not have been hit, but they were discouraged, because they quit firing. Perhaps they were working around the hill to flank me.

By this time, the Kenyans had seen the half-track and were firing at it from behind the line of trees. The vehicle replied with shell and three machine guns. The other newcomers turned and advanced across the field toward the Kenyans.

My next three shells went down the line of Kenyans on the left, middle, and right, and put an indeterminate number out of the fight. They ran away then, some toward the distant forest to the north and some toward me. The half-track went at full speed to the north end of the line of trees and caught a number of the soldiers trying for the forest. The newcomers on foot cut toward my hill.

I turned the cannon and fired two rounds to the right on the lower slope of the smaller hill. This was to discourage the Kenyans from coming around that side.

I was working furiously and sweating and beginning to feel tired because I had had almost no food or liquid for twenty hours. I was loading the shell, slamming the breech block shut, turning the cannon by lifting the tailpiece of the carriage, revolving the wheel to depress or elevate the barrel, and yanking the lanyard, though not always in this order. I had glimpsed the two soldiers scuttling across the level ground between the two hills, one on each side of me. I had to take care of them before I got rid of the last two shells.

One emerged from the shadows into the moonlight briefly, and I tossed a grenade his way. It fell a few feet from him; he froze; then he dived away from it. The explosion caught him in mid-air. He did not get up. I ran a stream of rifle fire across him to make sure he stayed down.

The other soldier was a brave man. He came up the hill at a run, zigzagging, and firing. I shot once; he fell backward. I approached him warily and put a bullet through his head.

With each death, I was numbly aware of my swelling penis and the rising tide of seminal fluid.

During this fight, the other soldiers came around both sides of the little hill and started up the big one toward me. They were desperate to get the cannon. With it, they could decimate the newcomers. They would, however, have to get me first and then bring up other caissons, because there were only two rounds left. I did not have time to fire these. I pushed the cannon over the lip of the hill and had the satisfaction of seeing a number running and screaming to get out of its way. Then I lobbed five grenades down the hill and took off down the other side with a BAR, a magazine belt, and three grenades.

Ten minutes later, I came up from behind one of the soldiers looking for me. I slit his throat, cut out his liver, and ate while I walked away from the others.

The cutting out of the liver finally evoked the orgasm that had been threatening, if I may use such a word. It was exquisite, but it was also disturbing.

(Those who have not read Volume I of my Memoirs, but who

are familiar with the first of the romanticized biographies, will object that I am not a cannibal. My biographer, when describing how I had killed the first human I ever encountered, said that I had first thought of eating him. Then I had rejected the idea because of an *instinctive* horror of cannibalism. This is one of the several cases of romantic nonsense and genetic misinformation that he believed in. The truth (which he did not know) is that I devoured the killer of the only being I had greatly loved. I did not like the taste, but I ate him as a matter of revenge. I have eaten other human beings since, but only when I could get no other food.)

Strengthened, I set out to torment the soldiers. These had pulled the cannon back up onto the hill and brought another caisson of shells up. The half-track, meanwhile, had taken a station behind a tree. The artillery duel began. A number of shells exploded around the vehicle, and one blew the tree in half. But eventually the recoilless .88 succeeded in hitting close enough to the Kenyan cannon to kill its crew and to blow up the other shells. The vehicle waited a moment, and then, probably receiving orders via walkie-talkie, started across the level ground toward the hill.

At that moment, I threw a grenade onto the platform. The crew died, but the shells failed to go off, as I had expected. Two men fell out of the cab and staggered away. I shot one and stunned the other with the butt of my rifle. It was easy to catch up with the vehicle, which was still rolling, and stop it. I put the two unconscious men on the platform and drove across the plain and as deeply as I could into the forest.

One man looked as if he would not recover. The other gained his senses with nothing but a headache from the blow. He was a muscular Arab, black-haired, clean-shaven, eagle-nosed, with two large but close-set eyes. He seemed to be about thirty years of age. He was dressed in khaki but wore no military insignia. He looked bravely enough at me, but he was shaking and was pale under his sallow skin.

The cannon and the grenades had again deafened me. However, I am an excellent lip reader in French, English, Arabic, Swahili, and a number of Bantu languages and dialects (if the latter are not tone languages).

I questioned him in Egyptian Arabic. He replied in Syrian Arabic. He said his name was Ibrahim Abdul el Mariyaka. He did not know what he was doing here or anything else. He felt brave enough to call me a dog of a Nasrani.

He ran his gaze up and down me and then licked his drying lips. He was standing with his back against a tree, both of them gray in the dawn. He was about six feet tall, but I was three inches higher and outweighed him about eighty pounds. I was naked, and my skin was smoke-blackened, but my gray eyes must have gleamed palely and wildly out of my dark face. Dried blood covered my mouth and chin and splotched my chest and hands, and there was dried blood and spermatic fluid on my belly and genitals. In addition, as I gestured at him with my knife, my penis rose slowly like a leech swelling with sucked blood.

Being an Arab, he must have been sure I was going to sexually assault him. In a way, he was right.

I kicked him in the stomach, and while he writhed, retching drily on the ground, I drank from a canteen of water I had taken from the cab. Then I removed some rope from the platform and tied him up. After propping him against the tree, I dragged the other man from the platform and sat him up against a wheel. He was gray-blue and breathing shallowly, but his blood pressure was high enough to drive a geyser into my face when I cut off his penis. I stuck it in his mouth and then drove his knife up through his chin to keep his jaw from falling open. Eyes open, limp bloody penis protruding from his mouth, he sat opposite the other man.

I cut out the liver, chewed off a piece, and swallowed it.

The Arab by the tree turned as gray-blue as the dead man when he saw me ejaculate on slicing into the man. He tried to retch but was unsuccessful. I waited. I had made no threats. None were needed. When he had quit trying to throw up, he leaned his head against the tree. His black eyes were dull below the half-closed lids. A snake of spittle ran down his chin.

I said, "I will ask. You will reply."

He knew, probably from experience in torturing others, that very few men can hold out against prolonged torture. He was willing to settle for a quick death. He answered my questions fully, and his information seemed to be valid.

The leader and organizer of this expedition was an Albanian. He went under the Arabic name of Muhmud abu Shawarib. His real name was Enver Noli. The others were mostly Arabs, although a few were Bulgarians who had fled to Albania because of their Red Chinese sympathies.

Noli had promised every man in his army that he would have enough gold to support him and four wives for the rest of his life. That is, if the Englishman, John Cloamby, Lord Grandrith, were captured alive.

"He talked only of gold?" I said.

"Yes. Was there anything else?"

Noli was not likely to promise his men the secret of prolonged youth, even if he believed that I possessed it. They would think him crazy and would not follow him. It was possible that he had no thought of the elixir, but I have encountered other men, all dead now, who believed, with good reason, that I had an elixir and were prepared to do anything to get the secret from me.

The Arab said, "You can kill me, Nasrani. But Noli will find you and inflict great pain upon you until you tell him where your gold is hidden. He is a very determined man, very cunning, and very strong."

"That may be," I said. I stabbed him in the solar plexus. Now I failed to have a sexual reaction, and I hoped that the aberration was, for some reason, gone. I doubted it. The truth was that I had only so much jism, and it had been used up for the time being.

I booby-trapped the vehicle with some wire and grenades so that three shells—one by the gas tank—would go off if the cab doors or the hood were opened. Then I went into the woods and up a tree and waited. The sounds of battle had died out. Presently, as I knew they would, the invaders came on the track of the vehicle. Two jeeps drove up; behind them straggled a mob, the survivors of the battle with the Kenyans.

CHAPTER SIX

Enver Noli was a huge man with a large belly, a shaven head, and great drooping moustaches that fell to his chest. His nose was immense, curved like a scimitar. He wore green coveralls and paratrooper's boots. He held his kepi in one tremendous fist and whacked it across the palm of the other hand. When he gave an order, he bellowed.

A soldier ran out from the main body of the troops and warily approached the vehicle. When he looked into the cab, he saw the wires I had gone to some pains to hide. He reported this to Enver, who stood up in the jeep, which was about seventy feet from the half-track. The soldier raised the hood to check the motor for traps there, and the grenade exploded and then the three shells. The vehicle and the soldier disappeared in smoke and flame. Noli was knocked off the jeep, but he bounded up and ran away with the rest. Unfortunately, nobody was hit by the shells or splashed by the gas. I did shoot two during the noise and panic.

Noli stopped running and managed to halt the twenty or so of his men. He got them to line up and to begin firing with two machine guns and fifteen rifles into the woods. While the bullets were flying around me, whipping the leaves and knocking off chunks of bark, I shot two more Arabs. Immediately after, I descended the tree and ran off in the direction opposite the invaders and then curved around until I was some distance behind them. The field, where the main fighting between the Kenyans and newcomers had taken place, was now being held by the jackals, hyenas, and vultures.

The two hills yielded more dead. The wounded had either been taken away or put out of their pain. The carrion eaters were busy here, too.

The village was entirely burned down, and of the survivors there was no sign. I knew they were hiding in the forest. They had fled to the forest more than once from Arab slave-raiders, though not until after great losses. I had been the one who had led them to victory against the Arab invaders and then led them across the country to terrorize the slavers so much that they never again dared enter Bandili country. I had led them against the Germans in World War I. I had led them in a great raid into Gekoyo. Now they were hiding again, and if they came out once more and fought, they would do it without me.

For 60 years I had been a Bandili and the great father, the elephant who charges, for the Bandili. Now, I was truly exiled. This was no temporary loss. It was forever.

I wept then. I had loved these people as much as I could any group of humans. I was far more Bandili than I was English. I had had true friends among them. But all that was ended. Although this village was the only one of the ten Bandili villages that had betrayed me, the others would be no better. The young were too hating and the old too feeble and too few.

Moreover, the Kenyan government had made it plain that I could no longer live in this country. Not in the open, at least.

I made a sentimental gesture. I waved my rifle at the ashes of the village and then at those hidden in the forest. It was the only good-bye I could give, and doubtless no one saw it.

Then I turned and began to trot across the savanna, toward the hills to the west.

My destination was the mountain range that lay far beyond the hills, approximately a hundred and fifty miles away, and twenty miles into Uganda. I trotted all night. The false dawn, the wolf's tail, was graying the savanna when I began to think about holing up for part of the day. The acacia trees in the distance looked like black cutouts of the monsters of Bandili myth. Then the sun leaned against the night and swung it away, and day padded in. A lion roared in the distance. The air was cool, moving gently from the mountains in the west. A wart hog trotted out of the tall grass, his tail held stiffly up. The sun gleamed on a yellow tusk.

I ran along easily with the savanna on my left and a clump of hills to my right. I carried the rifle in my right hand. I stopped for a moment because I saw the grasses move against the wind. Something big enough to be a lion or a man was approaching through the cover about thirty yards away.

The rifle soared up out of my hand, torn away by a blow like that from a crocodile's tail. It spun off, and then the sound of the shot came from the hills.

CHAPTER SEVEN

My arm was paralyzed by the transmission of shock through the rifle, but I did not find that out immediately. I dived toward the tall grass and rolled toward it. Dirt and grass flew up so close they fell over me. There were four gouts of earth and flocks of tiny pieces of grass, each followed by a shot ringing across the savanna.

I jumped up, and, zigzagging and bending low, ran. There was a growl, and a big yellowish brown body moved away from me. I smelled a lioness. She was gone, and I had the grass to myself except for the brief company of two bullets which cropped stalks only a few inches from me. I dived once more, and I stayed where I was.

Several minutes passed. My arm lost its numbness. More shots. More stalks cut in half, falling on me. The bugger had superb vision. I started crawling, though slowly. It was impossible to keep the grass from signaling my progress. More bullets slashed the grass.

When I had crossed about thirty-five yards, I was at the edge of the grass. I leaped up and ran away, still crouching. There were no more shots. Not for a second had I thought that the sharpshooter was a member of the Kenyans or of the band of the Albanian, Noli. A third party had dealt himself in.

I heard a roar behind and looked over my shoulder. A male lion was charging after me. I did not know how he could be in this neighborhood or why he was chasing me. He must have been very near but somehow hidden from me. The stimulus of seeing me run away from him had evoked the reaction of running after me. I knew every lion for 40 miles in any direction from my plantation. This one was a stranger and should not have been here out of his own territory.

He was the largest lion I'd ever seen. He weighed 650 or more pounds, and his mane was so thick that I knew at once that he had not been in the bush for long. He looked as if he had been bred for the purpose of eating me. He also looked as if he had not eaten lately; his ribs were getting close to the outside air.

I'm not often amazed, but this was one of the times. In my seventy-nine years, I've fought at most twelve lions, considerably less than my biographer records. Usually, a male lion is as eager to avoid a battle as I am. But I have killed them with only a knife, as my biographer records, though there have never been any of the face-to-face encounters shown in those very bad and lying movies. If I got into the situations those actors did, my bowels would have been scooped out or my back muscles plucked out or my head bitten off.

I crouched, waiting for the lion with my knife in my hand. The next thing that happened told me that the hitting of my rifle had been no lucky shot.

The knife was jerked out of my hand. Like a bright bird, it flew up and away. I heard the distant report of the rifle before the knife struck the ground.

My moment of shock almost cost me my life. The lion launched himself toward me on the final bound. I got to one side just in time; a paw flashed by, brushing the skin of my chest.

Getting onto the lion's back when he is in full charge requires very swift and unhesitating movements. If the slightest thing goes wrong—slipping a little, estimating the trajectory and speed of the final leap by too little or too much—it's over for the man. I had jumped to one side while he was still on the downcurve of the arc of his leap and stomped one foot and was bounced back in again and had grabbed the mane with my left hand. A savage yank pulled me along with the beast and also up into the air. Usually, I had to use one hand because my knife was in the other, but this time I had both free. And so I had a better hold and was on its back even more quickly than usual.

He reared up and then fell to one side. I went with him but twisted to keep from being crushed. Up he came again. I had my arms under his front legs, and when he rose I had my hands around the back of his neck and locked together.

His roaring had been loud. Now, from somewhere in that cavernous body, he got the force to double the noise. He rolled again—making me feel as if I were being spread out like a turtle under an elephant's hoof—but I managed to keep my legs locked around his belly. His hind feet moved up to tear my legs, but he could not get them under me or even touch my legs.

Then, as we lay in the dirt, slowly, slowly, his bones creaking, his head went down under the pressure of my arms. I realize that this is difficult to believe. A lion has truly enormous strength in those massive neck muscles. But I am not as other men, in degree or kind. Not in many things, anyway, and this was not the first time I had broken a big cat's neck with a full-Nelson, though the other had not been as huge as this one.

It was not easy. For a long time, the lion, growling much more softly now, resisted my utmost efforts, and his neck refused to bend any more. But the time came when the bones creaked again like a wooden ship in a heavy sea. My head was buried in the mane as I sweated and strove. The hairs stuck in my face like little spears. The green-yellow lion odor was strong, and, beneath it, was the stench of awareness of death. Not fear of death, awareness of its inevitability. The end had come for him, and he knew it. Everybody born in Africa—antelope, lion, Black man, Arab, Berber—knows when the time has come. The awareness is a legacy from this ancient land, the birthplace of mankind and of many many species of beast. Mother Africa lets her child know when he is about ready to fertilize her soil with the body she gave him. Everybody knows this except the descendants of Europeans—myself excepted.

As I felt the neck muscles weaken with this awareness, and my arm muscles gain in strength for the same reason, I became conscious of an approaching orgasm. I don't know when my penis had swelled and my testicles gathered themselves for the explosion. But my penis was jammed between the lion's back and my belly, and it was throbbing and beginning to jerk.

At that moment, the lion's neck gave way. As the muscles loosened, and the bones broke, I spurted, sliming the fur and my belly.

The lion moaned with a final outgoing of air, kicked, and himself spurted. I rose, unsteadily, after dragging my leg out from under him. I scooped up some of the lion sperm in the dust and swallowed it. This was a custom of The Folk, one which my biographer avoided describing. It is supposed to bestow the potency of the male lion upon the eater. I believe it does; no amount of European education has convinced me otherwise. Besides, I like the heavy big-feline taste and odor of it. It is, more than almost anything, African in its essence. There is everything in it. Let him who would envision the soul of this ancient continent, eat lion sperm.

Always, after making a kill of a beast of prey, I stand with one foot on the carcass and give a great yell of triumph. This, too, I learned from The Folk. But this time, the orgasm and the knowledge that I was a target for a sharpshooter, chopped off that cry.

CHAPTER EIGHT

Although the knife bore the dent of the bullet near the hilt and also had been twisted by the impact, it was still serviceable. Moreover, I would not have thrown it away if it had been useless. Though I am not sentimental, I could not bear to get rid of it. It had been my real father's in England, and he had given it to my uncle before he became mad. My first sight of the knife was my first knowledge of metal. And it had served me for seventy years and killed ten times that number of prey and enemies.

I put it in the sheath and looked toward the hills. The sun flashed now and then. The reflection of binoculars or cameras, possibly. Or of a telescope.

A puff of dirt struck immediately in front of me as I stopped to pick up the rifle; the sound of the shot came about a second later. The shooter was approximately 1,125 feet away. The second bullet struck a few inches to my left; the third, to my right. The fourth went between my legs. I was being told to run away onto the savanna and leave the rifle behind.

Instead, I cut the lion open and removed a piece of his heart and chewed on it. Four more shots, very close, enabled me to discern the exact location of the rifle. I also saw four men through the bush on the hill.

I left at a slow walk. I abandoned my rifle because its barrel had been bent by the bullet. I was angry because of the ease with which the rifleman was herding me and the contempt I felt he had for me. If he thought I was really dangerous, he would have killed me with his first shot. His actions seemed to say: Try your best, my dear Lord Grandrith. It won't be nearly good enough.

When I had walked a quarter of a mile, the shots ceased. From time to time, as I strode to the west, I looked back. Two miles away, a cloud of dust followed. When I stopped to bathe in a waterhole, the dust settled. I caught and ate several almost mouse-sized grasshoppers which inhabit this region. I threw a stone at a kingfisher but missed it by a wing's length. There are many kingfishers in this region, where there is little water except during the rainy season. But the kingfishers have abandoned an aquatic diet; they have adapted to catching grasshoppers and other insects.

When night came, I backtracked. Twenty minutes later, I had found the camp of the sharpshooter. It was on the flat top of a small hill in a clearing around which was an unusual growth of bush and number of trees. A depression beside it held some water, which accounted for the dense growth. In the clearing were two large trucks, one of which carried a very large camper, and two jeeps. Three tents were pitched; two fires had been built. Some Blacks were cooking over one fire, and coffee was boiling over both. There were six Blacks and two white men in sight. Then I saw a white man move behind the half-opened flap of a tent. The weak light from the lamp within gleamed on a bronze back for a moment.

I had smelled the coffee a long way off and had been salivating. I love coffee. If these people had not been shooting at me that afternoon, I would have been tempted to join them.

I moved around until I could get a better view of the man inside the tent. I still could not see much of him, but I got the impression of a very large and very solid man. He seemed to be doing some peculiar exercises. I caught glimpses of bronzed biceps, bunching and smoothing over and over again. The muscles looked like mongooses slipping back and forth in a wild play under a blanket woven of bronze wires. I know that that is a rather fanciful description, but that is what occurred to me.

The other two whites, old men, sat on folding chairs with their backs to me. The smaller was thin, quick-moving, wary as a bird, and had a face sharp as the neck of a broken-off bottle. He was dressed as if he had just stepped out of the most expensive safari outfitter's store in Nairobi. As he talked, he gestured frequently with a silver-headed black cane.

The other old man was so wide and had such abnormally long arms, thick neck, simian features, and low forehead, and his arms were so hairy, he could almost have passed for one of The Folk.

The Blacks had talked among themselves in Swahili, so I knew the names of all three whites. The man in the tent was a Doctor Caliban. The dapper old man was a Mr. Rivers. The apish old man was a Mr. Simmons. All three were from Manhattan Island.

I suspected that the old men were talking so loudly because they hoped to entice an eavesdropper—me, of course—to come closer. I found the trip wire which would have set off some kind of alarm and got over that without disturbing it. I also detected the two rocks, made of papier-mâché, which held electronic eye devices inside them. I had come close to wriggling between them, because that was the natural route to a depression in the ground behind a bush, an excellent place to hide while listening. Only because I happened to rub up against the false stone did I discover what it was.

I became even more cautious then. And I noticed that the flap of the tent in which Doctor Caliban had been exercising was now closed. For all I knew, he might be slipping out the rear of the tent to catch a spy.

If the two old men were part of a trap, they certainly took no care to keep silent on matters that an enemy should not know. And they talked about Caliban as if he were deaf.

I crawled around to one side where I could see their lips. This was not as informative as listening, because I missed words now and then, but it was safer.

". . . really know what's got into Doc?" the dapper Rivers said. "Something sure as shit is wrong."

"Looks as if he's gone ape," Simmons said.

Rivers laughed and spoke so loudly I could hear him. "Ape! Ape? You old Neanderthal, you're throwing stones at a glass house!"

"Listen, you sick legal eagle, you," Simmons said, "this is no time or place for your tired old bullshit. This is serious, I'm telling you. Doc has a screw loose somewhere. I think it's the elixir; it has to be. The side effects are finally coming through. I warned him years ago, when he offered it to us. I ain't one of the world's greatest chemists for nothing."

I had been intrigued before. Now I was caught, a crocodile on a hook. Elixir!

"You really think he's crazy? After all these years of doing good, combating evil, fixing up all those criminals we caught, and reforming them?" Rivers said.

The apish old man said, "That's another thing . . ."

I missed what he said next, then his cigar left his lips. ". . . operated on them, he said. Cut out the gland that made them evil, he said at first. Then later on he quit talking about that gland, because there ain't no such thing, and he started to talk about re-routing and short-circuiting neural circuits. Now, I ask you, do you really believe that shit? It was all right in the old days, because we didn't know much about the causes of crime then. But it's different now. We know it's caused mainly by psychosocioeconomic environments."

"Do we?" Rivers said. "What really do we know now more than we knew then, besides some things in the physical sciences and a little progress in the biological?"

"O.K., so they ain't as smart nowadays as they like to think they are," Simmons said. "But in the '30s, we could believe anything Doc told us because he told us it was so. But did you ever see him operate on a criminal? Not that I doubt he did something to them, handy as he is with a knife. But this crap about curing criminals with surgery . . . know as well as I do that a criminal is the product of genetic predisposition plus environment."

"Doc isn't the man we knew, that's for sure," Rivers said. "I don't know. It's like seeing Lucifer fall. Well, that's stretching it. Doc's no evil angel, but . . . if you want to get right down to the honest-to-God-call-it-shit-not-peanut-butter-reality, Doc may be right about the causes and cure of criminals."

Simmons looked as if he were grunting. He said, "Maybe. And maybe Doc was getting his kicks . . . well, I shouldn't say that, wouldn't, if it wasn't for his funny behavior now. You gotta admit he's been acting kinda peculiar lately. Now, I ain't saying he's become a Doctor Jekyll-Mr. Hyde . . . but . . ."

They were silent for a while. Simmons puffed on his cigar. Rivers lit a long cigarette in a long cigarette holder. After a while, Simmons pulled some rectangles—photographs, I presumed—from the pocket of his bush jacket. He held them up so that the firelight illuminated them.

He said, "Looka the whang on that wild man! Did you ever see such a prick on a white man?"

Rivers took one of the photos and studied it. "My tool is longer," he said. "Used to be, anyway. Eight inches. But it's skinny. I never saw such a shaft on a man except once."

"The son of a bitch is queer," Simmons said. "I was looking through the glasses when he got up after breaking that lion's neck. He had a hard-on you wouldn't believe outside a zoo. And he was coming like a Texas oil well."

"Yes, I know," Rivers said. "My choppers about dropped out. I saw Doc once, just once, and he's the only man I ever saw, Black or white, with a dong as big as that Englishman's. In fact, I'll swear his was even thicker and longer."

"You saw Doc's cock?" Simmons said. "When the hell was that?"

". . . adventure of the Tsar of . . ." Rivers said. "You remember, Doc and I'd been a long time hiding . . . had to piss . . . my eyes about flew the coop, believe me."

Simmons looked around uneasily. "Maybe we shouldn't be talking like this. Doc might . . ."

"You think he hasn't heard us a million times before? He knows how curious we've been. Personally, I think he's been listening to us for years. But what we said never seemed to bother him. You know what a button-down lip he's got. And he's the most self-controlled man in the world; he couldn't admit that anything we said would stick in his craw. And maybe it doesn't. He *knows* he's the superman's superman!"

"After what I seen today, I ain't so sure," Simmons said. "I've never seen anything like it! But I can understand now why Doc is so hot to tangle with him. He wants to test his mettle on somebody who looks as if he could give him a hard time!"

The little man said, as if he hadn't heard Simmons, "You know, I used to put it out of my mind, or tell myself that Doc was just keeping his private life entirely to himself. But he never lied to us, as far as I know. And he always said he led too dangerous a life and was too busy and always off on some quest or other. He couldn't afford to get married; it made him too vulnerable. That's understandable. But he went further. He said he didn't want to get involved with any woman because it wouldn't be fair to waste her time. That's understandable. But then he claimed he had nothing at all to do with women. Nothing at all! Now, didn't you ever think that was peculiar? No ass at all! No pussy, no nothing, for God's sakes!"

"Well," Simmons said, "he coulda been jerking off. But it just doesn't seem like Doc to be doing that. I always thought maybe he wasn't so perfect, after all. You know, maybe he was paying for his mental and physical superiority to the rest of us—to every fucking man in the world—by not being able to get a hard-on. Could be. Jesus Christ! There has to be some sort of compensation in this world!"

"There does?" Rivers said. "Who told you that, you shoddy imitation of a philosophizing orangutan!"

"One a these days, I'll orangutan it all the way up your decrepit asshole," Simmons said.

"No, you won't. I don't allow anything but high-quality shit up there," Rivers said.

They talked for a moment with their hands over their mouths as they held their smokes in their mouths. Then I saw Rivers' lips.

"You know, Doc and . . . as if they were brothers . . . coloring . . . black hair and gray eyes and a darker skin, but Doc has . . ."

They talked on, rambling much. I got the impression that these two octogenarians had known each other intimately for a long long time. They had been through much with each other, and they were very fond of each other. The abuses and insults they loosed at each other were good-natured, indeed, their second natures. And as I listened—read, rather—I understood that they were here on The Last Great Adventure. There had been three other men who had shared their exploits and dangers in the past. But these were dead now. The two old men expected to die soon, but they had insisted on coming to Africa with Caliban, and he had reluctantly agreed.

Now, they were sorry they had come. Or, at least, disturbed. Something had happened to the good doctor. He was here to hunt me down and to kill me. Not with guns. In bare-hand combat. This was not at all like Doc. He had always been averse to killing. He had only done so when he absolutely had to. And he had maintained that every man, no matter how evil, was worth saving.

Something had changed his mind. They knew what it was, but so far they had not named it. They referred to it circuitously.

Doc Caliban had told them that I was an abysmally evil man who should be obliterated. The two were not convinced. From what they had learned about me from other sources, they did not think I could be the monster that Doc described. Yet, all their adult lives, they had trusted Doc. They had regarded him as an oracle, as the fount of wisdom, as a doer of great good.

Doc had been born in 1903, I learned when the two were quarreling about the best sign in the zodiac. He was now sixty-five years old, but he looked as if he were still thirty.

They did not seem bitter that he had not shared his secret of prolonged youth with them. They spoke as if he had offered it to them, but they had turned it down.

I could not believe this. I assumed that I misunderstood them. There was the possibility that they had been over fifty when the offer was made. In that case, the elixir was only able to slow down aging somewhat. By the time they were ninety, they would have aged physically to about seventy. Perhaps, on considering the price they must pay for this slight prolongation of life, they had rejected it. What, after all, was an extra thirty years or so of life?

But when a man was offered a chance to live at least 30,000 years, then the price looked small.

I liked to think so.

But listening to them, I was forced to dwell a little on that which I had pushed away because it was too painful. Had I, by becoming a god, become less of a man?

CHAPTER NINE

Now I knew what Doc Caliban's ultimate goal might be. He meant to kill me, for some reason, but the end of his journey could lie in the mountains to the west, where I also intended to journey.

I began to get more uneasy. Not that I expected him to try to kill me now. It was obvious that he was "toying" with me. Also, it was obvious that the old men had instructions to talk as freely as they pleased. Caliban wanted me to learn much about him. The more I knew, the more "equal" would be the hunted and the hunter.

I felt angrier. Up to now, every enemy had done his best to make the situation as unequal as possible. But Caliban was treating me contemptuously.

Very well. Let him have his contempt. If he really intended to fight me to the death with only his bare hands, he was not going to frighten me.

I would leave now for the mountains, where I had an engagement for which I would be late if I did not start now. Doctor Caliban, if he was to make the same destination on time, would do better to start on the journey at once.

I inched backward. Then I stopped. A bronze cloud had scudded into the light of the campfire.

There were empty shadows. A second later, as if stepping from the wings of a stage, the man, the bronze cloud, was there.

The two old men started, even though they must have experienced this noiseless unannounced jack-in-the-boxery many times before.

Doctor Caliban was at least four inches taller than I. His body was superb, massive yet beautifully proportioned. The bones of skull and torso looked very thick, and his skull was long-shaped. He was the only other man, besides myself, and some of the Nine, who had such heavy bones. Which meant he had more foundation for muscular attachment and for larger muscles than most men.

His skin was a pale bronze. His hair, which was of medium length and parted on the right, was a darker bronze. It looked like a metal cap that had been welded onto his skull. And though he was too far away for me to determine accurately his eye color, I got the impression they were light-green.

His face was extremely handsome and regular. It was masculine, yet almost beautiful. It also looked familiar, though I had never seen him before.

He spoke in a deep resonant voice, like a bronze bell's. His speech was even and regular with none of the hesitations, pauses, vague exclamations, or broken off sentences and phrases that distinguish the speech of most humans.

"Lord Grandrith, the Noble Savage, the titled man-ape, is watching you two," he said.

He looked into the shadows at the exact spot where I lay. He laughed and pulled from his belt a round object I recognized a moment later as a grenade. He pulled the pin and with a swiftness that might have dazzled a leopard, tossed it at me.

It would have landed just out of arm's reach if I had not moved forward. I caught it and hurled it back at him and then was gone into the bush. I looked back. He was standing with his hands on his hips, his back bent backward, head thrown back, and laughing. The grenade was at his feet, and the two old men had dived away—very swiftly for eighty-year-olds—and were hugging the ground.

The Blacks were standing up and asking questions, but they could not see the grenade and so did not know what was causing the commotion. A big Negro stepped out of the tent with a rifle. I had not seen him before. He looked as if he were a Yankee.

Doc Caliban said, loudly, "It's a dummy! I just wanted to test his reactions! They're very good! The best I ever saw outside of my own!"

Simmons, getting up, spoke in a squeaky voice that was comical issuing from such a squat long-armed brutish man. "Doc! When're you going to cut out this crap! If he killed Trish, why don't you kill him and get it over with?"

CHAPTER TEN

U sually, I don't think in the human categories of good and evil. Those who would kill me are enemies. Just that and nothing more. I kill them without having to justify the deed by classifying them as evil.

But seeing this very handsome man, I experienced a feeling of genuine evil, of the anti-good. The hairs rose on the back of my neck as if a demon of a native African religion had pulled them up with his cold hands of wind.

It was a feeling I did not like.

I decided to leave for the mountains. However, about twenty yards from the camp, I came across a large aluminum-sided wooden-floored cage lying on its side, the door open. I sniffed at it, and I knew not only that it had held a lion, I knew which lion. I also knew why I had been attacked by a hungry lion that had no business in this area. Doc Caliban had not only loosed it at me, he had probably spent some time conditioning it to attack human beings.

If he had wanted an estimate of me, he now had it.

I lifted the cage above my head—it only weighed about 200 pounds—and carried it to a tree I had noticed a moment ago. This was tall and thin and had all the characteristics required for my sudden plan. I never learned its English name—if it had one—but knew it by the Bandili word, *ndangga*.

After lassoing its top with my rope, I pulled it down with much straining until its top almost touched the ground. After securing the rope around the trunk of another tree, I wove the branches of the bent tree into a rough net near the top. This required the breaking of a number of branches, which might bring Caliban running. That was a chance I not only would take but welcomed. He, however, did not appear.

The net of branches held the cage as well as I had hoped. I looked through the trees and saw that the two old men had returned to their chairs. They were talking so loudly that they covered any sound I might have made while constructing the catapult. A Black brought them glasses with some dark liquid in it, and, between sips, they shouted what must have been insults at each other. The Blacks were squatting on the other side of their fire and talking. The fire gleamed on their rolling eyeballs and teeth.

I waited a while. Caliban stuck his head out of the tent once to say something to the old men. At that moment, I whacked the rope in two with the knife. There was a hum, a crack as the rope snapped past me, another hum, deeper, and a loud whish as the tree straightened. The cage flew up and out in a trajectory that came from accident and hope more than skill. But the result was admirable.

The cage, turning over slowly, flew down toward Caliban's tent. He burst out of it like a bronze shell from a seventeenth century cannon. The two oldsters jumped up from their chairs, their drinks flying and their smokes falling out of their mouths as they looked around for the source of the noise. The Blacks scattered, some running toward Caliban's tent.

Caliban kept on running and disappeared into the darkness, undoubtedly looking for me. The Blacks were behind bushes and trees and looking at the crushed tent. Simmons was jumping up and down like an enraged chimpanzee and howling, "Oh, my God! My God! I shit in my pants! I was so scared, I shit in my pants!"

Rivers was on the ground and rolling back and forth and laughing hysterically.

For a moment, I thought of ambushing Caliban and getting this conflict over with. I was restrained by knowing that he probably had the same goal as I and that I would meet him there. I wanted to find out if he could continue to track and harass me. I also wanted him to be even more convinced that he was dealing with a buffalo in the bush, not with an antelope.

CHAPTER ELEVEN

The dawn was as gray as an old lion's hopes for fresh meat. It quickly enough became bright and quick and sent its golden roar out over the savanna. The gold melted over the world, and the day was hot and sluggish.

I trotted across the plain for an hour after the sun rose. I had been trotting all night and was thinking about holing up until late afternoon. The mountains, light-purplish and getting taller, were about thirty miles to the west now. Perhaps, if I pushed on, I could get there before dusk and even be part way up the flank of the nearest one.

I kept on going. After a while, I was within a half-mile of a Kitasi village, a collection of about thirty huts, round, double-domed, and built of sticks, grass, and dried mud. The Kitasi were cattle herders, drinkers of blood, many-wived, and of ancestors who had mixed their Negro genes with dark Caucasian somewhere in the north a long time ago. In 1920, when I first encountered them, they wore bark-fiber loin coverings which projected fore and aft, looking from a distance like the paper boats that schoolboys make. In the old days, the Kitasi had killed their king as soon as gray appeared in his hair. The British had forced a halt to this custom, but the king died by "accident." Then a white man had given the new king a bottle of hair dye, and the latest king might yet die of old age.

At one time the Kitasi had been a powerful people. They had warred with the Masai, the Agikuyu, and the Bandili. The thirty villages of 20,000 population, as a result, were now six with about a thousand inhabitants. The Kitasi hated many people, but they hated me most of all, and with good reason.

The men in the old stake-bed truck heading out from the village may have been told about me by radio and were looking for me. It was going southeast; I was going southwest. We were about a mile apart. Then they spotted me, and the truck swung around and raced toward me. I ran toward some acacia trees, a half a mile away, and got behind the nearest one as the truck pulled up, brakes screeching. It had stopped about a hundred yards away.

There were three men in the cab and six on the bed. All got out of the truck. Three were armed with rifles that looked, from my distance, like pre–World War I Enfields. One carried a heavy spear and a machete in a sheath. Two had bows and wore quivers of arrows on their backs. One had a revolver, and the other two carried big axes.

They talked awhile and then spread out in an ever-widening arc, the ends of which curved out toward me. A rifleman was on each end; the third rifleman was in the center. The two bowmen flanked him, and the spearman and the axemen were equidistant between the center man and the end men. The arc advanced slowly while the men shouted encouragement to each other or shouted insults and threats at me.

So far, they did not know whether or not I had a revolver, but they did know I had no rifle. There were nine of them, and they should have charged me in the truck, swung broadside when near me, and then let loose with a volley. Afterward, they could have jumped off the truck and charged me on foot. If they were brave and determined, they probably would have gotten me, even if I had killed a number of them.

They preferred to take it cautiously. My reputation probably made them extra careful. When they were within sixty feet, they stopped. I remained on the other side of the tree. The riflemen on the ends ran even further outward and then cut in so they could get behind me. I waited. I was naked and had only the knife, which had been worn down so much that it no longer had a good balance for throwing. I was going to have to depend upon speed, and I was not at my freshest after having run all night without eating and with little water.

Nearby were several stones, two of which were of the right size and shape for throwing. I put the knife between my teeth and picked up a stone in each hand. The riflemen on both ends seeing this, shouted the news to the others. Then they started shooting at me.

A bullet ricocheted off the tree. I darted around to the other side and started running at an angle from the men in the center of the arc. The rifleman there started to fire at me, and the bowmen shot their arrows. They missed. Immediately after the arrows were released, I cut back in the opposite direction. The second flight of arrows missed also, and though I heard some bullets, I was not hit.

All of these men had been raised on tales about me and so regarded me as some sort of demon. They were very excited and apprehensive, and the fact that I ran toward them instead of away additionally rattled them. Moreover, under these conditions, my zigzagging made it even more difficult to hit me. And I am swift; I have been clocked at 8.6 seconds in the 100-yard dash, and I was barefooted.

Yet they were brave men and stood their ground. (The Kitasi still eliminate their cowards before they reach eighteen, despite the watch that the British had kept on them.) They kept to their stations and fired at me, and the spearman and the two axemen ran toward me, shouting Kitasi war cries.

I stopped briefly and cast a stone. It caught the rifleman on his head. He fell backward, and I ran again, this time straight toward him. The youth with the revolver ran toward me, firing. I paid him no attention because he would hit me only by accident while he ran. The bowmen aimed again at me, while the axemen and spearman ran in toward me. I threw myself down and then jumped up and hurled my second stone. It struck the bowman on my left in the neck, and he fell down.

The riflemen on the ends were running back now and firing as they ran. One of their bullets struck an axeman, and he was out of the fight.

It had been nine. Suddenly, it was six. The spear went over my shoulder and thudded into the ground before me. I yanked it out, paused as bullets screamed by, and cast. The spear went through the shoulder of the youth with the revolver.

I dived for the rifle by the first man I'd hit, rolled, and came up with it. It still had an unfired cartridge in it. I took my time and aimed, and the rifleman on the right threw up his arms, his weapon flying, and fell on his face. I picked up a cartridge off the ground beside a spilled box and inserted it in the breech and jumped to one side, went to one knee, and fired again. The last of the riflemen clutched his leg and fell down and kicked and screamed. I removed the bandolier from the corpse and slipped it over my shoulder.

Sun flashed off an axehead as it turned over and over with me at the end of its arc through the air. I leaped to one side, inserted another cartridge, and killed the man who still had his axe. He fell a few feet from me; another two seconds and he might have split my skull.

The others ran away. Since I was between them and the truck, they went on foot. I drove off in the truck. The fuel meter was broken, so I could not know how much gas I had left. It did not matter. I would drive until it ran out.

I was happy. The fight had lifted me up, and I had a means for putting more distance more swiftly between me and my pursuers. I also noticed that I had not had an orgasm during the killings. This meant that the exertion and excitement had been too much for even that powerful aberrated behavior to appear, or it meant that I was still drained of seminal fluid, or it might mean that I was rid of my aberration. I was inclined to favor the second speculation.

But I had water in several canteens in the truck and could rest for a while. The bumpy ride was, to me, a relaxation. And I was headed at a speed faster than I had hoped to attain this morning toward the people who could give me an answer, if anyone could.

CHAPTER TWELVE

The shadow slashed across the truck like a knife cutting apart my hopes of escape.

The roar of the jets followed the shadow. Overhead, by thirty feet, the jet sped ahead, pulled up and around, and then came back in. In the brief look at it, I saw that it was a Kenyan Army plane, an English Huntley-Hawker.

The jet came back only twenty feet above the ground and about fifty yards to my right. The pilot was trying to see if I was in the truck. He shot by, his black face turned toward me. He grinned. Well he might. He carried rockets under his wings, pods of napalm, and, if these failed, or he did not want to waste them on one man, he could use his machine guns and the cannon.

I began evasive action. It looked, however, as if my evading days were over. I had no cover near. Even if I had, I would have been burned or blasted out.

The jet passed me and continued near the ground for perhaps 2,000 feet. Then it pulled up to about a thousand and circled so that it would come in straight at me. Undoubtedly, though I could not see his features, he was still grinning. He was happy to be obliterating the white man, the fabled Lord Grandrith. He probably did not know the reason for the Kenyan government's decision to destroy me. He may have heard stories about me, but, as an educated man, he would have been forced to laugh at the teller of them as an ignorant and superstitious man.

Whatever he believed, he must have thought he had me powerless.

He was the absolute master in this situation, and none of my demonic abilities would help me.

He came down swiftly. I pressed on the accelerator, ready to swing the truck to the left the moment the rockets or napalm pods were loosed. They would be going so swiftly that even my reflexes would be too slow. But I was going to try evasion. Something . . .

Overhead, something did develop. It was tiny and blue as the sky. It looked as if it were a bolt in the big door of the sky and someone had slammed it shut. It was blue and then it merged with the glitter of the sun on the jet, and both became a great red and white ball, expanding as the tiny missile and the rockets and the napalm and the fuel supply exploded.

The truck was going west and on a level. The fireball was going east and at a steep angle. I drove at full speed ahead; I could do nothing else. The light roared overhead. Heat struck in through the open windows and the broken windshield, and then the ball smashed into the ground behind me with a great noise, many in one. The heat intensified. I smelled paint and wood burning. There was light inside my head. The skin on my right arm and shoulder reddened with the sudden sear. I was already holding my breath and hoping my skin would not crisp and curl off me. And then I was out of the blast.

Some distance away, I stopped the truck and got out onto the top of the cab for a better look.

The wreckage was scattered over a half-mile square area. A hole in the midst of the flames could have been ten feet deep. Bushes and trees burned, and the grass was beginning to blaze in a fire that would sweep the savanna.

Far to the east, two clouds of dust rose. They were approximately the same distance from me but separated from each other by three or more miles.

One cloud would be rising from either the Albanian-Arabic party or Kenyan Army vehicles. The other would be from Doctor Caliban's group. I was sure that it was he who had fired that tiny but deadly missile. One of the trucks carried a camper that was more than a camper. It concealed a missile launcher and only Caliban knew what else.

I felt no gratitude. Instead, I burned as brightly inside as the wreckage outside. I burned with fury and frustration.

A Feast Unknown

After a while I cooled off, helped by the fact that the fire behind me would be frustrating my pursuers. It was racing across the savanna toward them, and they would be forced to run away from the flames—and so away from me. In the meantime, I would go ahead in as straight a line as the topography permitted. I would travel at thirty mph until the gas gave out or I reached the foothills.

I laughed. Caliban, momentarily at least, had checked himself when he had saved my life. A minute later, one of the worn old tires blew. I replaced it with an exhausted looking spare, and ten minutes afterward a stone went through that.

I continued on foot. Behind me, the world seemed to be going up in flames.

CHAPTER THIRTEEN

Six hours later, I was on the first of the foothills. Two hours later, I was on the top of the third large hill. The sunset was only two hours away. I felt tired and hungry, but first I had to survey the country behind me. The plains looked smooth from my altitude and distance, but I knew that they were very rocky for the last ten miles and crossed by a grid of wadis. Three dust clouds separated from each by about three miles, were slowly converging in the east. Dusk would fall before they got near each other, however.

I continued climbing through forest which was largely deciduous: oaks and maples. Though the savanna was dry, there was enough moisture here, mostly from underground sources, to supply a very thick growth. In fact, at many places, the trees were so close to each other that I could travel occasionally from tree to tree. Not in the fashion my biographer describes or as those lying movies portray. But adequately enough. My speed was faster in the trees, even though I went no faster than a slow walk, because I could avoid the almost impenetrable undergrowth. I could have made even better time if I had abandoned the rifle.

On the broad branch of a great oak which grew on an almost vertical slope, I waited for the dusk. I was tearing at the delicious meat of a scaly anteater and watching the dying dust from the three parties after me. They had gone as far as they could in their vehicles, and besides they had to camp for the night. Each was only about a mile apart from the next, but the hills barred their views. This did not mean that they were not aware of each other.

The Kenyan army personnel would stop where they were, if they observed national boundaries. I was now in Uganda. The Albanian-Arab party paid no attention to it, of course. Thirty tiny figures walked down a hill and then were lost. As nearly as I could determine, they carried no weapons heavier than rifles.

Doctor Caliban's party threaded down a narrow ravine. I counted them. Two Blacks were missing. They had stayed behind, probably to operate equipment in the camper. It was then that I decided to go back down the mountainside. This took into account the strong possibility that Caliban anticipated just such a move and had taken measures against it. He was the most dangerous man I had ever encountered, and I've run up against scores of the most cunning and vicious of killers. Although I knew little about him, I felt that he was by far the most intelligent and the best equipped, technologically, teleologically, and physically (in a neuromuscular sense).

The shadows had flooded that side of the mountain and stretched out to cover the smaller hills and some of the plains. Despite the growing dark, I saw a party leave the Kenyan camp. They did not intend to stop at the border.

I passed them on the way down. They were struggling through the undergrowth in a very narrow path which they enlarged with machetes. An officer said something about stopping soon, and they went on by me. We were separated by a few feet. I was tempted to approach the single file from the rear and cut a few throats before disappearing, but I resisted. To harass them for my own amusement would spoil my plans.

In the darkness, I watched the Kenyans that had stayed behind. They were busy. Evidently others were going to follow the first party in the morning. And from what I could hear of the radio operator's conversation, planes—transports and helicopters were bringing in other men and supplies. I did not know what they were after. Surely they would not be going to this trouble and expense, and risking un-pleasantness with Uganda, just to kill me. No, it had to be the gold. And they were acting as if they knew where they were going.

I went on to the camp of Doctor Caliban. The trucks and jeeps were parked to form a square in a clearing inside the woods. No men were in sight, and the camper shed no light. A small dish-shaped antenna on top of the camper turned around and around. This was probably only one of the devices for detecting intruders.

I waited. The night stretched out and blackened. Clouds were covering the stars. The moon was a dim irregular shape, like the just-beginning-to-form body of a chick in the yolk.

The door in the rear of the camper opened and shut. No light shone. Undoubtedly the door was connected to an off-switch so that the light would not give them away when they passed through.

Only one man had come out. He walked around the inside of the rectangle formed by the vehicles. He was smoking but took care to shield the fire in his palm. It would have been easy to get him with the rifle, but I did not want to alarm the other man or attract the Kenyans. He was pacing back and forth in the square, stopping short of one jeep and turning and striding back to the other and turning. He carried a submachine gun in his hand, as nearly as I could tell in the dark.

I timed him for a while and then leaped over the hood of the jeep, without touching it, as he turned away from it. He heard me and whirled, but I crashed down on him. Before he could cry out or trigger the gun, he was dead with my knife in his throat.

While I was waiting to launch myself, my penis had risen up, and as the man's blood spurted out, I spurted over him.

For a moment, I crouched, trying to recover my breath and also to listen for sounds within the camper. The orgasm had taken such violent possession of me, it had made me drop my knife and writhe as if I had been electrically shocked.

The aberration was getting more dangerous. How could I kill more than one person in a fight if the first kill made me momentarily helpless?

The submachine gun was of a make unknown to me. It was very compact, and the slender muzzle could eject nothing larger than .22 caliber, if that. It was probably custom-made for Caliban, and probably shot explosive bullets. I took the gun, felt it, inspected it as best I could in the dark, found out how to operate it, and then approached the camper. The antenna was still rotating.

I placed my ear against the metal of the camper but could hear nothing. Its walls were well insulated. I left the camper and explored the other truck. It was locked, but the keys were on the body of the Black. I unlocked it and went into the supply camper, and came out with several grenades. I pulled the pin on one and tossed it as far away as I could. I had decided I wanted to get the other man out as swiftly as possible, and I was not going to worry about the Kenyans. I hoped that the man in the camper would run out to see what the noise was. He could stay within and warn Caliban, of course, since I was sure he was in radio contact with him.

Immediately after the explosion, the camper door flew open and a big figure shot through. It landed on the ground crouching, a sub-machine gun in its hands. It called, "Hey, Ali! What's going on? Man, where you at?"

He may have sensed me. He whirled around. I chopped his neck as he was halfway around, and he kept on spinning but his knees were buckling and his body folding. I had not struck him with full force, however, because I wanted a prisoner. He was very strong; his neck was pyloned with muscles. He must have been partially stunned, but his fighting reflexes brought him back up and at me. I caught his wrist and turned it. His scream cut the night. Far off, a leopard coughed, but it may have been a coincidence, not a reply.

He dropped to his knees, his trunk bent backward, teeth white in the darkness. I brought my knee up against his chin, not too hard. He fell back on the ground.

Afterward, I noticed that I had a slight erection. Evidently my penis knew when I intended to kill and when I did not.

CHAPTER FOURTEEN

The man was the Negro I had thought was American. He was as tall as I and perhaps fifty pounds heavier. His shoulders were broad; his waist, narrow. His haircut was "natural," and he had a thick moustache and goatee. His skin was so light and his features so Caucasian, I suspected he was one-quarter white.

Tchaka Wilfred was born in Cleveland, Ohio. He had been a professional football player until he had been caught after holding up a bank to finance a militant black organization. He escaped from prison and joined another organization in Harlem. There he had run afoul of Doctor Caliban, who had taken Wilfred prisoner but had not turned him over to the police. Instead, he had sent Wilfred to the private sanatorium, where Caliban rehabilitated his criminals. By surgery.

This confirmed what the two old men had said.

I had little time for talk, but this information intrigued me. I have an M.D. and though my only practice has been among the Bandili, I read a certain amount of medical journals every year.

"What kind of surgery?" I asked.

"I don't know, honky," Wilfred said sullenly. "A cat under ether isn't too observant, you know."

"Obviously, he didn't tell you anything about his illegal tamperings with your brain. Didn't you ask him what he did?"

"Man, I asked till I was blue in the face, if you can imagine that!" Wilfred said. "Old Doc said it was a trade secret, and he wasn't about to let it out. Unscrupulous men might get hold of it and do great evil! Especially the Communists! Doc's really uptight on the Reds the last couple of years. He thinks they're out to take over and just about got it sewed up!"

That did not sound like a man who served the Nine. Loyalty to the Nine comes first, and the servant will get along no matter what the government. However, they do not care what a man's political beliefs are, as long as he obeys the Nine.

Wilfred laughed and said, "I thought maybe the bronze cat performed a prefrontal lobotomy, but I'm no zombie. And those old honkies, Rivers and Simmons, they say no. They think the Big Bwana Honky maybe installed a micro-miniature circuit board—one running off the electricity of my nerves—inside my head. Man, that's spooky! But . . ."

"Caliban threw me weaponless against that hungry lion," I said. "That doesn't sound like a man of irreproachable virtue to me."

"If the doc says you're evil, you're no fucking good! A-1 rotten. Essence of putridity. Evil as Lucifer after the Fall. Evil as the soul of an Alabaman Ku Kluxer!"

"Do you know who I am?"

Wilfred grinned, though the grin was nervous.

"Yeah. Doc told me. And I said, 'I hear you, Doc, but you just hung up my sense of credibility.' Doc didn't answer. He seldom does. And he could care less if I believe or not. Doc don't lie. Only honky I ever saw who don't. But I still didn't believe. He had to be putting me on. Then we came to Africa and caught that lion and let him loose at you, and there you were, big as life, and bigger. I saw you break that big cat's neck! But I still couldn't believe that, and I couldn't believe that you were really you. But I guess you really are. Man, you're something else!"

"It doesn't matter," I said. "I wonder why he hired you? For your muscle?"

He rubbed his wrist and winced.

"Yeah, partly for my muscle. But I'm an electronic technician and a damn good one, honky."

"But Doc is still, as you put it, a honky?"

"He's the only honky I wouldn't dare call honky to his face. That bronze cat was what Nietzsche was dreaming of before he flipped. A genuine Sooperdooperman! Sure a shame he isn't black!"

He was leaning with his back against the rear of the truck. I said, "I can see you're thinking about rushing me again. Here."

I held out my right hand.

He said, "What do you want?"

"Take it," I said. "Do whatever you want with it."

Instead, he advanced swiftly and tried to thrust his knuckles into my solar plexus. I seized the hand and squeezed on it. He screamed and fell to his knees.

"Do I make myself clear?" I said.

He moaned while he held the injured fist with the other hand. He said, "You're still a big donkey-pricked dirty stinking honky."

I admired his spirit but deplored his lack of intelligence in this situation. Obviously, he could gain nothing by antagonizing me.

And there was no use trying to tell him that I was outside his conflict of white and Black any more than there had been in telling Zabu. I was probably the only white in the world entirely free of prejudice toward men because of their color. Even if I could have convinced him of my attitude, I would not have bothered. What did I care what he thought?

"You will show me everything I want to see," I said. "Otherwise, I kill you."

We went inside the camper. It was crammed with equipment and instruments, most of it electronic. At the touch of a button, these sank away, and the top of the camper rose and split and folded to two sides. A pedestal with a bazooka-like tube rose up from the floor, and then the tube telescoped outward. At the same time, a section of the floor opened, and a replica of the tiny missile that had destroyed the jet appeared. This was about two feet long, was rocket-shaped, silvery, and weighed about forty pounds.

Wilfred adjusted the controls of an instrument with a cathode-ray screen. A section of the mountainside to the west sprang onto it.

A generator under the truck floor hummed.

The antenna turned southward as Wilfred rotated a dial. It stopped when it pointed almost south, and I saw part of the Kenyan army camp as if I were looking from the mountainside from a distance. In the daylight.

The picture was wavy and broken with jagged streaks, and almost immediately became so pale that I could see it only with difficulty.

Yet I should not have been able to see anything at all. The Kenyans were behind a tall hill about a mile and a half from us.

Wilfred explained that the antenna shot a beam against the mountainside. This bounced down over the Kenyans and then bounced up and against the ionosphere and back to the antenna. Unfortunately, the dark green of the mountain vegetation absorbed much of the energy, and the many irregularities of the tree-tops made for a broken picture.

I noticed that his attitude seemed to have changed, though he was unconscious of the change. He acted as if he actually respected me, and in addition, was in awe of me. He had become so interested in his explanations of the devices, he had forgotten to act as if he hated me because I was a "honky."

"Doc said he invented this beamer back in 1943, believe it or not," Wilfred said. "Hey, we need another transceiver!"

He opened a cabinet while I watched him closely for a trick. He brought out a deflated sausage-shaped balloon about a foot long and attached the open end to a nozzle. The balloon filled up and became a blimp about four feet long. He fastened a small blue cigar shape to four eyelets along the blimp to make a tiny gondola. He released the airship, and it rose swiftly, carried eastward by the wind. Wilfred adjusted controls on a board, and the airship, visible in the light streaming from the open top of the camper, turned southward.

I watched the picture on the screen. It was a bird's eye of the country beneath the balloon, as seen in the moonlight.

I asked how Caliban got such a bright picture in the dark.

Wilfred shrugged and said, "I don't know. He might use heat-radiation to help develop the images, but I don't know just how an ultra high-frequency beam could pick up heat images. I just don't know. I do know that the CIA and the Commies, Chinese and Russians, got wind of this device, and Doc was fighting his own people as well as the Commies. For some reason, he didn't want the U.S. to get it."

Apparently, Wilfred did not know about the Nine.

I watched the screen. Presently, the Kenyan camp was in view.

The balloon must have been directly over it.

"You mean it when you say you'll kill me if I don't show you how the missile-launcher works?" he said.

I did not reply, and he said, "You mean it." He grinned. "Doc doesn't care, anyway, if I get rid of a few Kenyans. He says they're interfering."

I said nothing. I had expected him to object because the Kenyans were Blacks, but he seemed to regard them as enemies, which, indeed, they were, if Caliban did not want interference with his hunt.

Wilfred loaded the missile into the tube. Another appeared in the opening in the floor.

The tube rotated and elevated in response to Wilfred's adjustments of the controls. A grid appeared on the screen. A white dot danced out and went past the intersection of the X and Y axes and then shot back to it.

Wilfred straightened up. "It's all automatic now. If you want Little Miss Annihilator to land dead smack in the middle of their camp, press that button there."

"What about the hot jets from the missile?" I said.

He grinned. He had been standing in one corner, as far away as possible from the flames which would issue. Undoubtedly, he had hoped I would be caught and burned. Moreover, I did not put it past the doctor to have a dummy button with a poisoned or drug-coated needle to pierce the thumb that pressed the button. I suspected that there were many traps which Wilfred was aching to use.

I picked up a pair of pliers with insulated handles—watch out for electrical shock, too—and pushed the button with the nose of the pliers. The missile flamed and whooshed away. The truck did not even rock with the take-off. The heat from the jet warmed my skin as I stood beside Wilfred. If I had been unwary enough to be closer, I might have gotten a bad burn and been off balance enough for him to attack me.

I was watching the screen but also flicking glances at Wilfred. He was staring wide-eyed at my penis, which had been rising as the rocket rose.

The missile shot up in a high arc which the eye might not have been able to follow if the jets were not burning so brightly. It curved over and behind the hill. I looked back at the screen. The missile appeared suddenly, and whiteness gouted and smoke roiled out and up. Bodies, pieces of bodies, a truck, a jeep, and pieces of vehicles and equipment flew out of the cloud.

I kept hold of my knife and my eye on Wilfred as I shook and groaned with the ecstasy. He moved away from me, his eyes on my spouting penis.

"Man, you got a beautiful setup!" he whispered. "But you're sure weird!"

I said, "Load another!"

He obeyed, while a third missile rose from the floor. He crouched beneath the tube, and I punched the button. The third missile completely destroyed the Kenyans.

Three times, I jetted. I writhed in powerful orgasms and waved my knife at Wilfred to keep him away. He stared with bulging eyes, and, after the third ejaculation had ceased, and my penis had drooped somewhat, shook his head.

"You're sick, man, real sick," he mumbled.

I came toward him. He backed away, hands out, and said, "You don't want to fuck me with that knobkerrie, do you? Don't, man! It'd split me wide open! Doc didn't say anything about you being queer!"

"Quit talking and scan that mountainside now," I said.

Since he could get a direct beam against the mountain, he switched off the balloon's transceiver but left the balloon cruising around in a circle. At that moment, we heard the distant but unmistakable noise of a helicopter. It became louder in a minute. Wilfred switched the transceiver back on, loaded another rocket in the tube, and this time, at my order, punched the button. I felt nothing then. Apparently, only killings directly done by me brought on the aberrated reaction.

The Kenyan helicopter went up in a great bloom of fire.

CHAPTER FIFTEEN

The beam probed the mountainside. The slope looked like solid vegetation, but the view could be squeezed down with the beam so that we could see a square of two feet from a seeming height of ten feet. Thus, we could look between the trees. It took an hour before we located Doctor Caliban and his party. I could see the dark bronze head of the doctor near a tree. He was holding a metallic box with an antenna.

"All right," I said to Wilfred. "Blow the good doctor and his colleagues to kingdom come or wherever they're going after death."

Wilfred howled and leaped at me. He tried a karate hand chop. Again, I grabbed the hand. I clamped down on it and jerked him past me and slammed him into a bank of instruments. He fell unconscious.

The little white ball came out on the grid of the screen and stopped at the center lines, which were cross-haired on Caliban.

Caliban looked up, and his mouth moved.

His voice came out of a cabinet behind me.

"Very well done, my dear Lord Grandrith. I underestimated you. I made certain that you were halfway up the mountain before I took off after you. I didn't think you'd sneak all the way back down and attack my camp. But I was wrong!

"How well you've performed! But not well enough! Don't you know I have only to press a button on this transceiver, and all four vehicles will explode, along with the remaining missiles in your truck?"

I froze. Caliban had been listening in, perhaps even watching, and I did not think that he was lying.

I said, "If you blow me up, you also blow up Wilfred."

"Too bad!"

Behind me, Wilfred groaned. He rose unsteadily, one arm limp, his eyes as red as if his brain had burst. He said, "Not you, Doc! You were the only good man I ever knew. I trusted you, Doc, even if you were a honky. I loved you, Doc, like I never loved a man before!"

"You always did flap your big lips too much," Caliban said. "Well, my lord, are you leaving peacefully, without pressing that button, or do I have to end it all now and cheat both of us?"

"He means it! He'd kill us both!" Wilfred moaned. "Old Rivers and Simmons were right. Doc has turned evil! He's a regular Jekyll and Hyde!"

"Shut up, Wilfred," Caliban said emotionlessly.

"My lord, I have to blow up the trucks and jeeps in any event. One of my Black colleagues, Ali Hamidu, has shinnied up a tree and scanned the scene with binoculars the power of which would astound even the scientists of this progressive century. He reports that the Albanian and his Arab mercenaries are sneaking up on you. They pulled the same trick you did, apparently. I think they spotted you when you came back down. Shame on you. Are you losing your touch? In any case, they see the light shining from the open roof of the camper."

I got out of the camper. Caliban's voice said, "Get back here! They've got the camp surrounded. You couldn't get two feet without being chopped down! I'm going to explode the two jeeps first, and then the supply truck! You stay in the camper until then, and take off under cover of the smoke! When you do, run like hell! The camper will be the biggest explosion by far!"

An automatic rifle began firing about fifty yards away. The bullets stitched the dirt and then ran across a jeep. Somebody shouted in Arabic; I thought it was a command to hold the fire. Probably, it was Noli shouting, because he wanted to take me alive.

I had no choice. I got back into the camper, the roof of which was closing up. Wilfred secured the door and the windows, and when the camper was tight, he said, "We're protected by double walls with fiber glass and steel wool insulation. It'd take a direct hit from a shell to get us."

100

He was watching the screen, which showed about thirty armed men slowly advancing through the bush. I said, "Didn't you see me when I was sneaking up on you?"

Wilfred curled back his lips and clenched his teeth. Then he said, "You were born under a lucky star, bwana honky. I was watching a leopard over the next hill and I didn't see you at all. When you got inside the camp, I couldn't use the beam to sight you then. You were too close. Otherwise . . ."

He paused, and then said, "I got orders not to kill you, anyway, unless it's absolutely necessary."

The first explosion rocked the camper, but the noise was muffled. The second came almost immediately after. And the third two seconds later. The last must have been the supply truck. The camper seemed to lift up and tilt at the same time, and the blast half-deafened us. If it had not been for the thick insulation, our eardrums would have been blown out.

Wilfred leaped up and opened the door and plunged out into the heavy smoke and the flames. He turned just before he disappeared and shouted at me. I could not hear him, but I could read his lips.

"Split, mother!"

CHAPTER SIXTEEN

I ran after Wilfred, but our courses diverged. My goal was to get down the slope of the hill as far as possible and to put as many trees behind me as possible. Wilfred had said there were ten missiles in the truck yet with a total explosive force equivalent to 400 pounds of TNT. There would not be much left of the hilltop after Caliban pressed the button.

I was about forty yards down the hill, out of the direct path of the blast, the greater energy of which would go upward. Then I felt the pressure; I did not hear it. I flew forward; a tree sprang up; I became unconscious.

When I regained my senses, I was still deaf. I could, however, hear the messages of pain in my eardrums, my head, and all my muscles.

The smoke was just beginning to clear away. The hilltop was gone. Most of the trees, branchless, splintered, uprooted, were halfway down the hill. One lay a foot from me. A little more force behind it would have dropped the trunk, heavy as a great boulder, on my head.

I rose slowly against the current of my pain. The moon was out behind the clouds now, and the sky seemed to be a peculiar shade of dark-blue. No doubt, I was furnishing the color, not the sky. The leaves of the trees were a sinister green, and the earth was a repulsive yellow-green. Everything was *stretched, elongated,* as if the world were a taut rubber band. The energy gathered in this band was waiting to be released when my hearing returned.

I was unarmed and naked except for the belt with its sheath and the knife.

Forty feet to my left, Wilfred lay face down. I turned him over. He had no visible wounds, but when I tore off his shirt, I saw on his lower back a bruise the size of a dinner plate. The bruise may have been caused by a truck wheel which lay about eight feet up the hill from him.

He opened his eyes and said something. I could not hear him, and it was too dark to read his lips. I found a match-folder in his pocket and struck a match. It may have been a foolish thing to do, but I did not think there would be any living men around for some time, and I wanted to know what he was trying to say.

The light was just enough for me to read his lips.

". . . not with a whimper but a bang, man . . . ain't life the shits . . . tell that bronze cat . . . no fucking good . . . God's a honky, you better believe it . . ." and then, "Mother!"

The last was not, I'm sure, a truncated pejorative. It was the final appeal to one who had answered his first appeal.

At that moment, I felt sad. If I had been able to know him under other circumstances, and if he could have abandoned all the masks, the mannerisms, the clichés which humans adopt for a group identity, then he and I might even have liked each other. But that was asking too much of most humans, and, moreover, I find that most humans have trouble being completely at ease when they're with me.

This, I suppose, is my fault.

I left him with mouth and eyes open. Before noon, the flies would be buzzing in and out of the mouth and the vultures would have plucked the eyes from the sockets.

The hilltop gave me nothing in the way of a weapon. I set off at a trot with the intention of going back up the mountain diagonally. I suspected that Caliban was even now racing down the mountain to check on my survival, unless he was able to see me through those super-binoculars. If I did lose him, I would do so only for a while. Eventually, he would be on my trail, for the simple reason that he was going where I was going. The two old men had told me that, although they probably did not know themselves. I doubted that Caliban would have said anything about the Nine to them, since it

A FEAST UNKNOWN

was forbidden. Also, he could take them only so far and then would have to go on alone. It was also forbidden to bring outsiders any closer than fifty miles to the caverns of the Nine.

I was thinking about this, and wishing that my deafness would clear up soon, when a piece of bark flew off a tree about a foot to my left. If I had not been looking in that direction, I would have been unaware of it, and the shooter might have been more accurate the second time.

So I thought at that moment. I dived to the ground and rolled beneath a bush in a slight hollow. When I peeked out, I saw a man, whose silhouette I recognized as the Albanian's, shooting a man with a burnoose, with a rifle. The man fell forward and did not get up. I jumped up to run away but by then Noli was only thirty feet away. I put my arms up in the air; the automatic could not have missed. I don't think he would have killed me, but he would have crippled me with bullets in the legs.

I did not know how he and the Arab had survived. They must have been further down the hill when the first jeep went up and they had managed to get away before the other explosions got to them. He said something to me. I shook my head and pointed at my ears. He pointed at his own, and I knew he was deaf, too. The Arab must have been deaf, and Noli had probably shouted at him that I was to be taken alive. Undoubtedly, the Arab had received orders to this effect more than once. But, shaken by the explosions, perhaps eager to revenge his fellows, he had fired at me. Noli was not close enough to knock him out with the rifle, so he had been forced to kill him.

He had to tie my hands and to do this required my cooperation, which I was not likely to give. He solved his problem by hitting me over the head with the barrel of the rifle. I ducked and so reduced some of the impact of the blow, but not enough.

When I awoke, my head ached as if it had sucked in every pain in the area for fifty miles around. My brain seemed to throb like a mangled and infected hand. My eyes hurt as if the optic nerves had been extruded into the eye-balls. My hands were connected behind me with what I later determined was a pair of handcuffs. A hangman's noose was around my neck, and the other end of the rope was tied to the handcuff's chain. My arms had been hauled up almost as far as they could behind me with the result that I pulled on the rope and choked myself unless I kept my arms up high. In this state, I could not test the strength of the handcuff's chain without strangling myself.

Later, Noli would remove the rope during the daytime, but at night he always replaced it.

Noli made signs which told me what he wanted. I would lead him to the source of the gold. And I would also tell him, when I was able, the secret of my juvenescence.

He was taking seriously what most people considered to be a tale of fantasy. He seemed to have done his research well, however, and was convinced that I had a hoard of gold somewhere in this area and that I really was eighty years old.

The facts about me—some, anyway—are available to certain people. The secret archives of many governments and some very powerful individuals contain pages of facts and of speculations, about me. These exist in Washington, London, Peking, Moscow, Paris, Rome, and other places. I know about them because the Nine told me of them.

Noli was either an agent of the Communist government of his country or a private agent. Or he was the former and had been sent to find the gold and was looking for the elixir for himself. I doubt that his government really believed in the elixir.

I transmitted to him my willingness to lead him to the gold. He was elated at this, and, at the same time, suspicious. He seemed to think I should have undergone at least a modicum of torture before agreeing to his demands.

I tried to tell him I did not think the torture was worth it, but I failed. He gave me the signal to precede him, and we went on down the hillside and then began climbing the mountain.

By dawn, we were near the top. Noli was puffing and panting. His mouth hung open, his chest rose and fell rapidly, sweat silvered his face and enormous mustachios, and sweat blackened his clothes. He was in good condition for a man of fifty-five, which I estimated his age to be. Even a young athlete would have been under a strain to keep up with my pace. Time and again, Noli jammed his rifle in my back and when I turned around, he gestured that he wanted to rest.

Twice, we ate and drank. He carried a canteen of water and had three cans of spam in his pocket. He gave me half a can while he ate one. I wondered what he intended to do after we ran out of food. He might be able to shoot some game, but he would dislike to do this, since it would advertise our presence.

Nightfall found us on the western side of the next mountain two hundred yards below the peak. My ankles were tied with a rope and my handcuffed hands were also tied to a rope the other end of which was around the trunk of a slim tree. The position was uncomfortable. My bowels had moved during the night, and I was able to get only a few inches from the mess, and I had to piss down my leg. Also, it got cold and wet. Mists and then chilling dew covered us. I have been used to worse much of my life. I did not intend to try to escape the first night, unless an irresistible opportunity came along. I would sleep and gather my strength while Noli slept uneasily and in much discomfort. He awoke frequently and sat up to inspect me or prowled around for a while before trying to seize a few more minutes of sleep. Or so he told me the next day. I slept very well.

Dawn was no more red-eyed than he, and it was much fresher.

He stood above me and pissed on me. Probably as revenge for having rested while he suffered and also part of his psychological warfare. It did not bother me. The urine was warm and felt pleasant, and I have been pissed on by others, all now as dead and as cold as last night's urine.

He untied the ropes and let me get up. I had to piss then. He watched me with an enigmatic look. But his penis was still hanging out of his pants, and, as he watched me, it swelled and grew hard. He looked down and then up at me and smiled. He then forced it within his pants and gestured for me to lead. I knew what he was thinking. The Albanians have been heavily influenced by the Turks, although it is not necessary to enlist history to account for certain attitudes. There are enough Enver Nolis in West Europe, the Americas, Africa, and Asia, none originating from Turkish influences.

At noon, we were at the foot of the mountain. He ate another can of spam, and I got a fourth of another. My stomach was growling, and I could feel my strength evaporating. My hearing was by then almost completely returned, and I could hear his stomach when he was close. He was hungry, despite getting the lion's share of the food.

The next morning, he was in worse condition. Hunger was beginning to erode him. He needed more food than he was getting even if he had been resting, but the loss of energy in climbing the mountains and in loss of sleep was great. At midnoon, his hunger got the best of his desire for concealment. A mountain pangolin ran out from behind a bush as we were going across a small plateau which was so rocky it contained less vegetation than other areas. The beast rolled over and over at the impact of the .38. The shot came from behind me and was unexpected. I jumped and whirled. He smiled. He had food and he also had discovered that I was not as deaf as I had pretended.

He picked up the animal, and we traveled three miles before he thought it safe to halt. With his own knife, he cut the beast out of its armor, threw the entrails away, and then dug a hole. He managed to get a small, relatively smokeless, fire going. He curled the armor of the pangolin into a bowl, filled it with water from a nearby cataract, put the bowl in the hole, and the hot stones into the water. He sliced the meat and threw it into the armor. He kept taking the stones out as they cooled and putting in hot ones.

The result was a lukewarm but meat-rich soup. There was enough for both of us and enough for another meal left over. He unlocked my hands from behind me, locked them again before me, and had me carry the armor-bowl with its soup contents. I had to give him credit for some ingenuity.

CHAPTER SEVENTEEN

That evening, after tying me even more tightly, Enver ate most of the soup and then slept for several hours. When he awoke, he looked up at the mists and the distorted moon behind them. He crawled over to me and said, in English, "I am cold. And I am also hot, my lord. Hot with passion."

This was the sort of monologue that my biographer might have put in his romances but which more discriminating readers would reject as absurd. They forget that books are often imitated by people.

I said nothing. Noli put his arms around me, and, shivering, clung to me for a while. Then he startled me by running his tongue up and down my spine from the nape of my neck to the base. He then lowered his hand and put it around in front of me and began playing with my penis. He moved the foreskin back and forth very softly and slowly. The heat of his breath on my back and the heat of his hand on my penis, and the lesser heat of his clothed body on my back felt pleasant.

I had not been so handled by a male since I was a youth and living with The Folk. Sexual experimentation among The Folk is permitted by the young from the time they feel like doing it until they pick a mate. The males of my age, from the time we could get a hard-on, stuck our penises in each other's anuses, and sucked on penises long before we could ejaculate. The females were right there with us, playing with each other and with the males. The hairy playmates of my childhood, however, had small penises. When they attained adulthood, and stood six feet and weighed three hundred pounds, they still had penises only about two inches long when erect.

Before the hair grew on my pubes, my *kq*, as it is called in their speech, was the marvel of the tribe. When I became a man, it was the desire of the females and the envy of the males and caused me much trouble from both.

When I became able to ejaculate, I still played sexually with the male and female young, buggered and was buggered, sucked and was sucked. This was not continuous, of course. Most of our play was the sort found among all young primates (man included), racing, wrestling, playing the jungle version of king-of-the-hill, harassing the very old, hunting for rodents, insects, and bird eggs, and playing leopard-and-victim. And so on. But we also spent at least half an hour a day in exciting each other sexually. We did much of this in full view of the elders and with their permission.

Only when pubescence began did the elders repress the juveniles, sometimes quite savagely.

The result is that I grew up with almost no sexual inhibitions. I was inhibited about using violence to gain a sexual end, since this was the one thing the elders stopped at once if they saw it. And they punished us severely.

When I came of sexual age, I had already lost any desire for the males. Not that, under the proper, or perhaps I should say improper, circumstances, I might not have resorted to homosexuality. But I was not a compulsive homosexual, nor did I know any among The Folk. Compulsive, that is, neurotic, homosexuality seems to be the characteristic of civilization, although there is some among the so-called savages. Compulsive behavior of any kind is neurotic. Which is why I was so disturbed about my orgasmic reactions to my killings.

Noli played skillfully with me. His hand was big, but it was almost as gentle and knowledgeable as my wife's. He must have had much practice.

I failed to respond in the slightest.

If my aberration had been absent, I might have had an erection and an orgasm eventually. Friction alone can do much, and I was not frightened of him. I was angry, but I doubt that this would have inhibited an erection.

After a while, he quit with an exclamation of disgust. He began to move his hard penis against my anus. He breathed harder, and then his hands clamped my buttocks and he spread them open. The huge glans was, however, denied entrance. I have a very powerful sphincter, which I closed as far as I could. He shoved for a long time. Then he said, "Let me in, or I knock you out."

I didn't want another headache and possible brain damage, so I said, "Very well."

He spit on the end of his penis, I supposed, and, slowly but insistently, pushed the head in. The shaft slid through immediately thereafter.

I hurt, and I also felt as if I had to get rid of a huge turd. He began to slide the penis back and forth, and the pain increased. He grunted with each lunge, and I could feel the thick stiff hairs against the bare skin of my buttocks. His hands were around me again, one on my penis and one cupping my testicles. He began squeezing on these. I clamped my teeth and endured the pain. Stoic as a wild beast, as my biographer would have said, if he had known about this, although he would have shut such a scene out of his mind, because it would have destroyed his image of me. I could be tortured in his romances, but I could not, of course, be buggered.

Noli was falsely sentimental as most of his kind, that is, Homo sapiens. After groaning loudly and jabbing rapidly in his orgasm, he lay quiet awhile except for his heavy breathing. Then he murmured something which sounded endearing, in Albanian, I suppose. He caressed my face with his hands (I resisted the temptation to bite off a finger) and kissed the back of my neck several times. I suppose he would have acted the same way with a prostitute, male or female. He did not care for me any more than he would have for a whore, but he had to carry out the ritual of love.

In about fifteen minutes, he repeated his assault. I endured it. He kissed me on the neck and then got around before me and kissed my penis and ran his fingers gently between my testicles and the hollows of my thighs. I did not respond except to spit at him. He struck me hard on the face, got up, made sure I was tied securely, and then lay down to snore. No doubt, he dreamed of former loves.

CHAPTER EIGHTEEN

That day, we put the water-rich green mountains behind us. We were in ranges as dry as a camel fossil. These mountains are subject to a local freak of climate, which diverts the rains to the mountains on the north and south. It is in this area that the valley which once held the gold was located.

We went down one mountainside and up another and the following day started down the other side. We were hungry because we had eaten nothing but a hare which Noli had killed with a shot that destroyed half of it. He put the carcass on top of a flat stone, tied me up, and then went to look for firewood.

I reached out a foot and closed my toes around the hare's ear and pulled the body to me. After shoving it against a bush to hold it, I got on my side and put my face against it and began eating on the part left open by the outgoing bullet.

When Noli returned, I had devoured everything but the skin, the entrails, and a goodly amount of meat barred from me by the bones. There was enough left for a meal for him, but he was furious. I think he had intended to let me have a leg and to keep the rest for himself. He called me a dirty bloody animal and beat me with the stock of his rifle. He did, however, pull his punches. Even in his rage he kept enough control to remember that I was the guide to wealth and immortality. The blows hurt, especially the ones over the kidneys. But I kept silent and did not move my face muscles.

"You're nothing but a wild beast," he said. "Look at you, with blood all over your mouth. You disgust me!"

I did not reply. Cursing, he turned to making a fire and to cooking the remains. After he had eaten, he felt better. We continued our journey.

The valley where the gold had been lay between two high, steep, and barren mountains. The topography resembles that described by my biographer as the site of the lost city which contained a secret underground chamber full of gold and jewels. My biographer also described the lovely high priestess of the sun cult of the degraded locals and her unrequited love for me. The basis for this romance was an actual ruined city. Or, I should say, about four acres of tumbled stone under earth and some stones uncovered by wind now and then, part of a wall, and the six foot high stub of a tower. It resembled the ruins of Zimbabwe in South Rhodesia. About four dozen people lived among the ruins in wattle-and-mud huts. With their peppercorn hair, yellow-brown skin, epicanthic folds, and tendency to female steatopygia, they resembled Bushmen. They may have been descended from the builders of the original city. They called the ruins *remog*, meaning *father-stones*. They spoke a language unrelated to any other, as far as I know.

In 1911, during one of my long wandering journeys across Africa, I found this valley and the ruins. I did some preliminary digging at random, and when I found a gold bracelet and a gold figurine not six inches below the surface, I named this place Ophir, after the Biblical city of treasures. I returned with some equipment a few months later and made some deep cuts. I found no more gold, although I did discover broken pottery, a few beads, some carved ivory, and some impressions of weapons which had left a bronze residue. I also found some primitive gold melting and refining equipment.

I explored the mountainside behind the ruins and found some caved-in mines. There was still gold ore worth extracting on the ground, and I was sure that richer deposits were in the mountain.

When I started to dig in the ancient burial ground near the ruins, the natives became angry and drove me off. I returned at night to dig some more. The moon was full, they saw me, and they called the entire adult male population, that is, nine men. These rushed me from downwind and surprised me. I fought with my shovel for a while and then when its edge remained wedged in a skull, I killed a man with a knife thrown into his solar plexus and, with his club, smashed in some skulls. Another club took me from behind, and I awoke with a headache and with my hands and feet tied. The shaman of the tribe was a young female whose face was not too unpleasant. She had enormously fat buttocks and full uptilting breasts. She also had a very large vagina and may have been disappointed in the ability of the males to fill her. She came to me that night and dismissed the guards. I was not very responsive, but she sucked on me and worked me up to a full erection. After this, she sat down on me and bobbed up and down like a balloon on a string until we both had come. This went on all night until just before dawn. I fell asleep for a while and awoke with a piss hard-on. A fly landed on my sensitive glans and precipitated another ejaculation. It was caught in the first spurt and died. I have never forgotten that. It may be the only one in the history of flies to have died in this manner.

The Ophirians were worshippers of the sun and the moon and a number of other natural bodies and forces. I never did find out just which deity I was intended to be sacrificed to, or, indeed, that I was being sacrificed to anything. It was apparent that they intended to kill me. First, though, the female shaman meant to get out of me all I had to give. She came to me for six nights straight. On the seventh day, she communicated to me, through signs, that I was to die at noon.

I had been straining against the leather ropes binding me whenever I got the chance. I finally managed to break those binding my wrists. I broke the shaman's neck and killed the guard carrying my uncle's knife and killed another guard with that and with the club I killed the rest of the males except for an old man who fled. The entire village followed him into the mountains. I never saw them again. I felt regret about this, because, at that time, I did not kill human beings unless they attacked me. I felt that if they had explained how strongly they felt about the burial ground, I would have abstained from digging.

Later, I dug in the cemetery again and found a number of gold bracelets, figurines, and symbols the meaning of which I did not know. These have remained in my private collection in my home in Cumberland.

The gold that made me one of the wealthiest men in the world—in potentia—came out of the mountain. It came out with much hard labor on my part. I did everything alone, the digging, the melting, the refining, and the final packing out of the mountains. I packed out golden ingots on my back for a hundred miles on the mountain trails, an ingot at a time, each ingot weighing a hundred pounds. And, of course, I handled the initial negotiations with the underground market.

More than once, I escaped abduction and murder at the hands of those who wanted to track me to the source or torture the information from me. My biographer had planned to use some of these episodes for his romances before he died. However, as he had done in some previous episodes, he would have altered the truth so the villains would be after the immense treasure of gold and jewels in the mighty ruins of the inconceivably ancient city peopled by the degraded descendants of a civilization which disappeared below the ocean 12,000 years ago. The male citizens would have been fantastically ugly and the women would have been fantastically beautiful. I am not ridiculing him. I can see why his readers would prefer his colorful imagination to the reality.

The gold gave out after I had amassed about twenty million pounds (in English currency), although I believe that there is more deeper in the mountain. I buried the ruins so that no one would suspect that anyone had ever lived in this desolate valley. First, I made extensive diggings, recordings, and photographs, just like a professional archeologist. I had a Master's in archaeology from Oxford by then.

(An aside, for the reader's benefit. I also have an M.D. from Johns Hopkins and a Ph.D. in African Linguistics from the University of Berlin. I have not been entirely idle in my almost eighty years.)

I had destroyed all evidences of mining, too. I thought that it would be a long time before anybody found anything. Even in these times, when Africa is relatively crowded and men are everywhere, few get to these rugged mountains. Moreover, the area has a reputation among the natives for being demon-haunted.

So I was surprised when we came over the mountain and looked down into the valley. At least a hundred men were digging on the site of the ruins or on the west side of the valley. Noli swore. He tied me to a tree and studied the valley through his binoculars for a long time. I took the opportunity to strain against the handcuffs, as I did every time his eyes were not on me. The metal was made of very tough material, otherwise I would have parted the links a long time ago. I stopped when Noli turned to untie me, and we went down the mountain, but away from the floor of the valley. When we had reached the top of the next mountain he again studied the intruders, after tying me to another tree.

"There's a strip of land which looks level enough for a plane to land on," he said. "Although from here you can't be sure. Is there a place where a plane could land?"

"There is," I said. "But these men may have come in by foot. I think someone told them where the gold is. Otherwise, they would have captured me first to make me tell. They would not have tried to kill me before they found out what they needed to know."

He looked through the glasses again. He said, "How did you know they were Kenyans?"

"It seemed likely," I said.

"They've removed their insignia because they're in Uganda, but they're Kenyan."

He put the binoculars down and turned to me. He was red-faced and scowling. The tips of his mustachios quivered.

"You said the gold was in the valley beyond this one!"

I did not answer. He began to beat me again. I kicked out against his shin and knocked him down and then kicked him in the chest with the sole of my foot. He rolled away and fought to regain his wind. I spat at him.

He looked as if he would like to kill me. He would have, since he knew, or thought he knew, where the gold was. But there was the elixir. He said, "You will pay dearly for this."

"I have paid," I said. "That kick was for the beating. But I still owe you for much more. And I am one who pays his debts."

"Is the gold really down there?" he said.

"They will find none," I said. "Not unless they dig much deeper than I did. The only way you, or they, can get my gold is to demand a ransom. My fortune is secure in fifty banks throughout the world."

He grimaced. He could walk only by limping. I had kicked him harder than I had intended.

"Caliban is down there," I said, "and he is showing himself so that the soldiers will chase him. But they won't catch him. They will catch us instead, unless we travel far and fast, because he will lead them to us."

He looked at the northern end of the valley, where we had crossed. The tiny figure should have been unidentifiable to the naked eye. He had, however, shed all his clothes. The sun gleamed on that metal-cap-like hair and the bronze skin. He moved as if he were a cloud driven by the wind.

A number of Kenyans were running toward him and firing, though he was so far from them they had no chance of hitting him. Others on the slope were after him, too. He angled in toward them. They may have been puzzled about that, but they took advantage of it.

He came up the mountainside like a great bronze-colored rock baboon. I have never seen a man run up such a steepness and rockiness so swiftly or bound so from projection to projection.

"He is leading them up to us," I said.

Noli had been watching him through the binoculars. He said, "Why is he doing that?"

He did not comment on Caliban's prodigious climbing. His expression was strange, however.

I saw no reason to tell Noli that Caliban was putting me to the test again.

"Unlock the handcuffs," I said. "I can't get away from you as long as I'm within range of your gun."

He smiled briefly and said, "You know I won't shoot unless I have to. No. You stay cuffed."

"At least let my hands be in front of me."

"No."

"You can't run very fast," I said. "The only way to stop them will be to roll rocks down and hope to start an avalanche. The slope here is a steep and loose talus. You'll need help. I can't help with my hands behind me."

He waved his rifle. "Let's go. We can still outrun them."

118

I saw no reason to go along with Noli an inch more. We had come to the parting of the ways.

I strained against the handcuffs. I thought I would rip out the muscles of my arms and the veins of my temples with my effort. There was a snap, and my hands came free. He backed away, his skin white and his eyes wide. He swore in Albanian.

I turned away from him and looked over the edge of the rock. Caliban was slowed down. The Kenyans had quit firing at him. About fifty were strung out in a rough line about three hundred yards long. The rest were still on the valley floor. They had stopped firing because they realized they could precipitate an avalanche.

I picked up a boulder which must have weighed three hundred pounds and lifted it above my head. I shouted at Caliban. He had stopped now. He was about forty feet below me. His feet were on a ledge so narrow that I could almost not see it, and his hands were gripping some projections invisible to me. His head was thrown back, and he stared straight up at me. He looked like a statue carved out of the mountain itself.

I shouted, "Catch, Caliban!" and heaved the boulder outward.

I don't think he expected us to be so close. He must have thought we would be at least a half-mile on and desperately striving to increase the distance.

The boulder fell for twenty feet, hit an out-cropping, bounded out, struck ten feet above Caliban, broke off rock and dust and bumped past him. I could see him dimly through the cloud.

I picked up a smaller boulder and tossed it after the first. It missed all the outcrops the first had struck and, as nearly as I could determine through the dust, should have hit Caliban. Or the place where he had been. Still was, I hoped. Or did I? I felt some sense of disappointment that the relationship was so soon over and that he had been so easily disposed of.

That is, if he had been. I would not have stayed a second in the same spot, and I doubted that he would.

The first boulder had leaped on down like a great legless kangaroo. It had hit something, a loose pile, an unstable boulder or cluster of boulders. The avalanche started. The dust rose so thickly that I could not see what was happening. A noise as of two clashing thunderstorms arose, and soon the flat rock on which I stood began to tremble. We retreated. The edge of the mountain did not, however, fall off. It remained firm, although it, too, became hidden in dust.

When the rumbling had ceased and the cloud had thinned, I crawled out onto the edge and looked down. The face of the mountain was somewhat changed. There were some fresh wounds in it, naked rock exposed by the slipping away of the massive piles. At the foot of the mountain, out across half of the valley, was a mass of rocks. No Kenyans were to be seen. Only their possessions, tents, supplies, and material, had escaped.

Nor was anything to be seen of Caliban.

Noli was still pale, but he managed a smile and said, "*We* certainly wiped them out, heh, Lord Grandrith?"

He was holding the rifle with both hands, and he was watching my hands. I said, "I know you have another pair of handcuffs in the pocket of your jacket. I will allow you to put them on me only if my hands are in front of me. There will be some very difficult climbing ahead, and it will be impossible for me to climb with my hands behind me. In fact, it may be impossible with handcuffs."

I held out my arms. He took the key out of his pocket and threw it to me. "Unlock those cuffs."

While I was doing so, he took out the other pair of cuffs.

"You will put them on yourself," he said. "You didn't really think I would get close enough to you for you to grab me, did you?"

"I thought I would try," I said.

He threw the cuffs at me and I caught them with one hand, spun, and released them as I completed the circle. The cuffs flew at him; he jerked the rifle up to ward them off; I was in at him, throwing myself like an American football blocker. The rifle blast seared my back; I hit him in the hips; he went down and over.

By the time he had gotten to his feet, I had the rifle.

At my order, he presented his back to me. I knocked him out with the rifle butt and chained his hands behind him. I put the key in his jacket pocket and sat down. When he regained consciousness, he groaned and fluttered his eyelids. I slapped his face to bring him to more quickly.

I lifted him up and passed a noose from his rope around his arms and body a few inches below his shoulders. I shoved him ahead. He balked but nevertheless went screaming over the edge. I pulled up on the rope so that it tightened before he had gone more than a body's length down. He dangled, his back scraping the perpendicular face of the cliff. He tried to look up at me, but the weight of his body and the pressure of the rock behind his head prevented him.

I lowered him slowly and gently. I did not want the rope to loosen and so drop him down the cliff. Then I jerked the rope and managed to turn him so he faced the cliff. He saw the tiny ledge below his feet. After some effort, he got his feet firmly placed on the narrow cropping. The heels of his boots hung over the air.

I let more slack into the rope and succeeded in working it loose from his body and pulling it back up. He must have wanted greatly to look upward, but he did not dare. He could maintain his position on the ledge only by pressing face and body in against the rock.

I called, "Noli! You can't go more than a few inches to the right or left! Yet, if you can get your hands in front of you, and somehow get the key out of your front pocket, and then unlock the cuffs, you can climb back up here!"

I paused. He said nothing. I said, "I'm giving you a chance to live, to get free! I'm leaving your rifle and bandolier and knife here, so that you might be able to get back to civilization, if you get out of your first predicament!

"Perhaps I'm being stupid! Maybe I should have tossed you over the edge, instead of giving you a chance to live! A very small chance, true, but still a chance!"

He did not say anything or move. He was probably afraid that the slightest motion would lose him his footing. Later, he would have to make the effort, no matter what the consequences. If he just remained there in paralysis, he would weaken, his legs would bend, and out and down he would go.

I relished that thought. It was so delightful, it gave me a semi-erection. For a moment, I was tempted to go back and drop stones on him until he did fall, just to find out if the fall itself would give me an orgasm.

I left the rifle as I had promised. First, I plugged the muzzle with dirt. If he should have the great nerve and limberness and strength and very good luck to get out of this situation, he would count himself very fortunate. He would inspect the rifle, of course, unless he was so upset or elated that he forgot his usual suspicions. If he did, and he fired it, he would lose his face.

I always check out any firearms that have been out of my sight for even a short time. Once, an enemy did the very thing to me that I was now doing to Noli.

CHAPTER NINETEEN

Before leaving, I surveyed the valley again. The dust had almost entirely settled. On the slope of the mountain on the other side, several figures appeared. I looked through the binoculars. I could not be sure at this distance, but it seemed that the party was the two old men and the Blacks.

I wondered how far Caliban intended to let them come. He knew the consequences if he deliberately brought outsiders anywhere near the next mountain.

That was his concern. I hurried on across the top of the mountain and halfway down found a sort of cave beneath three huge boulders. I slept uneasily on the cold hard stone. More than once I awoke, thinking I heard the rattle of a displaced rock or the scrape of a knife against stone. Twice, I dreamed that a huge shadowy figure was sneaking through the darkness toward me. Once, the eyes glowed with a strange swirling golden-flecked bronze light.

I dream, of course, as every human dreams. A psychologist once checked me out on that because I was convinced that I had had only one dream in my entire life. He awoke me when the proper eye movements told him I was dreaming, and I remembered my dreams.

That I now was aware of this dream indicated how deeply Doctor Caliban had affected me.

In the morning, I continued down the mountain. I was hungry and thirsty, and I wished I had cut Noli's liver and heart out instead of wasting him for the sake of revenge. I knocked over a rock hyrax with a stone and ate that. Later, I found some grubs under a pile of dirt and I scooped up several handfuls of ants. In the afternoon, I caught a gray lizard which looked much like an American horned toad.

I also came across some fresh goat droppings. I passed these up. I was not hungry enough for them yet. I have survived at various times by eating the spoor of animals. Antelope and elephant turds are not too distasteful. Zebra excrement is almost relishable. Lion shit and that of other meat eaters is very unpalatable and only as a last resort would I eat them. But I have. If I had not done so, I would not now be alive.

At the bottom of the next-to-last ascent was a number of scattered bones of men and women. Some were very old and might have been lying out under the African sun for fifty years or more. A few seemed to be recent. The vultures, jackals, and ants had quickly stripped the flesh after their owners died falling off the face of the mountain, and the animals and the winds had scattered their bones.

The mountain which had killed them was very steep and smooth. It required professional mountain-climbers equipment, if you did not know where to look. The Nine forbade any artificial aids whatsoever. There were places where a climber unafraid of heights, or with great courage, and equipped with strong fingers and toes, could clamber up the face of the 4,000 foot cliff. I do not know how old these digit-holds are, but I would not be surprised to find out that humans—and subhumans—have been using them for at least 30,000 years. The Nine could tell but have not, and no one dares ask.

Dusk fell when I was only 500 feet up. I crawled onto a ledge with a partial overhang and tried to sleep. The cold of the night did not bother me too much. I seem to be able to endure extremes of temperature that would dehydrate or give pneumonia to other men. What made my sleep fitful was the bronze giant with the glowing golden-bronze eyes and the big knife. He seemed to be prowling all night through the jungle of my dreams.

At dawn, I resumed climbing. The really difficult part of the ascent was behind me, and I went up like a monkey on a stick. Just as the sun began its slide down from the zenith, I reached the top of this cliff. There was a level stretch of rock about thirty yards square here, and another thousand feet of climbing. First, I had to get rid of all weapons and clothing. No one approached the Nine unless he or she was naked and empty-handed.

A shoulder-high granite boulder at one corner of the plateau looked as if it had fallen from above. A stranger would have passed it by without a second glance. I placed my hand three times in rapid succession on an egg-shaped projection on the boulder, waited nine seconds, and pressed six times. A section of the boulder slid up. A shelf inside contained a depression from which water bubbled. I drank deeply of this and then I put my belt, sheath, and knife and rope on the shelf beside a number of other articles. These had been left by predecessors. Among them was a bronze-colored belt with pockets which contained a number of interesting and puzzling devices. It had been worn, of course, by Doc Caliban. I thought he had been naked when last I saw him, but he was so far off I had not detected the belt. Now this was discarded.

Beside the belt was a bronze-colored square of paper. I picked it up. The handwriting was bold but beautiful:

I rescued your Albanian friend and sent him on an errand for me. I also detected the dirt in his rifle. He seemed shaken and grateful. I expect him to get over both states quickly. But I told him I would track him down and torture him as only a medical doctor with vast scientific resources could do if he failed me. He seemed to believe me. Also, my errand will enable him to revenge himself more than satisfactorily on you and will profit him monetarily. He will contact my agents, who will expedite his entry into England and thence to Castle Grandrith, where your wife now is. He will hold her until I get there. Of course, he may betray me and take matters into his own hands.

There was no signature, or need for one.

I bellowed with frustration and rage. Since I could not get my hands on Caliban, I attacked his possessions. I threw the belt, sheath, and knife over the ledge. I ripped the note to pieces and scattered them out over the face of the cliff. After that, I climbed swiftly, too swiftly, up the last cliff. Three times I almost fell off because of my lack of caution. With an effort, I cooled myself down, though it was some time before my shaking ceased.

The man's speed was very impressive. He had come along behind me and taken Noli from the ledge and then he had passed me. Of course I was not racing him; I had taken it relatively easy.

I told myself that I should turn back and get to England as swiftly as possible. However, Caliban might be lying to me so that I would do just that. If I failed to appear before the Nine at the appointed time, I would get no second chance for immortality. And the time I would have to stay in the caverns was very short compared to the time it would take Noli to get back to civilization. Unless Noli had been instructed to report to Simmons and Rivers, who would radio for a plane.

I knew that my wife would have insisted that I go on and let her take care of herself. She was extremely capable. If she had not been, she would long ago have been killed. She would not want me to lose the elixir for any reason and especially because of this situation.

There was also another reason, the strongest, for not turning back at once. Caliban would be waiting for me somewhere between here and the entrance to the caverns.

I had to make a decision which would take many civilized men days to agonize over. This decision took me two minutes, and that was the longest, slowest time I have ever taken.

Late that afternoon, I reached the top of the second cliff and drank from a small spring. The exit from the plateau led through a series of canyons several hundred feet deep and so narrow that both sides brushed my shoulders quite frequently. An hour's journey brought me out of them, but not before I caught a small snake that was in the act of swallowing a rodent. I ate both of them and, feeling much stronger, pushed on.

The canyon abruptly widened onto an apron of rock about thirty feet wide and sixty long. At its end was a crevasse which fell for three thousand feet to a river. The river was always in shadow at this point. It was between sister peaks, not over eighty feet apart at this height.

A natural bridge of granite spanned the abyss. It was twenty feet wide along the bottom and sixty feet deep. The Nine had had its upper portion carved away for a depth of twenty feet, so that, like the razor's edge bridge between the Heaven and Earth of the Muslims, a blade of rock was the only passage across. The only way across had to be on a surface three inches wide and eighty feet long.

At the other end of the arch was a broad ledge and an overhang and a blank wall of rock at the end of the ledge.

There was a seemingly natural fissure in the back of the recess. Behind this window stood a sentinel, one of whose duties was to make sure that every traveler walked across. Those who lost their nerves and sat down to scoot across were killed and tossed down into the river.

I have never seen anybody fall off the narrow arch or been thrown off, but then I have never seen anyone try to walk over it. I have always been unaccompanied when I made my required visits. I think that the Nine arrange matters so that the pilgrims of eternity do not see each other while on the way.

However, when I got into the caverns, I usually saw the same people. My wife always went at a different time, and I had never seen Caliban there. I suspected that the Nine, for reasons of their own, which I might or might not learn, had arranged our visits to coincide.

It did not matter. What did matter was that Caliban was waiting for me, as I had expected.

Naked, his arms extended for balance, he stood in the center of the bridge with one foot behind the other. He grinned when he saw me; the teeth were peculiarly white in the metallic reddish-brown face.

CHAPTER TWENTY

That penis was like a dark-bronze python sliding out of a nest of brown-red leaves. It gave me a slight shock to see it, it was so enormous. It was soft, yet it must have been at least three inches wide and eight inches long. The testicles were correspondingly huge.

The genitals were the one disproportion of the magnificent body. Revealed, they made him a freak.

CHAPTER TWENTY-ONE

I stopped at the edge of the abyss and set one foot on the bridge. The rock was black granite, smooth and cold when felt by the hand. My soles did not feel the stone, since the calluses on them were as thick and as tough as rhinoceros hide.

He seemed to expect me to say something, perhaps to ask him why he was after me. I saw no reason to talk. It was too late for words. The sooner I got him out of the way, the sooner I would get my business over with and the sooner I could get to England.

I stepped out on the bridge and slowly approached him, one foot behind the other, my hands held out. The wind blowing up from the river was cold. I was sweating despite the height and the lack of sun and the wind.

My penis was rising like a drawbridge.

Caliban looked at it and then shouted, savagely, "I will tear your prick off, my friend, and keep it for a trophy! It was with that that you raped my cousin, my beautiful Trish!"

I said nothing. I continued to advance.

"You killed her!" he shouted. "You raped and murdered her and you threw her body to the hyenas!"

I did not know what he was talking about. It was evident that he thought I had committed some crime upon someone he loved. I knew it was useless to reason with him, so I kept on walking toward him. And my penis was now rigid and at a forty-five-degree angle to my belly. It seemed ready to burst with blood. This bothered me, because I needed every bit of energy for the combat. Also, I must admit, I felt ridiculous and so was at a disadvantage. This feeling resulted in anger, and I did not want my judgment dissolved in its heat.

I was now close enough to see the color of those peculiar eyes. They were whirlpools of gold-flecked bronze, and they did not look quite human.

"You monster!" he shouted. "Don't you care? Doesn't it disturb you at all?"

It was no use telling him I was innocent, and I knew that he had put his weapons aside for the same reason that I would have. I was the only great challenge he had ever met among men.

I stopped, pulled in my arms from the side, and extended them before me. He stepped forward, halted, and put out his hands. I moved forward another step, and we gripped each other's hands. I exerted pressure to throw him off balance; he did the same to me.

This was not to be a long drawn out battle. There would be no kicking, gouging, kneeing, hitting with the fists or the edge of the palm. Our positions were far too precarious for those. Moreover, both of us, I believe, wanted to demonstrate his superior strength in a simple and undeniable manner.

I had never met so powerful a man. He was not as strong as a gorilla, but then neither am I. He was not quite as powerful as the strongest of the males among The Folk. But then neither am I.

We strained to throw the other to one side and so send him through the space between the mountains to the river three thousand feet below. Our muscles cracked; our bones creaked. Sweat oozed like our departing strength from our skin, stung our eyes, and ran coldly down our ribs and our crotches.

We swayed back and forth in this footless dance. He glared down at me, and I up at him. I don't know what he saw in the gray of mine, but I suspect that it was the same lust to kill that was in his gold-spotted bronze. We came closer and closer. Our arms were forced outward by the pressure we applied and forced backward, and we neared each other until our chests and noses were almost touching. His breath was hot on my wet face.

Then we came together. Our chests rubbed. Our bellies touched. And I felt that elephant trunk of a penis against mine.

I think that he was upset then. At least, his face changed from snarling hatred to an unreadable expression.

He looked as if he wanted to look down to verify what his other senses told him. He did not dare to do so, of course. He, no more than I, dared to change his attitude. The least unbalancing or weakening in one direction, and the other would upset him.

Eventually, one would weaken, and the end would be swift then.

Until that clasping of hands a few minutes before, I would not have believed that any human could withstand me so long. Now I knew that it was possible that I had met my match. More than my match.

I knew it, but I did not really believe it. If I had, I think I might have weakened just a trifle with the doubt and the surprise. And that would have been enough for him.

I was hoping that a similar doubt would corrode his strength just enough for my purposes. But there was nothing in the expression on his savagely handsome face or in those peculiar eyes or in the gracefully massive muscles to indicate that doubt was turning his bronze into lead.

By then, our peters were crossed like swords.

And I was beginning to feel the slow upbuild of an orgasm.

My aberrant condition was going to betray me. Kill me.

No matter how I fought it, I would be subject to a certain amount of transport and involuntary contraction of muscle and loss of force.

Caliban did not know what was happening, but he knew that something was occurring in me. He smiled thinly and said, "I am stronger than you, you filthy ape!"

I could feel the slight tremors in his belly and a slight jerking in his penis.

His eyes widened, and he said, "What the hell!"

He was beginning to feel the same sensations as I!

It was a question of who would ejaculate first, and I thought that it would be me.

I was about to release him, if possible, and throw myself backward and away. If I did it quickly enough, and he was seized in an orgasm, I might be able to keep away from him until we were both over the spurtings, and we could then resume the fight on equal terms.

He bit his lip and said, "God! What's going on?"

I tensed for my effort to break that metalled grip.

A voice bellowed in English, "Stop! In the name of the Nine!"

CHAPTER TWENTY-TWO

The granite slab covering the entrance to the caverns had slid into a recess. Nine people stood on the apron of rock near the other end of the bridge. Eight were of the Nine. The tall long-bearded old man with the black patch over one eye was missing. The ninth person was a tall Negro dressed in the blue Roman toga-like robes of the Speaker for the Nine. He held a wooden staff, nine feet high, on top of which was carved a crux ansata. A third of the length down was a carved representation of the symbol which the Finns call *hannunvaakuna*.

He shouted at us again so loudly that the mountain returned an echo. "No more fighting! Come to me, and I will give you the order of the day!"

Caliban backed away from me until I could not reach him. He would not turn away until I said, "It's over. For now."

His penis was beginning to shrink and to drop. Mine stayed erect for a much longer time. In fact, for a minute, I thought I was going to have the orgasm.

The eight of the Nine were dressed in differently colored robes with hoods. Their faces were hidden, and they turned away and were gone before I reached the ledge. This was the first time I had ever seen more than three at a time. During the many years I had served the Nine, I had seen all of them. But it had always been three one year, another trio the next year, a third trio the following year, and then, the fourth year, the cycle began anew.

I could not imagine why the old man whom we addressed

as *XauXaz* was not present. I did not ask. The Nine discouraged questions.

The Negro in blue was the majordomo, the Speaker for the Nine. He would serve for three months of the year and then go. I had been Speaker several years ago and my wife two years after that.

He said, "Peace between you two until the Nine say war. Follow me."

We halted in the first cave, where he went through the ritual of getting us through the guards. These were five men and five women, naked as everybody except the Nine and the Speaker, but armed with automatic rifles. Behind them were heavy-caliber machine guns, flame-throwers, a whippet tank, and a Bofors cannon. They were serving their four-hour duty, as did everyone who came through this entrance.

A woman took a sample of blood from our thumbs and disappeared into a wooden booth. She came out a moment later and handed two small cards to the Speaker. From a pocket in his robe he took two cards and matched them with the others. Then he handed all four to her and said, "Follow me!"

The next cavern, unlike the first, was not lit with batteries of lamps on the walls and overhead fluorescent cylinders. It was dark, and we progressed through it by placing our hands on the shoulders of the man before us. Since I had been the Speaker, I knew that he was following a narrow beam of sound transmitted through a small device in one ear. If he strayed to one side or the other, the sound would die out. I did not doubt that all sorts of scanning devices were studying us.

In the next cavern, which was empty, and was really a trap for any invader who got this far—the ceiling would fall on them and then the floor would drop out—I studied the Speaker. He was a tall, well-built, handsome Negro with a light-brown skin. He looked as if he were thirty.

Suddenly, I knew why he seemed so familiar. He was a New Yorker, a millionaire who had recently disappeared after the explosion of his yacht in Long Island Sound. Several people had been brought in for questioning, but no one had been arrested. The newspaper articles said he was sixty years old but looked remarkably younger.

He was supposed by the more superstitious in New York City to be using voodoo to prolong his youth. The black militants had accused him of being an Uncle Tom and of refusing to use any of his fortune to help his people. Furthermore, a million dollars was missing from his bank account.

It was easy to understand the explosion and the disappearance, now I had seen him here. He was getting to the age when questioning and astonishment about his youthful looks would increase geometrically in proportion with the passage of time. He could use makeup to seem older, but that had its annoyances and limitations. The Nine had ordered that he "die." He could start a new identity elsewhere after he had served his three months as the Speaker.

I wondered if the Nine were thinking of the same thing for me. I could not go on forever with my present identity. Only the fact that I spent so much of my time away from civilization, and my passion for obscurity, had prevented an order from the Nine. Even so, when I went to England or elsewhere, I whitened my black hair and wrinkled my face.

I suspected that Caliban was in my position. Rivers and Simmons had mentioned briefly that "Doc" had not been able to entirely hide his name and qualities from the world. A writer of pulps had somehow learned something of his strange rearing and training, his extraordinary, perhaps unique, qualities and abilities, and something of the hidden place where he rehabilitated criminals. The writer had used Caliban as the basis for a character, under another name, of course, in a series of wild science-fictional adventures, most of which were the result of his imagination. But there had been some fact in them. Apparently, the two old men had figured prominently in these adventures but also under different names.

CHAPTER TWENTY-THREE

The fourth cavern was enormous. It contained a village of pre-fabricated huts with bright lights on the end of tall stone pillars illuminating the lower part of the cave. The huts were provided with lighting, heaters, hot and cold running water, liquor, tobacco, and furniture.

Although I had learned much when I was the Speaker and had been in twenty caverns, I did not know where the supplies came from or where the water was pumped or the electrical generators were housed. Nor did I know what entrance the Nine used.

Caliban and I were marched into the central square of the village and dismissed. He went into the house marked with a card bearing his name: I went into the house prepared for me. Here I shaved, showered, and then ate a meal cooked by a famous Parisian chef. I wanted to gorge myself but I ate relatively little. I did not care to have a heavy bloated stomach when I went through the ceremony in the Council Cave of the Nine.

The woman who served me was a big titian-haired Dane with the greenest eyes and the softest thickest reddest pubic hairs I have ever seen. She was only an inch shorter than I and truly had the figure of a goddess. I knew her well, since she often came to the caves at the same time as I.

After I had eaten, I lay down on the bed. She lay down beside me and began to kiss me. I responded fervently and stroked and cupped her great shapely breasts, and gently rubbed the huge nipples. We went through the usual preludes of uninhibited and experienced couples, but when my penis failed to respond in the slightest to her skilled sucking, she stopped. She looked puzzled and hurt.

She said, "You must have been through something terrible."

"Nothing to talk about," I said.

"Nothing to talk about! That means nothing to you?"

I was silent. She said, "I heard about you and Caliban on the bridge." She shuddered. And then, surprisingly, she laughed.

"Cocks crossed," she said. "What is the matter with you two?"

"I wish I knew what is the matter with me," I said. "Is there something wrong with Caliban, too?"

"Aside from you, he's the most beautiful man I've ever seen. But he has that horsecock. He can only get it into very large women, you know."

That did not seem likely to me. I was a doctor and I had also read much in medical pathology. I had never heard of a single authenticated case of a man with a penis so large that he could not get it into a normally sized woman, provided that there was lubrication and the woman was not frightened and endowed with a powerful sphincter. I told the Countess Clara Aakjaer so.

She said, "You may be right. I told him to try me once, I thought I could take him. I was eager to try, but he said no, he knew it was no use. He wanted me to suck him off instead. I refused. I love to suck cock but only if it leads up to getting fucked. I'm funny that way.

"Anyway, I know that he has had a long love affair with his cousin, Trish Wilde."

"She's one of us?"

"Yes. She's an extraordinarily beautiful girl. She has his bronze coloring and even looks like a female Doc Caliban. But they never came here together. I just happened to be here once when she was. I knew her name but I didn't connect her with Doc until I happened to run into her when I was visiting New York. She took me up to Doc's apartments in the Empire State Building, and we had dinner together. We couldn't talk about our common interest in the Nine, of course, because his other guests were outsiders. But afterward we had a long talk. Trish, by the way, warned me to stay away from him. Outside the caves, he's hers, she says.

"But she was very frank. She said Doc could get into her but only with a lot of pain for her and she usually sucked him off. The worst of it is, Doc has great moral resistance to fellatio."

"What?" I said.

"He was given a peculiar training from the age of two on," she said. "It made him the greatest athlete and strongest man in the world—with the exception of yourself, of course. I don't suppose he would have gotten to that state if he hadn't had the physical foundation for it, he's got the biggest bones of any man I ever saw—except you, of course.

"He also was educated in the physical sciences and he became not only the greatest surgeon—under a different name by the way—but an extraordinary chemist, physicist, anthropologist, linguist, you name it. The man is disgustingly knowledgeable.

"His father raised him to be a superman, the primary purpose of which was to do good and combat evil."

"Sounds like a super Boy Scout," I said.

"In a way, you're right. His father hated evil with a passion you might call psychotic. His father was killed by criminals, you know."

"I didn't," I said.

"Yes. Anyway, Doc was given a rigid moral training, and for a while he was thinking of becoming a minister. Would you believe that he had no sexual experience with a woman until he was twenty-seven?"

"With a woman?" I said.

"I mean he didn't even masturbate. He suppressed his sexual feelings. He prides himself on his self-control above everything, you know. He never brags about it, of course, he never brags about anything. Not bragging is part of the self-control bit. But you can tell he's proud. I suppose that he may have been inhibited by the very size of his whang; it may have embarrassed him. This reinforced his moral reasons and ability to do without women. He told his colleagues, Rivers, Simmons, and the other three—I forget their names—that he was too busy to get involved with women. Besides, he didn't want to endanger them."

"They didn't accept all of that," I said.

"When Doc was twenty-seven, and was busting up a drug-smuggling ring in Los Angeles, he was captured. A woman, a member of the gang, the leader's moll in fact, slipped him a drug and he was tied up and carried off to a house up Topanga Canyon, I think Trish called it. Anyway, while the other gang members were gone, the woman—Big-Eyes Llewellyn, that was her name—raped Doc. She not only fucked him a number of times, she sucked his balls off."

"There was one woman who could get that bazooka in," I said.

"Yes, but Doc told Trish that she was a freak. Anyway, Doc tried not to respond but he failed hopelessly, abysmally. He found out what he was missing. The discovery did not delight him, it enraged him. He broke his bonds and killed the woman and escaped."

"He had to kill her?" I said.

"No. That was what sent Doc into the first sickness of his life. He almost went insane after that; his conscience almost killed him. He had lost self-control, and committed two evil acts, for the first time and in rapid succession. First, the woman had made him lose his self-control by fucking him and then sucking him off. Second, his reaction to this resulted in another loss of self-control, and he had killed the woman as you would kill a chicken, by wringing the neck until the head came off. He confessed to Trish, a few years later when he met her, that he had an orgasm when the blood jetted out of her neck. It splashed all over him and the room.

"He became very depressed and even suicidal for a year. He told no one what had happened. As far as his buddies were concerned, he had retired from society for a year to meditate and experiment. He went up to the Arctic Circle, somewhere in Canada, where he has a hideaway and stayed there for a long time. Then he came back with the intention of throwing himself into the battle against evil with a terrible fury. He would try to make up for what he had done by ridding the world of more evil.

"It was then that he met his cousin. Apparently, their fathers had not seen each other since they were teenagers. Trish's father had migrated from England to Canada and lost contact with the family. Doc's father also came from England but much later. It was only by accident that they met and then found out they were related.

"Doc and Trish fell in love. Doc told her all. Despite his moral prohibitions, he went to bed with her. She could take him, but it hurt her. She's a big girl with a small cunt, or so she said. Then Doc did a strange thing . . ."

"I saw that little Oriental greet him when he went into his house," I said. "She was very little."

I had not paid too much attention to her last few sentences. I had been thinking about his cousin and his accusations that I had murdered her. No wonder he hated me. But why did he think I had killed her?

"That's Patani. I hate her! She's so exquisite, so tiny and dainty. Don't worry. She won't try to take him into her cunt. She's a compulsive cocksucker. That's why she and Doc always get together when they're here."

She played with my penis for a while and then sucked on it a while. Again, it failed to respond. She said, "Have you really become impotent? No, that can't be so. You were crossing cocks with Doc, like Robin Hood and Little John with their quarter-staffs on the bridge. Say! You haven't gone fairy, have you?"

I said, "No."

There was no use trying to explain something I did not understand myself. If I told her I could get an enormous erection and jet all over her if I killed her, I would have frightened her. Or at least made her uneasy. Few of those admitted to the caves frighten without great cause.

She asked me if I would at least take the edge off of her, and I said I would. There were plenty of other men who would have done more for her, and so I felt complimented that she would prefer less with me than more with others. I used two fingers on her until she had a number of orgasms, and I also rammed her with my tongue until she had a dozen more orgasms. Aside from my wife, Clara had the sweetest vagina I've ever tasted.

I felt excited but it was a numb excitement.

Clara kissed me—she seemed to enjoy the taste of her own cunt—and left me.

Chapter Twenty-Four

I know that many of the aficionados of the romances about me will be shocked by what Clara and I did. Even outraged. My "biographer" has depicted me as a man of absolutely unyielding morality. According to him, I remained unswervingly chaste and faithful to my wife when being tempted by very beautiful and passionate young women after I'd gone through long periods of continence. Many aficionados of these romances firmly believe the accounts of my superhuman—or neurotic—moral behavior. Perhaps they like to believe in a man who has the strength they lack.

On the other hand, many readers scoff at this attitude. They deny that any well-sexed man could resist such beauty under such conditions. Even the Victorians were not that Victorian.

The strange thing about this is that my biographer did not exaggerate or lie. When I got married (I knew little as yet of human customs), I gave my word I would be faithful to my wife. She elaborated on this after the ceremony and made me swear again that I would bed no other woman as long as we lived.

We did not know then, of course, about the Nine or the elixir. I understood her attitude and what she required because The Folk have a similar attitude. However, among The Folk, a male can have more than one wife at a time. And divorce is easy for both male and female.

There have been long periods when I was roaming the jungle or off on some expedition or other or on some mission for the Nine, and I did not see my wife. At these times, I have masturbated. Or, for several years, in the jungle, I took along a pet, a beautiful female leopard. This was never written into his romances by my biographer. In fact, he never heard of it because I never told him. I liked him very much and did not want to offend him or to shatter his image of me any more than it had been by previous disclosures. He was one of the few really likeable humans I have known.

I fell in love with Kuta in an unconventional manner. Some day, I'll write about this peculiar man-feline relationship. The third year, she ran off with a male leopard, I suppose because I couldn't give her cubs. Or perhaps she could no longer endure her jealousy of my wife and was afraid that she would attack her. Up to the time that I first loved Kuta, in a glade on a mountainside shortly before dusk, she had been very fond of my wife.

I did not feel that I was breaking my vow by masturbating or by mounting Kuta. That vow only included human females. And certainly Clio would not be jealous of a leopardess. Or she shouldn't be. I did not, however, say anything about Kuta until after she deserted me. Clio and I were in our London house celebrating our seventh wedding anniversary and my birthday when I said something about it. It was November 21, 1920. We had been drinking champagne, and that was a mistake because I drink so seldom that a little alcohol quickly uninhibits me. I told her about Kuta and so had to endure several hours of tears and verbal abuse. I finally managed to convince her that I had not been really unfaithful or committed a terrible crime against Nature. As far as I was concerned, the only crime against Nature was against my nature, which suffers when I don't have a frequent discharge of sexual energy. In other words, if I don't come at least six times a week, I get nervous and mean.

She forgave me, or said she did, and she is very open and truthful, within limits. She forgave me because I had been raised by The Folk and so was not fully responsible for my "uncivilized" behavior. I said I took full responsibility, and my behavior could be justified far more by logic than hers could be. She ignored this and said that I must promise not to do any such thing again. Not only were humans off-limits, so were animals, no matter how beautiful and cooperative.

I asked her if that included "jacking off." She was startled and, also, red-faced. I told her about my masturbations. I was so "natural" about it, I suppose, that she overcame her inhibitions about it. After a few more glasses of bubbly, she confessed that she masturbated, too, when I had been away for a long time. It took much courage for her to tell me this. She came from an upper middle-class Southern family with a puritanical Protestant background. In addition, her Black "mammy," who had raised her since she was six, was a very strict Southern Baptist. Despite which, Clio managed to grow into a passionate not-particularly-prudish young woman with a tendency for what humans call "sexual experimentation." And she was able to free herself of those crippling conditioned reflexes that humans call racial prejudices. At least, as much as any North American white is able.

(I digress. But I tell my story as I wish. Moreover, the reader won't understand me or those I love if he doesn't see us three-dimensionally.)

Clio and I freely discussed our masturbations and the accompanying fantasies. She even made a joke about the size of the banana she needed to satisfy herself with after having had me for seven years.

This vow of fidelity did not hold during a part of the year. It was suspended for whoever was attending the ceremonies in the caverns of the Nine. When we accepted the elixir of prolonged youth, we also had to accept certain conditions laid down by the Nine. We spoke once about it and after that ignored the subject. We had agreed that the elixir could not be purchased without a very high price. Nothing comes free. The price was worth it, or so we thought at the time. I had my doubts now and then, but they were not powerful.

Clara interrupted my thoughts by returning. She said, "I just ran into the little Thai. She was very upset. She said she felt repulsed by Doc. He looked so absolutely *evil* to her. Something has happened to him. He is not the same Doc she has known for so many years. So she just walked out on him."

I said, "Did he have a hard-on?"

"No, he never does unless you suck on him a while."

I thought of our meeting on the bridge.

Clara looked hard at me for a moment and then said, "I had an uneasy feeling when we started to make love, John. Or I should say when *I* started to make love. You had changed, too. It wasn't just the soft-on. Do you know, you're *evil*, too!"

This was a peculiar thing for her to say. I wanted to ask her more about her feelings but she left quickly.

The silence had to be filled with my thoughts. They buzzed like flies in a dead mouth.

It seemed to me that anybody who accepted the gift of the Nine, and so accepted their terms, was, in some measure, evil. It was true that the Nine had never required me to do anything which I thought of as evil. As yet. They had the power, by the terms, to ask me to do anything they wished.

I thought of the inevitable parallel, the story of Faust and the devil. Faust, however, made a sorry bargain, a short-termed one, and regretted it. We, however, if we were lucky, would live for at least 30,000 years, and, once dead, that was the end of it. Also, some of us would probably become members of the Nine, because even they died now and then. The last one had died 2,000 years ago, and one of the servants of the Nine had taken his place. The next vacancy might not be for another 2,000 years or it might be today.

I would say that to be offered a multimilleniaed youth is to be tempted irresistibly. I can picture a mentally sick person, a depressed person, or a very old person, rejecting the offer. But not anyone who loves life.

Why should the Nine share this prolonged life with others? I suppose because the elixir is far more binding than money. And also because the Nine believe in tradition, in the continuity of their secret body of people, the oldest by far of any bodies.

The intercom buzzed nine times, and the Speaker's voice began to call our names. Mine was fifth. Caliban's was eighth. By this alone, I knew something unusual was happening. In the forty-eight years I had been attending, no more than one pilgrim at a time went into the ceremony cave.

CHAPTER TWENTY-FIVE

The entrance was carved out of rock, delta-shaped, and only large enough to admit one at a time. It was a tight squeeze for me.

The cave was well-lit only in the center. Elsewhere, it was dim dusk for the space of a few yards and then blackness. The rough granite floor sloped downward from all sides to the center. At the bottom was a tiny lake of black water, and in its center was a truncated cone of large rough-hewn oaken blocks and beams. On top of the island, which was about twelve feet high, was a circular oaken table, a ring. Inside the ring were nine high-backed intricately carved oak and ash chairs. The Nine entered through a trapdoor in the middle of the wooden cone.

The ceiling was covered with darkness except in the center, where nine massive crystalline stalactites hung down, like glowing hanged men, from the night of the ceiling. The light came from nine giant torches of wood and pitch projecting from moveable stone pillars set around the edges of the platform top.

We lesser beings stood on the slope—there were no chairs for us—throughout the ceremony. There was silence except for the inevitable coughing, occasioned by nervousness, not colds, since those who drink the elixir have no physical diseases. We were not allowed to speak except in reply to the Nine.

After a long time, the Speaker came up through the hole in the island and stood to one side of the chairs, leaning his staff with its ankh and *hannunvaakuna* outward from him.

Slowly, one by one, the Nine appeared from the hole and took their assigned chairs. The last to appear was the most important, the old woman Anana.

Only eight of the Nine were here. The chair just to the right of Anana's was empty. It belonged to the giant white-bearded old man who wore a double-headed raven headpiece and a black patch over a good eye. We knew him only as XauXaz.

The eight were dressed in their monkish robes, but the hoods were hanging behind their necks, and they wore their headpieces. Anana's was the head of a wild sow, and the others wore the heads of a bear, a wolf, a hyena, a ram, a jaguar, a badger, and an elk.

The woman Anana looked us over for a long time. I have been close to her many times, so I knew that she looked as if she were 125 and kept Death away only by scaring him. I had reason to believe that she was 30,000 years old.

Finally, she gestured at the Speaker. He walked to the empty chair beside her and lifted from its seat what the shadows had hidden. It was the two-headed raven headpiece of XauXaz. He placed it on the table before the chair and stamped the end of his staff against the oaken floor so that it boomed nine times.

He cried out in English in a loud voice that echoed back from the murkiness, "XauXaz has gone to his ancestors, as all must, even the Nine!"

The others picked up small stone cups and drank from them and set them down. There was another silence. Apparently, this was to be all that would be said about XauXaz, who had sat in that chair, or one like it elsewhere, for at least 5,000 years and perhaps for three times that long. The Nine may have had a previous ceremony during which they genuinely mourned him. I do not know. But when with us, they acted as if they believed in ceremony, but in a short one, only.

Anana seemed to shrink within herself, physically, though the force of her personality did not diminish. I was not joking when I said she was holding Death off by scaring him. I do not frighten easily, but I am very uneasy when in her presence.

After another painfully long pause, she stirred. She looked to her right at Ing, the old man who wore a bear's head, and to her left at Iwaldi, the gnomish old man who wore a badger's head. These two, with XauXaz, were, I believe, the oldest after Anana. I do not know what their age is, but I have been close enough more than once to hear the language which the three men spoke only among themselves. And I know enough of Indo-European linguistics to recognize several of the words. I have read them, in their hypothetical and reconstructed forms, though I had not, of course, heard them spoken by a native speaker. Until then, that is.

One word was "weraz," and the other was "taknwaz." I believe that these meant, respectively, "man" and "precious object." Ing, Iwaldi, and XauXaz were speaking a dialect of Primitive Germanic. This is the tongue from which is descended the modern Norse, English, High and Low German languages, and, earlier, Old English, Old Norse, Frankish, Gothic, Old Saxon, and so on.

The others ranged from seeming octogenarians to those who looked no more than fifty. I knew something of each, since I had had contact daily for several weeks when I had been Speaker. One was a Hebrew born shortly before 1 A.D. Two were Mongolian but spoke a language between themselves I could not identify. One was a very old, very huge Negro, and he sometimes talked to himself in a language that I am sure is the ancestor of all the Bantu tongues of modern Africa. The seventh looked as if he were a North American Indian. He also looked so Mongolian, however, that he could be an Olmec of ancient Mexico. Ing looked Nordic. Iwaldi was a dark-skinned dwarf with very broad shoulders, a huge head, slight epicanthic folds, long thick gnarled arms, great hands like the roots of an oak tree, and very short thick bowed legs. His white hair fell to his buttocks, and his white beard to his knees. He looked as if he belonged to a very different stock of Caucasian. Yet he spoke Primitive Germanic with Ing and XauXaz and seemed very close to them, as if they had known each other for a long time and had unusually common interests.

Anana said, "The mourning is over for us. And the chair is still empty. Who shall sit in the High's seat?"

The torches flickered on the naked men and women standing on the downslope. The light was dim, yet I could see the skin of the woman near me was goose-pimpled. It may have been the cold dampness of the cavern or the anticipation—apprehensive—of the ceremony, or it may have been the suddenly increased tension from

Anana's words. We knew, without having been told, that one of us was going to be nominated for a seat with the Nine.

I had counted forty-nine people, including myself. There were, I knew, many more than that in the organization. These people must be those whom the Nine considered their best candidates. Doctor Caliban stood on my left about twenty feet away. There was nothing between us to block the view. I studied him during the silence. He was indeed a magnificent man. By the peculiar light of the torches, he looked more than ever like a bronze statue. He was not, however, Hellenic. No Athenian sculptor would have created a male figure so divinely proportioned except for the genitals. They were gargantuan, and, for some reason, the penis was half-erect. It was of a far darker bronze than the surrounding skin, being engorged with blood.

At that moment, the statue came to life. Caliban shifted his weight to his left leg, and a second later he turned his head slightly and looked out of the corners of his eyes at me. His gaze was downward; a slight smile—not amused—made fluid the corners of the lips and the eyes seemed to light up from an inner explosion. This was, of course, an illusion of the flickering torchlight.

I looked down. Not until that moment had I realized that my hatred and my desire to kill him had erected my penis. I also realized that my own skin was almost as bronzish as Caliban's, even to the darker bronze of the penis.

The Danish countess, Clara, was staring at my erection. She was undoubtedly wondering why she had failed and what there was in this situation to arouse me.

The Speaker thumped his staff on the oaken floor again. It was as if a stalactite had fallen. Almost everybody jumped. I did; I react swiftly to stimuli unless I have some reason to control myself. Caliban did not jump. He merely smiled on seeing my response, and he looked utterly savage as he did so, and then he turned his head to look back at the Nine.

The Speaker told us, briefly, what we would do. Because of the death of XauXaz, we would go through the ceremony in the presence of the other servants. All except two would experience the same ceremony as before. These two were the final candidates, chosen from the group in this cavern. If the two candidates did not meet the requirements of the Nine, if both failed, then other candidates would be chosen from the rest of the group. That, however, would be at a later time, since the test would occupy the two for a while.

Silence fell again like a piece of darkness from the ceiling. The Nine seemed to be thinking of other things. Perhaps they were remembering the last time a new man had taken a seat.

The cry of the Speaker cracked the darkness.

"Lord Grandrith! Doctor Caliban! Approach! Wade through the waters! Climb the Tree to the Table of the Gods!"

We walked down the slope and into the lake. The waters were cold. The blood in my legs jelled, quivered, and was dead. This deadness went up my legs, up my thighs, and then the waters covered my testicles and my penis, which had lost its swelling as soon as it hit the water. The testicles tried to retreat into the cavity of my belly, and then they froze. My bowels became ice. The lower part of my spine was a tree with roots exposed to the Arctic sea.

Climbing up the oak logs to the top of the structure did not thaw me much. The ascent was not easy because of the partial paralysis and because the logs were slimy. I don't know what was the ultimate fate of anyone who slipped back into the water and then could not make the climb.

Caliban and I got to the top at the same time. At the low-voiced direction of the Speaker, we stood side by side and faced Anana across the table. She looked even more wrinkled than I remembered her, as if Time had folded up her face like a bag and then, changing his mind, had unfolded it to give her a chance to live longer. The dark blue eyes in that face like a fist were bright, however. And deep. The many thousands of years had drilled far into the region behind the eyes. There was something ineffably sphinx-like about her, and, at the same time, something unidentifiable. That nameless quality was frightening. She, and three others of the Nine, are the only human beings that ever made me feel touched with fear. These four may not be human. When a man lives past a thousand years, he may become more—or less—than human.

Anana's voice was a whisper. She spoke in English with echoes of a tongue that perished long before bronze was invented.

"What is your quarrel with him, Grandrith?"

I believed that she knew very well what my quarrel was. She probably knew far more than I, since she would also have the facts about Caliban. Also, I was beginning to wonder if she was not, in part at least, responsible for the state in which Caliban and I were enmeshed.

The Speaker bellowed out her question. The words flew back from the distant walls like invisible bats. I said, "Caliban attacked me without provocation."

Out of the corner of my eye, I saw the bronze figure shudder a little.

"Did you, Caliban?"

The Speaker shouted her words.

"No. He lies."

The Speaker repeated in a voice like a bull's, "No. He lies!"

I was beginning to get irritated by the thunderish repetitions and the bat-like echoes, which seemed to jeer. Ordinarily, such things do not bother me. The unusualness of the ceremony, its unknown and possibly sinister development, the irrational motives for Caliban's hatred, my desire to kill him and get him out of the way, and my nervousness to get to England to protect Clio combined to make me abnormally sensitive.

Anana said, "Why did you attack Grandrith?"

"He raped and murdered my cousin, Trish Wilde."

"You know this to be a fact?"

"She was with a botanical expedition near the Uganda-Kenya border. A naked man ran into the camp at night, knocked Trish out, and carried her off. Some of the natives identified the man as Grandrith. They tried to follow but lost the trail. They did run across two natives who had seen Grandrith raping my cousin."

He paused, and a sound like a suppressed sob came from him.

"They interrupted him; he took off with Trish over his shoulder, running like an antelope. She's a big woman, weighs 150 pounds. Who else could carry her off like that? And then Trish's colleagues found her two days later . . . what was left . . . the hyenas and the vultures . . ."

He drew in a deep breath, but his face was expressionless.

"There must have been enough to identify her."

"Only bones. Her skull was missing. But the bones were those of a Caucasian female of her age, that is, twenty-five, in appearance. Actually, she's sixty."

"The skull was never found?"

"No. It's presumed a hyena or perhaps a leopard carried it off."

"Do you know anything of Grandrith?" Anana said.

"Until 1948, I had thought he was a writer's creation, a character in a series of fantastic novels," Caliban said. "Not until then did I find out, by accident, that there was a factual basis to the fictions. I was curious and did some investigating through agents. I learned some things about him, not much, but enough to make me suspect that he was one of us. I did not follow up the investigation because I became occupied with other matters."

"Your brain transplant experiments," Anana whispered. She smiled a terrible smile, and she extended two fingers of her left hand. This was a sign to the Speaker not to repeat her words.

"We have learned a number of things about you recently. We suspect that you have also been researching with the idea of independently producing the elixir. So far, you have not succeeded. And we have good reason to think that you will never succeed. But this does not displease us. We have not forbidden our servants to try to make their own elixir. And if you had not tried, you would not have come up to our expectations of you.

"However, that is not my main point. I point out to you that your investigation showed that Grandrith was, in many respects, like you. You are undoubtedly the two greatest athletes that the world has produced for several thousand years. Which is the greatest remains to be tested. You two even resemble each other facially, though your different coloring tends to conceal it."

This was a long speech in public for one of the Nine. I wondered what she was getting at—or to—but did not say anything, of course.

She leaned forward and stretched out her skinny arms with the great veins like asphyxiated snakes. She said, "Come closer."

We, knowing what was expected, moved until our thighs pressed against the table edge and our testicles rested on the surface. My flesh had warmed up, but when Anana's hand cupped my testicles, they felt cold indeed. It seemed to me that anyone whose blood flowed that slowly could not have long to live.

Philip José Farmer

I did not flinch. I had never flinched when she had done this, even though I knew what she would soon be doing.

Then I saw that this procedure might be different. Certainly, she could not use a sharp flint knife on me with the other hand since it was holding Caliban's testicles.

She lifted the sacs as if she were estimating the weight and worth of meat in grocery bags. She said, "They are noble indeed. And warm with life. How many . . . ?"

Her voice trailed off. She looked up and smiled. Her teeth were black. Not from rottenness but from something she chewed. It was not betel; its odor was unidentifiable. I suspected that once all her people chewed this plant and that the plant had become extinct except in some garden in some very private well-guarded house somewhere.

"Today," she said, "you will not have to give up part of your flesh to the knife. You will eat with us in preparation for your contest. The next time we meet here to eat, only one of you will be at this table. Or at any table."

Apparently, there was to be no more discussion of our grievances or any arbitration of our case. They did not care who was wrong or wronged. They probably did not even acknowledge that wrong existed except in human minds. I say human because I do not think that they thought of themselves as human. Though they could die, they must have considered themselves as gods. No human could live that long and have such power and not think himself divine.

Would I, if I became one of the Nine, come to think as they?

Severed though I am from most human attitudes, or I should say, loosely connected, I still fully share some. The infrahuman has not entirely eaten out the human in me. I feel a certain—or uncertain—amount of sympathy and empathy for humans, for some humans. I would not wish to become even more alienated. I knew how it felt to see those with whom I most identified die away. As far as I knew, The Folk, never numerous, had become nothing.

"It has been two thousand years since this preseating ceremony was held," she said.

She gestured at the lean, dark-bearded, scimitar-nosed man with the ram's head. I had heard him speak of Caesar Augustus, Tiberius, and Herod Antipas when I was Speaker.

156

"At that time, Grandrith, your ancestral island was inhabited by the tattooed British and Picts and your English ancestors still lived in what was to be later called Denmark. And as for America, Doctor Caliban, no one knew of it—except the Nine and their servants. We kept the Phoenicians and the Romans and the Saracens from following up their discovery of the Americas, and we aborted the Norse colonization. We were thinking for a while about establishing an Iroquois-Cherokee empire. The first Europeans would have found a united people armed with firearms and riding horses. But the final decision was to let things happen as they would.

"The point is that when the last vacancy occurred, when Thrithjaz died . . ."

That would be Primitive Germanic for third, I thought.

". . . neither the English nor the Americans existed as such. But times change, even for us, and we have seen many nations and tongues born and die."

She lifted a finger at the Speaker. He directed me to stand at the far right, by the wrinkled, squat Negro with the hyena headpiece and Caliban at the far left, by the man with the ram headpiece. The Speaker then thudded the butt of the staff and began calling out names.

The ceremony was like those I had attended as one of the "eaten" and directed when I was Speaker. There were differences, however. Before, Anana had always fed first. Now, Caliban and I were treated as guests of honor. Anana took the testicles of a big mustachioed man with her left hand and cut the scrotum on one side with a long-bladed flint knife. The man looked down and did not look away even when the pinkish egg-shaped gland rolled out on the table. His dark skin did become pale and then gray; sweat rolled down his body; he gripped the table edge as if he were trying to leave his fingerprints in the wood.

As the Speaker, I had seen him go through this before and did not expect him to faint and fall off the structure into the cold black waters. I have seen some men faint. No one helps them. Usually, the water shocks them back into consciousness and most climb back up, however painful the ascent. Several could not, or would not, climb again. The guards took these away, and I never saw them again.

The ceremony must have been originated in the Old Stone Age, perhaps 300,000 years ago or more. It was probably old when Anana was born.

Anana picked up the testicle and placed it on the table before her after smelling it. The Speaker had stepped over the table; he now came around and smeared ointment from a jar onto the wound. While he did this, he chanted a few lines in an unknown language. The bleeding, which was not great, stopped altogether. Anana handed her stone cup to the Speaker, who gave the man a mouthful of the liquid. This tastes like mead to me, but I do not think it is. The pain would be gone within five minutes. Inside a month, provided the man got the proper food and rest, the testicle would be regrown. Not only did the elixir provide a prolonged youth and freedom from disease, it gave regenerative powers.

Anana sliced the gland into twelve more or less equal slices. She sent one to me via the Speaker and one to Caliban. One piece was thrown into the water and one was placed before the empty chair. Each of the Nine took a slice and ate it raw. I chewed and swallowed mine with gusto, because the testicle is one of the few pieces of human meat worth eating.

The mustachioed man, dismissed by the Speaker, climbed down slowly and painfully. The second person called was on top of the structure before the first had waded out through the waters.

CHAPTER TWENTY-SIX

I had only to turn my head to see Caliban because the table was curved and we sat, as it were, at the ends of opposite horns of a crescent moon. His face was expressionless; it did not show the repulsion I would have expected from a civilized man. Either he was in strong control of his emotions, which would agree with what his two colleagues said, or he was genuinely indifferent to, or perhaps even enjoying, the meat.

I was disappointed. I would have liked to have seen him disgrace himself by vomiting.

The next person summoned was a beautiful mulatto. Her hair was black and curly, *au naturel*, and her skin was as dark as a wild hare's eye. The eyes were a startling light blue. She was the wife of the Speaker and had disappeared with him when the explosion blew up the yacht. I recognized her because she had attended the ceremonies when I did. I had bedded her not infrequently and had, of course, tongued her all over.

I think Anana knew this. She seemed to know everything about us as if she were God and we were Her sparrows. Thus she knew I would have no objections to performing the ceremony with her. Caliban, however, was a white American born in 1903 and so more than probably had the usual conditioned reflexes of his "class." This may be why Anana designated Myra to go to him. If he did have any objections, he did not reveal them by expression.

He extended a hand to help her get up on the table, picked her up as if she were a hollow dummy and placed her on her back. She put her legs over his shoulders, and he spent some time with his face buried against the thick stiff hairs I knew so well and the slit dripping with honey-thick lubricating fluid.

Myra made an attempt to respond. She writhed and moaned a little, but I doubted that she was doing anything except acting. She must have been too tense to relax. The only woman whom I thought could in reality let loose and have an orgasm during this ceremony was the Danish giantess. I'm sure that the final act hurt her just as much as any of the women, but she could live for the moment as few can.

Finally, Caliban bit down. The woman stiffened, her fists driving the nails into the skin. (I saw the blood on the tips and palms when she got up.) Her feet bent and turned inward and her toes clenched. Her jaw clamped shut to keep the scream inside, although the Nine had not forbidden screaming.

Caliban lifted her up. He had some blood on his juice-smeared lips and chin, and he was chewing the clitoris. The Speaker, his face set, smeared some ointment on her wound. Myra, gray beneath the brown skin, walked across the table unsteadily and climbed painfully off the table and down the logs of the structure.

This was the first time that I had seen a husband and wife in the caverns at the same time. I thought that it must be rather hard on him to watch her with Caliban; I do not think that I could control my jealousy if Clio were doing this in front of me with him. I would have tried to kill him—perhaps. I knew that Clio was doing what the other women were doing. A man or a woman cannot keep their youth and vitality forever without wanting some variety, and I did not expect her to be a saint. But I also did not want to know what she was doing, even hear about it, let alone see it.

It may be that the Nine were punishing him for some reason. Or perhaps they were testing him.

I was given the honor of eating the next woman, a beauty from the Punjab. My experience in biting off clitorises was nil, but I succeeded quickly. The clitoris, aside from the delicious scent and taste of the moisture and fluid of a healthy woman's vagina, tasted like the man's testicle.

After her, a man was called up. His testicle was cut out and sliced and the pieces passed around. This time, each of us took only a small bite and then threw the remainder on the floor behind us. It was evident that we could not eat all the flesh of forty-seven people. The Nine had pets in their private chambers who would eat what we could not.

The third person called was Clara, and Anana licked at her until she came and then bit off the clitoris.

After that, the ceremony went swiftly with no foreplay for the women. There were too many to spend time dawdling.

At the end, the forty-seven men and women were sitting or standing on the slope across the waters. A few groaned. Several had passed out after making it back, but all regained consciousness and walked out, unaided, when the Speaker dismissed them. They were free to leave. Most would not hear from the Nine until the summons came for the yearly payment of flesh or their turn to be the Speaker.

Aside from these normal duties, I had heard from the Nine only seven times in forty-eight years. I was required to carry out assignments in Thailand, Rhodesia, Brazil, Czechoslovakia, the States, Jerusalem, and Berlin. One occupied me a year, during which I did not see my beloved Clio. I performed all missions to the full satisfaction of the Nine, although I came close to being killed several dozen times. Each assignment would have made a splendid book for my biographer. He never heard of them, of course, and he would have been forced to heavily censor them if he had. And he would have been horrified at the manner in which I did some things.

After the cavern was cleared of all but those on the oaken island, there was silence. The only sound was the sputtering of torches and an occasional licking of blood from lips and chins. The odor of blood and saliva and sweat and clitorises and testicles was strong. Caliban was gazing malignantly at me. I stared at him for a moment and then looked away, since I did not want to indulge in a childish I-can-out-stare-you contest.

Finally, Anana rustled her robes and said, "You two have experienced some very disturbing, highly abnormal reactions lately, haven't you?"

Simultaneously, we said, "Yes."

"Caliban," she said. "*Doctor* Caliban. What is your explanation?"

His slight smile showed that he had caught the sarcasm. He said, "I have no answer, except . . ."

"Continue."

"The elixir may have something to do with it."

He pointed at the stone cups and the stone pitcher with which the Speaker refilled the cups. That gesture meant that he believed that the elixir was in the mead-tasting liquid. He did not know that it was. None of the servants knew. We supposed that it was because we were given nothing else special to drink. The Nine referred to the elixir without telling us when we were getting it.

"I can't believe that any psychobiological mechanism could suddenly start operating after all these years unless it were released by the long-term action of the elixir. Of course, the mechanism must have been deeply buried in me, although I had not the slightest inkling that it existed. Grandrith also seems to be suffering from a similar aberration. Since he has been taking the elixir, too, it offers the only element common to us.

"I admit that I don't understand what this mechanism is or why he should have one also. I use the term mechanism, but I could just as well say trauma or engram."

That beautiful voice was so hypnotic that I almost nodded into sleep. For a moment, it lulled my hatred of him. When Anana spoke, she startled me.

"Grandrith. *Doctor* Grandrith. What is your explanation?"

Caliban's eyes opened just a trifle. I don't think he had known that I was an M.D.

"Unlike Caliban, I am not the greatest doctor in the world, or even in Kenya. But I can think, and that's doing more than most doctors I have known. I agree with Caliban that the elixir must be responsible for bringing an already-existing aberration to the surface. I seem to be incapable of getting an erection while loving a woman, unless I am inflicting pain on her. Perhaps you noticed that I had a slight erection while I was biting off that woman's clitoris. It was the idea of the pain she was having, which I was giving, not the sexual aspect that excited me. If I had thought I was going to kill her, I would have had a big hard-on.

"I am very disturbed. I have, however, been so busy keeping alive that I haven't had much time to think about it.

"If you know the answer, please tell me."

My petition indicated my desperation. Nobody asked the Nine, especially Anana, for anything without placing himself in peril.

She did not reply. I said, "It is possible that the elixir may have nothing to do with it. My aberration came with a shock, the explosions of the shells. Caliban may have suffered a shock, too. But it is strange that we suffer from much the same thing."

I was thinking of the news of his cousin's rape and death.

"The beautiful Patricia Wilde," Anana said. "So I will see her no more. Like flowers they . . . never mind. It's an old old story. We are not concerned with what our servants do to each other, as long as they are not disobeying us or interfering with our plans. But at the moment, Caliban, you have sent off a man to kidnap Grandrith's wife, in revenge for what you think he did to your cousin. This is not at all like you, who have combated evil all your life and traveled the world over doing good."

The sarcasm was so light in tone that I almost missed it.

"It seems the only right thing to do," Caliban said. "Grandrith must pay for the hideous evil he's done."

"Through more evil?"

"I don't consider it to be evil!" he said with the most heat in his voice I had yet heard.

"You admitted you have a psychic aberration."

"The aberration," Caliban said, "consists of this. And nothing else. I can't get an erection unless I inflict pain or death or am thinking about it."

He was one up on me. If I could just work up a hard-on while loving by thinking about murdering someone . . . but what kind of loving would that be? Responsive on the surface and inside totally removed from my Clio. Imagine forth terror and pain and death, while she thought I was melting into her with love.

Anana said nothing for a while. The others sat as if they were sleeping. The torches were beginning to burn out, and the blackness from the ceiling was sinking toward us. The blackness was gaining substance and, hence, weight. The air even seemed to be compressed beneath it. Instead of getting warmer, the denser air became colder.

Anana cleared her throat and said, "Grandrith, you had two uncles. One died in Africa, as you well know. The other went at an early age to America because he had assaulted and nearly killed one of his teachers. Your family never heard of him again. He took the name of Wilde and became a doctor."

Caliban could be startled. He jerked his head around to stare at Anana, and his eyes had become large.

"You know who your father was, Grandrith," Anana said. "Your uncle did not know what had happened to him; he left your father hiding somewhere in Whitechapel. The world knew of your father but it never knew his real name nor what became of him after the murders ceased. We knew, however, because he was one of us. He went to the States, too, and there he became a doctor. This was after the madness passed from him. He became a doctor, like his younger brother, and, indeed, some years afterward accidentally found him. The youngest brother had a daughter, and your father had a son in America."

She paused. My heart was clenching with the excitement and the anticipation. I also felt a little sick, because I knew what she was going to say.

"All were exceedingly strong men with tendencies to madnesses. All were doctors, too, as if the knife were your totem, your desire, your bliss. All lovers of violence."

She stopped speaking again. The silence was like that between the beats of a dying heart.

Then, from Caliban, softly, a weird rising-falling whistle, and, even more softly, "Incredible!"

"You two have the same father."

CHAPTER TWENTY-SEVEN

In less than a minute after Anana had made that statement, we two were blindfolded and led out through the trapdoor in the platform. A hypodermic knocked me out, and I regained consciousness in a single-motored plane. A short time later, the plane landed, and I was led out and the blindfold removed. The landing strip was at the bottom of a deep valley. The green-shielded mountains were everywhere around.

The pilot gave me brief instructions and flew away, leaving me naked and armed only with my hunting knife, which was still bent.

Caliban, I was told, had been taken to a place near the valley of Ophir and released. His instructions were the same as mine. One of us was to return within a month with the other's head and genitals. The victor would then take the seat left empty by XauXaz.

I knew my approximate location. If I stopped only to hunt when absolutely necessary and got only three hours of sleep at night, I could get through the mountains in five days to a strip used by a Ugandan mining company. A plane might not be available for some time, however.

I had wondered at first why the Nine had placed us so far apart. The area was so vast, we could have looked for a year for each other without success. The Nine, of course, did not expect us to do this. I was not going to waste time searching for Caliban while Clio was in danger in England. Caliban would know that, too. He was probably heading for the nearest air strip now, or had got into touch with his two old colleagues and had them radio for a plane. If this happened, he would outstrip me in the race by four or five days.

I set off. It was a half hour past dawn. A brightly feathered king-fisher swooped down and ahead of me and then soared back up. The native Blacks and The Folk would have taken this as a good omen, but I had long ago given up the idea of a higher being who was interested in me. Nevertheless, on seeing the kingfisher, I felt heartened. Perhaps, down there, where the childhood treasures are, I still believed.

I knew this area well. Some years ago, I had built a tree house here not too dissimilar to that shown in those bad and lying movies made about me. In fact, I got the idea from the movies. It was as comfortable as a house can be in the thin-air water-heavy atmosphere of the high mountain rain forest. Clio lived there with me for a while. The absence of a number of people to talk to, the silence, the cold, and the wet got to her nerves. After two months, she insisted that I take her back to the Kenyan plantation. Of the sixty days, three had been idyllic.

That day and part of the night, I climbed two mountains. The next day, I was only half a mile from my old tree house. I could not afford the time, but I detoured to see it anyway. I always have a nostalgia for any place in which I have lived any time at all, except for the town house in London, which is surrounded by too many people, too much noise, and too many unpleasant odors.

In the thickness, the air was not moving. When I smelled the dead body of a human adult male who had not been dead more than an hour, I knew he had to be close. A few steps this way and that showed me the direction to go.

My biographer has stated many times that I have nostrils as sensitive as an animal's. He described this as due to my upbringing in the jungle. This was nonsense, and he knew it. No amount of practice will increase the sensitivity of the human nose. My nose is, however, not normal. I am a mutant, as I have said in previous volumes, and I have described my several mutations in detail in Volume IV. My sense of smell is equivalent to a bloodhound's. This has its advantages. It also has its disadvantages. You humans have no idea of what the odor of gasoline fumes does to me.

Inside a minute, I came across broken bushes, plants stepped upon and just rising, squashed insects, and other evidences of a struggle. A leopard-skin loincloth was under a bush. Beyond it, the body of a male Caucasian lay on its side. He was about six feet six inches in height and must have weighed 300 pounds. He was very muscular but also fat and big-paunched. He was clean-shaven. His black hair was cut in bangs just above the eyes, and it grew shoulder-length behind. A leopard-skin band went around his head. The left side of his skull was bloody and caved in. His eyes were dark gray. His right arm, which had been torn off his body, was not in sight. Neither were his penis and testicles, which had been ripped off.

A trail of blood led from his body. I followed it and came across a big knife, much like my uncle's knife before long usage had worn it stiletto-thin. I deduced that the killer had knocked this out of the man's hand with the club which I found ten feet further on. Its end bore much blood.

When I came across two sets of tracks in some soft earth, my heart beat faster. I felt choked with a sense of homecoming and of love. They were the prints of two Folk, a female and male adult.

I hurried to catch up with them. Tears ran down my cheeks. I had thought that all The Folk were dead, their kind gone forever.

The trail led to the tree house so directly that I was sure the two were deliberately heading for it. Other tracks showed that the dead man had come from its direction less than sixty minutes ago.

When I was just outside the small clearing, in the center of which was the great tree with my house, I stopped. I looked through a break in the green wall and saw the female sitting with her back against a tree. She was holding an infant not quite a year old. I was close enough to smell them, and the infant was sweating the scent of near-death. Its eyes were closed, it was breathing shallowly and rapidly, and its lungs bubbled. Its body was wet.

The mother was stinking of grief and hopelessness. Her dull gaze was fixed on the male and the female under him by the big tree.

I was surprised when I saw what he was doing. In the first place, ferocious as a male of The Folk can be under some circumstances, he is shy when humans are in the area. If not cornered, he will run. But it was evident that this male had killed the man and at once gone to the tree house with his present activity in mind. I don't know what made this male behave so unusually. Perhaps, as I later speculated, his abnormal behavior was caused by a combination of long isolation from his tribe (all dead), the sickness of the infant and the female's concern for it and refusal to mate with him, and the lust aroused by observing the man's rapings of his woman prisoner.

Also, there was the sudden madness which sometimes grips the older adult males of The Folk. This results in their running amok, however. I have never seen the temporary insanity cause any kind of sexual behavior; it always causes a desire to kill all within reach. And this male was not trying to kill the woman unless it was with his cock.

If that was his intent, it was a failure. The woman was paralyzed with terror, but otherwise she was not being hurt. The largest erect penis I've ever seen among The Folk was two inches long and 3/8ths of an inch thick (estimated). If she had been a virgin, she would probably have remained one (technically so) no matter how many times he banged her.

He was on top of her and giving a short subdued scream and his body was shaking. A moment later, he renewed his thrustings.

The Folk have buttocks, which no true apes have, and hips constructed more like those of Homo sapiens than of the gorilla, just as their feet are more hominoid than simian. (Like a Neanderthal's, I should say.)

The woman's arms were behind and under her, by which I deduced that they were tied. Her ankles had been tied together. Someone had untied them, although one end of the rope was around an ankle and the other end tied to a bush. Her legs had been forced open and up over the shoulders of the male. The Folk normally use this position, unlike the apes, who usually favor the rear approach.

The skin of the woman had the peculiar beautiful bronze hue of Doctor Caliban, and the long hair spread out on the ground behind her was his dark metallic red-bronze. Her face was not visible.

I moved around the edge of the clearing until I could see that the male was kissing her. (This way of showing affection or sexual desire is customary among The Folk.)

This probably horrified her far more than the relatively innocuous rape. That great half-apish face had been thrust against hers, and those chimpanzee-thin lips had slobbered all over her face.

It was this that made me think he must be half-mad with sexual frustration. To one of The Folk, a human is a very ugly and repulsive creature. Only a perverted Folk would want to kiss a human.

I scouted around carefully, making sure that no one else was in the area. Then I stepped out of the bushes, seeing at the same time the arm of the dead man under a bush where the male had thrown it. The genitals had probably been eaten.

I gave a soft cry, "*Krhgh!*"

The male stiffened and came up off the woman so violently that her legs were thrown forward and she was momentarily jack-knifed. He whirled to face me.

CHAPTER TWENTY-EIGHT

He was one of the largest I'd ever seen. He was at least six feet two inches tall and weighed about three hundred and fifty pounds. He did not look as nearly gorilloid as my biographer has described The Folk. (As I have fully explained in Volume I, my biographer wrote his first story about me before he knew me. He got all his facts—and misinformation—from records and from a man who had known one of the persons who found me when I was eighteen. Using mainly his imagination, he described The Folk as much more apish than they are. By the time he knew the truth, he could not describe them correctly and maintain consistency in his novels.)

His arms, almost as thick with muscles as a gorilla's, were as short in proportion to his trunk as a man's. The legs were shorter, however, and bowed. The body was covered with thick straight rusty-red hair which formed a covering not as thick as a chimpanzee's. The skin was as black as a bush Negro's. The bones were approximately two and a half times as thick as a man's, thus giving a broad attachment for the massive muscles.

(My own bones are almost twice as thick as a modern man's. I could pass for a Cro-Magnon.)

The head was large and long and had a sagittal crest, like a gorilla's, for the attachment of the massive jaw muscles. The jaws were quite prognathous, and the canine teeth were as large as a gorilla's. The teeth had a "simian gap" for the accommodation of the tips of the lower canines. The Folk are primarily vegetarians, though they eat small animals frequently and the meat of large animals when

171

they get a chance. The chin was absent. The supraorbital ridges were massive, and the forehead was very low. (The average adult male cranium capacity is 800 cubic centimeters, an estimate based on my study of four skulls.)

The eyes were deep sunk and a russet red, although most of The Folk have dark or light brown eyes.

Under the lower jaw was a sac which swelled out when the male challenged another, or a predator, or just wanted to howl at the moon.

The male was sweating, although not as heavily as he would have if he had been a man. The Folk have always been forest dwellers and share a paucity of sweat glands with most forest animals.

All in all, he looked like a giant variety of Zinjanthropus, and he may have been a descendant of this supposedly extinct australopithecine.

The clearing seemed to crackle and to spark, like a cat's fur rubbed the wrong way. His hairs bristled; his eyes became even redder; his open mouth showed the thick yellow teeth and sharp canines and incisors, a red tongue, and the black pit of a throat. The sac on his neck swelled out.

The back of my neck felt as if my hairs were also bristling. I automatically adopted the stiff-legged sidewise walk of belligerency as I circled him. As soon as I became aware of it, I broke the stance, bent my knees, and opened my left hand. My right hand was empty, because I did not want to threaten him with the knife I had found in the grass. He might be talked into cooperation if I did not scare him with the bright human weapon.

The male growled and then said, "*Yh shth-tb.*" That is, "I am Leopard-Breaker."

I replied in the same whispering speech of The Folk, "*Yh tlhs.*" That is, "I am Worm."

The speech of The Folk does contain some voiced consonants, mostly back-of-the-throat sounds, but the majority of words consist of unvoiced consonants. They have only one vowel, similar to the sound of *u* in the English *cut* or of *o* in *done*, and this vowel is not often used.

Worm is the literal translation of my name. My biographer used a euphemistic translation, one which reflected his pigmentation orientation. The Folk, however, considered degrees of hairiness to be more important than color. I also had other names: Bird Nose, Big Cock, Smart Ass, Bright Eyes, Fat Mouth, and Monkey Shit. But I was generally known as *tlhs* or Worm. This name is not as derogatory as humans might think; The Folk consider the worm to be a beautiful creature and very tasty and nutritious. I could have taken a more dignified and impressive name after I came of age and killed the chief of our tribe, but I preferred Worm. To me, it meant the worm that turned.

He howled at me, "I am Leopard-Breaker!"

"I am Worm!" I shouted. "Leave the female alone. Or I will kill you."

"What? A worm would kill a breaker of leopards?"

"I have killed many many leopards," I said, flashing my fingers to indicate an immense number. "I have killed many of the great fighters of The Folk. I have killed many lions."

He looked puzzled, and I knew that he did not know the word which the west coast Folk use. He had probably never seen or heard of a lion.

"I will kill you!" he screamed.

I decided to brandish my knife. When he saw it, he looked around for another stick to knock the knife out of my hand as he had done to the first owner.

I said, "Let us be friends, Leopard-Breaker."

He screamed with all the air in his throat-sac, "Kill!"

And he charged.

I threw the knife. It should have gone in to the hilt in his paunch. He lowered his head, however, so swiftly that it protected his belly, though he did not do it on purpose, I'm sure. The knife struck the top of that thick-boned head, cut the scalp, and flew off. His head rammed into my belly, and his arms snapped together.

Not until I had thrown the knife had I become aware that my penis was bristling as much as my hair. Moreover, just as the knife left my hand, I became aware of an approaching orgasm. This disconcerted me and unbalanced my timing and coordination and slowed me. Otherwise, I would have sidestepped his arms.

He carried me up and backward, as he ran swiftly forward with the intention of crashing me into a tree trunk. My arms were free, so I interlocked my fingers and brought the edges of both palms down close to my belly and on top of that crest. Though he grunted, he drove on. Again, I came down with my hands but in a slanting blow on the back of that muscle-slabbed, heavy-vertebraed neck. He grunted and slowed down, and I slammed him again on the neck. If he had been a human, he would have had a broken, or at least fractured, neck.

He dropped me and then fell on top of me. I shoved him off and twisted away, seeing at the same time, a foot away, the tree against which he had meant to break my back.

He regained his senses very quickly and kicked out behind him. My feet went from under me, and my right leg between the knee and ankle felt numbed, as if a zebra had kicked it. He rolled over and bounded to his feet. Instead of leaping at me, which he should have done with my leg half-paralyzed, he ran off to get a thick heavy piece of thornwood, which was close to the woman.

She lifted her legs as he bent over to pick up the club, and she kicked. Her heels caught him on the side of his jaw. If it had been a man's jaw, it would have shattered. He dropped on his face without a sound.

Limping, I ran toward *shth-tb*, but he rose unsteadily and turned toward me. The woman, who had pulled herself along on her back with her heels—another indication of the strength in those long and beautifully shaped legs—kicked him in the ankle. This was done at the expense of a rope burn, because the rope around one ankle slid up her leg. It hurt her; her face twisted.

The male went down again. Roaring, though not as loudly as he had been, he again struggled to his feet. She smote him on the side of his jaw once more with her two feet, and then, after he had fallen, she rammed a heel into his nose.

I had picked up the knife. I rolled him over on his back. Blood ran from his nose, and his eyes were crossed. His jaw hung askew as if it were broken.

"*Kghd?*" I said.

He did not reply verbally. His big wrinkled hairy hand shot out and gripped the woman's ankle. She gasped and tried to kick loose but could not break the grip. He sat up and dragged her toward him, breaking the rope. He kept his crossed eyes on—or toward—me. He had acted so swiftly that he had caught me unaware; I had broken my own rule for just a few seconds and now must pay. Rather, she must pay for my lack of caution in approaching him.

He could break her neck before I could get to her, and if I raised the knife to throw it, he would crack it.

Despite this, I threw the knife. I could do nothing else. He was going to kill her no matter what I did.

My hurling the knife made him loose his grip for a moment, because he had thought he had me buffaloed. She bent her neck down instead of trying to jerk away and bit his penis. He screamed with surprise and agony and threw his hands up in the air. My knife went into his solar plexus with a sound as of an axe hitting soft wood. His eyes uncrossed, rolled up, the lids closed, and he fell on his back. His hands clenched, unclenched, clenched, and then were still.

I had lost control then. I was on my knees, holding myself up with both hands, and jerking with the spasms of the orgasm. The grass was puddled with the gray fluid. Of all my kills since this had started, this was the most intense ecstasy. It was as exquisite—and almost as tender and one-making—as when Clio and I loved.

I think it was because I had killed a great male of The Folk. I have always loved The Folk, but at the same time I have hated, deep down, the adult male. Too many of them caused me too much pain and terror when I was young. To me, killing one of them was a far greater feat than killing any number of human males. And there was the additional thrill (later, it was a deep sadness) of killing what was probably the last male of The Folk. I had paid them back fully and finally for the bullyings and horrors of my childhood.

CHAPTER TWENTY-NINE

The woman stared as if she could not believe what she had seen. I rose, pulled the knife from the belly, and wiped it on his hairy skin. The female still squatted at the other end of the clearing with her infant. Ignoring the woman's requests to cut the rope loose from her wrists, I walked to the female. She looked up with eyes black as the bottom of an open grave at night. The infant looked dead.

"I won't harm you," I said. "You may stay here and share my food, if you wish. I had to kill *shth-tb*. He forced me to."

She said nothing. Slowly, painfully, she got to her feet, looked once at the corpse of her mate, turned, and was gone into the jungle. I did not go after her. There was nothing I could do for her. Moreover, I did not have time to spare.

I cut the woman's ropes and helped her to her feet, since her arms and hands were in pain after the blood started circulating. She was at least six feet tall and very well formed. She had a fine haunch that curved out like an apple and looked almost as hard when she tensed her gluteus maximus on feeling my hand. I withdrew it and stepped back. She rubbed her wrists, said, "It hurts," and looked speculatively at me. The bronze hair was below her shoulders, wavy, and looked remarkably unmussed-up. She had no makeup but managed to look beautiful without it. Her pubic hairs were unusually thick and two shades darker than the metallic head hair.

She saw me looking at her and smiled slightly. I did not know what the smile was supposed to mean.

"If you're going to try to rape me," she said, "I hope you're not as inept as the last two. And let me rest first and eat something. I'm tired, sore, hungry, and shaken up. I've been abducted and mauled and chewed on and repeatedly splashed on the belly with the premature ejaculations of that demented creature. Or do you know whom I'm talking about?"

"He's dead," I said. "The ape killed him."

She said, "Oh!" and then, "That's no ape. It's a subhuman if ever I saw one, and I haven't, except in anthropology books. I didn't know that these things really existed, I'd always thought they were native myths. But it certainly isn't built for raping a female Homo sapiens. Not that it tickled me so I felt like laughing."

I had to admire her. Most women would have been hysterical, nor would I have blamed them.

"That monster—the human one—thought he was you, you know. So did I. You are he, aren't you? Could we eat? There's plenty of food in the tree-house. Canned," she added with another smile. "That wild man had a year's supply of everything."

I said, "Be at ease. I have no intention of raping you. I couldn't if I wanted to."

"Every male I run into is ejaculating all over the place," she said. Then she said something that startled me.

"It's almost as big as Doc's. And just about as useless, I'll bet."

She was very cool and very strange, though I suppose she must have thought me rather weird, too. I let her precede me to the house. She was a woman, but she had shown herself to be uncommonly dangerous. I did not want her behind me until I knew I could trust her.

The tree house was about fifty feet up and situated on a platform which ran entirely around the trunk and was supported by four huge branches radiating toward the cardinal points of the compass. It was built of bamboo and thatched with elephant's ear leaves and grasses. It had three rooms. The ascent to it had to be made by stainless steel rungs which I had hammered into the trunk. Wooden rungs would have rotted in a year or two.

Trish Wilde (she had not introduced herself yet) got a fire going in the stone fireplace and wrapped herself in a blanket before it.

The house was a mess. The floors were littered with opened cans, scraps of food covered by insects, and even a pile of excrement in one corner. If the crazy man had been imitating me, he must have thought I had the sanitary habits of a slum dweller. One of the bamboo and grass couches looked as if it had been taking punishment. One leg was broken off and the bottom was sagging.

The woman said, "Oh, by the way, I'm Trish Wilde, and I was assistant botanist to Doctor Everfields, a world-famous botanist, and we were searching for exotic plants when I was carried off. If the crazy man hadn't surprised me so, I would have kicked his kneecap loose and then smashed his balls and that would have been that.

"Once he got me up here, he hammered at me until he broke the couch. He never did get his thing into me. He kept coming on my belly. But he almost bit my nipples off."

"I can see that," I said.

"He stank, and he had a big belly, and he slobbered all over me. I think he wanted to stick his cock in my mouth, but he knew I'd bite it off if he did."

She was well educated but she talked like a wharf-dock whore. Certainly, she must moderate her talk in other situations. I did not know why she felt she could speak so uninhibitedly with me. Perhaps it was because she thought, and quite rightly, that my infrahuman rearing had left me without emotional reactions to the so-called "tabu" words.

"How tired are you?" I said.

"I have some energy left. Why?"

It was necessary to tell her part of my story if I were to get her to come with me voluntarily. I knew she was a member of the Nine's organization, so I would not be revealing secrets. I told her what had happened since the dawn the Kenyans attacked, but I left out all reference to her cousin. I also made it appear that Noli had escaped from me but had sworn to go to England and take revenge on Clio.

"Have you had this year's elixir?" I said.

"No," she said. "I'm not due for the caverns until next month."

Clio was also scheduled to go then. I did not tell her that. She would know that as soon as she saw Clio, who, presumably, had made the pilgrimage with her many times.

"I am leaving within the hour," I said. "I'll be traveling as swiftly as I can and sleeping little. If you want to come with me, you're welcome. It is easy for a stranger to get lost in these mountains, and I would not like to see you try to go it alone. Nevertheless, if you can't keep up with me, I will leave you behind."

"I could use a good night's sleep," she said. "But I don't want to wander around these mountains until I die or get picked up by some horny natives. I'll go with you."

I was glad that she said that, because I had made up my mind that she was coming with me no matter what she said. She could be a trade off if Caliban succeeded in getting hold of Clio.

We ate and drank and then made up a bundle for each. This consisted of a rainhat, poncho, blanket, a breakdown .22 rifle and cartridges, matches, and cans of food. Immediately after, we set off.

Despite our pace, which was rapid for the thick heavy growth of the rain forest, she had breath enough to chatter on and on. She told me of her childhood, her high school and college days, of meeting Doc, of the mysterious deaths of her father and her uncle. She had gone off with Doc and his five colleagues on several adventures. She owned a nation-wide chain of clothing shops and much property. She had a master's degree in psychology but had returned to school, after many years, and gotten a Ph.D. in botany.

I strongly suspected that this was at Doc's request. He was undoubtedly attempting to find the elixir, and he would have wanted her to help him. The ingredients for the elixir might be in plants unknown or little known.

She said, "I might still be tied up in the tree house if I hadn't talked him into letting me come down so I could walk around. After he let me lope around the clearing, like a dog on a leash, he tied me to the bush and tried to rape me again. Then he just happened to see the subhumans through a break in the vegetation; they'd been watching us all the while. He chased them, calling the male 'Brother!' and demanding that he stop and talk to him. Apparently, he winded the ape-man, or else the female couldn't go any more. So the big male must have turned and fought and killed him, and then he returned to the clearing. He saw that crazy man trying to fuck me, and it must have put ideas in his head.

"That weirdo really thought he was you. And that he was king of the jungle and all that."

"He wasn't the first," I said.

A number of questions directed my attention from her monologue. Even if the man were one of those poor devils who had brooded so long about me they had become me in their minds, how had he found my tree-house? And what about the body of the young Caucasian female which the others in the expedition had thought was Trish's? What about the story of the natives who said they had witnessed the naked man's raping and carrying off of Trish? And why had I been let loose by the Nine so near the house?

For the first time in this business, I began to consider seriously that I was being manipulated—or steered, at least—by the Nine.

Also, this sudden and compelling equation of killing with sexual intercourse could be a side effect of the elixir, and one expected by the Nine. Caliban had something similar and our father had been affected but in a different manner.

CHAPTER THIRTY

"Are we really trying to make fifty miles a day?" she said hours later. "In this dark and in this tangle? When do we start swinging through the trees?"

"When we weigh no more than a monkey," I said. "I know we can make that mileage. I've done it. Fifty miles in sixteen hours."

She sighed wearily and said, "Doc could do it, too. But I don't know about me."

She was strong, and she was game, but the time came when I was half-carrying her. There were times also when she was sleeping while walking. Finally, I let her slump under a tree, wrapped her up in her poncho and blanket, and then lay down near her. I awoke with a start, as vibrating as a suddenly awakened animal, and had my knife ready to stab the intruder. I realized then that she was crawling under my blanket.

"I'm cold and lonely," she murmured. "I want to snuggle against a warm body, nice male flesh. Don't get any wrong ideas, you big ape. Besides, I'm too tired."

She fell asleep and began snoring softly. I don't see how she expected me not to respond, since my penis was jammed between her buttocks and, after a while, when she turned, against the hairy slit. But she was safe. Although her softness and roundness and warmth and woman odor were very pleasant, they did not have the normal effect upon me. I drifted off to sleep, thinking of Trish and of Clio, but dreamed of my foster mother, *kl*, the female of The Folk who had raised me as her own and as more than her own and whom I had loved as the only being worth loving.

I slept longer than I had intended. The sun was slipping through the arms of the great tree over us. I had to urinate, and, as so often happens in the morning on awakening, my penis was rigid.

Trish, awakening when I rolled away, looked down and saw it. Her eyes widened, and she said, "Doc!" and then, "Oh!"

What happened after this was not predictable. If I'd been asked what I expected would happen, I would have replied that I would rise and step behind the tree to avoid offending her, and would have urinated. And the piss hard-on would have been gone.

At this point I am tempted to discuss what is, to me, the impossibility of a "state"—such as a "piss hard-on"—appearing or disappearing. But I resist. Besides, my psychological difficulties with the English language, with all human languages, with the self-contradictory *Weltanschauung* of English, is described fully in Volume II of my memoirs.

I repeat. The expected—almost logical—course of events did not take place.

It was to be taken for granted that Trish Wilde would not be attracted by the sight of my erection. She was no nymphomaniac, as far as I knew. She had been through many days of extremely trying, even distressing, and exhausting experiences. She had been exerting herself on the first day of our journey to such an extent that she might well have preferred to die rather than get up out of bed. Neither of us had bathed; we reeked of sweat, blood, and jism. I was a stranger who, though he had rescued her and offered her no threat, was still a mysterious and possibly sinister person. She had been in love with her cousin for many years. She had recently been the object of attempted rapes by a crazed man and a—to her—monstrous half-human. Hence, she could be expected to regard copulation with less than eagerness.

Moreover, she was hungry, her mouth must have been dry, and she undoubtedly had to piss.

And there had been no time for any warmth or tenderness to develop between us.

I could go on. I have made my point.

On the other hand, I did remind her of Doc (she was to tell me later). And the long love affair had resulted in much frustration for her. She had not suffered absolute sexual deprivation with Caliban. Although he could only get his giant penis into her somewhat small vagina by causing her pain, she was still able to have an orgasm. However, she usually substituted fellatio for coitus. This was to his great satisfaction, because he did not really like coitus. In the beginning, she had been excited by the act but had been left feeling unsatisfied. Then Doc had conditioned her, with much practice, verbal tricks, and some hypnotism, to have orgasms when she sucked on him. In fact, through his conditioning, she was able to have orgasms by manipulations of her nipples.

These climaxes were not, in some indefinable manner, as "satisfactory," even though they were often intense. She felt a craving for his penis in her womb. The other acts did not bring the "closeness" she felt when he was between her legs.

The other element making for a still unsatisfactory intercourse with Doc was that his own orgasms seemed to be too dull. He never "went out of his mind" or out of control.

Only now and then, when she "sucked him off, blew the fuse on his cock," as she so inelegantly phrased it, was he able to lose control enough to feel the exquisiteness he should feel. Afterward, he seemed ashamed of the feeling.

All this I learned later, of course.

At the moment, she was aware of my erection, and yet she had been told I would get none as response to a woman. She thought her mere proximity had done for me what the active labor of the Countess Clara had not been able to do. She felt flattered.

And she may have felt that she was giving me something in payment for having rescued her.

Whatever the reasons, they impelled her to kiss me on the mouth and at the same time to run her fingers down my chest to the pubic hairs and then to close them gently on my penis.

It may be that she had been denied sexual satisfaction so long that she would have taken on any man whom she could respect. She was a very passionate woman, and she had not been entirely faithful to Caliban. In the beginning she was, but during the past twelve years, she had bedded a dozen men. This was one of the almost inevitable results of prolonged youth.

I thought of Clio, of the time I was wasting in getting to her, and of my unfaithfulness. I was out of the cavern now, and so our normal relationship was, theoretically, in force.

But my desire to find out if my normal sexual responses were restored was too strong. I had to know that I was not permanently crippled.

I turned to her and kissed her lips. Then I kissed her eyes and her nose and the tips of her ears and stuck my tongue into her ear and kissed the side of her neck and so on down to her large, firm, great-nippled breasts, where I stayed for some time while I inserted a finger into her vagina and gently slid it back and forth until she lubricated fully and moaned and then had a number of shuddering orgasms. I then kissed her belly and tongued her clitoris and the insides of her labia.

After that, she sucked on my dong, running her tongue over its head. I hoped that the erection was now due to her, not to retention of urine. Certainly, I felt as if she were responsible.

Getting into her was not easy. I had to push, withdraw, push again, get up and apply some medical vaseline from our medicine box, and get down and push again. Slowly, the lips opened, and the head went halfway in, and then all the way in. The shaft followed easily after that. She kept her eyes closed and several times groaned and clenched her teeth. Truly, she seemed to have an organ the size of a small ten-year-old girl's. (I knew this from my internship while getting my M.D.)

I came several minutes after entry. Instead of withdrawing, I remained on top of her and left the semi-hard cock in her. She began to squeeze on it with her sphincter, which was powerful and, seemingly, tireless. It was like a weak but loving fist sending telegraphic messages. My peter swelled up again, and I began going back and forth with her legs over my shoulders and my hands around her hips and under her thighs so that the tips of my fingers caressed the edges of her labia. The second orgasm did not arrive until quite a few minutes later. I almost passed out from the intensity; I saw great red jungle flowers shooting up from green stalks, exploding in scarlet, and collapsing.

Tears came to her eyes. She had had a "flaming" orgasm, as she put it.

I said I was happy, and I kissed her. She responded warmly. Actually, I was feeling guilty. It was not being unfaithful that caused this. I have never—deep down—seen much sense in this oath of fidelity when a man and his woman are separated for long periods of time, but I had kept my word because it was my word. And would have kept it for always if I had aged as other men do.

I was feeling guilty because I had spent time in my own pleasure instead of traveling as swiftly as possible for England, where Clio *might* be in danger.

CHAPTER THIRTY-ONE

The rains started that night. We were miserable. Despite this, we slept well under the rain-proof ponchos and blankets. Trish was as worn out as an old knife by the grinding of the sixteen hours of battle to get through the cold wet tangle of the rain forest. She ate a few bites and dropped off, snuggling against me. And in the morning, after we had eaten and rolled up our supplies, we set off. There was no more loving beyond an abortive attempt by Trish one afternoon when we had rested a while and the sun had come out. It was a failure.

In three days, as I had projected, we were out of the mountains and at the mining company airstrip. This was used to shuttle executives to the capital and back.

The executives and the pilot of the twin-engined Cessna knew me, but they refused to let me go on the next scheduled trip. I would have to wait. And one commented that I was open to arrest for being in Uganda without a passport.

I took the plane anyway. After knocking the pilot out and yanking the three executives from the plane, with Trish's capable help, I piloted the craft downwind, toward the north. A few bullet holes appeared in the fuselage behind us as we left the ground, and the radio bleated in Buganda and English, warning us we would be shot down by military planes.

I swung west. And twenty hours later, I was approaching the southern shore of England (Land's End) about ten feet above the sea. We were fully dressed and armed and I was flying another plane, a two-motored turboprop craft. My connections and my good credit and name had secured the plane, gas, and supplies on the way. We were now entering England unnoticed (we hoped) and without passports.

Trish had demanded that we try to get into contact with Caliban while our plane was being refueled at an airport near Rabat, Morocco. I did not object. Caliban should know that she was with me. He would no longer have any reason to attack me or Clio. Or I should say Clio, since the Nine had decreed that one of us must kill the other. On thinking this over, I decided that the news that she was now alive would not reassure him. I had her, and he would not know what I planned to do with her. He thought I was mad, and he might think I meant to harm her.

I did if he killed Clio.

Or did I? I felt like it. Had felt like it, rather. But I now was very fond of her, respected her, and knew her as a human being. Moreover, I could not harbor the idea of revenge on Caliban through hurting her. He was the one I wanted to kill.

No, I could not harm her. But I could make Caliban think I would if he did not lay off of Clio.

So I made every effort to contact Caliban. I sent radio messages to London and Paris and I sent other messages via several underground organizations I had worked with during the war and during a mission for the Nine.

They reported back that no one had managed to find him.

This did not upset Trish. She had full confidence that he would get the message. He might have it now but had not replied, because he was often strangely reticent. He acted instead of talking. In fact, he might even now be on his way to Castle Grandrith to help me against Noli.

I smiled but said nothing.

As we passed Land's End on our right, she asked me a number of questions about our destination and its history. She had never been to the Lake District and knew little about it except that it was supposed to be England's "pocket Switzerland" and Wordsworth and Coleridge and Southey had lived there.

I told her that Cumberland County was in the extreme northwestern corner of England. The mountains (I would call them foothills) are remains of a massive dome-shaped earth movement which took place about forty million years ago. The mountains were deeply cut by lake-filled valleys. Cumberland County was one of the most densely wooded regions of England even long after the Norman conquest. The oak, ash, and birch were the principal indigenous trees, and sycamore and larch were common.

The earliest evidence of man there could be dated to the New Stone Age, about 2500 B.C. There were a number of "druid" circles of stone in the Lake District. There was a circle, in fact, on the estate of Grandrith. Looking west from the windows of Catstarn Hall, you could see the massive upright stone slabs on a hilltop beyond the castle. Looking north, you could see on top of a hill that huge and queerly shaped slab of granite which was called, for some reason, the High Chair. There was a local legend connected with it. The people of the village of Cloamby say that when the two ravens come back, the old man will sit. No one seems to know what this means.

My ancestors included the aboriginals, of course, the short dark people who might have been related to the Picts of Scotland, which is close by, and to the Firbolg of Ireland. The Celts invaded the island and exterminated or absorbed them. Later, Romans conquered much of Cumbria, but their investment was mainly military. This area, until the nineteenth century, was a back country somewhat aloof from the mainstream but not entirely. After the Romans left, the English Northumbrians held the country. The Vikings came in 875 A.D. and the majority of place names in Cumberland are of Norse origin.

An Eirik Randgrith, a Norwegian sea-king turned farmer, established a log-and-stone fort on the present site of the castle. This was near the small village of Graefwulf, which was destroyed fifty years later. The present village of Cloamby replaced it about thirty years afterward. These events took place between 900 and 980 A.D.

Randgrith means Shield-Destroyer. Randgrith was supposed to have been a huge man, very strong, and given to fits of melancholy and violence. His grandson was presumably converted to Christianity, but the Randgriths were suspected of heresy for a long long time. At least twenty of them over a period of 600 years were burned or hung for witchcraft. Despite this, the family managed to retain their lands and even add to them at times.

Cumberland was held alternately by the Scotch and Normans for a long time. In the seventeenth-century Civil War, the Cumbrians were generally loyal to the Stewarts.

Sometime in the thirteenth century, Randgrith became Grandrith by a metathesis probably influenced by the Norman "grand." The name is now pronounced Grunith.

The family was always distinguished by a large size, great strength, and a tendency to mental instability and eccentricity. It has usually been content to keep to its own part of the country or to go far abroad. It has been conservative, if not reactionary. It had clung to the old religions fiercely, although often secretly. The evidence is that the family privately worshipped the old Germanic gods long after Cumberland was ostensibly Catholic, and that it remained Catholic long after Cumberland was ostensibly Protestant.

I told Trish that the Grandriths were related to the Howards and the Russells and the royal family, not that that meant anything to me. I told her the story that William II, or Rufus, the Conqueror's son, had raped a Lady Ulrica Randgrith, who gave birth to his son. It is recorded in the family chronicle (but a hundred years after the event) that Rufus was responsible for the gray eyes of the family. (This is, of course, genetic nonsense.) It is also recorded that Rufus was killed in the New Forest, not by Walter Tirel or Ralph of Aix, but by the brother of the raped woman.

While I talked, the sun set behind the Atlantic to the left. England became a dark bulk with a few scattered lights, which were actually large towns. Then I swung out toward the middle of the sea, still only about ten feet above the moon-sparkling waters.

I thought of my ancestors and their country. When I first came there as lord of Grandrith Castle, Catstarn Hall, and Cloamby Village, I had not known my family history. Or even the history of England. Later, after much reading and travel, I understood much more. Yet I have never been entirely at ease on my estate or in England. I feel as if I were born of African earth and have no ancestors. The past was dissolved when I gave voice to my first cry on the seashore by the equatorial jungle.

CHAPTER THIRTY-TWO

My agent, stationed in the forest near the castle, responded to my call. Trish listened in.

I said, "Any news of Lady Grandrith yet?"

"Nothing, sir," the man said. "All we still know is that she left London to come here. She should have been here hours ago and may be. There were lights in the castle for about an hour, sir, but I couldn't get close enough to see who was using them. The drapes in the hall windows are closed tight, sir. I can't see any activity there, but I get the impression that there's much going on."

"Have you heard from the other man?" I said, referring to his companion.

"No, sir. The situation is the same as when I last reported. He went to investigate the castle and the hall; he said he might knock on the door and pretend to be a lost traveler; I never heard from him again."

"Have you found out anything about the two strangers who were buying such large supplies of food and liquor in Greystoke?" I said.

"Nothing, sir. They left before I heard about them so I couldn't put a tail on them. If Noli's men have moved in, as we suspect, then they may have been his."

"Ask him if he's heard anything from Doc or anything about him," Trish said eagerly.

The agent said he had heard nothing, but then he'd been out of contact with the London men for about six hours.

"Have you been able to look in the garage or the barns?" I said.

"No, sir. They're both still tightly locked and the windows are curtained. If there are an unusual number of cars in there, I can't find out without trying to break in. And as you said . . ."

"That's right," I said. "I don't want to let them know that anybody's on to their game."

His voice had not sounded quite right, but there was much static, due to the storm approaching from Ireland. I said, "We'll be landing on the strip in approximately one hour. You be ready to cover us, because if Noli is in the hall or the castle, he and his men will come swarming out. We'll run into the woods and then plan our strategy from there. Signals as arranged. Four blinks by me, six by you."

"Right, sir. Four and six."

I shut off the transceiver. The man had not quite sounded like my agent, but perhaps it was he, and he was taking this opportunity to warn me. The signals had been three blinks by me and five by him.

I told Trish what I suspected. She said, "If they've got him alive, they'll get everything out of him. And they'll kill him when they realize he's tricked them."

"They'll kill him, anyway. And he's probably already dead. They must have gotten everything from him. That voice was close to the real agent's, but not quite close enough."

I did not, of course, tell her that the man holding Catstarn Hall and Castle Grandrith might be Caliban, although I doubted it. Noli had a head start on him. If Noli was there, then Caliban might be in as much danger as I. Noli would try to double-cross Caliban, and Caliban must know that. Perhaps Caliban was amused by this, and stimulated, since it made the odds greater against him.

I turned the radio back on. We were approaching a black wall, the storm from Ireland. The weather reports said that its front was now over Keswick and moving east. The rain was heavy with winds at forty miles per hour. The plane bored into the blackness and began bucking. At the same time, I pulled her up, because I did not want to run into a vessel. At three thousand feet, I was picked up by the coastal radar, and the challenges started coming. I gave them a false identity, said I was an Irish flier blown off course. The identity lasted about six minutes. On receiving information from Ireland, the station challenged me again and told me to land or I would be shot down. I did not know how they were going to manage that, since I doubted they would send a missile against a small plane and no military plane would find me while the storm was progressing.

However, I pretended engine trouble, made a last-minute appeal, and dived the plane. The lights enabled me to pick up the sea surface just in time; even so we must have been licked on the underfuselage by the waves. Surface vessels or no, I clung to a twenty foot ceiling and did not pull her up until I saw lights. This should be Whitehaven, and from here on I had to maintain at least a five-thousand-foot ceiling. If the weather had been clear, I would have hedgehopped in. It was not, so there was nothing else to do. I could not help Clio—if she was not past helping already—if we smashed up against the Skiddaw or some other mountain.

"There's a small airport at Penrith," I said. "That's about five miles from Grandrith. The port doesn't have radar instruments to guide us in; we'll have to make a visual landing."

"And there's no visibility except when the lightning flashes," she said, peering through the rain at a massive upthrust revealed by a streak of whiteness. Thunder bellowed; the plane rocked.

She said, "Penrith. Is that name related to Grandrith?"

"No. Penrith is Celtic, one of the few Welsh place names in the Lake District. Grandrith, if you'll remember, comes from the Norse Randgrith."

She was trying to make small talk to cover up her nervousness. I went along with her to help her.

"Once we land," I said, "we have to move fast. There's no use in trying to convince the port authorities of a false identity. We'll just get out and into the closest available car and leave. If somebody recognizes me, I'll have to explain later."

She checked our automatics, my .38, her .32, the breakdown .22, six hand grenades, and a small crossbow. I wore a knife in a sheath back of my neck. She was similarly armed. In addition, she had a two-barreled derringer.

She put screwdrivers, pliers, and a jumper cable in the pocket of my raincoat.

"We could parachute down," Trish said. "The country is unpopulated back of your estate, you said. There'd be no danger of the plane crashing into a house."

"There are too many trees around there," I said. "Moreover, Noli will be looking for us to do just that, you can bet. And if I were able to make a landing on the road near Cloamby in this rain, you can bet that Noli would know it before we landed. He's listening in to the radar reports on us. He must have short-wave equipment. He'd have a car down on the road with his thugs and be ready for us."

"Then he'll have men waiting at Penrith for us."

"He won't know I'm going there until the last minute, if I have anything to say about it. He'll be able to send men then, but they'll be too late then, I hope."

"He may have figured out that that's the only place you *can* land," she said. "In which case, his men will be on the way now."

"That's possible. We'll see."

The radio reported that visibility was still zero but that the winds had dropped to twenty miles per hour. The airports in the entire county were closed except for emergency landings.

The military might be thinking like Noli and also have men waiting at Penrith. I did not tell Trish that; she was nervous enough.

I went by Keswick somewhere in the blackness below and over the lower edge of the great Skiddaw Forest and probably over Burnt Horse and then the Mungrisdale Common. The Bowscale Fell (peak height of 2,306 feet) was beneath us, if I reckoned correctly and if my own radar was functioning correctly. Then I was over my own estates but could see nothing, of course. I had taken this route instead of going directly to Penrith because I wanted to throw both Noli and the military off.

I cut in again to the frequency on which my presumed agent had been operating. I said, "Start signaling."

He sounded nervous. He said, "Surely, m'lord, you're not going to land here! It's impossible! You'll get killed!"

Noli and Caliban would say the same thing. Noli would want me alive for the elixir (unless Caliban had told him that the elixir could only be gotten from the Nine, and he was not likely to do that). Caliban would not want his cousin killed (if he knew that she was with me). Nor would he want me killed, since he intended to do that with his bare hands.

I wondered what the Nine would think if one of us died an

accidental death? Would the survivor then have to fight the next candidate? Or did the Nine want one of us dead for some unknown reason?

I replied to the man whom, by now, I was convinced was pretending to be the agent.

I said, "What do you advise?"

"The airport at Penrith is by far your best chance," he replied eagerly.

"I think I'll land on the road into Mungrisdale," I said. "I'll get a car there."

"You can't do that, m'lord!" he said. "It'd be suicide! At least Penrith has landing lights!"

"Mungrisdale it is, anyway," I said.

However, I agreed with him. My plan had been to lure Noli or Caliban into sending men down the road from Cloamby to Mungrisdale and detouring them from Penrith until it was too late. If Noli was intelligent, however, he would send men to Penrith anyway, if he had not done so already.

I realized then that I was convinced that it was Noli down there. Caliban might be close, but he was only on his way to, not in, Grandrith. The time element made this seem likely.

I put the plane into a steep dive from five thousand feet and did not begin to level out until the radar showed that I was 500 feet above ground level. Actually, we were probably much closer. There was just enough visibility for me to see several hundred feet ahead. Since the topography varied much within a short time, our progress resembled that of a very irregular sine wave. Trish gasped once and then closed her eyes. A moment later, she said, "I'm all right now. I just put my fate in the hands of the great god Old Crow."

I did not have much time to indulge in conversation. Nevertheless, I said, "Old Crow?"

"Yes. When I was very little, I heard my father say, more than once, that the greatest thing in the world was Old Crow. In my child's mind, I thought that Old Crow must be a great Indian chief, like Sitting Bull or Hiawatha. Then I thought that it must be the Great Spirit of the Indians and that my father had a place reserved for him in the Happy Hunting Grounds. So I started to pray to Old

Crow. Later, when I found out that it wasn't an Indian god but a whiskey, I refused to admit my mistake. A god was created in my mind, and it has stayed there since. And I am especially honored above all humankind, because only I have been admitted to the worship of the great god Old Crow."

By the time she had quit talking, we were close to Penrith. The radio was getting hysterical. Apparently the military had picked me up, and both frequencies, the port's and the military's, were screaming warnings, threats, and pleas at me.

I thought for a moment of crashing the plane on the Penrith golf course, which is a fairly large one, and parachuting in. I abandoned the idea at once, because I did not want to take a chance on killing someone. No, it would have to be the airport.

I dropped down fast, banked, and came in at the port as if I intended to strafe it. The lights suddenly became visible; I was coming in at the correct location and angle, though too swiftly. The lights along the strip were blurs, and the big lights on top of the control tower were diffused stars. I dropped the plane in from too great a height, not caring if I drove the wheels up through the wings. We struck hard but the wheels and gear held, and the tires did not blow. On the second bounce, I straightened her out and cut the engine speed and feathered the props more. The end of the runway still came up too swiftly, and I went past it, across the grass, and was able to stop it only just short of the parking lot fence.

There was no time to sit and gasp in air and take time to unjangle our nerves. We scrambled out with our bundles in our arms, opened them, put on the raincoats, stuck the automatics in our pockets, and ran toward the gate with the rest of the weapons in our arms.

The doors to the control tower and the passenger buildings were open; figures were running through them toward us, wildly waving their arms. The parking lot held six cars, none of them military or police. Perhaps they did not really think we would try to land there after all the foofaraw, or perhaps they had been delayed for some reason.

Trish used her pencil flashlight to light our path as we ran. We got to the cars well ahead of the people from the buildings. Moreover, these at first ran toward the plane; they did not know we were in the parking lot until a few minutes later. The six cars were a Hillman Minx, two Volkswagens, an MG, a Facel-Vega, and an Aston-Martin DB4. All were locked and none had keys in the ignition locks.

I smashed in the window of the Aston-Martin and reached in and unlocked the door. Then I raised the hood and, while Trish held the flashlight, went to work with screwdriver and pliers. It took only a minute to jump the wires, but by then we could hear voices, muffled by the wind and the rain. I completed the connections, put the hood down gently, and we scrambled into the car. At that moment, a pair of headlights swung around the corner of a building at the far end of the street which ended at the gates of the airport.

A man yelled, "Here! I say! What do you think you're doing there?"

Five men ran toward us. I put the car into gear and took off with a squealing of tires. Wet as the pavement was, the rubber burned. There was a pinging sound as we went through the open gates. A hole appeared in the windshield between us. I shifted to second. A second car had appeared behind the first down the street. In my rear view mirror I could see a pair of headlights come on in the parking lot.

Trish was busy taking the automatic from my pocket and laying it on the seat beside me, breaking open the .22, and assembling it.

Flames spurted from alongside the first auto heading for us. I began swerving but had little room to maneuver because the hundred-yard gap between us was narrowing swiftly. I was doing sixty mph by then, and the oncoming cars were probably doing forty mph. It swerved away when I did. The driver had acted defensively; he must have thought I intended to crash him or was playing "chicken" and he did not want a head-on crash with an impact of 100 mph.

In any event, we both skidded. I compensated properly but the Aston-Martin continued to turn, moving forward also and spinning around its vertical axis. The other also turned. Like two waltzers, or ice-skaters, we passed each other, our fronts missing by an inch or so. As we did so, Trish fired her automatic three times.

She said, "I think I got one! A hand flew up and dropped a gun out the window!"

Our car ended its whirl pointed in the right direction, so I just kept on going.

CHAPTER THIRTY-THREE

The second car must have put on its brakes. It was skidding but the driver apparently got off the brakes in time to regain control. Jets of fire leaped from its side as it went by. And then we were past each other.

Trish, looking through the rear window, said, "The first car has stopped; it's headed away from us. So's the other one. They'll have to turn around. But the one that was in the lot—it's coming. Watch out!"

The warning was not for me but for the third car. Its driver had tried to stop it when he saw the roadway blocked by the two vehicles. He skidded and slammed into one of the cars, their two sides, right and left, colliding, according to Trish. The lights of one went out.

I took the corner with a minor skid, straightened out, and was on my way for a straight shot for six blocks. I had to go through the "Square." I was on the A66, my immediate destination was the A594, leading westward out of town. The six blocks were traversed with no sign of pursuit. Since I slowed down before taking the corner, I did not skid much. Several cars honked angrily as I flew by. I was splashing water on both sides as if I were a motorboat trying for a speed record. Pedestrians, hearing me at a distance, raced for the sides of buildings, against which they flattened themselves. Their efforts to avoid getting hit were successful but they could not dodge the spray. I could imagine the fists and the curses. They were lucky they did not get run over. And, for all I knew, the pursuing cars would hit some.

Just before I turned the next corner for a shot at the central part of town, two cars came in sight behind us. One had only a single headlamp working.

A policeman stepped out of a pub and blew his whistle hysterically. I kept on, and he jumped back into the doorway as a blanket of water rose to cover him. I almost lost control again rounding another corner and then I was two blocks away from Market "Square." Trish, leaning out of the window, emptied a clip at the pursuers. The lead car swerved, and she exclaimed that she must have shot the driver. But it straightened out and flames jetted in reply from both sides of the car. As far as I knew, no bullets struck our vehicle.

Then I was roaring into the "Square" but double-clutching to gear down. At the end of the "Square" a large white board sign with the word ARNISONS shone in my beams. I swung left and, again, could not keep from skidding. Fifty miles an hour was too much for wet pavement and such an abrupt movement. As the car's rear end described its arc, my headlights passed across the black letters on the white plate. A594 KESWICK. This sign was on a black and white pole on a triangle of cement between three roads. A watchtower stood on the triangle behind the signpost.

The beams swung past that and illumined the front of the Midland Bank, and the car's rear went over the curbing of the triangle and struck the road sign. The pole bent with a crash; the car slid off it and continued on down the A594, past the bank and headed westerly.

I was lucky not to blow a tire or overturn. The pole must have damaged the side of the car, and I had been thrown against my seat and shoulder belt toward the right. She had been pressed against the door.

The first car to follow us was not as lucky. It was about forty feet behind us and going, I estimated at sixty mph. I don't think the driver was familiar with this town, otherwise, he would have been more cautious. It skidded, too, and went up over the curb of the island, completely bent the pole under it, and smashed broadside into the tower. Its lights went out, and I did not see it again.

The car behind it did not try to turn. It put on its brakes and skidded on down the street past the tower and out of sight behind the bank. However, it must have turned around swiftly, because a minute later I saw its lights a half-mile behind me.

The third car, which I presumed was driven by some of the airport personnel, did not appear again.

The A594 bent slightly southwest out of Penrith and then, near the Greystoke Pillar, a monument, turned northwesterly. Between Penrith and the village of Greystoke was a stretch of five miles with only farmhouses on either side of the road and not many of them. This was an excellent a Ministry of Transport road. Despite the driving rain and wind, I was going at eighty mph and occasionally at ninety. I traveled this fast only because I knew the road well. I was hoping that my pursuers had no local men among them.

Although I kept most of my mind on the driving, I could spare some for thinking about the situation. Those men had fired at me with intent to kill, not just to warn. It did not seem likely that Caliban's men would shoot at me if he knew his cousin was with me. Moreover, Caliban wanted to handle me personally.

Noli knew where the gold was, or where it had been. He wanted the elixir, however, and he needed me alive to tell him how to get it. Or did he? If he had Clio—I felt cold then—he could get the secret out of her. And so there was no reason for him to keep me alive except for personal vengeance. But he knew how dangerous I was and may have decided to let the torture go for an assurance that I was no longer a threat to him.

If I was right about Noli, then he was double-crossing Caliban. Noli was not only trying to frustrate Caliban's plans for me, he was trying to kill Trish.

I began to think that Noli was not so intelligent after all. Didn't he realize that Caliban was extremely dangerous? Noli's actions were those of a man who lets two tigers out of a cage, both of whom want to do nothing but kill him.

I topped a hill then and looked across the dip to the top of the next hill. I saw, fuzzily through the rain, lights on or near the top of the hill. And, at that moment, the rain ceased. The wipers cleared the windshield, and I saw that there must be more than one car on the other side of that hill. Two sets of beams turned sidewise, briefly shone out past the hill, and were turned off. If it hadn't been for the rain suddenly quitting, I might not have known that two cars were turned broadside to block the road.

The car behind me speeded up. Either the men in it felt more confident now that they could see better or they were in radio contact with those ahead. I suspected that both were true.

I did not increase my speed more than five mph going down the hill. The pursuer drew up behind me, doing approximately ninety-five mph. When about thirty feet away, its occupants fired six shots, one of which put a hole in the window behind me and in the windshield. I jerked because the bullet burned the top of my shoulder. I asked Trish to feel under my shirt, and she said that I was welted but there seemed to be no blood.

After that, the car dropped away. This convinced me that they were in radio contact. By the time I was almost to the crest of the hill, the car was only halfway up and still slowing down.

I took my foot off the gas pedal as I came over the hilltop. The hill ran at a forty-five-degree angle at this point. Bright in the glow of my lamps were the two barricading cars, only 180 feet ahead. They were in tandem with the rear of one off the road and the nose of the other sticking over the edge of the pavement. A hundred yards down, a third car was parked half on the road, facing us.

Nine men stood by the two broadside cars. Three were on the left beyond the ditch and holding submachine guns. Six were by the ditch to the right and holding pistols and rifles.

They began firing immediately. Trish crouched down but fired with her automatic at the men on the right. The hand grenades lay on the floor at her feet, ready for use.

Events happened so swiftly there was time only to react. I took the left side because there was more room on the wet clayey ground between the car and the ditch. Also, because there were only three weapons on that side, even if they were rapid-firing.

Gearing down, I ran at the left-hand car with my left wheels on the mire and my right on the pavement. I was crouched down as far as I could get and still see.

At this close range, we should have been riddled. But in the excitement and uncertainty, as almost always happens, the firing was anything but accurate. And the men must have been concerned about my crashing into them. Holes did appear in the plastic just above my head. Bullets whistled by. Something burning hit my neck. It was, I think, a deflected bullet that just touched the skin with its hot metal and then dropped onto my shoulder.

The three men with the submachine guns scattered because I could easily have slid across the mud and into them. They realized, too late, that I was not going to stop and let them shoot me and that I might be intent on running over them even if I got killed in the process. It was well for us that they broke, because if they had stood their ground they could have blasted us at point-blank range. I swung off the road onto the shoulder, there was a slight bump as my skidding rear struck the nose of the blocking car, and we were in the mud.

Just before that, Trish, with a coolness and precision that I had no time to admire then, tossed a grenade. She did not see where it struck, of course, but it must have been stopped by the wheels or some part of the car.

Our vehicle shot through the mud, toward the ditch. I geared down to first and we straightened out and slid close enough to the road for my right-side wheels to get back upon the pavement. I got back onto the road completely just as the grenade blew up. Trish said it exploded under the right-hand car, not the left-hand one, under which she had thrown it. It did not matter. Both cars went up in flames and smoke as their gas tanks exploded. Three of the men on the right side ran across the ditch to fire at us. They were caught by the outgush and set afire.

The third car, parked down the road on the right side, protected three men firing at us. Two men were on the other side of the hood, shooting rifles. A third was stationed behind the car and firing with a tommy. This, unlike the others, had tracer bullets.

We should have been skewered. But the explosions of the two cars must have shaken them up, even if they were hardened professionals. I further unnerved them by angling across the road, accelerating swiftly, as I aimed directly at them. The tracers hit the pavement to my right and behind us and then swung up toward us. I turned the front of the car away at the last moment, skidding again, while Trish continued firing with my .38. Just before the headlamps swung away from them, I saw one man behind the hood throw up his hands and fall backward. The man with the tommy, thinking I was going to ram the car, which I almost did anyway, ran to the left, and my rear, skidding around, knocked him into the air and against his car.

Then we were gone with the fires lighting our rear for many miles.

Trish began to shake. She held on to me and cried a little. I felt a little shakiness, too, but it was caused by my exultation.

I rejoiced too soon. Somehow, the car that had chased me from Penrith got by the burning cars. And the car down the road was manned by the survivors. I had not gone more than two miles before I saw the lights of two cars behind me. They were overtaking me swiftly. These were not the sort of men to be easily discouraged.

So far, my gas tank was three-quarters full and the oil pressure and engine temperature were normal. No tires had been struck, even if, surely, the tires had been shot at.

I passed Bunkers Hill, a farm with a three-quarters castellated house. This farm, with another, Fort Putnam, further down the road, were the works of the Duke of Greystoke in 1780. The then duke was pro-American and a militant Whig, and he built the two places to celebrate the Yankee victories after which they were named. The sight of them made me consider, for a moment, asking the resident of Greystoke Castle for help. He was my very good friend, and I can count those on my fingers. Then I remembered that he was in Alaska. Moreover, I could not, no matter how desperate the situation, bring this sort of trouble on him. For other reasons, I had not contacted the authorities to help me. I was certain that Clio would be killed if the constabulary or other slow-moving and cautious authorities showed up at Grandrith. Delivering her had to be done with a sudden attack.

Another reason for not bringing in the authorities was the Nine. This was a private, or internal, affair, and there should be as little publicity and as much obfuscation as possible. Of course, if it would have helped Clio, I would have defied the Nine. I was becoming half-convinced that neither of us would be in any trouble if the Nine had not shaped events for their own dark purposes.

Now, what with the business at the airport, the crash in Penrith, and the burning cars on the road, the authorities would be busy soon enough and on our trails.

A half-mile past Fort Putnam, the two cars began to overtake me. I could not get the Aston-Martin past eighty now, which convinced me that the car had been damaged by the bullets. Moreover, the two pursuers were doing 100 at least. They would gain more on me when I approached Greystoke, because I did not intend to enter it above fifty.

A quarter-mile outside the small village of Greystoke the engine temperature began to climb. Steam was pouring out from under the hood now. The radiator had been pierced, and I could not go much further before the engine locked. I told Trish to be ready to abandon the car and to start running.

There was no one on the streets and no lights visible when we drove into Greystoke. The pursuers were out of sight, down in a dip. For several seconds I thought of cutting north, quitting the Aston-Martin, and stealing another vehicle. The road north, which runs on the eastern side of Greystoke Forest, is not even a second-class motorway. It is crossed north of the forest by a similar road which goes westerly to another road which would take me southerly on the west side of Greystoke Forest to the road that leads eventually to my estate. This road is narrow and winding but tar-surfaced. The route would be much longer than the other way, but it had the advantage that my pursuers would not expect me to take it.

However, they would just go on to Grandrith and wait there for me, as they should have done in the first place. It was best to take the shortest route. I might be able to make my pursuers suffer more losses. The more opposition that was dead before I got to my destination, the better.

I would leave A594 in Greystoke and take the short-cut metalled road which paralleled an old Roman road and went by way of Barffs Wood. My pursuers could radio ahead and have a roadblock waiting for me at the junction of two roads, but they could do this no matter what way I went.

The road I would take out of the village met another running north from A594. This would take me past Berrier, Murrah, and Murrah Hall to a road which, in turn, would take me to my estate between the River Caldew and the Raven Crags.

As I sped into the middle of town, several things happened at once. The engine temperature indicator shot up. A door in a house by the road swung open and two men, dressed in motor-cyclist's clothes, stepped out. I had been in the middle of the road but I swung to the right to avoid them if they were going to cross the road. I saw a huge object, perhaps twenty feet high and eight broad. It was draped with a tarpaulin.

Just as I steered right, my front right tire blew.

Chapter Thirty-Four

The tire may have been weakened by a bullet or when it struck the curb at Penrith. I did not apply brakes, of course, but wrenched the wheel to direct us away from the tarpaulin-hidden object in the middle of the square. The car skidded and shuddered at the same time and slid nose-first into the base of the object. We were thrown forward but restrained by our seat and shoulder belts. The car hissed as the last of the water poured out of her smashed radiator.

We could see nothing because the tarpaulin had fallen over us. We got out of our belts, stuck the guns and ammo boxes in the pockets of our coats, and also took the bundle containing the crossbow, the bolts, and grenades. I shoved the .22 under the car.

The motor-cyclists, laughing and cursing at the same time, their North country accents even more thickened with liquor, were trying to pull the tarpaulin off us. Then they shouted with alarm and told each other to jump out of the way. Something gave a tremendous crash immediately before our car.

We got out from under. Our first concern was that our pursuers had not caught up with us. There were no lights as yet from their cars, but lights were going on in shops and houses by the road.

The thing under the tarpaulin had toppled over away from us, fortunately. For a few seconds I could not see what it was, and then when the lights came on and Trish's flashlight illuminated it, I did not understand what I was seeing. Then it became a configuration I recognized.

Several years before, a rich American aficionado of the author

Edgar Rice Burroughs had proposed to set up in the center of Greystoke a giant bronze statue of Tarzan battling a gorilla. As any reader of Burroughs knows, Tarzan was supposed to be an English viscount, "Lord" Greystoke. The American had decided that a statue of the ape-man should be put up in Greystoke to commemorate his ancestral town.

Many natives of Greystoke objected for various reasons. Some pointed out that Greystoke was not the real title of Tarzan. The first book in the series admitted that it was a name chosen to hide Tarzan's true identity. Thus, the real Greystoke had nothing to do with Tarzan. The pro-statue people admitted this but said it made no difference. The statue would bring the town much publicity, since everybody knew about Tarzan, even if many did not know that Burroughs was the author who had created him or that Tarzan was a titled Englishman. The tourists would flock in and the village would prosper.

The "Lord" of Greystoke was consulted for his opinion. Laughing, he said he did not object. He was not Tarzan, but this statue was all in good spirits and intent and it would bring in money, if that was what the villagers desired.

The last that I had heard, the issue had not been settled. But here was the statue, now on the ground and broken in several places. Though bronze and large, it did not weigh much. It was hollow and thin.

One of the motor-cyclists, seeing us emerge, cried, "Now you've done it! It was to be unveiled tomorrow noon, rain or no!"

The other said, "And bloody good riddance, too! I say the monster's a traffic hazard, right? Here's this poor couple running into it, and it not even properly blessed by the city fathers, God bless their drunken souls!"

"Don't talk that way, Arnie!" the other said, laughing.

I laughed; even though our car was wrecked, our pursuers might be on us any moment, and my stomach had a belt burn. If I survived, I would have another laugh in private with the owner of Greystoke.

The first of the chasers lit the end of narrow street. As yet, it was not on the straightaway.

I took out a number of bills, American money, and said, "You chaps. Here's over a thousand pounds. Will you rent me your bikes, immediately, no questions asked? Give me your names; I'll return the bikes later."

"No, why should we?" one said.

The other said, "This is very fishy, Tommy. Who're you running from?"

They weaved a little and stank of Guinness. I said to Trish, "No time to argue or bargain. And here come more people. Knock them out; get their keys."

We laid them out with chops of the palm edge on the neck. I did not like doing it, but we had to. I stuffed the money in the jacket of one, took his goggles off, took out his keys, and ran to the house outside which the two bikes were parked.

It was not necessary to ask Trish if she could operate a motor-cycle, because she had told me about her passion for them. The vehicles were BSA Lightnings, powerful brutes capable of 100 mph. We kicked over the motors, made sure that the bundle was secured tightly to the rack, thrummed the motors, and then tore out of the other end of the square as the first of the pursuers roared into the square. A quick backward look showed me that they would have to stop. There were too many people gathered around the statue, car, and unconscious motor-cyclists. A policeman's whistle shrilled above the roar of our motors, and then it was gone.

CHAPTER THIRTY-FIVE

Before we had gotten opposite Barffs Wood, the lights of Noli's men were a mile behind. Trish, who had been behind me about twenty yards, drew even and gestured at her fuel gauge. Then she held up a thumb and finger in an O. She was close to being out of gas.

She could transfer to my bike, but the weight would slow us down too much. I looked behind, estimated how quickly the two cars would get to us, and indicated to Trish that we would stop just as soon as we got over the crest of a hill. As we dipped on the downslope, I cut my light and she followed suit. When we had stopped, I said, "We'll put the bikes on the road, both lanes!"

It was a variation of the roadblock that they had set up for us. The bikes were let fall on their sides, and while Trish undid the bundle in response to my quick orders, I punched the gas tank of my bike with my screwdriver. Then I dragged the bike ten feet this way and that and back to its original spot. Trish, meanwhile, had gotten out the crossbow, a small type with a handle like the butt of a pistol. It could be fired with one hand and had no great range but could bury the full length of its bolt in a man within sixty feet.

Trish ran to take her station on the right-hand side of the road in a grove of trees. Behind her, hidden by the trees, were the ruins of the old Roman road. The lights of the first car came up swiftly. It was doing at least ninety mph. The second was about eight car lengths behind.

As the first came over the crest, I loosed a bolt at the left front tire.

The driver saw the bikes in the road before him; brakes screeched; the car began to skid; it struck the left-hand machine; and it rolled over and over. My bolt had apparently missed, but it did not matter. Its inclusion was a case of overkill, anyway.

I had dropped the crossbow, snatched out my automatic, and fired into the gas tank of my motorcycle. The tank exploded, and the fire spread out over the road. The second car was screeching as the driver pumped his brakes and swerved to the right side of the road to avoid the burning motorcycle. He struck the other motorcycle and was considerably slowed down. The motorcycle was sent spinning to one side, and the car kept on going. It stopped behind the upside down car. There was a silence and a motionlessness for a few seconds as the five men inside it stared at the wrecked vehicle, the two bodies thrown out of the road, and the four within the car.

I ran down the left side of the road along the ditch. Trish's automatic flamed twice from the trees. The car abruptly backed, its tires burning rubber and screaming. Then it shot along the left side of the road to pass the wreck, its right wheels on the pavement, its left in the mire.

The men in it were firing wildly in the general direction of Trish, whom they could not see. Despite this, she stepped out then from behind the big oak and tossed a grenade. It struck on the pavement in the path of the car. The explosion caused another screeching of brakes and a swerving from the road. Suddenly, the car was in the mire but still moving forward. It slid to one side, straightened as the driver fought it and then was back on the pavement. In the meantime, I had been firing at it and so had Trish. But it went on.

I bit my lip. We had lost all our transportation now the gamble had not paid off. I was hoping to get that car without wrecking it.

The lights of the car receded, then slowed, and suddenly they were no longer moving. I shouted to Trish to be careful, it might be a trick, and ran toward it. When I got closer, I could see those within silhouetted against the beams from the headlamps. The door by the driver's seat was open, and two men were pulling him out. He had been hit.

One man dropped the body and whirled. I fired, and Trish's shot came out of the darkness. He fell backward over the driver's body.

The other man was firing into the darkness with no idea of where we were. I shifted the crossbow to my right hand, aimed, and saw him throw the automatic up into the air and then double over, clutching his leg. When Trish and I moved in, we found that the bolt had gone through his thigh and several inches were sticking out in back.

I had intended to question him, but he died a moment later. A previous wound in the ribs, plus the shock of the bolt and more loss of blood, had put him out of our reach.

A voice speaking what I thought was Albanian was issuing from the car radio. It was questioning and, when no answer came, was threaded with rage and then with hysteria. There was no point in letting Noli know what had happened, so I repressed the temptation to crow over him. I turned it off and started to haul the other bodies out. Afterward, we collected all the arms and ammunition from the other car and put them in ours. Two men in the wrecked vehicle were unconscious but moaning. I put them out of their misery with a slash across the jugular vein.

The trunk of both cars contained flares, which I put on the floor of the rear of the big American car. They might have a use. We drove off at 11 P.M. The skies were still cloudy, and it was lightning and thundering again in the distant west, this side of Blencathra mountain.

CHAPTER THIRTY-SIX

Without incident, we drove all the way to the road at the foot of Raven Crags at the highest speed which the road conditions permitted. We kept a watch out for a copter. If Noli had one, he might send it off to find out why his men were not reporting in.

When we neared the fork of the road which led to the left to the village of Cloamby and straight ahead up the fell to Grandrith, we slowed down. I turned off the lights and poked along, because I suspected that Noli might have stationed men at the fork. A half a mile before the crossroads, I stopped at the bottom of a hill, and Trish and I proceeded on foot. This would delay us, but I was so sure that an ambush would be waiting for us I had to take extreme caution.

We circled through the heavy brush on higher ground. After intent observation, occupying ten minutes of quietly listening and peering, we found two men. They were on the north side of the road and a few yards below the fork. They were smoking, and, although they kept the flames cupped in their palms, I saw them. I also smelled the smoke. Reasonably certain that no others were around, I carefully approached them. They were on a slight eminence, screened by brush. Besides their tommies, they were armed with a bazooka. One had a walkie-talkie.

The road was only forty feet away; they could scarcely have missed us if we had driven by. I crawled back to Trish and told her what I had seen and what we should do. Before proceeding, I subjected the woods to another intent scrutiny by eye, ear, and nose. It was well that I did. A third man was fifteen feet up on the broad limb of a giant oak thirty feet behind the others. He had been stationed there, I presume, in case I was wily enough to do just what I was doing. He was facing away from them and had not seen or heard me because I am not one to make any noise in the woods. I found him because he sighed softly once and once moved his weapon against the bark.

It took some time to get Trish quietly into a position where she could get a good shot at him with the crossbow. I left her and crawled back to the three. They were talking softly in English. One was born within the sound of Bow Bells and one must have been born in Germany near the Dutch border.

I said, "Freeze! Don't make a sound!"

At my orders they turned around slowly, hands on their necks. I got behind them, and they advanced toward the man in the tree. One of them, at my softly spoken command, told him to throw his rifle down and then climb down. When the sniper hesitated, I told him he was covered on both sides. I did not add that I would kill his colleagues if he disobeyed. I doubted that he would care about them.

They were tough men but also, by *their* definition of reality, realists. They gave me information quickly enough. I told them I would kill a man for each unanswered question or unsatisfactory answer and torture the last one. They believed me. Perhaps they had been informed of the failures of the others to kill me.

Noli had recruited them through an agent, and they had been flown up here with ten men and landed on the meadow north of Catstarn. Others had come by car and on another flight of the big helicopter. There were probably thirty-five to forty men in Catstarn Hall and Castle Grandrith. Noli might not believe in God, but he certainly believed in overkill. Of course, he had Caliban to worry about, too.

Those of his men not Albanian—about half—had been paid $5,000 apiece and promised another $5,000 after the job was completed. That is, after I was killed.

Noli had told them they might have to deal with another enemy, a Doctor Caliban. But not if I was killed soon and they got away.

Where was my wife?

When I asked this, my heart was squeezing, and I was shaking a little. I expected the worst.

Their spokesman replied that she was holed up in the castle. When the copter had descended and the cars had come in in a two-pronged attack, she had fled to the castle with a rifle. She had wounded two men during her flight.

The castle was across the tarn from the hall. It had been in ruins since the time of Oliver Cromwell, but I had rebuilt part of it. The keep was massively constructed and built as a refuge for atom bomb attacks or an emergency like this. The great stone doors had been closed behind her, and she could not, as yet, be pried loose. Bazookas had launched missiles against it without success. Clio sat inside with an untouchable source of oxygen and plenty of supplies. She could be blasted out if enough powder and time were used, but Noli had quit trying. He was afraid of attracting the villagers. The five domestics were still alive but locked up in a storeroom.

This had happened two days ago at dawn.

The three men had been diverging, as if they were corners of a very slowly growing triangle, while I was questioning them. Perhaps they hoped that, since it was so dark and they were moving so slowly, I would not notice. Even if I had been blind, I could have told that they were moving away, since their body odors were getting slightly weaker.

I don't think that they would have tried anything if they had believed that I was going to let them go. But they must have decided that I would not dare to release them, since they could get to a phone in the nearby village of Cloamby or at a farmhouse on the secondary road and call Noli. It was possible that Noli had cut the telephone lines, but I could not trust them to tell me the truth about that.

One of them barked, "Take them!" and dived off to the left. The other two jumped for the right, one diving at my feet. There was a twang as Trish's crossbow cut loose. I fired four times. The top of the head of the man coming at me must have been blown off, because, as I later found out, my pants were wet with blood and brains. His head almost struck my leg as he fell. The fellow nearest me had his pistol out (I had suspected that they were carrying weapons under their coats but did not want to frisk them in the dark). My second bullet hit him in the shoulder; his pistol flamed to one side; he was hit two more times before he struck ground. The third, of course, had been pierced at point blank range with the crossbow bolt.

I made sure all three were dead by using my knife. Then we stood above the bodies, listening. There were no sounds, nothing to indicate that our shots had alarmed anybody.

I said, "Let's get back to the car."

We walked back, and then drove it up to where the men lay, loaded in the weapons and the walkie-talkie, and were on our way. The road was steep and narrow here and wound up and back and forth on the face of the mountain. At the top, it began to run through heavy woods, winding back and forth for a mile and then coming out on a fairly level stretch of 500 acres.

The tarn was a rough question mark-shaped lake about a half-mile long and two hundred yards wide. The castle was on the west side of the lower end of the tarn and the rather large chateau of Catstarn Hall was opposite the castle. The garages, servants quarters, and stables were north of the Hall. To the west, on a high hill, was the huge granite rock roughly shaped like a chair. This is the High Chair which I referred to before and which is connected with the enigmatic local saying. The original Randgrith is supposed to be buried by its base.

The walkie-talkie squawked as we drove into the woods, and a man said, in English, "Murray! What the hell's the matter with you? Report!"

Trish was driving. I imitated Murray's voice as best I could (I am an excellent mimic) and said, "Murray here. No sign of Grandrith yet."

There was silence. Then the man said, "Have you forgotten something, Murray?"

It was evident I had. I had forgotten to question Murray about passwords over the walkie-talkie. He had told me the code used for identification in getting into the Hall and the castle, but I had blundered in this respect. So now they would be even more on their guard.

In the distance was a faint whirring noise. It sounded like a helicopter rising, and it was probably coming to investigate.

We abandoned the car after maneuvering it on the narrow road to face the other way. I left the keys under a bush near it. If we had to, we might be able to race away in it.

A Feast Unknown

As I got out of the car, I heard another sound. It was quickly overridden by the chopping of the approaching helicopter, but not before I knew that a plane with propellers was nearby. Then we were in the woods, and the copter was hovering about fifty feet above the car, its searchlight poking around the woods. We made our way westward. Through breaks in the vegetation, I looked for the plane. I could see nothing, not even a darkness flitting across the sky. I suspected that the plane was Caliban's.

Another storm was advancing toward us. The thunder and lightning were nearer, and the wind had increased.

The copter continued to fly back and forth, its beam probing. It did not have much chance of spotting us in the very heavy undergrowth. I have always encouraged the opposite of park woods in my forests.

We got to the edge of the clearing. A hundred yards across the lawn was the back of Catstarn Hall. Its three-story rambling Tudor structure was splotched with white in the blackness. It looked unlit until someone briefly opened a door. Light jumped out like a lion from a cage.

At that moment, a distant flash of lightning revealed a two-motored amphibian descending from the south. It was landing broadside to the wind but had to do so because the tarn runs longest from south to north. It was crabbing to keep from drifting and also slipping in at a very-steep angle. Its lights were not on. Apparently the pilot was depending on the lightning flashes for his illumination, and also on his radar for the altitude detection.

There were more lightning flashes. The copter abruptly turned from the hunt and headed toward the tarn. Four men ran out of the house toward another copter, a smaller craft guyed down on the meadow between the Hall and the stables. Murray had not told me about this copter.

The amphibian's motors roared as it straightened out and flew up from the tarn, only thirty feet below it. Two more lightning flashes showed two small objects streaking from the plane. One struck near the copter on the ground. The other hit the big copter in the air. The machine on the ground was knocked over on its side by the explosion, which ripped the guy wires apart. The big copter became a great flaming globe and fell on the roof of the Hall.

By the light of the fire, the amphibian returned and landed on the tarn.

Trish and I took advantage of the confusion to run across the meadow south of the Hall. We went about sixty feet from the house, which was emptying itself of men as if it were vomiting them. The entire roof and the middle section of the Hall were burning brightly.

I carried two knives, an automatic, the bazooka, two grenades, and two bazooka missiles. Trish carried a knife, an automatic, the crossbow and six bolts, and another missile. Our destination was the castle.

By the time we got past the house, the amphibian had waddled out of the water and was proceeding swiftly on its wheels. It raced away from the south end of the lake, turned, and sped toward the men by the burning house. Submachine guns from the men and a heavy machine gun from the castle battlements pulsed flame at it. A rush of flame and a loud explosion came from the battlements where the machine gun had been. Briefly, by the firelight, I had seen the missile as a dark streak.

But forty feet away from the first explosion, a red jet shot out, something black whizzed toward the plane, and the nose was enveloped in smoke and it jumped a little. Smoke covered the amphibian, and when it was whisked away by the wind, a big hole in the belly, near the nose, was revealed. One of its wheels was gone, and the craft was listing.

The crew must have scrambled out on the other side and started running toward the castle. Red flame winked again on the battlements, and the amphibian, taking a direct hit, blew up with a roar and a white fifty-foot high gush. Ammunition inside it continued to explode. Trish and I were knocked off our feet and half-deafened and, for a minute, enveloped by smoke.

We got up, and I shouted for her to follow me. Something whooshed by us and ripped apart the air and shook the earth from fifty yards behind us (or so I estimated). We continued on around the plane. Noli's men must have seen us by the light of the burning, exploding plane, but intermittently, because we were veiled by puffs of smoke. A glance showed me that a number were running after us. They had to give the plane a wide skirting, however.

Ahead, three figures raced for the main entrance of the castle. The portcullis was up, and the drawbridge was down. The castle was surrounded by a moat which I had deepened and was supplied by the tarn through an underground pipe.

The giant in the lead was undoubtedly Doctor Caliban. The two behind him were the old men, Rivers and Simmons. Each carried a small submachine gun and wore dark coveralls and black coal-scuttle helmets.

I did not know why Caliban brought the old men along. Perhaps he did so because they were deeply attached to Trish and wanted to be in on her rescue. Perhaps they wished to die with their boots on, fighting to attain some sort of Valhalla. Perhaps Caliban had had so little warning that these two were the only ones available and their aid was better than none. Probably, they came along because of a combination of all the reasons I have suggested. I will say one thing for them. For men of eighty, they were remarkably agile and swift.

The third bazooka missile from the battlements, coming at a steep angle, blew up the end of the drawbridge behind them and hurled them forward and onto the floor of the bridge. They picked themselves up and ran through the great arch below the portcullis.

I did not like to use my bazooka yet, but I had to do so. We were now the targets of the men on the battlements, and we had much more ground to cross than Caliban and crew before we reached cover. After loading the bazooka, I put it on my shoulder and Trish aimed and fired it. The explosion was ten feet below the spot where I had seen the rocket's jet. We ran forward with the hope that the nearness of the hit would upset and delay them. But their missile exploded on the ground about forty feet behind us.

I halted again, and loaded, and Trish fired. This time the missile hit about ten feet to the right of their estimated location and approximately a foot below the crenellations. The crenellations disappeared, and so did the bazooka men.

Meanwhile, our pursuers had rounded the plane, which had ceased to explode but not to burn. They began shooting at us. I turned with the bazooka loaded with our last missile and fired at the group. They threw themselves on the ground, and the missile went over their heads and blew up a tree on the edge of the meadows.

However, they all jumped up and ran away behind the protection of the plane. I knew they would be back in a minute, so I threw the tube down, and we ran to the drawbridge.

We had to jump a gap of eight feet, which was easy for Trish even with her burden of weapons. A submachine gun in the battlements began firing at us. We got into the courtyard before he could bring his spray of lead around to catch us. The mob behind us, and the men above, were not all of Noli's forces. Explosions inside the castle told us that Caliban was meeting resistance from others.

I tried to raise the drawbridge, but the chains had been sawed apart. A head, silhouetted against the glare, appeared above us, and the short snout of a tommy poked out. Trish aimed carefully. The bullet screamed off the stone, and the head withdrew.

"Where's Doc?" Trish cried. "I want Doc!"

So far she had been as much aid as the best of men. But the time was to come when I would have to watch her because she might turn against me. That would not be, however, unless she got a chance to talk to him.

"We'll find him," I said.

We went through the closest of the nine entrances in the courtyard. This led up a narrow winding staircase for four stories, at which point an iron-bound oaken door blocked us. Noli's men had used the other two routes to the battlement walls. They had not found the key to unlock this and had refrained from blowing it open. I turned the huge dragon-headed knob six times to the right, pushed in on it, and turned it three times to the left. It opened slowly with a slight squeaking despite all my stealth.

There were three bodies on the stones and three men standing. One was on my right and looking down into the yard, presumably for us. The other two were looking toward the flames. They were manning a .50-caliber machine gun.

We stepped out. I shot the man with the tommy in the back with my crossbow. The other two did not hear or see us. I reloaded and aimed just as one man turned toward us. My bolt caught him in the belly, and Trish's two shots carried the other backward and against the stone wall.

I looked down at the bridge. The last of the men from the Hall was just entering the courtyard. I pulled the pins of two grenades in rapid succession and tossed them down on the bridge near the end of the gap. When the smoke cleared, a fifteen foot gap existed between the bridge end and the lip of the moat.

Trish and I poked the dead men's tommies over the embrasure within the yard and fired blindly down. A storm of bullets chipped stone off and one knocked Trish's weapon from her hand. It fell down into the yard. I think they must have emptied the clips in their automatics and rifles and reloaded and emptied them again. They shot as if they had an inexhaustible supply of ammunition.

CHAPTER THIRTY-SEVEN

Somebody suddenly realized that they were short of bullets. He shouted an order. I peeked over the edge and saw several men running into the castle. One body was sprawled on the stones. I leaned my tommy out and began firing but had to withdraw because they were not entirely out of bullets.

The next half-hour was one of siege. Noli's men came up the two stairways open to them. I kept an eye on the one through which we had entered, too, because it could be blasted open with a grenade. We used very short bursts to keep them from coming up the two ways; they replied with torrents of long bursts. It was amazing how so many bullets were expended with, as far as I knew, no casualties.

There was also shooting in the other part of the castle, way off. Then, silence.

After a while, we were silent, too, because we had used up the tommy's ammunition and all but five bullets apiece in our automatic pistols. I carried the machine gun and its tripod to the top of one of the stairways and waited.

The time came when I wondered if everybody was either out of ammunition or almost so. Noli and his men had been forced to run out of the Hall so swiftly that they could only scoop up the ammunition handy. Caliban and the two old men had been forced to run from the plane with little chance to get much ammunition. The men stationed in the castle had supplies, too, but these were probably limited.

I had seen no evidence of anything except tommies, rifles, and pistols. I had the only grenade in the place, as far as I knew. Of course, everybody must have a knife. And there were the maces, bludgeons, spears, and battleaxes on the walls of various rooms.

I fired several rounds from the heavy machine gun down the stairs. When the gun ceased, seven reports came from below. Stone chips stung my back and bullets shrilled. Trish, at my orders, fired once down her stairway and got eight in reply.

"They're out of ammunition, Trish!" I yelled. "I'm charging them!"

I threw an empty tommy down the stairs. Three shots were fired.

Trish did the same thing and got two bullets. They probably had at least a few more rounds.

Someone shouted, "Noli wants us! He's got Caliban cornered! Caliban's out of ammo! So are we! But we got the numbers!"

It was a trick. Otherwise, why let me know that they were withdrawing?

Possibly, most of them were out, and the few who still had some rounds would be left on guard.

I crept down the steps, going slowly, with the .50-caliber held in both arms. Faintly, the shuffling of many feet sounded. Then, silence. Most of those below had departed, though it might be just to the next room.

I went back up the stairs and did what I could have done before if I had had a good reason. I told Trish to patrol back and forth between the two staircases while I was gone. With my automatic in its holster and a grenade in my pocket, and my knives, I climbed down the wall on the outside above the moat. I used the half-brick projections, a provision of some ancestor who had wanted as many escape routes as possible.

At the first window I came to, an embrasure so narrow I would have scraped off my skin if I had gone through, I looked in. The room had been emptied except for two men. Each was stationed on the side of the entrance to the staircase, and each held an automatic. I fired twice through the window. One did not die immediately, and he looked very surprised. I had one bullet left.

After the silence of a minute was the sound of running shoes. The men stationed below Trish's staircase were coming to investigate.

Some of them, anyway. Evidently they thought the two shots were from their colleagues, who probably had orders to fire only if they actually saw me.

They ran into the room and stopped short. They were bewildered. It was incredible, I suppose, that I could have come down the stairs, killed the two ambushers, and gotten out without the others seeing me.

My last bullet took one in the chest. The other two fired blindly at the window as they ran from the room. I went through, scraping skin off beneath my clothes and for a second not sure that I wouldn't be stuck. I ran to the dead men, and ejected their clips. Their guns were all .45s, so the ammunition would not fit my .38. From the three, I got six bullets for one clip and inserted it in a .45.

I called back up to warn Trish and then went up. She took the automatic and the crossbow, while I carried the big machine gun. I descended one staircase. Trish took the other. The two men were standing out in the hall between the two rooms and discussing what they should do. I fired at the stone walls at an angle to richochet bullets at them without exposing myself. They ran away and Trish killed them with three shots. That left four rounds in her automatic and three bolts for the crossbow. I had twenty rounds in the belt of the .50-caliber.

It was inevitable that some of those who had left would return on hearing the firing. I emptied my machine gun down the steps and blew three apart. When a man stuck his head out through the door below, I threw the machine gun at him. He dodged back in time to avoid being hit.

"There must be more than one outside that door," I said. "We could go around them; there are at least five other staircases to the next story. But I don't like to have them behind us. I think I'll use the grenade."

I went down the stairs while Trish, from above, kept her .45 pointed at the door. She had insisted that she was an expert in using the big powerful weapon, but I have no faith in its accuracy, especially if handled by a woman who, though strong, is still not a strong man. I did not want to be shot by the .45 while she was trying to hit our enemies.

I listened a while and determined that at least three men were talking out there. I could not detect the odor of more than three, but the gunpowder was so strong I was handicapped.

"Jesus Christ!" a man said. "He can't have much ammo left, even if he did get all the stuff from the blokes upstairs. I say we ought to rush him."

"Don't be a dumbshit," another said.

"Well, hell, if we stay here, he can go down another flight of steps and come up behind us. Or just leave us sitting here."

"Fine," said a third. "Let Noli and his bunch handle him."

"Hell, they ain't got any ammo left! What'll they handle him with?"

"We got all that's left," the first man said, "and that ain't much. Six rounds between us three. Don't waste no more."

"If they got more than we think they got, our goose is cooked," the second said.

"We could take off," said one who sounded like a Yankee. "Shit, this ain't panning out like it was supposed to. This was supposed to be a breeze, a pushover. I ain't seen anything like this since I was in the Congo."

"We took Noli's money, and so we're staying," said another. "Besides, if we run out now, we'll lose the other five thousand and maybe a hell of a lot more. There's that gold he promised us."

"How you gonna spend all that money if you're six feet under?"

I pulled the pin on the grenade, counted to three, and tossed it. It struck with a metallic sound. There was a silence, then a series of yells and scuffle of feet. I flattened against the wall, turned my head away, and jammed my fingers in my ears. Even so, the roar half-deafened me, and the smoke billowing through the arch set me to coughing.

When the smoke was cleared, I looked in.

All three were dead against the walls, their clothes and parts of their bodies blown off. Unfortunately, the explosion had ruined two guns, bending their barrels slightly and set off the ammunition in the third and blowing it apart.

CHAPTER THIRTY-EIGHT

The crossbow bolts and the remaining bullets were disposed of inside the next two minutes. We were on the ground floor and crossing the great entry room, lit by a number of bulbs in artificial torches in sconces, when a shadow fell across us from above. I jumped and whirled; Trish screamed. A suit of armor that belonged to my fifteenth century ancestor, John Loamges de Clizieux William Cloamby, Baron of Grandrith, struck the floor beside Trish. She fired up at the dark gallery, and a shadowy figure ran along the hall of the gallery, hugging the wall as it crouched. The .45 was emptied, but a ricochet must have hit the man, because he staggered over and fell across the railing.

A man appeared at the far end of the entry room with a pistol in his hand and fired. My bolt took him in the shoulder and he whirled with the impact and fell. I loaded the crossbow again, while another man ran out from the hallway and dived to get the fallen automatic. He fired and missed, too, and I did not. That was his only chance, because the gun was now empty.

The wounded man was gray with shock. I said, "How many more ambushers?"

He stared at me with big pain-glazed eyes and said, "None. Everybody else is down there with Caliban and his men."

"Any guns among them?" I said.

"No. Noli let us have what was left because you were still armed. He's got enough men to run over three Calibans and then some."

"Don't be too sure of that," I said, and I cut his throat.

Trish became even paler and swayed. "Do you have to do that?" she whispered.

"I don't want live enemies at my back," I said.

We went through three rooms and down a hall toward the rear of the castle and then down a tightly corkscrewing case of stone steps. This led to the dungeon, which was a huge room with a number of cells with iron bars, some old torture machines, and, in one wall, the stone door to the atom bomb shelter. The room was well lit by a number of electric torches in sconces and several batteries of lamps overhead. It was a dead end room. The stone door to the shelter was pitted and gouged with Noli's efforts to blast it open.

The room was a babel of shouts and screams and a chaos of struggling men. I paused a few seconds. The chaos became a pattern, fluid, but still a pattern.

At the far end of the room was Caliban. He was not totally visible because he was immersed in bodies. About fourteen men were trying to get at him. Some were trying to get away, however, I quickly saw. They held knives, the butts of pistols, brass knuckles, and one had a mace taken from the wall upstairs. Some were armed only with their fists or were trying to use their feet or their hands, karate style.

The goal of their weapons seemed to be a whirlwind. He could not be halted long enough for anybody to get in a crippling blow or thrust. The flesh around him was a bag trying to contain one man, and when the man pushed, the bag swelled out on one side and collapsed on the other. His hands were a blur; they chopped, poked, and his elbows rammed, and his feet kicked frontward and backward. He did not seem to be holding a knife, but blood was spurting from stabs of his fingers. Shrieks of agony rose as he snapped wrist bones and fractured shinbones, crushed insteps, punctured an eye, tore an ear off, slammed a man so hard against three others that they all fell.

I have never seen a man move so swiftly or powerfully or skillfully. He seemed to be more of a natural force than a mere man. Yet, he was doomed. In a matter of seconds, a knife would go through a soft part or the butt of a gun slam into his skull and momentarily make him open to other weapons. Most of his clothes had been torn off, and he was splashed with blood everywhere.

There were unconscious or dead men on the floor around him. Eight at least. And six sitting up on the floor, too hurt to get up.

The two old men were halfway down the room, their backs against the wall. They were clubbing at the five men against them. Four men lay on the floor.

Simmons and Rivers went down even as I took stock of the situation. The slender Rivers succumbed to brass knuckles against his temple. The apish Simmons, bellowing as if he were enjoying the fight, fell several seconds later. A huge, black-haired, blue-jawed man stepped in just as Simmons brought the barrel of his weapon down on the head of a bandy-legged red-haired man. The huge man slammed Simmons on the side of the neck with the butt of a pistol. Simmons dropped his gun, and another man thrust a knife into the white-haired gorilla chest.

The old men were covered with blood, and their clothes were half-torn off. But they had given a battle of which young men would have been proud.

There was blood on the walls, on the floor, and on almost everybody in the room. Only Noli seemed untouched. He stood in the center of the room, his back to me, waving a long knife and bellowing orders, unheard, at those around Caliban. The men who had downed Simmons and Rivers joined the others. Nobody saw us standing at the foot of the stairs.

Trish, behind me, said, "Doc!"

"You stay here," I said.

I handed her the crossbow.

"One bolt only left."

I did not tell her not to waste it. It would have been an insult and a stupid thing to say.

I roared out like a male of The Folk challenging a leopard or defying a male of a strange band. I lacked the throat sac, but I have very powerful lungs.

That froze everybody except Caliban, who took advantage of the paralysis to twist a man's head until the neck snapped.

Nobody paid him any attention. Noli turned slowly as his bald head and face lost much of its redness.

I roared again and charged. Noli crouched with his knife up.

I don't really know what happened next. I did a bad thing, that is, a nonsurvival thing. I succumbed to my rage, to my desire to kill the man who had assaulted me and had endangered my wife. I saw through a red shot with black. And I recovered my senses only at the end.

Why his men did not interfere, I do not know. Perhaps things went too swiftly. Perhaps they, who had suffered so much from Caliban and his men while Noli stood aside, wanted to see how he would handle himself.

They saw.

I had taken his knife away from him. I had ripped his clothes off. He was entirely naked. Somehow, whether with the knife or with my fingers, I had cut around his anus, and severed it from the surrounding connecting tissues. And then, while he screamed, I raised him with one arm by a buttock, while holding the end of his bloody anus with the other. And I shot him away with my arm, giving him a half-spin.

Screaming, he soared. Every bit of adrenalin possible to my body must have surged through me, I threw him so far.

His intestines, approximately twenty-four feet long, trailed out behind him and then tore loose from his body.

He landed on his face and sprawled with arms out. He was still living, though gray with shock. His intestines were strung out on the floor behind him.

He jerked once and died.

I dropped the bloody end.

I had shocked even myself. I was not aware until then that I had ejaculated.

Since I had copulated with Trish, I had not had an orgasm. The several killings in between her and Noli had not, as before, resulted in ejaculations. I had been aware of semi-erections during them but had grown so accustomed that I had ignored them. If I thought about them at all, I hoped that the aberration was weakening.

I knew now that my unconscious forces had been summoning up a store, and conserving it, for just this.

The ecstasy had been missing or I had been so overcome with rage that I was unconscious of it.

CHAPTER THIRTY-NINE

Nobody moved. They could not accept what they had seen. And, when their senses thawed, they began to realize what they faced.

They were eighteen effectives. Behind them was Doc Caliban and before them was someone who, at that moment, must have seemed even more terrible.

Caliban, during the scene with Noli, had been as stone-struck as the others. He regained his volition first and struck twice, once with a kick in the base of a spine and immediately after with a chop on the side of a neck. The eighteen had become sixteen.

Nine turned toward him. I charged the remaining seven with a knife, and the room became a mêlée again. My knife went into a belly, but I took a gash from another across my shoulder. A throat got the first two inches of my knife, and a pair of brass knuckles banged and bloodied my cheek. The third man to get my knife took it in the solar plexus, and then it was knocked out of my hand by a blow from the butt of a rifle. The hand was paralyzed for a minute despite which I grabbed a wrist with my left hand while kicking a man's kneecap loose with my foot, jerked, and tore the man's arm loose from his socket. I whirled him around and into the bodies of two rushing me. All three went down. I leaped past a mace—but not without being gashed—kicked one of the men getting up off the floor and broke his neck, whirled, and leaped at the man with the mace.

He swung mightily; I dodged back and then in, felt the mace crack along one shoulder, rammed into him, and carried him backward against the wall where his skull was cracked. The mace was close enough for me to leap at it like a cat after a mouse and pick it up before the survivor could get it. He had a knife, but he backed away, and then flipped it up and caught it, adjusted it; and threw it. My mace was on its way; it hit the knife and both went off course. The man was able to duck the mace, and immediately thereafter he decided he had had more than enough. He tried to run away, but I caught him by the back of the neck and squeezed. His face turned purple, and he dangled at arm's length while I rammed him twice with my fist in the kidneys. When he was released, he sprawled motionless on the floor.

I whirled. Three of the nine were down. A man was stepping back, preparing to throw a knife at Caliban. Now that there were fewer to crowd around, the danger for Caliban was, paradoxically, greater. There was room to throw knives and wield rifles as clubs.

The man threw his arm back, and then he stiffened. The knife fell from his hand, and he was on the floor. I had heard the twang of the string and the *zzzt!* of the bolt. Trish had not wasted her one shot.

I was glad that it was gone, because I did not want her to have it when the end would come.

I charged in, ripped the ears off a man, and, as he turned screaming, chopped his ribs with the side of my palm. He fell forward, and I drove his chin up with my knee and cracked his neck.

Caliban had seized the wrist of a man stabbing at him with a knife, run ahead, turning the man, twisting the wrist so the knife dropped, and then stopped and pulled him over his back. The man cartwheeled through the air and slammed up against a wall.

Three were left. One charged me although I think he was more interested in getting by me than at me. I might have let them go but I did not think there should be anybody left who could testify about the events here. The man charging me was short but enormous of girth, weighing an estimated 340 pounds and with the short arms and legs of a champion weight-lifter. His nose had been smashed and he was bleeding from his chest. I ran toward him and kicked him in the belly. He went *oof!* as his air left him. Before he could recover, I broke three of his fingers and then chopped him again across the nose. Blood spurted from his nose and mouth. My knuckle drove his eye back into the socket, and my knee knocked him unconscious. I picked up a knife and split open the huge belly.

The other two had been caught by Caliban, who had smashed their heads together. They dangled at the end of each hand, while he held them by the necks and squeezed. When their life was gone, he dropped them.

Only then did I realize that he was wearing a metallic, razor-edged, sharp-pointed device on the middle finger of both hands. It was this that made so much blood spurt when he seemed to have barely touched them.

The only sound in the huge room was the labored breathing of Caliban and myself. Both of us were naked except for our shoes, bloodied all over, and bleeding from a dozen deep or minor gashes. The stench of sweat, blood, piss and shit was strong, exceeded only by the not-yet-gone odor of terror from the now dead men.

CHAPTER FORTY

Trish started toward Caliban. He gestured, indicating she should stay away, and said, "No matter what happens, Trish, you are not to interfere! Do you understand? You are not to interfere in any way until it's over!"

She shrank back, her bloody hand covering her bloody mouth. Her eyes were wide and fixed.

I backed away because I wanted a little time to try to bring him to his senses. He followed me, stalking like a huge bronze-skinned tiger.

"Caliban," I said, "*there* is your cousin. *Our* cousin. Alive and safe. She will tell you I had nothing whatsoever to do with her abduction. Or her rape. On the contrary, I saved her. Ask her! She will tell you what a terrible mistake you have made."

I did not care that the Nine had decreed that one must bring back the head and genitals of the other. In that moment, I had made the decision that I was no longer a servant of the Nine. I was their enemy, even if it meant losing immortality. I could no longer pay the price. Faust, you might say, wanted his soul back.

He said nothing but moved closer. Then he stopped and removed the finger-ring-knives and his shoes and socks. He wanted us to meet, naked and bare-handed, fighting as two males of The Folk fought for the chieftainship.

"Caliban," I said, "do not misunderstand me. I would never plead for myself. But I do not want us to be the tools and playthings of the Nine. I believe that the Nine have done us great evil for their

239

own cryptic reasons. They arranged for Trish to be abducted by that man pretending to be me. They arranged for the body of a woman to be found, and they probably had her killed just for that reason. The Nine probably had something to do with the Kenyans' attempt to obliterate me. You know what enormous, if invisible, power they have.

"Listen! I am convinced that my own birth, in its very extraordinary circumstances, was due to the Nine's machinations. There are some very puzzling things in my uncle's diary. I think he was the victim of the Nine, and that I am the result of an experiment by the Nine. I think that they arranged that I should be adopted by a female of The Folk and raised as a wild boy in the jungle among the subhumans.

"I am convinced that their designs have been even deeper. I think they had something to do with the madness of our father."

Trish gasped and said, "Your *father*? *Your* father?"

I moved a step backward. Caliban advanced by one step. His great hands, seemingly muscled with bridge cables beneath the glistening red-brown skin, were out and half-clenched. He was saying, as he had said on the natural bridge over the chasm, "No judo or karate or tricks. Power and speed only. We shall see who is the strongest and swiftest."

I wondered if he had heard anything I had said.

I refused to back any more. I waited.

I said, "Caliban, you haven't read the Grandrith family records. Your family's record. You don't know of the mystery surrounding our paternal grandfather, do you? He shot himself at the age of fifty-five. He looked as if he were thirty. He had three sons, but his wife, when she was very sick and thought she was dying, told an aunt that her husband had been sterile. The aunt wrote this in a diary in a code, which I cracked easily. The aunt said that she suspected a very tall, very powerful, very handsome but elderly gentleman from Norway who visited them quite frequently. The aunt wrote that she would think her suspicions insane, because the old gentleman looked as if he were over ninety. But he had a very strong personality, a strange, compelling, and sometimes repelling, radiation. Radiation is the word she used, I suppose, to communicate an outpouring of psychic strength. And she knew that he had seduced one of the maids in the wine cellar. The maid testified to that.

"The old gentleman, a Mister Bileyg, had a white beard that reached to his navel, and a patch over his right eye. And he was the biggest boned man she had ever seen."

Caliban frowned and said, "What are you talking about, Grandrith?"

"That man was our grandfather," I said. "The evidence may be peculiar, to say the least. It wouldn't stand up in court. But it tells the truth. Our grandfather was one of the Nine! The man we knew as XauXaz! Which, if you know your Primitive Germanic, means the High One!

"And the name he used when he visited Grandrith was Bileyg. That's Old Norse for One-Whose-Eye-Deceives-Him. Which is to say, One-Eyed!"

"What?" he said. Apparently, his reputedly wide and deep knowledge did not encompass Germanic linguistics. Or Germanic mythology.

"The man we knew as one of the Nine, XauXaz, must have been born in the Old Stone Age," I said. "I don't know how old he was. Perhaps 30,000. Perhaps 20,000. Who knows what his history was? At one time, he and two others, perhaps his brothers, who were also part of the Nine that then existed, went to lower Sweden. They were present when the Ursprache, the parent language of the Indo-Europeans, changed to what we call Common Germanic. The dialect that became the ancestor of all the Germanic tongues of today, English, High and Low German, Norse.

"In some way, perhaps because they had lived so long and knew so much, they became gods. Not actual gods, you know, but they were worshipped as such.

"What I'm saying is that XauXaz, and Ebnaz XauXaz and Thrithjaz—who died before we came along—High, Equally High, and the Third, were the old Germanic male trinity, later accounted as brothers. And, by the way, Iwaldi, that dwarf, gnome, or whatever, was contemporary with them. And he ruled his people, who dug deep into the earth and lived underground.

"Common Germanic died out, of course, but the three

continued to speak it among themselves as a sort of code. Sometime in man's history, they ceased to appear among men as gods. They shucked their role and retired to whatever identity the Nine required of them."

Caliban shook his head as if he were wondering about my sanity.

I said, "Our father got the elixir from the Nine. He was a Servant, as we are. As I was," I amended. "And then the same thing happened to him that happened later to us. The side effect of the elixir is to make the user mad, if only for a short time. Its effect is psychic, as well as physical. Something deeply disturbing, no matter how repressed, ruptures the surface, thrusts up from under. The particular form of the psychosis depends upon the character of the particular individual, of course.

"Take me, Caliban, or should I call you Doc, since I'm your brother? Take me. I had always thought my attitude toward killing was very healthy. And I'd always thought my attitude toward sex was extremely healthy. But somewhere in me was a linkage between the two. Something in me equated the act of coitus with killing, the thrust of the penis with the thrust of the knife, orgasm with *the bliss of the knife*, as Nietzsche called it.

"And take you, Doc. Brother. You have always, up until now, with one fatal exception, avoided killing. You never did it even to those most deserving being killed, if you could possibly avoid it. But you wanted to kill, Doc. And you equated coitus with killing. Down there, deep down there.

"And take our father, Doc. He went mad and was locked up in the castle. And he got loose and fled to London to hide in the big city. There his psychosis took the form of the grisly murders of prostitutes. Why, I don't know.

"He raped my mother. Which is why I was born. Later, he went to America. Something happened, the tide of evil reversed, siphoned off, as it were. He took the name of Caliban and devoted his life to good. Trying to make up in some measure for what he'd done in England, I presume.

"Note the name Caliban. Another name for a savage. Shakespeare's monster in *The Tempest*, and a literary archetype of the savage. An anagram of cannibal. It was to remind our father of what he had been.

"He raised you to devote your life to good. You were trained to become a superman of good. You were taught to hate evil and to fight it. But you were to love the evil-doer, not hate him. Hate the sin, not the sinner. Which is an extremely difficult, perhaps almost impossible, thing to do. This attitude has to lead to all sorts of conflict.

"You took a super-Boy Scout oath. You were reared by our father to be a physical and mental Ubermensch, though the development would not have been so successful if you had not been genetically superior. You have the bones and muscle of an Old Stone Age man because your grandfather *was* an Old Stone Age man.

"I suspect that our family is rather inbred, or at least has had more than a number of Paleolithic fathers and mothers. How do we know how many times Grandfather XauXaz, or his brothers, dropped in to resupply the archaic genes? Castle Grandrith may have been the Three's breeding farm.

"And you, Doc, like me and a number of others, were approached by the Nine. And you sold your soul, as we all did, for immortality."

"What soul?" Caliban said. The sneer was in his voice; his face had adopted its customary expressionlessness. But his green, gold-flecked eyes looked peculiar. I could not tell whether they were doubtful or murderous.

"A manner of speaking," I said. "You know well what I mean."

"You really think, then, that our grandfather, who may also be our great-great-grand-father and great-great-great-ancestor a number of times over, was the man-god known to the primitive Germanics as Wothenjaz and to later Germanics as Woden or Othinn or a dozen other names?"

"Yes," I said. "And I believe that the Nine are keeping the seat of our dead grandfather in the family. They made sure we would be trained to be what we are. Perhaps, I am their Wild Man of the Jungle candidate and you are their Man of the Metropolis candidate. It pleases them to pit us against each other. Perhaps, in the Old Stone Age, it was brother against brother in the ceremonial battle to the death for the chieftainship. Who knows? But they don't care who gets killed."

"I think you're trying to talk me to death," Caliban said.

Trish called, "Doc! Listen to him! He makes sense!"

"Not to me he doesn't," Caliban said in a low voice. "And even if he did, one of us has to die."

"I'm not fighting for a seat at the table of the Nine," I said.

He grinned slightly and said, "You're giving up?"

"I've eaten their shit long enough," I said. "I think our father decided that, too, and they killed him."

"I tracked down his murderers," Caliban said. The green-and-gold eyes seemed to pulse. "I did not kill them but I turned their traps for me against them, and they died. If I had to do it again today, I would kill them with my bare hands."

"How do you know they weren't agents of the Nine?" I said.

He had been inching forward now. He halted, and he shuddered. His bronze face, where it wasn't splashed with blood, had darkened with fury. His face twisted as if it were metal under great heat.

"You lie!" he screamed.

His penis rose so swiftly it looked as if it were being hauled up on a string. It swelled like a cobra, the blue veins pulsed, and the great red glans glistened.

I knew then that there was no talking him out of it. The fight was inevitable. I knew this deep down, and, perhaps, I had hoped deep down that it would take place. Whatever my true hopes, my penis rose also, though more slowly, and when fully erect, it looked pale and small against his.

He watched the organ swell and then he said, "I'm going to tear your balls and cock off, big brother!"

He sprang forward, swiftly as a tiger, and lashed out with one hand at my testicles. The other went up to catch whichever hand I extended for defense.

CHAPTER FORTY-ONE

I intercepted the hand and without flinching, which he had hoped I would do so he could throw me off balance if he missed my genitals. He came up swiftly then, though I almost threw him over, because he was crouched to one side and so off-balance.

We were again in the stance we had had when on the bridge. He glared down at me, six foot seven against my six foot three and his 300 pounds against my 240. I am a big wide man, thick-boned as a Cro-Magnon, as I have said, and greatly muscled, but my proportions are such that I do not look like a shot-putter. Alone, with no other humans by me for comparison, I look more like the Apollo Belvedere, although somewhat more broad-shouldered and deep-chested.

Caliban's proportions were also such that he did not look so massively constructed if he stood alone. But next to me, he seemed to be muscled with pythons. And I'm sure that we looked to Trish like a male African lion straining against an American mountain lion.

For what seemed minutes, we strained against each other. Both of us were bleeding from a dozen wounds and profusely from several. We had become weakened by the loss of blood and the energy expended. Our breathing was labored.

We strove. And then, slowly, oh, so slowly, but steadily, his arms were pushed back. His eyes widened slightly, and he breathed more harshly. The muscles of neck, shoulders, chest, and arms ridged. Blue veins pushed up the sweating bronze skin on his temples.

He bent forward and caught my nose in his teeth and bit. I jerked it out of his teeth, but it cost me a pain that seemed to run through my nose and split my brain. It shot down through the pit of my belly and down my legs, as if it were a streak of lightning. Part of it was torn off, and blood spurted.

Somehow, he jerked one hand loose and grabbed my testicles. It was done quickly, as savagely and powerfully as the swipe of a tiger's paw. Another sear of pain struck, like a spear head, between my legs. I screamed then, and I reacted half-unconsciously. We both were standing there with each other's ripped-off testicles in our hands.

Blood spurted from the torn skin and veins and arteries between his legs. I felt a warmth shooting down my leg but did not look down because that would have been fatal. There was not much time left before I became weak with shock and pain, and loss of blood.

I cast his testicles in his face and leaped. He dropped mine and tried to grab both my hands again, but this time I caught one of his hands and with the other made my own swipe. The penis, amazingly, was still huge and hard, though it was deflating. It twisted like a spigot in my grip; he screamed; I yanked with all my strength; the flesh tore like a piece of silk; the member, spurting blood at one end and jism at the other, was in my hand and before his face.

I dropped it; he stepped forward as if to pick it up. Then I was on his back and had a full-Nelson on him. He fell forward and crashed upon his face. The wind went out of him. Despite this, he still had enough vitality to resist my pressure. His neck muscles became as hard as wood. I could feel my own strength flapping away, like a sick bat into the night.

Yet, my penis was still hard and throbbing. It was up against his buttocks, which also felt as hard as oak.

I applied pressure with my hands against the back of his neck in a surge, knowing that if he could withstand that, he might yet win. Blackness was closing in on the edges of my consciousness.

His skin began to gray, even as the bones of his neck creaked like a ship's mast against the force of the wind.

I heard, faintly, a cry of protest from Trish. Caliban grunted once as if he were trying to force something out from him. His neck bent, and then the bones snapped.

I spurted over him with only a vague awareness of it. The Black rushed in as the fluid rushed out, and shortly thereafter I cared as little as Caliban about the world.

CHAPTER FORTY-TWO

The awakening was partial and blurred. I felt some pain, though it was everywhere, but so little that I realized—later—that I was drugged. The lights overhead were high and hexagonal. Dimly, I knew I was in bed in the atom-bomb shelter.

"Clio," I said but could not hear myself say it.

A head, framed in a bronze halo, blacked out the lights. It was smiling and weeping at the same time.

"Trish," I said. "Where's Clio?"

Another head, haloed in gold, appeared beside the bronze.

It leaned down and kissed me.

"Go back to sleep, dear."

I obeyed.

When I awoke again, I was still drugged. The pain had increased, however. It was wired throughout my body but centered from beneath my penis.

I turned my head. I *was* in the shelter. It was eighty feet wide, sixty long, and thirty high. Portable screens divided it into rooms, with the exception of a cement-block cube which housed the fuel cells and the converters. The air system was based on that used in manned space craft. There were supplies enough to last us six months. I had been against building it because we were so seldom in England. Clio had insisted that we construct it, and now I was glad that she was so stubborn.

I had many questions, but I asked first, in a weak voice, if she was all right. She told me to keep quiet and eat. She spoon fed me, and then I felt strong enough to put some questions to her. She began a lengthy account, during which, despite my intense curiosity, I fell asleep again.

On awakening the third time, I found Clio gone and Trish taking care of me. She said my wife had left the shelter to talk to the contractors about rebuilding Catstarn Hall.

I said, "I'm sorry, Trish. I tried to talk some sense into him. You heard me."

"I heard," she said. She shuddered. "I hope I never have to go through anything like that again if I live to ten thousand."

"Have you been contacted by the Nine yet?" I said.

She started and then said, slowly, "Yes. In the first place, we would have had worldwide publicity about this if the Nine hadn't pulled the strings of some highly placed puppets in the government. They clamped down on all reporters and police investigations, claimed security demanded it, and that was that. Oh, yes, the servants were told to be quiet, and threatened with severe penalties if they talked."

"The bodies?"

"We took care of . . . you . . . set up the intravenous and the blood. I didn't know Clio had had some medical training. Without her I'd have been lost. Then I drove like hell to Keswick and got Doctor Hengist, who is one of us. He'd already phoned to Whitehall before I got there. I'd phoned him I was coming. There were soldiers up here on the heels of the people from Cloamby and Greystoke."

"All those bodies," I said.

"The three of us worked like mules. We dragged every one of the bodies, except for those in the hall, of course, every one of the bodies outside and in here into a room in the castle and shut it up. That included dear old Jocko and Porky, too, but we'll give them a decent burial later, out on the hill by that big boulder. They'd like that."

There were tears in her eyes. For a moment, I did not realize that she was talking about the two old men.

"We washed off the blood as well as we could and covered up what wouldn't come off. Some high muckamuck is supposed to fly up here and make a complete report for the government, but he hasn't shown up yet. We'll tell him that a gang of criminals tried to kidnap us so they could force the location of the gold, which is nonexistent, of course, from us. We'll hint that the whole thing was a Communist plot. The only bodies for him to look at will be those in the crashed copter and in the ashes of the hall."

"What about the cars and the men on the road?" I said. "And the landing at Penrith, and so on?"

"We don't know anything about that."

She hesitated and then said, "We found out—we weren't officially notified—that one of the Nine is coming, too. One of Doc's friends dropped in—he's important enough to get through the military cordon—and he told us we're going to get a surprise visit."

"What about it? Why so alarmed?"

Clio entered then. I said, "What's so frightening about this visit from the Nine?"

"Who's scared?" she said.

"I've lived with you long enough to know you," I said. "Besides, I can smell the fear from both of you."

"Oh, Jack!" Clio said. "We were going to wait until you were stronger before we told you! But there's really not time now to put it off!"

Trish said, "Doc is alive!"

CHAPTER FORTY-THREE

It was a shock, but I felt glad. Perhaps, now that he was alive, he would have felt the same sense of the madness drained off which I had experienced. The third time I awoke, even with the pain, I felt an exultation. This resulted, not from the inflooding of sensation but from the departure of a sensation. I *knew* that the physical linkage between my sexual behavior and killing was gone. It was as if I were a bottle uncorked and turned upside down and emptied of a black stinking decayed fluid.

The shock of being castrated by Caliban may have done it. And perhaps—I hoped it was so—the shock of what I had done to him had had a similar effect on him.

I would not be absolutely certain that I was back to normal until my testicles had regenerated. That should not take much longer than the month required after the ritual excision of one testis. And it should take much less time than the six months required to regrow my right leg below the knee. I had lost this when the RAF bomber of which I was pilot crashed after a mission over Hamburg.

Trish said that Doc was sleeping on a bed behind a screen at the other end of the room. He would live. That is, until the Nine found out he was not dead.

"Doctor Hengist could not believe that Doc was still breathing. He said that he would have to die soon. It was just as well, because the Nine would not let him live. Neither Clio nor I knew that the Nine had decreed you two must fight to the death."

Trish began to cry. She said, "It's wrong—evil—to have to

murder each other. And it's hideously evil that the Nine can now say that Doc will have to be put out of his misery. Or that you two should have to fight again after you get back on your feet."

"I was weak once," I said. "I accepted the gift of immortality because the price seemed worth it. Not now. I intend to fight the Nine. But we have to be cunning until we are able to run."

"That's what Doc said," Trish cried, "when he was able to talk for a short time. Listen! Don't worry too much about losing the elixir. Doc has been working for thirty years on it. He couldn't get any samples of the elixir, of course, because the Nine controls it so rigorously. But he figured out that our tissues must be saturated with the elixir. Two years ago he cut off his own fingers and managed to isolate the elements of the elixir. He still hasn't been able to synthesize them correctly, but he says that it's only a matter of a short time until he will be able to do so."

"Is Caliban in good enough shape so that he could dispense with Hengist's services?" I said. "Could you and Trish take care of him, with remote-control advice from me? When I can get out of bed and take a look at him, I'll take over the active doctoring."

She nodded, and I said, "Very well. Wheel him into the room behind the fuel room. Hengist doesn't know about that, does he?"

Trish said, "I didn't know about it, either."

"When Hengist next comes, you tell him that Caliban died. He'll want to know where, because I am supposed to bring his head and genitals to the Nine."

Trish and Clio winced.

I said, "The Nine will have to be satisfied with what they can get. You tell Hengist that you two sunk Doc in the moat. If he insists that Doc be pulled out of the moat, then we're in for it. Knowing the Nine as I do, I imagine that they'll have to have positive evidence that he's dead. We may have to buy some time with an accident for Hengist or whoever acts as agent for the Nine."

"Oh, Jack!" Clio said. "*More* killings?"

"If we're going to resign from the ranks of the immortals, we will do it now," I said. "And we'll have to drop out of sight swiftly. You know that's increasingly difficult in this ever-narrowing world."

Trish and Clio left to wheel the sleeping Doc into the hidden room. An hour later, Hengist entered. He did not seem surprised that Caliban had died. Nor did he say anything about recovering the body. The next day, however, he notified us that the visit from one of the Nine had been cancelled. An agent, a Sir Ronald Hawthorpe, would bring me instructions and also interrogate me.

After he left, I tried to walk into Doc's room, but the pain between my legs discouraged this. I allowed Clio to wheel me in beside his bed. He was lying there with a stiff plastic collar around his neck. Clio had done a professional job in doctoring his broken neck. He was flat on his back and staring up at the ceiling. Tears formed pools with a deep golden-green bottom in his eye sockets, and tears ran down his cheeks. Trish was crying also, but at the same time she was smiling.

"He hasn't wept since he was a little child," she said. "Not even when his mother died or his father died, did he weep. He must have an ocean down there, and I thought it would never come. Oh, I'm so happy!"

If he did not stop crying, she would not be so happy. He could be suffering a complete breakdown, or he could be on the road to a healthiness he had never had.

I said, "Doctor Caliban, why are you crying?"

He did not answer. I waited a while and then repeated my question. After another long period of silence, he said, in a choked voice, "I am crying for Jocko and Porky and for the other wonderful friends I had. I am crying for many people, for Trish especially, because she loves me and I gave her almost nothing back. And I am crying most of all, and I cannot help it, for me."

Clio, always ready to be triggered with empathy, sniffled.

I said, "Then you must feel as I do, that you've suffered a strange sea-change, as it were?"

"I have," he said.

"Perhaps," I said, "we may be doing the Nine an injustice. Perhaps they knew that we would be all the better after having gotten through the effects of the elixir."

"I doubt it very much," Doc said. "They would not know exactly what the end-results would be. They must have gone through this themselves, though it's been so long ago they may have forgotten. You must not forget that they put us through hell before we met and that they ordered us to kill each other afterward. No, they are evil, evil!"

Clio said, "But won't we go through something like that, too?"

"Nobody can say, except the Nine," I replied. "And they're not talking, of course. It may be that only those descended from the Old Stone Age people, those who have the genes for it, react to the elixir in this fashion. But we'll never find out. The question now, Doc, is something only you can answer, though I can predict what your answer will be, I believe. Are you prepared to give up the elixir and fight the Nine?"

"Trish said she told you about my experiments. I think we'll have the elixir ourselves some day. But whether we do or don't, I am no longer obeying the Nine. And he who disobeys, you know, is their deadly enemy."

I wheeled closer and took his hand. "They divided us, brother," I said. "But united . . ." I did not feel brotherly, as yet, and I suppose he did not. But this was a man I could admire and respect and the best ally anyone could want. The odds were greatly against us, but if any two could put up a better fight, I did not know them.

Clio gave him another shot, and he was soon asleep. Trish stayed behind to watch him adoringly for a while. Clio and I returned to the room, where I slowly and painfully got back into bed.

Clio sat down and looked at me for a long time. Then she said, "Trish told me about you two."

"Oh?" I said.

My heart was beating faster than if I'd heard a leopard prowling in the African bush.

"When you two made love," she said.

"We weren't making love," I said. "We were loving each other. Fucking passionately and lovingly."

She reddened slightly. No matter how uninhibited her behavior, she still reacts to certain words.

"She said that nothing might have happened if you hadn't been so concerned about being crippled by your aberration."

"I did not explain to her why I was doing that," I said. "But she was essentially correct. Although I think the same thing would have happened even if I was not concerned about my aberration."

She did not go into a furious tirade or start weeping, as I had expected. She said, "The trouble with retaining complete youthfulness and its vigor is that a couple cannot grow old and fade away together. We're eighty and so should be weak and set in our ways and thoroughly accustomed to each, like a wheel in a rut. A wheel that doesn't want to leave the rut. But we know each other to the last atom, and, while we love each other very much, we are youthful and we are beginning to want some variety. So . . ."

"So?" I said.

"So I think we'll have to have some variety now and then. The little vacations in the caverns provided that, but those are gone."

Suddenly, she stood up and bent over and threw her arms around me.

"What am I saying?" she cried. "I love you and only you! I really want no other man!"

She was sincere, and I loved her very much at that moment. I always love her, although there are some moments when the intensity is less. And, certainly, when I was in Trish, I was not thinking about Clio. Fairness is fairness.

She really did not want another man—as her permanent mate. But she was right. Immortality has its price, and it is impossible to confine yourself to one mate forever if you have the vigor of youth.

This problem would have to work itself out whichever way it would go. At the moment, we had more vital business to attend to. Hawthorpe arrived that afternoon and, after some formalities, got to the instructions.

First, we must get Caliban's body up and remove the head and send it off to the Nine. Usually, the victor took the head himself, but since I would not be able to move for some time, that just could not be done. Hawthorpe would carry it to the Nine.

Second, I was to come to London as soon as I was able and not one second later. I would then be flown to Uganda and taken through the secret routes of the caverns. This time, I would not be blindfolded. After going through the ceremony of seating me, the Nine would hold a conference. This was the most serious meeting since 1945. Hawthorpe could not tell me much, but the discussion would be about the means used for solving the population problem.

The Nine did not intend to let the over-crowding and the pollution go on any longer. The only question was not when but how.

The Nine have a way with temptation.

For a minute, I visualized a world something like that into which I had been born but much better. The jungles and the savannas could return, and Africa would again have its millions upon millions of zebras, antelope, hippos, elephants, and its thousands upon thousands of leopards and lions. The human population would be few and scattered and living naked in thatched huts and fighting each other with spears. I would have vast areas to roam in. Perhaps, the gorilla could be saved from extinction, and if I could find just a few of The Folk left, their numbers could be increased to the point where they might become as numerous as they were 50,000 years ago.

It was a beautiful vision.

And, of course, it would have to be paid for, one way or another. I might not like the payment.

In fact, I didn't like it.

Moreover, I would have to buy an entrance ticket with Doc's head.

I said, "It may take a few days before we can get Caliban's body up."

"Oh, no," he said quickly. "I have two men fishing for it now. I'll take care of everything."

"That's decent of you," I said.

"Not at all, just carrying out orders," he said.

If I tried to convert him to our side, I would be warning the Nine. It would be of no use anyway.

I said, "Come here, Hawthorpe," and when he was close enough I grabbed his throat with one hand and the top of his head with the other. He was a big bull-necked man but squeaked like a mouse before I twisted his neck. I then sent Clio and Trish out after the other two. They called them inside and shot them, and then dropped the weighted bodies into the moat.

Both were shaken. Though they were old veterans and cool enough in defending themselves or attacking enemies on the alert, killing in cold blood was new. I told them that they'd have more of that before we were finished, one way or the other.

An hour later, after some difficulty in getting Doc into the back of a station wagon, we drove off. I stopped once before entering the woods to say farewell to the estate. I doubted that I would ever be able to return. I looked at the castle, the ashes of the Hall, the barns, garages, servants' quarters, the broad meadows and the question-shaped tarn, the woods beyond, and at the great boulder on the hill, beside which rested the first Randgrith. *The old man would sit when the two ravens returned*, the local saying went. I knew now what that meant. The old man, our grandfather, would never sit because he was forever dead, and the two ravens would not return.

Neither would I. Not for many years, anyway.

We drove away as the sun dropped behind the High Chair. The soldiers on sentinel duty let us through without delay. It would not be long before the Nine knew that the three of us had gone, however. Doc was hidden under some blankets and luggage. As soon as Hawthorpe failed to report in as scheduled, the Nine would investigate, and they would know that Caliban was still alive and with us.

Then the hunt would be on.

Hunter, beware the prey!

Before this is over, there may be more than one empty seat at the table of the Nine, and the world may be aware of its secret masters.

POSTSCRIPT

D o you know who they are?

Since Homer and Beowulf—and doubtlessly before—storytellers have found for themselves a hero-figure, and have with their audiences, discovered that just one story won't do, and a saga is born. The parallel between Homer and a long-running comic strip like *Gasoline Alley* is not often drawn, but it is a valid one. The hold of the continuing epic on its public is a firm one. People used to queue up to await delivery of the weekly papers in which they could find the latest chapter of a Charles Dickens novel. Ma and Pa Kettle had their countless thousands of faithful followers, and of course the success of a television series is based on this and nothing else.

The secret of the success of a saga lies in its reference to life—the very specific day-to-day, inside-the-skin life of the members of its audience. This is a matter of harmony or contrast; the narrative concerns itself meticulously with current and familiar events, like the Lanny Budd stories or the Forsyte Saga, or with events calculated to be exotic, like the legends of Bifrost or the Ring trilogy. (Dickens had the joyful genius of being able to do both at once.) Always, the most fascinating of all have been the stories which injected the superhuman into human events. This was the strength and magic of Homer—and also of The Shadow. Batman's adventures in Gotham City are nothing less.

Which bring us, of course, to the marvelous (one wishes, sometimes, that a word had never been overused to the point of total dilution: marvelous they were, marvelous they are) pulp-magazine heroes and the almost endless sword-and-sorcery serial novels and their unforgettable, unconquerable protagonists. With all my heart I pity those who have lived their lives without having been injected with the enchantment of Northwest Smith or Hawk Carse, Tarzan, John Carter, Doc Savage, Conan the Conqueror or any of their swashbuckling colleagues.

Almost without exception, however, the serial epics of the last couple of centuries have been bowdlerized to an extreme, and almost inexplicable, degree. To explain my use of that word, I must digress and tell you about the Man from Mars who follows me around.

I've never gotten a good look at him, so I can't describe him accurately. What he is, however, is not as significant as what he does. He asks me questions. He asks me the *damnedest* questions. There's no special penalty involved in giving him wrong answers or no answers—except the pressure of the question itself. He's not selling anything in particular, and what he asks may or may not reveal what he thinks is a right answer: I just don't know. But he keeps on asking questions that nobody else seems to ask, about all kinds of commonplace things and ideas. Why are our ground vehicles streamlined only where we can see them? Why is it I can walk, say, two miles down the boulevard howling curses, and/or punching a woman, but if I wear nothing but three yards of blue silk tied to my left forearm and carry a peacock feather, even if I walk sedately, I would be picked up in the first hundred and fifty yards? Why is it that most of our power plants are that category of machine called "heat engines," yet nobody seems to have designed one which can operate without a cooling system— that is, a device designed to dissipate heat? Why does society go to such extremes to protect the sacred life of an unborn child, and then send him off when he is seventeen to get his head blown off? Why, when the Health Department of a sophisticated modern city discovers an epidemic, and makes plans for a publicity campaign to stop it, does it find its funds cut in two? (The epidemic is venereal disease, but that isn't an answer—is it?) Anyway, he keeps on asking me these questions, and all too often I have to wag my head and say, well, sir, you see . . . uh.

One of his questions, then, is "Why don't your superhumans, your heroic fighters, leaders, battlers for good and against evil, so seldom have a sex life—or, indeed, sex organs?" Now, I don't know if Philip José Farmer has a Man from Mars like mine, but a book like *A Feast Unknown* is his riproaring answer—sure they have, and they refuse to be responsible for the misstatements of their bowdlerizing biographers. And if a man has been brought up by apes, he will eat like an ape and play sexually like an ape, and carry no burden of guilt for it, and will still continue to be a superman.

One of the most interesting aspects of this book is the absolutely direct and unconcealed connection between sex and violence. Surely it takes no specially trained perceptions to understand that the popularity of violence in the popular media is invariably a seasoning for sex, whenever it is not a substitute for it. If Farmer says nothing else in a work like this—and he says many other things—he makes it clear that unlimited violence coupled with unlimited sex is an unlimited absurdity. There is nothing in the pattern he presents that shakes my basic conviction that people who get enough sex—and enough is like enough food, enough water—cannot be obsessed by it and will need no substitutes, including violence. This is the healthy, constructive aspect of the new freedoms in sexual expression, and long may they wave. Freely enough expressed, described, and secured, human needs cease to be preoccupations, and we can go on to other things. I do not believe that violence is in itself such a need, it is merely the manifestation of denial—denial of food, of shelter, and of the phenomena surrounding procreation. This is the very core of the healthy truth expressed in the slogan, "Make love, not war."

There is one other profundity which, under the hyperbolic "chase" and the swashbuckle, Farmer explored with great acuity, and this is the function of the Nine—his name for something which has preoccupied humanity since it could be called human. It is the awareness of a controlling Presence or Entity of immense resource, merciless power, and a set of inexorable aims against which we mortals (they, of course, are immortal) must be tested. We are to be tested whether we understand those aims or not, and to fail the tests is to incur frightful punishments.

To identify this Power, to isolate its signs and symptoms, to recognize its agents, to comprehend its ends, and to assess its strength has been the basic chore of the philosophers and theologians since the first of them, in his snake-fang beads, glared redly at an approaching thunder-head and clubbed a neighbor in an act of propitiation. Farmer, with his Nine, brings out an extremely important point: that perhaps the ultimate aims of such a power are functionally Neolithic—which says two things: that it is in our blood and bone, and that it is hopelessly outdated—as good a description as any of the human predicament. It is gratifying to explain ourselves with naked apes and territorial imperatives. It is not wise to excuse ourselves with them.

Read *A Feast Unknown*, then, for its sprawling, brawling, shocking, suspenseful, hilarious self, and you will be well repaid in pure entertainment—which is true of all Farmer's work. True also, however, is that Farmer writes in symbols. His plays and his players are natural forces, natural people (by harmony and by contrast) and he is always questioning. He makes you recoil in horror and shock— but always in a manner that makes you ask yourself why you found it horrifying or shocking. He makes you laugh, and you wonder why you laughed; he makes you hope for certain outcomes, and you wonder why. He is, in short, continually asking you questions: questions about marital fidelity, questions about your fixed ideas about sexual practices, about violence, about prejudices—whether they involve eating worms or helping disadvantaged peoples, about clothing and hunting and passports and gratitude, and loving and atomic weapons.

My God. I never thought to ask him. Maybe he's a Man from Mars too.

Theodore Sturgeon
Sherman Oaks, California
1969

Afterword

In the summer of 1969, award winning science fiction author Phillip José Farmer published a short novel entitled *A Feast Unknown*. The publisher was Essex House which specialized in publishing pornographic novels in large type paperbacks. It included a postscript by fellow sci-fi author Theodore Sturgeon. The novel caused quite a stir. Farmer had always been an iconoclast over his entire writing career willing to take risks and to test the limits of propriety in his work. But *A Feast Unknown* was the most sexually explicit novel he had yet published. It also was hyperviolent and dealt with extremely controversial themes.

It was ostensibly the ninth volume in the autobiography of John Cloamby, Lord Grandrith (pronounced "Grunith") who was clearly a pastiche of Edgar Rice Burroughs' creation Tarzan of the Apes. His antagonist in the story was one Doctor James "Doc" Caliban who was clearly a pastiche of 1930s pulp hero, Doc Savage, whose adventures were primarily written by Lester Dent under the Street & Smith house name "Kenneth Robeson." But these two new characters were *not* like the iconic heroes upon whom they were based.

Burroughs' jungle lord was conceived as the exemplar of the noble savage raised in the wild by apes apart from the corrupting influence of human society. Doc Savage, on the other hand, was raised by scientists and other experts to be a renaissance man shaped by the highest ideals, education, and training available in modern civilization. They were classic good guys who embodied virtue, temperance, restraint, and moral rectitude as defined from their dialectically opposed perspectives. The ordinary faults and foibles of lesser men did not burden them. They were above all of that.

Farmer decided to depict his pastiches more realistically. Heroes were idealized in American culture. They were caricatures of human beings lacking the baser urges that plague mankind in general. Farmer challenged this sanitized image of the hero; it was his intention to deal with themes Burroughs and Dent would not have dared portray.

Lord Grandrith had the mind and personality of a man who was just a hair's breadth away from a wild animal. He had no compunction about disobeying political authority or killing his enemies in gruesome ways. He also had no hang-ups about sexuality and admitted to experimenting with masturbation, bestiality, and even homosexual activity during his feral upbringing. Furthermore, he did many things in his life that civilized people would have found disgusting, but which would have been second nature to the apes among whom he lived.

Doc Caliban was depicted as a Nietzschean superman who exploited his physical and mental abilities to achieve whatever ends suited him with little regard for other lesser human beings. In fairness, this was largely a side effect of an immortality elixir that he and Grandrith were receiving from the ancient order of the Nine, the secret rulers of the world. Prior to the events in *Feast* he seems to have been very much like the Doc Savage of the pulps, at least outwardly. In private he maintained an incestuous affair with his own cousin Trish Wilde and in one situation killed a woman who had essentially raped him. It was clear Farmer's Doc Caliban was not the self-effacing do-gooder Lester Dent had written about in the 1930s.

In his postscript, Theodore Sturgeon claimed Farmer was doing a send up of the pulp heroes who were undergoing a paperback renaissance at that time. As he put it, "ultimate sex combined with ultimate violence is ultimate absurdity." He saw *Feast* as just Phil Farmer's idea of a pulp story. Many other critics more or less agreed with this assessment. When it was first published, *A Feast Unknown* was seen among Farmer's fans and reviewers as an aberration: an excessively vulgar and disturbing story intended to shock and titillate, but of little importance in the grand scheme of his work.

With several decades of perspective behind us, including a large oeuvre of Farmer's subsequent work in the pulp realm, I think we need to reassess the meaning of *A Feast Unknown* and its place in his lifetime of writing.

Farmer's fiction was always preoccupied by sexuality: human and otherwise. His was not a prurient concern but more that of a biologist, an anthropologist, or a depth psychologist. He tried to portray sex as an integral part of life and of storytelling. Phil's portrayals were not "clinical" or merely mechanical. Nor were they particularly erotic. He tried to get behind what sexuality meant to his characters and how it functioned in his stories. Sex was often something that "just happened" to his characters in the course of the plot and was not exploited to titillate the reader.

This attitude was present in *A Feast Unknown*. Grandrith's tales of sex play and bestiality before—and after—meeting his wife Clio are told in a matter-of-fact manner. His incestuous coupling with his cousin Trish Wilde is something that Grandrith says made little or no sense in context. It was a spontaneous act that was neither planned nor intended by the participants. It just happened. The casual sexual dalliances between the candidates for immortality at the stronghold of the Nine were likewise spontaneous results of the isolation from one's real life and the nudity that the Nine demanded as signs of full submission of the candidates. The Nine required loyalty from them over and above all other allegiances, including spouses and families. Even the bizarre sexual cannibalism that is the tribute paid to the Nine for the elixir of immortality makes sense as the trading of one's natural relationships based on sex and its consequences (i.e., marriage and family) for immortal life in submission to the Nine. The painful mutilations reminded the candidates they had forsaken even the most deeply personal relationships in order to live forever.

Some commentators found the partial castration of the male candidates and the clitoridectomy of the females revolting, but they should be reminded that both male and female circumcision—which are forms of genital mutilation—have been rituals that are practiced by many cultures even today. Male circumcision is considered a *mitzvah* among most Jews and a *sunnah* by many Muslims. And the horrible mutilation of women in female circumcision for allegedly religious and moral reasons is an ongoing problem in the Third

World. The sacrifices required by the Nine were intended by Farmer to mimic and satirize these practices.

In many ways the use of sexuality in *Feast* is typically Farmerian, albeit more explicit than his earlier work. It is significant that in 1969, as an award-winning science fiction author, Farmer published this work with a company, Essex House, which was more tolerant of explicit material than his usual publishers. (It is possible that he was deliberately mimicking Kurt Vonnegut's fictional science fiction writer Kilgore Trout who was only able to get his work in print by pornographic publishers.) There were subsequent printings of *Feast* for popular consumption, starting with the 1980 Playboy Books edition (by the time of the 1983 reprint, Playboy had been acquired by Berkley), as well as a mass market release in the UK.

Community standards have changed quite a bit over forty-plus[1] years and now the content of *Feast* would not trouble most mainstream publishers.

Phil was a little ahead of his time in the explicitness of what he wrote, but I think the use of sex in his stories—including *Feast*—was consistent with his previous work.

One thing considered very controversial in 1969 was the mental illness that afflicted Grandrith and Caliban, in which they became sexually aroused with violence and achieved orgasm by killing. Many readers were disturbed by this, yet this mental disorder phenomenon was something well known among criminal psychologists for almost a century.

Some people—mostly men—derive sexual pleasure from torturing, raping, and killing other people. Jack the Ripper was the most notorious of these criminals. He has been retrospectively dubbed the first serial killer of modern times.

The concept of the serial killer was unknown in 1969. It came to public awareness in the 1970s especially after the arrest and trial of Ted Bundy. The concept is attributed to former FBI Special Agent Robert Ressler, who was the basis for the character of agent Will Grant in the Hannibal Lecter stories by Thomas Harris.

In *Feast*, Grandrith and Doc Caliban were the sons of Jack the Ripper by different mothers. This was no accident. Farmer wanted

---

[1] This afterword was originally published in 2012 in the Titan Books reprint.

AFTERWORD

to associate his protagonists with the same psychosexual dynamics as Jack the Ripper, which he considered an exaggeration of the pleasure that readers get from adventure fiction. Farmer knew that the appeal of the action hero was the vicarious thrill evoked in the reader by the story. That thrill in Freudian terms was libidinous and had to have a sexual component. More modern heroes in the 1960s like James Bond were openly portrayed as sexually active and Farmer followed the stereotype by portraying this as typical for men engaged in adventurous lifestyles.

Both Tarzan and Doc Savage were portrayed in their original stories as loving the thrill of adventure. Many times, Doc Savage said very clearly in the "Super Sagas" that he engaged in the fight to "right wrongs" for the thrill of it. Farmer was just letting us in on the dirty secret of what we really loved about our heroes and what would have motivated them in real life to take such great risks.

The particular aberration from which Lord Grandrith and Doc Caliban suffer is depicted as temporary due to the longevity elixir, but it is a direct consequence of their seeking immortality. In the story, the Nine demand absolute obedience from their candidates with no room for personal conscientious objection. Grandrith and Caliban loathe their aberration, but isn't it commensurate with the Faustian bargain they have made? They traded away everything in order to avoid their own deaths. Now it is only death that can give them the ultimate pleasure.

In the end, the climactic battle between them leads Grandrith and Caliban to break with the Nine. Their bond of blood as brothers comes to mean more to them than immortality itself. After they realize this, the strange orgasm-with-killing aberration goes away. They regain a moral focus and direct their wrath toward the annihilation of the Nine themselves. Their anger is redirected to the deaths of specific people for a specific moral reason.

We find similar rebellion against all powerful authorities in several of Farmer's works, such as the World of Tiers series, the Riverworld books, *The Lovers,* and *Dayworld.* Farmer rejected conformity and the claims of absolute power by one set of human beings over another. That is why so many of his books have Ragnarök—the death of the gods—as the ultimate solution to human problems.

Arthur C. Sippo

This brings us to the Farmerian hero. As already noted, Farmer was distrustful of authority and its claims on the individual, especially when such authority claimed to be ancient, venerable, and irresistible. It is no accident that the meeting room of the Nine is called "the Table of the Gods" and among the Nine are characters that seem to represent various deities from various mythologies and religions. XauXaz represented Odin, the Father God of the Norse Pantheon. Anana was like the Mother Goddess of Wicca and other nature religions. Iwaldi was like the Trickster archetype found in Amerindian lore. And another member of the Nine was described as "a Hebrew born shortly before 1 A.D." who sounds suspiciously like Jesus.

Every Farmerian hero from Peter Jairus Frigate, Sir Richard Francis Burton, and Samuel Clemens (the *Riverworld* series), to Two Hawks (*Two Hawks from Earth*), to Kickaha (the *World of Tiers* series), to Hadon (the *Ancient Opar/Khokarsa* series), to Jeff Caird (the *Dayworld* trilogy,) to John Gribardsun (*Time's Last Gift*) is a skeptic and a rebel who is not bound by social convention and who eventually takes a moral stand against the powers that be.

The Farmerian Hero is a man of personal integrity who stands up for what he believes and who does what he thinks is necessary even when it flies in the face of convention.

Lord Grandrith clearly has Phil's greatest sympathy in *Feast* because he is a human being unsullied by social mores. Doc Caliban is too inhibited by his civilized upbringing to be completely free until Grandrith "kills" him and he is "resurrected" to a new life as a rebel against the Nine.

Once again this is a theme that runs through virtually *all* of Farmer's work. *Feast* is not an aberration in his oeuvre, but rather is typically Farmerian.

There are several things in *Feast* that remain somewhat shocking even today. For example, early on in the story one of the natives at Grandrith's African estate rapes Grandrith's pet dog as revenge against the animal's master. Grandrith speaks about coprophagia (the eating of animal droppings) as something he did to survive, alleging that Zebra spoor was "almost relishable." He also describes a long standing sexual relationship with a female leopard named Kuta who eventually broke it off with him because "I could not give her cubs." And who could forget that climactic image of a naked Lord Grandrith and Doc Caliban wrestling with each other on the narrow ledge leading to the lair of the Nine with their erections crossing each other like swords *en garde*. I think these and some other references were intended to be a playful wink from Farmer who was pulling our legs. There was one scene at the end where Grandrith finishes off the villain Noli by making a strategic cut around his rectum and throwing him across the room, pulling out twenty-four feet of intestine. While this makes an evocative image, it is anatomically absurd and ultimately humorous in a grisly sort of way. I guess Farmer thought as long as he was pushing the envelope on 1960s standards he might as well have some fun with it.

But we should also recognize things like this actually do happen in the world. Bestiality, coprophagia, draw-and-quartering, and brutal encounters happen far more often than polite society wants to acknowledge. Philip José Farmer was well read in the dark side of human nature and in the practices of people in primitive cultures. While he may have had fun with his civilized readers, he was using horrific events that are not as uncommon as we would like to think.

Farmer also has Grandrith accidentally destroy a statue (i.e., a graven image) of Tarzan of the Apes that is being erected in the British town of Greystoke during the climactic car chase at the end of *Feast*. I think this is another "wink" from Phil letting us know he is deliberately destroying an idolized view of Tarzan with this story.

But we should not conclude he was just trashing Tarzan. Farmer grew up reading these stories and he would never do that. He was instead exploring the idea of the feral hero beyond the boundaries of our censorious and bourgeois imaginations. Grandrith is more like what a Tarzan would really be like. Doc Caliban, in his arrogance and lack of concern for others, is more like what a person bred to be a superman would become. In the end, Farmer loved these characters and redeemed them at a price. They needed to reassert their allegiance to personal moral integrity and stop being the standard bearers for the immortal secret elite who ruled the world from the depths of its past.

What no one knew in 1969 was that for several years Philip José Farmer had been doing research in Burke's *Peerage* trying to find the *real* Lord Greystoke. Phil later claimed that he had done so, and he published a series of articles and a full blown biography of the real jungle lord called *Tarzan Alive*.[2] In that same book, he found links between the ape-man and Doc Savage, along with other adventure characters such as Wolf Larsen, Ned Land, Sherlock Holmes, Nero Wolfe, Sam Spade, and The Shadow. This was the beginning of the Wold Newton Family, which has become a preoccupation of many writers and fans over the years.[3]

A Feast Unknown was the first major work in what would become known as Philip José Farmer's "Pulp Period." It is obvious in retrospect his research for the two biographies informed his writing of *A Feast Unknown*. In fact, the novel was clearly inspired by his research and the messages that Phil had been conveying in his work up to that time.

In his Pulp Period, Farmer would write several novels and stories (with some later completed by others with his and his estate's permission, based on prose fragments, outlines, and notes), all consequent of his seminal work in *A Feast Unknown*.[4]

- *Lord of the Trees* (Secrets of the Nine: Lord Grandrith novel, 1970)*
- *The Mad Goblin* (Secrets of the Nine: Doc Caliban novel, 1970)*
- *Lord Tyger* (novel, 1970)
- *Tarzan Alive: A Definitive Biography of Lord Greystoke* (Wold Newton biography, 1972)
- *Time's Last Gift* (a Wold Newton Prehistory novel, 1972)
- *The Other Log of Phileas Fogg* (Wold Newton novel, 1973)* [Meteor House edition includes Jules Verne's *Around the World in Eighty Days*]

---

[2] *Tarzan Alive: A Definitive Biography of Lord Greystoke*, Doubleday & Co., 1972; University of Nebraska Press Bison Books, 2006.

[3] In "A Tale of Two Universes," the afterword to *The Monster on Hold* (fourth in the Secrets of the Nine series, Meteor House, 2021), Win Scott Eckert discusses the similarities and differences between Grandrith and Greystoke, and Caliban and Savage, as well as how the Lord Grandrith/Doc Caliban novels relate to Wold Newton continuity.

[4] Those titles currently part of Meteor House's series of Farmer reissues are marked with an asterisk.

AFTERWORD

- *Doc Savage: His Apocalyptic life* (Wold Newton biography, 1973)*
- *The Adventure of the Peerless Peer* (Wold Newton novel: Sherlock Holmes/Lord Greystoke novel, 1974) [Rewritten as "The Adventure of the Three Madmen"—with Mowgli replacing Greystoke—in the collection *The Grand Adventure* (1984)]
- *Hadon of Ancient Opar* (Wold Newton Prehistory novel in the *Ancient Opar/Khokarsa* cycle, 1974)
- *Flight to Opar* (Wold Newton Prehistory novel in the *Khokarsa* cycle, 1976)* [Meteor House edition has restored text not included in original publication]
- *Greatheart Silver* (short story collection, 1982)*
- *Escape from Loki: Doc Savage's First Adventure* (authorized Doc Savage novel, 1991)
- *Tarzan and the Dark Heart of Time* (authorized Tarzan novel, 1999)* [original title *The Dark Heart of Time: A Tarzan Novel*]
- *The Evil in Pemberley House* (Wold Newton novel about "Doc Savage's" daughter, Patricia Wildman; with Win Scott Eckert, 2009)*
- *The Song of Kwasin* (Wold Newton Prehistory novel in the *Ancient Opar/Khokarsa* cycle; with Christopher Paul Carey, 2012)*
- *Exiles of Kho* ((Wold Newton Prehistory novella in the *Ancient Opar/Khokarsa* cycle by Christopher Paul Carey, 2012)*
- *The Scarlet Jaguar* (Wold Newton novella about Patricia Wildman by Win Scott Eckert, 2013)*
- *Hadon, King of Opar* (Wold Newton Prehistory novella in the *Ancient Opar/Khokarsa* cycle by Christopher Paul Carey, 2015)*
- *Blood of Ancient Opar* (Wold Newton Prehistory novella in the *Ancient Opar/Khokarsa* cycle by Christopher Paul Carey, 2016)*
- *The Monster on Hold* (Secrets of the Nine: Doc Caliban novel; with Win Scott Eckert, 2021)*

So, *A Feast Unknown* does not stand apart from Phil Farmer's literary legacy. It is the bridge between his earlier work and stories from his Pulp Period. We must understand *Feast* in order to properly comprehend his foray into the pulp world.

One final question is where Farmer got the title for his novel. It's based upon this short erotic poem by May Swenson, an American poet well known for her love poetry, which appears in the front matter of every edition of *Feast*:

> an Evolution
> Strange
> two tongues Touch
> exchange
> a Feast unknown
> to stone
> or tree or beast
> —May Swenson

A Feast Unknown was an integral part of Phillip José Farmer's literary output and marked the beginning of his Pulp Period and of the Wold Newton Family. It was not a mere indulgence in pornographic literature, but carried on the themes about human sexuality, morals, heroism, and distrust of authority that Farmer wrote about all of his life.

I disagree with Ted Sturgeon. Phil Farmer's message was not that "ultimate sex combined with ultimate violence is ultimate absurdity." Rather, I think it was that "ultimate allegiance to anything, person, persons, nations, or ideologies other than to one's own moral integrity is ultimate absurdity." In the end, even the greatest heroes of popular literature are merely human. They are sexual beings and through sex they form allegiances of family and blood to which they must remain loyal. They must not trade their moral responsibility to anyone else, even to attain the goal of eternal life. Both man in his natural state and man in his most civilized state cannot shirk moral responsibilities.

—Arthur C. Sippo MD, MPH
4 February 2012

LORD OF THE TREES

Volume X of
The Memoirs of Lord Grandrith

A Note From Philip José Farmer

Although the editors of this book insist upon publishing this work as a novel under my by-line, it is actually Volume X of the Memoirs of Lord Grandrith, as edited by me for publication. The British spellings and the anglicisms of Lord Grandrith have been changed by me for an easier understanding by American readers.

The location of the caves of the Nine and several other places have purposely been made inexact. This is for the benefit of any reader who might try to find these places.

LORD OF THE TREES

The Nine must have marked me off as dead beyond doubt.

I don't know whether or not the pilot of the fighter jet saw me fall into the ocean. If he did, he probably did not fly down for a closer look. He would have assumed that, if the explosion of my amphibian did not kill me, the fall surely would. After hurtling twelve hundred feet, I should have been smashed flat against the surface of the Atlantic off the coast of the West African nation of Gabon. The waters would be as hard as Sheffield steel when my body struck.

If the pilot had known that men had survived falls from airplanes at even greater heights, he might have swooped low over the surface just to make certain that I was not alive. In 1942, a Russian fell twenty-two thousand feet without a parachute into a snow-covered ravine and lived. And other men have fallen two thousand feet or higher into water or snow and lived. These were freak occurrences, of course.

The pilot would have reported that the twin-engine propellered amphibian I was flying to the *Parc National du Petit Loango* had gone up in a ball of flame at the first pass. The .50 caliber machine guns or rockets or whatever he had used had hit the fuel tanks and burning bits of wreckage had scattered everywhere. Among the bits was my body.

I recovered consciousness a few seconds later. Blue was screaming around me. My half-naked body was as cold as if the wind were ripping through my intestines. The explosion had ripped off most of my clothing or else they had been torn off when I went through the nose of the craft. I was falling toward the bright sea, though, at first I sometimes thought I was falling toward the sky. I whirled over and over, seeing the rapidly dwindling silvery jet speeding inland and the widely dispersed and flaming pieces describing smoky arcs.

I also saw the white rim of surf and flashing white beaches and, beyond, the green of the bush jungle.

There was no time or desire to think ironic thoughts then, of course. But if there had been, I would have thought how ironic it was that I was going to die only a few miles from my birthplace. If I had thought I was going to die, that is. I was still living, and until the final moment itself that is what I will always tell myself. *I live.*

I must have fallen about two hundred feet when I succeeded in spreading out my legs and arms. I have done much sky diving for fun and for survival value. It was this that enabled me to flatten out and gain a stable attitude. I was slowing down my rate of descent somewhat by presenting as wide an area as possible to the air, acting as my own parachute. And then I slipped into the vertical position during the last fifty feet, and I entered the water like a knife with my hands forming the knife's tip.

I struck exactly right. Even so, the impact knocked me out. I awoke coughing saltwater out of my nose and mouth. But I was on the surface, and if I had any broken bones or torn muscles, I did not feel them.

There was no sign of the killer plane or of my craft. The sky had swallowed one and the sea the other.

The shore was about a mile away. Between it and me were the fins of at least two sharks.

There wasn't much use trying to swim around the sharks. They would hear and smell me even if I made a wide detour. So I swam toward them, though not before I had assured myself that I had a knife. Most of my clothing had been ripped off, but my belt with its sheathed knife was still attached to me. This was an American knife with a five-inch blade, excellent for throwing. I left it in the sheath until I saw one of the fins swerve and drive toward me. Then I drew it out and placed it between my teeth.

The other fin continued to move southward.

The shark may have just happened to turn toward me in the beginning, but an increase of speed showed that it had detected me. The fin stayed on the surface, however, and turned to my right to circle me. I swam on, casting glances behind me. It was a great white shark, a species noted for attacking men. This one was wary; it circled me three times before deciding to rush me. I turned when it was about twenty feet from me. The surface water just ahead of it boiled, and it turned on its side just before trying to seize my leg. Or perhaps it only intended to make a dry run to get a closer look at what might be a dangerous prey.

I pulled my legs up and stabbed at it with both hands holding the hilt of the knife. The skin of the shark is as tough as cured hippo hide and covered with little jags—placoid scales—that can tear the skin off a man if he so much as rubs lightly against it. My only experience in fighting sharks was during World War II when my boat was sunk in the waters of the East Indian Ocean. The encounter with a freshwater shark in an African lake is fictional, the result of the sometimes over-romantic imagination of my biographer. Fortunately, my arms were out of the water and so unimpeded by the fluid. I heaved myself up to my waist and drove down with the knife and rammed it at least three inches into the corpse-colored eye. Blood spurted, and the shark raced away so swiftly that it almost tore the knife loose from my hands.

Its tail did curve out enough to scrape across my belly, and my blood was mingling with its blood.

I expected the shark to come back. Even if my knife had pierced that tiny brain, it would be far from dead, and the odor of blood would drive it mad.

It came back as swiftly as a torpedo and as deadly. I dived this time and was enclosed in a distorted world the visible radius of which was a few feet. Out of the distortion something fast as death almost hit me, and went by, and I shoved the knife up into the belly. But the tip only penetrated about an inch, and this time the knife was pulled from my grip. I had to dive for it at once; without it I was helpless. I caught it just before it sank out of reach of eye and hand, and I swam to the surface. I looked both ways and saw a shadow speeding toward me. Then another shadow caught up with it, and blood boiled out in a cloud that hid both sharks. I swam away with as little splash as possible, hoping that other sharks would not be drawn in by the blood and the thrash of the battle.

Before I had gone a half-mile, I saw three fins slicing the water to my left, but they were intent on following their noses to where the blood was flowing, where, as the Yanks say, the action was.

It was a few minutes to twelve P.M. when my plane blew up. About sixteen minutes later, according to my wristwatch, I reached the shore and staggered across the beach to the shade and a hiding place in a bush. The fall, the fight with the shark, and the swimming for a mile at near top speed, had taken some energy from me. I walked past thousands of sea gulls and pelicans and storks, which moved away from me without too much alarm. These would be the great-great-great-grandchildren of the birds that I had known when I was young. The almost completely landlocked lagoon on the beach was no longer there. It had been filled in and covered over years ago by the deposit of sand and dirt from the little river nearby and by the action of the Benguela Current. The original shore, where I had roamed as a boy, was almost two miles inland.

The jungle looked unchanged. No humans had settled down here. Gabon is still one of the least populated countries of Africa.

Inland were the low hills where a broad tongue of the tall closed-canopy equatorial forest had been home for me and The Folk and the myriad animals and insects I knew so well. Most of the jungle in what is now the National Park of the Little Loango is really bush. The rain forest grows only on the highlands many miles inland except for the freakish outthrust of high hill which distinguishes this coastal area.

After resting an hour, I got up and walked inland. I was headed toward the place where the log house of my human parents had once been, where I was born, where the Nine first interfered with my life and started me on that unique road, the highlights of which my biographer has presented in highly romanticized forms.

The jungle here looks like what the civilized person thinks of as jungle, when he thinks of it at all. His idea, of course, is mostly based on those very unrealistic and very bad movies made about me.

Knife in hand, I walked quietly through bush. Even if it wasn't the true jungle of my inland home, I still felt about ten times as happy and at ease as I do in London or even in the comparatively unpopulated, plenty-of-elbow-room environs of my Cumberland estate. The trees and bushes here were noisy with much monkey life, too many insects, and an abundance of snakes, water shrews, mongooses, and small wild cats or long-necked servals. I saw a scale-armored anteating pangolin scuttling ahead of me and glimpsed a tiny furry creature which might or might not have been a so-called "bushbaby." The bird life made the trees colorful and the air raucous. The salt air blowing in from the sea and the sight of the familiar plants made me tingle all over.

As I neared the site of the buildings my father had built eighty-two years ago, I saw that the mangrove swamp to the north had spread out. Its edge was only a quarter of a mile to my left.

I cast around and within a few minutes found the slight mounds which marked the place where I had been born. Once there had been a one-room house of logs and, next to it, a log building just as large, a storehouse. My biographer neglected to mention the store-room, because he ignored details if they did not contribute to the swift development of the story. But, since he did state that an enormous amount of supplies was landed with my parents, it must have been obvious to the reader that the one-room house could not have held more than a fraction of the materials.

Both buildings had fallen into a heap of dead wood and had been covered up by sand and dirt blown by the sea winds and by mud pouring down from the low ridge inland of the buildings. The ridge was no longer there; it had eroded years ago. A bush fire had taken away all the vegetation on it and then the rains had cut it down before new vegetation could grow.

On one side, six feet under the surface, would be four graves, but in this water-soaked, insect-infested soil the decayed bones had been eaten long ago.

I had known what to expect. The last time I'd been here, in 1947, the ravages of fifty-nine years had almost completed the destruction. It was only sentiment that had brought me back here. I may be infra-human in many of my attitudes, but I am still human enough to feel some sentiment toward my birthplace.

I had intended to stand there for a few minutes and think about my dead parents and the other two buried beside them. But mostly about what I had done inside the cabin with the books and the tools I had found in 1898, when I did not know what a book or a tool or a chronological date was, let alone the words for them in English or in any human tongue. And I especially wanted to recreate the day when I had first seen the long ash-blonde hair of Clio Jeanne de Carriol.

There were others with her, of course, and they were the first white-skinned males I had ever seen, outside of the illustrated books I had found in the storehouse. But Clio was a woman, and I was twenty, so my eyes were mainly for her. I did not know nor would have cared that she was the daughter of a retired college teacher. Nor that he had named his daughter Clio after the Muse of History. Nor that they were descended from Huguenots who had fled France after the Revocation of the Edict of Nantes and established plantations and horse farms in Georgia, Virginia, and Maryland. All I knew about the world outside a fifty-mile square area was what I had tried to understand in those books, and most of that I just could not grasp.

I suppose I was lost in thought for a little more than a minute. Then I turned a little to the east, because I'd heard a very faint and unidentifiable noise, and I saw a flash up in a tree about fifty yards away.

I dived into a bush and rolled into a slight depression. The report of the rifle and the bullet striking about ten feet from me came a second later. Three heavy machine guns and a number of automatic rifles raked through the bush. Somebody twenty yards to the north shouted, and a grenade blew up the earth exactly over the site of the storehouse.

I had to get out, and swiftly, but I could not move without being cut down, the fire was so heavy.

Leave it to the Nine to do a thorough job.

They had found out that I was flying a plane from Port-Gentil, ostensibly to Setté Cama. They—their agents, rather—had figured that I might be stopping off at the Parc National du Petit Loango for a sentimental pilgrimage. Actually, my main purpose was to leave the plane there and set off on foot across the continent to the mountains in Uganda. It would take me a long time to make the approach to the secret caves of the Nine, but it was better to travel through the jungle across the central part of Africa than to fly anywhere near it. In the jungle, I am silent and unseen, and even the Nine cannot distract me except by accident.

But the Nine had sent that outlaw fighter jet to shoot me out of the sky. And, as a backup for Death, they had arranged an ambush at my birthplace. When the jet pilot had reported in, as he surely must have, that I had gone down with my plane, the Nine had not pulled off their ambushers at once. I suppose they may have had orders to wait there a week. The Nine always were enthusiastic for overkill and overcaution, especially when one of their own—a traitor—was to be taken care of.

Even so, they must have been surprised, they must not have really expected me to come along so soon after being burned to death or smashed flat against the ocean and then eaten by sharks. But they had maintained a very good silence. The wind was blowing from the sea, so I had not heard or smelled them. I think I caught them by surprise; they may not have been sure that I was the one for whom they were waiting.

The grenade was close enough to half-deafen me but I was not confused or immobilized. I rolled away and then crawled toward the men shooting at me. Or shooting where they thought I should be. Gouts of dirt fell over my naked back and on my head. Bushes bent, and leaves fell on me. Another grenade exploded near the first. Bullets screamed off, and pieces of bark fell before me. But I did not believe they could see me. I would have been stitched with lead in a few seconds.

One thing, some of them must have seen that I was only armed with a knife, and that would make them brave.

Suddenly, there was silence except for a man shouting in English. He was telling them to form a ring, to advance slowly to contract the ring, and to fire downward if they saw me. They must not fire into each other. They must shoot at my legs, bring me down, and then finish me off.

If I'd been in his place, I would have done the same. It was an admirable plan and seemed to have a one hundred percent chance of success. I was as disgusted as I had time for. I should have approached more cautiously and scouted the area. I had made the same mistake they did, in essence, except that they were better equipped to rectify theirs.

I kept on going. I did not know how many men they had. I had determined that ten weapons had been firing. But others might be withholding their fire. It would take them some time to form a ring, since they had all been on one side of me. In this thick bush, they would have to proceed slowly and keep locating each other by calling out.

Men circled around swiftly and noisily. I could smell them; there were ten men on that side. So that meant there had to be as many or more ahead of me. Some had been holding back their fire.

I looked upward. I was close to the tree from which the flash had come as a sniper shifted his rifle. He was still about twenty feet up on a branch and waiting for me to make a break for it. I scrutinized the other trees around me for more snipers, but he seemed to be the only one.

I sprang out from under the broad leaves of the elephant's ear and threw my knife upward. It was a maneuver that had to be done without hesitation and which involved much danger, since it meant I would be revealed, if only for a moment.

It was, however, unexpected. And the only one who saw me before I ducked back under the plant was the sniper. His surprise did not last long. He saw me and the knife about the same time, and then the knife caught him in the throat. The rifle fell out of his hands and onto the top of a bush. He sagged forward but was held from falling by the rope around his waist, tied to the trunk. The knife had made a chunking and the rifle a thrashing as it slid through the branches of the bush. But the shouts of the men had covered it up.

The rifle was a Belgian FN light automatic rifle using the 7.62 mm cartridge. It could be set for semi-automatic or automatic fire, and its magazine when full contained twenty rounds. I set it for automatic fire, since I was likely to be needing a hose-like action in thick foliage. It was regrettable that I did not have the knife, but, for the moment, I would have to do without it. I did not want to climb up to the body and so expose myself to fire from below. At any moment one of them might see the corpse and know that I was on the loose with the firearm.

The voices of the men to the east came closer. The ones behind me and on my sides were not closing in so swiftly. One, or more, had grenades, and I especially had to watch out for them.

My heart was pumping hard, and I was quivering with the ecstasy of the hunt. Whether I am the hunter or the hunted, I feel the same. There is a delicious sense of peril; the most precious thing is at stake. You, a living being, may be dead very shortly. And since my life could last forever, or over thirty thousand years anyway, I have much more than most people to lose. But I didn't think of that. I am as willing to risk it now as I will be thirty millennia from now, if I live that long.

When the nearest man was within ten feet, he had a man on his right about twenty feet away and a man on his left about thirty. He had turned his head to say something to the man behind him. The butt of my rifle drove through the branches of a bush into his throat.

He fell backward and then I was on him and had squeezed his neck with my hands. I took his knife and a full magazine, which I carried clamped under my left arm. But another man about twenty feet behind him had noticed that his predecessor had disappeared.

He spoke in English with an Italian accent. "Hey, Brodie, where are you? You all right?"

I answered back in an imitation of Brodie's voice. "I fell down in this damned bush!"

The man advanced cautiously, then stopped and said, "Stand up so I can see you!"

I put on Brodie's green digger's hat—it was several sizes too small—and rose far enough so he could see the hat and the upper part of my face. He said something and came toward me, and I threw Brodie's knife into his solar plexus.

At the same, there was a yell from behind me. The dead sniper had been discovered.

The leader, bawling out in a Scots English, told everyone to stand still. They were not to start firing in a panic, or they would be killing each other. And they were to call out, in order, identifying themselves.

I waited, and when the time came, I called out with Brodie's voice and then the voice of the Italian. I did not know his name, and the leader could have tripped me up there. But he gave each man's name himself before requiring an answer.

I counted thirty-two men. Some of them were, like the Italian, backing up the enclosers in case I should break loose.

By then I had gotten close enough to the man on my left to cut his jugular vein from behind with the edge of the knife.

It seemed to me that I had an aisle of escape. I could get away and be miles inland, and once I was in the rain forest of the higher lands, I could not be caught.

But I have pride. I wanted to teach the Nine another lesson and also cut down the numbers opposing me. Also, it seemed to me their base must be nearby and that they must have a powerful short-wave transceiver there.

Still, there are times to be discreet, and this was one. I went on into the jungle. I had gotten about fifty yards when I heard muffled shouts. They had discovered the bodies, and they would be scared now. No doubt many, if not all of them, knew who I was. They would have known my abilities in the jungle by report and now they knew by experience. Moreover, adding to the desperation at having me loose would be the desperation at having to report failure to the Nine. They might as well be dead if I escaped.

I tried to figure where the radio would most likely be stationed. At one time, I could have told you, with my eyes shut, exactly where every tree and bush and open area were. But the place had changed too much; I might as well be in completely new territory. Finally, I took to the trees.

I carried the FN strapped over my shoulder, and in the foliage at the top I removed it. I could see ten of the thirty-one; the others were hidden in the bush. Nine were congregated around a tall thin man with a thick black moustache. His hands flew and his mouth worked as he gave orders.

I had seen him before, and now that I recreated his voice in my mind, I remembered it, too. I had heard it in the caves where the Nine hold their annual ceremonies, where the members of their ancient organization come for the grisly rites they must endure in order to get the elixir of youth. He had not had a moustache then and he had not been wearing clothes and it had been ten years ago, so I did not immediately recognize him.

LORD OF THE TREES

His name was James Murtagh, a name not too different from his real name or that of his notorious father. He was born in 1881 in Meiringen, Switzerland, but was raised from the age of eight in Wales. Like his father, he was an extremely talented mathematician, if not a genius, and he had taught higher mathematics at Oxford and the University of Tallinn. He looked as if he was about forty, so I suppose that it was in 1921 that he was invited by the Nine to join them.

Murtagh had not said a word about himself to me or to anyone that I knew. But the Countess Clara Aekjaer, the beautiful Danish Valkyrie who was my companion during the ceremonies over the years, knew much about him. She told me everything she knew. Perhaps she had been told to do so by the Nine, who were grooming me, without my knowing it, to become one of them if one died.

I could have gotten him with a single shot from my FN, but he might be a link to the next one higher up in the chain. So I set the rifle for automatic and sprayed about twelve rounds into the group. Five fell; the others dived into the bush. I dropped the rifle and slid down the tree before they could get reorganized and blast me from the treetops. I went through the bush southward. It did not seem likely that the base for the group would be in the mangrove swamp to the north.

By then the men were firing at the tree I had left. I continued to travel south while the sound of the weapons grew fainter. Then I heard a voice ahead and, a few minutes later, I peered through a bush at a large clearing. It may have been small a few days before, but axes and powersaws had cut trees and bushes down, and a jeep with a winch had dragged off the fallen plants. There were two large helicopters, Bristol 192s, at one end and six tents near my end. Inside the largest tent was radio equipment on a table; three men were by the equipment. An antenna reached high above the tent.

I scouted around the entire perimeter of the camp and found no hidden guards. I also was alert for booby traps and mines. Murtagh impressed me as the type of man who would think of such devices and smile while he was setting them. I appreciate that, since I also smile when engaged in similar activities.

There was a good chance that Murtagh would send men packing

back to the camp. He would figure that I would know a camp had to be close and would go looking for it. He had not set guards around it because he had not really expected that I would survive the attack by the jet. I had to work fast.

Even though much of the vegetation had been dragged away, there were still clumps of uprooted bushes and the stumps of trees in the clearing. I ran bent over across the clearing, approaching the big tent from its closed rear. There I listened to the operator relay orders from his superior officer. Someone in the group that had tried to ambush me had reported via wireless that I had escaped. So the big short-wave set was transmitting a request for two jets and two more helicopters. These would carry napalm bombs and would bring in more men and dogs.

The code name used for me was Tree Lord, which I thought both appropriate and amusing.

I was puzzled about where the jets and copters could be based. It did not seem likely that they would be at Port-Gentil. This was approximately one hundred and twenty-six miles to the north-east. The men in the tent talked as if they expected the craft in about ten minutes. Somewhere, probably in a man-made clearing in the interior, was a base. Had it been set up some time ago just for me? Or was it a multipurpose base? It seemed more probable that it was multipurpose. Otherwise, why had not all its personnel and machines been sent down here to terminate me?

I went around the side of the tent to the opening. Two shots sent the two officers spinning backward and onto the ground. The operator had a .45 automatic in a holster. But he made no motion toward it. He placed his palms flat against the table and stared at me with his mouth open. His huge round eyes, pale skin, shock of wheat-colored hair, sharp beaky nose, and the ear-phones made him look like a very frightened owl.

"Tell them to cancel the operation," I said. "Tell them I've been killed."

He hesitated, and I stepped closer to him. The muzzle of the rifle was only a few inches from his temple. He gulped and obeyed me.

After he had finished, he stared at me as if he expected me to blow his head off. He had a right to expect it, and I had a right to do it, though I have never bothered about rights as defined by human beings unless they happened to coincide with my beliefs. He was a member of an organization devoted to killing me; he knew it and had taken part in it; he deserved to die.

My own philosophy is simple and practical and not at all based on the idea that life is sacred. If a man is out to kill you, you kill him first. This has nothing to do with the rules of warfare as conducted by nations. When I was a member of the British forces in World War II, I observed the Geneva rules. That is, I did except in two cases, where I had orders from the Nine, and their orders superseded anybody's. In return for giving me a very extended youth, they demanded a high price sometimes. But I had had no qualms about killing the men the Nine wanted out of the way, especially since they were the enemy. If I were to tell you that several of them were the highest and most famous of our enemy, you might find it difficult to believe. Especially since the world believes that they committed suicide to keep from falling into the hands of the Russians.

"Do what I say, and quickly, and I'll spare you," I said. "And if you know anything about me, you know I don't go back on my word."

He gulped and nodded.

"Can you get Dakar?" I said.

He could do so, and he did at once, asking for Brass Bwana. He was operating illegally, of course, and what the authorities at Dakar thought, I did not know or care. The station was at the time out in the desert about thirty miles from Dakar, had been operating on a mobile basis for twenty-six years, and so far the police had not been able to come near it. I had used it when I worked for the Nine but had never told anyone else in the organization about it. Its operators were criminals, loyal to me, because I had rewarded them well. Now they were in contact with the organization that Doc Caliban had used when he was a disciple of the Nine. This station was somewhere in the Vosges and tied in with another in the Black Forest area of Germany.

I would have preferred to talk directly, but I could not do that and be free to look and listen for Murtagh and his men. The first thing I did was to tell the Dakar people that the code name for me was changed and that I would use the next name on the list the next time I contacted them. I also explained, briefly, that I had been forced to contact them through an enemy. I asked for Doc Caliban, using his code name of Brass Bwana, of course. A minute passed, and then Dakar relayed the message that Caliban could not answer himself. But my message would be passed on to him. However, he had left a message for me.

"The goblin has gone mad, and he is our enemy and the enemy of our enemies his former friends. The goblin is holed up, but we are digging him out."

I thanked Dakar and signed off.

"Do you know German?" I asked the operator.

He said he didn't, but he might have been lying. Not that it mattered. He was not likely to know that the goblin had to be Iwaldi, the old dwarf of the Nine. When I say old, I mean very ancient. He was at least ten thousand years old and possibly thirty thousand. If I understood Caliban's phrasing correctly, Iwaldi had gone insane and turned against the others of the Nine, too. Doc Caliban knew where he was and was going after him. Iwaldi was in the castle of Gramzdorf in the Black Forest. Though Caliban and I had been able to find out very little about any of the Nine's secret hideouts, we had discovered that Iwaldi lived at least part of the year in the castle near the village of Gramzdorf. Caliban had gone there with two of his men, recent recruits who were sons of the men who had been his aids in the old days. The fathers were dead now, but the sons had taken their places beside Doc.

I opened the case of the equipment and smashed the tubes with a hammer and ripped the wires out. Then I cut a slit through the back of the tent and ordered Smith, the operator, to step out ahead of me. We went swiftly to another tent which contained a number of firearms and belts on which to carry grenades. I put about seven grenades in hooks on a belt which I had secured across my chest. I tied Smith's hands behind him and secured him to a bush. It took me a minute to toss a grenade into each of the interiors of the two copters from a distance of two hundred feet. They exploded and burned furiously; they were indeed beautiful, though a little awing. I have never gotten over some feeling of awe for the larger machines that mankind makes. I suppose it's the residue of the first impact of civilization on me. When I blew those two fine but deadly machines, I was asserting the defiance of the savage against the complex and bewildering works of the technological man.

"Where is the base camp?" I asked Smith. "Don't stall. I haven't the time to play around."

"It's about thirty miles north-east of here," he said.

There wasn't time to find out if he was lying or not. I went into the bush by the edge of the camp.

The burning gasoline roared so that I could not hear Murtagh and his men, and the smoke was so intense that I could not have smelled them even if they had been upwind. But I could see quite well, and I smiled as I saw the scared or grim faces peeking from around bushes. They were not about to venture into the camp, since I might be waiting to ambush the ambushers.

Murtagh, of course, would wait until the two copters appeared and then bring them down for protection. But he did not do so. At least, not where I had thought he would. Instead, the men walked away. I had gone around them to come up behind them but by the time I got near the north end of camp, I found them gone. They were easy to track, which I did on a parallel path. It was well that I did, since the canny Murtagh had placed four men at two places to catch me if I came loping along after them. Each couple was back to back to make sure that I did not sneak up on them. I still could have wiped them out with short bursts from my concealment, but I did not see any reason to notify Murtagh that I was on to them. I passed them by and presently was alongside the double file of men heading for the beach. Murtagh was in the lead, and four men who kept watching over their shoulders were the rear guard.

Murtagh was about six feet five and had very rounded shoulders and a forehead that bulged out like the prow of a ship. He removed his hat once to wipe a completely bald pate. The hair that rimmed the back of his head was gray. His eyes were set deeply under a bulging supraorbital ridge. His jaws were so outthrust he might have been an aboriginal Australian. His long neck was bent forward so that he always seemed to be sniffing for something, like a snake. The snakishness was emphasized by the steady movement of his face from side to side.

Behind him was a man carrying a flame-thrower and about six men behind him was another man with a flame-thrower.

I went ahead to a point equidistant from both men and then I fired six bursts. The first shattered the equipment on the back of the first man, but the liquid did not catch fire. The men between the first target and the second went down, and then the flame-thrower on the second man exploded in a globe of fire that enveloped two men behind him.

I was away, rolling down a slight slope and then crawling into its bottom and along it until I reached a shallow ravine. The vegetation and the dirt above me whipped and flew as if a meteor stream had struck it. The firepower poured out in my direction was impressive and must have terrified the birds and the monkeys. But I was not hit.

I made a mistake by not killing Murtagh then. I should not have spared him because of wanting to take him prisoner for questioning later. But I did not regret not having killed him. Though I admit quite readily that I've made a mistake or erred, I never regret. What has been always will be and what is is. And what will be is unknown until the proper time.

Five minutes later, two huge helicopters settled down on the beach. The armed men in them got out and took their stations with the others along the edge of the beach and the jungle. Murtagh got new radio equipment from the helicopters, and the men of the Nine were ready to go into business.

My business was to get out as fast as I could, but I did not do so. I had been running so hard and so long from the Nine that I could not resist the temptation to give them even more punishment. I did, however, retreat to the north and into the swamp. I climbed to the top of a mangrove where I could get a good view. It was well that I did. While the men on the ground stayed on the beach, the two helicopters flew inward and dropped six napalm bombs. Two jets came in and shot six explosive rockets at random within a quarter-mile square area. Then they dropped napalm bombs and returned to strafe the jungle near the burning areas. After their ammunition was exhausted, they flew off, presumably to reload for another trip.

If I had been hanging around close to the men on the beach, I would have been burned to an ash. Still, they had no means of knowing that I was there, and it seemed a very inefficient and expensive method of trying to kill me. Not that the Nine care for expense or for inefficiency if the goal is attained.

With ten baying bloodhounds and six German Shepherds, the men on the ground split into two groups. Each went around the burning area. I did not know what garment of mine the dogs could have sniffed at, but I was sure that the Nine had located something in my castle at Grandrith. They weren't likely to pick up any odor from me near the napalmed area, since the smoke would deaden the nerves in their noses. But if they did pick up something near the edge of the swamp, the men would suppose that I was in there, and the mangroves would get a shower of the terrible jellied gasoline. The copters were overhead now, one over each group, waiting for orders.

I climbed down and waded through the brownish, vegetation-sticky waters between the massive buttress-rooted mangroves. After a mile of this, during which I saw several mambas and a large river otter, I went south and came out on dry ground, comparatively dry, that is. Though this was not the rainy season, it was still raining every day, and the soil around here seldom became dry. My footprints would have been evident if I had not been at such pains to walk only on fallen vegetation. Even so, I was leaving a trail which the dogs could pick up easily enough.

As I headed east toward the highlands and the rain forest, I heard the distant whirring of an approaching chopper. It came through the smoke in the distance and then was suddenly headed toward me. It had come at a bad time for me. I was in a natural clearing caused by erosion of the thin soil from a sloping sandstone mass.

The swamp was a quarter-mile to my left. The edge of the clearing on my right was about fifty yards. Ahead was thick bush with about a mile to go before I reached the foot of the cliff which reared up to about five hundred feet. This was the first of the heights which, a few miles inland, became a series of plateaus about five hundred to eighteen hundred feet high and which was covered with the closed-canopy rain forest. This was the tongue of the highlands which extended from the interior and was a freakish formation for this part of the land. Along the coast here, the land was generally flat for about eight to ten miles from the sea to the highlands.

I ran on ahead, glanced back once, and saw two dark objects streaking toward me. I threw myself on the ground, forgetting that I had to be careful not to dislodge the grenades attached to my belt by their pins. The explosions half-deafened me, and dirt showered me. But the rockets had overshot me by forty yards and blown up in a shallow depression. I was up and into the bush ahead and then into the smoke created by the explosions before the wind had a chance to clear it. The next two explosions came behind me. Apparently the rocket man in the chopper had compensated immediately for the overshooting, and if I had stayed in the same place, I would probably have been blown to bits.

As it was, the impact knocked me forward; I felt as if a log had been slapped across my back by a giant. But the impact was softened by the trees and bushes between me and the rockets, and I was up and going again. The smoke from the second volley was carried eastward by the wind and so veiled me from the chopper for a minute.

The huge helicopter came charging through the smoke, its pilot apparently assuming that I was either dead or incapacitated by the explosions. Perhaps, he did not release the napalm bombs because he had orders to take me alive if he could do so. Or perhaps he just wanted to make sure he could plant his bombs exactly on the spot where my body or its remnants were and so ensure obliteration of me.

Whatever his reasons, he brought the chopper down to fifty feet above the ground and at a speed of about fifty miles an hour. I was completely at his mercy or seemed to be, because he was suddenly about ten feet to the north of me. The gunners on the right side saw me a few seconds after I saw them, and the snouts of their .50 caliber machine guns began flaming.

They were not, as usual, accurate but they did not need to be, because they were bringing their fire around like water from a hose, and the intersection would be my body.

I did not try to run away, because they had spotted me, and I could not get away when they were that close. I stood up, while the gouts of dirt and pieces of bush torn by the bullets swung toward me. I yanked a grenade from the belt, leaving the pin attached to the belt, and I threw the grenade.

They would have expected me to fire back with my rifle, but this they had never expected. The grenade flew exactly as I had aimed it, went through the open port before the gunner on my right just as the bullets were on the point of intersecting, the scissors of lead about to close on my body.

But the gunner, or someone in the chopper, had been alert and cool enough to catch the grenade and start to throw it out the port. He was not, however, quite swift enough, and the grenade exploded in his hand. The covering of flesh was enough to soften its effect. He was killed and I suppose everybody else in the chopper was, too. But the fuel did not catch fire, not immediately, anyway. The chopper tilted and slid at a forty-five degree angle away from me and into a tree trunk about ten feet above the ground. By then I was running, and when I saw a gully, I dived into it. I was flying through the air when the fuel and napalm did go off, and I felt the heat pass over the gully. My bare back was almost seared.

My face was turned away, and I was breathing shallowly, because I did not want to sear my lungs. Then I was up and out, because if the first blast had not gotten me, I had a chance to get away.

The heat felt as if it were scorching the hairs off my legs and the back of my head, and smoke curled around me. But the explosion had taken place about a hundred and fifty yards away, and the heavy bush helped screen me. The napalm bombs were not large ones.

The other copter had hung back for some reason or other. Perhaps it was attached to the men with the dogs and was to play a part if the dogs treed me. But when the first chopper exploded, the second came up swiftly enough. It, however, stayed about three hundred feet up as its crew observed the wreck. They had no idea whether the copter had crashed accidentally or whether I had brought it down with my firearm.

I remained under the thick elephant's ear plant. An observer in the air can see much more than one on the ground in these conditions. Heavy as the bush was, it still had open spaces across which I had to cross, however briefly, and once I was seen I had little chance to get away.

The chopper did not hover long over the wreck. It began to swing in a wide circle around, apparently hoping to flush me out or catch sight of me. Then it went back west, and I left my hiding place and traveled swiftly eastward. Just before I reached the bottom of the first cliff, I had to conceal myself again. The chopper was returning. It went by about a hundred feet above me and two hundred yards to the north. It contained a number of men and dogs.

I could not see it, but I guessed that it had settled down on the edge of the cliff and that dogs and men were getting out of it. Their plans now were to push me east with one party and hope to catch me with the one now ahead. Then I was able to see the faces of some men as they watched from the lip of the cliff. The copter took off again and began circling around. Occasionally, the machine guns in it spat fire. I could not hear the guns above the roar of the copter, but some of the bullets struck close enough for me to hear their impact against the trees. They were probing in the hope they could scare me out.

If I stayed where I was, the dogs of the party behind me might pick up my scent. Their baying and barking was getting closer. It was difficult to determine in that muffling foliage, but it seemed that they were headed straight toward me.

I was beginning to feel that I had gone through enough for one day. To survive a twelve hundred foot fall into the ocean and a shark attack should be enough excitement for a month, anyway, not to mention blowing up two helicopters on the ground and lobbing a grenade into the port of another in the air. And getting through the firepower of thirty-five men and a rocket-carrying, napalm-bomb-dropping aircraft. I had had enough for some time; surely my luck must be running out. My anger was getting dangerous, dangerous for me, that is. I could not afford to lose control. But I was feeling a tiredness very new to me. Those who have read the volumes by my biographer, or Volume IX of my own memoirs, know that my energy is great. It can be called animal-like. But I had gone through an experience only two months ago which might be called unmanning. Afterward, I had had to go into hiding from the Nine with my wife and Doc Caliban and his cousin, Trish Wilde. I had been without adequate sleep for a week. I wanted to get back to the rain forest of my childhood and youth, to see the dark ceiling close over me, to hear the silence and feel the coolness of the green womb.

I crouched under the bush and tried to suppress my trembling.

I bit my lips and clutched the rifle as if I could squeeze in the stock with my fingers. I wanted to leap up and run toward the enemy with my gun blazing and, when that was empty, throw my grenades, and when those were gone, close in on them with the knife.

The images were vivid and satisfying, but they were deadly. I enjoyed them, then laughed to myself, and some of the shaking went away. I had to get out from the closing jaws by going north to the mangrove swamp or south through more bush. Men were already descending from the cliff on both sides and five dogs were with each column. Their ascent was slow and dangerous, but they were determined to extend the jaws of the trap. Other men stayed on top of the cliff to observe. And the dogs were getting closer now; I could hear them plainly because the chopper had traveled to my south. And then it rose and two objects fell from it, and the jungle to my right was a hemisphere of flame and a spire of inky smoke.

The chopper swung back and over me, past me, stopped high above the edge of the swamp, and two more bombs fell. The mangroves for a stretch of a hundred yards were burning fiercely.

Their plan was a good one. Of course, they did not know I was surrounded, but they were acting as if I were. And, as sometimes happens, the *as-if* hypothesis was going to bear a theory and then a fact. Unless I managed, like many a hard fact, to slip through the net of hypothesis.

There was only one thing to do. I crawled toward the left and into the edge of the smoke cloud. Though I was as close to the ground as I could get, I could not stay there long without coughing. Nor could I depend on the smoke to conceal me because of the vagaries of the wind. My purpose was to get where the dogs coming down from the cliff could not smell me or to get as close as possible to that area. Also, when I left that area, I would be reeking of smoke, which I hoped would cover up my body odor.

A man was saying something to a bloodhound, and then they were past me. I came up behind him, crouching, and broke his neck by twisting his head. Before he had fallen to the ground, I had also broken the neck of the dog. All this took place within twelve feet of the closest man and dog, but the roaring of the flames and the smoke swirling through the thick bush hid the noise and the sight of the dead. It took me a minute to get the dead man's clothes off and onto me. They fitted fairly well, since he was almost my height, six feet three inches, and he had a large frame.

The green digger's hat and the green shirt enabled me to get close to another man who did not have a dog, and he went down with a knife in his neck before he realized that I was the hunted. The next two victims were another man and a dog. I almost got caught, because a man was about ten paces behind them, but the bush concealed us long enough for me to be ready by the time he stumbled across the bodies.

They should have stayed back and let the helicopter saturate the area with napalm. They would have gotten me. But as long as they made the mistake of trying to roust me out with men and dogs in a bush in which I had lived a good part of my eighty-one years, they were bound to suffer. I then walked up the cliff, limping as if I'd hurt myself. I looked up twice and saw several men looking at me, and one was shouting at me, if his wide open and writhing mouth meant anything. I continued to limp and several times sat down as if I'd been badly hurt.

Halfway up the cliff, I saw two men coming down toward me. Apparently they were sent by their officer to find out if I had been wounded by their quarry. I sat down with my back to the descending men. The copter was circling tightly about two hundred yards away almost on a level with me. I could see some men and dogs two hundred feet below as they passed from bush to bush, but most of the enemy were concealed. Two men were coming toward me, and three men were on top of the cliff. I had to act swiftly.

My try at passing myself off as one of them failed. A man called down to me, "Cramer?" evidently thinking I must be the man whose clothes I'd taken. One look at my face would tell him his mistake.

I got up onto my legs as if it was painful to do so, with my face still turned away. The rifle was hanging from a strap over my shoulder, and my hands were empty, so that that must have lowered their guard, if indeed it was up at all.

"What the hell, Cramer," the man said in English with a Hungarian accent. "You know better than to leave your station! Did that wild man get you or did you just fall down, trip over your own feet, you clumsy lout?"

"Neither!" I said, and whirled around, the knife coming out of its sheath and through the air and into the Hungarian's solar plexus. The other man froze just long enough for me to pull the automatic from its open holster and shoot him in the chest.

Then I continued to fire up at the three faces hanging over the cliff's edge, three white faces with black O's of mouths. The Luger was a .45, the range was two hundred feet and at a difficult angle and at small targets, so I missed. I had expected this, but the faces did disappear, and I threw the automatic down, withdrew the knife and stuck it in its sheath, and ran up the steep and treacherous path—fit only for goat or baboons—removing my rifle as I did. A glance at the copter showed that, so far, the men in it had not noticed me. They were intent on something below them.

That would not last long. The men on top of the cliff had to have a transceiver of some sort, and they would notify the copter immediately.

By then, the top of the cliff was about one hundred and sixty feet away. I stopped, yanked out another grenade, and cast it. The grenade had to travel about fifty-five feet beyond the range most men can throw a standard hand grenade. It sailed just over the lip of the cliff as the three stuck their heads over to fire at me. The explosion threw rocks and dirt over me, but I saw one body sailing out of the smoke to crash against a projection, roll over and fall the rest of the way. I had to presume that the other two were out of the combat; if I was wrong, I would be dead. The copter had started to whirl around just before I threw the grenade. The pilot must have received the message from the man on the top of the cliff. I was ready for this, I'd yanked out another grenade, and I threw it.

It was probably the best throw of my life, as far as both distance and accuracy went. The grenade weighed about one and three-quarter pounds and the copter was about two hundred feet away when I threw the grenade. It had started to move before then and was coming swiftly. It was approaching nose first, so that its machine gunners could not aim at me. Its rockets had been launched during the first attack, otherwise it could have fired at point-blank range and disintegrated me and a good part of the face of the cliff.

But the pilot must have been jarred by the unexpected blast of the grenade, and he did not react to my pointing my rifle at him because I did not point it. Otherwise, I suppose he would have swung around so that the gunners on one side or the other could let loose.

By the time he decided to do that, the grenade was well launched, and just as he pivoted his craft around and stopped it, the grenade struck the vanes. The vanes and the body of the machine disappeared in a cloud of smoke, pieces of machinery came flying out, the machine dropped almost straight down and crashed. A second later, it was burning furiously, and it may have fallen on a number of men and the exploding fuel may have splashed on some. The men on the ground were shaken up; the fire directed at me as I raced on up the path was ragged and misdirected.

And then I was on top of the cliff, ready to fire at any survivors of the grenade I'd tossed up there. But there were none.

One of the corpses had six grenades attached to hooks on a belt. I tossed these, one at a time, into the bush below the cliff and had the satisfaction of knowing that I got at least two men and a dog. Then I picked up a rifle and left running because I did not want to be there if more copters were called in or if jets were used. As it was, I had just entered a thick bush on top of the next higher plateau when two jets screamed overhead about five hundred feet.

I kept on going and did not stop until I had reached the green cliff of seemingly impenetrable jungle that marks the border of the rain forest. I wormed my way through it and then it was as if I had stepped into a quiet twilight cathedral grown by God. I was home.

And now is as good a place as any to recapitulate the events leading up to those in this volume.

My name is known wherever books and movies are known, and that covers at least three-fourths of the habitable world. Even those who have never read the books or seen the movies know, in a general sense, what my name stands for. (When I say my name I mean the one that my "biographer" gave me to conceal my real identity.)

My biographer has stretched the truth, added things which never existed, and ignored others that did exist. But, in the main, the first two volumes of my life were based on reality, and the later ones at least springboarded from an actual event. My biographer did give a fairly accurate picture of my personality. Perhaps I should say he reported my basic attitudes, with much verisimilitude, though he softened some of these because he wanted reader identification with me. And he did not go into any depth about the infrahumanity of my thinking. (Although here I may not be fair with him. The creatures who raised me, The Folk, were subhuman, but they did have a language, and I wonder if anybody who uses a language can escape being classified as entirely human. I suppose the dolphins could, since they live in water and lack hands. But The Folk were anthropoids, probably a giant variety of the ancient hominids, Zinjanthropus or Paranthropus. And while their language reflected a very peculiar way of looking at the universe—to English speakers—it was no more peculiar than Shawnee would be to an Englishman. And in many ways their *Weltanschauung* was remarkably close to that of Sunset Strip inhabitants.)

In 1948, I decided to write my memoirs. I could not publish them because I was then serving the Nine, and they wanted no slightest word of their existence printed. Or even spoken of among the noncognoscenti. I could not have published the memoirs if I had omitted any reference to them. Certain obvious phenomena, such as looking as if I were only thirty when I had to be sixty, and the source of my enormous wealth (on a small fraction of which I paid income tax), could not be overlooked by the public or the authorities. Moreover, aside from all this, my statement that I was not a figment of a fiction writer's feverish brain would have resulted in enormous publicity and invasion of my privacy. Not to mention the possibility that I might have been certified.

Nevertheless, I started to write the memoirs. Some day they might be publishable. Also, I liked the idea of remembrance of things past. (Yes, I have read Proust and in French, my favorite human language.) I have an almost photographic memory but it sometimes results in pictures which startle the humans who lived through the same events. Volume I begins with the first day I can remember, when I was suckling and looking up into those beautiful rusty-brown eyes, into the eyes of the only being who loved me for eighteen years. Volume I ends at the age of ten, or what I calculate as the age of ten, the night I first used a knife. Volumes I through VIII covered seventy-eight years. Some of the manuscripts were slim, some were over a million words long. They corrected a number of distortions or omissions of events and told the true names behind the names my biographer used. They included many items of information which I suppose would repulse the readers of my "biography." I have never had any hesitation about eating human meat when the occasion demanded, contrary to what my biographer stated. Nor have I been rigorously Victorian in some aspects of my life, to say the least. And I suppose, in fact, I know, that many would condemn me for serving the Nine. They would equate this with Faustus' selling of his soul.

It is easy enough to scorn. Let the scorner be offered thirty thousand years or more of youth and then we shall hear what they have to say.

My wife and I took the oath under conditions that would make a Mau-Mau initiation look like a Sunday school Bible presentation. And I suppose we weren't honest or ethical even then, because we had unstated reservations. But we would remain with the Nine, and take their immortality, as long as we were not asked to do anything we just could not do and still respect ourselves. Fortunately, neither of us was asked, though I must admit that I am capable of much that would revolt most of the so-called civilized peoples. But then I have never really considered myself as part of humanity. This attitude can be for bad or good, depending on the circumstances.

Nevertheless, immortality brings a high price: It is true that you pay for everything valuable you get in this world. Nothing is really free. And so, for years, both Clio and myself felt a little less than "clean." That is the only word I can think of that is anywhere appropriate. Thirty thousand or more years ago, some Old Stone Age peoples discovered something that gave them an extremely extended youth. It also made them immune to any disease or to breakdown of the cells. Of course, they could fall down and break their necks or slit their throats or get clubbed to death. But if chance worked well for them, they could live for what must have seemed forever. They did age, but so slowly that a man who took the elixir at the age of twenty-five would only look fifty at the end of fifteen thousand years.

I don't know the history of what happened between 25,000 B.C. and 1913 when the agent of the Nine first introduced himself. By then, the Nine consisted of Anana, a thirty-millennia old Caucasian woman, XauXaz, Ing, Iwaldi, a dwarf, a Hebrew born about 3 B.C., an ancient proto-Bantu, two proto-Mongolians, and an Amerindian. They lived most of the year in various parts of the world, but once a year they held a ceremony which must have originated in the early part of the Paleolithic. This involved the giving up of flesh on the part of the servants of the Nine—a painful procedure—and the drinking of the elixir. The ceremonies were always held in a complex of caves in the remote mountains near Uganda.

Over a period of several months, the "candidates" drank the rejuvenation liquid. No samples were ever given out; the candidates entered the caverns naked and left naked. It meant a hideous death to be discovered trying to smuggle the stuff out.

We "candidates," I estimate, numbered about five hundred. We were the elite of the organization that, literally, ruled the world in secret. How many were enlisted in the lower echelons, I couldn't even begin to guess. The lower echelon, the "servants of the Nine," probably numbered half a million. None of these even knew of the elixir or had ever seen the Nine.

We candidates were those who might be chosen to replace one of the Nine if he or she died.

Volume IX of my memoirs opens with Clio in our estate at Grandrith, which includes a manor, a castle, a forest, and the village of Cloamby. (John Cloamby, Viscount Grandrith, is my true name and title.) I was in our house on the plantation in western Kenya. I was blasted out of my bed by a shell from a Kenyan Army artillery unit because old Jomo Kenyatta had given the order to wipe me off the face of the Earth. I had refused to become a Kenyan citizen or to leave Kenya, and he had put up with this for several years. Then he had decided to kill me (or perhaps somebody else in the Kenyan administration had). I survived and I escaped with the army on my tail. Not only that, an Albanian by the name of Enver Noli was after me with a band of heavily armed Arab bandits. He was hoping that I would lead him to the site of my gold mine in Uganda. I did, though the gold had long been gone. In the meantime, some mysterious enemy had let loose a lion on me. I found out that he was Doc Caliban, accompanied by two aged men, the last survivors of the band that had once helped him in his fight against evil.

Philip José Farmer

Doc Caliban was as strange a phenomenon as I. You might say I was the Feral Man, the Man of the Jungle, whereas Doctor Caliban was the Civilized Man, the Man of the Metropolis. He had been trained since an early age to develop to the fullest potentiality his physical and mental powers, which must have been considerable. In fact, they were probably, next to mine, the greatest. And no wonder, when you consider that our grandfather had been an Early Stone Age Man, XauXaz, the ancient who was second only to Anana in age and power at the round oaken table of the Nine. That was why my bones and Caliban's were so much thicker than modern man's, thus affording a broader base for the attachment of massive muscles.

But we did not know, at the time, that XauXaz was our ancestor.

Caliban was out to kill me because he thought I had killed his beautiful cousin, Patricia, when she was on a scientific expedition in East Africa.

Both of us were suffering the peculiar and unpredictable side effects of the immortality elixir. Ours occurred about the same time with the result that we each had very strange, and similar, psycho-neuroses. Those who are curious may read Volume IX of my memoirs.

Our first face-to-face encounter came on the natural bridge that leads to the caverns of the Nine. But the Nine stopped us from fighting. XauXaz had died, and we two had been picked out of the five hundred candidates to vie for his place. After the ceremony, we would be set free and one should kill the other.

It was then that Anana told us that we were half-brothers. Our father had also been a candidate, and the elixir had had an unfortunate side effect on him. Lord Grandrith had gone mad. He had, in fact, become that savage maniac known in history as Jack the Ripper.

But he had recovered and he had emigrated to the States, where he took the name of Caliban. The side effects had passed, but they left a consciousness of what he had done and a revulsion against himself. He swore to raise his son to fight evil. I think that he meant eventually to reveal his past to his American son and to turn him against the Nine. He did most of this in secret, and thus, though his child could have established athletic records that would still not be beaten (if I had also abstained), he never entered sports in high school or college.

LORD OF THE TREES

He did become the greatest surgeon in the world and he also was clearly the greatest in many fields: archaeology, chemistry, and a number of other sciences and professions. But he avoided publicity as much as possible. However, a writer found out something about him and used him and his band of aids as the basis for a semifictional series in a pulp magazine. Caliban's "biographies" deviated even more from reality than mine, yet many of the adventures did contain a kernel of truth.

I left the caves and went to a tree house I'd built in the rain forest wherein Clio and I had vacationed. I discovered a madman aping me. He it was who had abducted Trish Wilde, Doc Caliban's cousin. I rescued her, and we went on to England, where I knew that Enver Noli and Doc Caliban were going. Both were intent on getting hold of Clio and using her against me.

By then I was beginning to wonder if the whole situation had not been brought about by the Nine. They could have given both of us something to bring on the "side effects." They could have set up the abduction and supposed death of Trish to cause Caliban to want revenge. And I was sure that the mysterious death of our father was caused by the Nine. They must have discovered that he intended to turn against them and killed him. But his American son, Doc Caliban, did not know anything at all about the Nine and never suspected, until then, that the Nine were responsible. When they offered him immortality, he accepted it, just as I had. Just as, I am convinced, any human would.

At the estate, Caliban and I had killed off Noli's group and then we fought, though I tried to talk him out of it. We tore each other up like two leopard males at mating time, and we both almost died. But one of the properties of the elixir is the regeneration of organs, and we grew our lost ones back.

We also had recovered from the madness brought on by the side effect. We found out we had been duped, and we swore to fight against the Nine. We knew what little chance we had of ever winning. But I killed the men sent to summon us to a meeting of the Nine in London, and we fled.

All this is told in Volume IX of my memoirs.

Since then, Clio and I had been separated from Doc Caliban and his cousin. We had been around the world twice. During the first trip, I had dropped off the manuscript of Volume IX in a Los Angeles post office for your editor to publish. I had met him in Kansas City at the home of a common friend.

We went from Los Angeles to New York. Clio and I made an unchartered flight across the Atlantic in one of Doc Caliban's planes, which we got from a hangar near the tip of Long Island. We flew the jet all the way about twenty feet above the waves. We landed on an unattended strip in Devonshire on land owned by me, and we motored to London. I got in touch with Doc Caliban via the short-wave in our hideout in the apartment in Marylebone Borough. Doc reported that he now had two "sidekicks," sons of two of his former associates. The three men were on the trail of Iwaldi in Germany. He wanted me to come to Germany to join in the hunt, but I told him of my plans to scout out the caves of the Nine. I did not intend to attack anybody there, unless the chance of risk was slight enough to warrant it. I just wanted to map the area in my mind for the day when Doc and I would invade it.

I doubted very much that any of the Nine would be in the caves, since this was not the time for the ceremonies. But I did not know that. I suspected that there would be a formidable army of guards and that the entrances would be mined and booby-trapped. I did not know this, of course, but it seemed unlikely that the caves would be left unguarded. Though they were in a remote and arid mountain range, and the caves could be reached only with difficulty, there were bound to be gold or oil prospectors around there. The Nine had deliberately created a superstitious dread of the area among the natives just outside the mountains. And the Nine doubtless controlled in secret many of those high in the administration of Uganda and Kenya. These would take steps to declare the area officially off limits if the Nine had to kill so many that people got curious.

My plan was to approach the mountains from the west coast of Africa, on foot and alone. If I sailed or flew into the east coast, I might be spotted, and the skein of the Nine would be flung everywhere to catch me. Besides, too many people in Kenya and Uganda knew me. But if I landed quietly on the coast of Gabon and traveled as I like best to travel, alone and lightly armed, I could traverse the rain forests which stretch across much of central Africa. I would avoid all humanity, and I would come like a shadow out of the west. Nobody would expect me. And I should be comparatively free to investigate. It was the western end of the caves that I knew nothing about. All candidates had always been required to follow a strictly limited route from the east, and exploration of the area had been forbidden with a very painful existence and eventually death promised for those who broke the law.

Doc Caliban did not argue with me. He is very self-sufficient. Also, though I could be wrong, I think he preferred not to work with me. He was probably right, since we both are so strongly individualistic. It is not that we can't take orders, because he served with distinction as a commissioned officer in the U.S. Army in 1918. And I was a Squadron Leader and then a Group Captain in the RAF in World War II. And both of us were under the strictest sort of discipline from ourselves and others when we went through medical school.

But we each have our own way of doing things, and there was in both of us a residue of doubt about who was the strongest. This seems childish, and perhaps is, but after you have *known* for many years that you are the most athletic man alive, the swiftest, the strongest, and then you run across somebody who seems to be fully as strong, then you doubt. Doc and I had fought at Grandrith Castle, and you may read the results of that fight in Volume IX of my memoirs. But when two are so evenly matched, and one wins, the loser is entitled to wonder if the outcome would be different the next time. I'm sure that Doc thought about this at times, chided himself for his juvenility, and then could not keep from speculating again.

So it was best that we tackle the Nine separately, for the time being, anyway.

Clio objected to being left behind, but I did not want to be burdened when I traveled through the rain forest. Tough and strong as this delicate and beautiful little blonde is, she was not born in Africa nor raised ferally. The only human being whom I would have considered taking with me, because he could keep up with me under the primitive conditions, would be Doc Caliban.

So I kissed her goodbye and left London, which I hate because of the crowds and the noise and odors, and flew illegally to various ports. But I made a stop near Port-Gentil to check on some of my operatives, and it must have been there that the agents of the Nine detected me.

I had escaped where I had no right to by the usual mechanism and rules of probability of the universe. But, as I have said, I am convinced that I do have something about me that twists and distorts the odds against coincidence and good luck. It's what I call the "human magnetic moment," and it is what very few people possess. I am one, and Doc Caliban, from what he had told me, must be another. Of course, one day, the inevitable must happen. A bullet will plow into my brain or I'll fall off a tree or down the stairs or an automobile going through a stop sign will crush me or a faulty gas heater will asphyxiate me or . . . I remember a line from Merrill Moore's poem, "Warning To One": *Death is the strongest of all living things.*

It will come to me as to every man. But until the moment, I will live as if *I* were the strongest of all living things.

I was home again, and I breathed relief, though I knew it might not last long. For the first time in a long time, I could genuinely *breathe.* The air inside the closed-canopy tall equatorial forest is like that nowhere else. It sighs with the greenness of totally alive beings, animals or plants. Contrary to what most people think, this type of rain forest is not hot, even if it is on the equator. It may be staggeringly blistering just above the top of the forest. But below, where the ground is at the bottom of a deep well, roofed over by a tangle of layers and layers of branches and vines and lianas and leaves, it is cool. And the temperature does not vary much. Moreover, the area between the broad and tall trees is often park-like. It is free of that thick mass that can be penetrated only with difficulty by man and that people associate with the word *jungle* because of Hollywood's projections of what it thinks a jungle looks like.

In fact, if Murtagh's forces had caught me on the ground here, they could have blown me apart a dozen times before I fell. The area is too open for the sort of warfare through which I had just gone. Of course, if I had had a chance to get up a tree and into the various levels of the tanglery overhead, I might have gotten away.

Here, despite my two hundred and fifty pounds, I could travel from tree to tree for long distances. It wouldn't be by swinging from lianas. That is another Hollywood idea and utterly unrealistic. (Though I have done it several times under extreme emergency conditions.) On foot, and traveling not too swiftly, I have often gone for miles in this area without once setting foot on the ground. And when I was much younger and lighter, I could do it much more swiftly.

Now I stayed on the ground because I wanted to make speed. I trotted along until I found a small pool and drank from it. Then, feeling hungry, I hunted, and I finally saw a small half-grown tusker. I ran after him, and he took off speedily, but I am faster and have more endurance, and eventually he stopped, breathing hoarsely, facing me, his little eyes savage and desperate, saliva dripping from his tusks. I did not use my rifle because of the noise. I sprang in, he tried to wheel to one side, and my knife cut open his jugular. I drank the blood while it was still pumping out and then I butchered the beast. I ate him raw and then proceeded on my way with about half of him—the best half—wrapped up in his hide. There had to be water near, since the bushpig seldom strays too far from water. Then I remembered the small stream about a mile to the north and made for it. I drank and then ate some more of the pig. I was lucky in running across this creature, since they usually lie up in dense reed beds or tall grass by day and come out at night to feed. And they usually run in groups of twenty or so.

I have heard people who did not know that they were talking to me, scoff at my ability to survive in this area. They say that if I had eaten all that raw meat, I would have been infested with worms and other internal parasites.

They overlook that there are any number of natives who eat raw meat from which some get infested and some do not. However, it is my opinion that I never got sick because, one, I lived in a healthy area, the closed-canopy forest, and, two, far more significant, I probably had something in me which killed off all bacteria, viri, and parasites. I am convinced the Nine were dictating the course of my life before birth. I believe that I was injected with something which made me immune, just as I believe that the Nine deliberately set things up so that I was raised as a feral human by The Folk. (The factors which made me conclude this are detailed in Volume II of my memoirs, unpublished as yet.) Thus, my unique way of life was not entirely "natural," any more than Doc Caliban's was natural. This had made me wonder how many other men, known or unknown to history, have been "modified" by the Nine. How many geniuses owe their shaping to the grim ancients who pull the strings from their secret mansions?

I was walking along, noting that it was now twilight at ground level, which meant that the sun must be sinking close to the horizon. It was still comparatively quiet here, though some males of a troop of sooty mangabeys were occasionally giving their loud chattering cry. These were large long-tailed monkeys with gray fur especially long on the sides of the head and with pink faces speckled with gray-brown freckles. They make good eating, as I well know.

I was thinking about going up and making a nest in the middle level when I heard the baying of dogs behind me.

Doctor Murtagh had not given up. I don't know how he had managed to catch up, since I had traveled faster than ordinary men with dogs could, unless he called in more copters.

I dropped the hog, ran to the stream, which was a quarter of a mile away, and washed myself in it. Then I climbed a 150 foot high tree to the middle level. From there, I made my way across the tanglery to the source of the baying. I knew that they would find where I had gone up, and they would likely fire into the closed-canopy around there. They would be shooting for some distance eastward from where I had ascended on the theory that I was fleeing via the middle level. They would never, I hoped, believe that I had the guts to cross above them and travel behind them.

In about fifteen minutes, I stopped my cautiously slow travel. I hugged a branch which was almost entirely enclosed in lianas and vines and broad leaves. Down on the ground, it was so dark that the men were using flashlights and lamps. Where I was, the sunlight was still filtering down. By looking up, they could have seen me outlined against the lighter sky if it had not been for the dense green around me. My cloak of invisibility. Of course, I could not move now unless I did so very slowly, because my weight would bend the bridge of vegetation between the trees and the noise could be heard by the dogs or even by the less keen ears of the men. However, I could move while they were on the march as long as I trailed them by several hundred yards. They kept on my scent until the dogs broke into an eager baying and barking when they came onto the place where I had killed the bushpig. The dogs went swiftly after that, with the men stabbing their beams on every side. They would have liked to have camped for the night, I'm sure. They were in my territory, and they must have been spooked because of the day's events. But they drove on with Doctor Murtagh at their head and did not stop until they came to the tree up which I had climbed. A moment later, the gunfire that was aimed at the canopy aroused the monkeys and birds for miles around. The screeching continued long after Murtagh had given the cease-fire order.

If I had been hiding overhead anywhere within a hundred-yard square area, I would have been shot a dozen times. As it was, a number of bursts came my way, and I was two hundred yards back and behind a thick trunk. Then they probed the area with flashlights, hoping to find my corpse hanging from a tangle or fallen onto the ground.

Murtagh said nothing when his men reported no success. But his bearing, outlined in the flashlight, was a curse. He gave an order (which I could not hear at that distance, of course) and they pitched camp.

It did not take long. Every man except Murtagh carried a pack on his back. These consisted mainly of ammunition, food, water, medicine, and collapsible furniture and tents.

The tents were Doc Caliban's invention and known only to the servants of the Nine. The tents and the furniture could be likened only to that pocket-sized collapsible sailing ship of Norse mythology, *Skidbladnir*. A man would remove a neatly folded bundle of cloth about the size of a big handkerchief and snap it like a whip. Yards of green material unfolded, shot out like a flag in a breeze. The stuff was as thin and as light as spider webs, but it kept out light and cold, and it was as tough as an inch-thick sheet of aluminum. The framework of the supports for the tent slid out of a cylinder about two feet long and three inches thick and was set up within sixty seconds. Then the material of the tent was arranged over it and tied down at the ends to stakes driven into the thin forest soil. There wasn't much dead wood available for fires, but they did not care. They carried small metal boxes which unfolded and projected six large round rings at the ends of thin metal stalks. These burned a gas derived from a compressed liquid and furnished a fire for cooking or heating. Caliban had invented both the tents and the burners in 1937, but only the Nine had benefited from it then. Many of the things he invented in the '30s are still ahead of their time.

The lamps were set up to bathe the camp with additional illumination. Wires were strung and little buttons were stuck here and there outside and above the camp. The buttons would set off alarms in the camp through the wireless. They were set to react to any mass larger than a monkey which would get near the magnetic field they were radiating.

The tents were arranged in a circle with Murtagh's in the center. There were about fifty men and thirty dogs—enough evidence that copters had brought in additional forces. Double guards were stationed every forty feet outside the perimeter of the line formed by the tents. The area outside was bathed in a bright light, and the guards were relieved every hour. Of course, I could have dropped onto Murtagh's tent, but I didn't relish the idea of falling a hundred feet even after having survived a 1,200 foot fall that morning. Also, what was the use of killing Murtagh if I got shot to pieces?

For the same reason, I did not shoot him at a distance with my rifle. I had been extremely fortunate to have survived the concentrated fire in the bush. Here, where I had to travel slowly in the canopy, they could have overhauled me and gotten below me unless I was very lucky again. I did not want to stretch my good fortune too far.

I did want to hear what they were saying. Slowly, I crawled through the canopy. This was necessary not only to prevent noise but to test the stuff holding me up. It is not always anchored securely. I have fallen several times when I was a youth living in this area, twice saving myself by hanging onto a liana that did not break and once managing to grab the end of a branch as I fell toward the ground a hundred feet below. I have seen three of The Folk who were not so fortunate when they went through the green trapdoor; they broke most of their bones.

Every now and then the bright beam of a small searchlight fingered the tanglery where I was. The beam was being moved at random; it pierced the forest at ground level, lighting up the huge trunks of the trees, making them look like crudely carved pillars of a deep mine worked by gnomes. And then it would leap up onto the dark ceiling overhead, sometimes catching red in the eyes of the owls and bushbabies and servals.

The men not on guard were eating the food they had cooked in their cans over the gas fires. Murtagh sat on a folding chair by a folding table just inside his tent with several of his officers. When I was directly overhead, I could hear a few words, but most of the conversation in the leader's tent was lost. It would have been convenient if the tent had been under a tree with limbs sticking out only about twenty-five feet above.

Nevertheless, I lay flat on a net of lianas and leaves supported by a thin branch and stared down through the net at the camp. Some of the men had loud voices, and I hoped to learn from them. Two, a French Canadian and a mulatto Congolese, spoke in French, presumably on the theory that Murtagh couldn't understand them. Perhaps he didn't, but I think that an educated and cosmopolitan man such as Murtagh would have been very fluent in this tongue. Perhaps they were depending on him not to comprehend their two types of French. They may have been correct in their assumptions. The Canadian's French was only half-understood by me, and I doubt that a man skilled in Parisian French would understand the Congolese's patois. The two had to repeat much to make their own words clear.

The Congolese said, "If it is true that this white devil's plane was blown up, and he fell a thousand feet without a parachute, and swam ashore and then he got through us and killed half of us . . . then what are we doing here?"

"We are here because Murtagh said so, and because he is paying us very well," the Canadian said. "That *white* devil as you call him, is insane. He would have to be to take the chances he did. As for his falling that far from a plane, I do not believe that. And . . ."

"But I heard the report over the radio. I was standing behind Murtagh when the pilot reported. He said the plane exploded, and he saw Grandrith's body falling. He watched it until it disappeared, and there was no parachute."

"I read once about a man who fell two thousand feet into a snowbank and lived," the Canadian said. "It was a true story. It had to be, it was in the French edition of *The Reader's Digest*. It happened during World War II. And I heard about a man who fell a thousand feet into the sea and lived. So, why shouldn't this man live if others can?"

"And how do you explain that he also survived us?" the Congolese said. "Does a man have that much luck, to live through a fall like that and through our firepower and then burn four helicopters and kill fifteen men on the ground? Some with a knife while many others were only ten feet away? And kill dogs, too?"

While they were talking, moonlight fell on me. I was in the lower level of canopy, and above me was an opening in the upper level. I was not, of course, visible to those below me.

I listened carefully. The two discussed Murtagh and their officers and what they would do with their money when they returned to civilization. Then they said a few words about the base, which was apparently to the northeast somewhere, not too far away. The radio operator, Smith, had not lied.

I should have left then. The base was my next goal; I wanted to investigate that and perhaps harass its occupants. I could at least prowl around and pick up information by eavesdropping. Or perhaps abduct someone who might have valuable information which he would give, willingly or not.

But I stayed, hoping I would find out more. And then I heard a thrashing in the leaves behind me and turned swiftly, my knife ready. My rifle and belt with the grenades attached was stretched across a web of lianas. I saw a blurry form in the moonlight—a little guenon monkey, I think it was—and then a larger winged form after it. An eagle-owl had spiraled down through the opening in the upper canopy and spotted a tiny monkey and the monkey had seen it coming. It flashed across a liana and then was on me. I batted at it, struck it to one side; it gave a cry and clutched a twig and then was off, somewhere. I don't know where or care. The owl had been following it so closely that it did not see me until it was on me and then it screeched and its claws raked my chest.

I remember hearing shouting from below. A bright beam spun its cone around and then centered on me. This happened just as I fell with the owl. My perch had been precarious, and it did not take much to topple me, especially since I was so occupied with trying to tear the bird's claws loose from its painful clutch on my chest.

As I have said, there is something about me, my "magnetic moment," which has tended to cause coincidences which would be incredible in fiction to occur around me. It has given me very good luck many times.

But we have to pay with good for bad; for every action there is an opposite and equal reaction.

Bad fortune came, I fell a hundred feet, and this time, if my brain had not been frozen by the horror of it, I would have thought that I had come to the end of a long and unusually interesting trail. I could not expect to survive two long falls in the same day, even if this was much shorter than the first.

Rifles shot at me even as I fell. The owl screamed and tore itself loose and then it exploded in feathers. A bullet or two had hit it.

The bright lights and the dark green-black top of the tent expanded before me, whirled to one side, came back, shot away, the wind whistled through my ears, the rifles barked, and I kept my mouth closed, determined even then not to give them the pleasure of hearing me scream.

Then I was unconscious.

When I opened my eyes, I saw that it was still night. I was surprised, not because it was night but because I had expected to be dead.

By then the tent on which I had fallen had been set up again. I had hit it on my back with my legs and arms extended sidewise. The top had caved in but not lightly. I had hit the ground, but the impact had been considerably softened by the tent. Not enough so that my muscles did not ache but not enough to break any bones.

I was lying on my side inside a ring formed by six guards with rifles pointing at me. My hands were handcuffed behind me, and my legs just above the ankles had irons locked around them. The irons were connected by a thick chain of duraluminum or similar alloy. Moreover, something had been secured around my waist—it felt like another duraluminum chain—and a plastic disc about two inches in diameter and two-tenths of an inch thick was held against my belly by the belt. My belt with its knife had been removed, of course.

Murtagh stood near me but just outside the nearest guard. He bent over to look at me more closely. His eyes were as empty of light as a dead man's. His jaws protruded apishly, and his head moved from side to side, repulsively and, I am sure, compulsively.

"Lord Grandrith," he said. "The one and only. *Pelus blancus simiarum.* The demon of the jungle. Last of the wild men. Lord of the trees. Pristine spirit of darkest Africa. Member of the House of Lords and one of the wealthiest men in the world."

His voice was high and harsh. There was nothing about the man to like. He even had a bad odor, though I doubt if the others could have smelled it.

"Traitor, also!" he said. "And a corpse soon! Right now, if I had my say about it! You're far too dangerous to let live for a second!"

There did not seem to be anything to say in reply, so I glared at him.

"Before long you'll wish that I had had my way," he said. "Old Mubaniga wants you taken to the base, so taken you will be. And when the Nine get their hands on you, you know what to expect."

It was cool in the night on the soft dank ground of the rain forest, but I was sweating. I was not afraid, but I do have a vivid imagination and I could visualize some of the things that would be done to me.

Murtagh said, "The mathematical probabilities for your having survived just the explosion of the plane, let alone the fall into the sea, are so small that . . . well, and then . . . Do you know, you are the only man ever to have reduced me to stuttering. Congratulations for that. Though there will be nothing else from now on to congratulate you for."

He looked hard at me, turned, and went into the tent. A man pulled the flap of the tent down. I rolled over without objection from the guards and looked around. Beyond my six guards were four more, stationed as backups. There did not seem to be anything I could do. I did not even test the handcuffs, since I was sure that even I could not break the metal of the links. And if I could, then what?

I closed my eyes and in a short time was asleep. This ability to relax is beast-like, and, as my biographer pointed out innumerable times, I am half-beast.

A hand shook me awake. I should have heard the man approach and smelled him, but I was utterly exhausted. I had had a hard day.

The man was Murtagh. He had come out of his tent a few minutes after I was asleep. I wondered if keeping me awake was going to be the first part of the torture. But he only smiled, managing to look even more reptilian, and he said, "Aren't you curious about the disc attached to your belly?"

I did not reply. He sneered and said, "It's an explosive which contains a radio receiver. If you should by any chance get loose, you would not get far."

He took a small metal case and said, "If I snap the pseudo-lighter, the transmitter in the case will send out a frequency which will be detected by the receiver in the explosive. And your belly, and the rest of you, will be blown to little pieces. There will not be enough for the small birds to eat. And even if you should, somehow, get the handcuffs off, and then, somehow, detach the belt, you could not remove the disc without tearing off the skin of your belly. It is bonded with epoxy glue to your skin."

It seemed to me that the range of the transmitter would be limited. But I said nothing.

Murtagh hesitated and then said, grinning, "Oh, yes. I almost forgot. I was one of the ten candidates chosen to replace you and Caliban. If I capture or kill you, I was to be one of two. The other, I suppose, will be the man who gets Caliban. And that may be I, since I will be allowed to go after him once I've turned you over to the proper authority. In which case, I am bound to sit with the Nine."

I remained silent. He bared his lips, showing thick yellow teeth, and made a sucking noise as if he were going to spit on me. But he turned again, and the flap over the tent fell down. Within a few seconds, I was once more asleep.

At six in the morning, I was awakened. I had been half-awake for some time during the night because it had rained. The canopy kept much of the rain from falling directly onto me, but drops and occasional trickles startled me from a deep sleep. However, I am accustomed to this; even a more extreme change of temperature and humidity would not have made me suffer much. The guards around me complained about having to stand outside, but they did so in low voices that showed they did not wish Murtagh to hear.

A few minutes after the whistle sounded to wake the camp, Murtagh appeared from the tent. He stared at me a minute as if to satisfy himself that I was still there or to gloat over his reward for catching me. Then he went back in, and I heard the whirr of the electric razor. Breakfast was cooked in cans over the heater, and the cuffs were taken off my wrists so I could feed myself. Six men still guarded me. After eating, I rose and stretched and bent this way and that to get the kink and the pain out of my muscles. I was still sore from the fall, and being forced to sleep in the cramped chained-up position had not relieved me.

I submitted to having my hands cuffed behind me again, since there was nothing else I could do. My leg irons were taken off, and I was allowed to pace back and forth. During this time, the tents were quickly taken down and folded up into handkerchief size again, the support frames were collapsed, along with the furniture, and formed into small cylinders and stuck into the packs. The cans were pressed flat under the heavy boots of the men and then piled into a heap with other debris and garbage. A man sprinkled a fluid from a container onto the pile, smoke curled up from the pile material; the whole took on a gray cast, changed to ashes, and collapsed. The ashes were blown about, and we marched away with no sign of a large camp having been there. The footprints and the holes left by the stakes had been pressed down by men wearing broad discs on their boots.

The march was led by Murtagh, who frequently consulted his compass and also a small device which he held to his ear. These were guiding him through the rain forest, and it was fortunate that he had them. It is easy for anybody except a native to get lost in the forest. By native, I do not mean the average African native. He shuns these places; he hates to venture into the arched columnar world. The pygmies and the anthropoids and The Folk and the beasts of the quiet green mansions know their way around. And I know.

I did not understand why Murtagh did not lead us back the way he had come, since it was only about six miles to the edge of the forest. But he seemed to know what he was doing. And, after a half a day's journey, we broke out of the forest into a clearing. This was a recent, man-made well into which helicopters could drop. A few minutes later, a Sikorsky S-62 appeared and settled down. My leg irons were replaced, and I was forced to hop to the craft and climb awkwardly in. Murtagh and twelve of his officers got in, and we took off. Apparently the copter would return to pick up the others in several trips. It was some satisfaction to me that I had destroyed so many of their copters that they were reduced to one.

This was not true. After a twenty-minute trip, as registered by Murtagh's wristwatch, we came over another clearing. This was also man-made but much larger. There were about forty large tents arranged in concentric circles and, to one side, a space for copters. Two small craft squatted there. There was no sign of jets or of a landing strip for them.

Murtagh had sat ahead of me. He did not speak a single word during the flight. Once, he looked back at me and smiled. He seemed self-congratulatory, as a "great white hunter" would who was returning with the head of the largest elephant ever shot. The others did not speak either. I would have thought they would be much more jubilant, and then it occurred to me that they might be dreading reprimand or punishment of some kind. After all, they had not been so efficient; they had allowed one man to decimate them. And I had been caught, not through their cunning, but by sheer accident.

Why did Murtagh, their leader, the man responsible, not share their feelings?

Perhaps he did not care if he was reprimanded, since he had achieved his mission. And that, really, was all the Nine required of their servants.

After I had clambered out, my leg irons were removed. Murtagh removed the transmitter-activator from his pocket, showed it to me as he smiled slightly, and then gestured at my guards to conduct me ahead of him. We went through three circles of tents and stopped before the tent which was the center of the circles. This was also the largest, being thirty feet high. There were four guards in front and two at each corner outside the tent. When we went inside, I saw two at each interior corner.

A wall of cloth made two rooms. Murtagh reported to the officer at the table before the wall and presented a small plastic card. I'm sure that the officer knew Murtagh quite well, but he still went through the established procedures. He inserted the card into a small metal box with a screen above it. I could not see what the screen showed, but its presentation satisfied the officer. He picked up a wireless phone and said that he would send in Doctor Murtagh and the prisoner. He listened for a moment and then put up the phone.

"Give me the activator," the officer said, pointing at the device.

Murtagh did not say anything or move at all for a few seconds except for the sidewise oscillation of his head. He opened his mouth as if to protest but checked himself. The officer took the activator and went through the flap over the entrance in the wall. When he returned, he no longer had the device.

Evidently whoever was to receive us wanted to make sure that he controlled any detonation of the explosives in the disc glued to my belly. I admired his caution. If I had been he, I would have made certain that such an ambitious man as Murtagh did not get a chance to blow up the prisoner along with his superior and claim it was an accident or had to be done to keep me from escaping.

There was really little chance that Murtagh would do that, since he had half-won his seat at the table of the Nine. But the person within had survived so many millennia by not taking unnecessary chances. This was Mubaniga.

He sat in a high-backed folding chair at a large folding desk. Leopard skins cushioned his thin wrinkled flesh and frail millennia-old bones. His kinky hair was white, and his face and hands were valleys and ridges of grayish-black skin. The sunken eyes were black with red streaks mixed with yellow. His teeth were very thick and widely spaced. He wore a white jumpsuit with a black scarf around his age-corroded neck.

This was Mubaniga, one of the Nine. I had seen him at least once a year for fifty-seven years. Each time except one he had always been remote, and the meeting had been brief enough though painful for me. This was during the annual ceremony when a piece of flesh was extracted from the candidates and the elixir was given in return. But when I was the Speaker for the Nine, a sort of major-domo for several months, I came into more intimate contact with the Nine. Mubaniga had never talked to me except to give me orders now and then. But I had stood by and listened while the Nine talked among themselves. And often he talked to himself in a language which had to be the ancestor of all the Bantu and semi-Bantu languages spoken in Africa today.

I have the most intimate practical knowledge of African languages of any man, white or Black, and also have a Ph.D. in African Linguistics from the University of Berlin. My doctoral thesis (unpublished so far) was in fact derived from what I learned indirectly from Mubaniga. I got so I could understand some small part of what he muttered to himself, and I established a linguistic connection between proto-Bantu and the language of a small inland New Guinea tribe I had come across during World War II. My thesis was that the Negroids had originated in south-eastern Asia, possibly in some parts of south-eastern India, and had spread out in two directions. One branch had migrated to Africa and evolved into the Negro types we know now; the other had migrated to New Guinea and Melanesia and evolved into the types now existing. Those who had stayed in the land of origin had been absorbed into the Caucasoid and Mongoloid population.

Mubaniga, of course, had been born long after the migrations had taken place, even if he was twenty to twenty-five thousand years old. But he remembered the legends and the myths and the folk tales about those migrations in the days when there was a land bridge between south Arabia and Africa.

The Negroes had been diverted southward by the whites who lived in North Africa and had killed or absorbed the ancestors of the Hottentots and Bushmen.

My thesis was almost rejected. I knew it was based on valid evidence, but I could not produce Mubaniga as my witness. But the German doctors finally agreed that I did have some slight linguistic evidence, enough to call it brilliant but not really conclusive.

So now ancient Mubaniga sat before me and looked at me with eyes as fiery cold as a leopard's. He could speak a wretched English but addressed me in Swahili, which he spoke a little better. My own Swahili is perfect.

"At last," he said, "you have come to the end of the long road. Long for you, I suppose, but it seems a short one to me."

He could say that without contradiction.

I shrugged and said, "Once you're dead, what's the difference whether you have lived thirty thousand years or were born dead? To you, there is no difference. And if I have come to the end of my road, yours is not too far off."

Mubaniga crackled. He held up the activator and said, "Since the end is so close for me, I might as well press this. It will remove you and me and everybody in this tent and quite a few people outside."

Murtagh must have understood Swahili, because he drew in air with a hiss and paled.

The ancient put down the activator, though he kept his hand on it. He said, "You would have made a fine man to sit at the table. You are as cunning as the hare and as strong as the leopard, and you have a hyena's ability to survive. You might have sat at the table for thirty thousand years, as Anana has. But no, you had to throw away all that just because you could not stomach some deeds which have no significance for immortals. Don't you know that these people you pity will all be dead within a few years? Nothing you can do to them can really hurt them or deserves your pity. The only important thing is that you will live almost forever. What happens to the others does not matter."

"I understand the philosophy," I said. "But Caliban and I have self-respect, and we were choking on what you were shoving down our throats."

He shrugged and said. "Other candidates have felt the same way, and they died because they tried to fight us."

He spoke in Swahili to Murtagh. "You won't have to use the drugs to find out where Caliban is. Our agents have seen him in Gramzdorf, West Germany. But it is evident that both of them have an organization they're using against us. You will extract all the information from Grandrith about this. And then you will go to Germany to take charge of the hunt there, unless Caliban is caught before you are through with Grandrith, of course."

"Thank you very much, sir," Murtagh said. The only visible effect the news had was to slightly increase the sidewise oscillations of his head.

Mubaniga smiled and said, "You may thank me within the next hour, if you can."

Murtagh's oscillations stopped for a minute. I thought that his skin became even paler. I did not know what Mubaniga meant, but I soon found out. Contrary to what I'd expected, I was not at once conducted to a tent where the drugs would be injected. Instead, I was fed at noon, and then was conducted to one side of the clearing. A chair was brought outside for Mubaniga. He still held the activator. About forty feet before us were twenty-five eight-foot high posts. I was led toward the posts but was stopped by my guards ten feet from them.

Then Murtagh and twenty-four men, all stripped to the waist, were led out under guard. Smith, the radio operator whose life I'd spared, was among them. They faced the posts while their hands were tied above them to the tops. A man whose name I later found out was Greenrigg approached them with a long whip. He was six feet six and weighed probably three hundred. He had a paunch of no great size and a sheathing of fat, but if he had dieted he still would have weighed two hundred and seventy.

He raised the whip at a signal from Mubaniga. The first lash was on Murtagh's back and brought blood from a deep gash. Greenrigg then went on to the next man and down the line. He returned to Murtagh for the second round. Ten lashes were delivered to all except Smith. By then, some men were screaming and some were groaning and some had fainted. Murtagh stood upright and silent, and when he was untied he walked slowly and dignifiedly to the medical tent to have his wounds treated and bandaged. The others, however, were not permitted to leave immediately. They had to watch Greenrigg whip Smith until he died. No one told me why he was treated so, but I knew enough of the Nine to guess why. He had allowed himself to be taken prisoner by an enemy of the Nine, and they did not know what, if anything, he had told me. They could have found out by using the drugs they planned for me. But this would have taken time. Besides it was a good object lesson to the others to kill him so painfully.

Murtagh had not been relieved of his position, since he had attained the Nine's goal. But he had not conducted the operation to the complete satisfaction of the Nine and so must pay. Undoubtedly, if he did not do any better with Caliban, he might lose his candidate's position or even his life.

One of the men who had not been whipped because he had not been a member of the original force made a mistake. He taunted Murtagh with his inefficiency. Murtagh pulled out his automatic and put a .45 into his heart. Mubaniga said nothing about this. Murtagh was within his rights. He had paid for his mistakes and, since he had not been demoted, he was to be treated with the respect due an officer of the Nine.

I was immediately chained down by the legs to an eyebolt in the floor of one of the small helicopters. Murtagh and two others accompanied me. We lifted up while Mubaniga stood by the door of the big copter and watched us. The last I saw of him was a small black-faced white-suited figure. I wondered if I would ever see him again, and hoped that if I did I would be holding his neck between my hands. Even in that situation, I was still an optimist. I was not yet dead.

We flew about five hundred feet above the solid green roof for two hundred miles and then landed by the side of a strip cut out of the forest. We were transferred to a two-jet British plane which held six passengers. I was again chained by my leg irons to an eyebolt in the floor, but my hands were cuffed before me. Murtagh, I noticed, had the activator back. It must have been handed to him just before he stepped into the copter. He was not likely to use it on the plane, but I was even less likely to have a chance to force him to use it.

We ate. Night came. I slept. A man called my name, and I awoke just before the jet began to let down for a landing. This strip had also been cut out of rain forest. It originally had been fairly level land at the bottom of a valley. From the high mountains around us, the valley might still be far above sea level. The jet had to come in between two mountains forming a narrow pass and the strip itself was almost to the sides of the precipitous walls. There was barely room for the jet to taxi around so it could take off.

The strip was brilliantly lit, however, and a number of men, mostly blacks, received us. We got into a jeep and drove on a narrow road by the side of the strip out of the valley and to the right around the mountain. This took us up along the mountain. The driver, a Zanzibarian wearing a fez, sped like a maniac along the dangerous road with the right wheels often a few inches from a sheer dropoff. Finally Murtagh, whose back had been making him wince, told the driver to slow down. Murtagh was not suffering as much as he would if he had not been a servant of the Nine. The ointment was swiftly healing the lash wounds and deadened most of the pain. It was another product of Caliban's genius and would have been a boon to the world if it could have gotten it. But this, like so many of Caliban's inventions, was restricted for use among those who served the Nine. I suppose that the ancients of the oaken table liked to keep such things for themselves. Also, if Caliban had been allowed to reveal a small fraction of his inventions, he would have been the most famous man in the world. The Nine did not want him publicized. In fact, Caliban's original career as a brain surgeon at a prominent New York hospital had been cut short by the Nine. He had attracted too much attention with his great skill and the new techniques and tools he introduced.

The jeep went along so slowly then that we could talk easily. Murtagh said, "You answered every question and we have already radioed the information. Your men will be scooped up. Caliban will soon be caught."

"You mean that you drugged me on the plane?"

The reflection of the headlights from the grayish mountain walls on our left lit up his features. He smiled and said, "Yes. The drug was in your food. Even so, you were a reluctant subject. I had to use all my knowledge to dredge up the information. But you talked. And the men you've been using will be taken."

"They had no idea they were fighting the Nine," I said. "In fact, as far as I know, they have never heard of the Nine."

He shrugged. "It doesn't matter. They were helping you against us."

The men had known they could be in great danger if they helped me. They had been well paid, and they were expecting to die if things did not go well. But I still felt that, in some obscure sense, I had betrayed them. Rationally, I knew that I could not have helped talking. Knowing that did not erase a sense of guilt.

His statement that Caliban would soon be caught could not be based on anything I had told him. Caliban has his own organization, and while there was verbal contact between his men and mine, there was no way for Murtagh to find a path leading from my men to Caliban's.

Then I suppressed a groan. Murtagh must have seen some tremor and guessed the thought that made me sick.

"Oh, yes, you told us where your wife was."

He waited. Seeing that I would not reply, he added, "If it's any consolation to you, we'll be bringing her to you. We wouldn't want to separate a man and his wife."

There was always the chance that Clio might get away, but I told only myself that. He was not going to get any satisfaction out of my responses if I could help it.

But I was so furious—though more at myself than at him—that I might have seized him and jumped over the side of the trail and down the mountain, if I had been able. But my hands had been cuffed behind me and my legs were chained to an eyebolt on the jeep floor. And Murtagh and another man held pistols on me.

Murtagh said, "There is no doubt about the great capabilities of yourself and Caliban. Of course, you should have been candidates. But the fact that XauXaz was your grandfather must have been the main reason why you two were picked to fight for his seat."

He could not have known that unless he had questioned me while I was drugged. He was playing a dangerous game, since the Nine did not like inquiries into their personal business. But then any man who qualified as candidate for a seat at the table did not lack guts.

That he felt it necessary to reassure himself that nepotism was the chief basis for the choice of Caliban and me revealed much about his own self-doubts, however. That he could not resist telling me that he knew that XauXaz was our grandfather added more light to his character.

The sky began to pale above the jagged peaks on our right. The road led downward, and by the time we'd reached the bottom of the mountain, dawn had filled the valley. The road went through a semi-desert area. There was so little evidence of rainfall that I wondered if we were near the back parts of the mountains which hid the caverns of the Nine. There is rain forest on all sides of this range, but a freakish climatic condition carries rains over or around the mountains here.

Presently we were stopped by a gate in a wall which blocked the narrow valley. Above the mortared stone ramparts were sentinel towers, and three machine guns and a Bofors rapid-fire cannon stuck out from embrasures. The man on the driver's left got out and stuck a card through a slit in the wall. After a minute, the gates swung open. The jeep drove through; the metal gates, which were twelve feet high, swung shut. The road wound through a camp of the exceedingly light tents. I counted thirty men there and twenty at the wall. Then we were past the tents and going down. The mountains on both sides pressed in.

I had wondered why a copter had not lifted us over or around the mountain. But if this was indeed the rear entrance to the caves, then copters or any aircraft might be forbidden. That did not seem likely.

Murtagh, at that moment, answered a call on the radio and at the same time answered my question. Some observers ahead, who were hidden from us, were asking for identification again. The security measures here were very strict indeed, and this was one more piece of evidence that the caves were nearby. Murtagh identified himself and the party and then said something about when copters would arrive. It was evident from the conversation that followed that they were in short supply. I did not know why, but I surmised that important missions (among which may have been my capture) had taken them from this area.

We passed under a projection of gray, red-speckled granite. Holes had been cut in the face and in the bottom of the rock, and from these the white and black faces of guards looked. When I was past the projection, I looked back and upward. About a hundred feet above the outthrust was a dark opening containing armed men. That could be the rear entrance to the caves. The surface of the mountainside was so smooth that I suspected it was man-made. And from the opening to as high as I could see, the mountain leaned outward.

A helicopter could not have gotten close enough to the entrance to deliver passengers. Some sort of crane would have to drop a lift to hoist people up. If there was an elevator shaft within the mountain, its entrance at the base of the mountain was well-hidden.

The jeep drove on around the shoulder of the mountain. After two miles on a rough dirt road, the jeep stopped. Here the mountains were even closer. The sun would not be seen most of the day, and at this time a pale twilight filled the bottom of the valley with a seemingly liquid light.

The jeep stopped. The men got out. The chains through the eye-bolt were unlocked, and I was told to get out. We marched down the road, which was too narrow now for even a jeep to traverse. After two minutes, we were challenged again. The post here consisted of four men. A few feet beyond them, the path stopped. Beyond was a sheer dropoff of two hundred feet.

A thousand feet to the north, the two mountains merged.

Murtagh shoved his gun into my back and forced me to the edge. I looked down. The floor of the canyon was mostly bare rock with a few plants growing alongside a stream about six feet wide. The source of the stream was a small lake at the extreme end, and this derived from a spring, I supposed. The water ran down the middle of the canyon floor and then disappeared in the base of the cliff on which I stood. The only signs of habitation were three small huts built of stone halfway along the eastern wall.

A motor roared to my right. I turned to see a truck backing out of a cave. Its bed held a crane and a large drum of cable. At the end of the cable was a sling of leather. Evidently, I was supposed to sit in it so I could be lowered to the bottom of the canyon.

Murtagh, his face moving slightly from side to side, his thin lips pulled back to show long yellow teeth, watched while my cuffs were removed. I flexed my arms and did some knee bends. Then, at a gesture from him, I got into the sling. I could do nothing with all those guns aimed at me. The truck backed up until its wheels were close to the edge of the precipice, and I hung in the air past the edge. The motor and the cable drum worked, and I was lowered swiftly to the bottom. While I went down, I noted that the sides of the canyon inclined outward and were very smooth. If there had been any roughnesses which could be used for handholds, or any projections, they had been removed.

LORD OF THE TREES

I got out of the sling, and it rose up quickly. Faces sticking out over the edge were small white or black pie plates. This hole was to be my prison until the day of judgment. Evidently they were not worried that I would try to kill myself. They knew me well enough.

I smelled the water and tasted it. It seemed to be excellent drinking water. I started walking along the stream. When I came to a point opposite the stone huts, I stopped. I smelled a human female and that of another creature which I could not identify for a moment. Then the hackles on my neck rose, or felt as if they did, and I growled automatically. A male of The Folk was inside the hut.

A woman stuck her head out of the hut and seeing me, called "John!" She stepped out then, but I knew who she was as soon as I heard her voice. She was the six-foot one-inch high titian-haired beauty, the Danish Countess Clara Aekjaer. The last time I had seen her was at the annual ceremony eight months ago. She was dressed exactly as she had been then. She had no makeup, but she really did not need any.

She walked toward me with all the "vibrations made free" that Eve must have had for Adam. She was smiling as if she thought I had come to deliver her from this place.

I could not pay much attention to her just then because I was concentrating on the occupant of the other hut. He had stuck his head out, confirming what my sense of smell had informed me.

I did not know him, which was not surprising, since The Folk of the mountains in eastern Africa have always been very few and very shy. In fact, I had thought they were now extinct, with the possible exception of one female. Eight months ago, I had been forced to kill a male, *shth-tb* or Leopard-Breaker, as the name translates somewhat freely. He was the last male of his species, I had thought, and since his child was dying, his female would die without issue. But here was a big and apparently healthy male.

He came out into the twilight which filled the box canyon and stood before the entrance of the stone hut for a moment. He was about six feet three and probably carried three hundred and eighty pounds on that massive skeleton. Long russet hairs covered a dark brown skin. Actually, he had fewer hairs than a human, just as a chimpanzee has fewer, but their length made him seem hairier.

His body was humanoid except for the relatively shorter legs and longer arms. His feet were not those of an ape's but more like the feet of Neanderthal Man. He had the rounded buttocks and pelvic structure which would cause an anthropologist to unhesitatingly classify him as hominid. He never walked on fours, like a gorilla, as my biographer described the walking posture of The Folk. But my biographer did not know all the facts when he wrote the first two volumes of my life and so drew more on his imagination than on anything. Later, though he discovered his error, he clung to it to maintain consistency.

The neck was thick and powerful. The face was, at first glance, gorilloid, and I suppose a layman would continue to think of it as so after a long familiarity with it. Though I can't imagine any human except myself wanting to maintain close contact with it unless there were bars between him and the male. The immense ridges of bone above the eyes, the flat, wide-nostriled nose, the protruding jaws, the undeveloped chin, the thin black lips, and the long yellow canines, plus the low forehead and the roach of hair on top of his head would have frightened, or at least made uneasy, most humans. He looked much like the reconstructions of Paranthropus, the big vegetarian hominid that lived a million years ago in East Africa. He was basically vegetarian, too, but his teeth were more like those of the gorilla, who is not a meat eater. But The Folk eat meat whenever they can get it. He's an anomaly because his teeth are more apish than human, yet his brain is larger than a gorilla's. And he has a language. He is the living basis of African folk tales, a giant variety of the little hairy men the East African natives call *agogwe*.

He rolled toward me, swaying from side to side, his arms hanging loose but the huge black-brown hands working. His paunch stuck out before him, and the massive chest rose and fell swiftly.

I spoke to him in the whispering speech of The Folk. He stopped and blinked, then continued. I spoke again. He stopped again, and he said, "What language is that?"

I was astonished. No wonder. He spoke English. The pronunciation was not accurate, but the structure of his mouth would prevent the exact reproduction of a number of English phones. And he often did not voice his vowels of *u* in *untamed* or *o* in *son* or the second *a* in *galaxy.* But he spoke as fluently as if English were his native tongue, which it was. He had never heard the speech of The Folk before.

His bearing was not aggressive. I had just assumed it was, since all male of The Folk, on meeting strangers, act belligerently whether they feel so or not. He was merely approaching me to talk to me and was prepared to speak English or Swahili.

What he could not explain, Clara could. Twenty years ago, an agent of the Nine had brought him in when he was a few days old. The mother had died of some disease. Under direct orders of the Nine, Dick, as he was called, had been raised with the children of two Kenyans who were agents for the Nine. He had lived a good part of his twenty years on the edge of the rain forest of the mountains along the east Congo border. When he was twelve, he had been sent to this area.

For what purpose?

"Ah, John," Clara said, putting her long-fingered hand on my arm, "I suspect the Nine thought they would have some use for him eventually. And the eventual has come. I think they mean to put you two together in an arena of some sort, where you will be torn to pieces, if things work out as they expect."

"Is that true?" I said to Dick.

"I don't know," he said. "A man kept calling me names and throwing stones at me when he thought I wasn't looking. And he put stuff in my food to make me sick. I didn't see him do it, but I knew he did it. He hated me for some reason, though I had never done anything to him. I complained to my superior, and he told the man to lay off me. But this man, Scannon, he kept on bugging me. So, one day, when I crawled into bed and found a poisonous snake there, with no way for it to get there unless someone put it in my bed, I got very angry. I hit Scannon. I didn't mean to kill him, but I broke his jaw and his neck. And they put me down here, even though I told them it wasn't my fault."

It was strange to hear one of The Folk speaking English. Actually, though he was born of them, he could not be considered one of The Folk in any except a genetic sense.

Clara said, "I don't think he was put down here because he killed Scannon. That was just an excuse."

"And what do you think?"

"I think he's our jailer. Yours, rather, since they wouldn't really expect me to be able to escape from this place. And I think that it would be just like the Nine to pit Dick against you for their own amusement."

She could be right. On the other hand, he could be telling the truth, and *she* could have been set here to keep an eye on me. Or not so much to watch me as to pump me for information that Murtagh and the drug hadn't been able to get. The drug works well, but the one being questioned gives very restricted answers. And if the questioner doesn't ask the proper question, and word them just right, he isn't going to get much. Perhaps the Nine, knowing my fondness for Clara, hoped she would get me to talking.

I didn't ask her why she was imprisoned, expecting that she would volunteer soon enough. And so she did, though with a tone of exasperation at my seeming lack of curiosity.

She had been sent on a mission for the Nine to Rio de Janeiro. But she had delayed leaving London immediately because she was in love with an Englishman. So she had been drugged and put into a plane and shipped here. She supposed she would be an object lesson for the servants of the Nine in some hideous fashion. She did not seem to be frightened at the prospect, but Clara was a very courageous woman. Or perhaps she just did not care. She was a wild woman, one who lived intensely for every moment and was reckless of consequences. But she was intelligent and she must know what could be in store for her. Also, she could be a plant, as I said.

"You knew what would happen if you did not follow orders at once," I said. "You really have no one but yourself to blame."

"But I was passionately in love!" she cried.

I smiled. Clara was always in love, although she seldom stayed in that state long with one man.

At noon, the food was lowered to us in a net tied to the cable. We were given no utensils to use, on the theory that they might be adapted to make tools or weapons, I suppose. The food was good, though cooked too much for my taste. Dick was given meat along with the bamboo shoots, nuts, berries, and bananas. During the meal, I asked him if he wished to join me in an attempt to escape. It did not hurt to ask him, I thought, since even if he had been placed there to watch me, I would be expected to try escaping. And if he relayed the information to captors, he would have to be quick and sly about it to get by me.

The same reasoning applied to Clara.

"Yes," Dick said, peering out from under the massive frontal bones. "I want to escape. These are bad men. But where do we go? Even if we can get away, which we can't."

That was difficult to answer. He certainly couldn't settle down with any group of natives I knew. They would kill him or sell him to scientists. He could not go into the wilds, because he did not know how to survive there. He would have been as lost and helpless as a European astray in the rain forest.

"Well," I said, "if those canines were removed, and you were shaved all over and put into a suit of clothes, you might be able to pass for an unusually ugly specimen of humanity—no offence intended. You could make a fortune as a wrestler or boxer. I could introduce you to an honest manager, relatively honest, anyway. But you wouldn't be happy there, and sooner or later some zoologist would look closely at you, and the game would be up. Besides, city life would sicken you, you couldn't stand the gas fumes, the factory stinks, the noise, the crowds, but . . ."

I shouldn't have told him all that. I needed him, and it wouldn't help any to discourage him with the truth. If he had been a human being, I would have lied to him. But he was one of The Folk, and even though I have loved only two members of that genus, tolerated some others, and hated most, I could not lie to this simple trusting soul. That is, if he was as open and simple as he seemed to be. I had to remind myself that he could be a cunning agent for the Nine.

"There was a time when you could have lived with me on my plantation in Kenya," I said. "But I lost that, and I can't ever return to Kenya, not unless I'm disguised. But I'll think of something. The important thing is to get out of here. As soon as possible."

"If anyone could do it, you could," Clara said. "Or maybe Caliban. But nobody can. You'd have to be a bird to get out of here."

At dusk our supper was lowered. We went into a stone hut to eat and talk. There was no furniture there except for a pail to throw our garbage into. Our only bedding was a pile of old blankets, but these sufficed to keep us warm, with the help of each other's body heat. Back of the hut was a latrine ditch. As soon as night fell, and it fell early here, while the sky, three thousand feet above, was still a dark blue, we left the hut. The south end was lit by powerful beams, and a searchlight probed the valley. But we walked to the far north end, ignoring the light when it followed us. I plunged into the pool, sixty feet long and thirty wide, at the base of the northern wall. The water was icy, but I waded waist-deep until I got near to the wall, where I had to dive down. There were several openings in the rock through which water bubbled. But all were too small for me to get into.

After thoroughly exploring the bottom, I got out. I ran all the way to the other end to dry myself and warm up. Dick and Clara followed me at a brisk walk.

I was visible to the men above in the lights glaring down. They could see what I was doing, and if they wished to stop me, they had the means. But I think they were just laughing at me. I went into the tiny pool there and dived down to the bottom. This was about thirty feet deep, and the water flowed through an opening about six feet across. But a thick metal screen had been affixed to the rock with many metal spikes. I tugged at the screen about a dozen times, coming up for air each time. By the time I gave up, I was half-frozen, and it took me a long time to stop shivering. Somebody at the top of the cliff hooted at me for my efforts.

However, I did not feel that I had been foolish or wasted my time. That they had felt it necessary to screen the hole indicated that the hole might be an escape route.

After I had gotten warm under the blankets between Clara and Dick, I crawled out. Dick wanted to sleep; despite being raised by humans, he was one of The Folk in being unable to look far into the future. I told him he might lose more sleep before we got out of this, and if we didn't he'd have as long to sleep as anybody ever wished for. Grumbling, he followed me out. We sneaked past the probing searchlight to the detritus of flint I had seen at the north-east corner. Apparently, it had fallen there when a projection was blown off about fifty feet up.

Since there was no light, I could not work the flint. But when dawn came, I went to the door of the hut with a blanket over my shoulders. By the dim light there, I hammered and chipped away until I had several handaxes, long stabbing knives, scrapers, and choppers. I had learned the techniques from a French anthropologist who was once a guest at Grandrith Manor.

"What do you plan to do with your Early Paleolithic weapons, my cave man?" Clara said.

"I don't know yet," I said. That was true, but if I had a plan, I would not have told her until just before I initiated it.

"Well, at least you're keeping out of mischief."

The day passed just like it had before, except that Dick and I dived down to the bottom of the outlet pool and strove to pull the screen loose. When we came up for air, we could look up and see the faces of our guards there. They did not fire down to drive us away. It may be they felt there was no slightest chance of our loosening the screen. And if we wanted to exercise and to provide them with some slight amusement in a deadly dull job, so be it.

We gave up after a dozen dives. If our combined strength could not pull a corner of the screen loose with our bare hands, then tools were needed. I spent the rest of the day travelling around the base of the canyon and examining the walls. The north-east corner formed an almost square junction. By putting my back against one wall and pushing with my feet against the other, at a difficult angle, I might be able to inch my way up for the first hundred feet. After that the walls leaned slightly outward until, near the top, they were at an angle of about eighty-two degrees from the horizontal. The corner still maintained its squareness, but I would have to exert a tremendous pressure to keep from falling. I was not sure at all that I could do it.

As far as I could tell, there were no guards on that side.

Two hours before dusk, two men holding rapid-fire rifles were lowered. They stood guard while their officer, a Lal Singh, rode down. Then two other riflemen rode down. Then a man with scuba gear.

We three prisoners were allowed to stand within forty feet and watch them. The scubaman came up with a satisfactory report. Then our huts were examined. They did not find the flint weapons because I had hidden them beneath the surface of the north pool. The scubaman did not look into that pool. Evidently they knew that I could do nothing there.

After making searches at random in other parts of the canyon, they left. Just before he was hauled away, I asked Singh what had happened to Murtagh. He did not reply. I surmised that Murtagh had been sent to Germany after Caliban. Probably nothing would be done with me until he was killed or captured. But I could not bank on that. If Clio was caught and brought here, the Nine might think there were enough victims for a Roman holiday.

As soon as it was dark, I sneaked out and cut down some of the hardwood bushes. I trimmed them off and sharpened their points. I still did not know what to do with them, but if a situation arose where they would be handy, they would be waiting and ready. And they could be used as pitons, if I found a big enough crack.

I wanted to tell Clara and Dick what I planned. If their stories were true, then they should be with me. I did not think that Clara, strong though she was, could manage that climb. Dick was powerful enough, stronger than me, but he was also much heavier. And I just could not chance that they were spies. That the men had come down to search the area did not mean that either of my fellow prisoners had informed on me, of course. Almost everything I had done had been visible. And if my flint tools had been discovered, I might have suspected that I had been betrayed. No, they would say nothing about the flint.

An hour after nightfall, I slipped out from the blankets. Clara and Dick both stirred, and Dick said something, in Swahili, in his sleep. I stood there for a while, made sure they were deeply asleep, or else pretending to be, and left with my sticks. I waited a while by a bush to see if anybody would follow me. No one did. The beams probed around at random. I avoided them, went to the north pool, and recovered my flint weapons.

Before starting the climb, I had to get rid of the plastic bomb stuck to my belly with epoxy glue. I began chipping away at it with a flint dagger. The disc had a two-inch diameter and was two-tenths of an inch thick. The plastic was very hard and not easy to get at because of its snug position between my belly and the metal belt, which was two inches broad. I had to bring the flint down with considerable force to chip away the plastic. For all I knew, the concussion could set it off, though it did not seem likely that an unstable explosive would be used.

As I found out, the plastic was a rather thin shell around a tiny radio receiver and the tiny chemical detonating cylinder attached to the receiver. The problem became ticklish when I got to the detonator—not literally, of course. It was probable that a hard blow could set that off. So I pried away around it. The darkness and the angle at which I had to look at it made the task more difficult.

But, eventually, I pried both receiver and detonator loose and dropped them into the pool.

A shell of plastic was still adhering to my belly. It would have to stay there until I was able to find a chemical to cancel the bondage of the glue. And the belt was too tight for me to wriggle out of.

I had torn a strip of blanket off earlier that day. I tied this around my waist and shoved two daggers and six short sticks into a fold of the cloth. Since I would be bent forward with my back against the one wall and my legs drawn up with my feet against the other, I would keep the stone and wood from falling out.

The stone only got warmed up in winter time when the sun was directly overhead, and it lost its heat quickly. The skin of my back felt cold, at first. Later, as friction between skin and rock increased, the skin got too warm. And, of course, my back started to bleed. I left a trail of blood on the cliff wall as if I were some slug dying of hemorrhage.

To ease the rubbing away and cutting of the skin, I went slowly. But I got to the final fifty feet within an estimated twenty minutes. By then the strain was beginning to affect me. The pressure I had to maintain was draining my strength, and I was losing more blood than I had expected. Or at least it felt as if I were. The juncture of the two walls did not afford a perfect corner of a square. The walls were at oblique angles which varied, and this meant that often one leg had to be stretched out much further than the other. The unequal pressure sometimes brought me close to an uncontrollable shaking of my left leg.

Meantime, the beams continued to probe through the canyon, and several times they passed directly over me. When the cone got close, I stopped moving. The light, weak at this distance, did not reveal me to the men on the cliff, if they were watching. They must have been convinced that no one could escape. For all I knew, the searchlight was operated by a machine, and they only occasionally looked down from their card games or whatever occupied them.

I began the ascent on the part that projected outward. From that time on, I was like a fly on a ceiling. I had to be even more of a living wedge, one which proceeded by minute movements. The sliding of feet and the inching along of my back succeeded each other very slowly and very painfully. Now I bled more profusely, and my back became more slippery. The closer I got to the top, the more the cliff leaned outward. The only compensation for this was that the juncture of the two walls became more of an acute angle and thus gave me a better hold. I had planned on that, of course. If the corner had not become more narrow, I don't think I would have tried the climb. But the lesser space squeezed me down as if I were an embryo trying to give birth to myself.

I scraped across several narrow cracks in the rock but did not try to drive in any sticks as pitons. I did not need them, but when I got to the lip of the cliff, I might.

It seemed hours, but it must have been only fifteen minutes that it took me to get up the last fifty feet. Then I was hanging over the ground, wedged in tightly, with the edge of the cliff just above me. And here, where I was closest to safety, I was in the most danger. To reach up and over to clamp a hand down on the edge meant that I had to lose my grip on the corner. I could not leap out, because that would take me away from the edge. The only thing I could do was to reach up, place my hand on the lip, which was solid rock, let loose and hang by one hand, then reach up with the other, and pull myself up and over.

First, I had to get my daggers and sticks onto the edge, if I could. Otherwise, when I straightened out, they would fall out of the fold. This required a slow withdrawal of them, one by one, from the fold, and a quick throw with a looping motion. The two flint knives clinked on the edge. Two sticks also got onto the top, but four bounced off and fell. They seemed to be striking something.

Then, without hesitation, I reached up, bent my hand so it was at right angles to my arm, spread the fingers out on the rough granite stone, and let my body sag. I could not kick myself away because my grip was too precarious. Everything had to be done quickly, yet not violently. I swung out, and my weight started to pull my hand loose, since it had nothing to hold onto but was depending on pressure alone. And even though the rock was rough, it was not knobby. The surface friction was not much.

Despite my agonized efforts with my one hand, the hand slid away, tearing off skin against the rock. I reached up with the other hand, and got its palm flat against the rock, too. For the moment I hung there, and then I lifted myself up with a slow straining that made the muscles of my back, too long tense, crack as if they were splitting wood. When my chin was above the ledge, I used it to hold me up too. In fact, my chin supported the full weight of my body for about twenty seconds while I slid my arms forward until they were fully extended and flat against the surface.

Then, scraping the skin of my chest, I inched upward and over, my fingers digging into the rock, pulling me along like the legs of Lilliputian horses. Once my chest was fully over, I kicked with my legs, and gave a final convulsive effort that pulled me up and over the edge. To crawl all the rest of the way was easy, but it seemed to take a long time.

For some time, I lay there gasping for air. The cold air made me shiver, because I was covered with sweat and with blood on my back, my hands, my chin, and my chest.

When my breathing became regular, I sat up. Just ahead of me was a six-foot high rise of rock, a tiny cliff. It was against this that the four spinning sticks had struck and bounced back and fallen over the edge. The two knives had fallen close to the edge, and I had been forced to slide over them when I pulled myself over. They had ground into my chest, but they had not cut me.

I got up, stuck the one knife and the sticks into the cloth belt, held one knife in my hand, and started to work my way along the thin ridge of the canyon top. Close at hand were the higher walls of the mountains, and I could have tried to climb them to get away. If my suspicions that this area was the back end to the caves were correct, I could go over the mountains eastward and eventually get to the front entrance. Or I could take off to the west and be out of the dry desert area and into rain-forest covered mountains where the Nine would have no chance of tracking me down.

But my original intention had been to locate and spy on the back entrance to the caves. Having familiarized myself with it, I was to meet Caliban in Europe, or wherever we could, and then we would plan our campaign. Our idea was to attack the caves during the annual ceremonies, when we knew that all of the Nine would be there. Just how our small force was to make an effective attack was something we had not yet worked out.

I had given myself about a month and a half to traverse the central part of Africa on foot, from the coast of Gabon to these mountains. Due to my enemies' participation, I had arrived six weeks sooner than planned.

The moon sailed directly over the gap between the two mountains. I slid along like a ghost from shadow to shadow, hugging the base of the mountain with the top of the box canyon a few inches to my right. I also kept watching for mines or booby-traps, but if there were any along here, I was lucky and missed them.

It took me about an hour to get to the south end of the canyon. There were times when the ledge narrowed to nothing and I had to feel along with my face pressed against the rock, my toes groping for projections, my fingers hanging onto knobs and in fissures. Then the ledge came back to existence again, and I moved swiftly.

The battery of lights along the south end was directed downward, but there was enough reflection to reveal me when I got close to the end. I went swiftly, hoping that none of the guards would see me during my brief passage.

There were four. One was sitting on a chair by the big probing searchlight, which was, as I had suspected, randomly directed by a machine. He was bundled up and drinking coffee from a thermos. Two men were in the cab of the truck. Its motor was running, so that the heater could be operated, I presumed. The fourth man was inside a tent with all flaps closed. His head and shoulders were behind a small plastic window in the side. He seemed to be at a desk, reading something.

I took the man in the chair on the edge of the cliff first. It was easy, since the truck was facing away from him, and the two men in the cab were looking away. If one had looked into a rear view mirror, he might have seen me, but that was a chance I had to take.

I did not use my flint knife. I came from behind, gripped the man's head, and twisted. The crack of the snapping spine was sharp, but no one seemed to have heard it. I relieved the man of his knife and his belt, which held ammunition and a holster with a .38 automatic. There was also a Bren machine gun by the chair.

The knife had good balance. I pulled aside the flap of the tent; the man looked around to see who it was; then he jumped up, whirling. I threw the knife, and it went deep into this throat, shutting off his cry.

The tent held a desk and a shelf full of paperbacks, a coffee-making machine, and a short-wave radio. There were also automatic rifles and boxes of ammunition, magazines, a medicine chest, tins of food, biscuits, and a small gas stove of the Caliban type.

I munched on several biscuits and drank a cup of hot coffee, which I love. Then I went out to the truck.

I was the last thing the two men expected. They must have been tough to have been selected to work for the Nine. But one man stuttered, he was so flabbergasted. The other's voice shook. Both rallied quickly enough. By the time they had gotten out of the cab, one following the other out of the left side, their hands clasped on the backs of their necks, they were tense and wary-eyed. I made them lean forward with their hands against the side of the truck, their legs and arms stiff, and then I used my knife on one. The one who had stuttered I spared.

Under my directions, he backed the truck up and then showed me how to operate the cable, and then I cuffed his hands before him. I made him sit in the cradle at the end of the cable, and then told him what he must do if he wanted to live. I had to get into the truck then, and he could have tried to swing back onto the ground and run for a rifle. But he preferred not to try for a hero's grave, and he sat still while he was lowered into the canyon. I had to get out of the truck twice to check on how far down he was. Then he trotted away toward the stone huts. After a while, the huge dark figure of Dick and the blanket-wrapped figure of Clara appeared. Getting them back up took some time but eventually it was done. The man stayed in the stone hut; I assume to make sure that I did not try to shoot him.

Clara got into the clothes of a man I'd killed. They fitted fairly well, although the boots were too large. Dick put on a coat which restricted his movements but did warm him up. They drank coffee and spooned out hot thick soup while we talked in the tent. I watched them closely, because I still did not trust them. It would have been more realistic, from my viewpoint, to leave them in the canyon, since they could be very dangerous. But, like most human beings, I am not always realistic. I value friendship and love, and I have more concern for individual human beings than my biographer indicated. However, he was basing his evaluations on my early attitudes, when I had not yet adjusted to human society and still thought of myself as one of The Folk. I can be, from a civilized point of view, horrible, but that is only when I am dealing with my enemies.

Clara put one of Caliban's quick-healing and very soothing ointments on my torn and abraded skin, and then I fitted myself out in clothes as well as I could. Clara and Dick found my story of how I had escaped almost unbelievable, but that I had rescued them and therefore had gotten out of the canyon was undeniable.

We loaded the jeep with food and ammunition. Our plan for getting away was sketchy. We would just have to drive up to the main camp and improvise from then on. If I had been alone I would have tried to find out how to get into the caves themselves, but my immediate duty was to get Dick and Clara into the rain forest.

From then on, as far as I was concerned, they would be on their own, and I could return to this area.

I kept the pistol and the Bren handy at all times, and my knife was loose in its sheath. My main concern was treachery on Dick's part. Clara could be dangerous enough, but Dick, combining the enormous strength and quickness of a gorilloid hominid with all the human skills of karate and boxing and knowledge of firearms, could be the most deadly antagonist I had ever faced. So far, he had acted as if he were just what he said he was. But I wasn't going to turn my back on him.

Dick was quite capable of driving a jeep. In fact, I doubt that he could not handle anything mechanical that a human could handle. My conversations with him had been necessarily limited to practical matters, so I did not know how capable he was of really abstract thought. His brain was small, but the size of the brain is not an index of intelligence. Nor did it matter that he might not be able to appreciate the subtleties of Plato or Spinoza, Shakespeare or Joyce. How many humans can?

Clara sat in the front seat beside Dick. I was in the back seat. She drove at about twenty mph with the headlights on. We passed the cliff with the carved entrance a hundred feet up. The men stationed at the foot of the cliff did not come out to challenge us, nor was there any reason except excessive caution to make them do so. The road we were on was about sixty yards from the cliff base.

After a quarter of a mile, passing between cliffs so close we could almost reach out and touch them, we came into the open area of the main camp. There were lights at regular intervals around its perimeters; these came from lamps hung from poles. The tents all had closed flaps except one at the south end of the camp. There were four guards there, two on each side of the road, and an officer sitting at a desk within the tent.

Clara slowed down. We would stop—if we were challenged. If we were not, we would proceed at the same slow pace as long as nobody objected. The only illumination at this point came from the large lamps strung along a wire between two posts. They were quite bright, however, and it would be easy for the guards to see that Clara was a woman and that Dick was the man-ape.

I was hoping that the guards would be frozen by surprise for at least a few seconds. And so they were. Dick and Clara did not shout out a warning. But then they knew that I could easily blow both their heads off if they did.

A guard stepped in front of us, calling to us to halt, and then his eyes widened. Clara opened up with her automatic rifle on her right, as I had directed. I fired with my Bren to my left. Clara got the guard before us and the one on the right. I spun the two other guards around and brought up the fire, hose fashion, across the ground and then up. The officer had jumped up and started to run out through the front of the tent. My bullets caught him in the legs and then the belly.

Nobody at this point was going to stop us, but I wished it had been worked out otherwise. Now the men at the wall that ran from cliffside to cliffside would be alerted. And they could swivel their machine guns and Bofors rapidfire cannon around to face us and undoubtedly were doing so even now.

And the firing had also alerted the main camp behind us.

I should have sneaked around behind the tent and tried to get the drop on the guards while the jeep, with Clara and Dick, approached them. But I could not do that because I would have put myself in front of the jeep and the fire of Clara and Dick. I might have tried to keep the guards between me and the jeep, but if either Clara or Dick were loyal to the Nine, he or she would have been capable of killing his own men in order to get me.

Clara and Dick got out of the jeep and preceded me into the tent. There were loaded automatic rifles, and bazooka tubes with racks of rockets in the rear, and light machine guns on tripods, and hand grenades in the rear. I told Dick and Clara to slip the straps of their rifles over their shoulders so they could take a bazooka and several rockets. I could keep their hands occupied with the tube and the missiles. Dick took the tube. He said he did not know how to operate bazookas, but Clara said she knew all about them.

I attached about ten grenades to hooks on my belt so that all I had to do was to jerk them off to arm them. I yanked the phone wires loose from the short pole behind the tent. We got back into the jeep with me in the back seat again and drove until we were about an eighth of a mile from the wall. We stopped at the bottom of a dip which completely hid us, and Dick and Clara got out ahead of me. Both were sweating heavily with tension, and there was an additional element in Dick's sweat. I could not identify it then, but if I ever smell it again in one of The Folk, I'll know the odor of treachery.

The two searchlights on top of the wall ahead of us were swinging back and forth. No doubt the officer there had phoned into the camp, but they could not tell him anything as yet. When they got to the guard tent, they would know, and they would then switch to wireless.

Dick got down on one knee with the level of the road even with his chest. Clara loaded a rocket in. I fired a burst at both searchlights, and they went out. I shouted, Clara activated the rocket, and, its tail flaming, it arced down the road. It struck dead center and blew the gate apart. Clara immediately loaded and shot another one, this time at the fire-spitting muzzle of the Bofors. Its explosive shells danced across the earth but not directly at us. The rocket struck the wall below the gun emplacement, but it must have killed the crew.

The cannon started shooting again about thirty seconds later. Clara and Dick ducked down to load a third time. I stood up, firing at the dark area immediately around the Bofors until its shells were exploding fifty yards from me, and then I dived for cover.

We were lucky. One shell blew up near the edge of the dip and deafened us and covered us with a spray of dirt and a cloud of smoke. The shell just after it hit the edge behind us at such an angle that it struck a little distance beyond the edge. This explosion showered us, too, and increased our deafness, and, for a moment, numbed us. But I got to my knees, with my Bren pointed at Dick and Clara, and gestured. Even though it was dark, there was enough light from the lamps still operating along the wall for them to make out what I was doing. They got up and loaded and fired, just as the Bofors stopped. There was a heavy fire from two machine guns on one side and one from another—apparently the bazooka had taken out two machine guns, too—and about six automatic rifles.

They were firing blindly, fortunately, and when our fourth and last rocket struck, their fire was momentarily stopped. Clara was a superb bazookist. She placed that rocket just below the Bofors, and it disappeared in a cloud of smoke. We jumped back into the jeep then and roared up out of the dip, headed straight for the shattered gate. Clara fired with her rifle at the machine gun on her side, and I sprayed the left side of the wall. Then I dropped my weapon and threw two grenades in quick succession at the right and the left.

Bullets stitched across the top of the jeep, piercing the hood at an angle from left to right and shattering the glass of the windshield at the extreme upper right-hand side, just missing Clara. It seemed impossible to get through that hellish rain. But the grenades disconcerted them and may have killed or wounded some. Clara's cool firing, I am convinced, stopped several riflemen. Then we were through the gate, the jeep crashing into a piece still standing, and sending us off to one side of the road.

That was a touchy time, because now Clara would be entitled to turn around and fire past me. And she only had to move her rifle a little to cut me in two. But I crouched down so that she had to fire over my head and I could keep watch on her rifle out of the corner of my eye.

It was not as bad as it could have been. By the time the machine gunners could swing around, we were two hundred yards away. Two riflemen sent a stream after us; the tracer bullets spun along the ground as the streams swerved toward us. But our fire stopped them for a moment, and by then we were around a corner of the mountain.

After our first turn onto a higher level of the road, I told Dick to stop the jeep. We listened. Behind us was a roaring as of a dozen vehicles on the road, perhaps a half-mile away. Clara slipped forward and peered over the edge of the road.

"I can see their lights," she said. "There are exactly ten vehicles. Two trucks, the rest are jeeps."

"You two go ahead," I said.

They protested, but I said that I was running this ship. I jumped behind a big boulder on the left-hand side of the road, facing downward, so I could get out of line of the fire of Clara and Dick if they tried anything. But Dick drove off with Clara looking backward.

I ran across the road and down the side, slipping and sliding. I got behind a bush about twelve feet up above the road. And I waited. Presently, the first jeep skidded around the corner of the road, and I jerked a grenade loose and lobbed it into the floor of the jeep. I had one each inside the next two jeeps before the first went off.

The resultant explosions were quite satisfactory. I did not remain to assess the damage until I had gotten to the edge of the road above. By then the mountainside was bright with burning gasoline from the three vehicles. When I looked over, I saw that the road was blocked for some time. The lead vehicle was on its side, the one behind it was catty-cornered across the road, and the third was rammed nose first into it. If the truck behind them had tried to push them off the road, its crew would have been burned to a crisp. I wished they would try it.

However, the men, under the shouted orders of the officers, were climbing up the sides of the mountain to get to my level of the road. I lobbed four of my five remaining grenades down the slope.

That apparently killed or wounded many, because the fire from the survivors was feeble. It was strong enough to kill me if I remained, however, so I retreated up the side to the next level. But I was cautious about doing so, since the light from the burning wrecks was enough to illumine me as a dark figure to anybody above.

I still had one grenade, a .38 automatic with a full clip, a knife, and the Bren. The latter probably had very few rounds left. I had just gone behind a large boulder when I heard a muffled sound from above. It could have been Clara. I crouched for a moment and then there was a bellow of outrage and the clatter of a metallic object striking a rock and then slipping and sliding down the slope against other rocks. It sounded to me as if a rifle had been thrown down the mountain, and as if Dick was mad about this.

There were several interpretations I could put on these sounds. But whoever was in trouble would be needing my help. I went on up, though taking advantage of every bit of cover.

As I got closer, I could hear the shuffle of big feet in the earth of the road, pantings, and a woman muttering something. There was a slight swishing, which I interpreted, correctly, as a knife slashing air.

I stuck my head over the edge of the road. In the faint light cast by the fires far below, Dick was an enormous bulk advancing on Clara. He had his hands out ahead of him to grab her, but she was backing away with her knife slicing at him. The jeep, its headlights out, was a few yards up the road.

I stepped out, the Bren pointed at them, and said, "What's going on?"

They stopped. Dick backed away from her.

They both started talking at the same time. I said, "Ladies first. I mean you, Clara."

As usual, my attempt at humor was ignored or misunderstood. Maybe I should reserve them for situations less tense, but I have always thought that tense situations are those that most need humorous relief.

"This traitor, this thing, was going to shoot you!" she said in French. "I hit him over the head and threw the rifle away. He had no other weapon and I only had a knife handy. I couldn't get to my rifle, which is empty anyway, I think. I was trying to keep him away with my knife when you got here."

"That's a lie!" Dick said. "She was the one going to shoot you, when I grabbed the rifle and threw it away."

Dick had spoken in English.

I said, "Since when did you learn French, Dick?"

He stuttered then, and I said, "Why did you feel it necessary to lie to me about that?"

"I didn't lie!" he bellowed. "I can understand some French, even if I can't speak it! I didn't tell you I couldn't understand it!"

If he was innocent, then the omission was trivial, but if he were a loyal agent to the Nine, then this omission was one of a chain of very important facts.

Whatever the truth, I knew now that my caution had not been wasted. One of them was a spy, my enemy. And I could not abandon them to go on my own way because I owed one a debt of gratitude. And the other a debt of revenge. I don't walk away from those who would kill me.

Clara was reluctant, and she reproached me for lacking faith in her. But that was only to relieve her emotions. If she had been in my place she would have done the same, and she knew it. She dropped the knife and backed away so I could pick it up. I had her frisk Dick, and then he frisked her while I watched both. Neither found anything. I put her rifle in the back seat. They got into the front seat with Dick driving again. We went along the road at about fifteen miles, the maximum speed without lights on this narrow winding road.

We had gone about two miles when I saw lights ahead and below. Two vehicles were approaching us from about a mile and a half away. They had to be from the jet strip on the other side of the mountain. I stopped the jeep and watched the lights climb and wind, and then, suddenly, they went out. I returned to the jeep, warily, of course, and said, "Either they've stopped to ambush us or they figure they're getting so close they should turn off the lights. We'll proceed for a mile and then . . ."

We stopped every hundred yards to listen. Sound carried for miles along that high slope. We could hear shouts from far below us and the motors of the two vehicles approaching us below.

The third time we stopped, we failed to detect the jeeps. After a minute, I concluded they had heard us, and they had stopped to wait. I told Dick to shut the motor off. The slope of the road was steep enough so we could roll on down without pushing. In fact, it was necessary to apply the brake frequently to keep from picking up speed. We went for another half-mile, and then I had the jeep stopped. Our ambushers could hear the brakes from a distance.

I said, "I'm going up the side of the mountain and get above them, Clara. I'll leave your knife here, just in case you are telling the truth. I'm taking your rifle with me, though. You two stay here until I get back. That's an order."

"But he'll kill me!" Clara said.

"She'll knife me!" Dick said.

"I think both of you can take good care of yourselves," I said. "Just stay away from each other."

I went up the slope and left Clara's rifle behind a rock after determining that it had four rounds left in the magazine. It took me about fifteen minutes to work my way up the slope and then down, across the road at a point where Clara and Dick couldn't see me, work down the slope a distance, then along it, and then back up. I came out about thirty feet behind the jeeps we had heard. There were eight men crouching behind them. That left four men at the airstrip, if I had seen all of them when I left the jet.

"They must have seen us," an officer said. "We'll have to send out scouts."

He delegated three men to go ahead. They should fire at the first suspicious sign. If they ran into an ambush, they should take to the side of the roads.

The three left. I slipped along the slope, crouching, and then stuck my head over the edge. All five were standing together by the hood of the lead jeep. This made things very easy. My only regret was that I had not been in a position to catch all eight. But my grenade went off with a roar two seconds after it landed with a plop in their midst. They froze; they may not even have known what it was, but one of them suspected. He shouted, "Grenade!" and leaped away, but the explosion lifted him and sent him over the edge of the road to my right. He kept on sliding for a long time.

The blast had killed the others, too, and lifted the jeep up and slightly askew in relation to its former position. It had not caught fire but its two right tires and the metal from much of the right side were ripped apart.

The three came running back when they heard the explosion. By then I was up on the slope and I emptied my Bren in a burst that got all three even though they were strung out.

I went down the slope, picked up the rifles and automatics and knives and tossed them into the back seat of the undamaged jeep. I bent over just then fortunately for me. There was a metal box on the floor in the rear which I hoped contained grenades. Four shots sounded in rapid succession from the slope above me and bullets went through the metal of the door and over my head. I dropped flat onto the ground and the last two bullets would have pierced metal and me if I had remained in a crouch.

Then there was a whish of air and a thump as the empty rifle was thrown. It landed behind me in the dirt.

I doubted that Clara had the strength to throw the weapon that far. I doubted that any man except for Caliban and myself, could have cast it that far.

I felt cold then. What had happened to Clara?

"Come on down, you shambling mockery of a man! You ugly stinking ape!" I shouted. "Come on down! I won't shoot you! Use the knife you took from Clara, and I'll use my knife! I want the satisfaction of cutting your big belly open, you missing link! You treacherous beast! Lickling of the Nine!"

There was no answer. He was not going to give his location away. And well for him that he did not, because I had opened the door, removed an automatic rifle and then I let loose at the mountainside. I emptied that magazine and a second and a third, sixty rounds in all.

The echoes died away, the bullets quit ricocheting. There was silence except for a far-off harsh scream of some bird awakened by man's nocturnal activities.

At that moment, I heard the jet. It was high up and, until that moment, had been flying without lights. But they suddenly winked on, flashed, and then swung around. From around the corner of the mountain the light came. The big lamps along the strip had been turned on to guide the jet into the narrow valley.

I jumped into the jeep, turned on the motor, and roared away with a screeching of tires. I headed back up the road because I had to find out what had happened to Clara. I doubted that I had hit Dick. He would have hidden behind one of the many large boulders strewn over the slope. But he was armed with only a knife as far as I knew.

I even turned on the lights so I could go faster. I had gone not more than forty feet when a piece of the night detached itself and leaped from a great rock and landed in the back seat.

He came down in the back instead of on me because I had pressed the accelerator the second I saw him out of the corner of my eye. And I had estimated instantaneously that he would land just behind me. Which is why I rolled out from under the wheel and out of the jeep and onto the ground, leaving the vehicle to conduct itself wherever natural forces led it. If I had stayed there I would not have been able to turn around swiftly enough to defend myself, especially with the wheel cramping me. And he would have struck as soon as his feet hit the back seat.

He bellowed when he realized that I had slipped away. I was only half-aware of it because my head had struck a rock, and I was seeing sprays of light in the night.

If he had bounded out as soon as he had jumped in, he might have had me. But he crouched for a moment while the jeep turned toward the edge of the road. Only when it started to go over did he jump. He landed and rolled like a huge ball, and the vehicle, out of sight, crashed and clanged down the slope and then burst into flames. The glare from below illumined his silhouette, great and broad, long-armed and crest-headed. It also outlined the knife in his hand.

I sat up and groped for the butt of the .38 automatic that should have been sticking out of the holster at my belt. It was not there. I could not think why and then, as my head cleared, I remembered that I had placed it on the seat by me so I could grab it. The only weapon I had was a knife. That would have been enough at one time. I have killed males of The Folk with just a knife. But they were jungle-reared, ignorant of the use of such weapons, ignorant also of such refinements of fighting as judo and karate.

I got to my feet, unstrapped my belt and held the end in my left hand and the knife in my right. Crouching, Dick advanced on me. His knife gleamed dully, reflecting the brightness from below.

In the distance were shouts and, very faintly, the thud of running feet. The men from below were catching up.

From behind me, from around the corner of the mountain, came the thunder of jets as the plane lowered for the final approach.

My head was fully clear now. I stepped toward him and lashed out with the buckle end of the belt. He had not seen what I had behind my back, and so he was surprised. He leaped back, but the buckle hit the end of the knife. He did not lose the knife, but he was not as confident as he had been.

Then I lashed again, and he caught the buckle in his free hand. He was fast, faster than any man I'd ever fought and, of course, stronger than any man whatsoever, including myself. The belt was jerked out of my hand so violently it burned the skin. And it almost carried me into range of his knife.

He came in with a thrust for my belly, which he did not finish. My knife parried his blade and then I stepped back and threw it. It was all-or-none in this case. If he blocked it, he had me.

The knife sank into his paunch.

His own knife dropped. He staggered back, clutching at the hilt. Then he fell on his back, and air rattled in his throat.

Rifles exploded down the road. Bullets whizzed by me. Others raced along the dirt, just missing me. I had not time to pull my knife from Dick. I should have taken the time, have risked the bullets. If I had pulled that knife out . . . but I didn't, and what is done is done.

To have gone down the slope was to put myself in the twilight illumination from the burning jeep. I leaped across the road and was up the slope and crawling among the rocks. The men probed the slope with heavy firepower. However, they had seen me only at a distance and unclearly, and they had no idea where I was on the mountainside. They concentrated most of their fire on the area behind me, since they assumed that I would be travelling away from them. Then they quit, probably because they were running short of ammunition.

I went back down the road on a course about fifty yards parallel with it. There were no men where I wanted to cut down the slope to the lower level where I had left Clara, so I went swiftly there. The jeep was still standing where I'd left it. I did not understand why the pursuers had not used it. By it stood a single man with a rifle. On the road at his feet was a form. It was too dim there to see well, but I smelled her. She was still alive.

It was easy to come up behind the guard and break his neck. Once more, I was armed with rifle, pistol, and a knife.

Clara was bound hand and foot and gagged with strips torn from her shirt. Dick had taken her alive and tied her up so that she could pay properly for her defection. I untied and ungagged her.

"Can you climb up the hill?" I said.

She cleared her throat and said, "Yes. How in the world did you get away from them? And Dick?"

"He's dead. What's the matter with the jeep?"

"I don't know. The bullets must have damaged it somewhere. When the men came, they tried to start it, but the motor wouldn't even turn over."

I could not have used it anyway. I picked up a bag of canned food and two containers of water. I gave her a rifle and two magazines from the jeep's floor.

We started up over the mountain. A few minutes later, the sky grayed. We increased our pace. Within an hour, we were still going strong, though she was panting. Far below us, two jeeps carrying armed men stopped by the men who had been pursuing us. The jeeps evidently came from the airstrip on the other side of the mountain. They were too far away for me to identify the newcomers. So far, the jet had not taken off.

Crouching behind a rock, I watched the long conference. Occasionally, an officer turned his binoculars up the slope and swept the terrain. None stopped with me in their line of sight. Then the jeeps started toward the valley. If any of the Nine were in the jeeps, the men in charge at the camp would be lucky to get off alive. The Nine would never forgive them.

There was no more smoke from any of the burning vehicles. The roads were clear now, and jeeps full of armed men were coming up the roads. I counted eight. These were almost bumper to bumper as they raced along the dry earth, throwing up large clouds of dust.

Then they pulled over to the extreme edge, the wheels on the rim of the dropoff, to let the jeeps from the airstrip by. As soon as these had passed, the jeeps resumed their dangerous speed. I had assumed that the men in them were out to hunt me down, but the vehicles continued on around the mountain. Perhaps they were going to come up from the other side to cut me off.

They did not have enough men for that to adequately cover the area. If they had had a copter, they might have done it.

When we got to the top of the mountain, I saw what they were doing. The jeeps, so far away they were almost invisible, were parked near the two-motored passenger jet. Evidently the newcomers intended to leave soon, and they wanted to make sure I did not attack them at the plane or try to steal it.

We went on down the mountain and by late afternoon were near the bottom. The sun flashed frequently off the binoculars directed toward our slope. But if they saw us, they made no move. And I did not believe they would not come after us if they did see us.

Clara said, "Why are we heading straight toward them?"

"They don't expect us to do so," I said. "At least, I don't think they will. I'll admit I've been very aggressive, but that was because I was trying to escape. I want to get as close as possible because I suspect that one or more of the Nine came in on that plane. And it's obvious the plane is waiting to take them away again. Also, if we get a chance to steal the plane, we will."

Clara kissed me and said, "You're wonderful! A real Tarzan! A beautiful *Starkathr*! My loveable black-haired, gray-eyed *Übermensch*! Samson and Hercules and Odysseus rolled into one! Nobody but you could have gotten out of that canyon, and anybody else would have left us there! And then to get away and kill so many of them! And then to attack them when we could get away!"

"I *have* been pushing my luck these last few days," I said.

For some reason, she thought that was funny. She choked trying to repress her laughter.

Halfway down, we were forced to dive for the shelter of a large boulder. Mortar shells began exploding below us. We clung to the rock, our faces pressed into the hard ground, while at least thirty-five shells roared along the face of the mountain. The closest, however, was about forty yards below us. That was close enough, but, except for shaken nerves and insulted eardrums, we were not hurt.

After waiting for five minutes after the last of the shells, I looked out over the boulder. The tiny figures were engaged in doing something, but they were not attending the mortars, which glittered in the sun just before the shadows of the western mountain fell on them. Nor was there any movement toward us. I decided that they had lobbed the shells just to scare us out if we were anywhere in the neighborhood.

We stayed behind the boulder for another fifteen minutes and then started our descent again. By the time we were three-quarters of the way down, the shadows from the other mountain had fallen on us. We kept going in the twilight. When we were about a quarter-mile from the jet strip, we stopped to eat cold food from our cans.

Just before we finished the meal, a helicopter chuttered around the side of the mountain to the west. The lights along the strip flashed on, but the machine continued on over us and disappeared. There was no longer a lack of choppers. This one was going to pick up the newcomers and bring them to the jet, I was sure of that. That would avoid bringing them on the road in jeeps and so open to ambush from me.

Moreover, when daylight came, the chopper would undoubtedly be out looking for us. And other choppers might be on the way to aid in the hunt.

When night was fully alive, I left Clara behind a boulder near the foot of the mountain. The lights were on along the strip and around the four tents. I couldn't see them, but I had no doubt that mass-detection buttons were strung around the perimeters of the camp and the jet. Four men had just finished erecting a metal structure about thirty feet high on the tip of which was an antenna array. A minute later, the array began rotating. I stayed behind a bush. It looked as if it was a personnel detector, either radar or a heat-sensitive device. It must have been brought in by the jet. When detectors exist which can distinguish between the gait of a man or a woman at a range of twelve miles, the skulker at night has to be exceedingly careful and crafty. Clara and I had been lucky coming down the mountainside. If the detector had been installed then, we would not have been able to get away from the helicopter.

I watched for a while and determined that there were thirty-six men in all. Half were stationed as guards outside the camp and around the plane. The rest were cooking or lying down on sleeping bags on the ground or were doing something in the tents. I could smell their tension, and the infrequent but sharp laughter verified my nose.

There were two 60 mm mortars with piles of about sixty shells apiece. There were six .50 caliber machine guns along the perimeter of a circle described around the jet and the camp. Every man carried an automatic rifle. The jeeps were parked inside along the perimeter so that the men could fire from behind them.

The logical place for the choppers to land would be close to the jet so that the passengers could be transferred with the least exposure.

I crawled back to Clara, taking a long time because I had to keep behind boulders or in depressions as much as possible and when I could not I moved only when the antenna was turned away from me.

"The chopper will be coming back on one of two routes," I said. "Either all the way around the mountain, along the shoulder. Or directly over it, the shorter route. They know we have an M-15, so they will be flying high, either way. But maybe they won't be too high. They must figure that we won't be dumb enough to hang around here once our escape route was open. Especially since the chopper came. But they also must figure that they can't rely on me not to be dumb. Their experience must have convinced them that I don't always run."

She chuckled and kissed my cheek and said, "I think they don't know what to think."

I told her what I wanted her to do, if she wished to cooperate. If she didn't, she must leave. I did not want her around unless I knew exactly where she was and what she was supposed to do. She agreed, without hesitation, to obey me.

Even so, she was reluctant to part with me. She kissed me again, and she said she hoped she'd see me again. But she was happy, even if somewhat scared. She was out of what had seemed a hopeless situation, and she might yet get out of this one.

It would take most of the night for her to get stationed, since she had to go back over the mountain and then around to a place along the shoulder. I crawled back down to a position about a quarter-mile from the camp. If the chopper did come directly over the mountain, it would start lowering close enough for me to get it in my range. Of course, I would have to get the hell out immediately because the combined firepower would be directed at me.

The chance of getting the chopper was about a hundred to one, and the chance of getting away alive was about a thousand to one.

If the enemy had been anybody but one of the Nine, I would not have risked it. But I hated them so that I was willing to take the risk. Clara was out of range of fire from the camp, so that if she got the copter, she could get away.

The night fell to pieces, and the sun came up again. I had suspected that the chopper would carry the newcomers by day. It would be easier to spot us then, and it was also safer for the jet to take off. About a half hour after dawn, I heard the chutter of the machine. It was much lower than I had expected, about five hundred feet up. But it did not fly directly in a straight line. It zigzagged, and at first I thought it was taking evasive action. Then it came to me that this might be a dry run. It was not carrying VIPs; it held armed men. They were trying to fool us into exposing our positions by firing at them. Then, after dealing with us, they would go back for their passengers.

Trust the Nine to be supercautious!

I got under the overhang of the huge boulder and lay still. The machine passed almost directly overhead. It went as far as the camp and then it returned, but further to the north. It disappeared over the mountain. I suspected that it would come back again, this time around the shoulder, near where Clara was. I hoped she would not fire, that she would figure out that this was a dry run.

There was nothing to do except wait. The bulk of the mountain deadened any sound on the other side. I could not get up and climb to the top, because of the personnel radar. Therefore, wait it would be. My patience is great; I learned it in a hard school when I was young, hunting for meat. But this was the most painful watch I had ever put in.

An hour passed. Then the chopper came over the top, and this time it was even lower. Obviously, it was making another sweep, daring us to shoot. If we were lucky enough to bring it down, the Nine would have lost another helicopter and some servants, but they could then use the jeep to get to the jet. Or they could wait until another helicopter arrived. After ten thousand or so years, they had developed the ability to take the greatest of pains and to use as much time as needed.

I was certain that one of the Nine had to be involved. This much trouble would not have been taken for anyone lesser, not even for an important candidate for the empty seat.

It was not enough for the machine to be taken over this mountain. It went over the camp to the mountain on the opposite side and cruised up and down and back and forth for an hour. It seemed to be about only two hundred feet above the surface.

Then it rose straight up and flew back over my mountain maintaining several thousand feet height above ground level.

By then I decided that I had been wasting my time. I had taken a long shot and should have known better.

I waited. And I waited. The sun sank behind the western range. The camp showed no unusual activity. Several jeeps, which had left at noon, returned before dusk. These carried only the men who had left earlier and two bazookas and bazooka rockets.

I crawled to the top of the mountain and descended much more swiftly on the other side. I knew where Clara was and so called out softly to her and then waited for the counter-word. The wind was carrying the scent to me, and so I knew that she was alone.

"I don't know what he's doing," I said. She understood by *he* that I meant one or more of the Nine. "I'm sure he's inside the caves and probably sending out all sorts of messages. There must be a powerful shortwave set in there. I don't know when he's coming out, but you can be sure that we'll never get close enough to get the chopper that carries him unless we want to commit suicide."

"Perhaps it's too big a job for just us two," she said hopefully. "We can run away and fight again another day."

"We'll try one more day," I said. "If nothing happens we leave tomorrow night."

Part of that night we spent working our way down the mountain to the end of the valley into which the jet had flown. We approached the end of the strip by a shallow ravine. This lay about a hundred yards beyond the rammed earth of the end of the strip. Behind us was rough land with sparse bush for two hundred yards, and then a mountain began to curve gently up. The jet had to swing down over its two thousand foot height and come down close to the surface if it was to settle its wheels at this end. The strip was long enough to take the two-jet type but not a four-jet.

The personnel radar on top of the tower at the north end of the strip was undoubtedly able to detect us. And at this distance we would not have been able to see it if the lights had not been turned on. We crawled along out of the ravine until we were past the foot of the mountain on our right and out of the radar's line of sight.

I told Clara what I intended to do. She said that it sounded forlorn and, indeed, suicidal. I agreed and said I would try it, anyway.

The rest of the night we slept peacefully, except once, when I awoke and thought I had heard a leopard. But the scream was so far off, and I got in on the very end of it, so I could not be sure. If there were leopards here, they would not be man-eaters. I went back to sleep.

At dawn we ate the last of our food and drank the last of our water. An hour later, I heard the chopper. It rose high over the mountain and came down vertically exactly over the camp. The figures that got out of the machine were tiny, of course, because we were so far away. We were behind a rock at an angle to the camp, looking past the shoulder of the mountain west of the camp. But one of the figures was so bulky and long-armed and crest-skulled, it had to be Dick. I had not killed him after all. The knife must not have gone in as deeply as I had thought. And he may have been pretending to be dead so that I would approach to pull the knife out, and he could take me by surprise. He might well have done so, if those riflemen had not run me away. He was walking without any help, so he must have been quickly patched up. Caliban's medical inventions had long been of great service to the organization of the Nine.

The second figure that magnetized my attention was that of a broad-framed, black-skinned, white-haired man. His walk, distinctive even at that distance, identified him as Mubaniga.

The third figure was a tall skinny bald-headed man who could be none other than Doctor Murtagh.

For some reason, he had been called back from his journey to Germany.

Mubaniga got into the jet with a number of armed men. Dick and Murtagh remained on the ground. I knew then they had been left behind to hunt for us. Murtagh had been recalled to complete a job that he had erred in marking off. He undoubtedly would have liked to tell Mubaniga that I should have been executed the moment I was captured, but he would not have dared.

Two jeeps rode out along each side of the jet. At the end of the strip, they stopped, and the five occupants of each got out. They advanced with rifles ready and investigated the terrain for several hundred yards in each direction. Two men took stations on the edge of the ravine and faced outward. The others formed two lines near the end of the strip.

The jet took a long time warming up. I ducked down into the ravine at a point where it curved and so kept me from being seen by the two guards. My moves were dictated then solely by my hearing. I crouched there with the rifle in hand, the .45 in its holster, and the knife in its sheath.

Clara Aekjaer was in a hole beneath the overhang of a boulder set on the hillside but out of line of the personnel radar. She had her orders to come out when she saw me running.

The twin jets roared, but the pilot was still testing them. Then I heard something unexpected. The copter was swinging across the strip. I do not know why I had overlooked it in my plans. I suppose because I had regarded it solely as a carrier in the last stage of getting the jet away with its important passenger. But it was coming down the strip now and would then go up and down the gently sloping mountain to make doubly sure that no one was hidden there.

I shoved myself against the bank and tried to look like a rock. My skin was smeared with dirt, and my clothes were covered with clay, so I probably did look like a rock. And there was a projection above me to throw me into the shade.

The copter flew over about a hundred yards ahead of me. I dared to turn my head slowly to look over the opposite side of the ravine. The big chopper was zigzagging at only fifty feet above the ground. Its sides bristled with machine guns and rifles. It proceeded for about half a mile and then, its occupants believing that anybody beyond that could not harm the jet because it would be too high then, returned. It was on its way to land when the change in the noise of the jet showed that the plane was taking off.

That was my starting gun.

I ran down the rocky bed of the ravine, but I was still crouched over. Clara should have started to crawl out of the hole the moment she saw me go. She would get out just far enough to shoot down the nearest guard.

He, fortunately, had not resisted the temptation to turn and look at the jet for just a moment. Perhaps he wanted to reassure himself that he was not in its direct path. I had not been counting on him to do that, but it helped. It gave me a few more seconds to get down the ravine before I had to slow down and start shooting at the guard at the far end.

The copter was still coming down and its vanes, plus the roar of the jets, helped drown out Clara's fire.

The guard nearest me turned his head, saw me, froze, and then he crumpled to one side, dropped his rifle, and slid out over the ravine. He fell in front of me. I leaped over him, swinging my rifle up to point at the other guard, who had just become aware that his comrade had fallen. But he fell, too, hit by Clara's fire.

Halfway between the two corpses, I stopped. I listened and then, visualizing just how far down the strip the jet was, I bent down, gathered my leg muscles, and leaped to the top of the ravine, six feet up, and over it. My rifle was spitting as I came up and I caught every man on the right end of the strip. The burst stitched them together in death.

That they were facing outward and away from me helped the surprise.

The man at the nearest end of the line on my left side had seen the first guard fall. He had started to fire without warning the man on his right. This man, however, had heard the gun shooting even above the noises of the two craft. He had started shooting in Clara's direction, and then the others heard and began firing.

Clara's fire and mine were like two hoses started at each end, and they met in the middle.

The pilot of the jet must have seen what was happening. It was too late for him to stop. He could do nothing except try to get past us.

I crouched, Clara continued to fire at the oncoming plane. It lifted, perhaps prematurely in an effort to escape our bullets. I don't know. But I raised up and threw the rifle so that it spun once and then the barrel went straight into the plane's port jet.

I had not time to throw myself down. The wing shot a few inches above my head, and I was deafened by the roar.

Theoretically, the jet could fly with one engine dead. But things happened too fast. The rifle had wrecked the engine, the pilot had lifted the plane a trifle too early, and, for all I know, Clara's bullets had hit someone or something vital.

The jet plowed into the side of the mountain behind us and blew up. Pieces of metal spun through the air and fell around us. Fire shot up, and black smoke poured out a hundred feet high.

The people at the other end of the strip were paralyzed. I had banked on this. I leaned down, took Clara's hand and pulled her up onto the ground so swiftly that she cried out with pain. We ran to the nearest jeep. Clara got into the driver's seat and started the motor. By then the people in the copter had recovered some of their senses. It started to lift off, turned, and a machine gun and a rifle in its starboard bay began to shoot fire. And the men on the ground were piling into the jeeps there. In the first jeep were Dick and Murtagh.

If they had had any time to reflect, they would have fled without paying any attention to us. They had allowed one of the Nine to be killed, and their own lives were forfeit. Murtagh's candidacy was automatically cancelled, and he was as much the quarry of the Nine as I.

But they reacted with their reflexes only. They were still carrying out the Nine's orders, and they intended to kill the man who had thwarted them so much.

Clara wheeled the jeep around with tires screeching and headed toward the copter. He spun the copter around and started away, then stopped it and started back toward us. The fire from the gunners dug up the dirt on all sides of us and a few bullets pierced the hood. But Clara drove the jeep as if it were a bull with a nest of hornets hung under its tail. It swerved this way and that so violently that I had to jam my feet against the back of the seat in front of me and my back against the seat behind me. I fired as steadily as I could, and then the chopper veered away on its side and crashed in the path of the oncoming jeeps. It blew up, spraying flaming gasoline everywhere. Clara jammed on the brakes just in time to keep us from slamming into the inferno. She backed up quickly enough while our faces seared, turned around, and raced off.

The other jeeps backed up and went around the flames, and then the chopper exploded again. Presumably, it was the overheated ammunition. Fire like surf shot out and covered some of the jeeps. Men jumped out of the nearest vehicle while it was still going and rolled screaming on the ground.

Murtagh's jeep was partly splashed, but he and Dick got away. I shot at them but did not think I hit them.

Those behind, however, were occupied by determined men. They came around the flames and pursued us as if they had learned nothing from the past few minutes, not to mention the previous three days. And perhaps they were right in refusing to learn, since my good fortune could not last forever.

Clara took the jeep along the edge of the ravine, cut across its end, and we were loose on very rough country. We bounced high and hard, so violently that all I could do was hang on. But those behind us could not shoot either. Our course was strictly dictated by the terrain, which was as wrinkled as the face of a centenarian. The jeep cut back and forth, leaped out from the edge of ridges and slammed into the ground with bone-cracking and muscle-snapping force. Once she tried to stop the vehicle in time to keep it from going over another ravine, which was too broad for us to traverse. The jeep skidded toward the edge, stopped, teetered, and then went over on its side. Clara leaped out one way and I the other. I jumped up at once and looked down, expecting to see her crushed underneath the vehicle. But she was on its other side, flat against the earth. The jeep lay on its side.

I jumped down, picked her up, said, "Are you all right?"

She was white-faced, but she nodded. I handed her a rifle and said, "Keep them off while I fix this!"

"How can you fix that?" she said, but she moved on down the ravine and stood on top of a rock so she could fire over the edge.

I crouched down, got a good grip on the jeep, and slowly straightened up. The jeep, groaning, came up, I almost slipped, but not quite, and the jeep was upright.

Clara started shooting then. I ran up to her, tapped her shoulder, she turned, started, and then grinned. Some of the color was returning. The racket of gunfire and the gouting of earth along the edge of the ravine was still going on when we drove off along the bed of the cut. We did not go swiftly or too far. About three hundred yards down, we were stopped by a dropoff of about twenty feet. She drove the vehicle over, abandoning it just before it reached the lip of the little cliff. I had hoped that the jeep might survive the fall. But it dived into the dirt nose first, and the sturdy radiator, which had suffered so much, finally broke. Water pooled out from it.

Even so, we had a good headstart on the others. They were very cautious about approaching long after our fire had ceased. The steep ridge which had caused Clara to skid the jeep prevented their vehicles from going any further unless they went far to the north. They did follow us on foot, however, because I saw them coming out of the ravine when we were about five hundred feet up a mountain. This was partially covered with bush and trees. The rain forest would start just on the other side of this mountain, and the only one who could track us then would be Dick.

If he had been raised by The Folk, he would have been somebody to fear. His nose was keener than mine, but he had been raised by humans who lived on the edge of the rain forest but seldom went into it. He would be lost. And he could not travel as swiftly as Clara and I. He had too much weight to carry, and his legs were too short.

I kept on going with Clara panting heavily and having to stop now and then. The gap remained between us and the pursuers. But when, at evening, we plunged through the dense rim-growth into the cool and dark mansions of the rain forest, I stopped.

After getting Clara up into a tree, I returned to the tanglery by the border between bush and forest. From a branch a hundred and fifty feet high, I watched the tiny figures toil up the hill. They were lost from time to time in the bush, and then, as dusk fell, they became invisible.

LORD OF THE TREES

I had discarded one rifle when it ran out of ammunition. The other was with Clara, and it held only six rounds. I carried the .45 automatic and my knife. I was tired. I would have liked to hole up for the night. Clara and I had satisfied our thirst at a pothole and filled our canteens. She had eaten nothing since breakfast, and I had had only a small golden mouse I caught by the tail while I was on my way out.

But I had a job to finish.

I climbed down and went through the bush, though very cautiously. Dick's keen ears and nose made him worth all the others put together in the jungle, and I did not want to stumble over him lying in ambush.

About a hundred yards away, I heard a very strange noise.

They were all chanting my name.

"Lord Grandrith! Lord Grandrith!"

If it was a trick, and I did not know what else it could be, it was unique. It also whetted my curiosity to the point where I could not have stayed away.

At the last, I climbed a tree and peered down through the branches of two trees ahead of me at the camp.

They were cooking over Caliban's lightweight stoves. Eight of the ten were shouting out my name together. Dick squatted by the stove, his voice booming above the others. Murtagh stood in the center of the small open area with his hands held out.

I called out from behind the trunk during a pause in their chanting. "What do you want?"

Murtagh shouted back, "We want to parley with you."

"Why?"

"I think you know why. We failed, and so the Nine will kill us. We would like to team up with you. Some of us now believe that you and Caliban might actually have a chance against the Nine. And we have talents that you can use, since you can use every bit of help you can get, despite your fantastic success so far!"

"Throw your weapons into the bush! All of them! Knives and derringers, too, if you have them!"

They were reluctant to do so but only because they felt naked without them. And they could not be sure that I would not then mow them down.

When the last weapons, which did include two derringers, were tossed over a bush, I dropped from branch to branch, fell twelve feet to the ground, and then walked into the clearing. My pistol and knife were in their sheaths.

Murtagh was smiling now. I did not like him trying to be friendly any more than I had when he was trying to kill me. But alliances in wartime are not based on likes or dislikes. When he started to speak, I held up my hand.

"If you are to join me," I said, "you must make it worth my while to accept you. I need much information. What do you know about my wife? And what is the situation in regard to Caliban?"

"I am a candidate," he said, "but that does not mean I am fully in the confidence of the Nine. You know that. I have heard nothing at all about your wife. I do not even know the name of the man who is in charge of the business of getting her. As for Caliban, well, I was ordered to Germany to track him down after I had put you away in the canyon. I was told that he had been seen in the vicinity of Gramzdorf, a village and a castle in the Black Forest. I was told that he had been trying to kill Iwaldi. I was also told that we were to kill Iwaldi, if we got a chance, and . . ."

The world was certainly turning topsy-turvy. Here I was discussing an alliance with men who had been trying their best to kill me. And here I was being told that the Nine were trying to kill one of their own—old Iwaldi, the wrinkled dwarf whose white beard fell to his waist.

Joining forces with hated enemies was, of course, nothing new for mankind. Or even for me. I killed a number of Germans in East Africa during World War I, not for patriotism but for personal revenge. Then I found out that the atrocities that had set me on the blood trail were the work of a small band of criminals in the East African German forces. They would have been shot by their commander if he had known what they had done. Later, I became very good friends with Colonel Paul von Lettow-Vorbeck, who kept two hundred thousand British troops at bay with just eleven thousand men, most of them black Africans. Of course, anyone reading the volume of my biography dealing with this phase of my life would get the mistaken notion that it was the Germans whose hordes would have overwhelmed the British if it had not been for me. But my biographer was always more interested in dramatic values than in facts, and he was full of the intense anti-German feeling of that time. The truth is that von Lettow-Vorbeck was a greater guerrilla leader than Lawrence of Arabia, but he did not get any publicity. Besides, he was on the defeated side.

I doubted that there was anything admirable about the reptilian Murtagh to make me respect him as I had von Lettow-Vorbeck. But he was highly intelligent and ruthless, and he could be used, even if never fully trusted.

He said, "I was on my way to Germany when I got a message saying that I should go to Paris instead. Caliban had disappeared there. And then I got another message telling me to return. You had escaped. I couldn't believe it, but I had to. I met Mubaniga at a strip in the Congo, and we came here. He put me in charge of killing you, and then he took off, as you know. He did not say where he was going. But I got hold of a message which indicated that he would be going to Salisbury, England. Why, I don't know."

I smiled. If he was able to read an intercepted message, which he had no business doing, he had learned how to translate the language the Nine used among themselves. I have no idea what this language is or how ancient. But I got hold of a number of papers while I was the Speaker for the Nine during an annual ceremony, and I learned how to interpret that language, too. I surmised that Murtagh, when he was the Speaker, had done the same. He was a brave man or a foolhardy one to take that chance.

The language itself, as a side comment, seems to be distantly related to Basque. It is my guess that it was the original tongue of Anana, the terrible old woman who is chieftainess of the Nine. It is probably one of a superfamily that extended around the Mediterranean and possibly over much of Europe, before the Indo-Hittite speakers came out of the forests of what is today middle Germany.

"Where is this strip in the Congo?" I said. "Does it have a short-wave set that can reach Europe? Can we get there swiftly on foot? Or do we have to steal a copter or plane?"

He reached slowly into his jacket and pulled out a map. He unfolded it on the ground in the beam of a flashlight.

"It's there, in the Ituri forest," he said.

The map was French, and his finger hovered above a cross made of red ink in an area marked *Pygmées*.

It was about eighty miles from where we were. I could make it on foot in twenty-four hours if I knew exactly where it was. But if I let the others accompany me, I would take anywhere from six to eight days. I needed them. At least, I needed Murtagh, and I did not want to abandon Clara. Once we got to civilization, she could do what she wanted to do. But I had to get her out of the wilderness because I owed it to her.

"Are any more planes coming in to the strip back there?" I said, indicating the area outside the caves.

"Several choppers, at least," Murtagh said. They should be there now or coming in very soon. Oh, you have cost the Nine dearly!"

"Not as dearly as I plan," I said. "Wait here. I'll be back within twenty minutes."

I returned with Clara Aekjaer. While we ate, we went over my campaign. Murtagh tried to overrule me several times; he could not give up the idea that he was the leader. But I put him in his place without humiliating him, and after a while he saw that he could not push me around in any way. On the other hand, I did accept several suggestions of his for improving our plans.

Late at night, we all bedded down. I could have retired into the forest with Clara to make sure we weren't jumped on while we slept. But it was a case of full acceptance of partnership or none at all. I was ready to dissolve the alliance the moment I saw signs of treachery. Until then, I could not treat them as leopards ready to turn on me.

Even so, I had trouble getting to sleep. Perhaps it was Dick that kept my brain occupied. I did not know what to do with him. We could not take him to England with us. Even if we had shaved and clothed him and pulled his long canines, he still would have attracted attention we could not tolerate for one minute. I could have left him in the forest, but, as I said, he had been raised as a human, not as one of The Folk, and he would starve or go crazy from loneliness.

If I had had time, I could have gone into the wilderness with him, taught him how to hunt, how to build a nest against the rain and the cold. And the female I had seen last year might still be roaming the mountains in Uganda. We could find her and Dick could take her as his mate. And they could have young, and The Folk might not die out.

But that was a fantasy. Dick's tastes in food were set. He could not adapt to a diet of juicy white grubs, rodents, birds' eggs, raw birds, wild nuts and berries, and an occasional piece of meat, not always fresh by any means. In the wet and often chilly rain forest of the mountains, he would probably suffer from colds and he would likely die of pneumonia. He could migrate to the rain forest of the Gabon lowlands, but I doubted that he would get the female to go there with him, even if he could find and successfully woo her.

Besides, as I had found out when in the box canyon, Dick desired human females because he had been raised as a human. He probably would have thought the female of The Folk to be as ugly as a human thinks a gorilla is.

I told myself that I had no cause to worry about him. Though he had tried to kill me while pretending to be my friend, that was only something anybody would do to gain an advantage in war, and I did not hold it against him.

Then I fell into a fit of nostalgia. Suddenly, I wanted to shuck off this kind of life. I was tired, sick even, of killing and of being on the run or the attack. I wanted to get away from all these humans, and the subhuman, and travel deep into the forest. I wanted to go naked and hunt the pig and the antelope with only a knife. I wanted to sleep in a cozy nest in the trees, hear only the muted noise of the animals of the closed-canopy forest, be in the shadow and the silence. I did not want to see another human being for . . . for a long long time. I wanted to be free with an obligation only to myself. I could commune with the beasts, with Nature, as Whitman expresses it in several of his poems. I hated civilization, especially the big cities, especially London with its wet chilly air and coughs and sneezes and running noses, its blare and screech and roar, its citizens bumping into each other, the grit and rasp of hatred and madness fouling its air along with the physical poisons.

If it had not been for my wife, and for Caliban, I would have risen then and walked into the forest and left them to work out their own problems. As long as the Nine left me alone, I would not have bothered them, would not even have thought of them.

But Clio might be in danger. And Caliban, once my most dangerous enemy, was now my best friend.

I sighed deeply, turned over, and managed to fold in the night over my brain.

In the morning, Dick asked me if he could go with us to London. I told him why that was impossible. He finally admitted that all the logic was on my side. But he asked what he could do then. I replied that he should return to his foster parents, who lived in a hut near the edge of the rain forest. The time would come when Caliban and I would be ready to attack the Nine in the caves. Then we would need him, since he was a truly formidable antagonist. He grimaced and touched the bandage just above his navel. The next time someone came at him with a knife, and he himself had only a knife, he would throw it. He was not going to get tricked again.

My knife had not gone deeply because he had grabbed it even as it struck. He had cut his hands, too, but the pseudo-skin which Caliban had devised for wounds had been applied to the cuts. The knife wound had had to be glued after repairs were made, again with the use of one of Caliban's medical inventions. Dick could not exert himself fully yet without fear of tearing the wound open. The ride on the jeep when I was being chased had caused him considerable pain. But he would be completely healed within a week unless something broke open the wound.

Dick nodded when I said that they also served who waited. But he scowled, and that was a fearsome sight. The bulging bones above the sunken russet eyes, the blue-black skin, the protruding jaws with the long sharp yellow canines, all these looked fierce enough when he was smiling. On the way back to the jet strip, he was silent, except when addressed, and then he was curt and surly.

The first thing Murtagh did when we reached the jeeps was to report over the radio to the camp. The operator at the receiving end could not conceal his astonishment. He had supposed, along with everybody else, that Murtagh had either been killed when he took off after me or else had kept on going to put as much distance between himself and the Nine as he could.

"I have taken Lord Grandrith prisoner, and I am bringing him in," Murtagh said to the officer who had been summoned. "I also have the countess, Clara Aekjaer, prisoner."

LORD OF THE TREES

The officer, a man named ibn Khalim, was flabbergasted. Part of his reaction was because I had been taken alive. But the other part, which he would not admit if he had been asked, was amazement that Murtagh thought he would be forgiven now that he had me in custody. That he should have allowed Mubaniga, one of the Nine, to be killed was unforgivable. But if Murtagh was stupid enough to come back, so much the better.

Ibn Khalim quit talking for a moment, apparently to consult a higher authority. Then he ordered Murtagh to come in immediately. Clara and I were to be brought in alive. This was the personal order of Anana herself, relayed by radio from somewhere in Europe.

The ancient woman must have splendid things in mind for me. She might even be planning to save me for the annual ceremonies, when I could be tortured as an object lesson for the candidates. I could imagine her anger. And I smiled, though smiling at the thought of her is like being amused by the thought of Death Herself. If things worked out as I planned, she was going to be even angrier.

The journey back was much slower and more comfortable than that out. I sat in the front seat of the land jeep with two rifles at my head and my legs and arms seemingly tied together. Clara sat in the front seat of the second jeep, also seemingly bound. About a half-mile from the strip, a chopper met us. It flew about fifty feet above us all the way to the strip.

The mass of armed men I had expected to be waiting for us at the strip was not there. There were twenty men altogether, and six of these were stationed at the strip at all times. The others had come up by jeep from the big camp around the mountain. This small a number could mean that Murtagh and his men were to be treated as conquering heroes, so they would be put off their guard. Once Clara and I were turned over to the soldiers, Murtagh and his men would be separated. And then, dispersed, each would be arrested.

This would be a much less bloody way than attacking them while they were armed and organized. The Nine had lost so heavily that they were taking the subtle way.

This was more than I expected, especially since we had no plans for going deeper than the strip. We were prepared to open fire on whatever number of men was lined up to receive us. If we jumped the gun, we might be able to bull our way through. Now the task was so much easier.

The chopper settled down just as we drove up. An officer strode forward to greet Murtagh, who got out of the jeep and shot the officer through the chest.

We lost two dead and one wounded. But most of the others were cut down before they could bring their rifles into action.

I flew one chopper and Murtagh the other. We took off as soon as our men had climbed in and we had determined that we had enough fuel. We kept close to the tops of the forest once we got past the mountains, and we came into the strip in the middle of the Ituri forest with our wheels almost touching the treetops. There were one four-motored jet and two choppers near the small camp. The fighting was brief and bloody, and the four survivors ran into the jungle rather than surrender. We let them go.

While Murtagh was warming up the jet, and his men were placing dynamite to blow up the camp and the choppers, I sent a message to my men in Dakar. I did not expect to receive any acknowledgement, since Murtagh told me he assumed that my men had been located and killed. But they were a mobile unit—how mobile I won't reveal because I will be using them again. And they answered.

It was true that I had revealed the code to Murtagh under the influence of his drug. But, as I said, a questioner isn't going to get everything he should know unless he asks the right questions. Murtagh did not ask me if there was more than one code. He got the code for the particular day he questioned me. The Nine had transmitted a message on the following day, and so they had used the wrong code. My men had answered, given misleading information, and then had moved on.

Today was Wednesday, and so I transmitted the proper code for that day. I outlined what had happened, told them what I needed and how soon I'd be there. And then I asked if they had heard anything about my wife or from Caliban.

They knew nothing of Clio. But they had a reply to my first message sent some days ago.

It was from Doc Caliban. He was leaving for the county of Wiltshire in southern England. His ultimate destination was Stonehenge, the ancient ruins about seven and a half miles north of Salisbury. I was to get there as quickly as possible unless I considered events in Africa to have taken a very important turn. He was hot on the track of Iwaldi, and the business at hand might mean the end of the world—in a sense.

The message had been sent the day before.

If that proud and almost neurotically self-sufficient man was asking me for help, he must be in very hot waters indeed.

I sent him a message which I did not think he would get until it was too late, if he ever received it. Then I ran out of the station and signaled the others to get into the plane. Dick stopped me. He bellowed at me against the roar of the jets.

"Can't you take me with you? I could be of great help. Do you know anybody who has my strength?"

I shook my head and shouted back, "I'm sorry, I really am! But you can be of far more value to us if you stay here! When the time comes to go into the caves, we'll need you very much! And we just can't take you with us! You'd attract attention, which is the last thing we can stand! You might cause us to be killed by your very presence!"

"Then go to hell!" he bellowed, his throat sac swelling, and by that I knew he was almost insanely furious.

Logic told me to shoot him then and there, because there was no telling what he might do to hurt us. We could not afford to take the least chance. But I did not follow logic, of course, since I just could not kill him without adequate provocation. I even yelled at him to get into the jungle before the explosions.

Then I got into the plane, and the port was closed, we took off, and, as we swung back around, I pressed the button that transmitted a frequency to sets below. The two choppers and the tents blew up in a great cloud.

When the Nine heard of this, they would be doubly enraged, if that was possible. Never had they been so threatened, so outraged, so thumb-at-nosed-at, if I may use such a phrase. (It parallels the structure of Folk speech.) I hoped that old Anana's veins would swell up and up and she would die of a stroke.

But I knew that it was the end of the affair that mattered and that I might be dead, or wish I were dead, in a day or two. Or even sooner.

Philip José Farmer

Within fourteen hours, we were getting off a small boat on a beach near Bournemouth, a town of Hampshire. We walked up a steep flight of wooden steps to the top of a cliff. Four automobiles awaited us. It was four o'clock in the morning, and fog pressed heavily around us. Though the driver of my car could not see where he was going, he seemed to be trusting to instinct. He drove at what was a suicidal clip in the blindness, forty miles per hour, through the streets of Bournemouth. But a radar scope on the dashboard showed ghostly images of cars and people and street lamps and signposts, though we could not read the signs, of course.

Our trip had been smooth and speedy all the way. At Dakar, rather, at a strip in the desert many miles outside Dakar, the metal belt was cut off me and the shell of plastic explosive and the epoxy glue was removed. We were given new clothes and forged papers before transferring to a plane which took us around Spain to a small airport off the coast of southwestern France. From there we took an amphibian which set us down next to a small motor yacht twenty miles off the coast, just outside the fog. If you have enough money and have spent some years in building up your own organization, just in case you have a falling out with the Nine, you find that you can get much done quickly and quietly. As long as I could keep feeding my men money, and I had enough gold stashed away in Africa and elsewhere to do so, I had more than just myself to rely on in this battle. And, of course, Doc Caliban had his own organization, just as he had his own supply of gold.

It pays to be rich, as Clio often told me.

It was still dark and foggy when we were dropped off before a small hotel outside the city of Salisbury off the A338. Clara sat up in bed for a long time smoking until I asked her to quit or else go into the next room. I smoked heavily when I was first introduced to civilization, but that dissipation did not last long. It left too foul a taste and reduced my wind and was a nuisance altogether. Now I could not endure to have smoke anywhere near in an enclosed bedroom.

The maid woke me with a tap on the door at six. Clara was asleep but awoke shortly after I had shaved. She said, "I was trying to think last night why the Nine should be here. I know that they are supposed

376

to have tracked Iwaldi here. But why here? Then I remembered some years ago when I ran into a man I'd only seen twice before, both times at the caves. I was in London then, visiting friends. William Griffin, a son of Lord Braybroke, I believe, told me of overhearing a conversation between a Speaker and his woman. We candidates are great gossips, you know, trying to find out all we can about the Nine. The Speaker had overheard Shaumbim telling Tilatoc that the world had changed so much that it would be impossible to hold funeral rites at some of the places most closely associated with the Nine. Anana's birthplace, for instance, was now covered by a great office building in Spain."

Shaumbim was one of the two Mongolian members of the Nine. Tilatoc was the ancient Central American Indian.

"XauXaz was the one who died. Do you know anything about him at all? Could he have been associated with Stonehenge?"

"I've heard XauXaz speaking in an ancient tongue, some sort of proto-Germanic," I said. "And he spoke to me in English several times when I was Speaker, but only to give orders. Just before Caliban and I were sent from the caves with orders to fight each other to the death, Anana told me a few things about Caliban and myself. We're half-brothers, and our grandfather was XauXaz. He may also have been our great-great-grandfather. God knows how many times he was our ancestor. He used Grandrith Castle as a breeding farm in some kind of experiment. I suspect that his brothers, Ebn XauXaz and Thrithjaz, who are also dead, may have bred the Grandrith family, maybe a long time before the Grandriths came to England, when they were Norsemen. And maybe a long time before then, maybe they started when our ancestors were just forming their Germanic speech. I don't know, I'm guessing. I also suspect that old Ing, he whom the original Old English speakers worshiped as a living god, and he from whose name England was derived, may have taken a part in the breeding of the Grandrith line. Just as I suspect that my being raised by subhumans may have been an experiment of the Nine.

"But I'm digressing. I don't know what XauXaz had to do with Stonehenge. He was at least 18,500 years old when Stonehenge was built and maybe three times as old. He had been associated with the Germanic people from the beginning. And I doubt very much that the builders of Stonehenge, the 'Wessex' peoples, who probably descended from the Bronze Beaker peoples, were Germanic. The proto-Germanic language wouldn't even have existed then.

"But maybe he was associated with the Stonehenge people, maybe he was their living god. Maybe he supervised the building of Stonehenge. And then the Wessex people declined or he left them and went to the land between the Oder and the Elbe rivers. It is possible."

We might never know. But the Nine were here for what must be a very good reason for them.

Murtagh entered with a noticeable increase in the frequency of oscillations of face. His skin was pale, and his mouth was as thin as the edge of a fingernail.

"Are you exceptionally nervous?" I said.

"Exceptionally so," he replied. "But I always am when on the brink of an important action. You will find that my nerve won't desert me. I can be relied upon."

I told him what Clara and I had been discussing and asked him if he had any information.

"The Nine, as you well know, are sticklers for tradition," he said. "I suppose when you've lived as long as they have, you will be, too. Though the way you live I doubt you'll reach even a hundred. No offence!" he added sharply. Apparently, though he had thrown in with me, he still resented me.

"I rather believe that the ceremony will be the burial of XauXaz, if he is associated with this place. Not a genuine burial, because even the Nine don't have enough influence to bury him in the center of Stonehenge and keep all questions suppressed. But the funeral could be held there, and he could be buried nearby in some private land."

It seemed like a sound theory. I started to comment on it when the phone rang. I was closest, so I answered. A strange voice, deep as a hog grunting at the bottom of a well, spoke.

"J.C.? D.C. here!"

It was the proper challenge, and I gave the proper response. "Seedy? Seejay here!"

"Speaking for D.C.," the deep voice said. "Van Veelar. My friends call me Pauncho. Trish said to say hello. O.K.?"

By that he must have meant that the naming of Trish was an additional reassurance that he was sent by Caliban. Patricia Wilde was Doc's beautiful cousin, whom I was supposed to have killed but who was very much alive, as both Doc and I discovered.

"Meet you at the corner of Barnard and Gigant Streets," he said. "Be smoking a big cigar. You know what *G. beringei* looks like?"

That had to mean gorilla beringei, the mountain gorilla. I said, "Very well."

"That's me. A dead ringer for old beringei. You can't mistake me. Smoking a cigar in a big black Rolls. Always travel in style. See you. Hurry. This line may be tapped. Oh, and don't forget! Anybody with metal fillings in their teeth is out. Or with metal plates in their heads. Or anywhere in their bodies. Right? You got the message? Right!"

There was a click. I passed the word out, and in five minutes we had paid our bill and were driving away. The fog was as thick as ever. The sun was an exceedingly pale halo just above the housetops. The radio said that the fog had been in the area for two days and showed no signs of leaving. It was a freak phenomenon, extending inland for forty miles north of the coast.

I had been to Salisbury twenty years before, but I have a good memory for topography and direction. And we had a city map. So we found the corner of Barnard and Gigant and located the Silver Cloud in an illegal parking area. I approached the car from the sidewalk side while Clara and Murtagh came on him from the street side.

His window was open, and the collar of his thick black coat was up and his bowler hat was tipped forward. The cigar reeked in the heavy wet air. I bent down to look at him through the window. His profile was much like that of a male of The Folk.

Clara said something to him, and he motioned to me to come into the car. Clara and Murtagh went onto the sidewalk side and leaned in to hear through the window on the side, which he had opened. He turned on the ceiling lights. His eyebrows were the thickest I'd ever seen. His nose was a smudge; his upper lip was proportionately as long as an orangutan's; his jaws protruded; his teeth were thick but widely spaced. The eyes under those heavy supraorbital ridges were small and gray-blue. Despite his intense ugliness, he radiated likableness.

"Doc told me all about you," he said. "I don't know anything about our gang, but he said that you were the boss at your end of things, so I'm your obedient servant. I think we'd better get going, 'cause time is of the essence. You got pocket communicators so you can tell 'em back here to stick close to us. Easy to get lost in this soup."

I showed him the cigarette-lighter shaped transceivers which had a range of a half-mile. He was familiar with them, since Caliban had invented them. We got into the cars, I gave orders, and the four cars started up close on Pauncho's rear bumper. He had exceptionally long arms, and the body under the coat was keg-shaped. He talked out of the side of his mouth while the cigar bobbed up and down.

"I ain't got time to tell you everything that happened in Germany. Suffice it that we've tracked Iwaldi to this area. He's here because he knew the Nine would be holding XauXaz's funeral. They're on to his being here. They are also on to us being here, but all they know, so far, is that we are in the area, too. They've been looking for us; we've had some narrow escapes here. But that's all polluted water under the bridge. Listen, watch the road signs, will you? We got to take the A360 northwest out of town. I made a dry run last night, but in this fog . . . whoops! Watch it, you crazy fool!"

A dark form swerved away from us, its horn blaring.

"Listen, the radio last night interviewed some crackpot that claimed this fog was caused by witches. Said there was a coven lived near Stonehenge. I ain't so sure he was too far off the beam. Doc says old Anana has some strange powers that reach way back into the Old Stone Age. But I'm getting off the track. Here's the shape-up. Doc and Trish—what a dish!—and Barney, my dumb-dumb buddy, are near Stonehenge, by the long barrows at the crossing of A-three-six-o and A-three-o-three. Doc says if they're gone when we get there, we should proceed on to Stonehenge. The ceremony'll take place sometime today. The Nine won't be bothered by tourists on account of the fog or the local police. They've pulled strings to assure that. Doc thinks the police have been told that the British secret service wants the area kept clear while they run down enemy agents there. It's easy when you figure that some of the biggest big shots on Downing Street are servants of the Nine."

Pauncho added that Iwaldi was in the neighborhood, though Doc and his aides had not actually seen him. The battle would be three-way with my forces and Doc's definitely in the minority. But our strategy was to hit and run. If we could get just one of the Nine, we would feel happy.

Pauncho van Veelar told us to open the small chests on the floors. We did so and brought out chain mail shirts and loinguards and close-fitting helmets. All were of irradiated plastic.

"Put them on now," he said. "Once we get there, you won't have much time to change. Those shirts, by the way, resist a direct impact to a considerable degree.

"But if a man is strong enough—I am—he can tear the links apart."

We started to undress in the cramped quarters. I said, "Doc's message was rather curt. It said not to bring anyone with metal fillings in their teeth or with metal anywhere in their bodies. Now that I see this plastic amour, I'm beginning to get a vague idea of what was behind that cryptic order. Would you mind explaining so our mental fog isn't as thick as that out there?"

"Yeah, sure," he grunted. "Sorry. One thing at a time, I always say. You see, one of Doc's inventions is an inductive-field generator. It sends out a fan-shaped beam with an extreme range of half a mile. It's atomic-powered and eats up a lot of power but an amplifier enables it to radiate almost as much as it takes in. It heats up all metals within its field. Teeth fillings, rings, various articles such as watches, guns, knives, you name it. Copper telephone wires and aluminum high-tension power lines melt, and the towers get too hot to take hold of. The gas in a car's tank will explode from the heat of the metal.

"But we got weapons that we can use in the field in our trunks. Clubs—baseball bats—and plastic knives okay for stabbing but lousy for cutting. And small fiberglass crossbows with gut strings and wooden bolts with plastic points. And plastic grenades with compressed gas and detonators in them. Gunpowder, TNT, cordite, all types of explosives, become very unstable so you can't use them in plastic firearms or bombs. Even the gas in Doc's grenades is a special type of gas."

"So it's back to the primitive?" I said. "I like that."

It was ironic that the servants of the Nine and I had fought each other in the primeval forests of remotest Africa with helicopters, napalm bombs, automatic rifles, personnel detectors, and every up-to-date weapon available. Yet here in one of the most technologically advanced and most populated nations of the world, we were to engage in battle with clubs and knives and tiny bows. And with this heavy fog, we were liable to end up using only the clubs and knives and, indubitably, our hands and feet.

"Except for the materials, the weapons'll be primitive," Pauncho said. "And the inductor prevents the use of personnel radar or other detectors in this fog, too! The Nine'll have their own inductor going, you can bet on that, and the same kind of weapons we'll have, all of which Doc invented. And maybe Iwaldi'll have his inductor on, if he really shows. Of course, he won't unless he's crazy, but he's crazy, no doubt of that. The Nine'll have an army of thugs, and they'll be using them as a big net to catch Iwaldi, not to mention us, if they win the battle, that is.

"Oh, by the way, we'll have to hoof it a mile or so. We can't take the cars inside the inductor area. But Doc says that the Nine'll have cars, enough to carry them inside the area. They got three. Steam driven and plastic. Doc made them for the old geezers for just such a setup as this. Antipoetic justice, ain't it? We ride shank's mare, and they ride in style in cars Doc's genius built for them!"

We got onto A360, and Pauncho pushed the car at eighty all the way. He talked without letup. Ordinarily, such chatter would have rasped my nerves, but he provided much information which I desired. He told me that he was the son of "Jocko" Simmons and that Barney Banks, his *dumb-dumb buddy,* was the son of "Porky" Rivers. These were the old men who had accompanied Doc Caliban on their last adventure at the age of eighty. I have described them and their heroic deaths in Volume IX of my memoirs. They were the last survivors of a group of five who had dedicated their lives to helping Caliban in his battle against evildoers. (Never mind that Caliban was also working for the Nine because they offered him immortality. Caliban was given a free hand to battle crime as long as he did not interfere with the Nine. I do not condemn him for that; I succumbed to the temptation of immortality, too.)

Pauncho and Barney were born in 1932, shortly after their mothers divorced their fathers. Rivers and Simmons spent too much time with their leader and their wives, fed up, cut loose.

"I remember my father, the old ape, visiting me now and then," Pauncho said. "My mother remarried about two years after the divorce, and her husband adopted me. He was a great guy. But I was torn. I liked my father at the same time I hated him because he had, in a sense, deserted me. Now I can appreciate why he decided in favor of adventure. But I loathed chemistry even though my father was one of the world's greatest chemists. Maybe because of that."

Pauncho remembered visits from his "Uncle Doc" and visits to his wonderland laboratory in the eyrie of the Empire State Building. Pauncho and Barney had grown up together, since they lived three houses apart. They were in the same outfit in the Marines during the Korean War. They were visiting Doc after the deaths of their fathers, when he invited them to join him. Both had apparently inherited a love for adventure and combat from their fathers, and when they found out that Doc's own researches were close to the point where he would be able to reproduce the immortality elixir, they accepted his offer.

At the rate Pauncho was going, we would have reached the junction of the two highways in ten minutes. But we had to stop to avoid running into a pile-up of three cars. He slowed down to forty after that. Then, after a glance at the milometer, he crept along until the junction suddenly moved out from the fog. He turned right and drove for a few feet and then parked the car on the side of the road. The other cars followed. Two of the drivers got out swearing about the crazy fool Yank.

I could see no more than a few feet, but I knew that the country for miles around was as flat as Illinois farmland. A303 ran like a cannon barrel slightly northwest for about a mile and a quarter before crossing an untarred road. To get to Stonehenge, you turned left onto the untarred road and went about an eighth of a mile before passing Stonehenge, which was behind a fence in a field. At the junction of A344 and the small road, you turned left and then almost immediately were at the entrance to the "venerable and stupendous work on Salisbury Plain, vulgarly ascribed to Merlin, the Prophet," as described by John Wood, architect of Bath, in 1747.

If the air had been clear, we would have been able to see the white chalk wherever the soil had been cut away.

Pauncho got out of the car and removed his heavy overcoat. Since I was only a foot from him, I was able to see how he got his nickname. His belly stuck out as round as a gorilla's after a heavy meal of bamboo shoots. But it gave the impression of being as hard as a gorilla's chest. His arms were freakishly long, and his legs were very short. Even so, he stood six feet high, unlike his father, who had been not quite five feet high. Pauncho looked as if he weighed three hundred and twenty pounds or so.

He opened the trunk of his car and passed out the weapons to us. I took a baseball bat, a plastic seven-inch long stiletto, which I put in a sheath at my belt, a short quiver of bolts, also hung from my belt, and a crossbow. This was small and held with one hand, like a pistol, when fired. The bowstring was pulled back by hand, requiring a strong man to pull it all the way back. A catch secured the string, both of which were released when the trigger just ahead of the pistol-like butt was pulled.

"If the string is set at the extreme of the three positions and shot within a range of three feet," Pauncho said, "the bow will send a bolt through the armor we're wearing. Not very far, probably not more'n a half-inch into your flesh. But that'll smart, and if the bolt hits unprotected flesh, it'll go almost all the way through you."

The grenades looked like tennis balls. From the top of each protruded a half-inch long pin.

Twist the pin to the left as far as it'll go. Pull the pin and then throw." Pauncho said. "Don't dillydally. Six seconds later, the mingling of two gases produces an explosion equivalent to one and a quarter pound of TNT. The plastic shell is almost atomized, so these depend on concussion for main effect."

Two steps behind him, I followed Pauncho into the field. We sprang over a fence, the wire of which was warming up under the inductor's field, and walked a few steps. He stopped. The mound of the barrow had loomed out of the fog. Pauncho called softly, "Hey, Doc! It's me, Pauncho!"

There was no answer. The others, fanning out around the barrow, called quietly. I went up and over the mound and then along its other side. There was no one there. By bending down with my eyes close to the grass, I could see footprints in the wet earth.

We returned to the cars. Pauncho swore and blew on his enormous hands. "It's cold! That fog goes right through my bones!"

He called out, "Hey, Countess! You any good at warming up a man?"

Clara laughed softly and said, "You could chase me, my pithecanthropoid friend. That would warm you up! But save your strength!"

"We'll talk this over a martini sometime," he rumbled.

"I'll meet you after the fight," she said.

"Wait'll I tell that would-be-swinger, Barney, about this," Pauncho said, and he chuckled like a troll under a bridge.

I said, "Silence!"

Shouts were drifting through the gray wetness. Muffled cracks, as of bats striking bats or armor or, perhaps, bone, disturbed the cloud.

I called them in around me and told them what we should do for the moment. We started out just as a few more cracking noises came and then a scream which was cut off as if a knife had plunged into the throat. A grenade boomed three seconds later. Then silence returned.

If there were many people at Stonehenge, they were not conducting a full-scale battle. The sounds gave us the impression of blundering around, of probing activity by men who were not sure even after they had closed with another whether he was enemy or friend.

"We'll walk along the road until we're just opposite the first of the tumuli."

"What the hell's a tumuli?" someone muttered.

"A tumulus is an artificial mound, a round barrow," I said. "A grave for the ancients. This area is filled with them. We'll scout around there, take it easy, because Iwaldi or the Nine may have stationed people there. Keep close together. We don't want to get separated in this fog. Yes, I know bunching makes us better targets, but that can't be helped.

"And don't fire at the first person you see. He may be one of Doc's people. Now you've gotten the descriptions of Doc and Banks and his cousin. If you can identify them, sing out and identify yourself. Pongo is the code word."

"Identify them? In this fog soup?" a man muttered.

"Do your best," I said. "Outside of Caliban's group, everybody is our enemy."

I did not really expect Murtagh's men to refrain from shooting until they were one hundred percent certain.

They were all very tough and self-centered characters, and they were not about to wait until hit before they opened up. But at least they knew what their allies were supposed to look like.

We walked on the edge of the road with me in the lead. I held the butt of the crossbow in my right hand and the bat in my left.

The sounds had ceased but as soon as we reached the burial barrow three explosions deafened us. All of us dived for the wet ground, even though there was no indication that the grenades were being thrown our way. Then I rose, and, crouching, ran to the ditch around the outer wall of the barrow and dived into it. I fell on top of a man squatting on his heels. He grunted, I grunted, and I broke his jaw with a backhanded blow from the butt end of my bat.

Somebody nearby in the fog said, "What the hell is that? You all right, Meeters?"

The man I'd knocked out was not named Meeters, because he answered on my left about ten feet away.

At that moment Clara and Pauncho appeared in the fog, so I jumped up, yelling, and started swinging with the bat. I kept hold of the crossbow, which was loaded, until I was facing two at one time. One I shot through the mouth with the bolt and the other I knocked down with a blow that broke my bat, his bat, and his skull under his helmet.

I think I cleared the ditch on my side. But there were men on the other side of the barrow. Instead of charging around the ditch or coming over the top of the barrow, they took off. Somewhere in the fog some of them got down on the ground and began firing bolts back. All these did was to bury themselves in the dirt of the mound. But we scrambled into the ditch as if they could hit us. And of course they might flank us.

While I checked for dead or wounded among us, and found

that only two of us were out of the fight, Murtagh and Pauncho examined the enemy. All ten were dead or unconscious. But there was no way of determining if they were Iwaldi's or the Nine's. They were dressed in civilian clothes with a bright yellow band pinned across their chests. All had plastic chain mail shirts under cloth shirts, plastic loinguards, and helmets shaped exactly like ours.

Gbampwe, a black from Central Africa who said he was a champion spear thrower, and I cast grenades into the fog. I threw mine with a force which should have taken them about four hundred feet. They opened up the fog with a red roar. I couldn't tell if I hit anything because the only reply was a volley of bolts, some of which hit the soft earth of the barrow above us.

Somebody far away called. I could not make out the words, which were either garbled by the atmospheric conditions or were purposely distorted.

I bellowed, "Pongo! Pongo! Pongo!"

"Pongo your . . . !" somebody yelled, his last words lost in an uproar of shouts and screams and cracking bats.

Pauncho growled, "The farmers around here must be screaming their heads off for the police. And I'll bet they can hear those grenades clear on the other side of Amesbury. It's only two miles away."

It must have been a strain on the local police to give excuses for the explosions and for the loss of power. They must have wondered themselves just what the secret service was doing out around Stonehenge. But they would, of course, obey their orders. I took it for granted that the same orders had gone to the armed service posts in this area, of which there were many.

I threw another grenade. It went off almost exactly between the locations of the two previous blasts. Bolts whistled nearby after the explosion, but none struck us. It seemed reasonable that I might have killed the men we'd run out of the ditch, and that these missiles came from another group. On the other hand, they might be holding their fire, hoping we would think just that.

To our right, approximately at Stonehenge, another flurry of cracking noises came muffled through the fog.

I gave the order to get out of the ditch and to advance across the field. We would go parallel with the road on a course which would bring us near the so-called "slaughter stone." This lies outside the circle of the trilithons and sarsens and near the heel stone, which is named thus for no verifiable reason.

Suddenly, there was not a sound except for the rustle of our feet moving through the wet winter weeds and a slight sucking as feet were pulled up from mud. We were formed in three lines. I was in the lead with Clara, Pauncho, and Murtagh behind me at the limits of my sight. If I had stepped up my pace a trifle, I would have been all alone, as far as my ability to see was concerned. About halfway to the slaughter stone, or at a point which I believed to be halfway, I threw up my hand. The three behind me also signaled, and then the whole body was at rest. There was no more sound than if we had been at the bottom of a deep cave.

The only thing you could hear was the hum of nervous tension.

Out there were many men moving slowly, their eyes straining against the gray cloud, their breaths controlled, their feet descending and ascending slowly to avoid the suck of mud and brush of wet grass. Their ears were turning this way and that to catch a betraying sound.

My hearing and sense of smell are far keener than most humans, for reasons which I have explained in Volume II of my memoirs. But there was not a breath of wind, and the heavy droplet-ridden cloud seemed to be killing both sound and odor. I had a mental picture of enemy all around us, men who, if they knew where we were, could have cut us down with their crossbows or overwhelmed us with numbers alone. The blindness was to our advantage because of our very small force.

I gestured for us to advance. And then I heard a poofing sound, which I interpreted immediately, and correctly, as it turned out. I turned and gave the signal to hit the earth and then did so.

No sooner had I hugged the earth than an intensely bright light shot through the cloud above us. Somebody had sent up a flare. It had to be entirely nonmetallic, of course.

It did not turn night into day, but it did outline a mass of figures beyond the depression in which was the slaughter stone. And it showed me some vague figures gathered around the somewhat tilted sixteen-foot high heel stone to my right near the road.

There were six or more ahead and about eight to the right. None of them made the signal agreed upon if visibility should be restored.

But they had seen us stretched out on the ground. They had also seen each other.

We fired crossbow bolts back at both groups as they fired at us and at each other.

That seemed to be a signal for bedlam. Beyond, in the gray mists around the circle of Stonehenge, grenades opened the fog with flames. Men behind me screamed, and men ahead of me screamed.

And then there was silence again except for the groans of the wounded. These were shut up as quickly as we could with our hands over their mouths and then with morphine. I suppose the other groups had done the same, because I could not hear any wounded from any quarter.

Silence again.

If those two groups had not moved . . . I lobbed two grenades in quick order at where I thought they should be. The blasts came one after the other. There were screams and moans after the reverberations had died away. Then answering blasts, the flashes of which I could not see. The wounded quit making noises. By then I was up, crouching, and had told my men to follow me to the left, across the field. I was afraid that those not hit would retaliate with grenades. And while I doubted that anyone of them could throw a grenade as far as I had, we would still be within stunning range. Or one of them might run forward and toss the grenade.

It was a mistake on my part. A dark body suddenly appeared ahead of me, a crossbow string twanged, others near it let loose, and about six of my men, as I was to find out, were killed. I went down but not because I was shot. I fell forward, shooting my crossbow as I went. After I had hit the earth, I reloaded my weapon. The men ahead were silenced, and when I crawled forward, cautiously, I found three corpses and one wounded, unconscious. He had a bright yellow strip, splashed with blood, across his chest. I put him out of his misery with my stiletto.

Our outburst triggered off another in the vicinity of the ruins. Bolts whistled overhead. I think they were strays, but even so, one caught one of my men in the neck.

I crawled on and came across the first of many bodies within a narrow area. I counted twenty-five.

"Listen!" I said to Pauncho. "I don't know what is going on. But I doubt that any of the Nine would expose themselves as we have. They value their wrinkled hides far too much. But they must have come here because they would want to bring Iwaldi out in the open. And they *will* take chances. So they have to be here. I wonder if they could have exposed themselves long enough to bring Iwaldi's men out and then cut and run for it? Or they could be holed up in their cars."

But, cautious as they were, they were not cowards. And they were completists. They would want to make sure that Iwaldi had been killed. And if they knew that there were other forces operating in the grayness, they would be certain that these would be Doc or I or both. They would not rest until our heads had been brought before them.

I said, "I'm going to go back to the road and scout along it. You come along as far as the fence. Stay there for twenty minutes. If I'm not back by then, it's up to you what you do."

"Doc probably needs our help!" Pauncho said. There are a hell of a lot of men out there!"

As if to prove his statement, the fog was shattered with three grenade explosions somewhere to our left. And then we heard the whoosh of several bolts very near us. Somebody was shooting at random.

Clara wormed to me and said, "I want to go with you, John! I proved I can fight along with you!"

"All right," I said. "Let's make for the fence."

"Doc said I was to be under your orders while I was with you," Pauncho said. "But he told me I could rejoin him as soon as I got the chance. Well, now I got the chance. And that dumb-dumb Barney, he'd fall down and break his leg if I wasn't there to hold him up. And Doc may need me. No telling what's going on out there."

"You do whatever you think best," I said. I appreciated his loyalty and his concern for his comrades, and he had carried out his mission: to get us to the battlefield.

"Yeah, I'd like to stick with you, but I got a hunch they really need me," Pauncho said. "So long. Good luck."

He crawled away. I led the others to the road and ended up by the heel stone. This tilted to the south as if it were an ancient tombstone and the earth around it had yielded up its dead. Ten corpses lay around it. I looked them over and determined that about five had been killed by a blast, presumably from the grenade I had thrown. These men had yellow bands across their chests.

Murtagh said, "I would prefer that we all go together. If we don't, we're likely to end up shooting each other in this damned fog!"

At that moment, the firing stopped again for a few seconds, a pistol fired, there was some shouting, and then silence.

I said, "Clara and I'll go down the road. If you hear firing down there, stay here. I'll give you the code word when I come back. Pauncho knows where you are, so if he finds Doc he may bring them here."

Clara and I started to go down the dirt along the right side of the road. We had gone only a few feet when I heard the tires of a car accelerating swiftly, near the vicinity of the crossroads. There was no sound of a motor, so I knew it was a steam-driven car. And immediately after, grenades broke loose across the road from us. I don't know that they were throwing them directly at us on purpose, because they could not have seen across the road. But Murtagh and his men lobbed their grenades back across the road, and then suddenly figures loomed out of the fog. The roar of the car increased, and then I felt a hard blow against my chest. I looked down, dimly saw a grenade at my feet, leaned down and threw it back. It went off in the air and the grayness became black.

When I recovered consciousness, I was lying on my side on the cold wet earth. My ears rang, and my head felt as if it had swelled to pumpkin size. I put my hand on my head and felt a stickiness. I tasted my fingers. It was blood running out from a small cut on my throbbing head.

The noise level around me must have been high, because surely there were men screaming and groaning. Two bodies lay within touching distance, and when I got to my hands and knees and began crawling around, feeling for a club or a crossbow, I came across three more corpses. I found a crossbow and a quiver containing six bolts on a still body. I got to my feet and staggered across the road, stumbled over another body, fell down into a small depression, crawled out, and stopped. Something large and black and metallic-feeling was blocking my way.

I pulled myself up onto it, and then my senses, slowly clearing, told me it was the plastic steam car. It was lying on its side; the doors on the upper side were open. I looked into it and saw one body huddled down against the lower side in the back. I looked up across the car and saw a few flashes, like fireflies on a broad meadow. They were from grenade explosions, but I could not hear a thing.

Prowling around the car in the milky fog, I found a man in a chauffeur's uniform face-down on the road. He had been hit on the head with a bat and then stabbed in the throat.

I went back to the car. I hated to be trapped inside it, but I had to find out who that was in the rear seat. I climbed up and into the well with less than my usual suppleness and strength. The explosion had taken much out of me. By the corpse, I lit a match and shone it on the face for a moment.

He was one of the Mongolian members of the Nine, withered old Jiizfan. Those eyes, which had been young when there was still a land bridge between England and the continent, were closed. There was no sign of a wound except a dark mark on his forehead.

I put my ear against his chest and heard nothing. Then I placed a thumb on his skinny wrist and detected a very light pulse.

I raised my head and looked into the ragged pits of his eyes.

His hand moved. I caught it and squeezed. The bones ground together, and he screamed out.

It was a pitiful cry, but he had been responsible for the deaths of thousands, perhaps millions, during his multi-millennia-long life. God alone knew how many he had tortured. And he would have had me killed instantly if it was in his power.

I turned on the flashlight for just a moment, shining it on my face so he could see who it was. Then I cast the beam in his face. His eyes were wide open, his mouth was sagging.

Before I could reach up and twist his neck, his hand fell back and he slumped down. I felt his pulse. His heart had given out on seeing me.

However, a man who has lived that long, especially for so long in the Orient, may conceivably be able to stop his own heart for a while through mental means. When I climbed out, I carried his head by the long white hair. I wasn't sure what I was going to do with it. Toss it among his men if I could find them, I suppose. But I laid it down by the car while I investigated, and I never did pick it up again.

From the wounds on the bodies around the car, and the bashed-in rear, and the skid marks, I reconstructed the accident. Just as the men had charged across the road, to attack us or to run away from attackers, the lead car had plowed in among them. It had knocked several high into the air but its wheels had struck several bodies on the road, and it had turned over. It must have been going about sixty miles an hour when it hit. The car behind it had run over some bodies and rammed the rear of the first car just as it turned over on its side. Then the second car had backed up and taken off.

The occupants of the wrecked car, except for Jiizfan, had managed to crawl out, assisted by the chauffeur. (I suddenly remembered seeing him at one of the annual ceremonies.) He had been shot down, perhaps by his own people in the fog. The others, who I presumed were of the Nine, had gotten away. Whether they had gotten into the second car or were walking along the road through the fog was something I could only determine if I went after them.

I did not know how long I had been unconscious, I did not know whether or not Clara or Doc were within a few feet and shouting out the codeword.

I circled around and around and found all of my party dead except for Clara, Murtagh, and Szeleszny. The attack that had gotten me must have gotten them, too. One of the corpses was carrying a quiver with several bolts. I fitted one to my bow, picked up a bat, checked that I still had my knife and two grenades. The fog, which had started to turn whitish, was much darker. Apparently, above the fog, other clouds had moved in.

I went down the route I had started before being so violently interrupted. My head still felt as if somebody were pumping a very painful gas into it. My ears had not stopped ringing.

The fog became less dark again as I came to the junction of the two roads. I turned around in the slowly whitening mists to the left and cut across the road. Moving along the road on my right, I came to the entrance to the ruins. By then the ringing in my ears was not so loud, and my head did not feel quite so much like a balloon. But it still hurt.

Out of the thick milkiness, dark figures appeared, one by one. They were corpses on the white chalky path before me. Between the entrance at the northeast corner of the field and the flat stone at the perimeter of the ruins, just beyond the end of the path, I counted thirty-three bodies. I did not stop to investigate all of them, but many that I did had caved-in skulls, broken necks, or shattered jaws. Those with no marks of violence except swollen heads, bulging eyes, and bloody issues from nose, eye, and ear were the victims of grenades.

I stood for a while by the flat stone and tried to listen. I also sniffed the air, but could smell nothing but a wet wooliness. Then I advanced slowly to the left until two flat stones bulked out of the mist. These were broken stones lying on their sides. If I remembered correctly, just beyond the farthest was the first of the upright monoliths of the "gigantick pile." A few steps showed me that my memory had not failed me. The blackish-gray tablet seemed to drift out of the fog as if it were the mast of a stone ship.

Three bodies lay between its foot and the flat stone by it.

I determined, while I stood there, straining my senses to detect living bodies in the cloud, to go to the right, toward the center of the inner circle of trilithons and monolith. There the funeral ceremony for XauXaz would have been held, if the Nine had been allowed to hold it. And there his body might still be, if the Nine had been routed.

Then, to my right, a body did emerge from the milkiness. It put one foot before the other while it leaned forward, straining to see. It held something in front of it which, a second later, I saw was her crossbow.

We moved closer. Her bow was up, and her finger was ready to squeeze the trigger, and then she recognized me.

I did not speak because I did not want anyone else to hear us. And I could not hear Clara. I would have to read her lips, which would not be easy in the syrupiness.

Something came down out of the cloud. It seemed to have dropped from an airplane, but it must have been crouched on top of the monolith to my left, about fourteen feet high. It landed hard and rolled and disappeared and then was up on its feet and bounding toward Clara. She had jumped back, almost disappearing from my sight, and then she came forward again but with her right side turned to me. She loosed the arrow at the monstrous figure, which had been swallowed by the fog again but which she must have seen because she was closer.

Then the hulking shape leaped out of the fog as if vomited by it, grabbed her arm, went on, turning her upside down and then over. I ran up to her. I was too late. Her right arm had been twisted and torn off, along with the jacket and the chain mail shirt, by the enormous strength of that brute. The dark blood gushed out over the white chalk. She was dead.

My beautiful and brave and loving Clara was dead.

Her sudden death and its manner froze me. But I was additionally horrified because of the unexpectedness of the creature's appearance. I had thought that Dick was in Central Africa, waiting for me to return.

I did not know how he had gotten here, but the Nine had to have something to do with it. He had gotten into contact with them, and they had decided to use him against me instead of killing him. They needed somebody who was stronger than I and knew all the techniques of hand and foot fighting. And who, in an arena where gunpowder and metal were forbidden, would be like a lion loose. A lion with the mind of a man.

And while I stood over her and was as motionless and as dumb as those ancient piles around me, the huge shape dived out of the fog.

I went down. But, before he touched me, I came out of the horror as if I had been slid down a greased chute. I went onto my back and my feet kicked up. The bat and the crossbow were flung to one side. His hands were over my face—they would have taken my face off if they could have gotten a grip—and he went on over me and into the fog, propelled by the impact of my feet on the underside of his great paunch.

I grabbed the bat—the crossbow was lost in the mists—and I got on my feet and was ready when he came out of the wooliness again. But this time he was feet first, his body almost parallel with the ground, and those short but gorilla-powerful legs bent. They straightened out, and if they had hit my chest would have broken the bones. They did hit the club with enough force to knock it from my hands.

I rolled back and away into the fog and came down hard because I had not been fully prepared for that type of attack and I had slipped in Clara's blood.

He came down on Clara's body, then disappeared.

I was up and heading toward where I hoped the nearest monolith would be. I wanted to get my back to it, get my feet against it, and then launch myself at him, if he showed again. There was the chance that we would blunder by each other, perhaps not see each other again in this place. But his hearing was, as far as I knew, unaffected, and mine was still absent. That gave him an advantage. I wanted to stay in one spot, where he could not approach me from the rear, and wait for him. Even my breathing would have to be silent; I controlled the urge to suck in deep breaths.

At the foot of the rough pillar, blackish in the fog, the toe of my shoe nudged something. I knelt down and felt it. It was Clara's arm, thrown aside by the anthropoid.

I picked it up by the wrist with my right hand and drew my stiletto with my left hand. I waited. I could see about a foot before me. I wondered if there were sounds of a frantic battle going on around me. Perhaps Doc Caliban or his men or Trish Wilde or Murtagh were crying for aid only a few feet from me.

Suddenly, I smelled him. He had to be very close for me to detect him in the thick-dropleted cloud. And he would, of course, smell me.

I swung the arm as hard as I could before me, and it slapped his dark shoving-forward face just as it came like a black ghost out of the mists. But a powerful blow from him struck my wrist and knocked the stiletto into the mists.

The force of the blow from Clara's arm squeezed more blood out of it over his face. It blinded him, disconcerted him, and so the club he swung in his left hand missed me and broke against the stone where I had been. And I came up with my left fist with all my force into his belly, exactly against the wound I had given him on that mountain road in Africa.

He bent forward, clutching at his belly, and I slammed my right fist behind his left ear. He sagged forward and went down on his knees, and I hit the back side of that huge massively muscled neck with the edge of my palm.

If he had been a man, he would have died. But he was only half-stunned, and he came up and around with his right hand in a karate chop—though I think it was purely a reflex—and my left arm felt as if it, too, had been torn off.

The agony would come later. At that moment, the arm was numbed. I also hurt my knee so much that I could only hobble for a long time after that. But it was worth it.

He fell face-down, and I thought he surely must be dead. But he rolled over while I stared at him and I bit my lips to keep from groaning with the agony of my knee and my left arm. I stared while he got to a sitting position. I started forward, determined to kick him with my left foot, though I did not know how I could stand on my right while I was doing it. He looked at me moving through the fog at him and then he fell back and stared upward. Suspecting a trick, I circled him, with difficulty since I could not move without great pain. I approached him from behind. He did not move. Then I knelt down, again with difficulty, and closed my one good hand around his throat. I began to squeeze. His eyes opened. His tongue came out. He rolled his head slightly, but his arms did not move. And then that enormous chest quit rising and falling.

It could as easily have been me on the ground and probably would have been if he had not skidded in Clara's blood.

I released my hold on his throat and turned away. At that moment, announced by a grenade exploding in the distance, as if some dramatist in the sky had arranged matters, the first breeze cooled my face. The wind increased as I walked toward the inner circle of the ruins, and within a few strides I could see several feet away.

There were bodies everywhere, clubs, bows, arrows, and plastic knives. Murtagh was not among them.

In the center, lying on his back, his arms crossed, was XauXaz.

His catafalque was of ornately carved oak with affixed golden images. His enormous white beard covered his chest and his stomach.

The old wide-brimmed floppy hat lay above his head; his right eye was covered with a black patch held on by a thin black band. A huge black raven sat on each shoulder.

As I approached, they flew away, crying harshly.

Beyond, over the body, the mists were thinning.

There were more corpses past the trilithons.

I stood by the body of my grandfather, of the man who may have fathered many times in the Grandrith line, the millennia-old man who had once been worshiped as a god, as Wothenjaz by the first Germanic speakers, then as Wothen and Othinn and Wodan. The Mad One. He had many names, but in the caves of the Nine, he was called XauXaz, which meant, in proto-Germanic, High. And his brothers were Ebn XauXaz, or Just-As-High, and Thrithjaz, or Third. All dead now.

Soon the mists would be blown away. And the rude and massive and brooding stones would be revealed on this level land. And there would be visible this ancient, very ancient oaken catafalque and the body of the man who looked as if he were a hundred years old but had actually been born sometime between 10,000 B.C. and 20,000 B.C. And there would be the body of a creature that science had thought had perished a million and a half years ago. And there would be the other bodies, and the primitive weapons by which they had perished, the clubs and the bows and arrows with plastic tips and the plastic daggers.

Unless the Nine arranged to keep the area shut long enough to have the bodies hauled away, and all speculation hushed up, the story of the battle at Stonehenge would go around the world. And the mystery would be pondered on for years. Perhaps for as long as men were on this planet.

But I knew the Nine, and I knew that those who had gotten away, old Anana and Ing and the others, would arrange to cover up everything.

In fact, if I did not get out at once, I might be caught in the net they had undoubtedly spread to drag in all who would try to leave this area.

I hobbled past the great stones and out across the field. I thought I had seen, for a brief moment when the mists had parted, a number of bicycles on the edge of the field. These would be plastic, of course, and might have been brought here by Caliban. If I could pedal one of these, though handicapped by a useless left arm and a knee which it was agony to bend, then I could get to a car. I might have to steal one, but I knew how to do this, even though born and bred in the jungle.

It was then the fog split, and I saw the giant figure of a man with a peculiar bronzish hair and skin. By his side was a tall woman with the same coloring and a man with grotesquely broad shoulders and long arms, Pauncho. There were four men and a woman I did not recognize.

Bodies lay near them.

I hurried toward him, then had to slow down because of the pain.

Doc had stopped and was waiting for me. Then, seeing I was in such trouble, he ran toward me.

I smiled for the first time in a long time. We had gotten through, and we would get away. I would find out what had happened to Clio. And then we would go to the mountains which conceal the caves of the Nine and there do what had to be done.

The Mad Goblin

Dedication

For Jack Cordes, who sometimes lives in Peoria and
sometimes in the old-pulp Valhalla.

A Note From Philip José Farmer

Although the editors insist upon publishing this work as a novel under my by-line, it is really the work of James Caliban, M.D. Doc Caliban wrote this story in the third person singular, though it is autobiographical. He feels that this approach enables him to be more objective. My opinion is that the use of the first person singular would make him feel very uncomfortable. Doc Caliban does not like to get personal; at least, he doesn't like to do so with most people. Even the largest mountain throws a shadow.

THE MAD GOBLIN

Three figures moved in and out of the shadows of clouds and trees. The moon was riding high over the alpine mountain of Gramz in the Black Forest of southern Germany, only a few miles from the Swiss border. Long black clouds raced under it like lean wolves lashed by moonlight beams. Their shadow selves loped over the precipitous western side of Gramz Berg, bounding over the squat and massive stone pile of the castle on top of the mountain, writhing down the jagged slope toward the narrow sheen of the Toll River two thousand feet below.

The three figures were men toiling up the rock-strewn, pine-dotted slant. One was six feet seven inches high. He had the body of a Hercules. His bare head glinted dark-bronzish in the moonlight. If there had been more light, his eyes would have been a very light gray-green with many flecks of bright yellow.

The second man was about six feet tall but seemed much shorter because of the enormous breadth of shoulders and trunk. His arms were disproportionately long and his legs almost freakishly short. The forehead was low and backward slanting. The ridges of bone above his eyes were massive. His nose was a flat wide-nostriled blob, and his chin receded. His ears stuck out like the wings of an owl. His hair was the color of a rusty nail.

The last in line was also six feet tall, but he had the body of a greyhound. His face was that of a handsome fox. His hair was as black and as straight as an Apache's.

The lead man climbed swiftly, though he was burdened with an enormous backpack. The second man, huffing and puffing, called out. He sounded like the grunting of a bear at the end of a long hollow log.

"Have a heart, Doc! You're killing me!"

The third man said, "Yeah, Doc, maybe you ought to put him on your back, too! Carry old softy Pauncho van Veelar like the baby he is! Forget your pacifier, Pauncho? I brought one along just in case!"

The gorilla-bodied man turned and said, "Barney Banks! You gotta lotta guts! If it wasn't for you hanging onto my coattails, if I didn't have to drag you along, too, I wouldn't be near so tired! Besides, you ain't got the weight I got to carry, you scarecrow!"

"We'll rest," the big man said. His voice was deep and resonant, as if his throat contained many small bronze gongs. He sat down on a boulder and waited patiently. Though he could have kept on going without rest at twice the speed all the way to the top, he did not mind stopping. Nor did he mind the bickering of Pauncho van Veelar and Barney Banks. It reminded him of the old days, when their fathers, who looked and sounded so much like them, had carried on a similar running verbal battle.

While the two murmured blistering insults, he looked up the silver-and-black-brindled mountainside. A cloud whipped past the moon, and its lights shone again on the black many-turreted *schloss* still six hundred feet above. The lower wall looked as smooth as the palm of his hand from this distance. But, having gone near it in a helicopter in the daytime, he knew that there were projections and fissures on it. He had studied the photographs and planned the exact course he would take and alternate routes if circumstances barred him from the first.

Doc Caliban reached into a pocket of the vest under his thick jacket and pulled out two pills. He gave one to Barney Albany Banks and one to William Grier van Veelar. They popped them into their mouths and, a few seconds later, felt invigorated.

Doc Caliban began climbing again. The moon raced the clouds and lost but still gained distance across the starry arc. The last six hundred feet were the toughest. Here the mountain became solid perpendicular rock. The three put big flexible plastic discs on their hands and applied these to the rock. The degree of suction was controlled by the degree of pressure on the handles inside the discs.

They reached the junction of rock and the base of the castle. Here they clung to their discs. Their progress was slower from this point on. The alternation of exposed moon and concealing clouds flickered light over them. They seemed like lumps of stone, so minute was their ascent. But as time went by they gained their goal: a narrow opening about sixty feet from the base.

A minute before Doc Caliban pulled himself level with the bottom of the embrasure, a light shone in it.

Doc hung by one disc while he squeezed the other down into a small cylindrical form and stuck it in a pocket in his vest. He then took out a small handweapon from a pocket in his jacket. This was of .15 caliber and shot explosive bullets with a velocity of 4,000 feet a second. The accuracy was, of course, limited, but by holding on the trigger, the entire clip of fifty bullets would be emptied within six seconds. The butt contained a compressed liquid which became a gas ignited by a spurt of another gas into the firing chamber.

Doc Caliban held the gas repeater ready if someone should look out the window. But no sound was heard or object seen from the embrasure. The light, however, remained.

After a few seconds, Doc replaced the gun and took out the disc for his right hand and began his turtlelike climbing. When his chin was above the ledge of the opening, he stopped. The light showed him a narrow landing of stone within stone walls. Opposite was a narrow door of black wood with a tracery of red-painted iron. The embrasure had one vertical bar set in it and a window of glass which would have to be swung inward to be opened.

Hanging by his left disc, Doc Caliban withdrew two long wires about a twelfth of an inch in diameter. He tied one end around the lower part of the iron bar. Then he released the pressure of the disc. He pulled himself upward with one hand by the bar, reached up, and with one hand tied the end of the other wire around the upper part of the bar. After this, he lowered himself until he was below the embrasure, put a disc on his right hand so he could hang on the wall, and pressed a small button in a tiny device in a pocket in his vest.

Fire spurted from the wires around the bar. Doc went back up the embrasure, pulled the bar out and then laid it on the embrasure with its end sticking out. Inside the narrow opening, crouched with his back against one wall and his face almost touching the other, he tested the window with one hand. It did not seem likely that an alarm would be installed on this window, where only eagles could be expected to land. But there was only one way of finding out. He cut the glass with a diamond after applying a suction disc to it. When he had lowered it to the inner wall of the landing, he climbed through. A few minutes later, Pauncho's broad shoulders and big hard stomach came through. He groaned as his shoulders caught on the edges, and Barney, below him, said, "What's the matter, fatty?"

Barney could not see Pauncho, of course, but he guessed what was happening.

As Barney's head came above the ledge of the embrasure he found himself looking into the savagely grinning chimpanzee face of Pauncho.

"Who's a fatty, Bones?" he said.

"Quit clowning around!" Barney said. "I'm tired of hanging around here like a bat! I know you like it, since you're half-batty. But I don't! Let me in!"

Pauncho put a huge hand, the back of which was covered with thick dark-red hairs, against Barney's face. "One shove, and you can solo without wings."

Doc Caliban said, "We haven't time for that." Pauncho backed away, and Barney climbed in. Doc Caliban pulled up the latch of the door, but the door would not swing out. He then started down the steps, the little gas-operated gun in his big hand. Behind him on the stairway, which was too narrow for two men abreast, were Pauncho and Barney. Each held a gun like Doc's.

They went down three complete windings of the corkscrew staircase before coming onto a broader landing. Doc tried the wooden door here, and it opened noiselessly, its hinges having been recently oiled. The room beyond was huge, reached by a short flight of steps leading downward. At one end was a big canopied bed. The walls were naked granite blocks except where covered by huge tapestries. There were a few pieces of massive oak furniture. Heads glared down from the walls: elks, elephants, rhinoceros, African buffalo and American bison, wolf, lion, tiger, leopard, jaguar, kodiak bear. They were fine specimens but nothing extraordinary. They could be found in the game room of any man with money and time and the need to slaughter.

But on a table in a corner, near the huge fireplace on the western wall, was a mounted animal that he had never seen outside some drawings based on speculation and a photograph that could be faked.

"*Tatzelwurm*," he said.

It was a lizardlike reptile with a long slim snakelike body about five and a half feet long. The skin was brownish on top and somewhat lighter on the bottom. Its four legs were very short. The heavy and blunt-snouted head merged into the thick body with no bridge of a neck. The eyes were large and round and a light green.

"What's a *Tatzelwurm*?" Pauncho said. He stood beside the specimen, and the two, except for Pauncho's clothes, would have made a prehistoric tableau. He could have been a Neanderthal and the lizard a left-over from even earlier days.

"It's a reptile that's been reported as living in the Alps," Doc said. "There have been too many witnesses with similar descriptions over too long a period of time for any doubt about its existence. It could be a form of giant salamander or skink. But the longest ever seen was about three feet long. This is a monster. I wonder where Iwaldi got this? And I wonder how many years ago?"

There was enough dust on the furniture and specimens to indicate that this room was not much used. Nor was there anything of value for the business at hand.

Caliban, however, went over the room as swiftly as he could, looking for hidden entrances to tunnels and electronic detection devices. A few minutes later, he led Pauncho and Barney out of the room and down the winding staircase. On the next landing, they found a hallway running to the north and walked down it. There were three doors along the hall and one at the end. Caliban looked into the first three and found them empty rooms with piles of boxes and furniture. The door at the end revealed another huge bedroom. This was furnished with expensive tapestries and a bed and table like the one above, but it lacked the mounted heads. The fireplace was glowing with coals, and the bed was in disorder and still bore the impression of a body.

A closet door was behind a tall wooden screen on which was

painted a medieval battle scene. The clothes hanging in the closet were those of a woman, but the variety was amazing.

"She sure must go to a lot of costume balls," Pauncho said. "Or else she's a collector of historical clothes."

The closet was big enough to have made a satisfactory bedroom in most houses. By walking down the various racks, the three walked through history, starting approximately at the middle of the seventeenth century. Most of the clothing was preserved in airtight plastic bags filled with gas, probably helium.

This was interesting and somewhat puzzling, but they were not inside the castle for a Cook's tour. Caliban said, "Go!", being one who hates to waste words, and they left the closet and started toward the door to the hallway.

There was a slight chuffing sound behind them. It was heard only by Doc Caliban, whose ears had been sensitized by a chemical he had invented. He whirled, and the others began to turn as soon as he started to move. A section of the stone wall had slid smoothly aside and out of the blackness leaped huge gray forms. They were Canadian timber wolves, and they uttered no sound except for the click of nails on the stone floor. On top of each of their heads was a hemisphere of some gray material about the size of a ping-pong ball cut in half.

Ten bounded out of the hole, their jaws open and slavering, the white teeth ready to clamp down, driven by jaws powerful enough to take off a man's arm with one bite.

The first wolf, arcing toward Barney, who had been at the end of the line, suddenly found the giant with the dark red hair and the peculiar gray-green-and-yellow eyes at the end of its leap. A hand with muscles like pythons seized the wolf by the throat and Caliban whirled. The wolf shot out of the suddenly opened hand and went past Barney and Pauncho, its tail flicking Barney's face. It crashed into the door and fell in a limp heap.

Caliban kept on whirling, and the edge of his palm struck the second wolf in its midleap and broke its neck with a sound as of an axe chopping a tree.

Pauncho knew the necessity of silence, but he found it almost impossible to throttle himself when he was in a fight to the death.

His first cry was like a bull fiddle being strummed way down in a mountain hollow, and the strummings came faster and faster but somewhat higher as the struggle continued. His enormous fists smashed into the tender noses of the beasts or on top of their heads, crushing the delicate hemispheres and stunning the brains beneath. Twice he shot animals with the gun in his left hand. Twice he went down, bowled backward by a body the jaws of which closed on his jacketed plastic chain-mailed arm.

Barney had shifted his gun to his left hand too, and a six-inch knife had suddenly appeared in his right. Like a ballet dancer, he whirled among the wolves, bending, bounding, thrusting. Then he went down with the impact of a huge male on his shoulders, and two others jumped in to savage him.

Pauncho, roaring, kicked one of the wolves so hard in the rear that he raised it off the floor and sent it rolling over the tangle of Barney and wolves. The wolf did not get up again. Then Pauncho seized a tail and dragged the wolf, its legs pumping frantically to keep its grip on the floor, away from Barney. The wolf turned to bite Pauncho, but Pauncho fell on it with his hands around its throat. Another wolf leaped on his back only to be lifted up and smashed against the wall by Doc Caliban.

Barney yelled when the teeth of a wolf exerted very painful pressure on his calf. They would have cut through his muscles if it had not been for the plastic chain-mailed longjohns he was wearing. Barney shot the wolf, rolled away, put up his arm to ward off another wolf, and blew its eye and a good part of its brains out.

Caliban had grabbed two wolves by the throats as they leaped together at him and banged their heads together again and again. A third fastened its teeth around his leg, tearing the cloth of his pants. The pressure of the jaws hurt Doc's leg, but he made no sound. His face expressionless, he dropped the two unconscious wolves and seized the third beast by the ears. He jerked upward so violently he tore the animal's ears off, and it let loose of him and fled back to the hole. But before it reached it, it stopped, stood trembling for a moment, then wheeled and charged Doc again.

Caliban was amazed at its behavior. Its actions could only be accounted for by some influence from the hemisphere on top of its head.

He charged the wolf and as it rose upward toward his throat he bent over beneath it and then came up with his fist into the beast's belly. It kept on going, but its hind quarters flew up with the impact of the blow and it turned over and landed on its back. It did not get up.

Suddenly, the fight was over. There was silence except for the heavy breathing of Pauncho and Barney. Not once had the wolves uttered even a growl.

Doc Caliban smelled the sting of explosives and the rich under-current of blood. There had been a time when he had savored those odors, even though he had not liked killing. Only once in his life, when he had gone mad from the side effects of the immortality elixir, had he enjoyed killing. Now he could not tolerate the odors associated with death once the immediate need for being in their neighborhood was over. He said, "Let's go!" and they picked up their guns. The section of wall had slid back into place. It was obvious that whoever was controlling it was not going to open it again unless to release another form of death. It was possible that the opening was done automatically, and that they could find the controls to reopen it. But he wanted to get away from here in case the action was not automatic. Besides, alarms would be ringing somewhere in the castle.

Doc wrenched off several hemispheres from the dead animals heads, and they went down the corkscrew staircase again and came to another landing. For the first time they heard the muffled sounds of helicopters and of rapid fire rifles. Then there was a rumble—a bomb going off?—and, very faintly, screams.

Pauncho laughed one of his surprisingly shrill laughs—he had two different laughs—and said, "Iwaldi's giving two parties, and he didn't want either one, heh, Doc?"

Doc said, "It does sound as if he's being attacked on the front. We'll take advantage of whatever happens."

They walked swiftly down the spiral, their handguns ready. They went down four levels and still had not seen any other life. But the battle noises were louder and they were coming from the front of the castle. Through an open window they heard the *chuff-chuff* of a number of copters. There were several more booms. Grenades, probably.

The backside of the castle was on the edge of the 2,600 foot and almost perpendicular mountainside. The front of the castle was on a much less steep slope. A road ran from the drawbridge down the mountain, snaking back and forth between and through heavy woods. It eventually led to the village of Gramzdorf, where six hundred citizens supported themselves by working for several ski resorts in the winter and farming in the summertime. The ski runs were on the Heuschrecke mountain across the valley from the Gramz.

Wherever the choppers had come from, they had not come from Gramzdorf. Nor could Doc imagine who was attacking Iwaldi.

They went down another level and came out into a huge luxuriously furnished hall. It would have done credit to the magnificent palace of the mad King Ludwig of Bavaria. Iwaldi had been collecting artifacts for many hundreds of years, perhaps thousands of years, though this castle was not built until 1241, if the records were to be believed. But Doc had reason to think that there had been an older structure on which the *schloss* had been erected, and this may have gone back to Roman days. And he also believed that beneath that ancient building, inside the granite of the mountain itself, were extensive halls and shafts, many levels, most of them hacked out of the stone in an unimaginably distant age.

The staircase continued to wind on down, but Doc decided to go toward the source of the noise. He removed from the pack on his back six objects which looked like tennis balls with pins stuck in each. Two he put in his pocket and he gave two each to the others. They went on briskly through hall after hall and room after room, all with furnishings and *objets d'art* that would have astonished scholars in many fields.

Then he stepped behind a massive marble pillar covered with golden filigree. The deafening reports of rapid-fire rifles and pistols were coming from the next room. A man ran into the room and fell on his face. Blood spread out from beneath him.

Another man ran into the room, holding an FN automatic rifle. He stopped, looked around, and gestured to someone out of sight in the other room.

Doc whispered, "They're retreating, clearing the way for Iwaldi."

Doc could not believe that he would have Iwaldi in his sight so quickly. It had only been four days since an agent had reported seeing Iwaldi in Paris. It had been only three days since Doc had received a report that Iwaldi had flown, via chopper from Freiburg, to the castle of Gramz. Of course, organizing the search for Iwaldi and conducting it had taken five months of hard work. But the lair of Iwaldi had finally been located, and here the millennia-old man had been cornered. But Iwaldi had not survived this long by being careless or minus a sixth sense. It seemed to Caliban that things just could not be quite right if he got that ancient dwarf so quickly.

Part of this feeling came from the awe he could not help feeling for one of the Nine. It was they who had given him the elixir which enabled him, at the age of sixty-six, to be, physiologically, only twenty-five. It was they who had controlled the world for unknown thousands of years. If they did not actually rule it—and they might, for all he knew—they exercised a power that exceeded that of all the combined nations of the world. Doc Caliban, who had turned against them in disgust, could not tell the world the truth. He would not live for more than a day if he came out in the open to proclaim the truth. And, moreover, the world would not believe him. They would think he was insane.

Old Anana, thirty thousand years old at least, was the woman who headed the Nine, and it was she whom he would have liked to have had within the sights of his gun. With her dead, the others would not be quite as awesome and dreadful. But they were dreadful enough, and Iwaldi had killed thousands who had thought to kill him.

Three more men with rifles came in. Doc took one of the tennis-ball like objects from his pocket, waited while he peeked around the massive column, then saw the white hair and long whiskers of the squat dwarf. He got a flash of a face as wrinkled as the neck of a vulture turkey, and the long arms and short thick bowed legs. The dwarf was dressed in a peculiar suit that seemed to be made of badgerskin. Perhaps he wore this for some ritual reason. Or perhaps he was, being so old, hard put to keep warm.

Doc stepped halfway around the column, twisted and then pulled out the three-tenths-of-an-inch pin that extended from the north pole of the little globe, and tossed it. The riflemen began firing almost immediately, but he had whipped back behind the column. Bullets screamed off the marble; chips flew. The three men clung to the side of the column. Then there was a roar half-deafening them as the two gases in the plastic ball mixed. Doc leaped out at once, his gun ready. There was very little smoke from this type of grenade. The riflemen were all lying on their backs or sides, spread out in a sort of petal arrangement.

Iwaldi was nowhere in sight.

Doc at once pulled the pin from his other grenade and tossed it exactly through the middle of the wide and tall arch. It bounced on through, being as resilient as a tennis ball, and six seconds later, it exploded. But Iwaldi and his men were not in sight nor was there any sound of firing from them. Nor was the other party firing.

Doc ran to the archway and looked around its side. The room was a huge one, about one hundred feet by sixty. At the other end, the main entrance, a few heads were beginning to stick out from the side. A number of bodies lay here and there and chairs and massive tables with marble tops had been turned over to provide protection. But Iwaldi and his men were gone.

The men by the main entrance began to fire at him. He slipped back through the archway and gestured to Pauncho and Barney to follow him. Waiting for a pause in the firing, he leaped across so swiftly he must have seemed a blur to the invaders. They fired again but too late. And the other two, bending over, ran past the space where they would be exposed to the firing when there was another pause.

Someone shouted then. Many boots slapped on the marble floor. Pauncho spun and pulled a pin and bounced a grenade off the side of the archway and into the next room. Before the first had exploded, he had sent a second after it. All three were racing toward the exit at the far end of the room when the blasts came, one, two.

And then three, four.

The last two went off near or under an enormous table of mahogany and marble, twenty yards behind them. It broke in two and soared out of the smoke. The concussion pushed them on through the doorway out of the room and knocked them down.

They scrambled to their feet. Pauncho roared, "Our grenades and theirs passed each other!"

Doc gestured at Barney, who slipped out his two grenades and threw them, one after the other, at the far archway. One hit the edge and bounced back into the room. The other caromed off at the proper angle. The three stepped around the corner to be out of the direct influence of the explosion.

Two roars succeeded their two as someone tossed in grenades from the other side.

Doc signaled that they should keep on going. They passed through several large rooms and then Doc stopped. He had detected a slight crinkling of a large tapestry hanging on the wall to the right. Lifting the tapestry up, he looked behind it. The wall was of solid stone blocks bound in mortar. Or they seemed to be. But he had seen the stone-block wall in the bedroom upstairs slide away, and the tapestry might have been caught slightly, or bent, when a section behind it closed.

He quickly examined the area behind the tapestry and pressed here and there but nothing happened. Either the opening device was too well hidden, or certain spots had to be pressed in a certain sequence. Or possibly the activator for the opening mechanism was on the other side, and this opening was to be used as an exit only.

He went out from under the tapestry and started away when Barney's sharp metallic voice said, "Doc!"

Doc wheeled and saw that the tapestry was sagging in the middle. Understanding at once what was happening, he jerked his thumb at a group of large chairs against the opposite wall, and they quickly hid behind one of them. Doc passed out two more grenades to each of them but cautioned them in a whisper to use them only if they could not use their guns. Then he extended a slender flexible telescoping device under the chair and looked through it. But turning it on his end he could rotate the other end within 180 degrees and sweep the room. The end was uptilted, thus giving him a worm's eye view.

A red-headed man stuck his head out first. He was followed by six men, and then, through the doorway through which Doc and his friends had passed, twenty others came. Doc knew then how Iwaldi had disappeared so swiftly. He had taken a secret entrance in the wall of the outer room and gone through the tunnel to this room. The invaders had seen him and followed. Doc was glad that Iwaldi had not then cut back and taken Doc's party by surprise on the flank. But Iwaldi had not wanted to delay for anything. He had wanted to get away as fast as possible.

The invaders carried FN rifles and .45 automatic pistols, and four had hand grenades attached by the pins to their belts. There was even a bazooka team, one man with the tube and one carrying three rockets in a case on his back.

Doc made signs to Barney and Pauncho. They should let the invaders go on by. It was true that three grenades, thrown at once, could catch the whole party together and so dispose of them. But, though he had been compelled to fight them for the sake of survival, he did not know that they were basically hostile to him. Moreover, it would be best to use them to hound Iwaldi.

The party passed through the archway but left one man behind as a rearguard. Doc took out from a little box in his pack a ping-pong-sized, transparent ball and threw it when the man was looking the other way. The man spun on hearing the material break on the stone, looked around, then collapsed. Doc and his men had not even bothered to hold their breaths, since they were outside the influence of the vaporized curare. Doc sped to the man and applied the end of an air-operated syringe to his neck. He struck a sharp blow on the man's chest, and the man began to breathe again. But he was now unconscious and would remain so for half an hour.

Doc told Barney to return to the outer room and find where the secret entrance was. Pauncho appropriated all the man's weapons. Doc searched him for documents or other identification and found nothing. He was not even carrying a wallet.

The tapestry bulged, and Barney called out, "I've found it!"

"Who couldn't?" Pauncho said. "They left the door open, right?"

"I could tell you where to put the door, but I'm a gentleman," Barney said, coming out from behind the tapestry. "I'll define the term *gentleman* for you when we're not so busy."

"Would you mind spelling it for me?" Pauncho said. He grinned at Barney. He looked like a chimpanzee who'd just seen a fresh banana. "Hey, Doc, this Yale graduate's a real sooper-dooper speller.

Did you know we were in Korea six months before he found out you don't spell it C-H-O-R-E-A? Haw, haw! Of course, he wasn't too far wrong. Korea was a disease, as far as us marines were concerned."

"That's a disgusting lie!" Barney said. "As far as that goes, you thought Korea was in the South Pacific, and you're a Berkeley graduate!"

Doc said, "Stick something in that door under the tapestry. Not something big enough to make it stick out noticeably. We might want to use it for a getaway."

Barney looked disgusted, but he was angry at himself for not having thought of the idea. And he did not like Pauncho's grin. He knew his squat buddy was telling him, silently, that he was a dummy.

Doc was thinking how much the two resembled their fathers. Yet neither had gone to his father's college or taken up their professions. Perhaps this was because they resented or even hated their fathers at the same time that they loved them. Both Porky Rivers and Jocko Simmons had been divorced by their wives because they spent too much time away from home on their adventures with Doc Caliban. Both women had remarried, and their husbands had adopted their stepsons. But the real fathers still had visiting privileges, and they came about four or five times a year to take the boys on trips. Doc had met them and even entertained them in his apartment high up in the Empire State Building or on his Lake George estate. The boys had grown up imitating their real fathers because they were mysterious adventurers who roamed the world and did all sorts of fabulous and dangerous deeds. They were the sons of men who had married late in life, and so they had fantasized that they would replace their fathers when these grew too old for the man-killing exploits demanded of them by close relationship with Caliban. The old men had finally retired. But then they had come out of retirement for one last great adventure in Africa, when Doc Caliban was on the trail of the man he believed had killed his beloved cousin, Viscount Grandrith, a man whom most of the world believed to be a purely fictional character and whom the world knew largely by a name that had originated in a non-human language.

Grandrith had not killed Trish Wilde. He had not even known of her existence when she was reported murdered by him. But

Grandrith was mad at that time, insane in a peculiar way from the side effects of the elixir of immortality given to him by the Nine in return for certain services. Caliban was also insane because of the elixir's side effects. But he and Lord Grandrith discovered that they were half-brothers; and then Porky Rivers and Jocko Simmons died in their last battle at Castle Grandrith.

Pauncho van Veelar and Barney Banks had had a big shock when they saw Doc Caliban in 1968 after five years' absence. Of course, they had always remarked on how young their "Uncle Doc" looked. But seeing him again had brought up some very disturbing questions. How could a man born in 1901 still look thirty years old or younger? He should show *some* signs of ageing! And so Doc Caliban, who desperately missed his old sidekicks, no matter how self-sufficient he seemed to others, took their sons into his confidence. They would have joined him just to be able to get into the most exciting life on Earth and to follow in the footsteps of their beloved-hated fathers. But the chance of becoming immortal would have been more than enough inducement.

Barney had picked up two rifles and extra magazines of twenty rounds each. Doc said, "Thanks," and inspected his rifle for working order. Pauncho finished taping the mouth, wrists, and ankles of the sleeping guard. Doc said, "If my suspicions are correct, Iwaldi will be making for his underground labyrinth. He'll probably leave the way open so his enemies will follow him down. They'll find out why he's so hospitable."

They had just entered the next room when they heard and felt the explosion. The floor quivered, and air moved against their faces. Two rooms on, they came to an entrance made by a section of wall sliding back. Faint streamers of smoke and an odor of dynamite were being breathed from the dark mouth. Doc removed from his vest pocket a cap with a small tube atop it and put it on his head. Then he unfolded dark goggles from the same pocket and put them on. The others also put on caps and goggles, and then they went into the tunnel. This was unlit, but it did not impede them. The device atop the cap projected a "dark light" and their special goggles enabled them to see whatever the light hit. They had contact lenses which would do the same work, but these required time and effort to get in and out, and they preferred the goggles in this situation because they could be ripped off if the situation demanded.

The tunnel curved away from the entrance and then straightened out. The smoke got thicker. They inserted nose plugs to filter it. Thirty feet past the bend, they came to the entrance of a vertical shaft. Doc went down the steel ladder first, his backpack rubbing against the stone wall of the shaft behind him. He counted forty rungs about a foot apart before he stepped onto the bottom of the shaft. A horizontal shaft joined it, leading in an easterly direction. It was designed for dwarfs or designed to make men of normal stature uncomfortable. All three had to duckwalk for thirty yards before they came to a place where they could straighten up. This was a forty-foot square room, carved out of granite, furnished only with corpses.

These were near the opposite doorway. Apparently they had touched off some kind of trap loaded with explosives. Doc counted the bodies. Eight. That left eighteen. The bazooka team was not among them. He would have to be cautious about going too fast, since the survivors would be proceeding slowly now. However, the explosives in that confined area must have deafened and injured others, and the effective number of fighters in their party should be cut down. Also, it was possible that they would get cold feet, for which he could not blame them, and would return. To run head-on into them in these cramped tunnels could be fatal to his small party. But there was nothing to do but push on.

They walked bent-kneed through a thirty-five foot tunnel which ended when it joined another tunnel at right angles to it. Doc squirted some vapor for several yards down both directions. Suddenly, glowing foot-prints—glowing only because the goggles revealed them—sprang out. But the prints were in both directions, and Doc did not have any way of separating the Iwaldi party's prints from those of the invaders. It was true that Iwaldi was not over four feet five inches high, but his feet were disproportionately large. Nor was there any way of determining the weight of the person who had left prints. The vapor settled on the floor and was illuminated only where there was a difference in elevation of the material of the floor itself. Even a difference of two microns briefly illuminated the powder. There was enough dust on the floor for the boots to make some impressions.

The prints indicated that their makers had been going and coming on both sides of the tunnel at right angles to the one from which they had just emerged.

Doc cast up and down the tunnel for thirty yards. There were many more prints to the right, and then he found a stain of blood on the side of the wall to the right. He turned and beckoned to the two men, who could see him plainly in the radiation cast by their projectors.

"It's possible that they split up and some went the other way," he said.

Twenty yards further, the tunnel made a turn to the left. After another twenty yards, they found the tunnel almost completely blocked. A section of solid stone, three feet high and twenty long, had thrust itself out of the wall on the right and crushed a number of men against the left wall. Doc removed his pack and shoved it ahead of him while he crawled between the top of the block and the ceiling of the tunnel. He counted eight heads, most of which were above the stone, the bodies being squeezed into forms three inches wide. That left ten ahead, if the party had not split up.

"If I was them, and I'm glad I'm not," Pauncho said, "I woulda taken off by now."

"Maybe you shouldn't try to get through there," Barney said in a mock solicitous voice. "With that belly, you'll get stuck, and I won't be able to get by you. You stay here and guard my rear."

Pauncho chuckled, and the echoes came back from ahead. Doc said, *"Sh!"*, but Pauncho whispered, "Any time I get a chance—"

He stopped when Doc repeated his warning. Then he heard the noises, too.

Pauncho did have some trouble getting his huge belly through, and he was huffing and swearing when he fell off the other end of the block. By then the yelling and screaming of men and the weird shrill cries had increased. They duckwalked swiftly, Pauncho groaning softly and swearing that he would quit drinking beer if he ever got a chance to drink beer again. The tunnel bent at ninety degrees to the right, continued for ten yards, bent ninety degrees to the left, continued for twenty yards, and then they were at the arched entrance to a room so large it could almost be called a cavern.

It was lit only by the flashlights of the men inside but Doc's blacklight enabled him to see everything clearly. He removed the goggles for a moment so he could get an idea of how the situation looked to the men. The beams shot here and there and then dived for the floor, lay there shining, and were picked up again, though not always by the one who had dropped them. Some of the beams briefly illuminated large birds: white snow owls, golden eagles, bald eagles, African vultures. They swooped through the beams, their eyes flashing redly, their wings beating loudly, their talons outspread. Some closed in on the holders of the flashlights as if they were riding the beam down to their target. The butts of rifles flashed; one struck an eagle on the wing, and the great bird fell out of sight.

No rifles were being fired. Apparently the men were afraid of ricochets. They were using the weapons as clubs. But the birds did not seem discommoded by either the darkness or the lights shining in their eyes. They attacked from all angles, and men went down screaming under their beaks and talons.

Doc replaced his goggles.

The birds uttered no cries whatsoever. They were as silent as the wolves that had attacked Caliban's group in the bedroom. It was this that caused Caliban to look for the tiny hemispheres attached to the tops of the birds' heads.

Doc motioned to his colleagues to retreat with him. They duck-walked back to the end of the block and waited. Barney whispered, "What's going on, Doc?"

"Keep your rifles ready. We can shoot if we're attacked in here. As to the strange behavior of the animals and birds, I'll explain when I'm certain of its cause."

The screams went on for about ten minutes and then died out. The only sound was Pauncho's heavy breathing and the ripping of flesh as the birds tore at the corpses. Doc, not wanting to make any noise at all, put his hand on each man's arms and transmitted in Morse with the pressure of his fingers.

"The hemispheres may be electronic devices to control the animals by remote control. It's possible that the operator thinks his enemies are all dead and has shut down control. In which case, we might be able to stroll on by the birds without their attacking us. I say we should try it."

Barney and Pauncho simultaneously squeezed back, "You're the boss, Doc. You give the word."

He transmitted, "Ordinarily I would. But this is a very bad situation, and I would not blame you one bit if you decided to retreat now so we could fight later—in a situation more advantageous to us."

"If we go back, will you go back with us?" Barney transmitted.

Doc hesitated and then said, "No."

"Then we'll go on with you. Don't you like us, Doc, you want us to miss out on this? We have to earn our immortality."

Doc smiled slightly, and it was a measure of how deeply he was affected that he allowed his self-control to lapse even this much. Or perhaps it was a measure of his progress in getting rid of the too-rigid self-control of his past. He was trying to act more humanly, or more openly, since being too self-controlled was as human as not being self-controlled enough.

"O.K.," he squeezed back. "You cover me from the entrance. If they attack, I'll drop on my back and shoot upward, and you fire over my head."

He waddled into the room, straightened up, and walked toward the nearest body and the golden eagle feeding on it. The eagle looked fiercely at him and turned on top of the corpse, flapping its wings. Its beak opened as if it were uttering a silent cry. But it did not fly away. Nor did it attack. And the other birds continued to eat after glaring at him and assuring themselves that he was not belligerent.

Doc turned to signal to the two. Barney shouted, "Lookout, Doc!"

He wheeled, bringing up his rifle, having heard the flap of wings at the same time that Barney yelled. The vulture flew at him with beak and claws outspread, and behind him was the thunder of two dozen pairs of wings. All headed toward him.

He fell on his back, firing as he did. The vulture flew bloodily apart and spun to one side under the impact of the bullets. Blood and feathers and flesh spattered Doc. He continued to fire at the great birds, and then the explosions of his colleagues' FNs were added to his. Bullets ricocheted off the walls and the ceiling, wheeing by him, and his face stung from chips of stone. But the birds blew apart from the many high-velocity bullets striking them. And when Doc and the two men had emptied their magazines, they dropped the rifles and began firing with the 15-caliber explosive bullets from their gas guns. Able to see in the blacklight, they had no trouble aiming, and within sixty seconds all twenty-four birds were heaps of feathers.

Doc jumped up and ran toward the entrance of the tunnel as they quit firing and dived into its shelter.

Pauncho said, "What's up, Doc?" but Caliban did not reply.

He waited for some sign of action, knowing that the renewal of attack by the birds probably meant that the operator had happened to look into the room and see him. Or perhaps it meant that the operator had seen him from the first but had not stimulated the birds until he thought Doc was off his guard. It also meant that the operator could have a form of blacklight, since Doc had stayed out of range of the beams of the flashlight still operating.

Nowhere was there any evidence of TV cameras or one-way windows, but it would be easy to simulate rock.

There was a groaning behind them and a trembling of the floor. They turned to see the huge stone block withdrawing into the wall. The heads of the collapsing bodies struck the stone with a plop.

Doc nodded, and they got up and walked across the room, pausing only by the bodies to shove an extra magazine into their capacious jacket pockets. The exit was another archway at the far wall. They looked down its round length. Doc wondered why the tunnel was round instead of square, as all the others had been. It went for at least forty yards before making a turn. The roundness might preclude any section of the wall sliding out to crush them. At least the interior was smooth, seemingly carved out of the granite. But material in paste form, looking like stone, could have been spread over to cover up the lines of demarcation of a separate piece. He whispered to them, and they walked to the tunnel and entered, crouching. They held their rifles across their bellies so that the muzzle and stock extended past their sides.

They had gone ten yards when the wall to their right crumbled and flew outward, propelled by a block of stone. The mass squealed as it slid across the floor—but not loudly, indicating that the bottom was lubricated—and then the three were knocked side-wise. But the block stopped short with a crash; their rifles acted as rigid bars to hold the block back. And it was evident that there would be no more pressure put on them. The rifles had bent just a trifle but showed no signs of increasing buckling.

Doc crawled over his rifle and scooted on out past the block. He felt naked without the rifle to keep off the block, even though he knew that the three already wedged in were doing their work. Pauncho and Barney came after him with Pauncho snorting indignantly because Barney was making cracks about hippos in subways. But when they were out of danger, they sat down and wiped the sweat off.

Barney said, "Do you think—?" He stopped. Of course, Doc Caliban had no way of knowing whether or not there would be more such traps ahead. And they now had no rifles. They could go back and pick some more up. But, if they were being observed, the block could be withdrawn as soon as they went past the wedged rifles. And it could then be slammed in again with an excellent chance of catching them.

Barney and Pauncho had both thought of this, because Pauncho said, "I'll stay there holding on to a rifle and make sure that if the stone's moved, I'll be there to catch it again."

"Three rifles were strong enough to withstand it," Doc said. "I don't know that just one would do it."

"They're close enough I could reach out and grab two," Pauncho said. "And Barney could hold the other."

Doc looked at the block. This one was so much closer to the ceiling that crawling on its top was ruled out. It was as long as the other, and it had slid out when the three were halfway along its length.

"No," Doc said. "It could be withdrawn and slid out before we could reach the rifles. There's nothing to do except go ahead."

Barney and Pauncho looked dismal. Doc Caliban kept his face expressionless. It hurt him to see them express any kind of faint-heartedness or lack of faith in him. Yet his reaction was illogical whereas theirs was founded on a realistic attitude. They certainly were not cowards or easily downcast. His little experience with them had convinced him of that. Moreover, they had fought together in the worst of the Korean fighting, had escaped together from a Chinese prisoner-of-war camp, and both had won many medals for valor (though none for good conduct). After the war they had returned to school to get their higher degrees. And they had formed a business which had taken them into South America, where they had been captured by bandits and had again escaped. They did not lack courage or resourcefulness.

His own reaction was a hangover from the past, when he had gotten from their fathers a never-diminished gusto and optimism. They had never faltered. Or they had seemed not to falter. Perhaps they were more self-controlled and would have been ashamed to let him see their dismay. Their sons were more open, less vulnerable to shame. Moreover, if he, who prided himself on his logical behavior, was not doubtful about pushing on, then he must be missing something in his own character.

Doc Caliban thought, Well, not really. It's just that I know that I have more capabilities than they do.

Now was no time for soul-searching. He could do that when he retired to that hidden stronghold which had once been in the far north but which he had relocated at the bottom of a lake. Lately, when he had retreated, he had ceased to work on scientific devices and had taken to pursuing Oriental philosophies and their techniques.

He shook his head. Pauncho said, "What's the matter, Doc?"

Doc put his hands on their wrists and squeezed a message. Then he said, loudly, "We'll go ahead, take what comes, play it by ear!"

He turned and Pauncho got on one side and Barney on the other as they started across the room, which was about twenty feet high, sixty long, and forty wide.

Doc took two steps, whirled, and flashed back into the tunnel, sped crouching down it, and dived for the nearest rifle between the wall and the stone. Having seized it, he turned over and slid under it, releasing it only when Barney grabbed it. The two had started immediately after him but they were a few seconds behind since he was so swift. To any watcher he must have seemed almost a blur.

Pauncho, who was three times as strong as Barney but not as quick on his feet, caught up with Barney and grabbed his rifle. In a short time, they each had hold of a gun.

They waited for a moment. That the block had not withdrawn and then slammed in when Doc made his dive seemed to indicate that it was not being remote controlled. A watcher should have been startled by Doc's sudden return and operated the controls in sheer reflex.

It was also possible that the renewed hostility of the birds had come from an automatic mechanism. Doc had triggered off an alarm, perhaps by cutting across a beam.

While Pauncho braced himself between two rifles, and Barney gripped one, Doc slid out and then duck-ran back to the room. He returned with three more rifles. The two took them while Doc gripped the two rifles jammed against the wall and then he dived out and away, just in case there was a remote controller. The stone block did not move.

This room was without furniture or decoration except for a black, red-headed eagle, twice as large as a man, painted on a wall, and a ceramic container which might have been used for bathing small humans. The archway led to another round tunnel, but this was large enough for even Doc Caliban to stand erect in. At irregular intervals along the tunnel, about three feet up, were painted the symbols—squares with looped corners—which the Finns called *hannunkaavuna* and the Swedes *St. Hans's arms*. Doc knew this symbol well. It was carved on the staff which the Speaker for the Nine carried during the annual ceremonies in the caves in the mountains in Central Africa. The upper half of the staff bore a carved ankh, the cross with a circle on top, a symbol as ancient as Egypt.

The *hannunkaavuna* made him think briefly of Grandrith. That tall man with the black hair, gray eyes, handsome near-aquiline face, and Apollo-like body with its Herculean strength—his half-brother—should be near the coast of Gabon now. He would land there and proceed on foot across Central Africa, sticking largely to the belt of the rain forest, where few humans would see him. And then he would come up onto the bank of the mountains which held the caves of the Nine, and he would do what he could there. If he was confined to scouting and spying, he would wait until his brother could join him in an attack on the Nine during the annual ceremonies. If he had a chance to kill one of the Nine, he would do so.

The memory of pain twinged him in the back of the neck and elsewhere. His fight with Grandrith had not been without loss and agony.

They got out of the tunnel without incident. Pauncho wiped sweat off his shelving brow and said, "Whoo!"

Barney said, "I kept expecting the side of the wall to jump out at us."

Doc looked around. This room had hexagonal corners and was painted with many scenes of long-bearded squat little men fighting crocodile-sized creatures looking exactly like the stuffed *Tatzelwurm*. The focus of the battle was a big pile of gold rocks. A twilight illumination came from naked plastic bulbs set in widely separated brackets on the walls. Wires ran from them to black boxes on the floor.

Pauncho said, "Listen, Doc, do you think that once there may have been big whatchamaycallems, and these gave rise to the legends of the dragons?"

"Your guess is as good as mine," Caliban said, and he led them to the next archway. This was painted black, and the tunnel was black. They proceeded ten yards when they came to a hole in the center of the floor. Doc pointed his headlight down it, making sure that his rifle was still held at the proper angle across his belly. The shaft went straight down for about twenty feet and then became a hole in the ceiling of another tunnel. A section of wooden ladder lying flat on the floor was visible.

The atomizer revealed that someone had gone down the shaft by putting their back to one wall and their feet against the other. It also indicated footprints going on in this tunnel, but the light from the prints was not as bright as that on the walls of the shaft.

"It could be another trap," Doc squeezed on Barney's arm. Barney transmitted the same message to Pauncho.

"We're playing follow-the-leader," Barney squeezed back. His thin foxily handsome face looked eager. Pauncho was grinning like an orangutan dreaming of durian fruit.

Iwaldi seemed to be going to the lower levels. At least, that would be the natural direction for him to go when his home was invaded. Perhaps he did not know that his traps had killed all of one party of invaders and that just three men were tracking him. Perhaps he did, and he was crouching in some room and watching them even now, waiting for the proper moment so he could press a button or pull a lever or just watch while an automatic trap was sprung.

Doc leaned over and dropped his rifle, butt first. It struck and toppled over. He waited. Nothing happened. There was nothing to do but go down the shaft then. Near its bottom he removed a suction disc from his pocket, stuck it against the shaft wall, and lowered himself by his left hand down from the shaft, his legs drawn up. He swung like a gibbon from a branch, turning to take in the round tunnel which ran for ten yards in either direction and then curved out of sight. The ceiling was eleven feet from the floor, and the greatest distance between the walls was twelve. There were eight bulbs on brackets along the walls.

"How is it, Doc?" whispered Pauncho.

Caliban looked up. The ugly but congenial face hung over him.

"Only one way to find out," he said. He released his grip on the handle of the disc, it fell, he grabbed it, and he dropped down to the floor. But his other hand had his gasgun out before his feet struck the stone.

Pauncho came down, grunting, and then Barney.

The moment Barney landed, the world seemed to tilt. Doc made a leap forward for the shaft with his left hand, which still held the disc, extended. And when the disc slapped onto the inner edge of the lip of the shaft, he squeezed down on the handle. The disc held, and he hung there, while the ladder, his rifle, and his two friends went down the slope of the tunnel, which had suddenly dropped and was rapidly becoming vertical.

Sick, he looked down past his feet while Pauncho and Barney, their fingers grabbing for a hold on the smooth stone—or what seemed like stone but could not be—hurtled downward. And then they were gone around the bend, shot out of the gigantic chuteychute. The rifle went with them, and the ladder, bending at a number of places like a wooden snake, shot out by their side.

Panicked though they must have been, neither had screamed or yelled. Pauncho had groaned, and Barney had hissed between clamped teeth, but that was all.

Doc hung there, rotating slowly by the turning of his wrist. He could swing himself up and get his feet against the wall of the shaft and so climb back up to its top. Or he could swing out and back until he had enough momentum and then release the disc and land on the edge of the newly formed vertical shaft and go on down this tunnel. Or he could then climb down the chuteychute, using the discs and see what was down there. It seemed certain that Iwaldi would be waiting for him there, but he could not abandon his colleagues, not unless he knew for certain that he could help them by action elsewhere.

Within a minute, he was going down the shaft of the trap. When he came to the bend he proceeded more slowly. He lifted the goggles for a moment and, seeing that there was light ahead, left them up. He could see only a whitewashed wall ahead, but when he got to the end of the tube and looked down, he saw Pauncho and Barney.

Below them was another shaft about twenty feet wide and so deep he could not see the bottom. The shaft was in the center of a large room which seemed to be the storehouse for hundreds of wooden brightly painted statues. These ranged from beautiful nudes and fully clothed humans and dwarfish peoples to dragons to elk to wolves to badgers to monsters of various sorts. The light came from a dozen glass bulbs on top of stone lamps.

Pauncho and Barney were at the bottom of a net. This was composed of many thin and apparently sticky cords. Their weight had pulled the net, which originally had been stretched across the top of the shaft, to a bag-like shape with them at the bottom and about twenty feet down the shaft. They were struggling and cursing in low tones, but their efforts only entangled them more thoroughly in the cords. Seeing Doc Caliban, they stopped thrashing around.

"Get me out of here, Doc," Barney said. "This guy's so hairy, he's making me itch."

"Yeah, get me out of here," Pauncho said. "He's so bony he's cutting me."

Doc did not answer. He began to swing back and forth until he had enough momentum. He released the pressure on the disc handle as he started an outward swing, and he landed on the edge of the shaft. Neither of the two made a sound, though it might have been expected that Doc would teeter back and fall into the net with them. His toes only struck the lip of the shaft. But he snapped himself forward and then was solidly on the floor. He turned and began to pull on the net, hauling up the four hundred and seventy pounds of the two men and the hundred pounds of the net as if they were a minnow on a string.

The sticky cords clung to his hands, but he just walked backward, pulling the two over the edge with a bump and a scrape that brought groans from them. After they were on the floor, he managed to pull his hands loose and then he started the tedious and slow task of freeing them.

When they were out of the net, Pauncho and Barney were as dirty looking as coal miners at the end of a shift. The dark brown substance had smeared their clothes, faces, and hands.

"One thing I'll say," Barney muttered. "You look just as good dirty as you do clean. Maybe better because it's more natural."

Pauncho's thick teeth flashed in a grin. "As an authority on dirt, your opinion is to be valued. It takes one to know one, as they say."

"Takes one what to know what one?" Barney said.

"If you two will quit your clowning around now," Doc Caliban said, "we'll proceed. Though where I don't know."

From a pocket in his vest he took an object the size and shape of a large pocketwatch. Its face bore a number of dials and graduated markings and also a thin tube with a red column, like a thermometer. The others did not comment. They knew that this was a device with several functions. One of them was to detect objects of a certain shape and density. The device could be set to register when such and such an object was near its field of radiation. Doc now adjusted it by turning a small wheel on its back, and then he advanced down the room holding it out before him.

If there was anything immediately behind the walls or under the floors or above the ceiling, this detector would send a pulse of yellow light up and down the column on its face. The drawback of the detector was that it could not be used in the near vicinity of guns and knives or other considerable masses of metal. It registered the metal even if its radiating field was directed away from the metal. There was a certain amount of back radiation, an echo as it were, and this detected the metal. So Doc Caliban had to give his pistol and knife to Pauncho to carry while he preceded them by thirty feet.

He stopped at a wooden ladder sticking out of a shaft and the two halted with the same distance maintained between them and their leader. He swept the detector around and then went down the ladder. They followed a minute later. The next level down was a long corridor hewn out of solid granite. It ran for as far as they could see in both directions, and it was well lit with naked electric light bulbs on iron brackets about five feet from the floor and spaced about forty feet apart.

Doc sprayed some more of the atomized differential-level substance around. It revealed many footprints, but the freshest seemed to go off to the right, so he elected to go that way. They passed tools lying on the floor or propped against the walls: picks with broken handles or worn points; great sledges, bars with chiseled edges, brooms. Some of them looked as if they had been lying here a long time. Then they came to a broad staircase cut out of the rock. It led down for about sixty feet at a steep angle. They went down it, still guided by the electric light bulbs, and came to a room at least a hundred feet square and forty high.

Doc stopped, and Pauncho and Barney, forgetting that they were not to get close, almost bumped into him. The red column in the center of the face changed to a bright yellow light which pulsed.

Doc told them to move back, and the light went back to its quiescent state. Barney whistled softly and said, "Looks like they had a fight sometime ago, doesn't it? A long time ago!"

The footprints were plain here. The dust was so thick that it rose with every step. Pauncho almost strangled trying to keep from sneezing while Barney choked trying to keep from laughing at Pauncho's desperate grimaces.

There were about ten complete skeletons and parts of others scattered around the room. Rusty swords, knives, and double-headed axes lay under the dust, many still clutched by bony hands. Some of the skulls had been cracked or caved in; an axe was still wedged in the top of a skull.

Doc said, "Most of them were dwarfs. And an early type of *Homo sapiens.* Look at the thickness of those bones, the huge supra-orbital ridges."

The fresh footprints led through one of six archways. Doc went through this cautiously, ready to jump back at the slightest sign of anything suspicious. The room beyond was immense and lit by bulbs in brackets secured to the granite walls. There were more skeletons and axes and swords. And in the center of the room, sitting on an oaken high-backed ornately carved chair on a granite slab, was a figure.

They approached slowly, though it was obviously a corpse.

It was a very old corpse, a mummy. Its white hair fell over its shoulders and its white beard covered its lap and its knees. The dark eyes stared at them.

It wore a cap like a dunce's crown and leather garments and leather boots with curled-up toes. The brown, wrinkled, and heavily veined hand held a golden scepter with six diamonds inset on the polygonal knob of gold at the end of the scepter.

On the slab and around the oaken throne were many figurines of stone about a foot high. They represented a squat, hairy people: males and female adults and some children. They were dressed in clothes similar to that on the mummy. There were a few figurines of animals, mostly badgers, but two were of some sort of monster.

"What do you make of it, Doc?" Pauncho asked.

Pauncho did not expect an answer. But Doc said, "I am not sure. The mummy looks much like Iwaldi, as you know from my description and my sketch of him. And the figurines are modeled after his people. How this man came to his death, why he's been preserved, I don't know. But you must remember that Iwaldi's people are—were—some sort of dwarfish Caucasoids with a slight Mongolian mixture somewhere along the line. They're the little people who gave rise to the tales of gnomes, kobolds, and even trolls. I'm sure of that. They did a lot of mining and tunneling, and if my theory is correct, they survived in Germany and some parts of Scandinavia up to 1000 A.D. Then they were absorbed or just died out. Iwaldi kept on living. He would, of course, being one of the Nine. And he had this castle built over the ancient stronghold of his race during the medieval period. Though I think he also was the one who built the earlier fortress on which the castle was based.

"This man here may have been some king, perhaps a son of Iwaldi. If we get Iwaldi alive, maybe we can find out about all this. But I would prefer that we kill him. The moment we get the chance to. That old man is too wily, too dangerous, to let live for more than the time it takes to cut his throat."

He quit talking, and the oppressive silence returned. Pauncho shifted uneasily. The fierce-eyed and long-bearded figure seemed to have moved, though he knew it was an illusion. For the first time, he became aware of the millions of tons of stone over his head. The silence was as heavy as the stone. He was so awed by this that he whispered his feelings to Barney. Barney might have laughed at another time and place, but that he did not do so now showed that he felt much the same as Pauncho.

Doc gestured at them to follow him. He held the detector out ahead of him. Its light was flashing yellow, but the masses of iron weapons were responsible for that. He passed through a tall archway into another room which was filled with digging tools and swords and axes, all neatly stacked in piles along the wall. He chose to go down another broad staircase of stone steps. Footprints led away from it, but footprints also went down it and these seemed to be fresher. The stairs went on and on. Doc counted a hundred, then two hundred, then three hundred with no end in sight. The bottom was hidden somewhere in the shadows below. Along the wall there were bulbs which had been set much further apart.

Moreover, the walls began to move in closer, and the way slowly curved to the right. Then it straightened out for a hundred steps, after which it curved to the left.

"I wonder how far down these diggings go?" Pauncho whispered to Barney. "If this Iwaldi geezer is 10,000 years old, he may have started digging back then. The whole mountain could be honey-combed."

Abruptly, the stairs ceased. Doc waved the detector back and forth before the huge oaken door before them. The column in its face was red.

"Hey, Doc!" Pauncho said. "Those hinges are gold!"

Doc signaled and Barney handed him the knife. Doc touched the golden latch on the door with the knife as if he expected an electrical spark to leap out. Nothing happened. He slipped on the goggles and examined the door and the latch under the "blacklight." Then he raised the goggles and said, "We'll have to take a chance. Stand way back, you two."

The door swung outward, revealing a cavernous room beyond.

This was lit with the ubiquitous bulbs. It seemed to be a storehouse for many things: battle-axes, swords, cuirasses, and leggings, oaken and stone chests, many of them open and glinting with gold bars or gleaming with jewels. There were also statues, ranging from a foot high to life size, carved out of stone or formed from gold and silver. Some were of well-proportioned humans, some of the squat and muscular and thick-calved dwarfs, some of animals, of monsters.

The three walked slowly into the chamber, pausing to look at but not to touch the wealth strewn everywhere. Some of the chests contained coins and paper money of many nations.

Doc kept his attention on the fresh footprints in the dust. These led straight across the immense room toward a set of three arches at the far end. But before they reached them, they halted. On their right, set into the wall, was a steel framework with steel bars. This was at the entrance to a small cell cut out of the stone.

Pauncho and Barney said, simultaneously, "Wow!"

Doc Caliban's face did not lose its expressionlessness. But a close observer might have noticed those peculiar yellow-flecked eyes narrow.

A young man and a young woman were staring at them from behind the bars.

It was the woman who had caused the two men to express delight, surprise, admiration, and desire.

"Your cousin has finally got some real competition," Pauncho said to Caliban.

The woman's hair was long and loose and of an unusually deep red. Her skin was very clear and white, and her eyes were large and violet. Her only makeup was a bright red lipstick. She wore heavy hiking clothes and boots, but they were tight enough to reveal a superb figure.

The man was wide-shouldered and muscular but very short. He had black hair and brown eyes and a handsome face.

The woman's voice was throaty and caressing even though she was evidently under heavy stress. She gripped the bars and said, "My God, where did you come from?" and then, "Please get us out of here!"

The young man had also grabbed hold of the bars, but he did not say anything.

Doc Caliban looked past them. The cell was furnished with a double bunkbed and some light blankets and pillows, a washbowl with a pitcher of water and a glass, an open toilet bowl, and a stone shelf on which were two trays with dishes on which were the remnants of food.

"Did Iwaldi take the key to this lock with him?" Doc said.

"Who?" the man said.

"The old dwarf," Doc Caliban replied.

"He went thataway," the woman said, pointing her finger at the far end. She smiled, but she was evidently trying to be brave. Her fingers were white where she was clutching the bars.

"How many men did he have with him?" Doc said.

"Ten," the man said. His speech was, like the woman's, Received Standard English—that of an educated Londoner's.

Pauncho and Barney were pulling rolls of thin wires from their vest pockets. Doc raised his hand as if to check them, then let it drop. The cell and its prisoners might be an elaborate booby trap of some sort, but the only way to find out was to try to free them. The two wrapped several turns of the wires around the more slender bars which held the lock to the door. They pressed the button on the battery in their pockets; flame spurted out from around the wires; the bars and the lock were removed with a yank. Pauncho pulled the barred door open and said, *"Exitez-vous, madame."*

She smiled ravishingly at him; Pauncho, ravished, smiled back.

The man introduced himself as Carlos Cobbs and the woman as Barbara Villiers, his fiancée. They both taught archaeology at the university in London. They had been digging on the mountainslope three days ago when they were captured by the dwarf and his men.

Doc thought at first that they meant that Iwaldi's men had picked them up near the castle. But they said they had been digging in the woods near the bottom of the massive stone cap on which the castle rested. The earth had fallen in at the bottom of their trench, and they had gone in with it. Their shovels and picks had broken through the top of a tunnel. Exploring the tunnel, they found that it was part of an immense labyrinth of many levels.

They had pushed on, fascinated because they had come across stone figurines and the skeletons of men who were obviously early

Paleolithic. And then some men had captured them and brought them here, despite their protests. After a while, a strange long-bearded dwarf had appeared and questioned them. Barbara called him The Mountain King and said these were his halls.

"He wouldn't let us go," she said. "He—what'd you say his name was. Iwaldi?—said we were spies and that he'd kill us. But not before he found a use for us, since he didn't believe in wasting anything. He kept muttering something about the nine. Just the nine. Nine what?"

Doc did not reply. He entered the cell and prowled around with his detector in hand. Then he came out and said, "If I were you two, I wouldn't report this to the local authorities. Or any authorities. I'd just quietly get out of Germany and get back to London. I know you can't forget this, but you should act as if you had."

"Really?" Carlos Cobbs said. "Why should we?"

"You would probably die very soon after you started to talk about this. There is another group which is out after Iwaldi's hide—and mine—which would shut you up the hard way. Hard for you, easy for them."

"And who are you?" Barbara said.

"Your liberator," Doc said. He was thinking that he should send a radio message to his cousin in London to check on these two as soon as he got back to the village.

"Barbara Villiers?" Barney said, smiling. "An old and . . . uh . . . well-known name. You aren't related to the late Duchess of Cleveland, Countess Castlemaine, are you?"

The woman smiled back at him and became twice as beautiful. "You mean the wicked woman who was born in 1641, the daughter of Viscount Grandison? The mistress of Charles II, John Churchill, and William Wycherley, not to mention others common and great?"

"Yes," Barney said.

She laughed and said, "Yes, I'm related to her. But I don't have a title. I'm just a commoner."

"You're true royalty—aesthetically speaking," Pauncho said.

Barney glared at him.

"Don't you wish you'd said that?" Pauncho said, sneering at Barney.

"We're going after Iwaldi," Doc Caliban said. "That'll be very dangerous. Besides, I don't want to have to worry about you when the fireworks begin. I suggest that you go back the way we came."

"Won't that be dangerous, too?" Barbara said. She was looking him up and down and evidently liking what she saw. Doc felt uncomfortable and cursed himself for being weak enough to experience the feeling. He never got over it. He always attracted women, and he always felt uneasy at their admiration. What was worse, he now knew why he got uneasy, and he did not like that at all. After his final encounter with Lord Grandrith in that old castle in the Cumberland, when he had been invalided with a broken neck and was regrowing some rather roughly removed skin and flesh, he had done some deep self-probing.

"Either way is dangerous," he said. "But the trail blazed is always less dangerous than the trail to be blazed. Generally, anyway."

She looked at Carlos Cobbs. "I'd feel safer if we were with them even if we might run into that dirty old man and his gang."

Carlos Cobbs shrugged. He said, "Anything you say, my dear."

"We can't spare any guns," Doc said. "Pick up one of those swords or an axe and stay well behind us."

"Maybe one of us ought to stay close with the lady and see she doesn't come to any harm," Pauncho said. He grinned at the titian-haired beauty and managed to look even more like a baboon.

"If she stays with you she will come to harm," Barney said. "Just looking at you is enough to bring anybody down with a fatal case of the uglies."

Doc walked away with Barney and Pauncho a few steps behind and the couple following them. He halted before the archway, swept his detector back and forth, and then started through. He felt the floor dip and leaped high into the air like a scalded cat. The detector flew out of his hand as he grabbed for the rough stone along the edge of the point of the archway. Even though his leap took him above the heads of his two men, his fingers could not find a purchase on the stone. He fell back and into the hole below him and after Barney and Pauncho. Their yells were coming up the shaft even as he hurtled through the hole. He saw Cobbs and the woman staring open-mouthed and pale at him, and then the walls of the shaft were the only thing he could see.

Far below came a splash, then another splash. And then it was not so far below, and he plunged into icy water.

He went down deep, but his fall had been perhaps fifty feet, enough to kill a man if he struck the water at the wrong angle. His hard heavy boots took the major part of the energy of the impact. Even so, he was half-stunned. But he had secured the cap with the blacklight device onto his head by holding it with one hand, and he switched that on. Then he slipped his goggles down onto his eyes, sliding it over the skin to keep the water out, and held tightly with the other. As he rose toward the surface, he removed two plugs from a vest pocket and slipped these into his nose. He began breathing through them immediately. They strained oxygen from the water quite efficiently, and he breathed the carbon dioxide out through his mouth.

There was no light down here, and he would have been blind if it had not been for his blacklight projector and goggles. Even so, the water seemed to have a suspension of plant growth or perhaps of dirt and he could not see far. But he did make out Pauncho's form and when he had swum near enough for Pauncho to see him, Pauncho gestured outward. Doc swam even closer and could then make out Barney's shadowy figure. In a moment, Barney had swum close.

Both had retained their caps with the projector and their goggles, and they had also inserted into their nostrils the filters. But the icy water was rapidly numbing them.

Doc reached into another pocket and removed an object the size and shape of a boy's marble. He popped it into his mouth, chewed on it, and then swallowed it. A minute later, he began to feel warm. The sense of disorientation that had started to slip through him disappeared. The pill not only provided a source of energy the output of which was proportionate to the demand for warmth, but it fought shock.

He reached the surface but could not stick his head into the air. The water at this point boiled into the ceiling of rock. He and his two colleagues could only stay under and let themselves be taken away by the powerful current. There was no use fighting against it. Even Doc Caliban's massive muscles, anchored to a skeleton almost twice as thick as a normal human being's, could not have made progress against that force.

For approximately five minutes, as registered by the hands of his wristwatch, they were swept between stone walls that came closer and closer. This narrowing of the channel also increased the power of the current. They sped by walls of granite worn smooth by other rocks tumbled along in the past by the river. They kept hold of each other's hand so they would not be separated, and they went around and around as if they were on a dancing streamer around a maypole. But then they began to get cold again, and they had to swallow another energon.

He had one pill left apiece. After the effect of that was gone, their chance for survival was small. Unless—At that moment he heard a roar, and suddenly the water was boiling. A sharp ridge of stone passed a few inches below his drawn-up legs, then he was sliding on an apron of slick rock and then he was half in the air, half in the water, falling and turning over and over. Pauncho's hand was torn from his; a second later, he struck something. His ribs hurt so much that he could not repress a gasp, and water choked him.

When he awoke, he was lying on a muddy bank and was cold, cold, cold.

He sat up and began coughing. A shape appeared out of the darkness. He got to his feet as swiftly as he could but with agonizing slowness. A voice rumbled, "It's me, Doc. Take it easy."

He felt his head. His projector was still here. But his goggles were gone. Then his eyes became more adjusted to the dark and he saw that he was on a mud bank that sloped gently for several yards and then rose at ninety degrees for about forty feet. The sky was paler up there. The side of a mountain hung over them on the opposite side; the less precipitous slope was on the other side.

"Where's Barney?" he said.

Pauncho grunted like a sick hog and said, "He's trying to find a way out of here. You all right, Doc?"

Caliban felt his side. "I think I cracked some ribs. I won't know until I get back to Gramzdorf."

"I thought you were a goner. I saw you slam into that boulder at the bottom of the falls."

Doc could hear the muted roar of the cataract to his left. They must have gone quite a distance downstream before making this bank.

He swallowed another energon. When he started to feel warm again, he said, "Let's go after Barney."

They walked into a side street of the little village of Gramzdorf just before dawn. They were no longer cold and wet and dirty and hungry. But they went silently and stealthily and studied the outside of the inn, at which they were guests, for a long time before entering.

Doc had resumed his disguise of Mr. Sigurdsson, the old Norwegian tourist, and Barney was wearing a false red beard and red wig in his guise as a Mr. Benjamin. Pauncho wore contact lenses to change the color of his gray-blue eyes; he had a huge blue-black beard and his hat was jammed down to hide his enormous supraorbital ridges and his slanting forehead.

At this time of the year, when most of the snows were melted, there were few tourists. The locals, who stayed inside the village to work at the inns and the ski slides and associated businesses in winter, had retreated to their farm-houses. The clerk on duty in the lobby was asleep on his stool. The three walked past him and took the stairs to the third floor, the top floor. Doc inserted the slender tube of his see-around-a-corner and twisted it to inspect the front room from one wall to the next. Then he stuck another tube through the keyhole and pressed a bulb, pulled it out, and reinserted the *saac*, as he called it.

A little box attached to the opposite wall was flashing an orange light. That meant that it had photographed no one entering the room, and that, presumably, it was safe to enter.

Barney, who had been at the end of the hall and looking out of the window, signaled Doc. When Doc got there, he saw two figures coming down a side street: Carlos Cobbs and Barbara Villiers.

Doc Caliban was gone like a rabbit scared by a coyote. Though six feet seven and weighing more than three hundred, he moved as swiftly and as lightly as a tiger. He was down the hall, down the steps, and out onto the lobby just as the couple entered. His timing was precise. The two had no chance to get away if they had wanted to do so. Doc had considered not revealing himself so that he could watch the couple when they thought they were safe. But his own great size and difficulty of disguise for Pauncho van Veelar would also make it easy for the two to recognize them. Besides, he wanted information now, and he did not feel that the waiting game was the one to play at this time.

So he spoke to them in his own voice as they approached.

The jaws of both dropped, and their eyes were wide. But both recovered swiftly. Cobbs did not try to smile, but Barbara managed a brilliant and lovely smile. "I'm so glad!" she said, advancing with her arms open. "So glad! And so overwhelmed! I thought you were dead! You dropped into that awful hole and were gone! But the others? Are they . . . ?"

"All right," Doc said. "Would you mind coming to my room? There are some things we have to establish."

"Why not in the morning?" Cobbs said. "We're very tired. With good reason, as you know."

"I would think your curiosity would be too great for you to think of sleep," Doc Caliban replied. "You must have seen some things that you would have thought could not exist. And Iwaldi. Didn't—"

"Oh, yes, darling!" Barbara Villiers said, placing a lovely white hand on Cobbs' arm. "He's absolutely right! Besides, why is he disguised as an old man? I'm dying to find out! There must be some tremendous mystery here! I couldn't sleep thinking about that! I don't think I could sleep anyway, not with that mad goblin on the loose yet!"

Doc said, "The mad goblin. A good description indeed of Iwaldi. Will you go with me?" and he turned as if he fully expected that they could do nothing else.

They followed him up but stopped short when they saw Pauncho and Barney standing before the door. Cobbs said, "Who—?" and then, "Very good disguises those! But those long arms and that nose and mouth! No, I think I'd recognize him anywhere no matter what!"

Doc unlocked the door and let the others through and then locked the door and secured a little box against the upper part of the door with a disc. Barney had turned off the mechanism that was flashing a light and was removing the film.

Pauncho said, "What about a drink to warm us up and give us courage to face the morning sun? I thought I'd never see it again."

All took some brandy except for Doc, who never drank alcohol unless a disguise required it.

Pauncho lit up a long green Cuban cigar and said, "Doc, the floor is yours."

He added, "And the furniture, too, if you so desire."

Barney groaned. Cobbs and Villiers sat down before Doc could ask them to.

Doc said, "Did you two have any trouble getting out?"

"No," Cobbs replied. "We just walked out the front way. Everything was clear."

The titian-haired woman shuddered and said, "All those bodies . . ."

"You didn't tell the police here," Doc said. "Obviously you didn't have enough time; you got here so fast."

Cobbs said they had come straight down the mountain path to the inn. They did not know what was going on and they did not care to know. Their brief interviews with Iwaldi had scared them. The ancient dwarf—the "mad goblin"—had impressed them deeply. He seemed to be evil incarnate, and they were convinced that even if they had escaped him they would not be safe until they got to England.

"Just what were you digging for?" Doc said.

"Some years ago, when we were here on vacation, we heard about a shepherd who had discovered a stone with some strange markings on it. We investigated and found a rock with inscribed runic signs, made by some Germanic speaker by the name of, by a curious coincidence, Iwaldi. Probably the runes were incised between 600 A.D. and 800 A.D. We sniffed around that area and found a site of a small village. So, every now and then, we dig around here during our vacation. We're on sabbatical leave just now."

Doc made a mental note to check on their stories.

He could understand their fear. But what they had seen in the labyrinthal tunnels would establish them among the world's greatest archaeologists if they were to reveal their discovery. All they had to do was to get the police up there, and Iwaldi would have to run for cover.

On the other hand, they may have reasoned, quite correctly, that Iwaldi had enormous influence and could abort any attempt by the police to get into his castle.

Doc asked a few more questions. Cobbs said that the helicopters which had landed the invaders had left by the time they reached the castle's front door. But he was convinced that some of the invaders had gotten out alive. Apparently, the invaders must have split up, and the second party had survived. He thought so because he had seen the glow of cigarettes far below them on the mountainside path. It was true that the smokers could have been extremely early hikers or maybe forest rangers, but he doubted it.

"I'm asking you to stay here for a while. For today, anyway," Doc said. "If any of those invaders are now in the village, you could identify them for me."

"And what would you do to them?" Cobbs asked.

Doc did not answer. He looked at the young Englishman with all the intensity of his peculiar brass-shot gray-green eyes. Cobbs returned his stare with one just as unabashed though not as intense. Doc had been a practitioner of hypnosis for years and had been able to disturb many a man to the point of hysteria just by looking at him. But Cobbs was a tough and cool character.

Barbara Villiers, who looked devastatingly beautiful despite staying up all night, said, "I'll stay if you think it'll help you any."

"Babs!" Cobbs said reproachfully. "You might at least consider my feelings in this matter. After all, we are engaged! And we agreed that I am the head of the family!"

"There isn't any family yet!"

"Fabulous!" Pauncho said, grinning like a hungry monkey at her.

Cobbs sneered at Pauncho and said, "Discretion directs me to get out of here now! But I don't want you to think I'm a coward, and if my fiancée insists on behaving foolishly, then I'll stay too. But only long enough to look over the guests here and ascertain if we can identify any as the men we saw in the castle."

Barney had opened his mouth to say something, then he thought better of it. He looked as if he would explode if he did not get to ask Doc Caliban something at once.

Doc, guessing what he wanted to say, turned away from the couple and winked at Barney. Barney went into the bathroom. Doc said, "If you'll feel safer, you can sleep here in our beds. We'll make do on the sofa or the floor."

"I would prefer we do that," Cobbs said. To return to our own rooms now would be stupid. Of course, we have to go there to pack, but we can do that later."

Doc suddenly spoke to the two in a somewhat musical speech, low-pitched and with many glottal stops and fricatives.

The two only looked startled. Doc spoke in English. "Your profession hasn't taken you into the Central American jungles, then?"

"No," Cobbs said. "What was that for?"

Doc spoke to Pauncho, who listened intently and asked him to repeat several words. He and Barney had only recently learned the speech of the People of the Blue, a dialect of the "red skinned Athenians of Central America," and they were a long way from being as fluent in it as their fathers had been. Pauncho nodded and left the room for the lobby downstairs.

Cobbs said, "Look here! I don't like this mysterious conversation. If you have anything to say, speak English, man! We're not under suspicion, you know!"

"You're not innocent until proved guilty," Doc said. "Not in this affair. Everybody is suspect. You are not being detained by force, however. I must insist that you understand that. You may leave at any time you wish."

Doc removed his jacket and his vest. Barbara Villiers stared and then said, "I thought you looked awfully fat in the body, yet your face wasn't fat at all. And your friends looked incongruously bulky, too. Good heavens! You must be carrying enough weight in those vests to sink a battleship!"

Doc did not reply.

Cobbs and Villiers went into the large bedroom where he sprawled out on Doc's bed and she on Barney's. Barney came out of the bathroom and spoke softly in the speech of the People of the Blue.

"I sent out a message to Grandrith. His wife answered. She said he'd taken off for Africa a few hours before. She also said she might have to leave her rooms and go hide out in another place. She noticed a couple of suspicious characters hanging around in the street below. She said they might not be interested in her, but she's taking no chances."

"You told her about the events of the past few hours?"

"Everything. She said she'd pass it on to Grandrith when she got a chance. He's supposed to send her another message as soon as he's ready to leave the plane on the coast of Gabon."

There, near the place where he had been born, Grandrith would proceed on foot through the belt of rain forest stretching over a good part of Central Africa. He would live off the plants and the animals native to the land, killing them with arrows or his knife. He would avoid all human habitations; he would go like a shadow, like *the demon of the forest* as so many natives called him. Some used the name that an American writer had given him after accidentally finding out about him. On foot and almost naked, he would go faster than any human should through the silent closed-canopied, twilit rain forest where the only humans are the pygmies and where the pathetically few hairy and long-canined hominids, those beastmen of native legend, not long ago roamed.

Grandrith's wife, Clio, was staying in a slums district of London where she was operating a short-wave radio.

Caliban's cousin, Patricia Wilde, was also in London. She was on the trail of old Anana, the woman who headed the Nine. She believed that Anana lived at least part of the year in a town house in a wealthy residential district, and she was investigating a number of houses there. Caliban did not think she would have any luck, but at least it would keep her busy, and she did have a sharp nose for clues; she would have made an excellent private eye.

The phone rang. Doc was across the room like a bronze shark and had picked up the receiver before the second ring. Pauncho, speaking mainly in the language of the Blue People, said, "I checked out their registration here, Doc, after greasing the desk clerk's palm. Cobbs and the redhead have been registered here for a week. But the clerk says they aren't round much. I just saw two guys that looked pretty mean to me, like they could take care of themselves and others, too, if they were paid enough. They've been registered here for a week. They're Germans, Heinrich Zelner and Wilhelm Gafustimm. Zelner moves slow and careful, as if he's hurting. They're in room 215. You want—?"

Caliban asked for a detailed description. Zelner could have been one of the men he saw when he had looked into the room where the invaders were. He might have been wounded during the fighting.

"I'll be right down," he said. "Meet you outside their room."

He checked the pockets of his vest, which had dried out very quickly after he'd come out of the Toll River. He was short of anesthetic gas bombs, so he went into the bathroom and pulled a section of the wall aside. The short-wave radio and their supplies were stored here. Pauncho had cut out a piece of the wall and made a receptacle in less than fifteen minutes after they had moved in. His work on concealing the new door had been so skillful it would be doubtful that anyone would ever know about it until the inn was torn down.

The grenades were actually little plastic balls which shattered easily on impact. Their surface held a little nipple which could be squeezed off and a slender tube could be inserted into the hole created. Doc also took several of the tubes. Cobbs and Villiers seemed to be sleeping. The woman was heart-achingly beautiful.

"You stay here and keep an eye on them," Caliban said to Barney.

"Why does that *Pan satyrus* always have all the fun?" Barney said, more to himself than to his chief. But this time he was surprised. Doc did answer.

"Pauncho'll be jealous because you'll be with the woman," he said. "He'd like the job of guarding her."

"Some guard! But what good is that going to do me with that Cobbs fish . . . ?"

He stopped talking. Caliban had gone as silently and as swiftly as a wind-blown cloud across the face of the moon.

On the floor below, Pauncho came down the hall with the rolling gait of a gorilla unaccustomed to walking only on its hind legs. He was grinning, and he held a stethoscope device in one huge hairy hand."

"I listened in on them," he said. "They didn't talk much but I heard enough. They were up at the castle. They're waiting for orders from someone."

"We'll find out," Caliban said. His voice was level, but inwardly he was disturbed. What group could be fighting the Nine? Or was it some group that knew nothing about the Nine but had it in for

Iwaldi for some reason? They must really hate him to go in for such overkill tactics.

Doc decided not to transmit the gas via a tube through the keyhole. He knocked on the door and then Pauncho listened with the sound-amplifier applied to the door. He grinned and whispered, "They didn't say a word. But I'll bet one signaled the other to cover him while he answers."

A deep voice spoke in Austrian German. "Who is it?"

"Telegram, sir," Doc said in the local dialect and with an adolescent squeak.

"Slip it under the door."

"Sorry, sir, I can't. It has to be signed for."

There was a click, and the door swung open a few inches. An eye looked out. Doc seized the knob and jerked the door open with such force that the man was left staring at his hand. He had been holding onto it and had not expected that anybody short of a gorilla could have pulled the knob loose from his grip.

A second later what could have been the hypothetical gorilla charged into him, lifting him up and off his feet and doubling him over a hard shoulder. The man went *whoof*! Doc Caliban came in on Pauncho's tail, struck the man on the jaw as he went by, and then stopped. The other man, a tall skinny fellow with a shock of yellow hair, had stepped out from the bathroom. He held a .38 automatic in one hand.

Doc raised his hands. Pauncho dumped the unconscious man from his shoulder and also lifted his hands. A moment later, the skinny man looked surprised, and he started to open his mouth. Doc caught him as he sagged forward and eased him to the floor. By then, it was safe for him to begin breathing. He had broken two of the gas balls under his feet just as he stopped to raise his hands. It was an old trick that had been working for thirty-five years.

When Zelner and Gafustimm awoke, they were in chairs and their feet and hands were taped and their mouths were gagged. Doc was about to inject Zelner with fluid from a big hypodermic needle.

After he had shot both men in the arm, and they had gone back to sleep, he removed the gags. His questioning was swift and direct, because he did not know how much time he had. The inn was beginning to stir. Even though the ski season was long gone, there were a number of tourists who had come here to bathe in the mineral waters of Gramzdorf, which were reputed to have medicinal effects. It would be impossible to carry the two men up to Caliban's room without being observed now. And the two obviously expected visitors or a message that had to be answered soon.

The men replied to each question as all men did under the influence of calibanite. But they answered literally and only to the detail specifically required by the inquisitor. Both men told similar stories. They had been hired six years ago in Hamburg. They worked for an organization which they knew was larger than their immediate group. But that was all they knew of it. They had never heard of the Nine nor seen anyone answering to the description of the Nine. Their immediate superior on this job was a scar-faced Prussian known to them as Ruthenius von Zarndirl. He had led them into the castle last night but had disappeared during the fighting. When Zelner was wounded, Gafustimm had been ordered to go with him to the upper levels to route any stragglers while the others went off in two groups after Iwaldi. They had found no one, had returned to the ground floor, waited a while, then come down to Gramzdorf. On the way, they had run into van Zarndirl, who had told them to wait at the inn for instructions.

Doc removed the tapes and ordered them to go to bed. Like zombies, they shambled forward and climbed into their beds. After receiving a shot of a sleep-inducing drug, they began snoring loudly. Doc and Pauncho left the room, and Pauncho hung a DO NOT DISTURB sign on the knob.

They went back up the steps and down the hall to the door of their room. Pauncho rapped out the recognition code on the door with his knuckles. There was no answer.

Doc inserted the *saac* into the keyhole, twisted it as he held one end to an eye, and then quickly withdrew it.

"Barney's on the floor. Lots of blood." he said.

Pauncho grunted as if a big fist had slammed into his stomach. A second later, he was inside the room with Doc on his heels.

Doc Caliban said, "Some of the blood is his but most of it is somebody else's."

The bronze-skinned giant removed a case which looked exactly like a cigarette lighter from a pocket of his vest. He pressed down on the lever, and a humming emanated from it. He passed the device back and forth over Barney's head at a distance of two inches. After a minute, Barney's eyelids fluttered and then his eyes opened. Pauncho had brought a glass of water. Doc popped a pill into Barney's mouth and Pauncho held his head up while Barney drank.

The most serious wound was from a knife that had penetrated a half inch into Barney's shoulder. Instead of sewing up the wound, Doc held the edges of the skin together and sprayed it from a can. The spray dried and solidified quickly, looking just like a piece of Barney's skin. The other two wounds were treated similarly, and then Barney was given another pill. His color returned, and after a while he said he was hungry.

Pauncho complained that his mother did not raise him to be a cook or a bellboy, either. Doc told him to go down to the inn's kitchen and supervise the preparation of breakfast, and never mind if the chef thought he was acting peculiarly.

By then Barney had told his story.

A few minutes after Doc had gone down to the second floor, someone knocked on the door. Barney asked for identification. It identified its owner as Joachim Minter, chief of the local police.

"What do you want?" Barney said.

"We want to question Mr. Cobbs and Miss Villiers," Minter replied. "We have received some information about them from the Ministry." He did not say what ministry.

"Open up, please!" the voice said sternly.

Barney did not know what to do. To gain time he said that he would wake up the Englishmen and ask them what they wanted to do.

He turned to walk into the bedroom, heard a click, turned again, saw the door open, and three men enter. All three were in police uniform. The chief, a tall man with a big nose and several knife scars along his cheek, said, "You will please stand aside, Mr. Banks."

Barney started to protest when one of the policemen struck him on the chin with his fist. But Barney rolled with the punch and countered with a fist in the solar plexus. Then he felt a shock in his shoulder and was dully aware that he had been stabbed.

Barney brought his own switchblade knife out and stabbed the man who had stabbed him. The two grappled. Barney was aware that the pseudochief had gone into the bedroom, but he was too busy to determine what happened after that. He cut up both men but one hit him on the temple with his fist, and that was the last he remembered until he saw Doc above him.

"You were lucky you didn't get your throat cut," Doc said. "I suppose they didn't want the hounds called out after them. A corpse might get the authorities aroused."

"Then Cobbs and Barbara are gone?"

"Gone," Doc said. "You feel up to any violent activity yet?"

"I'm shaky, but breakfast will fix that up," Barney said. "Why?"

"The men who took them away are doing one of three things. They're holding them someplace in this inn or maybe in the village. Or they're taking them up to the castle. Or they're taking them out of the village to some other place. But I doubt that they'll try to keep them prisoners in the village itself for very long. That'd be too difficult. But they would have to change clothes immediately, because the real police are too well known. So the pseudochief—sounds from your description like von Zarndirl—and his men may be inside the inn yet, changing clothes and arranging for a getaway.

"If von Zarndirl is working for Iwaldi, then the two'll be taken up to the castle. I don't know what value Cobbs and Villiers have for Iwaldi. The fact that he didn't kill them when he caught them in his castle and that he wants them alive now—if von Zarndirl is working for him—shows that they've been holding out on us."

"You should have used calibanite on Cobbs and Villiers," Barney said.

"If I get my hands on them again, I will."

The phone rang. Doc was across the room as if the ringing was a starter's pistol in the hundred yard dash. "Doc," Pauncho's bottom-of-the-barrel voice said. "I just saw three men driving out of the courtyard with Cobbs and Barbara in the back seat!"

"Be right down!" Doc Caliban said. "Meet us at our car! Bring food; we'll eat on the run!"

Pauncho was standing by the car with a big cardboard box balanced on one huge hand. Doc lifted the hood of the Mercedes-

Benz and looked for bombs. Then he slid under and inspected the bottom for explosives or signs of sabotage. Satisfied, he got out from under and into the driver's seat. Barney got into the back seat and Pauncho sat down beside Doc.

There was only one way out of Gramzdorf. Doc drove as swiftly as he could through the narrow streets, which were occupied by enough locals that he had to take it easy. He used his horn when they showed a reluctance to get out of the way. But Gramzdorf was small, and within five minutes they were on the asphalt road which wound up the mountain for many miles and then would begin a descent. Von Zarndirl's car was not in sight yet, even though it had only about five minute's headstart. Doc was driving over the narrow road as if he were on the Indianapolis Speedway. Pauncho ate with a nonchalance that irked Barney, who did not care at all for the depths whizzing by a few inches from him.

"Karlskopf is twenty miles away," Doc said. "They can take a private plane from there."

The sky was blue above them, and the spring sun would be above the mountain across the valley to their right within an hour. But to the west black clouds were advancing. Pauncho stopped stuffing his mouth long enough to turn on the car radio. A German announcer verified the threat of the clouds. A storm was blowing in from France.

Barney moved over to the left side where he did not have to see the abysses springing up at him every time they took a curve. He said, "Pass some of that Wienerschnitzel or whatever it is back here."

"Very good stuff," Pauncho said. He lifted a bottle of dark beer from the box, tore off the cap with his thick teeth, and drank deeply. "Ah! Nectar!" he burped.

Barney said, "You're disgusting! What about it, Doc? You want Pauncho to feed you while you're driving?"

Doc shook his head. He did not want to be distracted by anything. Besides, he had just seen the car they were chasing, another Mercedes-Benz far ahead. It was on a higher level and just going around a corner of the mountain. It was moving suicidally fast, too.

The whole affair was puzzling. What group could be fighting the Nine? And why? Who were Cobbs and Villiers? Obviously, they were more than just archaeologists on a sabbatical.

Doc drove as if the car had become, in a mystical manner, a living thing that was also part of him. Eve -Barney felt this emanation from Doc and relaxed, though he still did not move back to the right.

Then their auto screamed around a curve and there, some fifty yards ahead, blocking the road, was von Zarndirl's car.

"Hey, Doc!" Pauncho said. "I saw Barbara going up the mountain-side! Up in the woods there!"

Caliban could not spare even a glance to look where Pauncho's finger was pointing. He was using the brakes to halt the Mercedes-Benz before the ambushers could fire at close range. He succeeded in stopping the vehicle, though not without some fishtailing and then backed it up with a roar. The expected gunfire did not materialize.

"What's going on?" Barney said.

Doc gestured with a thumb behind him. He had been looking in the rearview mirror. Barney and Pauncho turned their heads and saw two men coming out of the brush behind them about fifty yards away. One held a rifle; the other was looking down into a metal box he held before him.

Doc started the car forward with a surge that burned rubber and threw the others back against their seats. Brakes and tires screaming, he stopped the car with its nose almost touching the side of von Zarndirl's car. He threw open his door and fell out, was on his feet, and racing around to the other side of the car blocking their path. Von Zarndirl could be in the bushes just above waiting to catch them when they retreated from his aides, but he had to take that chance. He opened the right-hand door in the front and looked inside. The keys were still in the ignition lock.

Pauncho, looking in on the other side, said, "Hey, Doc! Why don't we just drive this—?"

A crack from up in the hills made him dive to the road. A bullet struck the pavement near him and screamed off. The report of the second shot came almost immediately after.

Doc leaped up, ran to the front of the car, lifted the hood, and then dived back to the pavement by the side of the car. The hood was perforated twice and the windshield once. But Doc was up and looking down over the side of the car at the motor. He rolled away as three more bullets went through the raised hood and through the windshield. Then, fluid bronze, he was back again, had reached in and yanked loose a wire and dived away again.

Pauncho and Barney were firing at the two men far down the road with their automatics. Seeing that the range was too far for accuracy and that the men were not even bothering to fire back, the two stopped shooting.

"What are you doing, Doc?" Pauncho called.

"I just disabled a bomb under the hood," Caliban said. "They expected us to drive their car out of the way; we'd have been blown to kingdom come!"

There was a trail up the mountainside. It was visible only in a few places, and in one of these Doc saw Villiers' red hair and Cobbs' black hair for a moment. His gaze kept going up the slope until it stopped on a whitish object. This could be the front of a house perhaps a thousand feet up.

Doc Caliban relayed this information to his men. "They didn't pick this spot for an ambush just by accident," he said. "They've got a place up there!"

If that was true, then the group von Zarndirl represented had planned well ahead. The two men Caliban had questioned probably knew of this place. But they would have said nothing about it unless they had been asked about it. And since Doc did not know about it, he could not have asked about it. Doc swore to present future prisoners with some general questions which might turn up items like this.

"Look out!" Pauncho yelled.

Doc stuck his head up, risking another bullet from the sniper, to see what Pauncho was alarmed about. He did not hear the bullets, but he did hear the two reports coming from somewhere in that mass of evergreens above. And he saw the thirty or so ravens and hawks swooping down the mountainside toward them. They were so close together they almost formed a solid black ball, and they were only a few feet above the tips of the trees. They made no cries, and they bore little white objects on top of their heads.

All three men began firing, then stopped as a dip in the ground took the birds out of their view. The man with the rifle down the road began firing slowly, forcing Pauncho and Barney to get between the two cars and lie flat on the road. The sniper in the trees continued to shoot at Doc. And then the birds, wings beating, beaks open, were on them.

THE MAD GOBLIN

It was impossible to stay out of sight of the two riflemen and fight the birds at the same time. Barney and Pauncho tried; they rolled over on their backs and shot straight up into the feathery avalanche that hurtled on them. Doc hosed the eight ravens and three hawks that came at him with the .15 caliber bullets from his gasgun, and the lead birds exploded in blood, bone, and feathers. But five birds got to him, and he had to drop the gun and defend himself with his bare hands. All of them tried for his head, and in so doing they got in each other's way: wings beating against wings knocked them down, talons extended to sink into his flesh touched another bird and automatically sank and beaks snapping for eyes and nose closed on wings and legs and heads.

Ignoring the sniper because he had to, Doc reared up like a whale coming from the deeps, sending ravens and hawks flying off him. He whirled around and around, his hands chopping out, breaking wings, cracking necks, smashing thin skulls. But one hawk got through and its talons sank into his face. He fell forward and rolled over and over and then began to unhook the agonizing steel-sharp claws from his cheeks. Blood flowed down his face and over his chest as he cast the body of the hawk away from him. He had twisted its head off with one turn of the wrist.

Barney and Pauncho were killing the last of their attackers with their bare hands, too. Like Doc, they were bleeding profusely from deep gashes on their faces.

Doc had two of the plastic tennis-ball-sized gas grenades in a pocket of his coat. He removed them, twisted the pin of one to the left, and pulled it from the ball. Then he stood up, exposing himself to the fire of the sniper in the hills. He threw the ball as hard as he could over the top of his car. It soared in a high arc as the rifleman down the road shot at it. And while he was doing that, Doc, .15 caliber gasgun in one hand and the second grenade in the other, was racing toward the rifleman.

To explode within effective range of its target, the grenades had to travel one hundred yards. The rifleman did not expect the ball to get anywhere near him. Not at first. But he was trying to explode the grenade in the air to make sure it didn't get close enough to make him even uncomfortable. And so Doc was speeding toward him while the magazine of the rifle was being emptied at the ball. When the rifleman realized this, he aimed at Doc. One round was left, and this missed Doc, who had bounded to one side.

Then the grenade blew up before it hit the ground sixty feet from the rifleman and the man with the box. Doc threw the second grenade then, as the rifleman dropped his FN and pulled out his automatic pistol. Doc continued to zigzag, firing with the gasgun. The second grenade struck the ground and bounced high and exploded a few feet above the heads of the two men.

Doc raced in while bullets from the sniper in the hills *whee*-ed by him or struck the road near him. Then he had picked up the FN, fitted it with a new magazine, stuck two more in his jacket pockets, put the metal box under his arm, and was running back to the car. Even with his heavy hiking shoes and clothes, burdened with a rifle and a metal control box, and on a tarred road, he was running swiftly enough to have breathed down the neck of an Olympic dasher.

When he reached the cars, Barney and Pauncho were in the one that had blocked them, and Barney had the motor going. Caliban dived into the back seat—Pauncho had left the door open—and the car backed up, stopped with a screech, and then screamed away down the road and around the curve of the hill while bullets struck the car or the road nearby.

About three hundred yards down the road, Barney pulled the car off onto the side of the road, where a stone fence had been erected to keep sightseers from falling off the edge. There were also a little stone restroom and two wooden picnic tables there. Doc gave quick first aid to everybody, himself last. They popped blood-building pills into their mouths and felt the pseudoskin he had sprayed over their wounds.

"Almost as good as new," Barney said, but he was exaggerating.

The blood-building pills, however, had to be taken with food to do much good. They ate the rest of the breakfast that Pauncho had brought along, even though their appetites were gone. The fight had shaken the two up, and Doc, though he looked calm enough, did not down his food with any pleasure. The pills would send their temperature up by a degree for half an hour and make them feel a little woozy. But their lost blood would have been replaced.

Caliban said, "Von Zarndirl will've arranged matters for us in Karlskopf. At least, I'm presuming he will have. Another ambush might not find us so lucky. Besides, I'm not going to bypass that house; it may contain the key to this puzzling affair."

Barney felt his shoulder and winced a little bit. Doc said, "You up to climbing that mountain and maybe mixing it up with those baboons?"

"You know I am, Doc," Barney said. He took the FN rifle held out by Caliban.

Doc Caliban untaped the six sticks of dynamite from the chassis next to the motor, saying, "We might use these."

"Hoist them on their own petard!" Pauncho rumbled. "I like that!"

They crossed the road and began climbing. The woods were heavy with firs and pines, but the underbrush had not begun to leaf out yet. Within an hour they were on top of the ridge on which the house rested. This was about half a mile to the south. From there on they proceeded even more cautiously because there was always the chance of mines or ambushers. Doc went on ahead to allow his puffing and panting compatriots to get their strength back. He saw the white house through the trees a hundred yards away from it. He also detected the gray slice of a partly hidden wire stretched across the path that wandered up from the road. He went around the tree to which one end of the wire was fixed and approached within twenty feet of the rear of the house. It was a one-story frame house with a big stone fireplace at the north end, the end near which he crouched. It was built in the form of an L and had about four narrow windows on each side. The blinds were pulled down almost to the bottom of the windows.

He returned to his men. "There's no sign of life," he said, "but you can bet they're all in there, waiting. Of course, they don't know we've come up here, but they can't afford to ignore the possibility."

Each of them had two of the bouncing gas grenades, the last of their supply. Doc said, "Let's go," and he seemed to the others to have dissolved into the forest.

Pauncho said, "Don't foul things up in your usual slap-happy manner, Barney. Try to keep from falling over your own feet."

"You low-browed hairy monstrosity!" Barney said. "I hope you can keep from swinging from the trees; they must really be tempting you! Keep your mind on our business and don't shoot me by accident!"

Pauncho grinned and said, "It wouldn't be any accident."

They saluted each other with fingers to noses and, still grinning, slipped into the woods. Barney went east, below the house, and cut across the path. Though he was not the equal of Caliban in moving swiftly and quietly through a forest, he was superior to most men. His rapier form moved past naked-branched bushes and over twigs with not a sound. Pauncho, even though he went much more slowly, made more noise. He cut to the west on the back side of the ridge and far enough below the house to make sure he wasn't seen. Then he worked his way up to the south end.

There was a silence for a long time. Only the faint cries of ravens and the screech of a hawk disturbed the air. The sun reached the zenith and began to slide down the blue steps. The storm that had been in the west showed no signs of coming closer; it seemed to have run into a wall.

Doc waited. He studied the windows for signs of life, but the thick curtains and the lack of light inside the house hid any faces looking from under the blinds. He was sure that armed men waited there. They had probably called for help; helicopters might appear at any time. The machines that had been used in the attack against Iwaldi could not be too far away. He could not wait until night or until they got so tense that they sent men out to poke around.

Doc cupped his hands close to his mouth and gave the cry of the lark native to these mountains. A few seconds later, the call was answered. Perhaps the men inside the house were fooled, but Doc knew that Barney was returning his signal.

He wormed between the little fir plank outhouse and a small log house from which came the odor of birds of prey.

The piles of lumber and firewood there made for good cover. That would have occurred to the men in the house, too, and they would be keeping a bright eye on the piles.

A third cry of the lark came. This was even less convincing than Barney's.

Doc wormed along the ground until he came behind the outhouse, and he stood up. He could see the limestone chimney on the north easily enough. He stepped back, estimated the distance and the wind again, and tossed the gas grenade underhanded. It flew up in a high arc and came down almost in its target, the square hole on top of the chimney.

It struck the edge, however, bounced up and down onto the sloping roof, bounded along and leaped from the roof's edge and fell onto the ground just below a window. Doc had stepped behind the outhouse by then and put his fingers on his ears. The blast was still getting echoes from the mountain behind him and across the valley when he tossed his second grenade. This disappeared down the chimney and exploded before it reached the bottom. At least, it should have done so. He had sent it higher than the first so that the six-second interval between pulling the pin and the mingling of gases would result in a blast halfway down the stone shaft.

There was the chance that Cobbs and Villiers might get hurt, but they would certainly be hurt if their captors got clean away with them. They would have to take chances, too. They were adults who knew very well what the consequences of this game might be if they lost.

The echoes of the second explosion had just died when a third, Barney's, blew up just outside the front porch—if Barney had thrown accurately. Doc charged toward the house just as Pauncho's grenade, thrown from the south, blew up the side porch.

Doc was hoping that the rapid succession of blasts would stun the defenders and yet would not kill the prisoners. He ran with the bundle of dynamite sticks held by a cord in one hand. He threw it ahead of him so it landed on the roof, leaped up, grabbed the edge, and swung himself up with the agility of a leopard. An automatic rifle began firing immediately afterward, and the muzzle, stuck from the window, tried to follow him up. But it was too late.

Somebody began to shoot through the roof. The bullets did penetrate the three-inch thick planks, but he had moved on to a station just beside the chimney. When the firing ceased, he yelled down the shaft.

"Come on out with your hands behind your necks! Or I'll drop this dynamite down the chimney!"

"If you do, you'll kill Cobbs and the girl!" a man shouted.

Doc said, "So what?"

There was a pause. He resisted the temptation to put his head over the mouth of the chimney to hear what they were saying. Somebody might be down there waiting to shoot his face off.

"O.K.!" the same voice shouted. "We know when we're licked! We'll come out with our hands up!"

"Send the prisoners out first!"

There was another pause. Then the man said, "Here they come!"

A banging as of the front door being violently opened announced the exit of somebody. He could not see who it was, but Barney suddenly stuck his head out from behind a tree and signaled. Cobbs and Villiers were being released. A few seconds later, he saw them walking toward Barney, who was waving an arm at them. They looked disheveled, dusty, and a little bloody. Their hands were tied behind them.

Two men came out of the back, three through the front door, and two through the hole blown in the south side of the house by Barney's grenade. They came out shooting wildly. Cobbs and Villiers threw themselves on the ground, but von Zarndirl's men did not care to waste bullets on them. They wanted to get Doc and his men first.

Doc, knowing that some of them would turn and shoot at him, tossed the bundle of dynamite toward the rear door to panic them. Then he leaped past the chimney and down to the ground, landing on both feet but going forward to the ground and rolling. His massive muscles and thick bones enabled him to take the shock without injury. He came up onto his feet, his gasgun spewing at the men in the front, two of whom had run to the north so they could get him in their line of fire. His little bullets ran across their chests, sending up gouts of flesh and blood.

Barney's FN had cut the third man almost in half.

The men in the back had taken off when the dynamite fell near them. They did not know that it had no fuse. They kept on running and so were caught in Pauncho's gasgun fire.

The two men who had gone out through the hole in the south side had been wounded in the legs by Pauncho's first few bullets. One got to his elbows and started to shoot, and Pauncho had to kill him.

The other man put up his hands, though he was unable to stand up when Pauncho ordered him to.

Barney had untied the hands of Cobbs and the redhead. She did not look so beautiful now what with the dust and the blood and the grayish skin. But, seeing Doc, she smiled, and at that moment, disheveled and shocked or not, she was beautiful.

Pauncho came around from the side of the house dragging a man along behind him, by the jacket collar. He dropped him before Doc, and said, "We're in luck! Von Zarndirl, if those scars mean anything!"

Caliban gathered together the metal box and the weapons, and Pauncho dragged von Zarndirl into the house. It was necessary to give him three of the blood-building pills. There was food in the house, and the German ate after the initial effects of the pills had energized and deshocked him. Doc put Barney on guard outside with orders to watch especially for helicopters. There was a transceiver by which they could have called for help. It had been on a table near the fireplace, and it and the operator lay in two heaps on the floor. Doc's grenade had blown out the upper part of the fireplace, and the stone fragments had shattered the radio and driven a sharp piece into the operator's neck.

The interior of the house was a mess. Shattered glass, ripped blinds, curtains, overturned tables, and pieces of stone and dust lay over the single big room.

Doc injected calibanite into the arm of von Zarndirl. Within fifteen minutes he had cleared up some of the mystery.

Von Zarndirl was working for an organization which had to be the Nine, though he did not know what its name was or even that it had a name.

Doc's face did not show it, but he was shocked. Even though he and Grandrith had turned against the Nine, he had never thought about others doing so. And Iwaldi himself was one of the Nine who sat at the table of power.

Von Zarndirl was too far down in the echelon of the Nine to be a "candidate." He did not know that Iwaldi was one of the millennia-old rulers of the organization for which he worked as cutthroat or whatever job was required of him. All he knew was that orders had come through to get the white-bearded old dwarf, Graf von Gramz. Von Zarndirl was lucky. He had led his group upstairs and lost some men to wolves and owls, and then he had gone down to the ground level to look for the other group. They had found a concealed entrance to the underground passages, but this was not the one which the first group had gone through. (Von Zarndirl did not know this, of course, but his description told Caliban that he had missed the obvious trail. How he had managed to do this, Caliban could not know. He supposed that the man had simply found an entrance before he had gotten to that left open by Caliban.)

Almost immediately, three-fourths of the group had been crushed against the wall by a sliding stone block. Van Zarndirl, in the lead, had escaped by an inch. The survivors, five men, had refused to go on. Von Zarndirl had returned to Gramzdorf (the choppers having departed long before by prearrangement), and he had reported via radio to a Herr Schmidt, whom he had never seen. His men had observed Caliban's group, but whoever it was that received the report did not recognize any of them. Or if he did, he did not tell von Zarndirl their identities. Schmidt ordered that Cobbs or Villiers be taken for questioning. The old Norwegian, Sigurdsson, and his two companions were to be kept under close observation. If a chance arose, they were to be taken alive. But if they looked as if they might get away, they were to be killed.

Doc Caliban was puzzled. Schmidt knew that the two Englishmen were somehow connected to the old Norwegian (Doc Caliban) and his cronies. But what of it? Unless Schmidt knew that Caliban was in Gramzdorf in disguise, he would have no reason to suspect Cobbs or Villiers. He did not know that they had been Iwaldi's prisoners or that Caliban had helped them escape. Although von Zarndirl's men had seen the two Englishmen go to Caliban's room, that would not mean anything.

And if any of the servants of the Nine had suspected that Sigurdsson was really Caliban, von Zarndirl would have been ordered to attack Caliban without thought of consequences. Cut him down in public, in front of the police station and a hundred witnesses if you have to! We'll get you off later, you can be assured of that. And you'll never have to work again or want for anything, short of a seat at the table of the Nine.

His disguise had not been penetrated. But he had been gone from the inn during the night of the attack, and that may have been what aroused suspicion.

He asked von Zarndirl if this were true. The scar-faced German, sitting on a chair, staring glassily straight ahead, replied in a hollow voice. He did not know. One man had been left behind to observe the village during the attack and to warn the attackers if the villagers became aware of what was going on at the *schloss*. He had reported the disappearance of the Norwegian and his companions. Von Zarndirl had passed this information on.

And Cobbs and Villiers had disappeared for three days. Anything out of the ordinary, anything unexplained, was to be reported.

He continued to question von Zarndirl. Yes, he supposed that the next time many more men would be used. Yes, he did not think it likely that Iwaldi would remain in the castle now, but such decisions were not up to him. If they were to attack an empty castle, they would do so. Whatever his boss, Schmidt, ordered, they would do.

Doc took one of the plastic hemispheres from a pocket and showed it to von Zarndirl. He asked him a few questions and received answers which confirmed his guesses.

The metal box and the plastic hemispheres were developments of devices Caliban had been working on when he had gone mad from the side effects of the elixir. The hemisphere housed electronic microcircuits which were connected to the brain of an animal through tiny holes drilled into the skull. The electrodes were inserted into those areas of the brain controlling specific behavior and also were connected with the visual neural system. The hemisphere transmitted a line-of-sight beam of what the animal saw to the transceiver of the metal box. This had a screen which displayed a picture of everything that came within the animal's vision. This was fine in the case of sharp-eyed birds, but the images were often fuzzy in the case of dogs or other near-sighted animals.

An animal or a group of animals could be roughly controlled by moving dials on the face of the control box. An animal could be driven to attack by stimulating the part of the brain which controlled aggression. But if it saw two persons before it, and the operator wanted it to attack only one, the animal was likely to attack both anyway. A fast operator could alternate states of aggressiveness and of fear very swiftly in the animal and so crudely stimulate or inhibit its attacks when it was confronted by more than one person.

The screen of the control box was also capable of producing up to twenty different simultaneous views, and a skilled operator could control that many individually, though not to the degree wished. Or the operator could control the entire group as one.

Doc Caliban had been close to finishing his prototype just before he went insane. After he had turned against the Nine, their agents had taken over his laboratory in the Empire State Building and his research facilities in his estate near Lake George. They had studied all his notes and the plans for many devices which he had perfected but had not yet released for use by the Nine.

Doc Caliban had guessed all this when the wolves had attacked him in the bedroom of the castle. Iwaldi had—or once had—his own animals, and the others of the Nine had theirs. Doc wondered where the man who had directed the wolves first and then the birds in Iwaldi's castle had been stationed. Of course, though the transmission was only on a direct line-of-sight and very limited range basis, the beams could be detected by transceivers and transmitted by wire to remote control posts.

Doc Caliban asked von Zarndirl what frequency his group used when directing their animals. The German did not know. This did not disturb Caliban, because he would examine the control box himself.

Barney came into the door—after calling out that he was entering—and said, "A chopper's coming. There may be more than one. It's hard to tell. The storm must be coming closer, too."

Doc Caliban looked out the window. The grayish-black western skies had broken loose from whatever was restraining them. The ominous clouds were spreading eastward as if chased by furies.

He saw the flash of sunlight in the air above the distant peak just before the sun was veiled by the clouds. Then he saw three tiny objects.

He turned and said, "Let's get out of here. Pauncho, you take care of von Zarndirl."

Pauncho said, "What do you mean, take care of him, Doc? Bring him along or shoot him?"

"Bring him along. He's of no use to us anymore, but . . ."

This was a war in which no rules of humanity applied. Or had been applied. But Caliban was getting increasingly reluctant to kill his enemies in cold blood. It was one thing to kill during combat. But to shoot a helpless prisoner was another thing. Not that he had not done that nor that Barney and Pauncho had not. When Doc was only seventeen and a lieutenant in World War I, he had captured two German soldiers at the same time that he had been cut off by the advance of the enemy. It had been necessary for him to get back to his own lines and yet he could not do so with the burden of the two prisoners. He could turn them loose or tie them up and leave them. While he was trying to make up his mind, he was joined by a captain and two sergeants, also cut off.

The captain had said that he was sorry, but they could not take the prisoners back. It would be too risky; they would be lucky to rejoin their forces without the burden of the prisoners. And it would not do to release two men who would soon be shooting at them again. The captain ordered the prisoners shot.

Doc had told the captain that he should perform the execution himself. If he couldn't do it himself, he should not ask his men to do so. The captain became furious and threatened Caliban with a court martial when they returned. Caliban replied that he had not disobeyed an order. He had merely stated an opinion. Besides, he doubted that the generals would permit such a charge to be made. The last thing they wanted was the civilian populace to know that such deeds were not rare. It did not matter that the French, British, Italian, Turkish, and German armies were all doing this under similar circumstances or even when there was no good reason.

The captain ordered Lt. Caliban to shoot the prisoners.

Caliban had never forgotten the faces of the two Germans. One, a tall brown-haired man with a black stubble of beard, had not said a word. He had glared at Caliban and then spat at him.

The other, probably even younger than Caliban, was a slight tow-headed man with greenish eyes. He had tried to be brave but, as Caliban raised his pistol, he had fallen to his knees and begged for mercy. The .45 in his chest knocked him backward into the mud. The other German, screaming his hate, rushed Caliban with his bare

Philip José Farmer

hands. Caliban shot him in the forehead and stepped aside to let the body, carried by the charge, slide on its face down a slope and into a shellhole full of water.

"There," Caliban had said to Captain Wheeler. "I have done the job you weren't man enough to do."

Wheeler was white with rage, but he said nothing. They started to sneak through the German lines. Caliban halted suddenly, and, for one of three times only in his life—that he remembered—wept. He sobbed for ten minutes and then continued on his way. When he was close to the American lines, he was shot at. The bullets were close, but he got away and then came up on the would-be killer from behind. The man was Captain Wheeler.

Caliban took his automatic away from him. Wheeler said he would charge Caliban with trying to murder him. Caliban said he did not think so, since a dead man could not bring charges. He stuck Wheeler's face into the mud and held it there until Wheeler quit breathing.

That was when he first met Barney's and Pauncho's fathers. Rivers was a colonel then and Simmons was a major. (Both were to be promoted shortly after.) They had been captured by three soldiers but had escaped. They came up just in time to see Wheeler try to murder Caliban and his execution afterward. At first, they were hostile, even though they knew that Caliban had been provoked.

He explained exactly what had happened, expecting to be put under arrest. But these two were not the dyed-in-the-wool military type; they were highly unconventional, and both had gotten into trouble because of some of their antics and their outspokenness. They told him to forget it, that Wheeler had it coming. As for the shooting of the prisoners, that had been necessary and it was doubtful that the sergeants would report it. Or, if they did, that their report would get very far.

Rivers (Barney's father) got Caliban attached to his staff. He recognized even then the genius of this young giant. In the few months that Caliban remained in the infantry (his true age was discovered and he was discharged), Caliban came to dominate the two older men. Or, perhaps, it would be better to say that he fascinated them.

Caliban kept in touch with the two after the war. He went to

Harvard (Rivers' school) and graduated in two years. He had never competed in athletics because it would not be fair, and he did not want the publicity to interfere with his studies. Even though he was capable of getting through medical school (Johns Hopkins) with the highest grades in two years, he had to take the normal amount of time. But he had plenty of opportunity to study many other subjects than those required, and his friendship with many professors enabled him to use the laboratories. In 1926, he completed his internship, but he had the equivalent of several Ph.D.s in widely separated fields. And he continued his studies in them and took up new subjects even while he was practicing brain surgery.

In 1927, the Nine made their first contact with him. In 1928, he was formally invited to join, and in 1929 he first attended the grisly and horrifying ceremonies in the caves of the Nine in east central Africa. But he was now immortal, barring accident, suicide, or homicide. His life would end by homicide if he did not obey the Nine in everything they ordered—he was assured of that. In matters which did not concern them, he could do exactly as he pleased. He could carry on his battle against crime as he wished, could perform brain operations on criminals to eliminate their compulsive anti-social attitudes. There were, he found out, times when he had fought and eliminated certain great criminals who were servants of the Nine and, in two cases, candidates. But the Nine had not seen fit to interfere with him since he was not interfering with any of their projects at that time.

Caliban's father had trained him from infancy to be a superman dedicated to fighting evil. Of course, if his son had not had the potentiality, he could not have developed into a superman no matter how much training he had had. But Caliban's heritage would have made him the greatest athlete of the modern world—except for one— even if his childhood had been normal. His grandfather had been one of the Nine. XauXaz had been born about 10,000 years ago—or more. And XauXaz's father had been born about 40,000 B.C. (here Caliban was speculating), so that old XauXaz was actually one of those Old Stone Age men whose massive skeleton and muscles made them much stronger than the strongest of modern man. Moreover, there was some evidence that XauXaz and his two brothers had been contributing their genes for a long, long time to the family which eventually became known as Grandrith.

Caliban's father, a candidate of the Nine, had gone mad from the side effects of the elixir in 1888. He had become that infamous murderer, Jack the Ripper, for a short period, and then, recovering his senses, had fled to the States. But not before fathering John Cloamby, the future Lord Grandrith, known also by The Folk as *tls* and in the human world by the anglicized name his "biographer" had given him.

Caliban's father had been so horrified by what he had done when insane that he had sworn to make amends. He had raised his second son as a deadly weapon of retribution against evil. And this extreme physical and mental and moral education had resulted in a superman.

But you get nothing without paying for it, Caliban thought.

The universe was a check and balance system from macrocosmos through microcosmos. Man, intermediate in size between the two, atom and the star, but the most complex of all objects, is no exception. James Caliban had paid. His high ideals and his high goals had resulted in too much self-control. Too much inhibition. And, admit it, a feeling of superiority, no matter how carefully he hid that feeling from others and, worse, from himself. That superiority— which did exist—had alienated him in many respects.

A stranger in a world he had never made; his father had made it.

And his father had intended to turn him against the Nine eventually, he was certain of that. His father must have blamed the Nine for that period of murderous insanity and for the price they sometimes exacted for their immortality. His father had prepared him not only to fight the obvious criminals of the world. He had secretly waited for the day when he would launch him against the Nine.

But the Nine had offered the elixir to the son before the father could reveal his plans. Caliban, who prided himself on his invulnerable morality, had said yes to evil when offered a chance to live for 30,000 years. His father had not known that, any more than Caliban had known that his father was also a candidate. Neither had ever attended the ceremonies at the same time, and neither had had reason to tell the other that he was a candidate.

And so the Nine had found out that his father was planning treason. Or his father had failed the Nine in some way. And they had killed him. Caliban had no proof of that, but he was sure that they had. The circumstances of his death were such that only the Nine would have been responsible.

Caliban had tracked down his father's murderers, but these had not known that they were working for the Nine. And the man who had transmitted the orders from the higher-ups had died without revealing that he was not the originator of the murder.

It was his father's death that had caused Caliban to devote himself wholly to the fight against evil—except where the Nine decreed otherwise. The lust for immortality had made him schizophrenic. He knew that now. He had known it then, but he had pushed that knowledge down into the mass of his unconscious.

He had gathered around him men who were highly knowledgeable and multiskilled and who had a thirst for adventure. Rivers and Simmons and Williams and Shorthans and Kidfast. He had met the other three a few months before he was discharged. He had kept contact with them while at Harvard and Hopkins, met them now and then. His father became good friends with them, and they sorrowed almost as much as Doc when his father died. It was then that they had accepted his invitation to join him in his crusades, and the first thing they had done was to help him run down his father's murderers. And—

"Doc! Hey, Doc!" Pauncho growled. "What's the matter, Doc?"

Caliban shook his head and blinked. He said, "I was thinking . . ."

"The choppers are coming fast," Barney said.

Caliban went out swiftly with the others behind him, Pauncho behind von Zarndirl, guiding the somnambulist with a word now and then. They went down the path for fifty yards and then cut into the woods, the cars their destination. Doc returned up the slope and climbed up a fir as agilely as a young gorilla.

One of the choppers settled down in the space north of the house, and men carrying rifles scrambled out. Another landed near it; more men got out. Then a man carrying a black box got out and turned some knobs. About twenty hawks flew out of a port of the second chopper. They spread out in all directions, two flying toward his area. He dropped from branch to branch swiftly and fell the last twenty feet to the ground.

The party was still making its way down the mountain toward the road. Doc Caliban caught up with them, appearing so suddenly that Cobbs and Villiers jumped.

"Give me the box," Doc said. Von Zarndirl handed it to him, and he quickly checked out the operations of the controls, all of which were marked with their functions. The power gauge indicated that the battery was almost discharged, and he had no other.

There was a flutter above a tree to their right. They moved backward to crowd behind a tree, but Doc did not think that the hawk would miss them. The dial had been set at a frequency which he supposed was the one being used when the original operator had dropped the box. He adjusted two dials beneath the four-inch square screen, and then pointed the red arrow marked on the center of the upper edge of the top of the box at the bird.

One of the disadvantages of this was that the beam between animal and box was tight. A fast moving bird was hard to keep track of. This device, however, bore a dial which moved to indicate the direction in which the animal had moved when the beam lost contact with it. Also, it continued to move in the same general direction of the target if the operator pressed a button. This activated a broadcast pulse which triggered off a mechanism in the hemisphere, and the operator, by moving the box and noting the swing of the needle, could narrow down the area in which the target was.

Then it was up to him to catch the tight beam again.

An operator needed lengthy training to be skilled. Doc Caliban, after a minute of experimenting, acted as if he had been through the required courses. But he had an advantage in that he had originated the theory of the TV-controlled animal.

The whiteness of the screen was suddenly a green and black picture—no color-blindness in a hawk—of branches and the ground seen between the branches sliding by swiftly. And then there was a bronzed face down by a tree. Other faces and parts of bodies. The hawk had spotted them and was coming toward them.

Doc looked up from the screen, saw the wide wings spread out stiffly as it sailed between two trees, and he said, "Get him, Barney!"

The FN banged three times. The hawk flew apart under the impact of at least two bullets.

Doc pulled out his handydandy, a combination knife, corkscrew, screwdriver, crescent wrench, and you-name-it. He quickly unscrewed the four screws holding the instrument panel to the box and ran his gaze over the circuits. It would have taken him much time to ascertain the function of each if he had not designed the prototype himself. He pried up four connections and exchanged them, and then said, "Down to the cars! I'll be behind you!"

The chutter of a helicopter became louder. They retreated under several bushes and stayed motionless while the craft circled around and around near them. Suddenly, a hawk flying at near top speed flew over them, turned, and shot back. But it had spied the dead hawk on the ground. It flew around and around until the chopper nudged it away and hovered over the spot.

"They know we're close!" Pauncho said.

Doc did not reply. He had moved the box around and now had zeroed in on the hawk. He pressed a button, and the hawk, zigzagging crazily, flew off. But it returned a moment later on a straight course.

"I set up the circuit to trigger its fear center," Doc said. "There isn't any button on this particular instrument panel for that, but the circuits can be arranged to stimulate fear if the button is pushed."

The hawk circled again, apparently again under control by the enemy. The copter moved toward them with rifle and heavy machine gun barrels sticking out of the ports. Doc pressed the button again, and the hawk wheeled swiftly and ran head-on into the nose of the craft. It bounced off and fell suddenly into a tree.

Doc spoke to Barney while still looking at the screen as he moved the box to try to pick up another bird. "Move slowly. Give me a grenade."

Barney extracted a pressed-down grenade from a big pocket in his vest. It expanded to its tennis ball size as he opened his fist to hand it over. Caliban slowly squatted down, laid the box on the ground, and took the grenade. He waited for the chopper to come close enough so that the men in it could discern them under the bushes. Pauncho and Barney had readied their FN's. Doc Caliban said, "Save your ammunition unless I miss. We'll need all we have if the other choppers come after us."

But the chopper swung away westward. They got away as fast as they could at an angle down the mountainside. The roar of a chopper was suddenly on them, and then, a moment later, a wind struck the forest. It was the storm.

Lightning veined the dark eye of the sky. Thunder cannonaded. The chopper dipped as the first fist of the wind struck it. It went on over the two cars parked on the other side of the road, swung out over the valley, rose straight up, and then beat a path against the increasing wind back up the mountain slope.

The air whistled through the limbs of the trees, which thrashed like the arms of men trying to keep warm. Pauncho yelled, "Good thing that storm hit when it did! They must have known we were here when they saw those cars! Anyway, they would've landed and checked out the registration and then they wouldn't have stopped till they found us!"

"Why always tell us the obvious?" Barney howled. He and Pauncho grinned at each other, happy because the storm had saved them.

Doc told the others they should wait until it got even darker or until rain came. Though the choppers were probably being tied down in the clearing by the house, men might have been sent up into a tree to survey the road. And if they saw the two cars driving away, they might send a chopper out after them, wind or no wind.

In ten minutes the rain came down half-frozen. The black asphalted road became grayish white with the first drops and then black as the drops melted. They left the woods and got into the cars. Doc ordered that they return to Gramzdorf, since that was the last thing that the enemy would expect them to do. Their rooms were still available, since they had not cancelled them.

Doc drove his own car with Carlos Cobbs and Barbara Villiers as passengers. He was silent for half the journey back and then he said, "Are you up to going with us tonight?"

"Where are you going?" Cobbs said.

"I intend to get into Iwaldi's place again. I could find the place where you two fell in when you were digging, but it would be quicker if you pointed it out for me."

"I'll be glad to!" Cobbs said. He lit up an American cigarette. "I owe that insane goblin a debt. But I still don't know why you don't just call in the authorities."

"They would just come in and look around and then depart without doing a thing," Doc said. "Unless we had some evidence that they could not overlook. You can bet that Iwaldi has cleaned up the mess in the castle and buried the bodies some place. And you can bet that he would bring pressure to bear in the highest political circles to keep the police out. What must be done will be done by us."

"Or by this organization that von Zarndirl belongs to?"

"They may try again tonight, storm or no," Doc said.

The car rocked with the wind's buffets. The half-rain, half-snow splopped on the windshield and was carved away by the wipers. Doc was driving at about fifteen miles an hour because of the limited visibility and the wetness of the road.

"I don't want to be left behind just because I'm a woman," Barbara said.

"The invitation included you."

He turned on the headlights.

She patted Caliban's huge arm and said, "I like your trusting a frail vessel such as myself."

Doc flicked a sidewise look at her but he did not reply. She had not shown the slightest sign of fear or hysteria, and outside the house she had picked up an automatic rifle and checked it out as if she were a veteran soldier.

He drove for several miles more in silence, wondering why they did not ask more questions. He was taking a chance by bringing them along if they were agents for the Nine. They might get an opportunity to trip him up. But if he left them at the village, he would not be able to keep his eye on them.

The storm continued for hours after they got back to the inn in Gramzdorf. Cobbs and Villiers went to their rooms. Barney immediately set up the radio in the bathroom. The contact man in Paris reported that no word from Lady Grandrith had been received. But he did have a message from Lord Grandrith. It had been sent by an operator for the Nine while Grandrith held a gun to his head.

Grandrith's communications, as usual, were more than cut to the bone. They went all the way to the marrow. He had been met by a big party of men out to kill him, and he had eluded them so far. He would be going on, as planned, on foot. It was doubtful that Caliban would hear from him again for several months. Caliban wished that Grandrith had added more details. Then he smiled slightly. His half-brother was no more taciturn than he was. Both talked as little as possible. But his brother did so because he had been raised in the jungle with sentients who did not converse much after they became adults. And he had spent much time with himself during the formative years. Grandrith's close-mouthedness was "natural." Caliban's was the result of his father's training and was "artificial." And also "neurotic." There were times when it was clearly to everyone's benefit to talk much, and he found it difficult to do so then. He did, however, talk vicariously through the pseudohateful banter of Barney and Pauncho, as he had done with their fathers. Though their insults sometimes irritated him, he needed the two men.

Von Zarndirl, having received another injection, slept on Doc's bed. Pauncho brought up more food from the kitchen after observing its preparation. He grinned as he told about the curious looks that the chefs gave him and how he had pacified a waiter with a huge tip.

"They think we're crazy, and of course they're talking about us. Half the village must know we're acting very peculiarly."

"We'll move out at nine o'clock," Doc said. "According to Cobbs, the cave-in is only two miles from here, on the north side of the mountain and about 2,000 feet below the castle."

At nine o'clock the storm had been dead for an hour. The wind was gentle but icy; the clouds were ragged, passing below the moon slowly as if they were battle-torn veterans on parade.

Von Zarndirl, taped and gagged, slept on the floor of the bathroom. The others, bundled up in climbing clothes, carrying alpenstocks and various boxes, went out a side door of the inn. They tromped through the slushy streets to where they had left the cars. After examining them for booby traps, they opened the doors and got out their rifles. They put on the caps with the blacklight projectors and their goggles and began tramping up the mountain, Cobbs leading. Water fell on them as they passed under the low branches of trees or by bushes. The earth was often slippery under them, but they dug in with their stocks and slogged on up.

Cobbs stopped for a moment and said, "It's about a quarter mile ahead."

"We'll go more cautiously now," Doc Caliban said. "Iwaldi is no dummy. He'll have backtracked after he caught you and either shut up the entrance or stationed a guard there."

They started walking again. The moon came out. Doc, looking up, saw the first of the big winged shapes. The broad beam from the projector revealed *lammergeiers,* the eagles of the Alps. There seemed to be dozens, and all were heading toward them.

He said, "Look out above!" and shifted the metal box he had been carrying on a strap around his shoulder to a position on his chest. "Don't fire!" he said. He pressed a button on the top of the box and held it there.

None of the humans could hear the noise that was broadcast from the box, but the eagles turned and flapped away swiftly to escape the eardrum-paining frequencies.

Immediately after, Barney said, "Doc! Wolves!"

Doc looked up and saw the first of the big beasts bounding over a bush to their left. But it was not a wolf. It was a large blackish German Shepherd dog. Behind him came three more and behind them six big Doberman Pinschers. Their mouths were open, revealing their sharp teeth, but they uttered no sounds.

A few minutes later, they turned and bounded away as if they had seen a pack of tigers.

Doc and his party climbed on toward the excavation, taking advantage of every bit of cover. The eagles and the dogs would undoubtedly be back. The noise had momentarily overcome the stimulus of the microcurrent in the hostility area of their brain. But once they were out of the influence of the supersonic frequencies, they would return.

"How can they see us, Doc?" Pauncho said. "I mean, how can the operators of the control boxes see much through the eyes of the animals in this dark?"

"I doubt they're using TV tonight," he said. "It's too hard to keep the narrow beams locked in under these conditions. They probably are just transmitting the code that turns on the juice to the aggression areas of the brain and letting the animals attack whatever they come across."

"I hope so, Doc," Pauncho said. "If they can spot us through the eyes of the birds, we're going to have a hard time."

"Here they come again," Caliban said. He had turned the sound generator off so that the animals would not be affected until they got close.

The eagles, their only noise the flapping of their wings, and the dogs, their only noise the brushing aside of the wet rain-covered plants, came in swiftly. They had but one intention: to tear apart these strangers in the dark.

Then Doc pressed the button, and the dogs whirled so fast they slipped in the mud and fell on their sides or scrabbled desperately to keep from sliding on down the slope. The eagles veered away and were swallowed by the night.

A minute later, the birds and the dogs were charging in again.

Thirty seconds later, they were frenziedly trying to get away from the invisible agony.

"How long's this going on, Doc?"

"Until something—or somebody—breaks," Caliban said.

Pauncho knew it was useless to ask him to elaborate.

The next time, the birds came in first and the dogs did not appear until the birds had been turned away.

"They're catching on," Barney muttered.

"And probably moving in on us," Pauncho said.

"Isn't it really too risky to stay in this one spot?" Cobbs said. "I think we should be moving about a bit."

"That's up to you," Doc said. He pressed the button again as the first of the birds appeared. This time they kept on coming and had almost reached them, with Doc saying, "Hold your fire!" when they broke and flew upward.

The dogs bounded down the slope again, just as the birds turned away. Doc said, "Hold your fire on these, too, unless you can stick your guns down their throats."

"The whites of their eyes, heh, only closer yet?" Pauncho said.

Some of the dogs slipped in the mud and slid into them. The others turned away just before the final leaps and went crashing into or over the bushes and down the hill.

Three dogs hurtled in, sidewise or fangs first, and Pauncho and Barney slammed one each over the head or the back and then kicked them on down the hill. Cobbs and Villiers hit a dog at the same time with the barrel of their rifles, breaking its ribs.

Doc said, "It ought to be over soon, one way or the other."

"What makes them voiceless?" Pauncho said. "I looked in the neck of a bird with its throat cut open back at the house on the mountain, and its vocal cords were all there."

"I saw you," Doc said. "But I supposed you'd guessed the answer. There are a number of electrodes at various areas of the brain. During the time that the animal is released for attack, its voice centers are inhibited."

"I wondered about that," Cobbs said. "But things have been happening so fast, I didn't have time to ask about it."

"I just supposed their vocal cords had been cut," Barbara said.

The others did not comment. Pauncho had asked Doc about the lack of voice after the attack by the wolves in the castle and Doc had given his opinion. But after the attack of the birds at the house on the mountain, he had told his colleagues not to mention anything about the characteristics of the animals. He had wanted to determine if the English couple would be curious about the strange lack of cries from the animals. If they did not comment, they might refrain because they knew the reason.

On the other hand, it was true that events had come one after the other and might have distracted them. But Barbara seemed to be a very stable and self-possessed person, and Cobbs, though he showed some apprehension, was far from hysterical.

The birds came first and the surviving dogs, going much slower because they had to climb uphill in muddy earth, attacked simultaneously. This time the wings of the eagles beat so close that the tips of some touched their faces. But the birds swerved again and shot back overhead. The dogs turned tail when they were still a few feet from closing with the party.

"I'd think they'd go crazy," Barney said. "They're being pulled apart by the opposing drives."

"They may yet," Doc answered.

About two minutes later the birds came in again, and this time Caliban turned off the sound generator for a few seconds after they had wheeled around to go in the other direction. The dogs then had nothing to stop them except the weapons of the party. While the others knocked the dogs on the head as they struggled uphill to get at them, Doc Caliban pressed a button on the other box, which had been on the ground by him. He had rearranged its circuits so that the aggressive areas of the brains would be stimulated.

The others did not notice what he was doing since they were concentrating on smashing in the dogs' skulls or backbones and doing a good job of it. He had not told them his plan, since he never confided to anyone unless he needed co-operation.

There were yells and screams to the right up the mountain, and then rifles and pistols banged away. Doc indulged himself with a broad smile. The others had their backs turned and would not be able to see him.

He switched off the aggression transmitter and turned on the sound generator. The two surviving dogs leaped backward down the hill as if they had stepped on a red-hot plate. One turned over and kept on sliding. The other regained his feet and fled.

"What's going on, Doc?" Pauncho said, jerking a thumb in the direction of the gunfire.

"As soon as the birds were deflected again, and presumably heading back toward the men who'd launched them, I switched off the noise generator and turned the aggression stimulation on. The birds, of course, attacked the first living things they saw, which were our enemies."

"Fabulous!" Pauncho rumbled. "I wish I had one of those hemispheres stuck on Barney's head. Then I could keep him from making a monkey of himself."

"Since when does a monkey's uncle know anything about proper behavior?" Barney said.

"The conflict of noise generator versus aggression stimulation might have driven them mad, anyway," Doc said. He led the way toward the groanings and whimperings drifting ghostily through the bushes. Approaching cautiously, they found six men on the ground, all alive but three totally unconscious and the others semiconscious. The birds were all dead, since they had not ceased to attack until killed. The onslaught had been so unexpected that none of the men had had time, or opportunity, to turn off the aggression stimulator. The birds had tried for the face and the throat and had blinded four. One man died of a ripped jugular vein while Doc was examining him.

After giving the survivors a shot to ensure that they would be unconscious for a long time, the party picked up some more magazines for their rifles and stuffed them in their capacious pockets. Pauncho and Barney threw the extra rifles down the mountain, and they continued climbing. They did not have far to go. Cobbs stopped suddenly, grunted, and said, "There it is."

In the blacklight of their projectors they could see the trenches that the two archaeologists had dug.

"Where's the cave-in?" Pauncho said.

"It's not there any more," Barbara Villiers said.

Doc began to poke his alpenstock into the bottoms of the trenches but stopped. He had heard the far-off chutter of helicopter vanes. He resumed probing and then said, "It's been walled up."

"Where'd those men come from?" Villiers said.

Doc did not reply. He took from a side pocket of his vest a tiny instrument and, holding it in his hand, began to walk back and forth for twenty yards each way. He worked his way up the mountain while she wondered aloud what he was doing. Since neither of his colleagues were sure, they did not answer her.

Ten minutes later, Caliban reappeared so suddenly from behind a tree that Barbara jumped and Cobbs wheeled around swiftly, bringing his rifle up.

Doc stepped back behind the tree and said, "Don't shoot."

"Doc, you shouldn't do that," Cobbs said. "You're likely to get shot."

Caliban said, "Follow me."

He led them upward to the right for about twenty yards and stopped. They were facing a fairly smooth outcropping of rock. Doc Caliban walked forward on the apron of the rock extending from its base and pushed on a small boulder at one side. The boulder rocked; there was a grinding noise and a section of the outcropping slid to one side.

"How'd you find it, Doc?" Pauncho said.

Doc tapped at the pocket which now held the small device he had used when casting back and forth. "It indicates small changes in the local magnetic fields. It detected the hollow behind that rock, and so I looked for something that would be the entrance activator."

They went into the chamber which had been cut out of the solid granite. Doc pulled a lever sticking out of a box in a corner, and the ponderous section of rock slid back into place. Immediately after, electric light bulbs fixed to brackets about four feet from the floor, and about thirty feet from each other, lit up. These were connected to wires which, in turn, occasionally descended the wall to the generator on the floor. Doc recognized the foot-square metal boxes as his own invention. They stored electricity derived by amplification of the flux of the earth's magnetic lines of force. They could not provide much current for very long, but the bulbs probably did not get much use in these corridors. They became extinguished as soon as the last person passed them, and they lit up as soon as the first person got within ten feet of them.

Each one in the party held his rifle across his belly. Doc held his with one hand while the other was extended with the magnetic-field discriminator.

Whenever it was a question of going to left or right, Doc looked at the juncture of floor and wall. Cobbs had carefully made tiny markings with a pen the first time he had come here. These indicated their previous route so that they would be able to find their way out.

They went up steps cut out of stone to upper levels four times before Cobbs finally called a halt.

"We're getting close to the place where the dwarf captured us."

They were standing in a round chamber about forty feet across. It contained a dozen large boxes of oak on which were carved hunting and battle scenes. The costumes of the dwarfs and the humans in the scenes were those worn circa 800-900 A.D.

"They look like coffins," Pauncho said to the woman.

"They are coffins," she said.

She tried to raise a lid but could not manage it. "It's so heavy," she said. "But you should see the mummified body and the jewelry and gold it's decorated with."

"Here, let me help you!" Barney and Pauncho said. They collided with each other in their eagerness to get to the coffin.

"Leave it alone!" Doc said. "They might be booby-trapped now!"

But Pauncho, grinning because he had shoved Barney out of the way, had started to raise the lid. Barney dived for the floor as if he expected the coffin to explode. Barbara gave a small scream. Pauncho had stepped back and dropped the lid, which was raised about eight inches. It did not drop. Instead, it continued to rise, and the figure in it sat up. He held an automatic pistol in one hand.

At the same time, the lids of the other coffins screeched upward, and other figures sat up aiming automatic pistols at them.

A voice behind them said, "Freeze!" A voice ahead of them said, "Not a move!"

"A beauty of a trap!" Pauncho whispered. He looked at Doc Caliban. The huge man was obeying instructions. He had no choice. The fire from three sides would have cut them all down within a few seconds.

Ten minutes later, their hands cuffed behind them, they went up stone steps onto another level. The twenty men who accompanied them kept pistols pressed against their backs. They marched down a long tunnel on the walls of which were hung many paintings done in a very primitive but forceful manner. It looked as if this were the place Iwaldi had chosen as his ancestral gallery. The paintings were mainly of long-bearded fierce-faced men with beetling brows, bushy eyebrows, round blobs of noses, and very broad shoulders.

Doc Caliban remembered, however, that Iwaldi had been born long before portrait painting of this sort was known. These dwarfs must be men who had inhabited this underground fortress; perhaps they were Iwaldi's descendants, not his grandsires.

Except for the paintings, the tunnel was bare rock.

They were marched into a square chamber and here all the prisoners were forced to undress. The inspection that followed was thorough and included probing for concealed objects. Doc's wig and facial pseudoskin was pulled off. Two false teeth containing explosives and a coil of very thin wire were removed from his mouth.

Barbara Villiers said nothing. She was as dignified as if she were wearing a formal at the opera. Out of regard for her, Barney and Pauncho repressed the ribald comments they would have made at each other's expense.

They were marched into a chamber about fifty feet square. Stone steps cut into the sides of the walls led up to three levels of runways carved out of the rock. A man led the way up on to the second level.

Just past the nearest of many entrances was a room divided by two sections of thick iron bars. The man opened a door set in the first by inserting a thin metal rod into a hole and pressing a button on the rod. The door swung back, and the party was marched up to the next section of iron bars. This was opened in the same manner, and Caliban, van Veelar, and Banks were locked behind it. But Barbara Villiers and Carlos Cobbs were left outside. The men conducted them out onto the overhanging runway and around the corner. An iron door clanged. The men marched away. Presumably, the English couple had been locked in a cell facing the runway.

"I wonder why they separated us?" Pauncho said.

Doc did not answer.

Days passed. At least, it seemed that many days passed. They had no way of determining time except by the number of meals, and they got so hungry in between these that they were sure many were being skipped. They exercised and slept and talked much, though when they did not want to be understood they talked in the language of the People of the Blue.

The only person they saw was the man who brought their meals, and he never said a word.

Then, three or four or five days after they were captured, two men entered the outside cage. Both were walking backward and holding a box with a short antenna directed at the beast which shambled around the corner. Two men came behind the animal, one of whom also held a box with an antenna directed at the beast.

This was a huge grizzly, the North American *Ursus horribilis*. Its head swung low, and its eyes were a bright red. Its open mouth dripped saliva.

The man with the box in front backed up to the wall, keeping his antenna pointed at the grizzly's head. Then he pressed a button, and the grizzly lay down and went to sleep.

The great head was only three feet from the prisoners, who could see the tiny hemisphere on top of it.

The two men got out of the cell quickly and closed the door with a loud clang. The grizzly quivered at the sound but continued sleeping.

One of the men holding a box pointed it at the beast, and,

suddenly, the ponderous animal was on its feet and roaring. It reared upon its hind legs and advanced toward the prisoners as if it intended to go through the bars to get them. The man pressed another button, and the beast dropped to all fours. It no longer seemed angry; it was just curious as it prowled around the cell, sniffing here and there and stopping for some time to gaze at the prisoners.

Barney said, "Do you think Iwaldi intends to let that bear loose on us?"

Doc Caliban called loudly, "Mr. Cobbs! Miss Villiers! Can you hear me!"

Cobbs' voice was faint but distinct. "Yeah, I can hear you!"

"Just testing!" Doc Caliban said. "Can you see anything of note?"

"Just some of Iwaldi's men! Nothing of Iwaldi!"

A moment later, "Correction! Here comes Iwaldi!"

Doc Caliban looked through the double set of bars but did not see the old dwarf appear as he had expected. About ten minutes afterward, the long-bearded hunched figure appeared from the right. Evidently, he had come up steps to the right instead of taking the closer steps to the left.

The grizzly roared on seeing him and pressed against the bars as if it were trying to get its muzzle through and bite him.

Two boxes with antennae were pointed at the bear, which immediately backed away and stayed in a corner while Iwaldi and four men entered. Two kept their antennae directed at the grizzly, during the conversation that followed.

Iwaldi rolled forward like a sailor, his body hunched forward and his arms swinging at his sides. His long white hair fell to his shoulders and his white beard swung like bleached Spanish moss in a wind. The wrinkled face came close to the bars but not so close that Doc Caliban could reach through and grab him.

Iwaldi stood for two minutes staring at them while his thin lips slowly opened into a wide smile. The eyes were as red as the grizzly's.

Finally, the thin and cracked voice spoke.

"You'll not get out of this, Doctor Caliban!"

"And why not, ancient fossil?" Caliban replied evenly.

Iwaldi cackled. "Do you think that you, a baby, a born-just-yesterday, could anger me with your puerile words? So I'm a fossil?

Well in a way, you're right, since fossils endure while flesh dies. And you'll die, Caliban, and soon! Very soon!"

Doc Caliban shrugged and said, "Maybe I will. Since you think I am going to die, it wouldn't hurt you to tell me what's going on. Are you and the Nine really at war? Or did I make a bad guess?"

Iwaldi fingered his beard with a deeply seamed and swollen-veined hand for a minute. Then he said, "It can't hurt to indulge an ephemera such as yourself. And the knowledge might make your end even less endurable to you.

"Yes, old Anana and her sycophants are at war with me! But it was I who declared war, not them! I almost got Anana and Shaumbim and Ing! We were to meet in Paris, and I arranged to have the walls of the house loaded with explosives! I was to arrive a few minutes late to the meeting, just after the smoke cleared away!

"But that Anana! She hasn't survived for over 30,000 years by being insensitive. She smelled death in that house! That's the only way I can account for it! She sniffed out the odor of coming death! And she left the house and took Shaumbim and Ing with her and was only a block away when the house blew up!

"She should have blamed you or Grandrith for that, since she knows you're capable of doing that! But the fact that I was late made her suspicious, and she sent me word to come to a house in London. She did not say why, but I knew. I was to be put on trial! Iwaldi! On trial!

"I sent her a letter impregnated with chemicals which would release a poison gas when the envelope was opened! But she had someone else open it, and that person died, of course! From then on, it has been a battle! I finally decided to hole up here in my ancient stronghold, this mountain that was the property of some of my ancestors, the kings of the southern branch of the Gbabuld family! But I'm getting out now—for the time being—and leaving you here to face whatever you must! And whatever you must will be a matter of choice! So thank me for giving you a choice of deaths, Caliban!"

"Why the war at all?" Caliban said, ignoring the reference to deaths.

"Because the others have opposed me! They have sided with Anana! I wanted to let the mortals poison themselves and so eliminate themselves in time! I wanted to permit pollution to continue, the air to be fouled, the waters to be fouled, the fish to die, the ocean plants to die, the trees to die! In a few years, most of mankind will be dying of starvation! You know that! You said so in your report to us in 1946. You extrapolated almost one hundred percent what would happen, what is happening now and what will happen! You stated that enough people would become alarmed that measures would be taken to combat pollution! But it would be too late! The politicians would take over the fight against pollution and use it for their own advancement! And most measures would be band-aids whereas deep excisions and grafts were required! Those were your own words!

"So, in about twenty years from now, a flicker of an eyelid in my lifetime, mortal, the sea life will be dying and there will be the very good chance that the world's oxygen supply will be seriously reduced.

"I wanted the Nine to keep their hands off! Let the mortals kill themselves off! Not that all of them would die, which is a pity, though it would be nice to have servants. But so many would die that civilization would collapse, and then the planet could begin the process of cleansing itself. Once again, we'd have pure air and pure water and trees would cover the land and the animals would return in great numbers. And we could set ourselves up as gods, as we did in the old days, and this time ensure that the mortals stayed few in numbers and poor in science. We wouldn't make the same mistake all over again of letting them multiply and invent until suddenly the entire Earth was threatened!

"But Anana said no. She said that if we let them go, we might die, too. The whole Earth might die. Only the most primitive forms of life would survive.

"I said that we had the means to restore the proper balance when we wished. Your report said that your own researchers had come up with a means whereby the phytoplankton balance could be restored and the chief source of the world's oxygen would thrive again. We could use that after the mortals had become savages again and the cities were being uprooted by the plants and being buried under the good earth.

"But they overruled me. Anana said that we could not afford to take a chance. We did not want to die, too, though she admitted that the prospect of a return to the good old days was tempting. She is very, very old, as you know, Caliban, but she remembers when the great forests covered Europe and even the isles of Greece were green with trees. She remembers when North Africa was wet and verdant. She remembers when you could travel for days in what is now France and not encounter a single human being. She remembers the great and the small beasts that lived in the forests.

"But she decided that we would not let things take their course as determined by the mortals. She said that we must start using our influence on the governments to determine the effective course in fighting pollution. Action had to be taken now, and we would start planning our campaign immediately. Not for the sake of you ephemerae, you know that. But for the sake of the blessed green Earth. And for our sake.

"So I appeared to agree, and I left. But Anana found out that I was secretly preparing countermeasures, and she summoned me to that house in Paris. And I set the trap, and it failed. But I will win. Old Iwaldi won't fail! Although you won't be around to witness my victory!"

"And that is the only reason why you have deserted the ancient table of the Nine?" Caliban said.

Iwaldi stared for a moment and then said, "Is that *all?* What do you mean?"

"There isn't some other reason you haven't told me?"

Iwaldi laughed so hard he had to bend over, and his beard almost touched the floor. When he managed to straighten up, he wiped the tears from his bloodshot eyes with the tip of his beard, and he said, "You're very clever, indeed, mortal! Very perceptive! It is too bad . . . if I could trust you . . . if only . . . but no, I can't! Yes, there is another reason, but even though you are to die, I won't tell you that! It'll give me some pleasure to know that you'll be wondering what that other reason is up to the moment that you start suffering so much you'll have no thought for anything but the pain!"

"Does this other reason have something to do with the English couple?"

"Why do you ask that?"

"Because they must have some value to you, otherwise you

would have killed them the first time you had them. It would be easy to find out if they were spies for Anana by injecting calibanite. And once you found out, you would kill them whether they were innocent or guilty."

Iwaldi made a smacking sound and said, "Very well reasoned out! You are indeed a worthy descendant of mine!"

It was Caliban's turn to be surprised, but he did not betray it with any change of expression. He said, "I know that XauXaz was my ancestor and I had suspected that his brothers were, too. But I did not suspect . . ."

"The Grandrith family tree has more than one god in its branches," Iwaldi said. "Even Anana was one of your ancestors, though she provided a son a long time ago, about the time the primitive Germanic speech was starting to split up into its North, West, and East branches. Which means that you have none of her genes, of course. But her sons became heroes of their people. They were as strong as you or your half-brother. But I was your great-grandfather, Doctor Caliban, though my genes seem to have been most prominent in another branch of your family, not in your direct heritage. Didn't you know that Simmons, your colleague, was my grandson? Haven't you thought about his extreme shortness, his massive trunk, his abnormally long arms and short legs? His Neanderthalish supraorbital ridges? All of which characteristics, except for his height, have been inherited by his son, Mr. van Veelar, doomed to die with you also. Then there is another illustrious descendant of mine, a second cousin of yours and of Simmons, a scientist who brought back some rather strange specimens from a high plateau in South America in the early part of this century. He also looked much like me."

"Cousin George Edward!" Caliban said.

"Grandpa!" Pauncho said, sinking to one knee and spreading his arms out wide. "Grandpa!"

Iwaldi stared at him and then smiled thinly.

"Very well! Clown away to the last minute! Very admirable! I wouldn't like to think that my great-grandson was a coward, though it doesn't really matter."

"And you'd kill your own flesh and blood?" Pauncho said, rising.

"Why not? It wouldn't be the first time. An ephemeral is an ephemeral."

A man appeared at the outside bars. The grizzly growled but did not move from the corner. The man said, "Pardon, sir, but the invaders are getting closer. They'll soon be on the third level."

Iwaldi said, "In a moment the servants of the Nine will find out they will have to keep on going down. A river of flame will appear behind them. Napalm is being forced by pumps into the tunnels. They'll try to take tunnels leading away but will find their route barred by big blocks of stone. They'll be herded, as it were, down to this level.

"In the meantime, I've opened a vein of water, and the tunnels below this are filling with water. They'll flood this level—unless the river of napalm gets here first. It'll be quite a race between the two, and if you prefer drowning to burning to death, you had better start praying."

He stopped. Caliban, van Veelar, and Banks returned his gaze. He said, "I like spirit in a man except when it's turned against me, and even then it affords me a challenge, however brief—a break from the boredom of mundane life. Do you see that?"

He pointed at a metal box protruding from the corner of the ceiling and the right wall.

"That's a movie camera. It will record your last moments, and then the front end will be automatically covered by a metal plate. When I return, I'll recover it and run off the film. It'll be a pleasure to review your deaths."

He gestured at the two men with the boxes directed at the grizzly. They stepped backward, and the men with the rifles followed them. Iwaldi walked backward for a few steps, too.

"I've made a little arrangement here. Possibly even given you a chance to escape from this cell, though I don't really think so. But if you should get out, Caliban, you will then only have the choice of throwing yourself into the flames or into the water. You can't get past them."

He turned and walked through the outer door, which a man clanged shut. The grizzly roared and charged the men behind the bars. They flinched, but Iwaldi did not move back, though the grizzly's paw was slashing the air only a few inches from his face. He said something, and the men with the boxes turned the antennae toward the bear again. He sat down and became quite docile, Iwaldi spoke loudly.

"Caliban, at any time you wish, you can slide your door aside and enter the cell with the bear! But the moment you move that door, a mechanism will radiate a frequency which will cause the bear to become insane with a desire to kill. Nor can you all go through the door and then shut it with the hopes that the grizzly won't attack you once the stimulus is removed. That frequency will keep operating even if the door is shut again.

"This outer door can be opened by you, if you can get to it. But it won't open immediately when you pull on it. A delay mechanism will keep it closed until five minutes have passed after pressure is applied. Which means that two of you can't keep the bear occupied while one opens the door and then all of you escape. The bear will be driven with the desire to kill every living thing in sight. He's nine and a half feet long and weighs one thousand one hundred and twenty pounds.

"You can stay in your cell and wait to be burned or drowned. Or you can fight your way out, and then be burned or drowned, but you'll have a choice. And this time, you'll have nothing but your bare hands and feet, Caliban! Use them well!"

He was silent for a moment as he stared at them and, doubtless, was hoping for a reaction of some sort. But the three were stony-faced.

"I'm going now," Iwaldi said. "It can't hurt to tell you that I'll be in Stonehenge for the winter solstice to attend XauXaz's funeral!"

Doc Caliban was surprised when he heard this, but he did not show it.

"Yes, XauXaz's funeral!" Iwaldi snarled. "You didn't know that, did you! His body has been kept in a big box in a London warehouse. It'll be shipped to Salisbury and then taken to the ruins of Stonehenge, where the Nine will hold the funeral ceremonies for him! And I'll be there, though uninvited! I'll kill all of them! Old Anana! Ing! All of them!

"And then I'll be free to release my biobomb! While the mortals are starving to death and also gasping for oxygen, I'll be in my mountain retreat, snug and safe, eating well, breathing a rich air! After it's over for the mortals, then I and a few of my servants, mostly female, and my stock of beasts and plants, will come out!

"What do you think of that?"

The prisoners continued to stare without expression.

"You can pretend to be unconcerned!" he shouted. "But you are naked, and I can see your hearts thumping! A long goodnight to you, mortals!"

He spat and walked away, two men preceding him, the others trailing.

Pauncho broke the long silence. "Maybe the invaders will take pity on us."

"Yeah," Barney said. "They might shoot us. At that, they'd be doing us a favor."

Pauncho looked at Doc and said, "I didn't know we were related. That makes me several cuts superior to this proletarian peasant, heh, Doc? I got the blood of English nobility in my veins, right? And the blood of ancient Viking sea kings. And what's more, the blood of men and women that were once gods and goddesses to the common herd, lowly swine like Barney. Say, Doc, what about that hero stuff? Who do you think were those ancient Germanic heroes he was talking about?"

"I don't know. Maybe the men whose exploits formed the basis of the *Volsunga* and *Nibelungenlied* epics. Or maybe the man or men who were the originals of the *Beowulf* stories. I'm more concerned about his descendants, three in particular."

Pauncho's small eyes widened. "Three?"

"Yes. That man's descendants have to include most of the present populace of north Europe or anybody descended from north Europeans and probably from south Europeans, and many Africans and Asiatics, too. Figure it out mathematically, if you ever get a chance."

Barney haw-hawed but quit when the grizzly, roaring, hurled himself against the bars.

Doc said, "Iwaldi didn't say whether or not pressure has to be maintained on that door. We can't afford to take a chance, so one man should keep pulling on it."

"If I had a pocket, I'd pull out a coin and we could flip it to see who's the lucky guy," Pauncho said. "But I'll be magnanimous, Barney. I'll handle the door while you help Doc with the bear."

Pauncho's voice was steady and he was grinning, but his reddish skin had turned pale.

"No," Caliban said firmly. "We'd be stupid to reduce our strength by one-third. We either put the grizzly out of commission and then open the door—provided Iwaldi wasn't lying to us—or we don't make it at all."

"Well, Barney, you always said you might be skinny but you could lick your weight in wildcats," Pauncho said. "Here's your chance to prove it."

"I said cats not bears," Barney replied. "Anyway, the three of us total about seven hundred and seventy so that gives the grizzly an edge of three hundred and fifty pounds. And he's got teeth and claws a hell of a lot sharper than ours."

"Tell me something I don't know," Pauncho said. "Like how're we going to take him?"

He pressed his blobbish nose against a bar and stared at the grizzly. It was pacing back and forth, its head low and swinging, the brownish silver-tipped fur beautiful but the beauty lost on the watcher. There was fat under that loose glossy hide but there were also giant bones and the strength of two gorillas.

"I want you two to hang back in here until I give the word to join me," Doc Caliban said. "I'm going to make him chase me until he gets tired."

Barney and Pauncho looked at the cell, forty feet square, and they said, at the same time, *"Chase* you?"

"It's worth a try," Caliban said. For him, that was equivalent to a long speech by Hector urging the discouraged Trojans to venture out against the Achaeans again.

He pulled back on the door and slipped through. The grizzly bellowed and whirled around, glared at Caliban, and then charged. It went so swiftly that it was a blur to Pauncho and Barney.

But the reddish-brown golden-tinted skin and dark auburn metallic-looking hair of Doc Caliban was a blur, too. He sprang to one side just before the grizzly was on him, ran at the wall, and bounced off it like a handball.

The grizzly rammed head-on into the bars with a crash that shook the bars and quivered the iron floor under the feet of the two men. But the enormous and clumsy-looking beast recovered swiftly, whirled, and was after Caliban, who had sped to the corner where the wall and the outside barred wall met. Again, he leaped to one side, and again the beast crashed with wall-quivering impact.

"If that grizzly's smart, and he doesn't look dumb," Barney said, "he'll be watching for Doc's sidewise maneuver."

"Yeah, but his thinking processes may be overwhelmed by the aggression stimulation," Pauncho said. "It may make him all fury and no brains at all."

The third time, Doc startled his aides by suddenly running at the bear just after it had started its charge. Events happened so swiftly that they looked as if they were being run by a speeded-up projector. The bronze blur and the brownish silver-tipped blur met. But Doc had leaped up and leveled out, and his legs shot out. His bare feet struck the grizzly on the nose and the sides of the head. The two bulks stopped. Doc fell backward but rolled and landed on his side and then was up and away. The bear, roaring, shook his head, while blood flowed from his nostrils, and launched himself at Caliban. The man did not quite succeed in escaping untouched. Claws, backed by a great paw swinging with strength enough to remove a man's head, barely nicked the back of his right leg. The skin came off in a wide band across the back of his calf, and blood ran down his leg.

Caliban spun and ran straight into the bear. The grizzly heaved himself up, coming up off all fours like a killer whale bursting from the sea's surface, and opened his front legs to receive the foolhardy human.

Doc Caliban went on in as if he had lost his desire to live.

Pauncho and Barney cried out, "Doc!" and Pauncho yanked at the door to pull it back. He and Barney would go out there now; surely this was the time.

But Doc had planted a blow with his huge fist with all the power of his left arm and his back and legs. The arm sank into the fur of the animal's belly, into the fat, and into the muscle.

The grizzly went, *"Oof,"* and it fell backward.

Doc Caliban leaped back, then, but even as it fell the grizzly's left paw raked the top of Caliban's head, and blood gushed out from a torn scalp.

Doc was momentarily blinded. He turned and ran, judging the distance to the wall by memory, stopped there three paces away, and turned. He wiped away the blood from his eyes, but more flowed down.

The grizzly had gotten to all fours and stood for a minute while it sucked in air. Its belly heaved, and its tongue dangled far out.

Then it charged, more slowly than it had before but still fast enough to have kept pace with many Olympic dashers.

Doc waited until it was very close and then, putting his feet against the wall behind as a springboard, dived under the beast.

It was completely taken by surprise by this maneuver. It whirled around but Caliban had gone between its legs, come up behind it, and was on its back. He seized its ears as it reared up on its hind legs and whirled around and around as if it could catch the man clinging to its back.

Pauncho and Barney, knowing that it would roll over in a minute and crush Caliban, went through the door. Yelling, their hands waving, they charged the bear. It roared and batted at them as it kept on dancing with its partner in his strange position on its back. They danced, too, around the perimeter described by its long claws. Once, the tip of a claw caught the end of Barney's long slender nose, and blood squirted out. A second later, he slipped in the blood which had spilled on the floor from Caliban's wounds and the nose of the bear. The grizzly was so close that it could have dropped on all fours and covered him, but it whirled away.

Doc's hand stabbed out and plucked the hemisphere from its head.

Pauncho lifted up Barney, who was half-stunned when the back of his head had hit the metal floor. Then Pauncho, looking something like a bear with the mange, charged the grizzly. He came diving in just as the animal was half-turned away, and his three hundred and twenty pounds slammed into the side of the bear's right leg.

The grizzly toppled over on its side, which was just what Caliban did not want. But he hung on to the ears and then bent his body back, his muscles cracking with the effort, and tore the ears of the grizzly off with a sound like the ripping of a sail under an overwhelming wind.

The beast bellowed so loudly that it half-deafened the three men. It spun around, and its jaws clamped down on Caliban's leg as he was trying to crawl away through a pool of blood.

Doc, instead of continuing to try to get away, twisted around and brought both fists down hard on the grizzly's skull. And then he hammered the big wet bloody nose with his fists.

The twisting around resulted in great pain and more loss of blood. It was so painful, he felt faint. The grizzly, if it had been able to seize him then, might have finished him in a few seconds.

But Pauncho, roaring, leaped up in the air and came down with both feet on the back of the grizzly's massive neck. The impact of those feet, driven by those two extremely powerful legs, stunned the creature, even if only for a very short time. Its jaws opened enough for Doc to pull his leg loose. He rolled away but without his customary speed. Barney, imitating Pauncho's example, leaped into the air and came down on the bear's back. He did not have the weight nor the strength of his partner, but he did the bear some damage.

It coughed and then got to its feet slowly. Blood was running from its nose, from the places where the ears had been, and its eyes were crossed. It stood for a minute, looking at Doc Caliban, who was now crawling away, leaving a red trail.

Pauncho came up from behind the grizzly and kicked him beneath the tail with his right foot. The bear was turned into a maniac again by the kick. It whirled so swiftly that it caught Pauncho by surprise. He tried to run away, but it charged and grabbed him with both its front paws. Pauncho went down screaming under the bear.

Barney, yelling, leaped upon the huge shaggy back and, his legs clamped around the body, dug his thumbs into the eyes. The grizzly, bellowing, released Pauncho and reared up on its hind legs and then fell back, apparently by design, to crush Barney.

Barney fell off and rolled away but not before a paw, batting blindly, scraped his left leg from the top of the thigh to the knee. His blood mingled with Caliban's and the bear's on the floor.

Barney was slight compared to Caliban or van Veelar, but he had a wiry strength that had surprised many a large man who had tackled him. His hands were slender, even delicate looking, but he could double a steel poker. And his hands were strong enough to have dug into the sockets of the skull and popped out the bear's eyes. These were now hanging from the nerve cables on its cheeks.

It was blind, but it could smell, though not efficiently because of the damage to its nose; and it could hear, though not efficiently, because of the pain from the tearing off of its ears. But it located Caliban and went after him, ignoring the others. Doc, hearing the warning cries, turned and got to his feet, though not without difficulty and not without gritting his teeth to suppress a groan.

The bear charged straight into him. Doc reached out and jerked the eyes loose and cast them on the floor and then, as he went down under the beast, rammed his arm all the way into the bear's mouth. It choked, and its paws tore at his back, and then it backed away swiftly. Its jaws opened, to get rid of the object that was strangling it, and Doc's hand came out, closed on the huge wet tongue. The slipperiness almost balked him, but he managed to keep his grip. Only one other man in the world could have done what he did.

When the tongue came out by the roots, the grizzly shot blood all over Caliban and the wall of the room. And then it turned and charged blindly across the floor until it rammed its head into the bars of the inner door. It collapsed there, wailing until blood choked it and it died.

But Doc Caliban had lost much skin and his back muscles were so torn up they were causing him intense pain.

Doc sat up and waved Barney's helping hand away. "Open the door!" he said. "We have to get out of here!"

Pauncho was there before Barney. He pulled the sliding door back and said, "No five minute wait."

Doc Caliban tried to get to his feet, but he slipped twice. Barney, standing by his side, made no move to help him because he did not think that Doc would like it. It was Doc who always helped others; he never needed anybody else.

Doc wiped the blood from his forehead, looked at Barney with the yellow-flecked verdigris eyes, and said, "You too weak to assist me?"

"Hell, no, Doc, glad to do it!"

Barney leaned down and let Doc put a massive arm around his shoulder and then he straightened up. Doc came up slowly but not with the full weight of his three hundred plus pounds on Barney's slim shoulder.

"Now I'm up, I can make it by myself," Doc said. Then he clamped his teeth and pressed his lips together.

"I think I hear something!" Pauncho said. "Yeah! And I smell something! Smoke! Hey, there's somebody down that way!"

He pointed to the left.

"The invaders," Doc said. "Anana's men. Driven here by the flowing napalm, I suppose. We'd better go the other way. Barney, check on Cobbs and Villiers. I don't think they're still here, but . . ."

When Barney returned he said, "Not there. And there's nothing we can use for a weapon. I didn't see our stuff either. You'd think Iwaldi wouldn't have bothered to hide it, since he didn't figure we'd even get out of the cell."

"He knew it wasn't impossible for us to get out," Caliban replied. "But he must have figured we'd never get out of the cave even if we somehow got past the bear."

They went down the runway to the nearest stone steps on the right and descended to the floor of the chamber. There were a number of exits. Doc picked the middle central one, and they went down a tunnel. Smoke was pouring out of several of the entrances behind them, and Doc could hear, faintly, coughing from one. They went down the tunnel and came to a shaft which contained no ladder. Caliban, looking down it, saw ankle-deep water on the floor of the tunnel under the shaft. It was rising swiftly.

"This is the tunnel we came up after being captured," he said. "It should still hold Cobbs' marks, unless Iwaldi rubbed them out. We'll have to chance that; it's our only hope."

Slowly, because he felt weak and because the movements pained him considerably, he let himself down the shaft and dropped. The impact almost made him faint. His colleagues dropped down, too, and they went toward the direction which—he hoped—was the right way. The lights along the tunnel were still on but might soon go out. However, since this system was based on one he had originated, it was possible that the lights would operate long after the tunnel was flooded.

"Hold it a minute!" Pauncho said.

They stopped. Seemingly from faraway came voices. But if they could be heard there, they would not be too far distant.

"They've probably seen our blood by now and are trailing us," Caliban said. "If only we could ambush some of them. They have guns and they may have first-aid kits; and they must have blacklight projectors and just possibly underwater breathing plugs."

"Wouldn't Iwaldi know that and take care of that possibility?" Barney said.

"Yes. But we know the way, and we know what kind of traps Iwaldi has sprung," Doc said. He did not mention the probability that Iwaldi had closed off all exits.

They went on, splashing. The water around their feet was tinged with red. Doc suddenly stopped at a corner where the tunnel ran into another. He bent over, peering, and said, "There's Cobbs' marks."

They went down the tunnel, turned right, walked ten yards, turned left, and were confronted with a stairway the top of which was a foot under water. The marking at the corner of the wall was still visible through the water. It indicated that the way led down the steps.

"There are three levels to go before we get to the exit," Pauncho said.

Doc help up his hand for silence. A splashing was coming from far around the corner.

"We can't make it unless we have breathing plugs," he said. "And there's only one source for them. Here's what we'll do."

Barney walked back to the far end of the tunnel and looked around the corner. Within a minute, he jerked his head back, turned, and waved at them. Then he trotted toward them. By the time he reached them, the water was up to his calves.

"Ten of them," he said. "Automatic rifles and pistols. Blacklight projectors on their caps but they're not using their goggles. It's impossible to tell if they have breathing plugs."

He added, "And I smelled smoke. The napalm can't be too far behind."

The invaders would not know about Cobbs' markings, of course, so they would go on down the tunnel. They would be looking for a way out which would not force them to submerge. Doc had looked down the corridor and seen the hole in the middle of the floor. There was a shaft there which the ancient kobolds had made apparently for quick exits, as if they were human-sized mouse holes. This was the pivotal point of his attack.

He waded down the steps until the water was up to his waist and then he swam along the wall. The bulbs along the wall guided his path and enabled Barney to see him. When Doc was opposite the shaft, Barney signaled him. Doc dived, was visible in the lights until he went under the ceiling, and then popped up in the well in the middle of the tunnel. Pauncho went down the tunnel to the end and around the corner. Doc Caliban submerged and came back up in the other tunnel. He hung on to a light bulb while Barney sat on the steps with his ear placed near the juncture of wall and steps.

In a few seconds, Barney heard the loud splashing of the ten men. He waited until he judged that the lead man was just about to come opposite the stairway, and he slid off the stairs into the water and down alongside it. When he reached the bottom, he flattened himself against the side. Now all he could do was to hold his breath and hope that the leader would not take time out for a glance into this tunnel before deciding to go on. If anybody leaned out and looked down the side of the steps, he would see Barney in the light of the closest bulb.

Doc had submerged also and swam the few feet necessary to get to the bottom of the well. Here he placed one hand on the ceiling next to the lip of the shaft and waited. He hoped the bleeding would slow down enough so the men would not notice that the waters were reddened. And he hoped the enemy would not loiter in that corridor. Normally, he could hold his breath for fifteen minutes if he hyperventilated for thirty minutes (the official world's record was 13 minutes, 42.5 seconds). But he had no time to hyperventilate and he was too weakened to hold his breath for much more than two minutes.

Fortunately, the lighting was such that the men above cast their shadows over the well as they passed on its right. He counted ten and swam up with all his strength as the last shadow passed. He came out of the shaft without making any noise and pulled himself with one fluid motion onto the floor. The water was then a foot and a half high and the splashing made by the men drowned out any noise he made. He stood up and quickly approached the rear man whose eyes were straight ahead. He hit him in the back of the neck and caught the rifle as it fell. By then Barney was coming down the hall behind him, and he threw the rifle to him and then waded up and knocked out the next man.

He did not fire at once. He waited until the lead man got to the corner and he saw Pauncho's long thick arm reach out and grab the rifle and pluck it out of the man's hands. The stock of the rifle, reversed, caught the man under the chin, and he went down.

Doc called, "Freeze!"

Pauncho stuck the barrel of the rifle around the corner and said, "Don't move!"

The shock held the others in its grip long enough for them to see that they could only die if they tried to resist. They dropped their rifles into the water and put their hands, slowly, behind their necks.

Pauncho stepped out from the corner and said, "You there!" indicating the man now at the head of the line. "Drop your belt! Slowly! Then get the nose plugs off this guy!" He tilted his head to indicate the man he had knocked out. This one lay face down on the floor, covered entirely by the water. He had drowned, but he would have drowned in any event, since Pauncho was taking his breathers away from him. Three men had to be sacrificed. The survivors could consider themselves lucky that they had had the right positions in the line.

While Barney kept the rifle on the men, Doc felt through the pockets of the two men he had knocked out, who had also drowned. He came up with the plugs and handed two to Barney. The enemy were dropping their belts, which held knives and pistols and bullets, into the water. At Pauncho's command, they completely undressed.

One of the men carried a medical kit. Doc opened this and popped hemenerogen tablets into his mouth. Barney swallowed some, and one man carried some to Pauncho and then returned to his place in line. There were also ointments and some pseudoprotein dressings which Doc and Pauncho applied while Barney held his rifle on the prisoners. Both immediately felt better though far from being in one hundred percent good health.

While they were doing this, the water had risen three inches.

Doc Caliban explained to the prisoners what they would have to do if they wanted to survive. They did not like the idea, but a gush of smoke and a steady rise in the air temperature convinced them that they had no other choice.

Caliban removed the ammunition from the rifles and gave one to each man. They went back to the entranceway and down the steps, shivering at the coldness of the water. The only clothing they wore were the blacklight projectors and the goggles around their necks in case they came to dark tunnels. Their captors wore only belts with sheathed knives, and they carried rifles.

The three stayed behind the seven men, who moved through the water, swimming with one hand while they held the rifles against their bellies and at right angles to the longitudinal axis of their bodies. This made for slow swimming, but it also made for safe swimming, as they found out. On the last level down, a section of the wall slid out, displacing much water as the first four men went by. Three of the rifles caught as they were supposed to do; the fourth was dropped as the man swam away in a panic. The movement of the block had been impeded by the water and the displacement of the water had warned the defenders.

There was no other incident. They reached the chamber where they had entered. By then, they were all so numb that they could hardly feel anything with their hands. Their strength was spurting out swiftly.

Doc Caliban had told his colleagues what to expect while they were getting ready to ambush the enemy. He gestured at them to make ready, and they swam to him and clung to the pipe protruding from the wall. He hoped that the massive wall of stone would slide back; the pressure of the water was immense against it. It was true that Iwaldi and his party had probably gone through this way. But they would have done so when the pressure was much less.

He turned the valve. The screaking of the stone against stone was shrill in the water. It hurt their ears. But the wall was moving slowly to the right, and then they felt the current as the water began to spurt out of the opening. The current became stronger as the opening widened. Doc clung to the valve until, seeing that the exit was now broad enough, he tapped the others on the shoulders. He let loose and was swept toward the opening, scraped against the edge of the still moving wall, and was shot out into the mountainside. Pauncho and Barney were close behind him.

The others had become momentarily jammed in the opening when it was only two feet wide. Then, as the wall withdrew, one went out and the others had followed. Since they had not come in this way, they did not know what to expect. They went out across the ledge and were carried over the edge and down the mountainside. This was not so steep that they were in a free fall, but the slope was rough with rocks where it was not muddy.

Caliban and his friends straightened themselves out, letting the current shoot them across the stone ledge and on down the incline. They became their own toboggans, though not without loss of more skin on their backs. The pseudoprotein that Doc had spread over his back was torn loose again, and the agony of his back would have been worse if he had not been so anesthetized by the icy water.

They managed to stop themselves by grabbing hold of bushes about forty feet down the slope. Though the water struck them hard, they held on, half-drowned and almost completely frozen. Then, frighteningly, they began to slide on down even though they kept their grips on the branches. The earth had become loosened under the pressure of the water and was now moving.

Below them came yells as their seven predecessors saw the large mass sludging above them. These men had managed to stand up, even though the water was up to their knees and threatening to knock them down and roll them for another bruising, banging slide. Now, seeing what looked like the beginning of an avalanche, they tried to run away. Their feet slid out, and they were carried away by the water and the loose mud under them.

They did not, however, go far. About forty feet further, a ledge stopped them, and they managed to grab bushes. A moment later, they screamed as the cliff of mud and rocks and bushes bearing Caliban and his aides flowed around them and then began to cover them up.

Suddenly, the flow of water became a trickle. The wall of stone had shut, and the water was penned up in the mountain again.

The seven, half-buried, struggled to pull themselves free. Caliban and his colleagues, shivering with the cold and with repugnance, took out their knives and did what had to be done. They could not afford to let the Nine know that they were here and that they had gotten free.

Just before dawn three men, covered with dried mud and nothing else, walked into the side door. Nobody saw them, which was fortunate, because the police would have been called. The three found themselves locked out, but the biggest rammed the heel of his bare foot against the door, and it flew inward with a crash. They entered, showered, shaved, ordered food sent up, dressed, and the apish-looking man went down to pay the bill. The clerk was surprised that his ugly guest no longer wore a moustache, and he noted several other lost characteristics. But he said nothing except the customary pleasantries.

The three drove off with Barney, in the back seat, operating the shortwave set.

"Trish says that Lady Grandrith has disappeared," Barney said. "She tried to phone her, didn't get an answer, and went over to see for herself if anything was wrong. She saw two suspicious-looking characters hanging around and went in the back way. A guy tried to knife her on the second floor; she broke his arm and stuck his own knife in his ribs; but he got away. Clio wasn't in her room. She hadn't packed; so if she took off it was in a hurry. Trish'll keep trying to get into contact with her."

Doc Caliban took the microphone and said, "Trish! We'll let you know, in the usual way, when we've arrived. But you send a message to Grandrith. Tell him to come to Salisbury by way of Bournemouth. Make the arrangements; we'll have somebody meet him if he can make it. Tell him the Nine will be at Stonehenge. If he can get there, he should do so by all means. The end of the world may come if Iwaldi isn't stopped."

Trish had a husky voice that sent delicious chills up a man's spine. "O.K., Doc. I gave my love to Barney. Tell that big ape Pauncho I love him—like a sister. Please hurry. It's so lonely, especially since Clio disappeared. We didn't see each other, but we did have phone conversations now and then."

"We'll be there soon. So long," Doc said, and handed the microphone back to Barney.

"That's the first time I ever heard Trish complain," Barney said. The tension is really getting her down. But then she's been through so much for so long. Ever since that nut that thought he was Tarzan kidnapped her. Things have been coming one after the other, like bad news was an endless snake, a Midgard serpent."

Barney put on a fake beard and thick glasses and took over the driving while Pauncho and Caliban crouched down on the floor after covering themselves with blankets. Barney drove through Karlskopf slowly. If there were any agents of the Nine here, they would see only a hairy-faced old man who looked as if he taught philosophy at the University of Heidelberg. Moreover, the license plates on the Benz had been changed, so that if the agents knew the old number, they would see at a glance that this could not be Caliban's car.

Once out of Karlskopf, the two got up off the floor. Barney kept on driving, headed toward Kieselsfuss, a small town which had an airstrip nearby.

The following day, three men met near Charing Cross station. Each had come in on a separate airliner, twenty minutes apart. Each was disguised. They took the taxi to Marylebone Borough, went past the building where Clio Cloamby, Lady Grandrith, had a room, and stopped outside another building six blocks away. They were confident that they had not been tailed. They removed their suitcases and went into the building. After the taxi had left, they came out, walked two blocks, flagged down another taxi, and drove off to an apartment on Portobello Road. They were admitted by the doorman, who had been told to expect them, went up the elevator to the third floor, and knocked on Trish's door. She opened it and was in Doc's arms and kissing him, though complaining about the bristly salt-and-pepper moustache he was wearing.

"I don't have one," Pauncho said. "Here, give us a kiss."

"Both of you?" Trish said, turning and grabbing Pauncho around the neck.

"Yeah, I'm man enough to make two," Pauncho said.

"Two gorillas, maybe," Barney said. "Kiss me first, Trish. I come in second to no *Pan satyrus*. And speaking of pans, did you ever see an uglier one?"

"You two remind me so much of your fathers!" Trish said. She hugged and kissed them both and a few tears ran down her cheeks. "It's almost like having them back again!"

Barney and Pauncho did not look too pleased, though they knew that Trish meant nothing derogatory. Also, it was still difficult for them to realize that Patricia Wilde, though she looked a fresh twenty-five, had been born in 1911 and that their fathers had courted her.

Doc and the others began to remove their disguises. In a short time, they would put on others, and Trish would become a blue-eyed ash blonde, concealing her bronzish yellow-flecked eyes and deep metallic auburn hair, so much like her cousin's.

"Well, at least you don't have to conceal that superb build!" Pauncho said, as she put on a Kelly green miniskirt. "And them legs! Whoo! Whoo!" He blew her a kiss. "I'm sure glad you didn't inherit the Grandrith muscles!"

"I did," she said. "But their quality, not their quantity, as you well know, you big orangutan. Just don't ever get fresh with me again, unless I tell you you can."

Barney grinned when Pauncho blushed. Pauncho had been high on something—vodka, which he loved on the rocks or rum-soaked pot, which he also loved, or maybe both—when he had lost his inhibitions about Trish and tried to make love to her. Trish had been in a bad mood that night—she and Doc had had an argument—and she had thrown Pauncho's three hundred and twenty pounds over her back and halfway across the room. Pauncho had acted as Krazy Kat does when Ignatz Mouse brains her with a brick, that is, as if violence and pain expressed deepest love. He had come back for more and gotten it, this time knocking plaster off the wall with his head as he sailed through the air for a short distance.

"Don't look so sheepish," Trish said. "You know I love you," and she slapped him on the back. Pauncho leaped into the air, bellowing with pain. Barney laughed so hard he fell on the floor. Doc had taken off his shirt and undershirt, revealing the patches of pseudoprotein on his back and chest. He smiled slightly and said, "Take it easy when you touch us, Trish."

An hour later, the first one left the building. No one who had seen any of them enter would have recognized them, though the simian body and features of Pauncho and the giant body of Caliban were difficult to disguise. Doc, however, was a bent-over old man with the palsy, and Pauncho looked like a fat middle-aged man with definitely feminine characteristics. Barney wore a waxed handlebar moustache and very long sideburns. His eyes bulged out as if he had goiter disease. Trish was a blonde with a big nose and big ears.

None of their disguises were designed to make them merge into the woodwork. They did not care if they were noticed as long as they were not recognized. They left at intervals of ten minutes apart and took taxis to Charing Cross station. They went into the restrooms and when they emerged they had shed their former disguises. Now Doc was a big American mulatto tourist with a camera hung from his neck. Pauncho was a rather brutal-looking turbaned Sikh. Barney was a racetrack toff. It hurt him to dress so flashily, since he had inherited his father's delight in sartorial elegance. Trish was a bulky-bodied, wattle-chinned, dowdily dressed, middle-aged woman with messy gray hair.

As she passed Doc, she said, "Called Clio. No answer."

Doc Caliban took a taxi to a rental car agency and, using the forged papers and credit cards, rented an automobile under the name of Mr. Joshua King. He drove away, picked up the others one by one at different places and then drove into a large warehouse. A man wheeled several large boxes on a cart out of an office. Doc gave him some money after the boxes were loaded into the trunk of the big Cadillac.

Mr. Sargent was a tall, thin, heavily moustached, middle-aged man. He had once been one of the best safecrackers in the world, operating in the States and England. Doc had caught him one night when he was trying to open a safe in Doc's laboratory in the Empire State Building. Doc had taken him to the Lake George sanatorium after finding out who had hired him. He had performed the usual operation, implanting a microcircuit in his brain and then putting him through a series of hypnotic treatments. The man was unable thereafter to crack safes, even under legitimate circumstances. He got a job as a salesman for burglar alarm systems and seemed well on the way to being a completely honest citizen. But, as had happened more than once before, the ex-criminal backslid. Not into his former profession. That was forever barred to him. Sargent became a dope addict and a pusher. To raise money for his habit, he became a lowly stickup man.

Doc Caliban heard about him and again sent him to his sanatorium. He cured him of his dope habit and gave him more hypnotic treatments. Sargent went to England to work as manager of a warehouse which Caliban owned in London. (Caliban owned businesses all over the world.) He was one of Doc's most trusted agents. He had done much for Caliban when Caliban was in the Nine but the Nine did not know of his existence (as far as Doc knew).

Sargent was also the last man on whom Doc had ever operated to change his criminal ways. It was just too discouraging to implant a repulsion against one form of criminality only to have the man take up another. Or, sometimes, to go insane from, apparently, a subconscious conflict.

Sargent pulled an envelope from his coat pocket and handed it to Caliban. "Gilligan not only saw them getting off an airliner, he took their photos," he said.

Doc opened the envelope. Pauncho, looking over his broad shoulder, said, "Cobbs! And Barbara!"

Trish looked over Doc's shoulder, too. "No wonder you said she was so beautiful! Makes me jealous just to look at her!"

"She looks a lot like you," Pauncho said. "That's why I flipped over her."

"I heard him say he'd leave anybody, even you, for her," Barney said.

"You should've been a lawyer like your father," Pauncho snarled. "The truth is not in you."

Doc turned the photo over. On the back was the address of a Carlton House Terrace mansion.

"They left yesterday, late last night," Sargent said. "Crothers didn't know where. He asked around but the servants were mum."

"Salisbury," Caliban said.

A minute later, the four drove out with Caliban at the wheel. The trip was mainly occupied with telling Trish what had happened at Gramzdorf and with Doc going over their plans for Stonehenge. Pauncho kept coming back to Barbara Villiers as if he could not believe that she could be guilty of collaboration with Iwaldi.

"That Cobbs cat, yeah, he's pretty oily. I could believe it of him. But that Barbara, she's just too beautiful to be anything other than an angel. Besides, Doc, you haven't got any real proof! Maybe Iwaldi is forcing them to help him. They know what he's capable of; they don't want to be tortured."

"They could go to the police," Trish said.

"A man with Iwaldi's connections and organization could get them, police protection or not," Barney said.

"I had Sargent check them out at the university," Caliban said. "A Villiers and a Cobbs are on leave from the archaeology department. Their photos resemble those of the Cobbs and Villiers we know. But they're not the same. And the university said they're supposed to be digging in Austria, not Germany."

"What do you make of that?" Pauncho said. He did not ask Caliban if he was sure. Caliban never made a statement unless he was sure or he had defined it as speculation.

An hour later, they pulled into a farm off the highway and drove the Cadillac into the barn. Leaving by the back door, they went down a tree-covered path to a small hangar on the edge of a meadow. The two men here assured Caliban that the plane was ready.

On the way, they disguised themselves again. Doc was an English businessman with brown hair and eyes, a crooked nose, and a walrus moustache. Trish became a housewife with a more conservative mini-skirt. Barney and Pauncho became informally dressed Americans.

Forty miles from the southern coast, the gray day suddenly became gray night. The plane flew into a dense fog, and from then on it was on instruments. They circled a while above the airport at Salisbury and then made a perfect landing.

"How long has this fog been here, Doc?" Trish said.

"Since two days ago. It's extraordinary for it to go so far inland for so long. The papers have been full of stories of letters from cranks who insist that a coven of witches near Amesbury are responsible for it. Or so the radio says. I wouldn't be surprised if old Anana had something to do with it. Not with the coven. With the fog. She's the most ancient and most powerful of witches."

They were tramping down the sidewalk to report in at the office before driving away. Trish could not see his face, so she did not know if he was kidding or not. Her cousin was not the least bit superstitious, but he admitted that some superstitions might turn out not to be such.

"Whatever is responsible for the fog," Doc said, "it'll suit the purpose of the Nine fine. They can hold the funeral of XauXaz without being observed. Of course, the Nine can bring enough pressure so they could get Stonehenge to themselves even during the winter solstice tomorrow. But this way nobody will be spying on them with binoculars. The good thing about it is, we'll have a better chance to get close to them."

"And Iwaldi'll have a better chance to sneak in a bomb," Pauncho said.

"Everything has its checks and balances," Barney said. "Except maybe you, Pauncho. Aren't you overdrawn at the bank?"

"My patience is overdrawn!"

While at the airport, Doc showed an official a photo of Cobbs and Villiers and asked if they had landed there that day. The official said no, not while he was on duty. Doc was satisfied that they had probably motored down, unless the official had been bribed to deny that they had flown in, or unless the two had been disguised.

Caliban did not plan to send his people around to hotels in Salisbury and Amesbury to find out if any of the Nine were staying there. It would arouse suspicion, since it could be assumed that the servants of the Nine would be looking for too-nosy strangers. Also, it was doubtful that any of the Nine would trust themselves to a hotel. With their immense wealth, they probably owned houses all over England. These would be left unoccupied most of the time, waiting for whenever the owners needed them.

They got two hotel rooms under their aliases, Mr. and Mrs. Clark and John Booth and William Dunlap. A half hour later, a man phoned in a message for Mr. Clark. It was from a Mr. T. Lord (the T. was for Tree) and said he and his party would be arriving at Bournemouth at the stipulated time. The landing would be made at the agreed-upon spot.

Caliban called the two men in. "We'll go up to Stonehenge late tonight after we get some sleep," he said. "You'll go with us, Pauncho, but you'll leave as soon as you know how to get back to us. Then you'll go to Bournemouth. Crothers will handle the first meeting with Grandrith; you'll pick him up and bring him to us. Barney, Trish, and I and six of my men will be waiting for you to join us."

When they awoke—having put themselves to sleep with the hypnotic techniques taught them by Caliban—they were refreshed. They ate and dressed and then left the hotel. Their equipment had remained in a rented Rolls Royce. Two more cars, filled with men and equipment, joined them. They drove away swiftly in the fog with Doc at the wheel of the first car, watching the big radar screen he had affixed to the instrument panel. They drove on A360 out of Salisbury and in fifteen minutes had slowed down for a right turn onto A303(T). They could see the signposts quite clearly when they were close because they were wearing the blacklight projectors and the goggles. Doc drove onto the side of the road near a fence a few yards past the junction and stopped. The goggles enabled them to see the ancient burial mounds, the long barrows beyond the fence.

Doc advanced cautiously, a mass detector held out before him. Pauncho held a small box with several other instruments before him, and others carried shovels and pickaxes and weapons. They went over the fence on a folding stile brought from the car and walked about twenty yards past the barrow. Here two men started digging.

Others made several trips back to the cars, each time bringing parts of a device switch that, put together by Doc, made a metal box two feet high, four feet broad, and six feet long. Two short antennae stuck out of the top of the box. The device went into a hole and was covered with dirt with the antenna tips barely sticking up.

"No doubt the Nine have already buried theirs or will soon," Doc said. "And if Iwaldi shows, he'll bury his somewhere around here. Which one of us activates his first is anybody's guess. But you can bet it'll be some hours before the ceremony starts."

He stuck a device in his pocket. When the time came for it to be used, it would activate the buried equipment, which was an atomic-powered generator of an extremely powerful inductive field. In its field of influence, a cone-shaped beam with a range of a mile and a half, metal objects turned hot. Copper wires and aluminum wires would eventually melt. Gasoline was ignited and explosives were detonated because of their metal containers. Radar and heat-detectors would be unusable in its field because the circuits would melt and then the cases, if they were thin.

Doc had already ascertained that no one in the party had any metal fillings in his teeth or metal plates in his skull.

Tomorrow, when the ceremony began, the only weapons would be the baseball bats, plastic knives, crossbows, and the gas grenades that Doc had brought along. They were wearing plastic helmets and chain mail under their clothes. The crossbows were of wood and plastic and gut, a small type with a pistol-like butt held in one hand. They fired wooden bolts with sharp plastic tips.

If the fog held, the battle would be conducted by almost blind soldiers.

Doc looked at his Watch and then removed it. A man was putting everything metal in a bag which would be taken away in a car.

Pauncho shook Barney's and Doc's hands and kissed Trish before he left. He hated to go, but he did not complain. If Doc wanted him to carry out his mission, so be it.

"We won't be staying here," Doc said, "since the Nine will undoubtedly send men through here ahead of them. We'll be hiding out across the road north of Stonehenge. But I'll be back by the long barrow by the time you return with Grandrith's party, unless something prevents me. In which case you and Grandrith just come on up to the ruins. That'll be where it's at."

Pauncho drove off. The other cars were driven away to a point half a mile away along A303(T) to the west. Doc figured that they would be outside the range of all three of the inductors he expected to be operating by morning. The men would bicycle back on the plastic collapsible vehicles they had brought along in the trunks of the cars. The others had been unloaded.

They waited. Presently, they heard footsteps and issued soft challenges, ready to fire if they proved to be the enemy. But the proper codeword—Pongo—was returned, and the men joined them. Then they went across the field, blindly, the wet grayness allowing them to see only a few inches. They carried their weapons in their hands and packs on their backs. These contained pup tents, which could be folded into the space of a large box of kitchen matches, and cans of self-heating food and water and medical kits.

After a walk of about four-fifths of a mile, they came to the fence along A344. They crossed it and the road and went over another fence into a field near the Fargo Plantation and The Cursus, that strange roadway that the builders of Stonehenge had made. There they bedded down for the night.

"The servants of the Nine will be poking around," Doc said, "but they'll probably confine their scouting to the triangle formed by the three main roads. Then the old ones will be coming in their plastic steam-driven cars—my invention, ironically enough, and made for just such occasions—and they'll start the ceremony, fog or no fog. They won't be able to bury XauXaz in the circle of Stonehenge. Not even the Nine could do that without causing embarrassing questions. So they'll probably bury him someplace close by."

"Why hold the ceremony here?" Trish said. "I thought XauXaz was at least 10,000 years old when Stonehenge was built. What's his association with it?"

"I don't know. Stonehenge was built in three phases from about 1900 B.C. to about 1600 B.C. by the Wessex People (so named by the archaeologists). It may have been built as a temple to some deity. No one knows except the Nine. It does seem that, whatever else the *rude, enormous monoliths* were, they did form a sort of calendar to predict seasons, and they could be used to predict lunar and solar eclipses. Those circles of monoliths and trilithons made a prehistoric computer.

"XauXaz may have been a living god of the Wessex People. He may have supervised the building of Stonehenge. His name would not then have been XauXaz, since this was a primitive Germanic name meaning *High*. In fact, our English word *high* is directly evolved from XauXaz. But primitive Germanic did not even exist then. It hadn't developed out of Indo-Hittite yet."

After a system of guards were arranged, they got into their sleeping bags. At 5 A.M., Doc was awakened to stand his watch, the length of which was determined by the time it took sand to fill the bottom of an hourglass. He squatted on top of his sleeping bag by the fence for a while, then got up and walked slowly back and forth. The fog showed no sign of thinning out; he was in a cold and wet world without light. Though his party was only a few feet away, he could not see them. He could see nothing. He could hear the snores of a few men and, once, far off, muffled by the fog, the barking of a farm dog. This was the world after death, and he was a soul floating around in the mists of eternity, cut off from the sight and touch of other beings but tortured by being able to hear them in the distance.

When would the struggle stop? When would the killing cease? When would he be able to live as he wished; peacefully, studying, researching, inventing devices to help mankind?

Probably never. The only long-lasting peace was in death.

His sense of time was almost perfect. When he lit a match and held it by the hourglass, he saw that only a few grains remained in the upper part. The match went out, and suddenly the activator in his pants pocket began to get warm. He knew then that either the Nine or Iwaldi were in the area and had turned on an inductor. He removed the activator from his pocket with his bare hand, since it was not yet too hot to hold. He pressed its button and then threw it into the fog. It had done its work and its circuits would, in a few minutes, be melting.

He awoke everybody and told them what was happening. They bundled up their bags and ate a light breakfast from their cans. About fifteen minutes after Doc had noticed the activator's warmth, they heard shouts down the road.

They went over the fence, which was becoming hot, and ran across the road to the fence on the other side. After climbing over this, which was by then red-hot, they proceeded slowly along it. It was the only guide to the east. If it were out of sight, they could just as easily have turned around and gone westward or southward within a few steps.

Doc suddenly stopped and held up his gloved hand, though those behind him could not see it until they had bumped into him. More shouts and a few screams had come from ahead. He estimated that their sources were about a hundred yards away, but it was difficult to be accurate because of the distortions caused by the heavy fog. Underneath the cries was a strange note, a heavy grinding noise.

He moved on, and within a few yards he thought he could identify the strange noise. It was the growling of many dogs.

It would be a good thing to use dogs in this fog. They could not see, but they could smell, and this would lead them quickly to the enemy.

But the hemispherical devices could not be used because of the inductive fields. The metal in the circuits of the hemispheres and the controlling boxes and the wires inserted into the brains would get too hot. The dogs were being used without cerebral regulators.

His guess was confirmed a moment later when a dog yelped sharply. He went on, and then two more dogs cried out in agony. The crack of clubs against bone and flesh pierced the fog. And then a loud boom made them stop.

"They must be out of their minds, using grenades!" Trish said. "They have to be throwing blindly!"

Doc Caliban did not think that they were so insane. As long as a group stayed closely together, so that its members knew that the others were in an area near him, they could throw the grenades anywhere else. They could hope that the little bombs would strike by chance among the enemy.

He pulled from the bulging pocket of his jacket one of the tennis-ball-sized plastic gas grenades. He twisted the pin in its north pole to the left and then yanked it out and heaved the grenade into the fog. Six seconds later, a roar and a faint orange flash came through the fog.

He removed another grenade and pulled the pin but he never had a chance to throw it. Dark figures suddenly appeared ahead of him. And something struck him in the shoulder and spun him around.

He staggered backward then. His shoulder and arm felt as if they had been cut off. But he knew even in the shock that a bolt from a small crossbow had hit him. The plastic chain mail beneath its covering of shirt and jacket had kept the plastic point from piercing him. The shock of the impact from the bolt, fired at about five feet or so, had paralyzed his side for a moment.

He had dropped the grenade, and it had rolled to one side out of his sight. He staggered back away from where he thought it was, shouting to the others to run. They did not hear him because they were struggling with the people who had run into them.

The grenade had bounced and rolled further away than he had

expected. It split the fog in a blaze of light and a wave that half-deafened Caliban. He saw the body of a man flying, turning as it arced toward him, its legs and arms spread out as if it were sky diving. The body struck near him, but the light was gone, and he could not see it.

A large man, striking out with a baseball bat, sprang at him. Doc jumped to one side, lost the man, jumped back in as the man was turning around to locate him or perhaps to make sure that no one was sneaking up on him. Doc still could not use his right arm, but his left drove in with the plastic dagger he had pulled from its sheath on his belt, and the sharp point went over the man's raised right arm and into his jugular vein. Doc stepped back, pulling the knife out, whirled in case anybody was behind him, crouched, and caught another man in the throat as this man flew out of the fog. The man dropped his crossbow. Doc picked it up—he suddenly remembered having dropped his when the bolt hit him—and he waited. Because he was still partly deafened, the sounds of battle came dimly from all around him: shouts, snarls, shrieks, bats hitting helmets and flesh or other bats, the twang of a released crossbow string, the grunt of a man hit with something.

Then a woman came running through the fog, and Doc, instead of shooting, threw himself in a football player's block at her legs and knocked her over. Then he was sitting on Barbara Villiers' chest and twisting her wrist with his left hand to force her to drop her dagger.

Another figure shot out of the fog. Doc knocked Barbara out with a left to the jaw and sprang up and rammed his head into that man's stomach.

The man went, *"Oof!"* and staggered back. A released crossbow gut twanged and the bolt touched his ear, burning it. The crossbow fell to the ground, and then the man was on the ground. Doc's left hand gripped the man's throat and squeezed just as the point of a plastic dagger drove through his shirt into the chain mail undershirt. The dagger fell, and the man choked and then became still. However, he was not dead. Even in the gray wetness, Doc Caliban had recognized the man was Carlos Cobbs. His hair was short and yellowish, and his nose was long and his chin too jutting. But the gait had been Cobbs'. Even though he had had only a second to see his manner of carrying himself, he had identified it.

Trish loomed out of the pearly mists. She put her mouth close to his ear, and said, "You deaf, Doc?"

"Partly. But my hearing is coming back. I'm taping these two up. Get her before she comes to, will you?"

Carlos Cobbs, sitting on the ground and bending over, his wrists bound behind him, coughed and choked for a minute. Finally he gasped, "So it's you, Caliban! I thought . . . !"

"Thought what?" Caliban said. He was squatting so he could see Cobbs' expressions better.

He had to keep twisting his neck to look around because the struggle around him, though much diminished, was still going on. From the shouts he could hear, as the victors identified themselves to others, his men seemed to be winning. Then Barney Banks appeared with the announcement that the group they'd run into had either been killed or had run off into the fog. As far as he could tell, they had three men left who could fight, not counting Trish, and Caliban and himself, of course.

"You started to say that you thought that . . . ?" Doc Caliban said to Cobbs.

"Never mind that!" Cobbs said. "Let me go! And you get out of here! Fast! If you don't, we'll all get killed! I'm telling you this because I have to! Get out of here!"

"Why?" Caliban said. Cobbs did not seem to be acting; his voice shook with urgency and with dread.

Barbara suddenly sat up. She said, "You fool! He's left a bomb back there that'll go off in fifteen minutes, in less now, and blow everybody for a half a mile around to kingdom come!"

"That's right!" Cobbs said. "It'll take the Nine with it! They'll not get away this time! Anana and Ing and Yeshua and Shaumbim and Jiizfan and Tilatoc, they'll all go out in a blaze of glory! And I, I will have done it! Listen, Caliban, we don't have time to talk about this here! We have to get going! Now! I've got plastic bicycles waiting on the road and we can get away on them to my steam cars only a quarter mile down the road and get out of here before the bomb goes off! Don't delay, man! I cut it close as it was, too close! But I didn't want them to get suspicious and take off! You know how Anana is! She's got a nose for anything that smells of death!"

A grenade cracked about forty yards behind him. More screams and yells.

Brightness dispelled some of the fog high up in the mists. (The flare was non-metallic, of course.) Doc could see for at least a hundred feet. Shadowy figures struggled at the edge of his vision, and then, when he turned his head, the flare died.

"We could all take off and talk at my leisure," Doc Caliban said. "But friends of mine are out there fighting, and if we ran they'd die with the Nine. They might say that the sacrifice would be worth it. But I can't ask them, and if I could, I wouldn't. You tell me what kind of bomb it is and where we can find it. Now! Either I stop it from going off or we all die!"

"You stupid mortal!" Cobbs screamed. "What do you care what happens to your friends if you can live forever? Listen, I can get you the elixir! I'll give you the formula! I know you've been cut off, and that the ageing has started! And you'll die in a few years because you'll never have the elixir unless one of . . . The Nine gives it to you!"

"One of . . . us?" Caliban said. "What's your part in this, Cobbs? It's obvious you're hand in hand with Iwaldi. You were just pretending to be prisoners of Iwaldi, for some reason I can't comprehend, unless it was to infiltrate into my organization and catch us all when you had us cold."

"Time's running out!" Cobbs said, his voice cracking. "Would you throw away eternity, man?"

Caliban reached out and pulled Cobbs' large nose loose. It came off with a slight tearing sound, and the rest of the pseudoskin over his face followed. When the wig came off, the Cobbs he knew looked out of the fog.

Barbara Villiers said, "For God's sake, Caliban! We don't have time to play around! Get us out of here and then we'll give you whatever you want! The elixir! The map of the caves of the Nine and the traps set in it! Even some of the addresses of the Nine, though they won't go near there anymore, of course, unless they think we're all dead!"

"For two who are just candidates, or maybe just servants, you know a great deal," Caliban said. "Old Iwaldi must have taken you into his deepest confidences. By the way, where is Iwaldi? He wouldn't have let you go running off while he fought a rearguard action. Not old Iwaldi. He may be a mad goblin, but he's not that mad. Unless he thinks you double-crossed him figuring to blow him up with the rest of the Nine and then you two would take over. Did you plan on carrying out his ideas, releasing the phytoplankton bomb? Or did you plan to kill him so you could stop that but still get the elixir and his wealth?"

Cobbs bent over so he could get his face closer to Caliban's. His features were twisted with agony, and the moisture on his face seemed to be even heavier than the fog droplets could account for.

"Get us out of here, and I'll tell you where you can lay your hands on Iwaldi!"

"You'd betray him?"

"Why not? He'd betray anyone if it meant saving his life!"

"Where is he?"

Barbara Villiers' voice cracked, too. "We can't tell you at this moment. He sent us in to do his dirty work for him. But we'll show you where you can ambush him. Just get us out of here!"

"What kind of bomb?" Caliban said.

"It's a heavy irradiated plastic box containing the explosive in liquid form! The dial and the time mechanism are all plastic or hard wood, too! I set it to go off in fifteen minutes! The mechanism pulls a pin out of a vial of plastic containing the gas that'll mix with the liquid and set it off! There won't be anybody living left within a half a mile radius and it'll kill many outside that area! The stone monuments of Stonehenge will be knocked down and maybe shattered! Old XauXaz's body and his coffin and the stones he set up as a temple for the sun god—himself—will be gone! Along with the rest of the Nine! Even old Anana, who said she was going to defeat death!"

"Who's fighting the Nine out there?" Caliban said. "Or are they blundering around fighting among themselves? Grandrith can't be responsible for all that!"

"I left most of my men there to hold them, keep them occupied!"

"Doublecrossing your own men, too? Well, that's to be expected, *Iwaldi!*"

Trish and Barney said, "What?"

Villiers gasped. Cobbs' jaw dropped.

"He can do what I can do," Caliban said. "He has enough control of his muscles to pull his spine and add or subtract inches to his height. I've done it plenty of times myself. It takes much practice and knowledge. But what I can do in my short lifetime, Iwaldi has had many lifetimes to learn."

He pulled on Cobbs' nose and when that would not come pulled on the skin of the face and then on the dark hair.

"That won't do any good, you fool!" Barbara Villiers said. "That is his own skin and hair! The old goblin you knew was the false one! The wrinkled skin and the redshot eyes and the long white hair and beard, those were the fakes! They were true enough once, but when he regained his youth—"

"Shut up!" Iwaldi yelled.

"We haven't got time to carry this deception out!" Villiers said. "Besides, there's no sense in not telling him that we have the rejuvenation elixir. He won't leave us here to die if he knows that he has to take us away to get the elixir! You should have known that, you greedy old man! It was our main card, and you've wasted too much time holding out! It may be too late because of your stupidity!"

"You can't talk to me that way, my dear Countess Cleveland!"

Caliban's eyebrows went up. He said, "Then Barney was telling the truth, not kidding you as he thought he was, when he said you must be the Lady Castlemaine whose petticoats hanging out to dry made Pepys flip? Charles the Second's mistress, mother of his three sons? You did not die as history said, but you used makeup to look as if you were getting older and then you pretended to die and some woman died so that you could be buried, and you—"

"Yes!" Barbara Villiers snarled. "Yes! How many candidates have done that? Hundreds, thousands? You and Grandrith are my own descendants! My grandson had a child by a Grandrith woman; so I'm your many times great-grandmother! For the sake of us all, for the sake of eternal life for you and your friends, and for me, your ancestress, get us out of here! You will not only have eternal life but eternal youth!"

"I appropriated your notes, after you turned against us," Iwaldi said. "I knew you'd been working on rejuvenation and I hired the best scientists in the world to develop the elixir from the information in your notes. One did develop it, and I got rid of him in an 'accident.' In two years' time, I became a young man again! The wrinkles and the white hair and the ropy veins disappeared! But I used makeup so that the others would not know! But . . . *must* I talk away our lives! Let's get out of here! Plenty of time for talk later!"

The old man—now turned young man—knew that even if he was taken out of the explosion area, he was in grave danger from Caliban. But he was wily, and he had survived so many millennia by being more tricky than his contemporaries. He must have something up his sleeve besides sheer desperation.

"It's too late!" Barbara Villiers wailed. "We can't get away in time now!"

"Then give me the combination!" Caliban said.

"Why not *make* him do it?" Trish said.

There was the sound of running feet nearby, a twang, a cry, and a man slid across the cold wet winter grass on his face. He stopped so close to Caliban that he could see the crossbow bolt sticking out of the back of his neck.

"We might not even be able to find the bomb!" Caliban said. "Quickly, Iwaldi! The combination! It does have a combination to turn it off, I hope?"

"If I tell you, you'll kill me!" Iwaldi said. The voice of Cobbs had become the familiar deep growling voice of Iwaldi. The panic and the cracking were gone.

"I promise to release you and Villiers," Caliban said. "After you give me the formulae, of course. But my word is not to be given lightly and will not be broken. I will let you two go free, give you twelve hours' headstart, after which I will try to kill you, Iwaldi. Villiers can go with you if she chooses, in which case I'll try to kill her, too. But if she wants to work with me, and I decide I can trust her, well, I don't like the idea of breaking the neck of my own grandmother several times removed, even if she's so distant I couldn't possibly have any of her genes."

"Talk our lives away!" Villiers said. "Iwaldi, tell him the combination! Now! There isn't much time left! He doesn't even know where the bomb is! He may not even be able to get to it in time!"

"Hey, Doc! Trish! Barney!" a deep grunting voice said somewhere in the fog. "Pongo! Pongo!"

"Pongo! Pongo! You hairy ape!" Barney called out joyfully. "This way!"

The squat and monstrous form of Pauncho van Veelar appeared. He rolled toward them and then stopped. "What the hell's going on? Cobbs! Barbara!"

Barney capsuled what had happened, but Doc listened to Iwaldi.

"There are ten numbers on the dial," Iwaldi said. "You set the dial on each number from 1 to 10. Then go right to 3. Then back to 9. If you do that in time, you can make the mechanism push the pin back into the gas vial container. *But* you'll have to *push in* on the dial while you're working the combination. Push in hard! If you don't, the mechanism not only won't reinsert the pin, it'll pull the pin immediately. And you'll have to keep the pressure applied for five minutes after you have worked the combination."

"Why all those provisions?" Caliban said.

"You never know when they can be used to your advantage. Now, if I could have gotten away in time, you would have set off the explosion trying to stop it. But it didn't work out that way. Also—"

"Never mind. Later." Doc stood up, then said, "Pauncho, where's Grandrith?"

"Out there. I left him to find you. Why weren't you at the long barrow?"

"I sent Rickson to meet you."

"He must've been killed before he got there."

"Watch these two," Doc Caliban said. "I'm going after the bomb. Watch for Grandrith."

He picked up a crossbow, fitted a bolt to the string and pulled it back to the third notch and locked it. Then he walked off into the fog while Trish said, "Doc! I want to go with you!"

He did not answer. He did not want to be hampered. He ran back and forth, bent over, looking at the ground between glances on all sides. No grenades had burst for several minutes, but the crack of bats and yells were still filtering through the woody dampness. And then, as the dim figure of a trilithon—two upright stones with a third laid across them—solidified out of the grayness, he saw a body with a plastic shovel beside it. There were other bodies near it, but this one was the one that Iwaldi had told him to look for. It was that of the man who had dug the hole into which the bomb had been put. A bolt from out of the fog had caught him in the right eye as he straightened up, and he had fallen across the heap of dirt.

Caliban rolled him over and then began digging. The box was buried under a few inches of dirt, so it did not take him long to unearth it from its chalky cavity. While he was working, the grayness became luminous, as if the sun had appeared and was striving to burn the fog away. At the same time, a grenade boomed about thirty yards away, and he dived for the ground. He was up at once but heard cries from near the ruins. He faced toward the trilithon but kept on digging. Then he got down on his knees and pried out the box. It was about eleven inches square and was smooth except for the dial and the numbers around it on its top.

He had to bend close to distinguish the numbers, which was lucky for him. A bolt whizzed over his head. Two figures, interlocked, whirled by him and were swallowed up in the grayness. One of them cried out a minute later, and then Doc heard footsteps on the wet earth. He wanted to start working the combination, because he had no idea of how much time was left before the pin would be entirely pulled out of the detonating gas container. But he could not start turning the dial unless he knew that he would not be disturbed. If he had to release the pressure, he and everybody here were done for.

The man suddenly came out of the fog. Doc said, "Pongo?" and the man cursed and jumped back. Doc could not afford to wait any longer; he fired at where the man had been, aiming so the bolt would hit the belly, if it hit at all.

The gut twanged; the bolt leaped out; a thud came; a man groaned. And immediately after, Doc heard the slight squishing of feet in wet earth and the rustle of weeds. He turned, and a giant was on him, striking out at him with a baseball bat.

Doc hurled the box at him. The man ducked but not quickly enough. He staggered as the impact sent him back, and then Doc was at him with his plastic knife in his left hand. His right arm had recovered enough for him to use it, but it was still far from having regained all its strength. The giant stepped up to him and swung with both hands on the bat, bringing it around so that it caught Doc against the side of his helmet even though he had almost ducked entirely under it. Doc saw phosphene streaks but kept on lunging, and his knife drove up. The man had dropped the club after it glanced off Doc's helmet and had put out his hands. The knife went through one; the giant roared. Doc jerked the knife out. The man brought his knee up and caught Doc in the chest. If it had hit him in the chin, it would have shattered even his massive bones. The man was wearing irradiated plastic knee guards.

The knee hurt Doc's chest and knocked the wind out of him. But his right arm closed around the leg, and he brought the knife up between the man's legs. It tore the man's pocket and slid off the plastic groinguard and then off the plastic chain mail around his leg. The man brought both fists down against the top of Doc's helmet, half-stunning him. The man howled, because the blow had hurt his fist hand. But Doc fell backward, not knowing exactly what was going on. The dagger did not fall from his hand; many years of fighting had built in a conditional reflex so that he would have had to be entirely unconscious or dead before his hand would have relaxed. And his wind quickly came back.

The giant charged in, roaring. Doc Caliban rolled over, not realizing consciously what he was doing, and he was out of sight of the man. But a few seconds later, the giant thrust out of the fog, and seeing Doc starting to get onto his feet, cried, "No, you don't!" and rushed him, his huge hands clasped to bring them down on top of Caliban's helmet again.

Doc bent his legs and leaped outward as if he had been shot from a cannon in a circus. His head drove into the man's big paunch with an impact that did not help Doc regain his senses. But the breath went out of the man—who must have weighed three hundred and thirty—and he went backward. Stunned, Doc did not act as quickly as he should have, and the man, though struggling for breath, knocked the dagger from Caliban's hand with a blow of his arm against Caliban's wrist.

Their faces were close enough that Doc could distinguish his features in the milky grayness.

"Krotonides!" Doc said.

He was one of the candidates, a bodyguard for old Ing. Doc had seen him a number of times at the caves during the annual ceremonies. He had endured the boastings of Krotonides that he was the strongest and fastest human in the world when it came to hand-to-hand combat and that Caliban's reputation was overrated.

"Caliban!" Krotonides said. His dark, big-nosed, bushy-eye-browed face hung in the fog. "I always said I could take you!"

Caliban's hand with fingers stiffly extended stabbed him in the eye, and Krotonides bellowed with agony. He rolled away, but as Caliban got to his feet the giant leaped out of the fog, his hands in the classical position to deliver a karate chop.

Doc snatched off his helmet and threw it with all the force of his left arm and the body behind it. There was a thud, and Krotonides staggered, slowly rotating around and around, while dark blood gushed from his nose, which had been almost severed by the sharp edge of the helmet. Caliban moved in swiftly though not incautiously, since Krotonides was still a very dangerous man. Before he could reach him, three figures advanced through the mists, and he felt it discreet to withdraw. Besides, he had to get to the box as quickly as possible.

Suddenly, he heard steps behind him. He whirled and then a rumbling voice said, "Pongo! Pongo!"

"Pongo! It's me, Doc," Caliban said. "Help me find that bomb before it's too late!"

The three men had been engulfed in the fog, but they were still in the immediate neighborhood, so Doc and Pauncho had to keep an eye out for them. Doc hoped that none of them would toss out a grenade in their general direction.

Pauncho suddenly cursed, and then he said, "I fell over it, Doc! Hey, Doc! Quick! Over here!"

Caliban found him squatting by the box with his crossbow ready. Caliban got down on his knees and put his face close to the face of the dial. "I'm starting now," he said. "Once I get going, I can't stop. I have to hang on to this for five minutes at least. So you'll have to handle anybody that shows up. But as soon as I get the combination worked, we'll run away from here. I can hang on to the box. We'll worry about killing the old geezers some other time."

He started to turn the dials, stopping them briefly on each number, starting with 1, advancing to 2 when the mechanism clicked at 1. He kept pressure on the dial, which had sunk within a recess about one-tenth of an inch deep when he had first pushed. He clicked the dial through each of the numbers, and at 10 reversed the dial quickly to 3 and then turned it back again to 9. On reaching this, he breathed deeply and then started to count. "One thousand and one. One thousand and two. One thousand and three."

When he got to "One thousand and three hundred," he would have counted out five minutes, but he would go to one thousand and four hundred just to make sure before he let the dial push back to its level with the box.

He stood up, holding one corner of the box with his giant hand and pressing in on the dial with the other.

"Run, Doc!" Pauncho said. "Here comes a whole army!"

Caliban twisted his head. A number of dark figures were emerging from the fog. He said, "Follow me! Don't stand and fight!" and he trotted away. He dared not run at full speed because he might stumble over a body or slip on the half-frozen mud. Behind him feet slapped as Pauncho kept on his heels. Somebody shouted and then about forty feet ahead of them, the fog opened up with an orange-bordered roar. Doc's feet slipped from under him as the blast hit, and he fell on his back. But he kept hold of the box and his pressure on the dial.

Pauncho was bellowing in his ear, "Hey, Doc! Can you hear me? You all right? I'm half-deaf, Doc!"

"Quiet!" Doc shouted back.

He put his mouth close to Pauncho's ear. "Get rid of all your grenades, and mine, too, fast as you can. Maybe you can get those guys before—"

The second grenade from the enemy was about three feet closer, and it was followed by a third which landed almost on the same spot. Since they were on level ground, the impact of the blasts was not softened. They were rolled over, and their heads sang and their ears were dead. But the plastic bombs depended almost entirely on concussion for effect, since the explosion reduced the plastic shell to dust. And they were not within the killing range of the blasts.

They would be if the enemy continued to lob grenades at random. They got to their feet and ran on. Pauncho stopped to toss grenades behind him, and Doc lost sight of him. Suddenly, he saw a body ahead of him. He tried to dodge to one side, slipped, and fell on his side. He came down heavily because his primary concern was keeping pressure on the dial. He called, "Pongo!" and then rolled away, holding the box up, hoping that if it was the enemy it would fire at where he had been. He wasn't worried about the person tossing a grenade, since he'd be committing suicide if he threw one that close to himself.

"Pongo!" Trish said. She looked as if she were shouting, yet he could barely hear her.

He got up and approached her cautiously, since it was possible the situation had changed and she was being forced to lure him in. He preferred to believe that she would die before doing that, but she might be depending on him to get her out of the situation, no matter how bad it looked. She tended to think of him as a superman, despite his lectures to her that he might be a superior man but he was also flesh and blood and one little .22 bullet or a slip on a piece of soap in the shower could make him just as dead as anybody else.

He peered through the fog. "Talk loudly. I'm almost deaf. Pauncho may be coming along, so don't shoot without giving the codeword. Where's Barney?"

"He went after you," she said, shouting in his ear. "Well, not exactly *after* you. He said he was going to make contact with the enemy and explain the situation. He thought that if they knew about the bomb, and that you were trying to keep it from going off, they'd quit fighting. They might even take off and leave us alone."

"Doesn't sound like it," Caliban said. The crump of grenades going off in the distance—somewhere around the Stonehenge circle—was still continuing. But there were no blasts nearer, where Pauncho and the three men should have been.

Suddenly, there was a silence. From far off, as if behind piles of wood, a voice cried. It was saying something. And then another voice cried. And then he heard, very faintly—dimmed by distance or by his injured hearing, or both—a rushing sound.

"Tires," his cousin said. "It could be the Nine taking off in their steam cars."

"Maybe Barney got to them," Caliban said. "He disobeyed orders, but he was doing something I should have thought of. Pauncho disobeyed, too, luckily for me."

A form like a truncated monolith from Stonehenge stepped out of the fog. Trish shouted the codeword back at him. Pauncho walked up to them and said, "Where's Barney?"

Trish told him. Doc had resumed his interrupted counting. He stared at Iwaldi and Villiers, who were standing up now. One of the three men, Elmus, was holding a loaded crossbow on them.

"It's ironic that I came here to kill the Nine and now I have to let them go, even Iwaldi," he thought, managing to count at the same time.

Trish stopped talking to Pauncho. They had heard the squeal of tires as they suddenly accelerated and then the screams of men and the thump of a massive swiftly moving object striking flesh and bone. Then a grenade boomed, and immediately thereafter was another screech as of tires sliding on pavement. Then there was a crash, and a series of bangs. More screeches as a vehicle accelerated again and sped away. Another boom of a grenade. Then, silence.

Doc continued to count. Barney came like a ghost out of the ectoplasmic pearliness. "I thought I'd lost you," he said. "I've been wandering around, afraid to go too fast or to yell out. Even though I think most of the enemy has gone. They didn't know whether or not to believe me, but they must've decided they couldn't take a chance. Besides, as one said, it'd be just the thing the crazy old dwarf would do. They think he's insane; no doubt of that."

Doc Caliban did not ask him if he had seen anything of the Grandrith party. If Barney had, he would have said something about it.

Doc kept on counting. Undoubtedly, five minutes were passed, at least seven minutes had gone by, but he preferred not to take a chance. The blasts had hurt his head, so that his sense of timing might have been disturbed. But he could put it off for only so long, and he finally decided to take his hand off the dial. He could see Cobbs—no, Iwaldi—and Barbara Villiers watching him. When they saw his hand drop away, and nothing happened, they sighed. At least, they looked as if they had. He could not hear them. He still could hear only loud sounds.

Trish put a hand on his shoulder, causing him to jump. She put her mouth close to his ear and said, "There's something still going on out there. In the ruins, I think. I heard a woman scream."

They waited. There was no more evidence that a fight was still occurring among the stones, but they had a feeling that something important was taking place under the monoliths and the trilithons standing like the ghosts of ghosts in the mists.

A faraway hoarse bellow, the cry of something not quite human, reached him. Silence again.

"You said we could go free," Barbara Villiers said.

"Leave. Or stay here," Doc Caliban said. "Do whatever you wish. You have a twelve-hour headstart."

"Untie us," she said. Iwaldi merely glared.

"I said you could go free," Caliban replied. "I wouldn't feel easy with you in this fog and your hands free to pick up some weapons. Come on, the rest of you. We'll find the bicycles and then the steam car."

"I'll come with you as far as the car," Villiers said. "Iwaldi told me he'd kill me because I betrayed him, though I don't know how he figures that."

"You want to throw in with us?" Doc said. He was not inclined to trust her one bit, but she undoubtedly had very valuable information about Iwaldi's organization.

She hesitated, then said, "Why not? I know a winner when I see one."

"Thank you, Benedictine Arnold," Trish said.

Iwaldi strode off into the fog. The others started to walk away, staying close to each other so they would not lose sight of each other. But they had not gone more than five steps when Doc stopped. Trish had put a hand on his shoulder. She said in his ear, "There was a low cry! I think Iwaldi—"

They walked in the direction Iwaldi had taken. Suddenly, he was on the ground at their feet. His throat was still pumping blood through the broad wound.

Something came through the fog, and only Caliban would have been quick enough to see it and to react with the swiftness of a leopard. He batted at the round object as if he were playing handball;

his hand struck it and sent it back into the fog with terrific force. There was a roar. The blast knocked them all down, and his ears hurt even more, and his head felt as if it had been squeezed in a vice.

They got to their feet with Doc assisting Villiers, whose hands were still taped behind her. They went ahead slowly, and then they felt the breeze, and before they had gone thirty feet, the fog began to fall apart. The sun dropped through in pale golden threads and then the threads coalesced into a blazing ball.

A wisp of fog, like a snake, moved across the face of a man on the ground, seeming to disappear into his open mouth. Doc approached him cautiously, though the fellow looked dead. His clothes were half-ripped off by the explosion, and blood ran down from his nose, ears, and mouth. A bloody plastic knife lay near his outflung hand. His helmet had been blown off, revealing an extraordinary high forehead. He was bald, and his jaws thrust outward, giving the lower part of his face an apish appearance. His body was tall and skinny.

"I think I know him," Caliban murmured. "I've seen him at one or more of the annual ceremonies in the caves."

The name would come, though it would not matter to the man, who was dead. He had come across Iwaldi and cut his throat, though he could not have recognized him as Iwaldi. But he did not know him, and that meant that he was an enemy. Then he had heard the others and tossed the grenade and it had come back so swiftly he must have thought for a horrified moment that he had bounced it off a nearby wall.

"Hey, Doc!" Pauncho bellowed. "I think that's Grandrith inside the ruins! He's waving at us!"

A FEAST REVEALED

A CHRONOLOGY OF MAJOR EVENTS PERTINENT TO THE SECRETS OF THE NINE SERIES

With selected entries from Philip José Farmer's *Tarzan Alive: A Definitive Biography of Lord Greystoke*, *Doc Savage: His Apocalyptic Life*, and other sources

WIN SCOTT ECKERT

In "A Tale of Two Universes,"[1] I made the case that Farmer's Nine novels, featuring the ape-man Lord Grandrith and his half-brother Doc Caliban, the man of bronze, take place in a parallel universe to the Wold Newton Universe.[2] I also suggested that "Depending on whether the two universes diverged at some common point in the distant past, or whether they have always been coexistent, the Nine in each universe might conceivably have had some members in common, immortal members who were alive when the universes divided."

Keeping these points in mind, what follows is a timeline of the Nine Universe of Lord Grandrith and Doc Caliban. Relevant

---

[1] *The Monster on Hold* by Philip José Farmer and Win Scott Eckert, Meteor House, 2021.

[2] Philip José Farmer's Wold Newton Universe novels and biographies are: *Tarzan Alive: A Definitive Biography of Lord Greystoke*, *Doc Savage: His Apocalyptic Life*, *The Other Log of Phileas Fogg*, *Time's Last Gift*, *The Adventure of the Peerless Peer*, the Khokarsa series (*Hadon of Ancient Opar*, *Flight to Opar*, and *The Song of Kwasin* [with Christopher Paul Carey]), *Ironcastle*, *Escape from Loki: Doc Savage's First Adventure*, *Tarzan and the Dark Heart of Time*, and *The Evil in Pemberley House* (with Win Scott Eckert).

information from *Tarzan Alive* and other sources is included, as well as a few speculative additions.

Some of the entries below take place in the Wold Newton Universe, but have direct bearing on the continuity of the universe of Lord Grandrith and Doc Caliban.

Due to the influence of time travel and dimensional breaches on the Grandrith/Caliban continuity, the Chronology is presented in causal order rather than strict chronological order.

PRE-DIVERGENCE EVENTS

The following events take place before a quantum event causes the universe to divide into two parallel universes, which then diverge somewhat over the millennia.

Thus, the events described here are part of a shared common past of the two parallel universes.

Approx. 40,000 B.C.E.

An Old Stone Age people discover an elixir giving them an extremely extended youth, as well as immunity to any disease and to breakdown of their cells. They do age, but so slowly that someone taking the elixir at age twenty-five looks only fifty after 15,000 years, or one hundred after 30,000 years. (*Lord of the Trees*)

Approx. 40,000 B.C.E.

Birth of XauXaz's father. (*The Mad Goblin*)

Approx. 30,000 B.C.E.

Birth of Anana, chieftainess of the Nine. (*A Feast Unknown*)

Approx. 30,000 B.C.E.

Birth of XauXaz and his brothers, Ebn XauXaz and Thrithjaz. (*A Feast Unknown*)

Approx. 26,000 B.C.E.

A quantum event causes the universe to split into two

parallel universes; the continuities of these universes diverge as the millennia pass, creating two parallel timelines.

EVENTS IN THE WOLD NEWTON UNIVERSE

The post-divergence entries described here take place in the continuity known as the **WOLD NEWTON UNIVERSE**.

Mid 1600s

Two rival extraterrestrial races, the Eridaneans and the Capelleans, arrive on Earth and are stranded. Over the centuries, the warring alien races, which are very long-lived, are forced to adopt human guise; they covertly continue their rivalry while living amongst humans. The two races use "distorters," very powerful personal teleporters, in furtherance of their conflict. As the aliens die off, many humans are secretly inducted into the ranks of both the Eridaneans and the Capelleans, in furtherance of the conflict. These humans are given an elixir allowing them to live at least one thousand years, barring accidental death. (*The Other Log of Phileas Fogg*)

Early 1700s

The use of distorters by the Eridaneans and the Capelleans in the Wold Newton Universe creates tiny tears in the pluriverse, weakening the dimensional barrier between the Wold Newton Universe and the Grandrith/Caliban Universe. ("The Wild Huntsman")

1720

The Nine in the Wold Newton Universe become aware of the Shrassk entity (which was invoked by their counterparts in the Grandrith/Caliban Universe) and place guards around the deep caves in Maine where it's located to prevent her and her Children from escaping into their world.

November 22, 1888, a few minutes after midnight

John Clayton III (the future eighth duke of Greystoke) is

born on the coast of French Equatorial Africa (Gabon). He becomes the eponymous hero of *Tarzan Alive* and is a member of the Wold Newton Family. (*Tarzan Alive*)

November 12, 1901

James Clarke "Doc" Wildman, Jr., a Wold Newton Family member, is born on the schooner *Orion* in a cove off the northern tip of Andros Island, Bahamas. His parents are James Clarke Wildman, Sr. and Arronaxe Larsen. (*Doc Savage: His Apocalyptic Life*)

He later acquires the nickname "Doc." Doc's maternal grandparents are the notorious Wolf Larsen (from Jack London's *The Sea Wolf*) and Arronaxe Land, who is the daughter of Ned Land (from Jules Verne's *20,000 Leagues under the Sea*).

Hubert Robertson and Ned Land are also present. It is possible that they, along with Wildman, Sr., have gathered to discuss their plans against the Nine.

(See Christopher Paul Carey's essay "The Green Eyes Have It—Or Are They Blue? or Another Case of Identity Recased," in his *The Grandest Adventure: Writings on Philip José Farmer*, Leaky Boot Press, 2018, wherein he proposes that Wolf Larsen and Baron von Hessel [from Farmer's *Escape from Loki*], among others, are all the same man, and indeed may also be the historical Woden [Odin], the immortal member of the Nine known as XauXaz.)

March 31–July 1918

Sixteen-year-old James Clarke Wildman is captured during the Great War and sent to prison camp Loki where he battles Baron von Hessel and meets future colleagues in his forthcoming battle against evil. (*Escape from Loki: Doc Savage's First Adventure*)

Unknown to Wildman, Baron von Hessel is Wildman's grandfather and an immortal member of the Nine. (Carey's "The Green Eyes Have It"; Eckert's "The Wild Huntsman")

1925

> James Clarke Wildman joins an Antarctic expedition as meteorologist and second-in-command ("a bronze giant of a man"). (*Who Goes There?* revised as *Frozen Hell*; *The Monster on Hold*)

1926

> Wildman, Jr., takes his M.D. at Johns Hopkins.

1929

> The leader of the Miskatonic University expedition to Antarctica, "Professor Dyer," is really Professor Littlejohn, one of Doc Wildman's five assistants. (*At the Mountains of Madness*; *Doc Savage: His Apocalyptic Life*)

Early 1930s

> Doc Wildman begins conducting brain operations on criminals in an effort to cure them of criminality.

November 1948

> Doc Wildman descends into the depths of New England caverns and has a terrifying adventure which cannot be explained by rational means. (*Up from Earth's Center*, a Doc Savage novel by Lester Dent)

Late 1949

> Doc Wildman "retires" from public view.

February 1950

> Marriage of Doctor James Clarke Wildman, Jr., and Adélaïde Johnston Lupin.

November 12, 1950

> Birth of Patricia Clarke Lupin Wildman.

1972

> Lord Greystoke ("the Englishman") and Doc Wildman

defeat the Nine in the Wold Newton Universe; unbeknownst to them, the Wold Newton Universe version of XauXaz survives.

Wildman and Greystoke spread stories and rumors that they were also killed in the battle that wiped out the Nine. (*The Monster on Hold*)

Greystoke, his wife Jane, and various family members fake their deaths and take new identities in order to avoid unwanted questions. (*Tarzan Alive*)

Wildman fully retires and devotes himself to scientific research. A short time later, Wildman and his wife Adélaïde Lupin Wildman fake their deaths in a plane crash, somewhere in the Arctic, possibly to evade . . . something. Shortly thereafter, their daughter, Patricia, becomes heir to a great legacy upon the deaths of John Clayton III and his wife Jane. (*The Evil in Pemberley House*; "The Wild Huntsman")

The near-simultaneous demises of these accomplished men, Wildman and Clayton, are not noted by the public as generally remarkable . . . although perhaps they should be.

1977 / 1984 / 1993

The events of *The Monster on Hold*.

In 1984, in the caverns beneath Maine, which he last visited in 1948, Doc Wildman sees a man who looks remarkably like him from across the dimensional void. The other man is Doc Caliban. (*The Monster on Hold*)

2070–12,000 B.C.E.

The jungle lord, John Clayton III, now calling himself John Gribardsun, is part of the expedition of the time vessel *H. G. Wells I* which travels back in time from 2070 to 12,000 B.C.E. (*Time's Last Gift*)

Gribardsun lives 14,000 years without aging, as noted in the canonical books about the jungle lord and by Gribardsun himself: "As you know now, I was fortunate enough to be given an elixir by a witch doctor who was the last man of his tribe. He belonged to a family the original head of which, some generations before, had discovered how to make the elixir, a vile-tasting devil's brew, from certain African herbs, blood, and several other constituents I will not even hint at. He had a high regard for me because I saved his life and also because he thought I was some sort of a demigod. He knew of my rather peculiar upbringing." (*Time's Last Gift*)

It is important to note that this elixir differs from that of the Nine in that it bestows true eternal youth as well as immortality. Imbibers of the Nine's elixir age about one hundred biological years over 20,000 to 30,000 years.

(See "Gribardsun through the Ages: A Chronology of Major Events Pertinent to *Time's Last Gift*" by Win Scott Eckert and Dennis E. Power in the Titan Books edition of *Time's Last Gift* for complete information on this time-traveling immortal jungle lord.)

10,814 B.C.E.

Gribardsun encounters Nine member XauXaz (who calls himself Kethnu at this point in time) near Khokarsa in ancient Africa; Kethnu acquires Gribardsun's immortality elixir. Gribardsun's elixir prevents any aging whatsoever, whereas with the Nine's elixir, the user's body will age perhaps one hundred years over tens of thousands of years, and the user will still eventually die. Kethnu/XauXaz does not share this improved elixir with his fellow Nine members. ("The Wild Huntsman")

December 13, 1795

The immortal John Gribardsun, still living forward through time from 12,000 B.C.E., comes to witness the Wold Newton meteor strike, which imbued his ancestors with, and passed on to him, the qualities of supermen. He is an invitee at the Conclave called by Sir Percy Blakeney, and held in Wold Newton, in December 1795.

XauXaz is also present, having time-traveled to the event from the year 1972.

(See Eckert's short stories "Is He in Hell?" [*The Worlds*

of Philip José Farmer 1: Protean Dimensions, Meteor House, 2010] and "The Wild Huntsman")

2070

The *H. G. Wells I* time-travel expedition occurs again, attempting to reach a point 14,000 years in the past:

"When the *H. G. Wells I* voyaged into time (again), he felt sorry for John II, Rachel, Drummond, and Robert. This trip would not take them to the France of 12,000 B.C. Somewhere along the transit, the vessel and its passengers would disappear. He did not know how or to where. But the same time barrier that had existed from 1872 to 2070 would prevent the vessel from existing in 12,000 B.C.

It was supposed to appear the same day that he, John I, had appeared. His cells had not replaced themselves yet, which meant that the ship and its passengers would go elsewhere.

He liked to think that Rachel and the others had not just disintegrated. ***Perhaps they were shunted off into a parallel world.***

The temporal obstacle was removed the moment the vessel was launched. There would be no more John II's, John III's, John IV's, and so on. Ad infinitum.

If it were not for the time barrier, John II would also have lived 14,000 years or so and have waited in the wings while John III prepared to board the vessel. And then John IV and then John V. Until the world was crowded with them.

The circuit of time was broken now. No need to worry about those others."

(*Time's Last Gift*, emphasis added)

26,000 B.C.E.

Owing to the impossibility of arriving in 12,000 B.C.E. (see prior entry), John Gribardsun and the expedition in the time vessel *H. G. Wells I* are "bounced" an additional 14,000 years into the past, arriving in 26,000 B.C.E.

(See the short story "Into Time's Abyss" by John Allen

Small in *The Worlds of Philip José Farmer 2: Of Dust and Soul*, Meteor House, 2011)

The time travelers' arrival in a different time period causes a quantum division and creates two parallel universes, which diverge over time.

The Nine organization already exists at the time of the quantum split, and the group's membership includes the Nine's leader Anana; XauXaz; and XauXaz's brothers, Ebn XauXaz and Thrithjaz.

Since these Nine members are already alive and immortal at the time of the quantum split, these doppelgängers live on through the millennia in parallel universes: the Wold Newton Universe and the universe of Lord Grandrith and Doc Caliban.

Through the ages, the two universes diverge somewhat, and the membership of the Nine in each universe mirrors that divergence. By 1720, both XauXazs are still alive in each universe; XauXaz's brothers in the Grandrith/Caliban Universe are deceased (their status in the Wold Newton Universe is unknown, but it is likely they are deceased); and Anana is still alive in the Grandrith/Caliban Universe (it is unknown if she is still alive in the Wold Newton Universe).

Events in the Grandrith/Caliban Universe

The post-divergence entries described here take place in the continuity known as the **Grandrith/Caliban Universe** unless otherwise indicated.

Approx. 10,000 B.C.E.
> Birth of Iwaldi. (*The Mad Goblin*)

1900 B.C.E.–1600 B.C.E.
> Stonehenge is built in three phases by the Wessex People, supervised by XauXaz. (*Lord of the Trees*, *The Mad Goblin*)
>
> (Presumably the XauXaz counterpart in the Wold Newton Universe also plays a part in the building of Stonehenge in that universe.)

1241

Iwaldi's castle is built in Gramzdorf, Germany, upon an even more ancient keep and series of caves. (*The Mad Goblin*)

1641

Birth of Barbara Villiers, 1st Duchess of Cleveland, Countess Castlemaine. (*The Mad Goblin*)

Early 1700s

The use of distorters by the Eridaneans and the Capelleans in the Wold Newton Universe creates tiny tears in the pluriverse, weakening the dimensional barrier between the Wold Newton Universe and the Grandrith/Caliban Universe. ("The Wild Huntsman")

1709

Barbara Villiers, a candidate of the Nine, fakes her death. (*The Mad Goblin*)

(Barbara Villiers also has a counterpart in the Wold Newton Universe with the same name and titles, but it is unknown if the doppelgänger was also recruited by the Nine in that dimension.)

1720

The Nine in the Grandrith/Caliban Universe become aware of Shrassk, a multidimensional entity, and invoke the creature to quell a rebellion among three candidates of the Nine. Shrassk has the power, perhaps uncontrolled by it, a wild talent, to touch the subconscious of some sensitive human receptors and cause nightmares. After the rebellion, recognizing the danger posed by the entity, the Nine imprison Shrassk. Shrassk and her Children are suspended in a nether space, with the potential to act as a sort of bridge between the Grandrith/ Caliban Universe and the Wold Newton Universe. The Nine place guards around the deep caves in Maine where Shrassk is located to prevent her and her Children from escaping into their world. (*The Monster on Hold*)

1720

Wold Newton Universe

The Nine in the Wold Newton Universe become aware of the Shrassk entity (which was invoked by their counterparts in the Grandrith/Caliban Universe) and place guards around the deep caves in Maine where it's located to prevent her and her Children from escaping into their world.

1720–1968

Wold Newton Universe and
Grandrith/Caliban Universe

XauXaz from the Wold Newton Universe discovers and utilizes the "bridge" created by Shrassk to travel back and forth between the universes; he accesses the bridge using a Capellean distorter (there are no distorters in the Grandrith/Caliban Universe because the Eridanean/Capellean conflict on Earth has not happened there). Shrassk taps XauXaz's subconscious, but XauXaz is the only human to overcome Shrassk's influence and thus use Shrassk's dimension bridge for his own purposes.

XauXaz is the counterpart, but much younger appearing, of the XauXaz from the Grandrith/Caliban Universe; unlike XauXaz or any member of the Nine in either universe, the Wold Newton Universe's XauXaz had not aged one hundred years over tens of thousands of years. This is because he has, or at least once had, access to an elixir like John Gribardsun's, which functions differently than the Nine's elixir.

The Wold Newton Universe's XauXaz crosses over to the Grandrith/Caliban Universe and murders his counterpart—the Grandrith/Caliban Universe's XauXaz. Between 1720 and 1968, he travels back and forth between the dimensions, playing the part of XauXaz in both universes, with both groups of the Nine. ("The Wild Huntsman")

Late 1850s–Early 1860s

XauXaz, during his many crossover trips from the Wold Newton Universe ("The Wild Huntsman"), takes the guise of elderly Swedish gentlemen "Mister Bileyg" and over the course of a few years pays several midnight visits to Catstarn Hall on the Grandrith Estate, and to the woman who will become the mother of three brothers: James, John, and Patrick Cloamby. (*A Feast Unknown*)

The woman's sterile husband, Viscount Grandrith, who is fifty-five but looks thirty, commits suicide after his wife takes her own life. He suspected that her own suicide was brought on by a guilty conscience due to her infidelity. (*A Feast Unknown*)

Thus, the XauXaz of the Wold Newton Universe is the grandfather of the Grandrith/Caliban Universe's John Cloamby, aka Lord Grandrith; James "Doc" Caliban; and Trish Wilde. (*A Feast Unknown*; "The Wild Huntsman")

He is also the grandfather of the Wold Newton Universe's James Clarke "Doc" Wildman (Carey's "The Green Eyes Have It") and the ancestor many times over of Greystoke the jungle lord and other members of the Wold Newton Family. ("The Wild Huntsman")

1881

James Murtagh is born in Meiringen, Switzerland, and is raised from the age of eight in Wales. Like his notorious father, he goes on to become an extremely talented mathematician, a genius, who teaches higher mathematics at Oxford and the University of Talinn. He is also a candidate of the Nine. (*The Mad Goblin*)

March 21, 1888

Alexandra Applethwaite's brother-in-law, John Cloamby, rapes her in the streets of Whitechapel while suffering insanity under the influence of the Nine's elixir. She becomes pregnant. (*A Feast Unknown*)

John Cloamby goes on to commit more murders, and is

known as Jack the Ripper. Finally, the insanity subsides and, remorse-stricken, he changes his surname to Caliban and disappears to America, eventually fathering James "Doc" Caliban. (*A Feast Unknown*)

May or June, 1888

James Cloamby, Viscount Grandrith, and wife Alexandra Applethwaite sail for West Africa, where James is assigned to conduct a secret investigation for the Colonial Office. They are later marooned on the coast of French Equatorial Africa. (*A Feast Unknown*)

November 21, 1888 at 11:45 P.M.

John Cloamby (the future Lord Grandrith) is born prematurely on the coast of French Equatorial Africa (Gabon). He becomes the lord of the trees. (*A Feast Unknown*)

1889

Deaths of James Cloamby and Alexandra Applethwaite; John Cloamby is adopted and raised by The Folk. (*A Feast Unknown*)

1898

John Cloamby discovers his mother and legal father/uncle's (James Cloamby) cabin along with books and tools. (*Lord of the Trees*)

1901

Birth of James Caliban, later known as "Doc" Caliban. He is the half-brother of John Cloamby, Lord Grandrith. (*The Mad Goblin*)

A Feast Unknown gives Caliban's birth year as 1903. The 1901 date from *The Mad Goblin* makes more sense, as Grandrith mentions in *Lord of the Trees* that Caliban fought in the Great War: ". . . he served with distinction as a commissioned officer in the U.S. Army in 1918." And in *The Mad Goblin*, it's noted that, "When Doc was only seventeen and a lieutenant in World War I, he had captured two German soldiers at the same time that he had been cut off by the advance of the enemy."

In *A Feast Unknown*, Grandrith spied upon Caliban's elderly aides, Rivers and Simmons, and learned the 1903 date. Either they misspoke, or Grandrith misheard them.

1908

John Cloamby first lays eyes on Clio Jeanne de Carriol. (*Lord of the Trees*)

1911

Birth of Patricia "Trish" Wilde, cousin of James "Doc" Caliban and John Cloamby, Lord Grandrith. (*The Mad Goblin*)

Trish's father is Patrick Cloamby, who traveled to Canada at a very young age, after assaulting and nearly killing a teacher; this presumably occurred sometime before 1888. Patrick Cloamby changed his surname to Wilde and became a doctor. (*A Feast Unknown*)

Lord Grandrith discovers a hidden valley containing a ruined city in Africa; the gold he uncovers at the site, which he names Ophir, becomes the source of his immense wealth. (*A Feast Unknown*)

November 21, 1913

Marriage of John Cloamby and Clio Jeanne de Carriol. (*A Feast Unknown*)

December 1913

An agent of the Nine approaches John Cloamby and his wife Clio. (*Lord of the Trees*)

At this point, the Nine consist of Anana, a thirty-millennia-old Caucasian woman; XauXaz; Ing, a Nordic; Iwaldi, a dwarf; Yeshua, a Hebrew born about 3 B.C.E.; Mubaniga, an ancient proto-Bantu; two proto-Mongolians, Jiizfan and Shaumbim; and Tilatoc, an Amerindian from Central America or perhaps North America. (*Lord of the Trees*)

1918

The underage James Caliban serves as a Lieutenant during the Great War. (*Lord of the Trees, The Mad Goblin*)

1920

Lord Grandrith and his wife Clio are formally inducted into the Nine as "candidates" and they begin attending the annual ceremonies to receive the elixir. (*A Feast Unknown*)

According to Grandrith, the "candidates of the Nine" number five hundred or more, and are the elite of the organization with whom the elixir is shared. A lower echelon, the "servants of the Nine," number perhaps half a million and are not aware of the elixir. (*Lord of the Trees*)

1921

James Murtagh is inducted as a candidate of the Nine. (*Lord of the Trees*)

1925

James Caliban joins an Antarctic expedition as meteorologist and second-in-command ("a bronze giant of a man"). (*Who Goes There?* revised as *Frozen Hell; The Monster on Hold*)

1926

Doc Caliban completes his medical internship. He already has several Ph.D.s in a variety of disciplines, and a law degree from Harvard. (*The Mad Goblin*)

1927

Caliban takes his M.D. at Johns Hopkins.

The Nine make first contact with Caliban. (*The Mad Goblin*)

1928

Doc Caliban is formally invited to join the Nine. (*The Mad Goblin*)

Doc Caliban kills a gangster's moll, Big-Eyes Llewellyn, while breaking up a drug-smuggling ring in Los Angeles. His remorse over this act sends him into a suicidal depression. He withdraws from society for almost a year, retreating to a hideaway in the Arctic Circle. (*A Feast Unknown*; *The Monster on Hold*)

1929

Doc Caliban, upon returning to civilization, meets his cousin Trish Wilde for the first time. (*A Feast Unknown*)

Caliban (and presumably also Trish Wilde) undergoes the first of the terrible annual ceremonies in order to receive the Nine's elixir. (*The Mad Goblin*)

Caliban secretly accompanies the Miskatonic University expedition to Antarctica; the group's leader, "Professor Dyer," is really Professor Williams, one of Caliban's five assistants. (*At the Mountains of Madness*; *The Monster on Hold*)

1932

Births of William Grier "Pauncho" van Veelar (son of "Jocko" Simmons) and Barney Albany Banks (son of "Porky" Rivers). (*Lord of the Trees*)

Simmons and Rivers are two of Doc Caliban's five adventurous aides, the other three being Williams, Shorthans, and Kidfast. (*The Mad Goblin*)

Early 1930s

Doc Caliban begins conducting brain operations on criminals in an effort to cure them of criminality.

Late 1930s

Doc Caliban secretly begins researches into independently creating the Nine's elixir—or an elixir superior to that of the Nine. (*A Feast Unknown*)

1943

Grandrith loses his right leg below the knee after the RAF

bomber he's piloting crashes after a mission over Hamburg. The leg regrows in six months due to the Nine's elixir. (*A Feast Unknown*)

1944

Grandrith's boat is sunk in the Indian Ocean, giving him his first experience fighting sharks. (*Lord of the Trees*)

1945

The Nine hold a highly important meeting, presumably regarding World War II. (*A Feast Unknown*)

The result of this meeting may have been a mission assigned to Lord Grandrith:

"My own philosophy is simple and practical and not at all based on the idea that life is sacred. If a man is out to kill you, you kill him first. This has nothing to do with the rules of warfare as conducted by nations. When I was a member of the British forces in World War II, I observed the Geneva rules. That is, I did except in two cases, where I had orders from the Nine, and their orders superseded anybody's. In return for giving me a very extended youth, they demanded a high price sometimes. But I had had no qualms about killing the men the Nine wanted out of the way, especially since they were the enemy. If I were to tell you that several of them were the highest and most famous of our enemy, you might find it difficult to believe. Especially since the world believes that they committed suicide to keep from falling into the hands of the Russians." (*Lord of the Trees*)

Farmer and pulp expert Rick Lai reasons that "the highest and most famous of our enemy" were Adolph Hitler and Joseph Goebbels: "Grandrith says that both high-ranking Axis officials supposedly committed suicide because they were afraid of being captured by the Russians. This fits Hitler and Goebbels. Goering and Himmler committed suicide in American custody, and are ruled out. Grandrith also says both leaders were men. Therefore, Eva Braun and Mrs. Magda Goebbels aren't being directly referenced.

Japanese leaders like Sugiyama knew that the USA, not the USSR, would judge them. The only possible exceptions might be Japanese officials in Manchuria which the Russians invaded after the Nazis surrendered. It isn't difficult to reconcile the 'suicide pact' deaths of Goebbels's wife and children with Grandrith's statement. Magda Goebbels could have gone crazy after seeing Grandrith kill her husband, and then killed her children and then herself. All Grandrith then had to do was make it look like Joseph Goebbels was part of Magda's suicide pact. Whether the Eva Braun of the Grandrith/Caliban universe killed herself or was executed by Grandrith is debatable."

1946

Doc Caliban issues a report to the Nine regarding mankind's eventual destruction of the earth through pollution and mass starvation. (*The Mad Goblin*)

1947

Lord Grandrith once again visits his parents' cabin on the coast of Gabon. (*Lord of the Trees*)

1948

Up until this point in time, Doc Caliban believes that Lord Grandrith is a fictional character in a series of fantastic novels. In this year, Caliban also begins brain transplant experiments. (*A Feast Unknown*)

Lord Grandrith decides to secretly begin writing his memoirs, knowing they are unpublishable due to his membership in the Nine. (*Lord of the Trees*)

An agent of the Nine discovers an orphaned baby of The Folk; the Nine order the baby to be raised with the children of two Kenyan agents of the Nine. (*Lord of the Trees*)

November 1948

Doc Caliban descends into the deep New England caverns and battles terrifying shapeless creatures and tentacled beings. (*The Monster on Hold*)

Early 1950s
> Pauncho van Veelar and Barney Banks serve in the same
> Marine outfit during the Korean War. (*Lord of the Trees*)

1958
> Lord Grandrith first sees James Murtagh during the Nine's
> grisly annual rites, held in the caves deep in east central
> Africa. (*Lord of the Trees*)

1966
> Doc Caliban cuts off some of his fingers in an effort to
> isolate elements of the elixir. The fingers regrow, of course.
> (*A Feast Unknown*)

March 21–April 1968
> Events of *A Feast Unknown*.
>
> Death of one member of the Nine, XauXaz, due to
> extreme old age. He is the first member of the Nine to die
> in about two thousand years. The last member was XauXaz's
> brother Thrithjaz, and the "preseating" ceremony which
> Grandrith, Caliban, and seven other candidates attend is the
> first to be held since then. (*A Feast Unknown*)
>
> Grandrith and Caliban discover they are half-brothers,
> and after overcoming the madness brought on by the Nine's
> elixir, they turn against the Nine. (*A Feast Unknown*)
>
> In "The Wild Huntsman," it is revealed that the
> XauXaz who appeared to die in 1968 in *A Feast Unknown*
> was actually murdered by his counterpart from the Wold
> Newton Universe about 250 years earlier, and the parallel
> universe counterpart had been impersonating him ever
> since. With the Nine in Grandrith's universe starting to
> become suspicious of him, the doppelgänger faked his death
> in 1968, thus setting off the chain of events in the Secrets of
> the Nine series.

May 1968
> In Los Angeles, Lord Grandrith mails the manuscript for

Volume IX of his memoirs (published as *A Feast Unknown*) to a man he believes to be his editor. (*Lord of the Trees*)

In reality, the man is XauXaz from the parallel dimension known as the Wold Newton Universe.

XauXaz travels back to the Wold Newton dimension and, pretending to be a man calling himself "James Claymore," mails the manuscript from Western Samoa (see *A Feast Unknown*) to science-fiction author Philip José Farmer for publication.

Mid 1968

Pauncho van Veelar and Barney Banks, who have not seen their "uncle" Doc Caliban since 1963, are shocked to see that he has still not aged. Caliban recruits them into the fight against the Nine. (*The Mad Goblin*)

1968–1969

Lord Grandrith and Clio circle the globe twice in an effort to shake the Nine from their trail, while Doc Caliban, Trish Wilde, Pauncho, and Barney lie in wait, planning their next move.

Eventually, Doc and company get a line on the location of one of the Nine, Iwaldi, and prepare to go after him. (*The Mad Goblin*)

Meanwhile, Grandrith leaves Clio safely ensconced in a London hideaway (or so he thinks) and heads to Africa to scout out the caves of the Nine. (*Lord of the Trees*)

1969

Events of the intertwined sequels to *A Feast Unknown*: *Lord of the Trees*/*The Mad Goblin*.

Lord Grandrith kills a member of the Nine, Mubaniga, and another, Jiizfan, dies in the battle at Stonehenge. (*Lord of the Trees*)

Another member, Iwaldi, is killed by James Murtagh during the Stonehenge battle. Murtagh also dies. (*The Mad Goblin*)

With the deaths of XauXaz, Mubaniga, Jiizfan, and Iwaldi, the Nine are left with four empty spots to fill. Surviving members of the Nine are Anana, Ing, Yeshua, Shaumbim, and Tilatoc.

There are ambiguous and sometimes contradictory references to the amount of time that has passed since the events of *A Feast Unknown*—understandable, given that the follow-up manuscripts were separately written by Grandrith (*Lord of the Trees*) and Caliban (*The Mad Goblin*).

Some descriptions in *Lord of the Trees* of the amount of time passed since *A Feast Unknown* indicate that it is still 1968 and that only two months, or eight months, have passed, but other references in both *Lord of the Trees* and *The Mad Goblin* indicate a year has passed, pointing to a 1969 date. There is a reference to "spring" in *The Mad Goblin*, but also two references to the "winter solstice." The conflicting time references—surely purposeful on the part of Grandrith, Caliban, and their editor, Farmer—have resulted in a general 1969 date for these adventures in this Chronology.

1977 / 1984 / 1993

The events of *The Monster on Hold*.

In 1984, in the caverns beneath Maine, which he last visited in 1948, Doc Caliban sees a man who looks remarkably like him from across the dimensional void. The other man is Doc Wildman. (*The Monster on Hold*)

A Brief Sketch of the Wold Newton Universe's XauXaz

Mythological/Religious
Woden/Wotan/Odin.

10,814 b.c.e.

Kethnu. "The Wild Huntsman." Wants Gribardsun's "witch doctor" elixir (it's better than the Nine's elixir; in fact, it's the most effective immortality elixir in two universes).

1720

XauXaz from 1972 (using time distorter based on Eridanean teleportation distorter) travels to the Grandrith/Caliban Universe, kills that universe's XauXaz, and takes his place from 1720 to 1968.

13 December 1795

XauXaz. "The Wild Huntsman." Present at Wold Newton meteor strike (via time travel from 1972); battles Gribardsun; manipulates events to ensure Wold Newton Family comes into existence, knowing he may need their scientific genius in the future.

c. 1810s

Lars Ulf Larsson (in the Grandrith/Caliban Universe). *Image of the Beast*. Norwegian sailor involved with Dolores del Osorojo.

c. 1880s

Wolf Larsen. *The Sea-Wolf*. Marries and abandons Doc Wildman's grandmother.

1912

"Witch doctor." *Tarzan and the Foreign Legion*. Gives Greystoke (later known as Gribardsun) the elixir with blood sharing, so that his younger self can get it back in 10,814 B.C.E.

1917

Baron Ulf von Waldman. "The Adventure of the Fallen Stone." Gribardsun's "witch doctor" elixir doesn't work quite as well on him as it does/did on Gribardsun/Greystoke, and it's starting to wear off; he's seeking help in recreating the elixir.

Undocumented time period

Karl Woldheim. "The Adventure of the Fallen Stone."

Undocumented time period

    Carl Waldhaus. "The Adventure of the Fallen Stone."

1918

    Baron von Hessel. *Escape from Loki.* Trying to recruit his grandson Wildman to help recreate the "witch doctor" elixir, among other things.

1929–1930

    Larsen, the sailor. *At the Mountains of Madness.* Just tagging along . . .

1930s

Acquires an Eridanean distorter.

1937

    Baron Karl. *Fortress of Solitude.* Keeping tabs on his grandson (the son of Lili Bugov) battling Wildman in the Wold Newton Universe, as well as his daughter/son (aka Lili Bugov) battling Caliban in the Grandrith/Caliban Universe.

1939

    Captain Larsen of the transport ship *Saigon. Tarzan and the Castaways.* Probably trying to capture Greystoke to get another blood sample.

1939

    Baron Orrest Karl Lestzky. *The Golden Man.* Noted brain surgeon rivaling Doc Wildman.

1944–1946

    Dr. Karl Walden. *Hunt the Avenger.* Trying to recruit and strongarm The Avenger into helping recreate the "witch doctor" elixir. The Countess Lilya Zarov, aka Lili Bugov, also is involved.

1948

    Dr. Karl Linningen ("Dr. Karl"). *Up from Earth's Center.*

Manipulating Doc Wildman into penetrating the cavernous depths which lead to Shrassk; he also traveled to the Grandrith/Caliban Universe and similarly manipulated Doc Caliban (as "Dr. Carlos").

1967

Dr. Karl Stipier. *Honey West and T.H.E. Cat: A Girl and Her Cat.* Sidelining in selling bioweapons and advanced technology to the highest bidders.

1968

Masquerading as the XauXaz of the Grandrith/Caliban Universe, he fakes his death as that version of XauXaz (XauXaz's death noted in *A Feast Unknown*).

1972

Succeeds in modifying Eridanean teleportation distorter to function as a time distorter ("The Wild Huntsman"). Makes many trips to Grandrith/Caliban universe (each year, 1720–1968), as well as other time periods in the Wold Newton Universe (see prior entries, such as 13 December 1795), and even other "pocket universes" within the pluriverse.

1974

Behind some of the events of *The Scarlet Jaguar.*

1984

Arnie/XauXaz. *The Monster on Hold.*

SPOILERS OF THE NINE
Completing Philip José Farmer's *The Monster on Hold*

Note: A fair warning to those who have not yet read The Monster on Hold, *the fourth book in the Secrets of the Nine series by Philip José Farmer and Win Scott Eckert (published by Meteor House in 2021): "spoilers" does indeed mean spoilers.*

Philip José Farmer's *The Monster on Hold* is a direct, if unofficial, sequel to Lester Dent's final Doc Savage novel, *Up from Earth's Center*. Unofficial, because *The Monster on Hold* (TMOH) is not an official Doc Savage novel, licensed by Condé Nast—and because it does not feature Doc Savage, at least not by name. As long ago as 1973, Farmer speculated about such a sequel, with Doc returning to the mysterious New England caverns to confront the denizens of Hell:

> Doc, after long meditation and a firm decision and much preparation, would have led an expedition against the things. With him would have been his five aides and perhaps Pat. The expedition would have been loaded, not for bear but for the Forebear of All Evil. And it would have expended all the hundreds of gadgets in a final apocalyptic onslaught....
>
> We can be sure that he would have used as his most formidable weapon the one thing that evil can't face: Light.
>
> If the cavern dwellers were indeed lost souls encased in strange forms, Doc may have lost. And Hell is as strong as ever. If they were extraterrestrials, subject to natural laws, they might have lost. If they had won, it seems likely that

they would have come out into the open by now in an all-out war. They haven't, so perhaps Doc won. Or perhaps they are among us as reasonable facsimiles of human beings.
(Farmer, writing about *Up from Earth's Center* in *Doc Savage: His Apocalyptic Life*, Doubleday, 1973; Meteor House revised edition, 2013, 2023)

What has been perhaps less clear is that TMOH is also a sequel to Farmer's official Doc Savage novel, *Escape from Loki* (EFL), the origin story of Doc and his crew. In turn, retrospectively it seems fairly obvious that Farmer, noted for his use of coding and symbolism, intended EFL to be the beginning "bookend" to the official Doc Savage series, complementing *Up from Earth's Center* as the concluding bookend. This is coded to readers in the fourth sentence of EFL: "What seems Up may be Down." Young Clark Savage seems to be shot up into the atmosphere. His career of 180-plus supersagas is just beginning, on the upswing.

His officially documented lifetime of adventuring (at least as recounted by Lester Dent and the other original pulpsters who wrote for *Doc Savage* magazine) will come to an end—Down—at Earth's Center.

Yet, he will escape, Up, and then, as Farmer speculated above, later go back Down for one final confrontation: *The Monster on Hold*.

It is telling to note that in addition to the well-known outline and chapter for TMOH which Farmer presented at the 1983 World Fantasy Convention, he wrote another three short chapters, located in his "Magic Filing Cabinet," which featured working titles "The Leasor of Two Evils," "The Unspeakable Dweller," and "Down to Earth's Centre." The latter two became titles for sections one and three of the completed final novel, TMOH: "Some Unspeakable Dweller" and "Down to Earth's Centre."

The phrase "Some Unspeakable Dweller" is from one of Sherlock Holmes' most terrifying cases:

A thick, black cloud swirled before my eyes, and my mind told me that within this cloud, unseen as yet, but about to spring out upon my appalled senses, lurked all that was vaguely horrible, all that was monstrous and inconceivably wicked in the universe. Vague shapes swirled and swam amid the dark cloud-bank, each a menace and a warning of something coming, the advent of some unspeakable dweller upon the threshold, whose very shadow would blast my soul. ("The Adventure of the Devil's Foot" by Dr. John H. Watson, M.D., London, *His Last Bow*, Sir Arthur Conan Doyle, ed.)

"The Devil's Foot" takes place at Poldhu Bay, on the Cornish peninsula, in the hamlet of Tredannick Wollas, and features a West African root, the toxic smoke of which induces transcendental experiences—if one survives the inhalation. The smoke evokes Baron von Hessel's cigar smoke in EFL, which Christopher Paul Carey has theorized may be the secret delivery mechanism for a life-extension elixir.

Poldhu Bay, and the hamlet of Tredannick Wollas, are both mentioned in Farmer's Cthulhu Mythos tale "The Freshman." This is Farmer casting a Lovecraftian shadow on Watson's tale. The Sigal of Dembron is from Farmer's notes; the Sigal takes its name from a thirteenth-century French wizard, Dembron, who is undoubtedly related to the Marquis Manuel de Dembron mentioned in "The Freshman."

The title of section two of TMOH, "The Guardian at the Threshold," is lifted from "The Dweller on the Threshold" from Edward Bulwer-Lytton's *Zanoni*; the phrase from *Zanoni* also appears in the television series *Twin Peaks*. According to occultist and mystic Max Heindel:

> The real "Dweller on the Threshold" is the composite elemental entity created on the invisible planes by all our untransmuted evil thoughts and acts during all the past period of our evolution. This "dweller" stands guard at the entrance to the invisible worlds and challenges our right to enter therein. This entity must be redeemed or transmuted eventually. We must generate poise and willpower sufficient to face and command it before we can consciously enter the super-physical worlds.
> (Heindel, *The Web of Destiny*, The Rosicrucian Fellowship, 1928)

Heindel's description perfectly illustrates the secret journey that Doc Caliban (and his "Other" aspect, Lacewing, aka Doc Wildman, aka Doc Savage) must take in order to confront, once more, not only the terrifying things deep in a New England cave (*Up from Earth's*

Center), but also the entity that waits beyond the threshold, at the intersection of the pluriverse: Shrassk. Shrassk is Farmer's female version of Lovecraft's deity Yog-Sothoth, whose titles include "the Lurker at the Threshold," "the All-in-One," and "the One-in-All," combined with some aspects of Lovecraft's female deity, Shub-Niggurath.

In Lovecraft's "The Dunwich Horror," Yog-Sothoth impregnates a human woman, resulting in twins: a mostly humanoid child, and an unspeakably monstrous child. An aspect of this is seen in TMOH's Children of Shrassk: "The monster on hold reproduced asexually, always generating twins: one an unutterably monstrous and dangerous Child, and one a vaguely humanoid bloblike thing that could take on many shapes." The theme of duality is carried on throughout TMOH with Doc Caliban and The Other; the two Xau-Xazs; the two Lili Bugovs, and the two groups of the Nine.

It is also revealed that Lili Bugov is a human-shapeshifter hybrid, very closely related to the shapeshifter who plagued both A. J. Raffles and Sherlock Holmes in 1895 (Farmer's "The Problem of the Sore Bridge—Among Others"). These, and many other associated shape-shifters, are related to and/or descended from the bloblike children of Shrassk:

> "I don't know where we come from. We've been around for millennia, and some of our ancient ancestors escaped to other planets. Some of their descendants evolved on different paths and have even ended up back on Earth in different times and places."
>
> "All right. Tell me everything you can about your species."
>
> "We are shapeshifters."
>
> "Obviously," Caliban said dryly.
>
> (Farmer and Eckert, *The Monster on Hold*, Meteor House, 2021)

Of course, we cannot overlook the "worm unknown to science," first noted in the Sherlock Holmes tale "The Problem of Thor Bridge," and later seen in Harry "Bunny" Manders and Farmer's "The Problem of the Sore Bridge—Among Others," as well as *Escape from Loki*. One cannot help but think that the eerie whitish worm was a child of Shrassk in its infancy.

SPOILERS OF THE NINE

Other related shape-changing beings are the antagonists in "Who Goes There?"/*Frozen Hell* by John W. Campbell and *At the Mountains of Madness* by H. P. Lovecraft. Both Caliban and Wildman were on the Antarctic expeditions, in their respective universes, described in Campbell's "Who Goes There?"/*Frozen Hell*. And Wildman's archaeologist colleague, Johnny Littlejohn, led a follow-up expedition, whereas in Caliban's universe, Caliban himself was on the second Antarctic mission; the second expedition (in both universes) are described in Lovecraft's *At the Mountains of Madness*.

It's also not hard to imagine that the Eridaneans and Capelleans—whose true visages are never revealed in Farmer's *The Other Log of Phileas Fogg*—are also shape-altering offshoots:

> The [Capellean] Old Ones were just completing their report on Earth when the Eridaneans landed. There had been war, and both spaceships had been damaged beyond repair. And so both forces had gone underground. With surgery, they had remodified their bodies to pass for humans.
> (Farmer, *The Other Log of Phileas Fogg*, most recently reprinted by Meteor House in 2024 as *The Full Account*, a combined edition with Jules Verne's *Around the World in Eighty Days*)

Speaking of Verne, Farmer's notes indicate Johnny Littlejohn's grandfather was Jeorling, the narrator of *An Antarctic Mystery; or, The Sphinx of the Ice Fields: A Sequel to The Narrative of Arthur Gordon Pym* (*Le Sphinx de Glaces*). And so, in TMOH, Johnny's analogue in Caliban's universe, Professor Williams, is the grandson of Jeorling.

The cry "Tekeli-li!" is from Edgar Allan Poe's *The Narrative of Arthur Gordon Pym of Nantucket*, Verne's *Sphinx of the Ice Fields*, and H. P. Lovecraft's *At the Mountains of Madness*. The *Grampus*, the island of Tsalal, and the *Jane Guy* are from *Arthur Gordon Pym*. The *Halbrane* and Captain Len Guy are from *Sphinx of the Ice Fields*. The character of Dirk Peters also appears in both of these works. The star-headed creatures (the Elder Things) and the pulsating pustule-like mass (a shoggoth) are from *At the Mountains of Madness*.

Philip José Farmer lived in Los Angeles, California from 1965 to 1970. I refer to this as Farmer's "California period," in which he produced many of his best-known, and controversial, works, including the first four novels in the World of Tiers series, the beginnings of the Riverworld series, *A Feast Unknown*, *Lord of the Trees*, *The Mad Goblin*, *Lord Tyger*, *Image of the Beast*, *Blown*, and *Love Song*, among others. It struck me, reading the aforementioned three short chapters entitled "Down to Earth's Centre," in which Lacewing is in Los Angeles, that the writing had the same vibe as some other works in Farmer's California period. Controversial, boundary-pushing, and even otherworldly.

With that in mind, and given Farmer's own penchant for referencing his own and others' works, I included references to *Image of the Beast/Blown*, *Love Song*, and *Up from the Bottomless Pit*, the latter of which was written in the 1970s but not published until much later. (The latest edition is from Meteor House, 2020.) A California setting was not the only criterion, but was merely a starting point. Another common point among these works (with the exception of *Love Song*) is that they cannot be smoothly incorporated into Farmer's main pulp continuity, the Wold Newton Family/Universe. But they all could certainly occur in Doc Caliban's realm.

Don Pedro del Osorojo, Trolling House, Michel Le Garrault, and *Les Murs ecroules* (*The Collapsed Walls*) are from *Image of the Beast/Blown*.

> Le Garrault was a nineteenth-century Belgian scholar and occultist and the first to propose the existence of parallel or alternate dimensions occupying the same space as our own—not just worlds that were very much like our own, with subtle divergences, but other planets occupying the same physical space as Earth did, existing in dimensions that had wildly different laws of physics. Le Garrault also proposed that the walls between the universes could be broached, and had, in fact, already been broached, and that there were gates—perhaps accidental breaks or flaws, or perhaps created purposefully—via which a dweller of one dimension might travel to another.
>
> (Farmer and Eckert, *The Monster on Hold*)

Readers of *The Monster on Hold* know that the concepts of multiple realities are central to that work. The inclusion of Le Garrault was an "aha" moment that almost wrote itself.

Incidentally, when Caliban trails the Soldiers of Jehovah flunkey through the streets of Los Angeles, they drive by Phil Farmer's former home at 824 S. Burnside. Caliban also wonders, since the SOJ man is also an agent of the Nine, if the Nine were not ultimately behind the Cal-Pax oil disaster (*Up from the Bottomless Pit*).

The description of the Norwegian sea captain Tors Lundgren (*Love Song*) is reminiscent of XauXaz—who, in his long immortal life has taken many identities, including Wolf Larsen from Jack London's *The Sea-Wolf* and Baron von Hessel from Farmer's *Escape from Loki*. Casting Tors Lundgren as yet another of these aliases was not a bridge too far, and set the stage for the inclusion of *Love Song*'s Victoria and Barbara Lundgren as candidates of the Nine.

Other references and ideas directly from Farmer's chapters, notes, interviews, or letters found in his Magic Filing Cabinet are:

• Story idea: "The Nine using Caliban's college to turn out super-criminals now?"

• The name of the commandant of Camp Loki in Caliban's universe is Colonel Arnold Etzel von Bissell, whereas the commandant in Doc Savage's (aka Lacewing, aka Doc Wildman) universe, as seen in EFL, is Baron von Hessel. The von Bissell name appears in a pitch letter for EFL from Farmer to Bantam Doubleday dated August 30, 1988.

• The gray-eyed, sun-brown-skinned giant, an Australian by birth named Gordon, who accompanies Lacewing on the return descent into the New England caves, is John Gordon, aka Jongor, a Tarzan-like hero of a series of novels by Robert Moore Williams. Jongor is a Wold Newton Family member, just as Doc is: "If Doc did mount an expedition back to Earth's Center . . . a member of the family might have volunteered, if Doc could have located him. This was Jongor (John Gordon)."

(Farmer, "The Fabulous Family Tree of Doc Savage [Another Excursion into Creative Mythography]" in *Doc Savage: His Apocalyptic Life,* Meteor House revised edition, 2013, 2023)

• Scott Free in Caliban's universe is the counterpart to the enigmatic Mr. Wail in Doc Savage's dimension (Wail is from Dent's *Up from Earth's Center*). In TMOH, Mr. Wail is now known as Mr. Cri.

Other references I slipped in, from the wealth of material that comprises Farmer's Wold Newton Family/Universe, and other sources:

- Doc Wildman's beloved professor who was murdered is from Lester Dent's Doc Savage novel *The Land of Terror*.
- The giant ape, the aftermath of whose fall from the top of the Empire State Building Lacewing/Wildman/Savage witnessed is from Farmer's short story "After King Kong Fell."
- Lacewing's daughter, who joins him on the return expedition into the New England caves, is Patricia Clarke "Pat" Wildman from *The Evil in Pemberley House* by Farmer and Eckert.
- The black-haired beauty who captured Lacewing's heart is Lacewing/Wildman's wife, Adélaïde Lupin, from *The Evil in Pemberley House*. She is the daughter of Maurice Leblanc's gentleman thief Arsène Lupin.
- Lacewing faking his and his wife's deaths in a plane crash in 1972 is from *The Evil in Pemberley House*.
- The "certain Englishman" with whom Lacewing/Wildman/ Savage partnered in battling against the version of the Nine in Doc Savage's universe (the Wold Newton Universe) is John Clayton III, otherwise known as Tarzan of the Apes.
- The sea captain, who is also a mathematical genius, is Jules Verne's Captain Nemo from *Twenty Thousand Leagues under the Seas*. H. W. Starr, a Sherlockian scholar, identified Captain Nemo as being the same person as Sherlock Holmes' rival, Professor James Moriarty, in his essay "A Submersible Subterfuge or Proof Impositive," found in the back pages of Farmer's *The Other Log of Phileas Fogg*.
- XauXaz's pocket watch is a modified Capellean distorter from Farmer's *The Other Log of Phileas Fogg*.
- The modern XauXaz is an aficionado of the psychedelic phase of The Beatles, specifically "I Am the Walrus." (Eckert's story "The Wild Huntsman," included in *The Monster on Hold*.)
- Tilatoc, one of the Nine, is known by many other names, including Misquaneqes; this is a variant on Misquamacus, an ageless Native American whose devilries are described in the book *Of Evill Sorceries Done in New-England of Daemons in No Humane Shape*. (August Derleth and H. P. Lovecraft, *The Lurker at the Threshold*.)

- Doc Caliban wonders if Lestski, the Vienna-based surgeon with exceptional skills, and the only other person who understands the critical steps and secrets of Doc's brain surgery and hypnosis techniques, has perhaps given the Nine the information necessary to reverse the operations and produce super criminals. Lestski is the Nine Universe counterpart of Baron Orrest Karl Lestzky from Lester Dent's Doc Savage novel *The Golden Man.*

- Langston Dupont and Virgil Sol are from Frank Schildiner's Secrets of the Nine novella *It's Always Darkest.* Dupont is the Nine Universe's conflated version of several pulp heroes such as The Shadow, The Green Lama, and The Spider. Sol is the son of Virgil "The Turk" Sollozzo from Mario Puzo's *The Godfather.*

- In 1984, Doc Caliban drives up Topanga Canyon and is pleased to see that the house where he was assaulted in 1928 was destroyed in the massive mudslides that plagued the Los Angeles area and Southern California during the incredible deluge of never-ending rainstorms about a decade prior. The mudslides, never-ending rainstorms, and the house that was destroyed—the mansion that was the headquarters of the Ogs—are from *Image of the Beast/Blown.*

- Anana, the ancient leader of the Nine, has a namesake in Farmer's World of Tiers series. The man who appears through a dimensional gate in the epilogue of TMOH and tells Doc Caliban that he is looking for Anana is none other than Kickaha, the primary protagonist of the World of Tiers series. How the two Ananas (or are they one?) are connected has yet to be revealed.

- Just before Kickaha appears, Caliban is meditating at a mountainside retreat. Although no music is referenced in this epilogue, The Police's "Secret Journey" plays in my head when I reread this scene. Indeed, the song is reflective of Caliban's entire character arc.

Perhaps the most serendipitous reference in *The Monster on Hold* pertains to *The Rubáiyát of Omar Khayyám.* Lester Dent included quatrain thirty-one at the beginning of *Up from Earth's Center.* This, in itself, is remarkable, given the lack of literary merit commonly attributed to the pulps and their authors.

Up from Earth's Centre through the Seventh Gate
I rose, and on the Throne of Saturn sate,
And many Knots unravel'd by the Road;
But not the Knot of Human Death and Fate.
(Edward FitzGerald translation, 1859)

I had long settled on the idea of the two Docs—Caliban and Savage—merging into a Doc unity in order to pierce the veil, cross the unspeakable threshold, and ultimately defeat Xau-Xaz and Shrassk:

> But the two Docs, of one mind, also could not shake the notion that they were more than simply alternate universe versions of each other, but rather they were somehow different manifestations of the same being.
> The two Docs had coalesced, merged, into one, each superimposed over the other, slightly out of phase, but acting as a monoentity, the Doc unity. They were, essentially, the same person. Their different dimensional origins, family backgrounds, life histories, were irrelevant.
> (Farmer and Eckert, *The Monster on Hold*)

As I reviewed *The Rubáiyát of Omar Khayyám* once again—for I always continued to research as I worked to complete the novel proper—my eyes settled on quatrain thirty-two—the quatrain *immediately following that which Dent had quoted*:

> There was a Door to which I found no Key:
> There was a Veil past which I could not see:
>   Some little Talk awhile of ME and THEE
> There seemed—and then no more of THEE and ME.

It wrote itself. I was a mere conduit.

—Win Scott Eckert
In the mountains of Colorado
May 2024

References

Philip José Farmer

- "The Adventure of the Sore Bridge—Among Others"
- "After King Kong Fell"
- *Doc Savage: His Apocalyptic Life*
- *Escape from Loki*
- *The Evil in Pemberley House* (with Win Scott Eckert)
- *A Feast Unknown*
- "The Freshman"
- *Image of the Beast/Blown*
- *Lord of the Trees*
- *Love Song*
- *The Mad Goblin*
- *The Other Log of Phileas Fogg*
- *Up from the Bottomless Pit*
- The World of Tiers series

Lester Dent ("Kenneth Robeson" the house byline for the Doc Savage pulp novels)

- *Fortress of Solitude*
- *The Golden Man*
- *The Land of Terror*
- *The Man of Bronze*
- *Up from Earth's Center*

H. P. Lovecraft

- *At the Mountains of Madness*
- "The Dunwich Horror"
- *The Lurker at the Threshold* by August Derleth and H. P. Lovecraft

Jules Verne

- *An Antarctic Mystery; or, The Sphinx of the Ice Fields: A Sequel to The Narrative of Arthur Gordon Pym* (*Le Sphinx de Glaces*)
- *Twenty Thousand Leagues under the Seas*

Christopher Paul Carey: two "Creative Mythography" essays which were invaluable and provided much critical background. Both can be found in Carey's book *The Grandest Adventure: Writings on Philip José Farmer* (Leaky Boot Press, 2018)

- "Farmer's Escape from Loki: A Closer Look"
- "The Green Eyes Have It—Or Are They Blue? or Another Case of Identity Recased"

Other

- "The Adventure of the Devil's Foot" by Sir Arthur Conan Doyle
- "I Am the Walrus" by The Beatles (Lennon/McCartney)
- *The Narrative of Arthur Gordon Pym* by Edgar Allan Poe
- *The Rubáiyát of Omar Khayyám*
- *The Sea-Wolf* by Jack London
- "Secret Journey" by The Police (Sting [Gordon Sumner])
- *Tarzan and the Castaways* by Edgar Rice Burroughs
- "Who Goes There?"/Frozen Hell by John W. Campbell
- *Zanoni* by Edward Bulwer-Lytton

ABOUT THE AUTHORS

Philip José Farmer was born on January 26, 1918 in North Terre Haute, Indiana. He grew up in Peoria, Illinois where he spent much of his childhood reading everything from the Bible and books on mythology to the classics by Baum, Carroll, Cervantes, Defoe, Dickens, Homer, London, Swift, and Twain to popular works by Burroughs, Doyle, Haggard, Verne, and Wells.

He sold his first story, a mainstream tale titled "O'Brien and Obrenov," to *Adventure* in 1946 before he decided to try his hand at science fiction. His next published story, "The Lovers," appeared in the August 1952 issue of *Startling Stories*, and is noted for breaking the taboo on sex in science fiction, as well as for earning Farmer a Hugo Award for "Most Promising New Talent."

Married and with two children, he soon quit his job to become a full-time writer, but after selling several more stories to the science fiction pulps, his career hit a stumbling block when he "won" the Shasta Prize Novel Contest. The grand prize was four thousand dollars (a lot of money in 1953), but he never received his winnings. Instead, the publisher asked Farmer for rewrites while the prize money was invested in another book, which bombed. By the time the truth came out, Farmer had lost his house and was forced to take up full time employment.

Farmer left Peoria with his family in 1956 and moved around the country working as a technical writer for the space-defense industry, eventually ending up in Beverly Hills, California in 1965. All the while he continued to write and sell science fiction short stories and novels, launching his popular World of Tiers series and even winning a second Hugo Award for the novella "Riders of the Purple Wage." Then, just before the moon landing in 1969, he was laid off from his technical writing job, so he decided to write fiction full time once again. This time it stuck.

In 1970, Farmer moved back to Peoria with his family and again his career began to take off, this time with a third Hugo Award win, for *To Your Scattered Bodies Go*, the opening novel in his bestselling Riverworld series. For the next few years Farmer sought inspiration from the popular literature he so loved, writing novels such as *The Mad Goblin* (a Doc Savage pastiche), *Lord of the Trees* and *Lord Tyger* (both Tarzan pastiches), *The Wind Whales of Ishmael* (a science fiction sequel to *Moby Dick*), *Venus on the Half-Shell* (written as if by Kilgore Trout, a character from the works of Kurt Vonnegut), and one of Farmer's greatest achievements, writing *The Other Log of Phileas Fogg* (the "true" story behind Jules Verne's *Around the World in Eighty Days*), the merged stories presented here for the first time. He also wrote two "biographies" during this period: *Tarzan Alive: A Definitive Biography of Lord Greystoke* and *Doc Savage: His Apocalyptic Life*.

The next two decades saw the publication of the Dayworld trilogy, as well as further installments in the Riverworld and World of Tiers series. Farmer also fulfilled his lifelong ambition to write an Oz novel, and authorized Doc Savage and Tarzan novels, with the publication of *A Barnstormer in Oz*, *Escape from Loki*, and *Tarzan and the Dark Heart of Time*. Late in his career, Farmer tried his hand at a different genre with *Nothing Burns in Hell*, a detective novel set in his hometown of Peoria.

After Farmer retired from writing in 1999, new collections such as *Pearls from Peoria* and *Venus on the Half-Shell and Others* continued to appear, as did new collaborative works such as *The Evil in Pemberley House* and *The Monster on Hold* (with Win Scott Eckert), *The Song of Kwasin* (with Christopher Paul Carey), and *The City Beyond Play* and *Dayworld: A Hole in Wednesday* (with Danny Adams).

Farmer passed on February 25, 2009, but his fan base is as ardent as ever, still gathering at annual FarmerCons.

Win Scott Eckert is a novelist, editor, essayist, and writer of short fiction. He is steeped in the works of famed science fiction writer Philip José Farmer, particularly Farmer's shared universe literary-crossover Wold Newton cycle and the Lord Grandrith/Doc Caliban series. He has a deep interest in studying fictional biographies, creating detailed chronologies of fictional characters and universes, and exploring the metafictional connections between seemingly unrelated works, which resulted in *Myths for the Modern Age: Philip José Farmer's Wold Newton Universe* (MonkeyBrain Books, 2005), a 2007 Locus Awards finalist, and the critically acclaimed, encyclopedic *Crossovers: A Secret Chronology of the World 1 & 2* (Black Coat Press, 2010).

Eckert has also chronicled the exploits of popular characters, including Zorro, Sexton Blake, the Phantom, Honey West, the Scarlet Pimpernel, the Domino Lady, and the Green Hornet, all of which can be found in the pages of anthologies from Moonstone Books, Meteor House (*The Worlds of Philip José Farmer*), Black Coat Press (*Tales of the Shadowmen*), and Titan Books (*Tales of the Wold Newton Universe*).

He contributed a new foreword to the 2006 edition of Farmer's well-known fictional biography, *Tarzan Alive: A Definitive Biography of Lord Greystoke* (University of Nebraska/Bison Books), as well as several forewords and afterwords to Titan Books' reissues of Farmer's novels. He played a key role in reissuing Meteor House's definitive editions of Farmer's fictional biography *Doc Savage: His Apocalyptic Life* (2013), and Farmer's authorized Burroughs novel, *Tarzan and the Dark Heart of Time* (2018).

Eckert is the authorized legacy author of Farmer's Patricia Wildman series (*The Evil in Pemberley House*, *The Scarlet Jaguar*). His latest releases are an authorized Avenger book from Moonstone, *Hunt the Avenger* (2019); two authorized novels in the new Edgar Rice Burroughs Universe, *Tarzan: Battle for Pellucidar* (2020) and *Korak at the Earth's Core* (2024), and, as coauthor with Farmer, the fourth novel in Farmer's Secrets of the Nine series, *The Monster on Hold* (2021), furthering the titanic saga of Doc Caliban's battle against the dark manipulators who hold the secret to eternal life, the Nine.

Find him online at www.winscotteckert.com.

R Paul Sardanas has been exploring innovative forms of creativity since the 1970s. He is the author of over fifty books, ranging from scholarly works on Shakespearean and historical topics, to poetry collections, to thrillers and erotica. He has been nominated ten times for the Science Fiction Poetry Association Rhysling Award, which recognizes outstanding speculative fiction poetic works. His philanthropic work includes publishing support for new, gifted authors, and since 2004 benefit events through his nonprofit Gromagon Press to raise awareness and offer tangible support to organizations working to fight illiteracy and domestic abuse. Since 2015, in partnership with Iason Ragnar Bellerophon, he has been authoring the ongoing Talos Chronicle, which seeks to elevate pulp fiction by melding it to the techniques of fine art and literature. Lists and samples of his work can be viewed at http://www.doctalos.com.

A rthur C. Sippo is a medical doctor who served in the U.S. Army and the National Guard for over twenty years. He is board certified in Aerospace and Occupational Medicine. Art has a bachelor's degree in Chemistry from St. Peter's College (Magna Cum Laude), a medical degree from Vanderbilt, and a Masters in Public Health from Johns Hopkins. He was a Flight Surgeon for the 101st Airborne Division, Director of the Biodynamics Research Division at the U.S. Army Aeromedical Research Laboratory, an exchange officer with the RAF Institute of Aviation Medicine in Farnborough, England, the Commander of the 145th MASH, the Assistant State Surgeon for the Ohio National Guard, and vice president of the Occupational Care Consultants in Toledo, Ohio. Currently he is the Medical Director of Express Medical Care in Fairview Heights, Illinois. He is also the cohost of The Book Cave Podcast series that covers pulp fiction, comics, Sci-Fi, and adventure stories. Art has been a fan of Philip José Farmer since reading *A Feast Unknown* in 1969. He has been married to his beloved Katherine for twenty-five years and they have five children.

METEOR HOUSE TITLES

THE WORLDS OF PHILIP JOSÉ FARMER
Anthology Series edited by Michael Croteau
Volume 1: Protean Dimensions
Volume 2: Of Dust and Soul
Volume 3: Portraits of a Trickster
Volume 4: Voyages to Strange Days

Jesus on Mars by Philip José Farmer
The Stone God Awakens by Philip José Farmer
The Man Who Met Tarzan by Philip José Farmer
A Rough Knight for the Queen by Philip José Farmer
The Best of Farmerphile edited by Michael Croteau
The Philip José Farmer Centennial Collection edited by Michael Croteau
Greatheart Silver and Other Pulp Heroes by Philip José Farmer
Up from the Bottomless Pit by Philip José Farmer

SECRETS OF THE NINE SERIES
Secrets of the Nine Omnibus
(*A Feast Unknown, Lord of the Trees,* and
The Mad Goblin by Philip José Farmer)
The Monster on Hold by Philip José Farmer & Win Scott Eckert
It's Always Darkest by Frank Schildiner

WOLD NEWTON SERIES
Doc Savage: His Apocalyptic Life by Philip José Farmer
Tarzan and the Dark Heart of Time by Philip José Farmer
Ironcastle by J.-H. Rosny & Philip José Farmer

THE PHILEAS FOGG SERIES
The Full Account (Around the World in Eighty Days and *The Other
Log of Phileas Fogg)* by Jules Verne and Philip José Farmer
Phileas Fogg and the War of Shadows by Josh Reynolds
Phileas Fogg and the Heart of Osra by Josh Reynolds